The Hungry Road

www.penguin.co.uk

The Hungry Road

Marita Conlon-McKenna

TRANSWORLD IRELAND

TRANSWORLD IRELAND
Penguin Random House Ireland, Morrison Chambers,
32 Nassau Street, Dublin 2, Ireland
www.transworldireland.ie

Transworld Ireland is part of the Penguin Random House group of companies
whose addresses can be found at global.penguinrandomhouse.com

First published in the UK and Ireland in 2020
by Transworld Ireland
an imprint of Transworld Publishers

A CIP catalogue record for this book
is available from the British Library.

ISBN 9781848271975

Typeset in 12/15 pt Ehrhardt MT by Jouve (UK), Milton Keynes
Printed and bound in Great Britain by Clays Ltd, Elcograf S.p.A.

Penguin Random House is committed to a sustainable
future for our business, our readers and our planet. This book
is made from Forest Stewardship Council® certified paper.

MIX
Paper from
responsible sources
FSC
www.fsc.org FSC® C018179

1 3 5 7 9 10 8 6 4 2

For my family

Part One

Chapter 1

FROM EVERY FIELD AND FARM, LANE AND STREET, VILLAGE AND TOWN–land in West Cork, the people came. Some in groups, some alone, they walked in heavy boots or barefoot to witness their great hero, Daniel O'Connell, speak at the Monster Repeal Meeting in Skibbereen.

Mary Sullivan was among them, for she was determined to see the Great Liberator, who had done so much for Ireland and her people. She had been anxious about leaving her children, but her kind neighbour Brigid had offered to mind them.

Band music filled the stilly June air as she, her husband John, his brother Pat and uncle Flor neared the market town. The crowded streets of Skibbereen were bedecked with welcome flags and brightly coloured bunting, and every store, stall and merchant was busy. Mary laughed, caught up in the heady excitement and gaiety of it all.

Filled with anticipation, they joined the slow, winding snake of men and women of all ages as they pushed forward towards Curragh Hill, where their champion would address them.

Since sunrise, Father John Fitzpatrick had been watching the crowds arriving in Skibbereen. The people were like pilgrims travelling from afar, arriving in carts and coaches. Some were staying in the town's hotels and boarding houses, and many had walked miles to get there.

The numbers were huge – thousands and thousands – far greater than he and his fellow priests had hoped for when they sent out word to the people of Carbery that all were welcome to attend a meeting where the great Daniel O'Connell would speak of repealing the hated Act of Union, which had merged the parliaments of Great Britain and Ireland. He gave a silent prayer to the Lord to grant them a fine dry day for their endeavours.

After he returned home from saying mass, Father Fitzpatrick checked that his housekeeper, Bridey, had the spare room ready. He had informed her that a guest would be staying with him in the parish house that evening. The brass bed was made up with their finest linen, the wardrobe and chest of drawers were freshly polished with beeswax, the glass in the window was sparkling.

'I suppose they are going to the big meeting too?' Bridey asked the priest as he came downstairs. 'Will the two of you be eating here afterwards?'

'No, Bridey, don't trouble yourself. We're attending the Repeal Banquet in the Temperance Hall tonight. But I'm sure my guest would enjoy a good breakfast with some of your soda bread tomorrow morning before he sets off on his travels.'

'Father, I've never seen such a palaver in the town. But don't worry, I'll be up early to cook a few fresh eggs for the good father too.'

He laughed at her assumption that it was a man of the cloth who was coming to stay. He felt disingenuous, keeping the identity of his guest from her, but Bridey couldn't be trusted not to brag and boast around the town.

Father Fitzpatrick had had to admit to being rather surprised that Daniel O'Connell had rejected the Repeal committee's offer to take a room in the comfort of the nearby Becher Arms Hotel and requested to stay with him instead. Perhaps the great man preferred the privacy and quiet of a simple priest's home to more luxurious surroundings where he would be approached constantly by admirers.

He would do his utmost to ensure Daniel O'Connell found rest and peace here in the parish house if that was what he desired.

Satisfied that everything was in order, Father Fitzpatrick left to join the large welcome procession of parishioners, carpenters, shoe-makers, weavers, other tradesmen and musical bands getting ready to escort O'Connell and his carriage to the packed meeting place.

Dr Daniel Donovan was finishing his rounds of the Skibbereen Union Workhouse when the young midwife came running after him.

'The matron ordered me to fetch you,' she called, out of breath.

With O'Connell's visit to the town later that day, Dan was pressed for time, but he knew well that the matron would not request he attend unless she was in need of medical assistance.

The young mother-to-be in need of attention looked no more than eighteen years old; a pretty girl with thick dark hair that clung to her head with sweat.

'I am fearful for her and the child,' the middle-aged matron confided.

'I am here to help you,' he tried to reassure the girl. Her brown eyes were filled with fear, and she was too exhausted to take notice of him, let alone deliver a child.

As he examined her, it became clear that the baby was breech. Instead of presenting head down, one of the unborn child's tiny feet was beginning to appear first. Difficult and risky in any case, breech deliveries often resulted in the loss of mother and child.

Dan thought back to his medical school days in Edinburgh when his professor would lecture him and his fellow students on such cases. He would drive home the vital importance of judicious and decisive assistance with such problematic births to try to ensure both lives were saved.

O'Connell would have to wait, for the mother was near collapse and he needed to deliver the baby immediately. Dan ordered the two women to help him hold the mother as he attempted to extract the baby as swiftly as he could.

'I know you are tired—'

'Her name is Maggie Hayes,' interjected the matron.

'Maggie, let me help your baby.'

A foot, a leg, a thigh, the buttocks . . . Somehow he managed to hold the child's lower limbs steady and guide them as they emerged. Then, holding its body firmly, he quickly proceeded to ease the baby's neck and small head downwards, trying to ensure he did not damage the neck or spine. The infant was blue and still. Dan untangled and cut the cord quickly, willing the boy to take his first breath.

The silence was ominous as he caught the little fellow and held him up, clearing the mucus and blood from his face. Suddenly the baby stirred and moved his hands before giving a low, faint cry. Dan held and rubbed the child, relieved as the infant began to give a stronger cry, his lungs filling with air and his colour improving.

'You have a fine son,' he told Maggie, placing the baby into her waiting arms, 'but you must rest awhile.'

He nodded to the matron who was tending to her, before glancing at his fob watch and realizing how late he was.

Maggie smiled weakly.

'I am naming him William after my late father and Daniel for the Liberator who is in town this very day, his birth day,' she said proudly, kissing the baby's head.

'A day all of us will remember,' Dan acknowledged as he took his leave.

'I'm sorry for delaying you,' apologized the matron as she escorted him to the door, 'but thank you for your assistance.'

'You did the right thing,' he assured her, 'for both the mother and baby are healthy.'

'There is no mention of a father,' Matron sighed. 'The girl will have to stay here and nurse and mind the child.'

'At least they are both in your good care, Matron,' Dan said as he climbed up into his horse and trap, and set off home with great haste.

Henrietta Donovan was growing anxious, for her husband had promised to return for the meeting in plenty of time. Seeing such crowds, she fretted that they wouldn't get there soon enough. What could possibly be delaying Dan on such an important day? Suddenly, she heard his rapid footsteps on the stair.

'Where were you?' she scolded lightly. 'I was getting worried that—'

'Hush,' he soothed. 'I'm here now, just let me change my shirt and jacket. I was delayed in the Union, assisting a difficult birth. Fortunately, both mother and child are well.'

'Thank the Lord for that.'

She knew there was no point in rebuking Dan, for his patients would always come first. Her husband, the physician for the recently opened Skibbereen Union Workhouse and the town's dispensary, was possessed of a kind nature and an utter dedication to the care of the sick.

As they set off in the horse and trap, Dan took his wife's hand.

'You look pretty, my dear, in that new lace dress,' he offered.

Henrietta was delighted, for she had taken great care in curling her dark brown hair and applying a very slight touch of rouge to her lips, as well as purchasing a new dress for the occasion. She was gladdened by his compliment as Dan never usually noticed fashion!

The crowds had thinned as they made their way through town. Skibbereen's bars and taverns were all closed, for O'Connell was an outspoken advocate for the Temperance movement and did not want his Monster Meetings marred by the raucous behaviour of a few drunks.

Before long, Dan and Henrietta joined the line of horse-drawn vehicles pulling up at the enormous meeting place. Henrietta's heart pounded with the reverberation of the drums as she and Dan were escorted to a position near the large podium. All around them were townspeople and tradesmen, tenants and labourers, united in the hope that O'Connell would help restore an Irish parliament to Dublin that would govern the Irish people fairly.

'Did we ever think that we would see this day?' laughed Daniel McCarthy, the wealthy brewer, unable to disguise the pride and emotion in his voice. 'The most famous man alive and, thanks to our own good efforts, here he is in Skibbereen.'

'We knew the people would come.' Dan gazed around him at the huge crowds. 'For O'Connell speaks of what is in every man's heart.'

'And woman's,' Henrietta reminded her husband, squeezing his arm.

There was a flurry of movement as carriages and a procession of people bearing tall, billowing banners began to approach the enormous gathering. As the band struck up loudly in the distance, she was overcome with a frisson of excitement.

Chapter 2

GAZING OUT ACROSS THE FLOWING RIVER ILEN, MARY SULLIVAN WAS overwhelmed by the sight of tens of thousands of people gathered together on Curragh Hill. The sea of O'Connell's supporters shimmered in a haze before her.

'Keep a hold of my hand,' urged John as he propelled her forward.

A regiment of soldiers stood to the side at the ready, observant and unflinching, as the couple manoeuvred their way through the waves of bodies towards the large wooden podium positioned at one end of the field.

A massive roar of welcome broke from the near seventy-thousand-strong crowd as three marching bands, followed by four stagecoaches bearing Daniel O'Connell and his entourage, arrived in the grounds. As the bands played a loud triumphant march, a procession of priests, parishioners and local tradesmen led the coaches up the field to cheers and applause. There was such a din that Mary worried how the drivers would control the horses.

The coaches finally came to a stop and the tall, heavy-set figure of Daniel O'Connell in his black cape stepped out and up on to the podium. He was an imposing figure, with a broad face and a head of dark curls. His eyes roved appreciatively over the huge crowd.

A hush fell as a man with pride in his voice welcomed the Liberator to Skibbereen, citing O'Connell's achievement in securing

Catholic emancipation and his fight now to repeal the despised Act of Union.

The crowd began to cheer wildly as O'Connell threw off his cape with a confident swagger. In grand style he stepped forward and flung open his arms, greeting his supporters warmly in a clear, booming voice. There came a roar of approval as he began to speak in Gaelic, and laughter at the bewilderment of the large force of British military and constabulary that had surrounded the field. The redcoats were left scratching their heads, wondering what he was saying.

'I am honoured to be your representative in Parliament,' O'Connell continued, his eyes shining, 'even though it is a Parliament packed against me.'

The cheers echoed through the still summer's day as he spoke of the achievement of Catholic emancipation, which had finally given Catholics the right to hold important offices and serve as members of the British parliament.

O'Connell's voice filled with emotion as he looked down at the crowd.

'I may have been at the head of the battle, but victory could not have been won without you, the people, behind me.'

A profound silence fell as he outlined his new Repeal campaign to regain Irish freedom and self-government with the return of an Irish parliament to Dublin.

'It is the right of every Irish man over twenty years of age to have a house and to vote.'

O'Connell's voice carried loud and clear across the field, filling the spectators' parched hearts with the hope of change. They latched on to his words, all tiredness and soreness in their feet and legs forgotten. The prospect of freedom hung in the air, blowing tantalizingly among them, along with the cherished hope of regaining the right to own the roof over their head and the land on which they raised their crops. Many were ready to rally to his call and take up arms to fight if need be!

However, O'Connell soon made his opposition to violence clear.

'This battle will be fought in Parliament peacefully and legally, with justice and equality as our swords. Good people, I call on you to support the Repeal movement, for we intend to grow it. Lastly, I ask you all to give three cheers for the Queen, Victoria who rules the empire. The Queen!'

John and Pat remained stubbornly silent, their eyes cast down as the cheers echoed across the fields and hills.

'Hurrah! Queen Victoria! Hurrah!'

As O'Connell brought his speech to a close, he thanked the crowd for travelling so far – from all over Cork, Kerry and Tipperary – before bidding them farewell. The band struck up again loudly and, in only a few short minutes, the coaches and horses departed the field to more cheers as the Liberator's carriage passed.

As the crowds began to disperse slowly, Mary felt strangely bereft.

'He has the men, so why doesn't he organize us instead of sending us home with only words?' Pat remarked angrily as the coaches disappeared from view. 'Words won't win back our cottages and our land.'

'Hush, or you'll get us all into trouble,' cautioned Flor, noticing a soldier standing nearby.

'Will we all go into town for a pint of porter to mark the day?' suggested Pat. 'Hopefully one or two public houses will be open.'

Mary had no interest in joining the men in one of the town's noisy hostelries. Instead, she decided to call on her sister, who lived in the crowded, rundown lanes of Bridgetown on the far edge of Skibbereen.

'I'll meet you in Kathleen's later,' promised John, 'and we'll walk home together.'

Chapter 3

AS THE PEOPLE STREAMED BACK INTO SKIBBEREEN, MANY OF THE SHOPS and stalls had re-opened. Mary paused as she passed Honora Barry's dressmaking shop where she had worked as a seamstress before her marriage. It was still closed but Miss Barry had wisely placed a pretty sprigged-cotton dress in the window to attract customers.

She continued on her way and turned in to the narrow streets of Bridgetown, with its rows of small low cottages and cabins built almost on top of each other. Children played in the dirt and a group of women in shawls chatted loudly about the handsome Liberator.

The Caseys' cottage was down the end of a lane. Outside, her nephews and niece – Michael, Jude and Sarah – were busy with a piece of old rope they had found, and some sticks and a plank of wood.

'We're making a boat to float on the river,' boasted eleven-year-old Michael as Mary ruffled his thick curly hair.

Kathleen welcomed her younger sister warmly as she stepped inside.

'You were up at the Liberator like Joe and the rest of them?' she asked. 'I'd a mind to go myself but Lizzie is teething and she'd have roared the place down.'

Mary could see the baby's hot red cheeks and felt an immediate sympathy for her once-beautiful sister, who now looked worn out.

Things were hard for Kathleen as her husband, Joseph Casey, who had charmed her with his handsome looks, grand talk and promises to make a fortune, was a simple labourer who went from one job to another. He had been employed on building the large Union work-house, but had had little work since then.

Mary did not know how Kathleen could bear such circumstances. The small, one-roomed cottage with its half-door was in the worst part of town. It was cramped and gloomy. The three older children slept in a low space under the thatch roof, while Kathleen and Joseph slept on a pallet bed placed against one wall, with Lizzie in a make-shift crib near by.

Kathleen flung more turf on the fire and brewed some leaves for tea while Mary told her excitedly about O'Connell and his stirring words.

'I've no use for politicking.' Kathleen shrugged. 'What have all these members of parliament ever done for the likes of us?'

She called the children in and insisted that Mary share their family meal of spuds and buttermilk.

'There will be better eating in a few weeks,' she apologized as they dipped the old, greyish spuds in salt and mustard. 'Once Joe gets harvest work.'

By the time John called to collect Mary it had grown dark and Kathleen was putting the children down to sleep. After saying their goodbyes, Mary and John took the road for home together.

The stars shone high above them and John reached for her hand.

'That was the grandest day ever.' Mary's heart was full of hope from the Liberator's words. 'One I will always remember.'

'Aye, so many people gathered together,' John agreed. 'But it will all come to nothing if no one listens to us!'

'Daniel O'Connell will win them over.'

'I fear no matter what he promises, it's the landowners of England who will decide our fate.'

Even in the darkness Mary could sense her husband's doubt.

'Believe me, they will fight tooth and nail to stop Repeal,' he warned her.

'But we will win!' She'd no intention of letting John dampen her enthusiasm.

He reached down impulsively and kissed her. His lips tasted of porter, and as she responded he pulled her even closer to him, holding her so near that she could hear the steady beat of his heart. She ran her hand along his face tenderly, her fingers touching the stubble of his cheek and jaw.

'*Mo ghrá.*' He gave in, kissing her again, this time gently. 'I pray that you are right.'

They walked along the starlit road until they neared the familiar potato fields with the tall willow trees and scraggy hedges.

'One day this will be ours,' she affirmed as they walked towards the low thatched cottage where their children slept. 'Every root, stalk and blade of grass, and every bit of earth beneath our feet will belong to us.'

'Sullivans' fields,' John shouted, spinning her round and round in the darkness. 'Sullivans' fields.'

Chapter 4

THOUGH THE HOUR WAS LATE ON THEIR RETURN FROM THE DINNER IN the town's large Temperance Hall, Father John Fitzpatrick sat talking with his guest by the fireside.

A huge crowd had attended the Repeal Banquet and people had milled around, keen to be introduced to the great man. After dinner, a toast had been proposed to O'Connell and Repeal, which had nearly raised the roof.

One young Irelander had declared boldly his determination to shed his blood for Repeal, even if it was on the scaffold. O'Connell had told young John Shea Lawlor that rather than die for Ireland, he would rather live for Ireland, for one living repealer is worth a churchyard full of dead ones! It had been inspiring to listen to the great orator.

'You must be tired after such a successful day,' Father John ventured as they sat back in their chairs. 'And then to have to go and meet and talk to so many people again tonight.'

'Father, that is what is expected of me in every town the length and breadth of the country.' O'Connell yawned as he stretched out his legs in front of the fireplace. 'But it does help to raise contributions and funds for the movement.'

Father John could see his guest was weary. The man's eyes were heavy and his face was slightly flushed. He looked every bit of his near seventy years of age.

O'Connell chose that moment to confide in the priest that although he was often surrounded by crowds, he was lonely. He had his sons and grandchildren, but he desperately missed his late wife, Mary, and her conversation and company.

'You of all men must understand. Here you are with a large parish yet come home at night to sit at a lonely hearth?'

Father John did indeed know all too well. Answering the call to the priesthood meant that he would always remain a man alone with no wife or child of his own.

The two men continued to chat easily. O'Connell sighed heavily as he reeled off a list of places that he was still to visit to speak at before the largest Monster Meeting of all.

'It will be in October, in Clontarf in Dublin. I hope that you will join us, Father John, for there will be Repeal supporters coming from all over the country.'

'I and a few of the Skibbereen committee will certainly try to attend,' the priest promised.

'We need to demonstrate – to Peel and to Parliament – the massive support our movement enjoys, and force them to respond to the demands and will of the Irish people,' said O'Connell with fervour.

'Such a large-scale event in Dublin will certainly attract their attention.'

'I fear the authorities and Dublin Castle are already opposed to it. No doubt the military will be out in full force,' O'Connell confided. 'But I believe that Clontarf, the place where the great Brian Boru vanquished the Vikings, will be the place where we may gain our own victory. We will have such numbers that they will have no alternative but to grant us Repeal and the return of an Irish parliament to Dublin.'

The next morning, Father John was glad to see that his guest looked more refreshed after a good night's sleep. Bridey almost scalded herself with hot tea when she recognized the Liberator sitting at the dining table.

'I'm sure Mr O'Connell would enjoy some of your bread and an egg or two before he sets off on his travels,' said Father John with a smile.

Ever the gentleman, O'Connell complimented the blushing house-keeper on her soda bread and begged her for a few slices more before he left.

'Father John, until we meet again in Dublin,' Daniel O'Connell said, shaking the priest's hand and thanking him warmly for his kindness and hospitality.

As the priest watched O'Connell's carriage drive down North Street, he could not help but wonder how much longer the Liberator could continue his fight for Ireland and her people. Surely the time was coming for a new, younger generation to take up the mantle and battle for the change Ireland needed so desperately.

Chapter 5

Creagh, County Cork
October 1843

AS MARY TIDIED HER SMALL VEGETABLE PATCH, SHE COULD FEEL THE warm autumn sun on her back. John teased her about growing cabbages, turnips and onions, saying it would be far better to plant potatoes there, but her mother had always grown a few vegetables and she wanted to do the same.

When she had married John Sullivan, Mary had moved out of Skibbereen to the holding near Creagh that John shared with his father, Cornelius. The old man had welcomed his new daughter-in-law and had insisted she and John take the room he had shared with John's late mother, Anne. He had also been glad, she suspected, to have a woman around again to clean the place and cook the meals.

Little by little, Mary had made some changes. She had convinced John to mend the cottage's thatch roof and wash its walls with lime, and to build a wooden pen for the pig to stop it from wandering about and destroying the place. Encouraged, she had even persuaded him to make a small hen-house to hold their hens.

'With all these improvements, we will have the landlord down on us looking for more rent,' John had said, worried.

'They are only small things,' Mary had assured him. 'Things any bride would want.'

Old Corney Sullivan's eyes had filled with tears when he held his first grandchild, Cornelius John Sullivan, in his arms. He was a wonderful grandfather, who loved young Con – and his little sister, Nora, who followed soon after – dearly.

Following his father's death, John had been heartbroken. The only consolation was that his parents were finally reunited, buried together in the nearby graveyard.

Soon after, John had gone to Henry Marmion, the land agent for their landlord, Sir William Wrixon Becher, and asked to take over his father's holding. The tenancy was agreed but the rent was increased.

'A young man like you should be well able to work harder and earn more than the old man ever did,' Mr Marmion had told him as he gazed about the Sullivans' well-ordered fields and cottage.

Mary had felt guilty that her husband's fears had been well-founded and that her few improvements had somehow caused the increase.

'This is no fault of yours, Mary,' John had reassured her. 'That man has been waiting many a day for my father to die so he could do this and try to squeeze even more money and work from us.'

In the years that followed, Mary and John had worked hard, raising Con, Nora and their third child, little Tim, and tending their holding of one and a half acres. They now fattened two pigs – one for the market and one for themselves – and kept a few sheep. She even had twelve hens, and supplemented the family's small income by selling some of their eggs.

Looking up from her work weeding the vegetable patch, Mary laughed as she watched the children play with Patch, their black-and-white collie. Eight-year-old Con was throwing a stick for him to fetch, but the dog began to bark as he spotted John and Pat returning from town in Pat's small, horse-drawn wooden cart.

'There is bad news,' John called as he climbed down. 'O'Connell's Monster Meeting in Dublin was cancelled.'

'The Lord Lieutenant had the military and the police surround the city,' said Pat angrily. 'They even had warships at the ready in Dublin Bay to attack the crowds. They are all afraid of O'Connell and the millions who follow him!'

'O'Connell had no choice but to call it off, for many might have been injured or killed,' John explained as he lifted a sack of oats from the cart.

'There is talk that O'Connell himself will be arrested! Parliament and the authorities detest him and the Repeal movement.'

'The Liberator will fight on,' Mary insisted.

'Then he should have fought earlier when he had the chance,' Pat said sarcastically, urging the horse on as he headed across the fields to his own small dwelling.

Later that night, as she and John sat by the fire, Mary's thoughts were with the proud, strong man who had stood on Curragh Hill and promised to champion the cause of poor tenants like them.

John stared into the glowing turf. 'O'Connell may well be arrested, but he has shown us that we have the numbers. Pat and his Young Irelander friends are right. The time is coming that we should forget politics and fight properly for what is ours.'

Mary loved her husband dearly but was suddenly afraid of what he might become involved in.

'John, we have the children and the farm. Promise me that you will not—'

'Hush,' he said, placing his finger on her lips. 'I cannot make a promise I may not be able to keep.'

Even in the dull firelight she could see that he would brook no more discussion on the matter.

Chapter 6

Skibbereen
September 1844

'GRAND DAY, FATHER!' BEAMED TIM MCCARTHY DOWNING.

Father John Fitzpatrick had stopped in front of the large site on North Street where he hoped in time to build a much-needed new school for the town.

'Like myself, you must be delighted to see Daniel O'Connell released from prison and a free man again,' the local solicitor ventured.

'Indeed I am, Mr McCarthy Downing, for his imprisonment was a travesty.'

The priest, along with most people, had been deeply troubled by O'Connell's arrest the previous year on charges of conspiracy. Following the ban of last autumn's Monster Repeal Meeting in Clontarf, the great man had been treated like a common criminal. Along with his son, John, and five followers, he'd been sentenced to a year in Richmond Prison.

Father John had written to his former house guest, and his heart had lifted on hearing that O'Connell was in good spirits. He received news that he was being treated fairly, and his family and friends were permitted to visit him. Then, earlier that month, the House of Lords had thankfully deemed the trial unfair and O'Connell was released.

'By all accounts, he's had a hero's welcome in Dublin, with over two hundred thousand supporters coming out to cheer him. It must have been a fine sight to see,' laughed Tim McCarthy Downing. 'The Liberator transported through the streets of Dublin in that gilded carriage drawn by six horses!'

'It is only what the man deserves,' the priest acknowledged.

'How are the plans for the new school here going?' enquired McCarthy Downing.

'I'm afraid there are still funds to be raised and a great deal of paperwork and planning details to be worked out before we begin,' Father Fitzpatrick admitted honestly, 'but we will persist until we get our school.'

'If there is any assistance I can give, please call on me, Father,' the solicitor offered.

'I may well take you up on that, Mr McCarthy Downing.'

The construction of St Fachtna's School had been a long-cherished hope of Father John's. In his eyes, the children of Skibbereen deserved a good education and to attend a school where they would learn to read and write. In his mind, it was the only way to a fairer society.

'Father Fitzpatrick, if you are free on Sunday would you care to join us for lunch?'

'That is most kind of you,' he said, accepting the offer, for McCarthy Downing was a generous man and a most considerate host with a beautiful home. 'I shall look forward to it.'

'We can celebrate O'Connell's release,' the other man said with a smile, and took his leave.

There was indeed much to celebrate, but the priest's delight at Daniel O'Connell's freedom was tempered somewhat upon hearing that some considered the Liberator's health to have deteriorated during his incarceration, and there was the suggestion that he was a changed man. Father John prayed that Ireland's great leader would be restored in strength of mind and body before long and, with his usual courage and conviction, would soon take up the fight for Repeal once again.

Chapter 7

Creagh
August 1845

ALL AROUND MARY, THE WHITE POTATO BLOSSOM FLUTTERED IN THE fields. The pale flowers crowned each lazy bed of the crop, for the drills were nearly ready to be dug. The air was heavy and warm. Patch lumbered over to sit near her feet, panting with the strange, intense heat of the day. Mary pulled up her streels of light-brown hair as it was so warm, and closed her eyes momentarily as Con, Nora and Tim played together, while ten-month-old Annie slept in her crib inside the cottage. She was roused from her moment of stillness by Nora, whose freckled face was flushed from running.

'Ma, it's too hot for us. Can we get some water?'

The hens clucked around Mary as she walked to the well and filled the bucket with cold, clear water. She dipped the can into it again and again as she and the children drank their fill and splashed water on their faces and arms to cool down. Each time she refilled the bucket and tipped it into the hens' dish, Patch lapped up the spilt liquid.

Within half an hour the heat of the day was gone, for the sun had disappeared behind a dark heavy cloud. Without warning, rain began to lash down and she called to the children to join her inside as they ran to escape the torrential downfall. As the heavy raindrops beat the ground and the straw roof, she worried how their plants would tolerate such a deluge.

It was the second time this week that the strange rain had come.

'Mam, there's a fierce bad smell outside,' announced Nora. ''Tis everywhere.'

Curious, Mary stood up immediately and, with Annie in her arms, went to investigate.

As she looked around, she could neither see nor smell anything except for the peaty scent of smoke from the fire. She was about to go back inside when she glanced towards their fields. Her attention was caught by the strange, sudden wilting of the tall potato stalks, which seemed to have blackened and collapsed. Row after row of their potato plants were stricken.

'Take your sister!' she ordered Nora as she made her way to the drills.

Within seconds, Mary too was assailed by a sickening stench – rotten and putrid. She had never smelt the like of it and was filled with apprehension. Taking the spade, she began to dig. As she reached with her fingers, she lifted a clump of shapeless blackened potatoes that resembled nothing she had seen before: the vegetables were a stinking mess in her hands.

Worried, she called for the boys to come and help her.

'Ugh!' grimaced Con, covering his nose with his hand.

'Run and fetch your father!' she urged. 'He's down in the lower woods with Flor, cutting logs. Tell him he's needed here!'

Her eldest son took off while she and seven-year-old Tim dug a few more plants.

'Mam, these are bad,' complained Tim, for the ones he lifted were marked with signs of some strange disease.

Before long, John returned from the woods with Con. Uncle Flor, out of breath, followed behind them with Smokey, the old donkey, and the little cart. John grabbed the shovel from Mary immediately, cleaving deep as he dug into one drill after another, checking the potatoes.

'God's truth, I've never seen the like of it,' he said with worry as he scrutinized the potatoes, his fingers touching the oozing softness of the blackened tubers.

'I'm away to our place,' declared Flor, his eyes filled with concern.

'Any potatoes you find that are white and hard, throw them in the bucket,' John told the boys as he turned the earth, searching the ridges desperately for any potatoes that could be saved from the pestilence that had fallen on their crop.

Mary could see in the neighbouring field that the Flynns' crop appeared to be in the same sorry state as their own. How could potato plants have turned so quickly from growing strong and healthy one minute to this state?

Over in the small field, the drills seemed a bit better and John dug quickly, the lug of the spade turning up clumps of firm white potatoes that seemed untouched, unlike the other tubers.

'Con, bring the buckets for me to fill!' he called out.

Side by side, the family worked together, examining every smooth round shape closely in the hope of finding healthy and edible potatoes. In the surrounding fields, Pat, Flor, his wife Molly and their neighbours were digging and kneeling in the earth, backs bent, doing the same.

When he came to some of the drills at the far end of the field, John gave a shout of triumph. Despite having black spots dotted on their leaves, the potatoes seemed firm and healthy. The family filled four or five buckets with them, then John layered those that bore no sign of disease carefully in the potato pit where they would be kept until they were needed.

Annie began to cry hungrily, and Mary sat down on the stone wall to feed her.

'Are ye all destroyed too?' asked their neighbour Nell Flynn, coming towards them. Her hair fell around her face in dirty streels, and her skirt, blouse and feet were covered in mud. 'There is divil a bit to eat in our patcheen of a field. I've never seen the like in all my years. What did we do to deserve this?'

Mary knew how hard things were for the Flynns, who lived with their three sons in a tiny cabin near the end of the lane. They had only a bare quarter-acre to feed them. Nell's husband, Tom, with his bad hip, was unable to do the same heavy work as the other men, and he and Nell constantly borrowed and begged off their neighbours.

'Nell, will you have some tea?' Mary offered her. 'It's too hot to be sitting here.'

The older woman followed Mary, who was glad to get away from the sight of the rotting stalks, into the cottage.

'The boys will go hungry for we've nothing to give them,' Nell complained as she sipped her tea noisily.

'They'll not go hungry tonight for you'll take a few eggs and a half of soda bread home with you,' Mary found herself offering, for she was used to Nell and her ways.

'But you might have need for them yourself,' Nell wheedled, looking around her.

'I have more flour in the barrel and my hens are good layers,' Mary insisted as Nell left, trying not to give in to the rising panic she felt at the loss of most of their potato crop.

John stayed outside, searching their fields for any more healthy-looking potatoes, as Mary prepared their evening meal. The children were quiet, their eyes big in their heads, as she served up a pot of the first crop of new potatoes with some salt. To her mind there was a slight taint to them.

'I think they taste grand,' said ten-year-old Con, who always made the best of things, as he helped himself to more.

'What are we going to do, Mammy, when the taties are all gone?' ventured Nora.

'Your daddy and I and all of you will be fine,' she assured them, trying to hide her worry and fear. 'We have three sacks and some in the pit. We have plenty of flour in the barrel and vegetables, pigs and sheep to sell at the market. We'll not go hungry, for your father will always get work.'

*

The children were gone to bed when John finally crossed the door, his black hair wet with sweat. Mary flung her arms around him and made him sit by the fire. She dished up the new potatoes with a mug of buttermilk, which he ate hungrily.

'At least we've three good sacks and some in the pit to feed us,' she said, serving him a few more.

'Near two-thirds. The best part of our crop is gone,' he said forlornly.

'It's not the end of the world,' she replied quietly. 'We've lost part of the crop before.'

'Nothing like this!' he said bitterly. 'It is like some quare disease that has fallen on them. Denis Leary says it is everywhere across the Mizen and that the pestilence came in the mist and the clouds and the rain.'

She thought of her brothers' fields in Goleen, and wondered if they too were badly affected.

'I don't know what we will do, Mary,' he said in despair, 'for we still have to find the rent money.'

'We can sell the animals,' she said reassuringly.

'Aye,' he agreed with a yawn. 'Besides, without potatoes we have nothing left to feed the pigs with.'

They were both worn out and so made ready for bed. John finally gave in to exhaustion and fell asleep beside her, but thoughts crowded Mary's mind. She stared up at the dirty thatch, wondering how, with so much of their crop gone, they would manage during the hungry months to come.

Chapter 8

Skibbereen
September 1845

AS DAN DONOVAN WAS DOING HIS DAILY ROUNDS OF THE SKIBBEREEN Union Workhouse, the master stopped him outside the small infirmary for the sick. A tall, imposing man with bushy eyebrows and whiskers, Mr Falvey appeared a rather intimidating figure, but Dan found him to be meticulous in his duties with a great concern for the fair treatment of those who entered the Union.

'Doctor, we've had a large increase in the number of admissions these past few days,' the master explained. 'No doubt the potato failure has contributed to it.'

'With so little to eat, some will have no recourse but to enter here,' Dan acknowledged. 'I fear that it will likely get worse, so the Union must prepare, Mr Falvey, for this increase in our numbers to continue.'

The Skibbereen Union Workhouse had opened only three years ago and housed far fewer inmates than it was built to hold, for local people had a huge fear of crossing its threshold. Who could blame them, for it provided little comfort and operated under the same strict rules as other workhouses built across the country and throughout England

28

and Wales. Men, women and children who entered were all separated and housed in different wings, and had little contact with each other.

Dan Donovan's role as physician was to ensure the inmates remained healthy, that they were cared for medically, if necessary, and that there was no outbreak of contagion or disease among them. He did his best to ameliorate their conditions, treating them in the same way he did all his patients, for the Union was the last resort of the sick, the homeless and the mentally ill, who had no family or friends to care for them.

'Then we are in agreement.' The master nodded seriously as Dan continued on his way to the women's ward.

There, he met with an elderly woman who begged him for help. Not for herself, but for her husband who was in the men's ward.

'He's blind, doctor. These past years I've minded him all this time, but with the potatoes gone how am I going to feed and keep the two of us?' she sobbed.

'Mrs Reilly, I promise that he will be fed and looked after here,' he assured her. 'You both will.'

The relief on her tired, wrinkled face was visible.

'Can I see him?' she begged. 'Tomás and I have never been parted and he will be afraid, for he knows nothing – only our small cabin and patch.'

'In time your husband will get used to being here, but I will arrange with the master that you can visit him.'

Continuing on his rounds, Dan's next stop was the men's ward to see Mrs Reilly's husband, Tomás. He found the poor man deeply upset, his hands clasped over his head and clearly terrified by his new surroundings.

'I talked to your wife and will arrange that you are allowed to see her,' Dan promised the elderly man, taking hold of his hands.

As he examined Mr Reilly, he could see the man was malnourished but otherwise well cared for by his wife. Both eyes showed cataracts, their lenses a dense milky white, but the right eye was slightly better than the left.

'I lost the sight near ten years ago,' Tomás sighed heavily. 'I prayed that it would come back but it never has.'

Disorders of the eye had always fascinated Dan and he had studied ophthalmology in Scotland. He had considered practising as an oculist, but instead had become a general physician. However, he still maintained a keen interest in researching and treating eye conditions, and had developed quite a reputation in that area. Patients came from all over to consult him and he wondered if there was any way to restore even a little of Tomás's vision.

Moving on to the children's nursery, he examined two sisters who had been found by neighbours. The little girls were unwashed, uncared for and clearly malnourished.

'The eldest girl told us her mother died and their father went away,' declared the nurse angrily. 'He left them like two unwanted puppies.'

Dan examined the children gently, for they were both terrified. Their matted hair was riddled with lice and scabies.

'I'm Dr Dan,' he told them kindly, 'and the nurse is going to wash you both. She's going to cut and comb your hair, and put a special lotion and ointment on your skin that will take away the terrible itch. I promise it will help you both to feel better.'

'Do we have to stay here, sir?' the older child asked tearfully.

'Yes, I think it is for the best,' he ventured, not trusting himself to say more. 'You will be safe here.'

It angered him deeply how people treated their children, with no regard for their feelings.

As he was leaving the ward, young Will Hayes ran over to greet him.

'Dan . . . Dan,' the boy called, gripping the doctor's leg.

Dan lifted up the two-year-old in the air. Will was a fine, sturdy fellow with straw-coloured hair and piercing blue eyes, and only a year younger than Dan's youngest son. Whenever he saw the little boy on his rounds, he made a point of talking and playing with him, for being a workhouse child was no easy thing.

Will's mother had absconded from the Union after six months, leaving her illegitimate child to be raised in the workhouse. His childhood would be one of hardship and work, with little affection shown to him. At twelve or thirteen, the boy would likely be apprenticed out to some local farmer or tradesman. Dan hoped that some day, far from the Union, little Will would find the love and happiness he deserved.

Riding back towards Skibbereen that evening, Dan stopped his horse and trap to survey the blighted fields all around him. Most of Carbery district had been affected by the murrain, with more than a good half of the crop ruined. Even the few acres he had purchased in Poundlick, where he grew mostly oats and barley, had seen heavy losses of potatoes.

He had ridden out there after church on Sunday to discover that most of the crop belonging to his tenants had been destroyed, leaving them fearful. They were decent men with families and he had assured them that, for the time being, he was prepared to forgo the rent payment, due to the circumstances in which they found themselves. As he told them, he had seen the gratitude and relief in their eyes.

Looking around him at the stinking, blackened potato stalks, he hoped that many of the local landowners were prepared do the same for their tenants.

Chapter 9

October 1845

HENRIETTA DONOVAN AND HER CHILDREN STROLLED HAPPILY AROUND the crowded Carbery Agriculture Society Show, admiring the prize-winning livestock on display.

Her eldest boys, Henry and Jerrie, and daughters Ellen, Fanny and Harriet were beside themselves with excitement at seeing all the animals. The big bulls that blew steam from their nostrils; the grunting, smelly pigs; the sheep; the flocks of fowl that squawked and quacked; and the gentle plough horses that let the children pat them. There were ploughs for sale and new items of farm equipment on display, and a tea tent for the ladies to enjoy. Henrietta took great pleasure at browsing the stalls with their rounds of creamy cheese and prize-winning displays of fruit preserves and pickles, to which she was partial.

The children ran around the showground, stopping to watch some small piglets squirming over each other in a pen, and pleaded for Dan to buy them one.

'Please, Dada,' begged Ellen. 'Can you buy us the middle one with the black tip on his ear?'

'Little pigs soon become big smelly ones.' Dan laughed before distracting them with a visit to the toffee-apple man.

*

Later that evening, Dan attended the Agriculture Society Dinner and Henrietta stayed awake until he arrived home at eleven, to see how he had enjoyed it.

'You should have heard them, Henrietta,' he fumed, unable to hide his annoyance. 'All the big landowners talked about was the progress and improvements being made in agriculture that could help them increase their tillage or livestock.'

'That is a good thing, surely?' Henrietta asked, confused.

'These men are blinkered!' he cried. 'The loss of the potato means little to them. How can they not see the devastation it is having on their tenants, who cannot feed their families?'

'Perhaps some of their lands have not been affected,' Henrietta suggested gently as she brushed her hair.

'I have travelled the six parishes in the county and the potatoes are destroyed most everywhere,' Dan explained forcefully. 'Attempts to store undamaged potatoes are proving hopeless. Reverend Traill from Schull and his landowner friend Mr Thomas Somerville have both devised some exacting new storage methods, using special pits to preserve whatever is left of the crop, but I doubt them.'

'Reverend Traill is a most intelligent man?' she ventured.

'Their method is useless! It makes no matter if the potatoes are stored in pits or in cabins or in outhouses, for I suspect they will likely carry the hidden disease that has caused this devastation. I've read reports that it is the same in England and Scotland, and on parts of the continent. Fortunately, these places do not have millions of poor people who depend on the crop like we do.'

'What will happen?' Henrietta asked, suddenly fearful.

'Unless they are helped, the people will go hungry,' Dan said as he undressed. 'It may even lead to famine.'

'Oh, Dan, don't say such a terrible thing!'

'I only speak the truth, but thank heaven that Henry Marmion, Mr Welply, and Mr Clerke from the bank have good sense. They suggested that we have a duty to buy corn to protect the county from famine and each pledged one hundred pounds. But I fear no matter what we try to do, it will not be enough as most have no means of buying food.'

Henrietta grew anxious thinking of their children and the new baby, dark-haired little Margaret, who lay asleep in the crib near her parents' bed.

'I'm sorry, my dear, I did not mean to distress you at this late hour, but I am distracted by it and we have always shared our concerns and worries.'

'Dan, I am here by your side always,' she assured him. 'I am glad that you told the tenants on our lands in Poundlick that you would not take rent from them while they are under such duress.'

'It was the least I could do.'

'My love, you are generous-hearted but are you sure that you can afford it?'

'I will not touch any money that should be used to buy grain for these men's families,' he insisted. 'They are good tenants and will no doubt repay me with their labours when I need it.'

As they kissed goodnight, Henrietta thanked heaven that she had followed her heart ten years ago and married the serious-minded young medical man with the long narrow face, intelligent eyes and quick wit who had swept her off her feet. She loved Dan dearly.

Chapter 10

Creagh

MARY HAD WATCHED AS JOHN AND PAT LOADED THE TWO SQUEALING pigs into the cart to sell at the busy market in Skibbereen.

'I didn't even get a fair price for them,' John had complained bitterly on his return.

Three weeks later he sold their few sheep to O'Driscoll's butchers on North Street.

'We should have got far more for them, but at least we have money in our pockets,' he pronounced firmly.

Mary was relieved that John had managed to collect money for the rent in this way, but worried all the same, for there was very little remaining from the sale of their livestock to keep them.

On his next visit, Henry Marmion, accompanied by his underagent George Hogan, made his position clear to all the tenants of Sir William Wrixon Becher.

'Potatoes or no potatoes, the rent is still to be paid,' he declared.

'But we have nothing to give you,' pleaded Nell Flynn. 'Would you have us take the food from our children's mouths to give to a man who has never known a day's hunger or hardship in his life?'

'Mrs Flynn, there are no exceptions to the rule,' George Hogan replied coldly. 'Those who do not like it know well what the result will be.'

Mary thanked heaven that, unlike Nell, she and John at least had their rent, though little else to feed their family with during the coming winter months.

'Everyone has bad years,' John consoled her, 'but we'll manage to get through the long lean months until we have next summer's potato crop.'

As the days grew shorter, Mary and the children foraged and scoured the hedgerows and shoreline. Early in the morning, she combed the fields for mushrooms, and gathered nettles and herbs. She even paid a secret visit to the orchard at Creagh House, for the house was empty, where she filled her apron and shawl with damaged windfall apples.

John worked all the hours that he was able, doing whatever rough labouring jobs he could get, but there was little enough work to be had with so many other men trying to keep their families fed.

The Sullivans' last sack of potatoes grew emptier by the day and Mary fed the children turnips and eggs. Now, even the poor hens were laying less for she had no meal to feed them.

All around her, the neighbours were beginning to sell their possessions to purchase food and pay their rent. Mary looked around her small cottage to see if she had anything worth selling or pawning.

There was her bristle brush, with its silver handle, that John had bought her when they were courting; a rough brush and a simple comb would suffice now. She studied the pair of fine, soft leather shoes that she rarely wore any more, for they were not sturdy enough to use on the farm. They could certainly go. Then there was John's mother's heavy, black woollen shawl with the tassels. It was far too big for Mary to wear, but it had sentimental value, as did the blue-and-white china jug and plate that had also been his mother's.

She opened the chest where her wedding dress lay carefully folded in the hope that, one day, one of her daughters would wear it. She wasn't ready to part with it yet and closed the lid firmly.

Pat offered to give her a lift into town as he had some business there. He made no comment on the fact that she intended to sell some of his late mother's things. As she climbed down from the cart they arranged to meet later.

Mary swiftly joined the queue of people outside Hegarty's pawn shop, waiting their turn to have their possessions assessed. The women around her carried shawls and dresses, blankets and shirts. Men carried wooden stools, cradles, frock coats and fishing tackle, their eyes downcast as they stood in line. All were ready to sell each and every item in order to buy oats, flour and grain with which to feed their families.

She watched the people ahead of her enter the shop, only to leave with disappointment etched on their faces as they counted the money in their hands before entering the provisions store next door, which was also owned by Denis Hegarty and run by his son.

'Bad cess to you,' an old man in a stained coat and hat shouted angrily as he left. 'Thieving off the poor in their misfortune!'

Mary tried to remain composed as she moved up the line and entered the busy pawn shop. A good-looking woman ahead of her held a blue satin hat trimmed with fine feathers, which she wanted to sell.

'Dublin-bought!' the woman claimed, tossing her hair.

'Fine feathers, but who is to wear them here, my dear?' sneered Mr Hegarty.

'Then what about this?' she asked, producing a golden locket which she dangled in front of him.

The shop owner studied it carefully, weighing it in the palm of his hand as the two of them haggled over the price.

'I could take it to Cork or Dublin,' she argued, her cheeks reddening.

Mary could see that, under her good coat, the woman's shoes were broken down and her dress well worn.

'That is your right, if you want to travel so far,' the pawnbroker said coldly. 'But my offer is eight shillings. That, of course, will include the hat.'

The woman nodded reluctantly. Stretching out her hand, she grabbed the money and pushed past Mary in her rush to escape the place.

Putting a smile on her face, Mary stepped forward, as if her business with Mr Hegarty was an ordinary, everyday matter. She did not want him to sense her nervousness.

'What have you got today, Mrs—'

'Sullivan,' she interjected, placing the shawl on the counter before her. 'A heavy woollen shawl, in perfect condition.'

He said nothing as he lifted up the item and inspected it.

'It was my late mother-in-law's. I would wear it myself but she was of a much taller and broader physique than me.'

She could sense Hegarty's eyes run over her neat, trim figure.

'Hmm,' he muttered, fingering the garment. 'I already have a store room of shawls.'

'But this is of far better quality than most,' Mary insisted, holding her ground. 'I also have a pair of fine leather shoes that are barely worn. I live out in the countryside now but used to work in the town.'

Hegarty feigned disinterest, but he knew the shoes were well made and would appeal to the ladies in the town.

Mary produced the jug and bowl next before finally placing the pretty silver-inlaid bristle hairbrush in front of him with a flourish. Denis Hegarty began to tally some figures, scratching them on a scrap of paper with a pencil he took from behind his ear.

'I can give you twelve shillings for the lot,' he said in his nasal tone. 'Though I'll likely be stuck with them, for who wants to buy such items these days?'

She flushed, for the amount being offered was far less than she had hoped for. Two women pushed and shoved behind her, awaiting their turn.

'I expected that the brush and shoes would be worth more?'

'That is all they are worth to me, Mrs Sullivan,' Hegarty said, the shillings already in his outstretched hand. 'Take it or leave it!'

He gestured for the next customer to come forward.

'Thank you, Mr Hegarty,' Mary said politely, taking the pawn tickets and coins in her palm.

There was enough to buy some grain and oats to sustain her family for a few weeks, but she would not give Denis Hegarty the satisfaction of spending it in his provisions store next door. He'd had enough of her business for one day, and she would go elsewhere for her purchases.

Skibbereen was crowded with people like herself trying to purchase food for their families, but despite their numbers the normal commerce of the town continued, with people still going about their business and visiting the bank and hotels, solicitors and tradesmen.

Out of force of habit, Mary stopped outside Honora Barry's and found herself pushing open the door and entering the dressmaker's shop where she had worked years before. Honora was busy with a customer so Mary stood quietly and watched the older woman narrow the fine pleats on the front bodice of a pretty satin dress. She then proceeded to pin up the cuffs of the gown as the sleeves needed shortening very slightly.

Before her marriage to Jeremiah Collins, Mary's mother had been a seamstress in a big house in Bantry. She used to work by the fireside in the evenings, when Mary and her siblings were children, taking up hems, making and mending garments. She had taught both her daughters how to sew, but Kathleen had no patience for it, injuring herself with the needle and scissors. Mary, on the other hand, enjoyed it and began to make clothes herself from scraps of material.

Her skill with the needle had led to her being hired as an apprentice seamstress at the age of sixteen by Honora Barry in her shop in Skibbereen. The hours were long but Mary soon learned how to cut patterns, sew satins, silks and lace, and make dresses, skirts and jackets. It was at the shop that she had met John Sullivan, the tall, dark-haired young man with the rather hesitant smile and a solitary dimple in his lower left cheek, who constantly seemed to need torn jackets, shirts and trousers mending.

39

It had taken months for him to finally summon the courage to ask if he could visit her at her parents' cottage on her Sunday off.

Within five months she had fallen in love with John, who, with his kind heart and steady way, declared he could not live without her. She had accepted his marriage proposal happily and that summer made her wedding dress. Honora had given her advice along the way and admired the beautiful garment Mary had designed and hand-sewn herself. A married woman, Mary left the shop to look after her husband and growing family.

Mary smiled as she watched her former employer fit the customer's satin gown expertly.

'The bodice and neckline are ideal for someone with your fine figure,' Miss Barry complimented.

'Will my dress be ready in time?' the dark-haired young woman fretted. 'We are visiting Dublin and attending a few balls.'

'Certainly, for it will take only two days to make these slight alterations,' the older woman promised, tapping the pincushion that was tied to her wrist.

'I'll be with you in a few minutes, Mary,' acknowledged Honora Barry as she escorted her customer to the discreet changing room to help her out of the gown.

The stylish young woman re-emerged soon after in a beautiful fitted coat with a velvet-trimmed collar and cuffs. Miss Barry accompanied her to the shop door before turning to her visitor.

'Motherhood suits you, Mary, for you look as pretty as ever,' she told her, before enquiring after John and the children.

Mary nodded. 'They are all well. Though we lost most of our crop and have had to sell our animals.'

'The government needs to step in and do something about giving assistance,' pronounced the dressmaker in sympathy.

'Miss Barry, I came to ask whether you have any spare work – alterations, repairs or mending – that I could do?'

Mary worried that she was being presumptuous, but could see that Miss Barry was considering her offer, knowing well that Mary was one of the finest seamstresses she had ever employed.

'I need the work,' Mary admitted, 'and could do it for a reasonable rate.'

'Normally I wouldn't have any spare work,' the dressmaker said, arching her grey eyebrows, 'but Catherine left me high and dry just last week. She's moved to Cork City where she and her betrothed are getting married next month. Her position is free, but with the way things are at present I do not intend taking on another employee for the workroom. There is, however, still work to be done.'

'Please, Miss Barry, give me the chance. I won't let you down.'

Honora Barry smiled. 'Mary, if there is one thing I know it is that you are a good, reliable worker. So perhaps such an arrangement might suit us both for the present.'

'Oh, that would be grand, Miss Barry. When will I start?'

'Well, you can start today, for I have this bundle of men's clothing that needs repairing. It's just sitting up in the workroom, and Jane and I are far too busy to attend to it at present. Would you be able to have it done and returned by next week?'

'Yes,' Mary promised.

The bag of mending was heavy and she was glad that Pat was still in town with his cart so she could get a lift home, for she still needed to go and purchase some oats and flour.

'Well, isn't that a piece of luck, getting some work?' congratulated her brother-in-law as they drove home. 'Though there is little enough for me except hauling and carting stuff.'

Mary knew how hard it was for Pat of late. A few times a week he came to the cottage to eat. They didn't have much but she could not begrudge him a share of what was in the pot, for when he could he provided them with a rabbit or hare, or even a fish to eat.

Passing Oldcourt, the small harbour and inlet overlooking the sea and the river, Pat and Mary watched two ships that had journeyed from Liverpool to West Cork's fishing port of Baltimore and then upriver, carrying grain bound for McCarthy's brewery. Men worked tirelessly unloading the stores of grain on to four smaller boats and barges that would transport it to the quays and the brewery's piers.

'O'Connell and his committee in Dublin called on the Lord Lieutenant and the authorities to stop the export of food and corn, and to halt brewing and distilling so that the grain can be used to feed the people,' Pat said in despair. 'But they refuse to do it.'

'How can they use grain for porter when people can't even afford to buy it?' Mary protested.

'Some day they'll pay for making the like of us scratch and scrape for food,' Pat said coldly, urging the horse homewards.

Chapter 11

November 1845

WHEN THE DAYS GREW SHORT, JOHN SULLIVAN DISCOVERED THAT THE few potatoes he had stored in the potato pit had all rotted.

'Bad cess, every single one of them has turned black,' he told his wife, disgusted. 'Even the smell of them would make you sick.'

Mary could not understand how such a thing could happen to saved healthy potatoes lifted from the ground, but the same thing had happened to all their neighbours'. Everyone was at their wits' end, for they still had the winter to endure and the long months of spring and summer ahead of them before the next potato harvest.

Mary sat darning and patching, and repairing hems and tears late into the night until her fingers grew tired and her eyes became heavy with sleep. The money she earned from Honora Barry was scarcely enough to buy a bag of meal each week and the odd jug of buttermilk or piece of smoked fish, but if she was frugal, she and her family would survive these hard times.

A few weeks later, with not a bag of oats or grain in the place, Mary decided without a second thought to take her wedding dress and a lace blouse to sell at Hegarty's. A sack of flour was now more valuable to her than any item of clothing.

She still had her hens but she suspected someone was stealing their eggs, for whenever she or John went to check on them, a few would be missing. She told the children to keep an eye on the birds and watch for anyone who was lurking around their field and hen-house.

To her dismay, it wasn't long before one of her good-laying hens disappeared too.

'Maybe a fox or dog or cat got her,' consoled John.

'It was no hungry animal,' she retorted. 'There is no sign of a feather even, so I know well 'tis a thief who took her and stole the food from under our noses.'

'Hush,' he said, trying to calm her. 'If it were a hungry person who was desperate, we cannot begrudge them.'

'Well, you may say that when all the hens I have kept are gone and we don't have even an egg for the children to eat or a hen for the pot, while others feast on them!' she said, angered by her husband's reaction.

She warned Con and Nora to be on the lookout for the culprit.

'Mark my words, they will come back again.'

'Mammy, I saw Paddy Flynn searching one of the nests under the bush,' Con confided in her. 'You know, the hen with the white speckles, and I think he took her egg. I tried to talk to him but he just ran away home.'

'Never fear, pet. I'll keep my eye on him and his brothers.'

Annoyance burned inside her that Nell Flynn, to whom they had always been good, would use them in such a fashion.

'They have little enough, God help them,' soothed John, 'and my mother was always fond of her.'

'Well, 'tis not your mother she'll be dealing with if they steal any more of my eggs!'

At night Mary listened, and during the day she watched. Then, one evening when she was about to lie down, Mary heard the hens squawking. She rushed outside in the darkness to find a figure just about to lift another protesting bird away from her roost.

'Who is that?' she called. 'Is that you, Nell, or one of your thieving family trying to rob us?'

Mary lunged at the figure and caught them by the shoulder. As she made them drop the hen and pushed them towards the cottage, they let out a sob.

In the gloom of the fire, Nell stood there, defiant.

'You have nine fat hens and my family have nothing,' she declared.

'At the rate you are going, soon I will have no hens,' Mary retorted angrily. 'They will all have found their way into your pot. What am I to feed my family with then?'

'It's just a hen,' Nell wheedled. 'A stupid old hen.'

'It's my hen and she's a fine layer.'

'There is not a pick of food in the place or even a few leaves for the tea!' Nell sobbed. 'And we have Hogan threatening to put us out for we have no rent. Poor Tom is addled with it.'

Mary felt guilty immediately, but she had her own family to think of.

'Nellie, don't let me catch you near our hens!' she warned.

'It won't happen again,' her neighbour promised.

'I am sorry for your troubles,' she offered as she watched the forlorn figure of Nell in her black shawl walk slowly back across the fields.

Overcome with pity for her neighbour, the next morning Mary sent Con over to Nell's with two turnips and a screw of tea leaves.

Chapter 12

Skibbereen
December 1845

'THEY SAY THAT A THIRD OF THE CROP IS LOST IN SOME PLACES,' TIM McCarthy Downing explained to the huge crowd at the packed public meeting in Skibbereen Courthouse to discuss the potato failure. 'But here it is far worse than in other parts of the county, with half or even two-thirds of the crop gone. Given such circumstances and the situation we face, I suggest that we set up a fund to make provision for famine in the coming months.'

There was instant approval for raising such a fund.

Dan's heart gladdened to see landlords, labourers, farmers, and both Protestant and Catholic clergymen coming together. They all knew that the state of affairs was grave.

Sir Robert Peel, the prime minister, had been forced to resign over the repeal of the Corn Laws, which would have permitted the import of duty-free grain. Peel at least had the decency to order a larger shipment of Indian corn from America to Ireland, and had appointed a Relief Commission for Ireland under Randolph Routh to distribute it.

Only a month ago, Daniel O'Connell and the Mansion House Committee in Dublin had made an appeal to the Queen herself, informing her of the situation across the country and the effect it was having on her poor subjects. Queen Victoria's reply had been to advise her Irish subjects that they were in her care constantly. To Dan's mind, that care was certainly not adequate!

'I propose that we appeal to the government for public works,' Reverend Robert Traill said, getting to his feet to address the meeting.

'Hear! Hear!'

'I have written to the heads of government in both England and Ireland concerning the scarcity, and also to all the landlords in my parish, requesting that they let their tenants keep their grain, in order to spare seed potatoes for planting next year's crop,' he continued. 'And I suggest to all the clergy present here that they do the same.'

Father John Fitzpatrick and the other church men present nodded heartily in agreement. Perhaps the landlords would listen to them!

'With regards to Reverend Traill's suggestion of public works, I propose that we apply to the government for assistance for the deepening of the river Ilen, which is badly needed, and for the construction of a military barracks,' Henry Townsend added. 'For these works would be productive and good for the town.'

Next, a young tradesman in the crowd stood up bravely.

'Property has its duties as well as its rights,' he reminded them, looking directly at the landowners and influential people present. 'I am speaking for the humblest, and I ask that landlords make a reduction on rents, for people cannot pay them.'

There came shouts of approval and applause, but a few regarded him stony-faced.

Dan admired the man's courage in speaking out at such a gathering, and hoped that his words would have some effect.

'Now I turn to medical matters,' Dan said, serious. 'There have been a few small outbreaks of scarlet fever and smallpox in the district. I recommend that a section of the fever hospital be isolated for such cases. Unfortunately, further building at Skibbereen workhouse has ceased due to lack of payment by the Board of Works.

However, this work must be done, for the people are in a poor state facing into the winter. Scarlet fever is spreading from the west and smallpox from the east!'

He could see the alarm in the eyes of all gathered at the mention of such contagion.

'Of course, Dr Donovan,' Tim McCarthy Downing responded. 'You must take whatever steps you believe are necessary.'

As the meeting came to an end, Thomas Somerville of Castle-townsend asked anyone present who was willing to set up and organize a relief committee in Skibbereen to remain behind. As a doctor, Dan felt it was his duty and volunteered immediately to become involved.

There was much work to be done if they were to alleviate the growing distress of the people of the district during the hard winter months ahead, for the many who had no income or food, Dan believed, now faced the very real threat of starvation.

Chapter 13

Creagh
July 1846

JOHN HAD PLANTED OUT THE SEED POTATOES IN MARCH, THE DAY AFTER St Patrick's Day.

'Mary, will you give up your old vegetable patch?' he'd pleaded, 'so I can set more seed potatoes?'

'No, I need it for the vegetables!' she had refused stubbornly, for after last year she intended to grow even more cabbages and turnips.

The winter had been the worst since they had married, for they had little to eat except what they foraged or what Mary could purchase with the money she made. She'd killed the last of their hens over three weeks ago as the bird was better in her family's bellies than in her neighbours'.

They had cleared their two fields of any last trace of the diseased potato crop. They had raked up and burned the stalks and debris, and turned the soil, before John dug fresh new drills for planting. He and Pat had carted heavy loads of iodine-rich seaweed to their fields from the rocky shoreline, and spread it over the beds to fertilize them and feed the plants. They hoped that it would give them a better yield of potatoes.

She and John were like two broody hens with a clutch of eggs as they watched over this year's new crop. They inspected their plants nervously for any sign of blight or leaf damage, but were relieved as the months passed and the drills grew tall and strong.

'This will be the best harvest ever,' boasted Flor, sitting on the wall across from his cottage. He sucked at his clay pipe as he and grey-haired Molly surveyed the potato plants all around them. 'It will be a fine crop to make up for last year.'

'They say it promises to be good, but we must not take the crop for granted,' John warned, unable to shake off the nagging fear that the blight would return.

'Brother, you are worrying over nothing,' teased Pat. 'For it is clear to all eyes that this year's potatoes are thriving.'

Looking out across the fields at the pale pink-and-white potato blossom which blew and danced like a wave, Mary was reassured that their potato pits and sacks soon would be full again with this year's harvest. Once their crop was stored for the year ahead, it would not be long before the hard times were behind them.

John and Pat were busy getting in the barley and wheat crop for their landlord.

'The grain stores will be full,' John remarked as they sat around the fire, sharing a pot of gruel and griddle cakes. 'Though most of this year's crop is bound for Liverpool, Leeds and London.'

'Why must we feed the factories and workers of Britain,' pondered Pat angrily, 'when all we have is gruel to keep us until our own crop comes in?'

'It has always been the way.' John shrugged. 'But it's the wrong way.'

'I'm telling you, it's time that things change.' Pat's eyes flashed angrily. 'We can no longer be like an old dog lying under its master's table, waiting for scraps. The time is coming for the hound to rise up and bite.'

'Will you hush up with your talk, Patrick?' Mary warned, noticing that young Con and Nora were glued to his words. 'Do you want to bring trouble down on this house and our children?'

'No!' He lapsed into silence and ate his gruel.

Con's eyes shone as he looked admiringly at his uncle and Mary thanked heaven that at least her son was too young to be involved with Pat and his group of Young Irelander friends.

Pat disappeared in a huff as soon as he had finished eating.

'Why did you chase him out of the place?' rebuked John later. 'You know it's lonely for him, being on his own.'

'He should have thought about that four years ago when he broke off his engagement to Frances McCarthy and chased after Julia Carmody.'

'Unfortunately, a man is ruled by his heart not his head.'

'I'm not sure that I would call it his heart!' Mary teased. 'He threw Frances over, with her father's ten acres of land and a cottage, for that black-haired beguiler he paraded around the town with.'

'Julia was not the woman for him,' John admitted. 'She'd not live on Pat's scrapeen of land.'

'Well, Frances is happy now, and her husband has charge of the land since her father took ill last year and died. I hear she is due a second child soon.'

'It upsets him thinking of what he lost.'

'Maybe Pat will find another girl.'

She felt a surge of pity for her handsome brother-in-law. With his long dark eyelashes, deep-brown eyes and easy smile, he had a certain way with women, but still lived alone in a small cabin and spent many of his nights drinking porter or talking politics and rebellion in the local *síbín* with another few wild men like himself.

'He will be a lucky man if he finds himself a girl as beautiful and kind hearted as the one I found.'

Mary laughed. She had forgotten what a charmer her husband could be!

Dusk had fallen, and together they listened to the unexpected rain which had begun to patter on the thatch roof. John ran outside to look at the drills and returned soaked to the skin but happy.

'Will you stop your worrying?' Mary urged him as she pulled off his sodden shirt and made him sit by the glowing turf. 'The potatoes are grand, just grand.'

Chapter 14

August 1846

MARY WOKE TO THE AWFUL CLOYING SMELL OF LAST SUMMER. DREAD filled her heart, for John was already racing outside, pulling on his britches as he went. Gripped with fear, she ran after him across the fields, for she could see the potato stalks drooping, their leaves already spotted with black.

Her mouth dry and heart pounding, she knelt down and began to dig frantically with her hands to unearth the potatoes. Her fingers closed around what seemed like three or four large, healthy ones, but as she lifted them out of the soil Mary could feel their flesh was already putrid and foul. She tried another plant, and another. It was useless. Every clump she touched was marked with disease. The potatoes in their mud-stained skins were already decaying, rotting in her hand.

As she shook off the clay, she could see the lumper potatoes were black in parts, soft and oozing, the stench so pervasive that it made her queasy. She looked over at her husband, despair already written on his face.

'Look at them!' he shouted, back bent digging in the earth with his shovel as he tried desperately to save their potatoes from the deadly blight that had spread through their crop overnight. 'They're destroyed.'

How could this happen again, she asked herself, when John had been more than vigilant and had tended their crop with such care!

The children had been woken by the commotion and ran outside. Con, Nora and Tim's faces went white with shock as their father, streaked with mud and the stinking sludge, shouted at them to help dig and lift the potatoes from the ground.

'Help us to save them!' John ordered loudly.

Nora began to cry at the memory of it all.

'Any good potato, even if it is very small but is firm and hard,' he said, softening his tone, 'throw it in the bucket.'

Little Annie, terrified by the smell and strangeness of it all, clung tightly to her mother as Mary took in the disaster around her, for every field as far as she could see was the same.

Con went on his knees in the dirt, digging at the plants to see what could be saved. Somehow, like a thief in the night, the pestilence had returned to poison their crop. John, meanwhile, had crossed to their other field. From the slump of his shoulders, Mary could tell that it too had been affected.

'Rotten! Every one of them!' he shouted despairingly as he checked each line of drills.

Nora worked beside her mother. Her little hands and face were spattered with the filthy slime. Tim went down the rows, checking the fetid piles for any healthy potato they might have overlooked, and Annie trailed behind him with a little bucket. Mary continued to pull at plants, lifting the potatoes. The stench around them had worsened and hung heavy in the air, over their fields, and the acres and acres of land. It clung to her hair and skin, and was so bad that she could taste it.

Surely to God, somewhere here there must be a few of their crop untouched by the murrain; a few that they could harvest and use!

Someone was crying, and it was a terrible sound in the stillness.

The family worked for hours. Mary's nails were broken, and her fingers were red and sore. Every plant, stalk and drill was checked, and the few hard lumpers that were found were put carefully in the tin bucket.

The children were caked in mud, going from row to row with their heads and backs bent, like blackbirds searching the festering stalks and clumps for a small, firm pearly potato.

Mary's back ached, but she couldn't give up.

In the distance she could see Pat, digging his patch. She prayed that he had been luckier than they had. Flor and Molly were moving from drill to drill, carefully doing the same. In the fields all about her, Denis and Brigid and their children, and Nell, Tom and their sons were all digging frantically, searching their drills in vain. Every holding as far as the eye could see was already ravaged by the fast-spreading murrain.

Mary went inside and returned with two cans of water and some leftover griddle cake, which she shared between her family.

'John, you must take a rest,' she begged, passing him the can of water. She had never seen him in such a state. Soaked in sweat and covered in mud.

'I cannot stop.'

He took a few gulps of water and threw the rest over his face and head.

Con, also sweating and filthy, stood shoulder to shoulder with his father, trying to help him. Nora looked as if she were about to collapse, and usually carefree Tim was grim-faced as he searched through every clutch of potatoes, desperate to find a few that they could eat.

'Da, I got four,' he proclaimed proudly, carrying them carefully to the near-empty tin bucket.

Mary tried not to give in to the mounting panic she was feeling at the devastation of their two fields and the complete loss of their crop this time.

John, agitated, continued with his shovel. Digging, digging and digging . . .

Eventually, Mary sat down and told the exhausted children to rest.

At last, John too put his shovel down and looked out over their fields. There was nothing more they could do.

The children were scared, their eyes full of fear. As they huddled together, Mary vowed that she would not let her children go hungry . . .

Part Two

Chapter 15

MARY STARED OUT AT HER FAMILY'S DEVASTATED LAND AND THE stinking acres all around them, unable to believe that such a calamity had befallen them again.

In the bright morning sunlight things looked worse. The foul stench still hung in the air, and the drills were filled with the rotting mass of stalks and potatoes where they had dug and laboured the previous day. How in God's name would they survive this?

All night John had thrashed and turned beside her in the bed, restless yet exhausted. The children still lay asleep, curled up in their rough blankets like little mice.

Tears welled in Mary's eyes as she surveyed everything the blight had taken from them. This time it had left them with nothing . . . Nothing to eat, sell, or pay their rent with. A deep fear at what lay ahead gripped her heart. She and John no longer had a purse of hidden money, nor even a penny or a shilling to call their own. Everything had depended on them raising this new potato crop.

She watched the smoke begin to curl from her neighbours' chimneys as people began to rise and process the full extent of the catastrophe wreaked upon them. From what she could see, nobody had escaped the destruction of their crop.

John came outside to join her, gathering his thoughts as he assessed the damage.

'If it is all across the county, I don't know what we can do, for we are all ruined.'

'We will manage somehow,' she said, resting against him. 'We are both strong and good workers. That has to count for something.'

'It will count for nothing when the landlord sends his men for the rent, or when the children cry with hunger pains in their bellies.'

'Don't say such a thing!'

'It is the truth.' John sounded utterly forlorn.

In all the years she had loved him and slept beside him and borne his children, Mary had never heard such despair in his voice. Her husband was the one who usually rallied her when she felt low or worried, or was tired out from the children.

'John Sullivan, I will not have you speak like that! We will do what we need to survive. I will not have us put out of this cottage and off the land, or see our children go hungry.'

His blue eyes held hers and she could tell he sensed her fury.

'You are right. We must act quickly and make ready for the hungry months ahead. The Sullivans have always fought for this place, and I'll not be the one to give it up to Wrixon Becher or anyone else!'

Relief washed over Mary and she took his rough hand in hers.

'Aren't we are a grand pair?' John said, leaning over and kissing her gently, as if they hadn't a care in the world.

She felt overwhelmed with emotion momentarily. They both knew well that this time, with no animals or possessions to sell, terrible times lay ahead, but at least they were together.

Brigid Leary called down to her, red-eyed and weary.

'The children are so upset that I'm awake half the night,' she confided. 'Denis was weeping like a boy over the potatoes. I've never seen him like that before.'

Mary hugged her, glad of their friendship, as they shared their fears and worries.

'I don't know what Denis and I will do, for we haven't a penny to our name. If he doesn't get work, there is no saying what will happen to us.'

'He and John will both find something,' Mary encouraged her, not wanting to see Brigid more upset.

Around midday Pat came over. He looked rough and dishevelled, and clearly had been drinking.

'Drowning my sorrows, like most of the men in the district,' he admitted, gulping down two cans of cold water and pleading for half a griddle cake to set him right.

'You are a saint of a woman,' he thanked Mary as he ate quickly.

Mary said little in return but resolved there would be no more food for him under their roof when he was still in the throes of drink. A man who wasted his money on porter would not be welcome at her table any longer, for she had the children to think of.

'I was down in the *sibín* last night. The pestilence is through the district. Not a field or a farm in the whole of Carbery is untouched. I tell you, there was a good crowd of us, all destroyed after yesterday. Not a man among us will be able to pay the gale rent when Marmion comes looking for it.'

'We've not a penny either,' John admitted angrily. 'I have to get work.'

'First thing in the morning we'll take the horse and cart and set off to search,' Pat agreed. 'Two strong men with a cart must have some chance of paid labour.'

Mary hoped that her brother-in-law was right.

She was intent on travelling to town tomorrow to ask Honora Barry – nay, beg her – if she had any more sewing or mending for her. Every penny she earned would be needed to help feed the family. She had no intention of sitting by idly and watching her children weaken and starve.

The Sullivan children were fretful and anxious. They could sense how bad things were and Annie clung to her mother like a little shadow. Mary did her best to reassure them that all would be well. She could not destroy their innocence and let them know the seriousness of their situation and the distress they might face.

'Stop mooning around like a load of sick lambs. Let's go up the fields and hunt for early blackberries,' she coaxed, despite the strange heavy weariness and fear that assailed her, for she was desperate to distract them. 'Now, grab a tin bucket and some cans, and we'll be off!'

No matter the scrapes and scratches from the thorns and brambles, the children enjoyed themselves. Patch barked with excitement as he ran among them. Little Annie opened her mouth like a baby bird to eat the fruits, getting used to the sweet but tart taste, her face stained with blackberry juice.

'I wish we had blackberries to eat all year round.' Tim grinned, his tin overflowing with plump berries.

Back home, the smell of the pestilence lingered everywhere, awful in its intensity. Mary went to boil the few remaining potatoes but they had already turned grey and sludgy in the bottom of the bucket. Nausea washed over her as she threw them out.

As she fetched a few turnips from her patch, she thanked heaven that they looked healthy and seemed not to have been affected by the murrain. At least she had something to put in the pot and feed the children with in the hungry days ahead.

Chapter 16

Poundlick, County Cork

AS HE RODE AROUND THE DISTRICT VISITING THE UNION AND HIS patients, Dan grew accustomed to the sulphuric smell of rotting potatoes that emanated from field after field. It lingered heavily in the warm air and was nauseating.

The signs of destruction were everywhere. He could see where tenants had tried to dig and pull the rotting crop from the rows of potato drills with their wilted blackened stalks and leaves. They had hoped to save some of the crop only to discover the putrid potatoes that broke apart in their hands and on their spades. Such was their atrocious state they could not be used even to feed an animal.

From Ballydehob to Skeaghanore, Caheragh to Roscarbery, Glandore to Union Hall, Creagh to Baltimore, everywhere he rode it was a terrible sight to see. Most of the tenants grew nothing else in their small fields – no barley, no corn, not even turnips. Looking across the acres and acres of destroyed potato fields, he worried how the people would manage to feed themselves, let alone pay their rent, which was now due.

Dan had then ridden out to Poundlick to inspect his own lands. Every single potato field there had been affected, and he could see fear and desperation written in the wary eyes of his tenants. His

63

acres of barley had flourished and were due to be harvested, but in the small potato fields beside each cabin and cottage lay the rotting detritus of the crop upon which his tenants depended.

'Dr Donovan, you can see yourself that all is lost to us,' admitted Tim Driscoll – one of the tenant farmers – approaching Dan as he got down from his horse. 'The murrain has destroyed us, for we have nothing.'

'I can see that, Mr Driscoll,' the doctor said, looking at the neatly kept holding where five small, stick-thin children gazed out at him nervously.

'I'm afraid, sir, that I cannot keep my promise to pay the rent due to you at this time,' the farmer said, his gaze clear and unwavering, man to man, one father to another.

Tim Driscoll was a good worker, who took pride in his holding and was not one to shirk his responsibility. Dan had respect for the already gaunt-looking man. How could he possibly insist that this fellow pay his long-overdue rent when he had a wife and children to care for!

It was the same for the rest of his tenants – the McCarthys, the Lynches and the Murphys – who all had large families to feed. The half-year rent was due, but looking at the ravaged fields around him and knowing the men and women who tilled and tended this land, Dan could not put any extra demand on them this time. He knew well there was not a penny to pay him. These people lived hand to mouth at the best of times.

This trouble was no fault of theirs, so the only decent thing he could do to ease their burden was to forgo his rent again this year. It would affect his finances badly, which no doubt would displease his bank manager, but Dan would not impose such penury on his tenants or threaten to evict them.

'The barley has done well this year, but given the failure of the potato crop and your need to sustain and feed your families, there will be no rent collected here,' he reassured them.

Men shook his hands warmly with relief and gratitude.

'You're a gentleman, Dr Donovan,' pronounced Michael McCarthy, his eyes filled with tears. 'God bless you.'

The men would help to harvest his barley and he would make sure that each received a large bag of grain in return for their work.

As he bade them farewell, he turned his horse and set off for Skibbereen, for he had an important meeting that evening with the relief committee.

Chapter 17

Skibbereen

'I'VE NEVER SEEN SUCH PANIC AND FEAR, FOR THE PEOPLE ARE ALREADY weak and starving,' Dan said, enraged, at the urgent meeting being held in the Union workhouse. 'Can the bureaucratic fools in London and Dublin not see that with nearly the entire Irish potato crop devastated, hunger is surely staring us in the face?'

'We have done our best to buy oatmeal and Indian corn from the Cork depot for the needy,' their designated chairman Thomas Somerville admitted as the committee members voiced their concerns. 'But without government assistance, I too fear we are facing impending disaster.'

'The potato crop is all but destroyed,' declared Father John Fitzpatrick, his voice racked with emotion, 'and hungry hordes of labourers travel the streets and countryside with poverty depicted on their countenance. Relief is urgently needed, and I deplore the many landlords who have not subscribed, and those who have given only stingily!'

'There are landlords here who get rental of two thousand pounds a year from Skibbereen and have only given a measly two hundred pounds in relief,' denounced Tim McCarthy Downing. 'That is less than they would spend at the races in Cheltenham! I appeal to those same landlords to reduce rents.'

'The government has sanctioned public works for Skibbereen, which will employ the destitute, but unfortunately, little work has commenced,' Michael Galwey, the local magistrate and a cousin of Dan's, complained.

'The men desperately need work,' added Reverend Fitzpatrick. 'I did my best to ensure that men from Bridgetown and Windmill Lane and the district were employed as labourers building the new school, but now, with the school finally finished, unfortunately there is no further work for those poor souls.'

'Without employment, the whole fabric of society may dissolve,' worried landlord Lionel Fleming.

'How are the people to buy food?' Father Fitzpatrick interjected. 'Are there any plans by the government to supply food and meal to the needy?'

'Unfortunately not,' said Thomas Somerville. 'The government food depots are instructed to remain closed until the end of the year, even though food supplies are already scarce in the town.'

'Gentlemen, we do not have months, or even weeks, to solve this!' Dan warned. 'If the authorities do not take action immediately to feed these people, there will be terrible consequences. I have already seen outbreaks of cholera, which I suspect were caused by eating rotten potatoes.'

He could see dismay written on the faces of the good men of the town.

'Over six hundred people have already been admitted to the workhouse, and we have doubled the number of patients in the fever hospital,' he informed them. 'Though they are very sick, some must sleep three to a bed. It is intolerable! Unless there is some sort of intervention, these numbers will continue to grow.'

'Doctor, we are all in agreement with you,' reassured Thomas Somerville. 'We have already written letters of appeal with regards to the crisis, to little avail. So I suggest instead that we send a delegation from here to meet the new Lord Lieutenant, Lord Bessborough, in Dublin to inform him of the alarming state of Skibbereen district and to request relief, to save it from anarchy.'

'What if the Lord Lieutenant does nothing?' Dan demanded.

'Then the delegation will go on to London, if necessary,' Somerville replied firmly, 'to meet the prime minister, Lord John Russell, and appeal to him for relief!'

There was unanimous approval for such action to be taken, though Dan worried that it would have little effect.

'Thank the Lord the public works are finally going to open,' declared a delighted Michael Galwey the following week, on hearing that the prime minister had introduced the new Labour Act, which would employ people on public works relief schemes. 'It's exactly what we hoped for.'

'We must apply immediately to the Board of Works' presentment sessions and put forward proposals for new roads, piers and harbours that will benefit the district,' urged Thomas Somerville.

When the relief committee discovered that many of the most useful and beneficial proposals had been rejected, Dan and his fellow committee members were perplexed.

'A road to a bit of a village? Building a new wall across from an empty field? It makes no sense!'

'Work is work,' Michael Galwey consoled. 'At least the men will be paid and able to buy food.'

Chapter 18

September 1846

FATHER FITZPATRICK WALKED PROUDLY AROUND THE RECENTLY OPENED St Fachtna's School on North Street. For the past two years he had put much work and effort into its planning, organization and construction.

Now the school was finished, it did his heart good to see the rows of new pupils, girls and boys. However, some were ragged and gaunt, poorly nourished with scabs around their lips. It was a sight different from that which he had expected – rows of healthy, energetic pupils – but, despite the calamity that raged around them, he could see a spark in the children's eyes that showed they were still eager and ready to learn.

The large girls' classroom upstairs was already half full, there were only a few places left in the boys' one downstairs, and the numbers were growing in the two smaller infant classes. The parents of Skibbereen, despite their troubles, were determined that their children would enjoy an education that few of them ever had.

As he listened to the young sing-song voices reciting the alphabet with their teacher, he gave thanks that these children had the opportunity to fill their hearts and minds with learning. Education had been the way forward for him. He had attended a small school for boys in Fermoy, run by his older brother James, a priest. With an aching thirst for knowledge and learning, he had decided to follow in his brother's footsteps and later study for the priesthood. A choice he had never regretted.

Bidding the children farewell, he returned home to discover a man in broken-down boots and a stained top coat that flapped about his bony legs waiting patiently for him.

'Come inside,' he offered, leading Jeremiah O'Driscoll into the dining room.

He asked Bridey to provide them both with a cup of tea, and gestured for Mr O'Driscoll to sit down. He listened considerately as the man outlined the dire circumstances in which he found himself: yet another rent demand from his landlord, Reverend Stephen Fitzgerald Townsend.

'I cannot read or write, Father,' the man admitted, embarrassed. 'So I am begging for your help to intercede on my behalf and write a letter from me to Reverend Fitzgerald Townsend, pleading for leniency.'

Father Fitzpatrick sighed, for he had heard this story from many tenants, repeated over and over again. So many were illiterate! Hopefully the new school would help to change things.

'I have done my best, Father. Last year I sold all we possess to pay rent, but now there is nothing left, and my wife and children are suffering distress, and the hunger—' The man's voice broke. 'I appealed to Reverend Fitzgerald Townsend's agent, but he insists that the rent must be paid or we will lose our holding and be put off it.'

Father John had grown up as part of a large family. His had been a relatively humble background, for he'd been raised on a smallholding and knew well the concerns of tenants such as Jeremiah O'Driscoll.

It had been almost eleven years since he'd been appointed parish priest here and he had already written officially to every landlord in the district – Lord Carbery and Reverend Stephen Fitzgerald Townsend, who owned nearly half the town and townlands between them, along with R. H. Becher and Sir William Wrixon Becher. He'd pleaded for leniency for their tenants and asked that rents be forgone during this time of affliction, citing the deplorable condition of the people, but all to no avail.

However, if writing a letter was the only hope this poor man had, Father John would not deny him the opportunity to state his case in yet another appeal to Reverend Stephen Fitzgerald Townsend, one of the largest and wealthiest landowners in Carbery district.

This so-called man of the church was another oppressive absentee landlord, who lived in England. He had demonstrated not a bit of interest or care for his tenants and their families in Ireland, and their deprived circumstances, but perhaps this time might be different.

'My father, my grandfather and great-grandfather were all tenants of the family,' Jeremiah O'Driscoll explained. 'We have always paid what is due, and I give my word to Reverend Fitzgerald Townsend that once things improve and our crops have returned, I will pay him the rent.'

Father John Fitzpatrick could see the man's sincerity and concentrated on writing down his words exactly, listing carefully all the relevant details.

Bridey appeared with a tray with the tea and two cups, and Jeremiah O'Driscoll stared as she poured their drinks.

'Is my meal ready yet?' Father John enquired.

'Aye, Father, I have it kept warm for you.'

'Then you can serve it now, Bridey. Please bring two plates, for Mr O'Driscoll and I will share my repast.'

He could see by his housekeeper's disgruntled expression that she did not approve, but she returned and served them with two plates of bacon, cabbage and mashed turnip.

Father John watched with satisfaction as his guest ate slowly, savouring every mouthful. Afterwards, he insisted that the man take the remaining bacon and vegetables home to his wife and children. Then he presented to Mr O'Driscoll the letter he had written for him to make his mark.

'I will send it to England tomorrow by post and shall contact you if I get a reply,' he promised.

The man nodded, full of hope that his letter writing would bear fruit as he bade the priest goodnight.

Father John yawned, for he had lost count of the number of similar letters he had written.

'I keep warning you, Father, not to let those people through the door, but you pay not a bit of heed to me,' Bridey sighed heavily, her plump face flushed as she tidied away the plates.

'I know you have only my interests at heart, Bridey, but Mr O'Driscoll is one of my parishioners,' he reminded her gently, as she flounced out of the room.

Chapter 19

Creagh

'THE TICKETS ARE BEING ISSUED FOR THE NEW RELIEF WORKS,' DENIS Leary had told John when he called in to the Sullivans' cottage to share the news with his neighbour. 'You and Pat and Flor should sign on, for everyone needs the work!'

The following day, Pat had taken the three of them in the horse and cart to register their names in the hope that they would get on the scheme. John and Pat returned with their tickets, but poor Flor was upset because an official had judged him too old for heavy labouring.

'There is more strength in me than in most men!' he complained bitterly.

A few days later Mary watched as John made ready to leave for his job on the new roadworks.

'The pay is said to be poor,' she said with worry, 'and the work very hard.'

'Will you whisht, Mary! Hard work never killed a man,' he said quietly, pulling on his brown jacket and worn leather boots. 'And 'tis better surely for me to earn the few pennies we need every day than to sit home and watch you and the children go hungry?'

'Of course.' She smiled and reached out to bid him well.

He set out to join a few of the neighbours who were walking to the works along with Pat, Denis and Tom Flynn. They had all been surprised when Tom, who complained of a bad hip, had been issued a ticket for the new scheme, but Flor had been refused.

Mary was filled with hope that now John was working, the huge burden of feeding and keeping their family would ease a little. At last there would be meal and oats for the pot, and perhaps a little bread to keep the starvation and hunger off them. The whole family was weak and badly in need of nourishment, and every penny he earned would give them a little more strength.

'Oh, you're soaked to the skin,' she fussed, when John returned that evening. She took off his jacket and shirt, and put them near the fire to dry.

'I'm fine,' he protested as she made him rest easy and warm himself in a blanket, huddled close to the turf fire.

'Where are you working?'

'Over beyond Oldcourt.'

'Are they putting a new road there?'

'Aye, some kind of road down near the harbour.' He shook his head heavily. 'They have us digging out the ground for it, while some are set to breaking stones.'

'At least you will earn some money.'

'Eight pence a day,' he said bitterly. 'That is all they are paying us, and the like of Tom Flynn get even less. All the Board of Works wants is for us to be employed doing some sort of heavy work. One man told me that the works schemes are designed to occupy the like of us building roads and walls to nowhere!'

'Why would they do such a thing?' Mary puzzled as she warmed up the yellow meal for him.

John was all done in, too tired to talk. He went to bed early, and fell into a heavy sleep, snoring as he lay against her.

Every day, John would set off early in the morning with his head down and only a cut of bread or a few spoons of gruel inside him. He would return home exhausted, saying little to Mary about the works. She would serve him an evening meal of stew with wild onion, turnip and cabbage, for there was little left to forage these days.

'We do the work they ask, yet they still haven't paid us,' John grumbled. 'Not a penny for any of the men. How can we keep on working and get nothing in return? A poor young fellow collapsed beside me this morning. He told me his belly was empty these past two days. A man cannot work on that!'

'What will happen?'

'We complained to the foreman but he cares not a toss for us. He just said that we had to wait for our wages.'

Mary grew alarmed that John was labouring for no reward. Digging, lifting, and the breaking of stones and laying them was backbreaking work. She could see it in the stiffness that had developed in his shoulders and arms, and in the taut look on his face, which betrayed how difficult the job truly was.

The following week, he finally got paid. The paltry few shillings he earned was used immediately to purchase a bag of meal and oats.

'Pat has gone to Maguire's,' he sighed.

'Well, I'm glad that you didn't join him there, drinking porter,' Mary said sharply.

'He has no wife or chicks to feed,' her husband said defensively, 'and deserves a few pints for all his hard work.'

Two days later Mary found it hard to stifle her annoyance and anger with Pat. He was back at their table, sitting across from them and eating their hard-earned food, as most of his wages were gone. She served him only a small portion of the soup, for no matter what John said, she had no intention of letting him steal the food from her children's mouths.

'This is no life for man,' he said, eating some of the bread she had made to go with the cabbage soup. 'I'll not stick this, for it's no life at all.'

Chapter 20

Skibbereen

AS DAN DONOVAN RODE THROUGH THE FALLING LEAVES, HE SLOWED
down his horse. Some distance away was a large group of men bearing shovels and spades that glinted in the autumn sunlight as the
men marched along the road. There were hundreds and hundreds of
them, a dishevelled rag bag, poorly clad and poorly fed. Stalwart
men now emaciated, likely employed on the new public roadworks
near Caheragh.

For the most part they looked too undernourished to lift a pick or
shovel and be set to hard physical labour. Dan had protested at the
treatment of these men, advising the authorities to feed them and
allow them to return to strength before employing them, but they
refused to listen.

Lately, Dan had heard of the failure to pay the men the subsist-
ence money they were due. No doubt this half-starved mob was
making its way to town en masse in some form of protest.

Dan feared what would happen when this massive army of nearly
a thousand men reached Skibbereen, where they would face the
armed military forces. Skibbereen had asked for food supplies but
instead they had been sent more soldiers, who were now stationed in
the town to protect the district's food stores.

There was little time and so Dan rode on quickly to forewarn Major Parker, the head of the Board of Works, about the workers.

'There are near a thousand of them,' he warned. 'I presume that they are in search of food or money. You must appease them, Major, or else there will be violence this day on the streets of Skibbereen.'

Dan could sense that the major was reluctant to believe him. Immediately, he turned his horse quickly and went to warn some of the townspeople, before heading home to alert his own family.

'My dear,' he told his wife, 'you must stay inside with the doors locked and make sure that the children do not go outside.'

'What is happening?' Henrietta cried, alarmed.

'Hundreds of men from the roadworks are marching into town, no doubt to protest to the head of the Board of Works, and I fear they will not be deterred in their purpose.'

'Promise me that you will be careful, Dan,' she cautioned, 'for you have done these people no wrong.'

As he headed back into town, Dan passed the courthouse. There he met his cousin, magistrate Michael Galwey, who had been attending court, and told him of the situation.

Confirming Dan's suspicions, within a short time hundreds and hundreds of angry workers poured into Skibbereen, protesting that they could not afford to buy food for their families as they were owed their pay by the Board of Public Works.

Terrified merchants, shopkeepers and the bank staff all rushed to close their doors, but many of the townspeople were sympathetic to the workers' plight.

The men kept coming, like some pale spectral army, and the intensity of their demands and anger seemed to grow and grow. Seventy soldiers, with their guns ready and loaded, awaited them in front of the town's new school.

'We are famished!' the men chanted again and again, clanging their shovels and spades on the ground.

'We have no food! Our wives and children are starving! We work and get not a penny in payment! Not even a piece of food!' they yelled, shouting out their grievances to the passers-by. 'The hunger is on us!'

'We'll have our money!' a grey-haired man shouted to the crowd, raising his shovel high in the air as the mob surged towards the bank.

The soldiers began to surround them, bayonets at the ready, but they were far outnumbered and would surely come under attack before long.

Dan pulled aside one of the soldiers.

'Go and tell Mr Hughes at the depot that he must distribute some food to them,' he told him. He abhorred the unfair treatment of these men and believed that they were justified in their actions.

'I'll speak to them,' offered Michael Galwey. 'Perhaps they will listen to me.'

He stood up in front of the school and the men came to a halt.

'As the local magistrate, I inform you that this riot is unlawful. You must all return to Caheragh and not disturb this town or, I warn you, the military here will be forced to use their weapons and take action against you.'

'We may as well be shot as starved!' they shouted back loudly. 'We have not eaten a morsel for twenty-four hours!'

Michael Galwey raised his voice and ordered the seventy soldiers to prepare to fire. The town fell silent. There were only slight mutters of dissent as the rioters took a few steps back.

The grim-faced soldiers held firm.

Afraid of the army that now faced them, with their guns raised and ready to fire, the protesters stopped. A voice declared loudly that there would be no trouble.

'Return to work and I promise that the money due to each of you will be distributed in a matter of days,' urged Michael Galwey.

At that point, Mr Hughes from the food depot appeared.

'Open the food store immediately, Mr Hughes,' the magistrate ordered, 'and issue these men with a quantity of biscuits. Three cheers for the Queen and plenty of employment tomorrow!'

A few half-hearted cheers rose from the crowd of workers, but most kept their heads down and said nothing. Their riot defeated, the exhausted men sat quietly and devoured hungrily the biscuits they were eventually served.

Dan had to assuage his own anger. How could the Board of Works not understand how desperate the men were for the eight pennies a day they were being paid? For them, it was the difference between life and death. He wished they had fought harder for their demands. They had strength in numbers and should have refused to leave the town till they were paid.

But Dan could see it everywhere: hunger and disease were slowly killing the people's spirit and their ability to fight for any kind of justice.

Chapter 21

HENRIETTA DONOVAN WAS MOVED AND UPSET BY THE GROUPS OF paupers who loitered constantly near her front door in the hope of seeing her husband. It had been the same scene every day since the hunger had come.

The hungry and sick were everywhere, flooding into town looking for work and food. They sought assistance from Dan as the Union's physician: a ticket for a visit to the dispensary with a sick child or wife, or for Dan to visit them in person; a ticket to be employed on the public roadworks; or a pass to be admitted to the Union workhouse. Desperate people during this desperate time!

Henrietta worried as she watched her husband set off every morning, dressed in his usual frock coat and tall black hat, sporting his neat side whiskers, his countenance filled with concern for the care of his patients. She and the children scarcely saw him, as Dan worked longer and longer hours, returning home later and later every day.

She had tried to persuade him to move away from the area for the sake of their family. He was a renowned oculist who not only had papers published regularly in *The Lancet* and other medical journals, but also had patients travel to consult him on his medical expertise in the area of eye diseases. They came from as far away as Dublin and Galway as well as from overseas.

'Dan, we could leave here and you could practise as an oculist in

Dublin or Edinburgh, such is your reputation,' she cajoled. 'Or you could take up a position in one of the big city hospitals, for you are a skilled surgeon.'

'Hetty, I have a rewarding position here,' he reminded her. 'And I have no intention of leaving it . . .'

At night, despite his tiredness, Dan sat at his desk for hours, writing his 'Diary of a Dispensary Doctor' and reporting truthfully on the state of affairs in the town and district. His accounts were now being published in the *Southern Reporter* and in other newspapers further afield. Henrietta was so proud of him and dearly hoped that his words would shame the authorities into providing the relief needed.

'Why does Dada not care for us any more?' puzzled Fanny, her brown eyes serious. She wore a tight little frown on her brow as she wondered what they had all done to upset him so.

'Your dada does love you all so much,' Henrietta tried to reassure her children. 'It is just that he is kept very busy looking after the sick.'

'And there are sick people everywhere,' Ellen pronounced knowledgeably.

'Yes, I'm afraid so,' her mother agreed.

'That is why we cannot go out to play like before?'

'Your father would prefer you to stay at home or play in the garden for the moment, until things improve.'

'When will that be?' Fanny pressed.

'Soon,' she tried to reassure them. 'Soon.'

She too found it suffocating to spend so much time confined to their home, trying to teach the children and amuse them. Glad to escape the confines of New Street, she welcomed invitations to visit Dan's relations. Visiting their country houses for afternoon tea or a walk in the nearby woods always cheered her. There, she could watch the children run and play and laugh and chase around like children should. For the most part, the youngsters of Skibbereen were now silent and quiet, all childhood fun and games for many banished by the hunger.

*

Of late, Dan had taken to entering their home via the back scullery door. He had requested that Henrietta or their maid, Sally, leave a clean shirt, waistcoat, topcoat and pair of shoes there for him to change into, following his visits to the decrepit cabins and cottages of his patients, which had become dens of effluent and human waste. She would watch as he removed his soiled and often foul-scented clothing meticulously, and washed and scrubbed his arms to the elbow in the scullery sink before re-dressing. A handsome man, he had always been a fastidious dresser, and took care of his appearance, with his starched white shirt and tailored top coat with its brass buttons and lined lapels.

On his return home, she felt Dan deserved the reward of a good meal after his work and endeavours throughout the day. He was partial to beef and so she tried to ensure it was served a few times a week. There were no potatoes for the present, but turnips, pastry, boiled onions and dumplings pleased him, followed by a pudding.

That evening there was beef and vegetable pie served with turnip, then an apple and raisin pudding, a favourite of his. Dan enjoyed the meal, but left the pudding untouched, and pushed the bowl away.

'Is it not to your taste?' she queried.

'I fear that I do not have the stomach for it. Perhaps one of the children will take it.'

She passed the bowl to their eldest son, Henry, a growing boy who was certainly partial to pudding. It concerned Henrietta that her husband's lack of appetite was perhaps a sign of some kind of illness.

'Are you feeling unwell, Dan?' she asked him in the drawing room, after the children were all in bed.

She was fearful that he might be developing a fever, like so many others in the town.

'I am not ill,' he reassured her, as if reading her mind. 'It is just that I cannot countenance enjoying such a rich table while all around us the people are starving. It is abhorrent to me.'

'What do you want me to do?' she demanded, upset by him.

'Empty our larder and pantry, and put the food and provision out on the street for the beggars to eat? Though I must remind you that we have a large family of our own that needs feeding . . . Our own flesh and blood, our children to care for.'

She could not hide her anger, for it was Dan who, despite her pleas to move away, insisted on remaining in Skibbereen so that he could minister to his patients and the people who thronged into the town.

'My dear,' he soothed. 'I do not intend to upset you. There is no better mother who cares more for her family than you. It is just that, given the present circumstances that pertain in the district, it would be better if no pudding or cake were served with meals under this roof. I believe the food should be kept plain and nourishing with no lavish, rich or luxury ingredients. Good meals simply served for the family.'

Immediately, Henrietta felt contrite. She was ashamed that she herself had not thought of such a matter, given the scenes she witnessed daily on her own doorstep. She was in agreement with him.

'Very well. I will instruct Sally and, if you wish, I will ensure that no more puddings and cakes will be served for the present,' she promised, knowing full well that Dan would miss such delicacies more than the rest of the household. 'No treacle pudding or slices of the ginger cake that you favour.'

She leaned over and kissed the worry line on his forehead that seemed to be there almost permanently these days, then his cheek and then his lips.

'Sometimes I think that you are far too good for your own good,' she teased him gently, 'but I wouldn't have it any other way.'

'I know how hard it must be for you and the children with my work and the constant demands on my time.'

'Dan, you are a doctor. I knew that when I married you and accepted what being a doctor's wife means.'

'But what is happening here is beyond any expectation!' He sighed heavily.

Tears welled in her eyes unbidden as she remembered the early days of their marriage when they lived near the coastal village of Union Hall. Much happier times!

'Hetty, you are an angel to put up with me,' Dan said as he pulled her gently on to his lap. Tenderly, he wiped the tears from her eyes. 'My own beloved angel.'

Chapter 22

Creagh

MARY WAS GROWING WORRIED FOR JOHN'S HEALTH. WORKING ON THE roads was taking a toll on him, sapping his strength, energy and spirit.

'They work us like slaves,' he admitted as he hunched over the fire, bone weary and exhausted.

'Well, I am no slave,' declared Pat angrily as he sipped a warming mug of tea she'd made with leftover tea leaves. 'They want to break us all – every man, woman and child – but I'll not let them break me. I'll leave this poisoned place and make a life somewhere else. I'll not die laying stones at the side of a road.'

'Ah, brother, how could you go? Where would you find the money?'

'I'll find it somehow,' he declared testily, refusing to be drawn any further.

Mary studied her brother-in-law and could see he was intent on it. He did not have the same ties to the land as she and John; his was only a smallholding, barely enough to support a family. He had no sweetheart or wife, or child to bind him here. Why would he stay amid such calamity when a better life beckoned him across the sea?

As Mary and John readied for bed that evening, John sighed.

'Patrick and his old talk of leaving! He'll never leave this place.'

'Don't be so sure. I think he means it,' she said, tracing the curve of her husband's bony shoulder. 'For there is nothing to keep him here any more.'

Every second or third day Pat called to the cottage, joining them to share whatever little they had. Shamefaced, he would some-times bring something at least to add to the pot. Mary was caught by surprise one evening when, with a flourish, he produced a big bag of meal and a large hare that he had somehow managed to catch.

'How this wily old fellow has managed to escape all this time.' He grinned and passed the skinned and cleaned hare to Mary. 'But today was not his lucky day. I got him fair and square lying in the ferns.'

'You are good to share him with us,' she thanked him apprecia-tively as she transferred the hare to cook slowly in the pot.

Of late, her brother-in-law had surprised them on several occa-sions with bags of meal, a small round of cheese, a box of salted herrings, a sack of oats, and now this!

'Don't ask where he gets it from,' warned John. 'It's better that we know nothing of where he and his wild boys get these goods.'

After they finished their feast, the children cleaned their bowls and licked their fingers. In the corner, Patch chewed hungrily at a bone and everyone sat around the warmth of the turf, talking. Pat then brought out a small bottle of *poitín*, which he insisted on shar-ing with his brother.

'It's grand stuff . . .'

'That will warm your heart and spirit,' Pat joked as the two brothers reminisced about their childhood.

Later, he confided in Mary and John about the cart of grain, bound for shipping to Liverpool, that he and two friends had man-aged to intercept.

'I promise you, those three bags that we took while the cartman went for a piss won't be missed until the sacks are unloaded in Liverpool!'

'What if they catch you?' Mary asked, worried.

'They won't.' He shrugged. 'Besides, grain grown here should stay here.'

As the hour grew late, John fell asleep in his chair. Mary walked Pat to the door and thanked him again for the hare and sack of meal.

'John is a lucky man to have found a woman like you. Truth to tell, I envy him.' Pat's hand reached up to touch her face. 'From the day we met, Mary, I wished that I was the one who had saw you first.'

'Hush,' she laughed. 'It's just the drink talking. Sure, you have been in love so many times, and have half the women of the parish mad about you.'

'But they are not you,' he said, emotion showing in his eyes.

'Pat, I am your sister-in-law,' she reminded him firmly. 'I love your brother with all my heart, and have always done so and always will.'

He stepped back, crestfallen and a little ashamed.

'Away home with you to your own bed,' she urged gently, watching him take the path for home.

There was no sign of Pat Sullivan for two days. Concerned, John went to his cottage, fearful his brother had fallen ill or, worse still, had been caught and arrested. Pat's horse and cart were gone from the smallholding and John carried home the note he had found there.

'I told you he would go away,' Mary said as John read Pat's words aloud.

The brief letter informed John that Pat would be taking the horse and cart, which were rightfully his to sell. He would be using the money to purchase a ticket to sail to Liverpool and then on to New York. He wanted a new life far from the hunger, and crossing the ocean to North America was his chance of a better future.

'I cannot believe that he has just left with not a word to us!' said John.

Mary was not surprised. She knew their last meal together had been a farewell of sorts as Pat had, in his own fashion, said goodbye to all of them. He had said nothing of his plans for he likely did not want them to stop him. She was angry, however, that the cart and the old horse were gone.

'Pat has little enough with the cottage and only a small patch of land,' her husband said in defence of his brother, 'but my father gave him the horse and cart when he died. Although I used them at times, they were always his to sell.'

'Then he was within his rights,' Mary sighed. 'Let's hope that he got a good price for them.'

'I'll miss Pat. It's likely we will never see him again, but I wish my brother good fortune wherever he travels.'

As she passed Pat's empty cottage to hunt for haws, sloes, rosehips and rowan berries, Mary thought of him. She knew in her heart that he had made a wise decision to escape the hunger while he still could. It was a decision she sometimes envied, as she watched John grow weaker and her children turn pale, the flesh beginning to melt from their bones.

Chapter 23

Oldcourt, County Cork
October 1846

DAN WAS OUT NEAR OLDCOURT, RETURNING FROM A VISIT TO A MAN, weak with hunger, who had fallen and broken his leg, when he stopped his horse. The ships, boats and low barges that plied their trade in the small but busy harbour were loading and unloading their cargo. This was a place where the sea and river met. Ships and boats arriving from Liverpool and Newport and Cardiff sailed as far up the river Ilen as they could before they transferred their goods to smaller row boats that would transport them upriver to the town.

He watched as large sacks of grain destined for McCarthy's brewery were moved to two waiting barges ready to sail upriver. Grain that could have fed hundreds being used instead to make beer and porter for the busy taverns of Dublin and Cork! It made no sense to him.

Protesting livestock, squealing pigs and a few sheep arrived and were loaded quickly into the hold of a large ship ready for their journey to England. Baskets of cheese and dried fish, and barrels of butter were stacked tightly on to another vessel, destined to feed the factory workers of Liverpool, London and Manchester.

As he stood on the small quay, Dan noticed that one ship, the

Mersey Lady, had not been reloaded, but the crew were hoisting the sail and making ready to leave.

'Are you casting off?' he called out.

'Aye, sir, we have to catch the tide or we'll be landed here till tonight.'

'But you have no cargo?'

'We delivered a cargo of corn for Swanton's and will return from Newport with another delivery next week.'

'Do you not usually return with a cargo from here?'

'Rarely,' replied the man whom he presumed to be the captain.

'You have an empty hold returning to Liverpool or Wales regularly?' he pressed.

'Aye.' The man nodded. 'Those are Mr Swanton's orders.'

An empty ship leaving Ireland was a lost opportunity. Surely such a vessel could provide passage to a new life in Liverpool, or another one of England's great cities, for those who had lost everything.

'Would you give consideration to taking a few passengers on your return journey from here next time?'

'This is not a passenger ship,' the man retorted gruffly. 'We transport grain from place to place, not people.'

'Even a few people desperate to escape from this ravaged place?'

'I am employed by Mr Swanton,' the captain replied brusquely. 'You would need to discuss the matter with him.'

James Swanton was one of the town's most prosperous businessmen. He owned a large mill and several warehouses, but unlike other local business owners, he had joined the relief committee and might be prepared to assist Dan.

'We are well acquainted.' Dan smiled at the captain. 'Thank you. I will, as you advise, discuss the matter with him and perhaps we can reach some agreement.'

Chapter 24

JAMES SWANTON WAS BUSY IN HIS OFFICE DOWN ON LEVIS QUAY, BUT greeted Dan warmly.

'Can I help you, doctor?' he asked, curious about the reason for this visit from his fellow committee member.

'I am not here on committee business but with regard to another matter,' Dan replied. 'I was riding to Oldcourt yesterday and I noticed one of your ships had unloaded corn, but was preparing to return to Newport with no cargo. I spoke to her captain.'

'The import of corn, grain and materials from Liverpool and Newport is the backbone of my milling business.' James Swanton leaned forward and fixed the doctor with his gaze. 'Despite this calamity, business must go on.'

'I understand that, Mr Swanton.' Dan had not meant to sound critical in any way, for he needed to get the merchant on his side. 'It is the empty cargo hold that I want to discuss with you.'

'I may be a businessman, Dr Donovan, but while Irish men and women starve I am not prepared to export any food goods from this country on the ship I have hired. Timber and fuel, yes, but no food-stuffs or livestock! I have considered using the hold to transport those who are willing to leave this sorry place but I'm not sure if any would accept such an offer.'

'Believe me, Mr Swanton, they most certainly would,' Dan declared firmly. 'If such an offer was made, would it be possible to use your empty ship to transport those desperate to escape from here with no fare payment?'

'It is not a passenger ship,' Swanton reminded him. 'There would be no comfort for people on such a voyage, but it would at least transport them quickly and with no charge.'

'That is most generous of you.'

'I need to talk to the captain about it, but I will not agree to provide passage to any who are sick or infirm. I don't want to risk the captain and crew falling ill or have them turned back at the docks.'

'I promise that I will medically examine every passenger travelling and ensure they are strong and well,' Dan assured him.

'Then I will find out from the captain how many passengers he can safely accommodate and agree dates for the sailings with him.'

Dan thanked him warmly and they agreed to meet up in a few days' time to organize things further.

James Swanton arranged free passage on his grain ship for a hundred people. Over the course of the long week that followed, Dan approached a number of orphaned young men to see if they were interested in his plan. He also spoke to Helena Collins, a widow with three boys who had planned to leave Ireland with her husband, and a desperate young couple who had been evicted and were sleeping rough in the fields. All were anxious to escape the hunger and desperate to begin a new life away from the sadness of their homeland.

Many he talked to were utterly destitute, with not even a coat on their back. They could not be sent to Newport or Liverpool in such a state and so, taking their pawn tickets, Dan redeemed them. Using some of the donations he received, he returned much-needed coats and shawls, boots and britches, and dresses to their rightful owners.

As word got around, Dan became inundated with requests from people wanting to take the free passage across the sea but regretfully he could only issue so many tickets.

*

Two weeks later, Dan returned to Oldcourt with the *Mersey Lady*'s first passengers. The water was choppy and a strong wind was blowing. The young men and women, and few children he had handpicked for this first voyage waited anxiously as the sailors unloaded their cargo on to the waiting barges and the captain shouted orders.

He waited patiently on the quay alongside James Swanton.

The relief committee had agreed to issue two shillings to each passenger just before their departure, for they would need it on their arrival in Liverpool. The waiting passengers had few other possessions with them, only a blanket and some oatcakes that Mr Swanton had donated to them.

'I am very glad to be of assistance.' The miller smiled as he introduced Dan to the ship's captain.

'Once we land these people I cannot provide any further assistance to them,' the captain explained. 'They must find work themselves or journey on across the Atlantic, but it is not my care what happens to them. The sea ports are filled with starving Irish, who do little to help themselves and plague the taverns and hostelries. Many of them are being returned to your shore.'

'That is understood, Captain, but I promise you that these people are willing to work.'

'Dr Donovan, I will only transport passengers who are strong, healthy and fit for a sea voyage.'

'That is only prudent and I have checked each one personally. Though they are malnourished, they are otherwise healthy,' he assured him. 'Captain, I thank you sincerely for agreeing to help these people.'

'We will sail in less than half an hour,' the captain announced peremptorily. 'We cannot tarry as rough weather is expected.'

The passengers soon began to board the vessel. Dan was filled with sympathy for Mrs Collins, who wept openly as she and her children stepped on the deck of the ship.

'Thank you, Dr Donovan. We will never forget it for you.' Michael and Jane Carmody, filled both with excitement and plans for their future, smiled as they shook his hand.

'Our uncle has a boot factory in the town,' grinned Donal Harrington, who was travelling with his brother Tommy. 'We hope to get work there.'

One of the doctor's own tenants, Michael McCarthy, had welcomed the opportunity to leave Cork with his family. A few of the other passengers were young men from the lanes of Skibbereen who were more than ready to work and escape their lowly background.

One of the crew untied the ship from its mooring and the sails were hoisted as the vessel moved off. Pulling his coat tightly around him as the wind blew, Dan watched from the harbour wall with James Swanton.

'I'm glad that we managed to assist a few souls today to escape from this place of hunger,' James Swanton declared firmly. 'Thank you, doctor, for your help in arranging such matters.'

'I was glad to do it.'

'Next time my grain ship is here, I'll see to it that it will transport a few more of those who you consider suitable for free passage,' he offered as the two men shook hands.

As he turned for home, Dan was already mentally drawing up a list of deserving passengers.

Chapter 25

Skibbereen

DAN STARED AT THE EMACIATED CORPSE OF DENIS MCKENNEDY, A labourer on the relief roadworks. As he prepared his instruments for the post mortem, he remembered his days as an undergraduate in Edinburgh. Many of his fellow medical students were overcome when confronted with a cadaver, but he had never been affected in that way. He was innately curious about the human body, discovering how it worked and why life had been taken from it. The examination of organs, tissue and bone revealed more than any textbook and usually provided proof of cause of death.

'I suppose another man from the works,' nodded Dr Patrick Dore, who was assisting him.

They both found this work difficult of late, for they had to carry out post mortems on some of the unfortunates found dead in the district's fields and ditches, roads and laneways. Men who had once been strong and able and willing to work, but had died of starvation and fever contracted from the poor conditions they were forced to endure.

Recently, Dan had carried out a post mortem on a similar case – Jeremiah Hegarty, another labourer discovered dead by the side of the road. On examination, his intestines had been found to be devoid

95

of food. At the official inquest, Dan had reported that Hegarty had died from lack of nourishment and exposure.

'I see this man died on the seventeenth of October,' noted Dr Dore as he consulted Mr McKennedy's notes. 'His body is in a worse state than most we have examined.'

Dan could see immediately that the corpse was lacking any sign of muscle or fatty tissue. It was one of the most attenuated that he had ever examined. There was no trace of fat anywhere around the abdomen and scarcely a vestige of omentum. All the adipose matter had been absorbed by the body.

'There is no food in the stomach or small intestine,' he remarked as he examined the man's innards, which were blanched and empty. 'And all I can see is what appears to be a small quantity of cabbage mixed with excrement in his bowel.'

The two doctors looked at each other, both moved by the plight of the man before them.

'How did this poor fellow manage to find the strength to work at all?' questioned Dr Dore.

'Apparently, Mr McKennedy had not been paid since the tenth of October,' Dan said angrily. 'It's appalling that another good man was forced to walk miles and do heavy labouring work for a pittance without any sustenance and nourishment. This travesty cannot continue!'

There were few in attendance at the inquest into Denis McKennedy's death held at the courthouse in Skibbereen. The Board of Works tried to lay the blame on a pay clerk, Mr Hungerford, who had made an administrative error, which had resulted in Mr McKennedy not being paid when due.

Dan took up his notes and began to read aloud the detailed record of the autopsy.

'The only sign of any form of food I could find in Mr McKennedy's bowels was some cabbage leaf.'

A woman near the back sobbed loudly and he could sense the embarrassment of the court officials.

'Therefore, following a full autopsy and examination of the body of the deceased, I find that Mr Denis McKennedy died of starvation owing to the gross negligence of the Board of Works.'

There was a stunned silence at his direct accusation of the Board, followed by a murmur of dissent from the officials. He could see the clerk cast his eyes to heaven, but Dan continued, for he was the court-appointed physician carrying out post mortems on such men.

'And this shall be entered in the records,' Dan concluded loudly, determined that the truth be told and written up officially.

Chapter 26

Creagh

AS MARY COOKED THE YELLOW MEAL IN THE POT, SHE TASTED A LITTLE of it on the wooden spoon. No matter how hard she tried to soak and grind and cook it, it had a terrible consistency. Nora and Tim both complained that it made them sick. After eating it a few days ago, they had doubled up from sharp pains in their stomachs, but she had cajoled them into eating more of it to give them some nourishment.

On the way from the dressmaker's earlier that day, she had called to see her sister, who had given her a narrow strip of dried-out fatty bacon.

'Use it to feed you and John and the children,' Kathleen had urged. Mary suspected that her sister or her husband, Joe, may have stolen it, but in these desperate times the poor had no other option but to look after their own.

Mary sliced the meat thinly. She would scrape a tiny bit on top of each plate in the hope that it would give the yellow meal some taste as well as a little extra sustenance. Most of it she would give to John, for her husband was fading before her eyes. His muscles were gone, and his arms were long and thin, like those of a boy. To see him lose his strength was enough to make her cry.

Poor old Patch watched her from the door. The collie was a changed animal, for there were no more scraps from the table and she hadn't seen him catch a rabbit in months. God knows what the wretched creature was living on, for they had nothing to give him.

The dog sidled up to her and Mary rubbed his black-and-white coat gently. His fur had begun to fall out, and she could feel his ribs. He was a good dog, who used to love to chase and roll around in the grass, but since the hunger had come all the playfulness had gone from him.

'You poor old thing, you are suffering like us all,' she soothed. The dog rolled over at the kindness of her words to have his scrawny belly rubbed.

'Aww,' she sighed, bending down to tickle him like he was a child.

She called the children and John to come and sit by the turf fire as she spooned out the yellow meal.

'I'll not take it,' protested Tim.

'You'll eat it or you'll feel the strap,' interjected John. 'None of us likes it, but there is nothing else and it will keep the hunger off us.'

'There is a scrapeen of some nice salt bacon that your auntie gave me. It will make it taste a bit better,' she promised them.

Tim looked dubious, his bottom lip stuck out as if he was going to cry. Lifting the bacon off her own helping, she passed the grey-looking strip towards her son's bowl. Though she was hungry, the fatty meat turned her stomach.

As Tim reached to put it into his mouth, Patch sprang up and flung himself at the boy. He grabbed the bacon, growling and biting, as he dragged it literally from the child's mouth.

'No! No!' Mary shrieked as Con, Annie and Nora all began to cry and scream.

Terrified, young Tim dropped his food as he tried to push the snarling dog from him.

John caught Patch with a kick but the dog kept going, crazed with hunger, gobbling at the meal and bacon that was spilt on Tim's clothes and lap. He bared his teeth at John as his master tried to pull him away.

John kicked Patch again, catching the animal's scrawny body. Despite the dog's biting and snapping, John somehow managed to get him to the other side of the room, where Patch hunched, a deep low growling coming from him. Mary grabbed the willow switch brush and forced the collie out the door.

Tim was as white as a ghost. He was bleeding from the corner of his mouth and there was a gash on his lower lip. His right hand bore the imprint of the dog's teeth.

'Why did Patch do that?' sobbed Nora. 'He loves Tim.'

'He's hungry, pet,' Mary explained sadly. 'And when dogs are hungry, they get fierce and dangerous and forget that you love them.'

She lifted Tim on to her lap and told John to get some water. She began to wash her son's lip, face and hands. He was shaking, terrified that the dog would come back and attack him again.

'Dada and I won't let him near you,' she promised. 'He's not coming back in here ever again.'

John disappeared outside.

The children were quiet as they finished the meal. Con was still upset and asked her if he could go outside to see Patch.

'You are all staying here with me till your father returns.'

'We love Patch,' said Nora softly. 'It's not his fault that he's hungry like the rest of us.'

An hour later, John returned. His shoulders were slumped and his eyes red-rimmed. She could tell he was deeply saddened by what he had had to do, but he'd had no choice.

'Where's Patch?' demanded Con. 'What did you do to him?'

'I put the poor creature out of his misery,' he explained haltingly as the children stared wide-eyed at him. 'It was the kindest thing to do.'

'You had no right to do that!' protested Con, upset. 'Patch is our dog and we care for him.'

'We all cared for him,' John explained gently. 'He was a fine dog, but what would you have me do? Let him attack Nora or Annie like he attacked Tim? We have little enough to eat and there is not a scrap to give the dog when we are hungry ourselves. Would you have us watch Patch starve to death?'

'No,' said Tim. 'Dada is right. I wouldn't want Patch here with us, biting and attacking me again.'

'But I'll miss him.' Nora began to cry, sobbing loudly.

Mary tried to steel herself as she looked at the tear-stained faces of her children. Truth to tell, she felt like crying herself, for the dog was part of their lives.

Later, as she lay beside John while the children slept, he told her about Patch.

'The poor dog was terrified. He knew that he had overstepped himself and that we could never trust him again. He was licking my hands the way he always does and looking at me with those big eyes of his as if to say sorry. I kept thinking of when he was a puppy.'

'He was always a good dog,' she agreed sadly.

'I took him over near the trees and sat down with him. I got him with two quick blows to the head. I buried him there—' His voice broke as he told her. 'I was always fond of that collie.'

'I know,' Mary soothed, 'but it had to be done.'

'The children are fierce upset, but when things are better next year we'll get them a new pup.'

'John Sullivan, you are the kindest-hearted man I know,' she said, kissing him and pulling him into the warm comfort of her arms.

Chapter 27

Skibbereen

DAN CALLED TO A SICK FAMILY IN CORONEA, MOST OF THEM SIMPLY weak with hunger, and then to a young boy who was suffering from bad seizures in Bridgetown. His last ticket was to visit the Murphys' cabin in Windmill Lane. Julia Murphy was a gentle type of woman, a young widow who had last come to him when her son had fallen and broken his arm. He was one of two children and Dan wondered who in the family was ailing and required a visit from him on this occasion.

'Mrs Murphy?' he called as he knocked lightly on the low door of the small cabin.

A young girl of five or six appeared in filthy rags and held the door for him. In the dim, smoky light of the one room Dan's senses were overwhelmed by the obvious smell of putrefaction.

'Where is your mother?' he asked the child.

'There.'

She pointed nervously at a hunched figure that lay sleeping on the floor among the filthy straw.

'Julia, it's Dr Donovan,' he called softly.

There was no response. As he approached her a voice moaned, and he bent down to look more closely.

'Julia?'

He stopped suddenly, realizing that there was also a boy of about four years old under the blanket, sobbing tearfully. Beside him lay his mother, cold and pale. He moved her gently and checked, but there was no pulse or sign of life. Her body was already beginning to decay. He lifted up the half-starved child.

'It's all right, little man,' he soothed the scared child. 'You are safe.'

The small girl ran over to join her brother.

Neither of them was anything more than bones, their small stomachs swollen. Lord knows when they had last eaten. Dan searched the damp cabin and found no trace of any type of food. How long had poor Julia Murphy gone without eating? No doubt the little she had she had given to her children while she grew weaker.

Overcome with sadness, he stared at the once-beautiful woman who had lain down and died here in her own home. There was no furniture, no comfort, and she and her children had little clothing. Likely she had pawned their every last possession.

Was there no one in the town who might have helped her or her children? If only they had come to the dispensary, he could have at least had them admitted to the Union! Perhaps pride or fear or shame had prevented Julia Murphy from seeking help.

The small boy clung to Dan's neck. Both children needed to be cared for, so he resolved to take them to the workhouse straight away. Following a proper examination, he would make arrangements for the burial of their poor mother.

'What are your names?' he asked the girl.

'I'm Maria and he's Owen,' she said as she stared at the doctor, her eyes sunken in her face.

'Well, Maria and Owen, I have a fine horse and trap, and I am going to take you to a place where you will be fed and looked after as your mother cannot do that any more,' Dan tried to explain.

'Is my mama dead?'

'Yes, I'm afraid so. But she would want the two of you to be well cared for.'

As he took the children by the hand and led them down to where

103

he had tethered his horse, one or two curious neighbours appeared at their doorways.

'Mrs Murphy is unfortunately deceased, so please do not enter there,' he warned. 'On my return I will attend to things.'

As he drove the young Murphys to the workhouse, Dan thought of his own children and prayed that they would never face such sadness. No boy or girl deserved to see their beloved mother meet her end in this terrible way.

Chapter 28

November 1846

'GENTLEMEN, I HAVE SEEN TERRIBLE THINGS RECENTLY,' DAN ADMIT-
ted, trying to control his emotions as he recalled the tragic deaths of
poor Julia Murphy and Denis McKennedy. 'Women and children
in a weakened and perilous state, hungry men who are not fit to
work on the public relief schemes. It is incumbent upon we who sit
on the relief committee to find some other means to assist them, for
we can no longer stand by and watch our people as they starve and
die before our very eyes.'

'Dr Donovan is right,' agreed chairman Thomas Somerville as
they sat around the table in the meeting room of the workhouse. 'We
can no longer wait for Charles Trevelyan and his cronies in the
Treasury to act. We must try to find an affordable solution.'

'Perhaps here could be further utilized for such urgent assistance?' suggested Michael Galwey, looking in Dan's direction.

'I'm sorry, Michael, but the workhouse is already full,' Dan admitted regretfully. 'There is talk of us having to procure more buildings
here in town, to house the additional sick and destitute.'

'Then what can we do to help the hungry?' Father Fitzpatrick
demanded.

'The roadworks are oversubscribed. The men flocked to them

only because they needed to be fed,' interjected Daniel McCarthy. 'Food is what is urgently needed!'

'Then it is our Christian duty to find some way to feed them,' insisted Reverend Richard Boyle Townsend.

'We must provide relief that does not involve hard labour or people agreeing to enter the workhouse,' Dan proposed.

'I agree with the good doctor.' Reverend Townsend nodded, his thin features animated. 'If we provide food for the poor, there must be no conditions. It must be gratuitous relief.'

'Gentlemen, you do realize the enormous task we may be under-taking here?' warned Daniel McCarthy. 'We may have to feed hundreds – nay, thousands – of poor souls a day.'

'The workhouse serves soup or gruel to the inmates mostly every day, along with bread or some rice,' Dan informed them. 'I believe there is great need to provide a similar type of meal once a day for the hungry here in the town. Miss Penn of the Society of Friends told me of large soup kitchens in Manchester and London which the society ran. They kept thousands of poor people alive by serving similar gallons of soup and rice.'

'Providing a soup kitchen here in town to feed the hungry is exactly what is needed.' Reverend Townsend nodded, excited.

'There must be no charge for the soup,' warned Father Fitzpat-rick. 'We must provide gratuitous relief, as Reverend Townsend suggested, with no conditions.'

'No charge? But feeding such a large number will be costly,' reminded the town's brewery owner.

'Mr McCarthy, you know well that they have not a penny to pur-chase food.'

'That I do. God help us, I see them every day, hungering. But how are we to raise the funds ourselves for such a large endeavour?'

'By subscription, rates money and, of course, charitable dona-tions,' Tim McCarthy Downing said slowly and deliberately, looking around the group. 'The money will have to come from that.'

A low mumble passed around the committee.

'A large soup kitchen will cost a tidy sum to operate, what with ingredients and a few cooks or servers. Then there is the business of having to find suitable premises to hold such numbers!' Daniel McCarthy reminded the room.

'I would offer my church grounds, but we have no building large enough to house such a kitchen,' sighed Reverend Townsend. 'My church will fully support it, however, and contribute towards the running cost.'

'I am in a similar position,' nodded Father Fitzpatrick, 'in that we have only the church itself, which is the house of God.'

'What about that property on the river? The new steam mill?' ventured Michael Galwey.

'The steam mill is not yet in use,' suggested Tom Marmion, the land agent for Stephen Fitzgerald Townsend, one of the largest absentee landowners in the district. 'It might be suitable for such a venture.'

'Tom, I cannot see Reverend Fitzgerald Townsend agreeing for it to be used for such an endeavour when he refuses even to consider forgoing rent payments from his suffering tenants during this calamity.'

'I suspect there is little generosity or charity in the man.' Father Fitzpatrick sighed despondently.

'This matter does not concern Reverend Fitzgerald Townsend,' Tom Marmion responded. 'The property does not belong to him.'

'Then to whom does it belong?' quizzed the chairman. 'Who do we approach?'

'I am the proprietor of the mill.' Tom Marmion's cheeks flushed. He knew full well that he had surprised the assembled gathering. 'I had hoped that it would be busy milling these past few months. However, given the situation, it is not the proper time to open such a venture. That is why I would like to offer it for use temporarily. To serve as a distribution centre, be it for soup or as a food depot, or whatever is considered necessary by the committee.'

'That is most generous of you, Tom,' Father Fitzpatrick offered.

Dan nodded in agreement. Though he suspected that the purchase of land and construction of a new mill must have cost Tom a pretty penny, money likely amassed from the large rents he collected for Reverend Stephen Fitzgerald Townsend and his like.

'You are a good fellow,' cheered Daniel McCarthy. 'The mill would be ideal for such a venture to feed the people. Perhaps the good doctor can enquire at the Union about the composition of a soup or meal to sustain the hungry of the town during this time of crisis. And we will endeavour to purchase large boilers and such like.'

The soup provided by the large Union kitchen to the workhouse inmates was unappetizing but cheaply produced. It provided the necessary sustenance, though to Dan's mind many of them still suffered from poor nutrition.

'I'm sorry not to be able to help further, doctor,' the cook apologized when he consulted her, 'but we are already overstretched here with the huge numbers that must be fed.'

Mrs Hegarty from the Becher Arms offered to assist them, but the soup usually served in her hotel was too rich and expensive for their needs.

'But it is no problem to make a cheaper standard soup,' she advised, 'that will be both filling and nutritious.'

Henrietta and the Donovans' maid, Sally, had both been intrigued when he questioned them on the merits of the good restorative soup that he regularly enjoyed in his own home.

'We use some meat – often left over from another meal – turnips, parsnips, onion and carrot, doctor,' explained Sally. 'We used to have potato but now barley or another form of meal has to suffice.'

Dan made a note of the quantities needed.

'Mary McCarthy and Elizabeth Townsend both told me that their husbands have got a sudden notion for soup and tasting it,' Henrietta teased him as she spooned some oxtail broth into his bowl. 'Abigail Penn kindly provided us with a recipe that the Society of Friends has used successfully to make gallons of soup for the needy.'

Although the provision of adequate nutrition for an adult was the aim of his research, Dan soon realized that taste and texture were also important. The soup they provided must be palatable to those who desperately needed it. Good cuts of meat would be impossible to obtain, but Sally assured him that poorer quality meat, and even offal, was just as good once some sort of seasoning was added during the cooking process.

Dan, along with Father Fitzpatrick and Michael Galwey, Tim McCarthy Downing, Reverend Townsend, Daniel McCarthy and Tom Marmion retired to the Becher Arms. There, Mrs Hegarty, after much consultation and perusing of the recipes of the Union, Miss Penn and others, had agreed to prepare and serve them each a bowl of standard soup that would be nutritious and suitable for serving the large numbers required at a reasonable cost.

Though he felt the meat had become rather stringy, Dan declared that the soup itself, which was thick and similar to a stew in its consistency, was good to taste.

'I like it,' agreed Father Fitzpatrick.

'It's a nourishing meal,' proclaimed Michael Galwey as he spooned the last of it from his bowl.

'A little more barley, perhaps,' suggested Daniel McCarthy, 'will make it more filling.'

'Dr Donovan, it is a good soup to fill a hungry belly,' enthused Reverend Townsend.

Mrs Hegarty and her cook were both proud that they had managed to provide a nourishing basic soup capable of feeding so many.

A few days later, escaping the heavy rain, Dan joined the committee at the large, impressive steam mill which stood at the side of the river.

'The first thing we need is to find someone who will agree to organize and manage the soup kitchen. Someone who is available to do it on a full-time basis,' proposed Thomas Somerville. 'We are all busy men. Unless there is someone here, ready to take on such a task . . .'

Dan looked around him. Who among them could give up their own work for such an onerous duty?

'I may know somcone,' interjected Reverend Townsend. 'A fine clergyman of my acquaintance who may be available. That is, if he has not already been assigned to a new parish. Reverend Frederick Trench has great strength of character and determination, and I believe he would be the type of man to take on such a challenge as part of his Christian duty. I will write to him immediately to inform him of our plans and see if the position here is of interest to him.'

The chairman nodded in agreement. 'We will await his reply eagerly and, if he is so disposed, arrange to meet him.'

'We will need a huge boiler, and large cooking pots and ladles, and a big preparation area in order to feed such numbers,' warned Daniel McCarthy. 'I am willing to provide a boiler and the like, but we are going to need people to prepare the soup, and then cook and serve it, and clean up and keep order.'

'We will need long tables and benches for people to sit at and eat,' added Tom Marmion. 'I will be happy to provide them.'

'The people should be given a daily ticket to attend the soup kitchen and must show it, otherwise we risk people returning again and again,' suggested their treasurer, bank manager John Clerke.

'Mrs Hegarty from the Becher Arms has kindly offered us a cook and some of her kitchen staff to assist us temporarily. Her business has suffered greatly with all that has happened, for these days there are few visitors willing to stay in the town for more than a day or two,' Thomas Somerville explained.

'I'm sure more ladies from the town will volunteer to help once we open,' added Father Fitzpatrick.

'Then let us waste no more time. Let us plan to open the soup kitchen to the public as soon as it is possible,' declared Reverend Townsend. 'For every day we hesitate, more poor souls are lost.'

Chapter 29

FATHER JOHN FITZPATRICK WAS DEEPLY MOVED BY THE HUGE CROWDS HE observed along Ilen Street as they converged on the mill. Despite the freezing chill of the November day and its biting wind, the gaunt and poorly clad figures all walked with great purpose towards the newly opened soup kitchen to be fed. Gaunt-faced men carried scrawny, stick-like children on their backs.

The grand opening of the soup kitchen had attracted much attention, and many of Skibbereen's traders and merchants were both curious and concerned to see how this kitchen might help alleviate the terrible hunger suffered by so many. Word must have spread quickly, for all through the town, along the river's edge and across the bridge the hungry walked in their hundreds: barefoot mothers and young children; fathers in ragged coats, carrying infants; elderly men bent over sticks and skeletal old women. Their desperation was etched on their faces.

A few in the parish had raised fears that the relief committee's soup kitchen might attract indigents from the surrounding areas, with more beggars and sick crowding into Skibbereen than before. But looking around him, Father Fitzpatrick felt nothing but pride in what the committee had accomplished.

The enticing smell of the soup was carried on the wind. As he made his way to the back entrance of the mill, the priest saw the tall figure of Reverend Trench in full command of the situation as three women stirred the soup in an enormous boiler. Others were serving it from large cooking pots into tin bowls and cups, and whatever rusty mugs and containers the people carried with them. Those who did not have a suitable receptacle for their portion were given a tin bowl, which was rinsed quickly when they had finished eating so that it might be reused.

The serving women's faces were flushed from the heat and effort of their work, unaware that hundreds more people were queuing outside, desperate to be fed.

Following Reverend Frederick Trench's orders, requests for an extra serving were refused.

'Come again tomorrow,' the servers urged. 'The soup pots will be full again then.'

'This is a good day's work we have done here, Father Fitzpatrick.' Reverend Townsend smiled as he approached the parish priest.

'You are right, Reverend Townsend. We have saved lives this day.'

They watched as the long lines of hungry people continued to swell and grow.

'What if they run out of soup?' he asked, worried. 'We can't turn people away.'

'They won't,' reassured Reverend Townsend. 'Reverend Trench assures me that the women have another two huge pots cooking, ready to use when needed.'

'I never imagined that so many were going hungry. We will have to raise additional funds if we are to feed all these people day after day.'

'Reverend Caulfield and I are set to travel to London as part of a delegation from the relief committee to lodge an official appeal to all those in authority with regards to the situation and relief needed here in West Cork.'

'The government must surely intervene, Richard, for things cannot continue in such a vein.'

'We hope to have a meeting with Charles Trevelyan in which we can inform him first hand of the calamity and terrible conditions we witness daily.'

'I pray that you manage to exert some influence on the treasurer and all those in London who can provide assistance here,' Father John offered sincerely, for he had a high regard for the Protestant minister and his devotion to the people of the town.

Chapter 30

MARY WRAPPED UP THE CHILDREN WARMLY, FOR IT WAS BITTERLY COLD outside as they prepared to set off on the long walk to Skibbereen.

'Where are we going, Mammy?' asked Nora, curious.

'We are walking all the way into town to get the soup,' she tried to explain.

Kathleen and Honora Barry had both told her of the big soup kitchen that had opened in the mill by the river. Nell and her family had gone there twice already, joining the long lines of people waiting for a portion.

'It's the grandest soup ever,' Nell had declared. 'There was enough even to help fill those hungry boys of mine!'

Brigid had announced shortly after that she too was taking her children into town to take the soup as there was nothing in their cottage for them.

'My heart is scalded with it, Mary, watching them all go hungry!' she had fretted.

So the two friends decided to journey the four miles to town together, their nine children walking along beside them.

After only a mile or two, Annie demanded to be lifted up and carried.

'She has you wrapped around her little finger,' teased Brigid.

They passed close to the roadworks at Oldcourt, near the pier where John and Denis were employed, but caught no sight of their husbands.

Growing tired, the children slowed down . . . for none of them had the strength or energy for walking they had before the hunger came.

'It's only another two miles,' Mary cajoled them, 'and then there is a grand feed of soup waiting for you.'

'I'm tired,' complained Brigid's youngest, wanting to sit down and rest only a half-mile later.

'It's only a little bit further,' promised her mother.

As they neared the town, the road began to get busier. Hundreds of people were all making their way to the soup kitchen. The children huddled close to their mothers for fear of getting lost.

'We need to get a ticket at the dispensary first,' explained Brigid.

They then joined the long line of people all along Bridge Street, making their way slowly towards the mill . . .

Mary had never seen the like of it as they turned on to Ilen Street. Old and young, hungry and weak, all were lined up, some with their tin cups, to enter the soup kitchen. Some were so exhausted and starved that they could barely walk. Their legs and arms were like sticks dressed in rags. Hunger was etched on their thin faces. A man checked their tickets and beckoned them forwards.

Inside the mill was hot and steamy and packed. They could see a huge boiler, and two large serving pots, filled with soup. Behind that, a group of women in aprons were cutting and preparing more vegetables to put in the boiler.

The children grew nervous as they neared the server, a red-faced woman who ladled out a half-bowl of soup for each of them. She gave Con and James – Brigid's eldest boy – a larger ration than the younger ones. She then filled Mary's can with a pint of soup and pointed out where they could get a hunk of bread each before sitting down at the long narrow dining tables to eat.

'Can I get some extra to take home for my husband, please?' Mary begged.

'We can't be doing that,' the woman said, shaking her head. 'Or else there wouldn't be a drop of soup left for all the people here.'

Mary took her seat with Brigid and the children, and made sure that Tim and Annie ate.

The soup was salty, made with carrots and turnip, onion, rice, barley and a little beef. She ate it slowly, not wanting to turn her stomach as she had eaten little for the past two days. The bread she would save for John. Brigid's three boys gulped it down quickly, as did Con, while Nora said little but took it spoonful by spoonful, savouring it. There was little conversation around them as everyone concentrated on their meal.

At the table next to theirs, a pale-faced boy of about eight was shaking his head. Despite his mother's pleas he refused to take the soup, telling her he was no longer hungry. The poor woman dipped her finger into the bowl and made him suck it as if he were a baby.

'Suck, my little *peata*,' she crooned. 'Suck, my little lamb child.'

Before long, a bell rang to signal that all those eating must move on and make way for the next group. A tall young woman came over to collect their bowls and spoons for washing, and urged them to leave.

The soup had warmed them and filled their stomachs, and Mary felt better for it.

Con shouted out when he caught a glimpse of his cousin Jude in the distance, lining up on Ilen Street with his mother, Kathleen.

Mary ran over to speak to them.

'Even though it's near on our doorstep, we'll be here a good two hours or more, waiting.' Kathleen shrugged. 'Take your children home before it rains and sure, I'll see you the next day.'

Walking the long miles home took an age, for the younger ones complained. Tim kept saying that his foot hurt, while Brigid's youngest, Sally, claimed the soup had made her stomach sick!

'Aren't they the grand family we have, after them all being fed!' Brigid sighed as the rain began to fall, soaking them all through.

*

Mary was glad to get home and sit at the warmth of her own fire. Taking out her scissors, needle and thread, she began to fashion a special pocket concealed in the folds of her wide skirt where she would hide her can on their next visit to the soup kitchen. She would use a lid made of thick cloth to contain a half-pint of leftover soup, which she would save for John.

Every day the children complained about the long miles they now walked to Skibbereen, but Mary would hear none of it. The soup would take the worst of the hunger off them. She would not let them starve like others around them or watch the flesh fall from their young bones. So they walked the hungry road . . .

Chapter 31

HENRIETTA WOULD NEVER GET USED TO THE SIGHT OF SO MANY MEN, women and children waiting patiently at the mill to be fed. Thousands now flocked to the soup kitchen every day, coming from all over West Cork. From Aughadown, Creagh, Kilcoe, Rath, Baltimore, Ballydehob and Union Hall, they swamped the streets, lanes and roads leading to Skibbereen. Some were so weak that they could barely walk.

'Henrietta, I see we are in the same mind coming to visit here.' Elizabeth Townsend, the rector's wife, smiled at her in greeting. 'It is heartening to see that at long last something is being done to help these poor people.'

'But it is so bitterly cold, and most of them have no shoes or coats, or even shawls to keep them warm,' Henrietta sighed, unable to hide her distress.

'Richard says that they have sold or pawned all they possess in order to buy food. They now face the winter with nothing but rags to wear.'

'Poor things, they will surely get severe chills and colds with this weather,' Henrietta said with worry as she looked at a shivering mother, her two little girls and baby boy.

'Perhaps the women among us could do something to get them some old clothes,' suggested Elizabeth. 'An unused dress or shawl for the women, maybe, and trousers, shirts, jackets and dresses for the children to wear. The minute I get home I will look to see if I can find any warm clothing I can pass on to them.'

'I will search our wardrobes and chests too,' Henrietta promised. 'There must surely be something that we have that would prove useful.'

'Do you think the other wives of the committee and people in town might be interested in organizing such a relief collection of clothing and warm items?'

'I do hope so. Most people are kind hearted and should be willing to give something.'

'Many have been very charitable already,' Elizabeth reminded her gently.

Henrietta felt somewhat guilty, as Elizabeth was a most dedicated and helpful wife to a busy church minister. She, on the other hand, was caught up with running a busy household, taking care of a baby, her young children and the constant stream of patients all anxious to see her husband.

'Henrietta, will you come to the Glebe to have tea with me tomorrow and we can discuss it further?'

Henrietta had never been invited to their home before, but she knew that their husbands were united in their efforts on the relief committee.

'Your children are welcome to come along too,' Elizabeth added.

'They are noisy and rather troublesome,' warned Henrietta.

'I always enjoy having little ones in the rectory,' coaxed Elizabeth.

Henrietta decided the boys would be better at home, but she dressed up the three girls and baby Margaret and took them along to the rectory with her the following day.

Elizabeth welcomed them into her drawing room warmly.

'What pretty daughters you and Dan have!' she said, admiring Fanny and Harriet, who with only a year between them looked almost like twins in their matching pink dresses. 'They are like two little rosebuds.'

'Thank you.' Henrietta knew that it must be difficult for Elizabeth. She and Richard had not been blessed with any family of their own, yet with good grace she had organized many events for the children of the parish over the years, from Bible plays and pageants to the annual Easter party.

Elizabeth rang the bell and her maid, Jane, came along to serve them tea. She also carried a pretty plate of hot buttered scones with jam and a few small slices of cake.

'Cake! Good-ee!' shouted Fanny loudly. 'We are not allowed to eat it at home any more.'

'Dada doesn't like it,' added Harriet sagely.

'It's just with the situation at the moment,' Henrietta tried to explain. 'He feels that we must not be wasteful or indulgent.'

'Don't worry, these days we rarely have such things either,' Elizabeth admitted. 'But having you and the girls come to visit gives me a chance to be hospitable.'

'Well, we very much appreciate the invitation,' Henrietta replied, helping herself to a scone and some jam.

'Besides, it is nice for me to have a little company while my husband is away. He and Reverend Caulfield have travelled to London to appeal for assistance on behalf of this district,' she explained. 'Richard intends to talk to people at the highest level. He is hopeful of an opportunity to meet Charles Trevelyan and convince him of the urgent necessity for government intervention and support for immediate relief efforts.'

'Well, I pray that their mission is successful.'

'All our prayers are with them!'

Henrietta looked enviously around the neat drawing room, which was a haven of peace. There were shelves filled with books, a piano, and Elizabeth's embroidery hoop lay on a side table.

'Do you embroider?' her host asked, following Henrietta's gaze.

'No, I am afraid that I am all fingers and thumbs.'

'At night I find it relaxing to sit by the fire and embroider while Richard writes his sermons or does some parish work.'

The children, curious, had ventured over to the piano.

'Do the girls play?'

'No, I'm afraid we don't have one,' she told her regretfully.

'Richard and I both play a little.' Elizabeth smiled. 'I find that music is good for the soul.'

Elizabeth crossed the room to the instrument and demonstrated to Harriet and Fanny how to play a few notes. She encouraged Harriet to sit at the piano stool and guided her in touching the keys gently to produce a scale. Delighted, the girls played away. Their playing was tuneless but their enjoyment was evident as they ran their fingers up and down the black and white keys.

Jane came into the room with more tea. She was a pretty little thing, not more than fifteen years old, with fair hair and a pert nose.

'Will I bring more cake, ma'am?'

'Yes, please. Finely cut for my young guests.'

Jane nodded and left the room.

'Although she is young, she is proving to be a fine maid,' Henrietta's host confided. 'And Kate, our cook, is happy to have young Jane here to assist her.'

On her return, the maid offered to take baby Margaret and the children for a while so that the two women could talk in peace about their plan to ask the wives of the committee members and other friends to consider a clothing appeal. The baby settled happily in Jane's arms as she shepherded the other girls down to the kitchen.

'I have already unearthed almost a box of clothes that neither Richard nor I need any longer, which we intend to donate,' Elizabeth began.

'I found two coats – one of mine and one of my husband's – and a boys' jacket, some clothes from our son Daniel that I can give, and I'm sure I have some warm stockings and a dress or two that the girls no longer need, and three pairs of sturdy boots.'

'Well done, Henrietta, for I'm sure that, like many large families, most of the clothes get passed down between the children, much as my own parents did.'

'Mostly, but I still managed to find a few items that hopefully will be useful. And I'm intent on finding more.'

'We have not been idle but must ask others to join us,' Elizabeth said, taking out a sheet of paper and starting to write a list of names that they should each approach.

'I have so enjoyed our visit,' thanked Henrietta, as she and the children got ready to leave. It had turned bitterly cold outside so she buttoned up the children's coats and wrapped their scarves around them tightly.

Elizabeth smiled. 'You are welcome here any time.'

'The next time, perhaps you will come and visit me. Though I'm afraid our home will certainly not be as quiet and peaceful as yours.'

'I will look forward to it,' said the rector's wife graciously as she bid goodbye to Henrietta and the children.

'Mama!' called Harriet and Fanny excitedly, as they ran outside. 'Look, it's snowing!'

Snowflakes tumbled from the sky like feathers, whirling and swirling all around them. The children held out their hands to catch them as they walked back to New Street. The falling snow continued all through the long night and by morning had blanketed the streets and lanes, roads and fields and entire countryside with thick, deep, white cover.

Chapter 32

THE FALLEN SNOW LAY DEEP AND HEAVY ON THE GROUND. HENRIETTA laced up her boots and grabbed her heavy wool coat. She pulled on her hat, gloves and scarf as she set off to brave the elements, for there were some errands she needed to run.

The streets of Skibbereen were icy, and the hungry who were sheltering from the cold in doorways and gateways begged and pulled at every passer-by for food or money. A small group of them were hunkered down near the Donovans' doorway.

'Bit of food, ma'am, for the hungry?' pleaded a stick-thin man with his wife and two boys.

'I'm sorry but I have no food on me,' she apologized, moved by their plight as she eased her way past them gently as they called after her. How these poor families could endure such weather, dressed only in tattered rags with their feet bare, shamed her. Dan was run ragged looking after such people day after day, and always showed such constant care and consideration for them that it made her love and admire him even more.

She had made a list, for she had to purchase some necessary household items. She would dearly love to order a new dress to see her through the winter and Christmas season but Dan, she knew, would not countenance such extravagance, especially in the face of the distress suffered by their fellow man.

As she had sorted through clothes to donate, she had realized that young Dan was in sore need of breeches, shirts and a new warm jacket, for he had outgrown his infant clothes and was becoming quite a little boy! Her husband could not expect her to dress their small son in the worn hand-me-downs of his two brothers.

She also needed desperately to purchase a book. She got bored being at home so much, and longed to read the latest work of Mr Dickens if it were available. She also was in need of writing paper and some ink of her own, for Dan was forever at his desk writing letters. She dearly wanted to correspond with her family and friends, and to hear some good news, if there were any.

Groups of the poor and hungry huddled together everywhere – in the doorway of the bank, outside the Becher Arms, near the brewery – trying to escape the bitter cold. A small boy tugged at her coat like a frightened sparrow. He held out the palm of his hand, too tired even to say a word. His face was covered with a downy layer of hair.

Poor child! She reached into her pocket and produced a penny, which she handed to him in silence, then watched him scurry away, no doubt to spend it immediately.

At the stationer's she collected the new pen that she had ordered for Dan and some writing paper and ink. One part of the shop held newspapers, periodicals and a small display of books, which she browsed. There were a few of Maria Edgeworth's books and she was drawn to the latest work of Charles Dickens, *A Christmas Carol*, which she decided to purchase. It would definitely hold her attention and might even interest Dan.

She then moved on to Hayes' drapery on Main Street to purchase clothing for young Daniel: three pairs of breeches, three shirts, a warm navy wool coat, some undergarments and woollen socks.

'A growing boy, Mrs Donovan.' Mr Hayes laughed as he parcelled them up. 'Anything that doesn't fit the young lad, just return them and we'll find something more suitable.'

Normally, Henrietta enjoyed looking around the shops, but it was far too cold to dawdle. She had just turned off Market Lane when she almost tripped over a woman sitting on the icy ground. The woman's legs were outstretched and she held a baby in her arms. Dressed only in a threadbare shift, Henrietta could see her bare breasts and skinny torso, her shoulder bones and ribs clearly visible. Her legs were like mottled sticks, and her feet were swollen and dirty.

The baby lay crookedly in her arms, when the woman pitched forward suddenly. Overcome with pity, Henrietta rushed to prevent her from falling to the ground and tried to save the small baby that was wrapped in a filthy bit of blanket.

'Are you all right?' she asked, alarmed by the woman's condition.

The woman said nothing but leaned back and tried to straighten herself up.

'I am weak with the hunger,' she whispered.

Henrietta was filled with concern for her and was about to hand the child back when she realized how still it was. A terrible fear gripped her when she gazed down and saw that the small face was waxy, the skin almost translucent, with a blue sheen around its delicate lips and closed eyes. The child was stone cold, dead, all the life gone from it. No matter what Henrietta did, there was no saving this child.

The mother's hands reached out for her baby and Henrietta passed her the infant. She felt a strange chill inside her own heart and did not know what to say to this poor mother. Was she aware of what had happened?

'You must stay here,' she begged the woman. 'I am going to get some help for you.'

She took off so quickly that she nearly lost her footing on the ice.

All she wanted was to find Dan and get him to help this unfortunate woman and her child. She had no idea what to do but Dan would know. She gasped as she ran home, trying not to cry as she thought of the poor frozen baby.

Dan was sitting at his desk, writing, puzzled by her disturbance.

'Dan, you must come with me quickly. Get your coat and hat!' she pleaded. 'There is a woman on the street with a dead child in her arms. We have to help her.'

In a matter of minutes Dan was making his way with Henrietta to the street where the woman still sat with her eyes closed, one hand outstretched, the child still in her arms.

'I brought my husband,' Henrietta explained.

'I am a doctor,' Dan said gently, kneeling down beside the woman. 'This lady is my wife and she was concerned for your child. May I take a look, please?'

Wordlessly, the woman passed the bundle into Dan's arms.

Dan looked carefully at the lifeless baby before turning his attention to the mother.

'I'm afraid that your baby is very poorly and you yourself are very weak. The best thing I can advise is that you be admitted immediately to the Union workhouse. I am the medical officer there. I will arrange it. Have you any family?'

'No.' She shook her head. 'Everyone died these past weeks.'

'As you are in a weakened state, I will fetch my horse and carriage and bring you myself.'

Tears of relief slid down the woman's exhausted face and Henrietta tried to control her own emotions in the face of her husband's kindness.

'My wife will stay with you for a few minutes while I go and fetch it.'

Henrietta crouched beside the woman, aware that the few people who passed them averted their gaze as they did not want to be accosted or get involved. She unwound her own knitted scarf from her neck and arranged it gently around the woman's shoulders, covering the child.

The day was growing ever colder. On Dan's return she assisted him in helping the woman – who had told her that her name was Catherine Driscoll – and her baby up into the carriage.

'Will I come with you?' Henrietta offered.

'No, my dear, it is better you return home,' Dan said softly. 'I will take care of Mrs Driscoll and ensure that she is admitted and looked after.'

*

Back at home, Henrietta fed the children and, despite her worry and distraction, prepared them for bed. They said their prayers and she read a story to them from the Bible. The younger ones' preference was for Noah's ark or Daniel in the lions' den. As she hugged their warm bodies, brushed their curling hair and tucked them in their beds, she prayed for God to keep all the children in the town safe and well that night.

'How is Mrs Driscoll?' she probed as Dan ate his meal that evening.

'Poorly, for she has typhus.'

'What about the baby?'

'Nurse Lynch managed to get her to give up the infant. She told her that it was with the rest of her family in heaven.'

'Oh, that poor woman. How could such a terrible thing happen, Dan?'

'Please, my dear, you must not distress yourself.'

'Of course I must distress myself. Witnessing what happened to that mother and her baby is something that I will never forget . . .' She tried to keep the growing sense of hysteria she was feeling from her voice. 'That woman lost her only living child.'

Dan ate his food slowly and meticulously.

'I'm sorry,' she apologized. 'I know this is what you see every day, but Dan, how can you bear it?'

'Henrietta, it is my duty. And besides, I have you and the children to consider.'

As she lay in his arms before sleep, Daniel soothed his wife and tried to calm her fears.

'Everything will be well soon,' he promised, treating her like a child.

Her dreams that night were haunted by Catherine Driscoll and her baby, and she could not put them from her mind, despite her best efforts.

The following day she enquired about Mrs Driscoll's health. Dan said little, only that she was ill in the fever ward. Three days later he broke the news that she had succumbed to typhus and would be buried with her child.

'You mean they will both be in the pit in Abbeystrewery grave-yard?' Henrietta demanded angrily.

'Yes, such are the daily burials,' he said quietly. 'But take comfort in the fact that they are both united in the afterlife, away from this torment.'

'It is small comfort, Dan, for I would far prefer to see her happy with her child, walking the streets of Skibbereen with her head held high, than lying in that cold place.'

That afternoon she lay down on their bed and cried, pulling the blankets around her as the snow began to fall again. A deep weari-ness possessed her, which she could not shake off and so gave in to sleep.

Hours later she awoke from her slumber. She had slept for so long that she had missed tea and putting the children to bed. She chas-tised herself! How could she do such a thing when she was a strong young woman, with a husband and family who needed her? Dan deserved a better wife, one who was resolute and steady, who could be relied upon and who would be a constant support to him and his work.

She stretched and got up, re-buttoned her dress and fixed her dark wavy hair. She dabbed a little lavender water on her wrists and neck before slipping on her shoes and making her way downstairs to join her husband who was sitting at the fire.

'I told Sally to tend to the children and let you rest,' he said gently.

His kindness near overwhelmed her and she felt close to tears again.

'It's all right, Hetty dearest.' Dan got up and wrapped his arms around her. 'I am here with you, and I promise that you have noth-ing to fear. I will always guard and protect you and our children.'

She could hear in his voice the care, concern and love that had always been between them. Without a word, Henrietta found herself sitting beside him, her head on his shoulder, watching the flames flicker in the grate.

'I am better now,' she said a long while later.

'Good,' he said, reaching for her. 'For you know that I cannot bear to see you so upset.'

Chapter 33

December 1846

DAN GAZED OUT THE WINDOW OF THE OFFICE BESIDE THE MILL. THE crowds below, like pale ghosts, struggled in the snow and icy conditions to reach the soup kitchen.

'God help them, for this is the worst winter in my memory!' Henry Marmion lamented as the relief committee gathered for its regular Monday meeting.

'It is hard to believe that we are already feeding between a thousand and fifteen hundred people a day,' reported John Clerke, the bank manager. 'The costs, as you can imagine, are enormous, and the numbers taking the soup continue to grow. We have decided to issue tickets that are to be used at different times of the day, which will make controlling such large numbers easier. Reverend Trench has also asked us to order two more boilers. Fortunately, we are receiving donations from generous-hearted Englishmen and a few charitable organizations, but we still need to raise far more money if we are to continue . . .'

The rest of the committee nodded in agreement.

'We must congratulate Reverend Townsend on his successful visit to London, which has already borne fruit.' Thomas Somerville smiled. 'The food depot in town has just opened and will remain open three days a week, while all other depots are to remain closed until after Christmas.'

'Reverend Caulfield and I did our best to inform those whom we met of the terrible conditions that prevail here,' Reverend Townsend admitted modestly. 'We had a good hearing with Mr Trevelyan, but he gave us little indication of his thoughts. However, his recent decision to divert a portion of the money due to Ceylon to aid the destitute here instead is most welcome. Apparently, the Queen has also indicated her intention to write a letter of appeal in the coming weeks to raise funds for her starving subjects.'

'We are very appreciative, Reverend,' thanked the chairman. 'You have done much to help the cause of Skibbereen and her people.'

Two days later, as he was about to leave the dispensary, Dan was appalled to see at least three hundred starving men from the road-works out by Lisheen, marching along the street in the freezing snow, demanding payment for their work. Most were severely emaciated, shivering with the cold and begging like some spectral army.

'Issue them each with a ticket for the soup kitchen,' he ordered the dispensary clerk, as he led the men to the mill where they were admitted immediately and served a pint of warm soup and a large portion of bread.

The local Board of Works commissioner and his man finally appeared and tried to appease the men with the promise of payment in a few days' time.

'They should hang their heads in shame,' Tim McCarthy Downing sighed as they watched the commissioner try to squirm his way out of responsibility for the men's poor treatment.

'It's the bureaucracy and ineptitude of those running the scheme that is to blame!' Dan raged, unable to hide his anger.

On the recommendation of Dan's cousin Michael Galwey, Nicholas Cummins, a justice of the peace from Cork, had asked if he could accompany Dan on a few visits to his patients. He wanted to assess the true state of affairs in West Cork and, if necessary, report on it.

'Dr Donovan, I have heard stories of terrible deprivation among the people here, which if they were true shame our government and officials,' he explained. 'Yet others say such claims are exaggerated. It behoves those of us in a position of influence to make our own investigation of such matters.'

'I have my rounds to do, Mr Cummins. You are welcome to come with me,' agreed Dan, 'but I must remind you that my duty is to my patients.'

It was clear that Nicholas Cummins was well intentioned, for only the day before he had visited the little village of South Reen.

'I brought loaves of bread for the people but the place seemed deserted. I went into what appeared an empty cabin only to discover six skeletons lying on the floor. I presumed the family were dead, until I heard moaning.' His voice began to shake. 'They were all sick with fever, Dr Donovan, and it was the same in one cabin after another.'

'It is a frightening thing to see,' Dan sympathized, 'but I'm afraid fever is rampant.'

'Then a gang of nearly two hundred starved, crazed creatures appeared, grabbing at me and pulling at my clothes. I tell you, I was lucky to escape them!'

Dan could see Mr Cummins was still deeply shocked by what he had seen.

As they walked around Skibbereen, Dan pointed out the corpse of a girl that had been dragged out of a cabin and into the street by her sick mother. It lay there, half covered with stones.

'She will be buried later in Abbeystrewery,' he reassured the justice of the peace.

They visited cabin after cabin of the sick and dying, finally stopping at one near the town's cavalry station. Dan warned Mr Cummins to stay at the door. Inside, seven people lay together under a cloak, a young man among them already dead, but the others near death and too weak to move.

'I will arrange to transfer the sick to the fever sheds in the workhouse,' Dan said quietly as he came back outside, for he could see his companion was deeply upset.

'I had never imagined such things in a Christian country,' Mr Cummins declared fervently as Dan finished his rounds. 'It's disgraceful and shames us that people are left to suffer like this. But I promise you, doctor, that I will endeavour to alert those in a position of influence to the horrific state of affairs here.'

Much to the surprise of the committee, only a few days before Christmas they received a visit from the Assistant Commissary-General, Mr Inglis.

'He's been sent by Randolph Routh himself to meet with us and to help us organize a plan for the relief of Skibbereen,' explained Thomas Somerville.

Mr Inglis could not hide his dismay at the scenes that greeted him, not only at the soup kitchen but on every street corner and lane. The committee members were more than pleased when, before his departure, he pledged eighty-five pounds towards the running of the soup kitchen, as it was the first government assistance they had received!

Henrietta begged Dan to take Christmas Day off at least and spend it with his family.

'What of my patients?' he protested. 'I can't leave them.'

'You must rest,' she insisted. 'Or you will fall ill!'

They had celebrated the birth of Jesus at a crowded mass, which many of his patients also attended. Excited, the children had fun outside in the snow with some friends and neighbours, before they returned home for their Christmas meal.

Dan stretched out in front of the fire as they played some new board and card games with the children, and read a few chapters of Mr Dickens' wonderful new book.

'Look at this.'

He called Henrietta over to read a long letter that had been published on the front page of *The Times* on Christmas Eve. Nicholas

Cummins had kept his word and had written to the Duke of Wellington. He had told in great detail of his harrowing visit to Skibbereen and implored the duke, in the name of the starving thousands, to break the frigid and flimsy chain of etiquette and save the land of his birth, and the paper had published it in full!

'That letter must have caused quite a stir at many a Christmas table,' Henrietta mused. 'For Mr Cummins requested that a copy of it also be given to the Queen.'

Dan smiled and began to re-read the piece. 'This one voice can say more than a thousand.'

Chapter 34

ON HIS RETURN TO WORK IN THE DISPENSARY, DAN WAS CALLED OUT TO Bridgetown immediately, where there had been serious outbreaks of both typhus and dysentery. Nearly every cabin in one lane was affected. In Windmill Lane the police had found the body of a man which had turned green and been left to rot for at least five days. His wife and children – a boy and a girl – lay ill on the filthy floor near him.

'Why didn't you bury him?' he asked the wife gently.

'I have no coffin,' she sobbed.

Seeing her shame at her near-naked state of undress, it was clear that the sick woman wanted to be left to die with her husband.

Dan was torn between anger at her situation and pity for her as he arranged for the children to be moved immediately to the fever hospital.

Back in the dispensary, a large crowd of patients waited to see him, most of whom were suffering from fever and bowel complaints too. They all clamoured for his attention and Dan's heart sank when he saw Mr Hughes, the commissariat officer, arriving to enquire about the latest statistics for disease in the neighbourhood. Could the man not see he was inundated and had no time to give him?

'Mr Hughes, as of this morning there are about eighty-five cases of fever on a single lane in Bridgetown,' he reported succinctly.

The other figures were similarly grim and he could see the anxiety on the other man's face as he listed them.

'Also, Mr Hughes, I must inform you officially that many of the men employed on the public relief schemes are now succumbing to a new classification of sickness which I call "road fever". It is prevalent among the famished and weakened labourers who are engaged in this work at the expense of their own lives.'

'I will note your concerns, Dr Donovan,' Mr Hughes returned coldly.

Dan was barely able to conceal his frustration. Not only did he battle against disease and hunger but also against a wall of hypocrisy and petty administration that had no intention of acting on any of his medical recommendations.

'You must forgive me, but I am due soon at the Union and fever hospital,' he said brusquely, dismissing the official and returning to his duties.

Over Christmas the workhouse had been overwhelmed by new admissions. Both the women's and men's sections were now so crowded that there was hardly a space in which to stand, let alone in which to lie down and rest or sleep. In the fever wards, the sick were forced to share their soiled straw pallets with other patients.

'I'm sorry, Dr Donovan, but what are we to do?' pleaded the matron. 'My staff and I are doing what we can, but there are no blankets or even pallets left.'

He knew the good woman was trying to manage, but having so many patients packed together was no doubt contributing to the spread of disease. He was also concerned for the welfare of the exhausted staff, some of whom clearly were unwell.

'Matron, I will speak with Mr Falvey and inform the Union guardians officially that we urgently need to acquire more buildings in the town in which to place inmates.'

In the children's wing, a number of young children had also been admitted. He examined them and all were malnourished, with a few showing clear symptoms of dysentery too. They should have been placed in the fever ward, instead of there, where they were mingling with the other children.

Young Will Hayes ran over to Dan, who gave the boy a small red ball he'd kept for him. His own children had received a number of toys for Christmas and he had encouraged them to be generous with their gifts.

The three-year-old's eyes lit up, as he was unused to presents and playthings. Dan showed him how to catch the ball and roll it back and throw it himself. The boy laughed as he caught it successfully. It was heartwarming to see him play.

'Now, I must leave you as I have to work,' Dan said ruefully, bending down to his level.

The child reached out to touch him, and Dan lifted him up and spun him around in his arms, the way he did with his own children, before lowering him slowly to the floor.

'Thank you,' Will said, as he ran off to play with his new ball, followed by two other small boys.

On his leaving the workhouse, the waiting crowd outside assailed Dan, begging for his help to admit them.

'Go home,' Dan pleaded with them. 'Take shelter somewhere else. There is no admittance as the workhouse is full, and many inside are sick with fever.'

It made no matter what he said. They refused to budge.

He arrived home to find Henrietta in a terrible state, weeping into her hands.

'Dan,' she said, throwing herself into his arms. 'Poor Margaret Murphy has just died.'

'What happened to her?' He was shocked to hear of their good neighbour's death.

'Her daughter tells me she caught the fever. She sickened soon after visiting me here only a few days ago. It's entirely my fault!'

'My dear, why would you think or say such a thing?'

'Because it is true. While she was here I opened the door to a patient of yours, Mr O'Shea. He wanted help to buy a coffin for his young son. The poor man was clearly ill and distressed, and Margaret, who as you know was always so kind, made him sit down here and consoled him.'

Henrietta broke down again tearfully as Sally, their maid, tried to calm her.

'Margaret's kindness to that poor man has killed her.' His wife sniffed, her eyes and nose red. 'If she had not crossed this door she might still be alive. Her children would still have their good mother, her husband his wife.'

'Hush, my love, we do not know that for sure,' he soothed, kneeling down beside her, taking her hand in his.

'It is so, Dan,' she said bitterly, taking the handkerchief from his hand. 'Margaret came here because we are friends, and then was stricken.'

Henrietta broke down again, inconsolable.

As he held her hand, Dan's mind was racing. He was growing increasingly worried about the safety of his own family. What would happen should Henrietta or any of the children fall ill, as their neighbour had?

If anyone was to blame it was he, for Patrick O'Shea and his son had been his patients. The child had died of typhus and, frantic to find a coffin in which to bury him, his bereaved father had left his own sick bed to come here for assistance, putting Dan's own family at risk.

These past weeks it had been his greatest fear that the fever somehow would spread from the poor and starving to the rest of the town's population. Now, here in his own home, that fear had come to pass . . .

Chapter 35

January 1847

MARY CAREFULLY FOLDED THE SMALL BUNDLE OF CLOTHES SHE HAD
patched and mended, ready to return them to Honora Barry. Of
late, the dressmaker had been giving her less and less work but despite that, the good woman often parcelled up a cut of soda bread, a
piece of cheese or a salted herring for Mary to take home to the
children, insisting that she had more than enough to eat.

The fields around the cottage were blanketed with thick drifts of
heavy snow, for it had fallen again these past two days. It was far too
deep for Annie and Tim to walk into town, but despite the fierce
weather, John was still working every day.

Taking down her heavy shawl, Mary wrapped it around her shoulders and told Con and Nora to stay inside in the warm and mind
their younger siblings.

By the time she reached Honora's shop, her fingers and feet were
frozen with the cold. The window looked dusty and the same dress
that had been in the window a few weeks earlier was still there. She
rang the bell but no one answered. She tried to push the door but it
was locked. Peering through the glass, she saw the dressmaker inside,
sewing, her head bent in concentration. Mary knocked briskly on the
window pane until she got her attention.

'I have to be careful these days,' Honora apologized as she opened the door. 'The town is full of beggars.'

Mary blushed as she followed Honora inside, for by all appearances she herself was no better. The older lady gestured for her to sit down as Mary passed her the small bit of mending she had done.

'Your usual good work, Mary,' she thanked, examining it briefly.

Mary could tell she was distracted and upset.

'I'm so sorry, but I won't be able to give you any more work, for I have little enough of it myself these days.'

Mary was gutted with disappointment but had suspected as much as Jane had stopped working there in November and returned home to Bantry.

'Will you have a cup of tea with me?' the dressmaker offered.

Mary nodded, for a warming drink would hopefully take the chill out of her.

'Business is bad these past months,' Honora admitted as they sat in the back room and she poured the tea. 'The good ladies who used to come to me for their style are fearful of being seen to be extravagant or frivolous in these hardest of times. So, any repair or alteration work for my customers I will now do myself.'

'I understand.' Mary nodded, trying to remain calm and not give in to the fear and sense of foreboding that gripped at her heart.

'I should have moved to Dublin or Cork last year,' the dressmaker said ruefully. 'Closed up my shop and gone like many others. But alas, now it is too late for that.'

She paid Mary a shilling – a bit more than she owed her – taking the money from the tin box that was kept in a drawer in the dresser, and also gave her a half loaf of oaten bread.

''Tis too big for a woman on her own,' she said with a smile as they said their farewells. 'Hopefully we will both soon see better times.'

Back on the street, Mary felt faint and so went to the dispensary to get a ticket for that day's soup kitchen. Clutching the piece of paper, she made her way to the large mill and joined the long line waiting to be fed. Once she'd eaten, she bought a small bag of oats and some flour with the little money she had, before calling briefly to her sister.

Kathleen commiserated with her when Mary broke the news to her about Honora Barry not being able to give her any more work.

'I don't know how we will manage without the money,' she said tearfully.

'Things will get better,' promised Kathleen, telling her the good news that Michael, her fifteen-year-old son, had found employment as a servant in Mr O'Brien's house in Clonakilty.

'The boy who worked for him took sick, so Michael will replace him. To tell the truth, I'm happy for him not to be labouring on the roadworks like his poor father,' she admitted.

'At least they both have work.'

'Though they earn divil a bit for it,' Kathleen said bitterly. 'Not enough to keep a family. At least with Michael away there will be one less mouth to feed, for the boys have me scalded looking for food!'

'Con and Tim are the same, but at least you have the soup kitchen close by,' Mary said enviously. 'The icy roads are too bad these days for the children to walk them.'

'Half the town would be dead without it, for near every soul in Bridgetown has a ticket for it.'

Despite the soup, Mary could not help but notice that her three-year-old niece Lizzie's face was as pale as the snow outside and her stomach distended. Realizing it would soon get dark, Mary wrapped herself up warmly, said goodbye to her sister and set off home.

Chapter 36

DAN TOOK A DEEP BREATH AND FILLED HIS LUNGS WITH FRESH AIR before he entered the workhouse where the conditions were increasingly deplorable. Every square foot and yard of floor space was taken up by a mother, child or decrepit old man near to his end of days. Crowded and stinking, there was little space for a body to stretch or move, and certainly there was no comfort here for the ill or weak. Was it any wonder that in this festering environment, typhus fever and dysentery were rampant among the inmates?

Dan's heart sank in the fever hospital when he spotted three-year-old Will Hayes. The little boy was hunched up under a badly soiled blanket with two other children, all sick with dysentery. His skin was hot to touch, his heartbeat rapid and his breathing shallow.

'Come on now, Will, try to take a little water for me,' Dan coaxed.

At the sound of Dan's voice, the small boy slowly opened his blue eyes. He was seriously ill and Dan asked the assistant to bring him a clean blanket and damp cloth so that he could try to cool him down.

'Will, when you are well again, I promise that I will bring you another ball to play with,' he said, stroking his hand.

The boy gripped the doctor's forefinger and Dan could see he was trying to fight this illness, just as he had once fought to come into the world and to survive in this place.

'You are such a brave boy, Will,' he urged him as he sat quietly by his side. 'Stay strong!'

A short while later, with great reluctance, Dan had to leave his young friend as the matron needed him. The nurses and assistants were doing what they could to help the living and dying, but Dan could see that they too were exhausted and worn out.

'We endeavour to do our best for them, Dr Donovan, but we are overwhelmed and do not have enough beds or blankets, or buckets even,' the usually stalwart matron confided in him, close to tears. 'One of my nurses is sick and I fear another will leave.'

Mr Falvey was equally concerned and called Dan into the privacy of his office.

'The situation here is intolerable,' he said. 'We cannot continue like this, trying to manage such numbers. Some of our staff have fallen ill and others are threatening to leave.'

Dan could see that the poor man was grey-faced and near the end of his tether.

'And such is our dire financial situation, Dr Donovan, that by tomorrow the kitchen will not be able to serve even a small bowl of gruel to the inmates, for we do not have enough money to replenish our stores.'

Shocked to hear of the perilous and precarious position of the workhouse, Dan called an urgent meeting of the Board of Guardians of the Union, deciding to move the meeting from their usual boardroom in the workhouse to the courthouse – for their own safety.

'We have one thousand, one hundred and sixty-nine inmates. Three hundred and thirty-two of them have fever and are in either the infirmary or the hospital,' Mr Falvey explained nervously as he addressed the board. 'Gentlemen, these numbers are far greater than the Union was built to hold, and I have no other choice but to request that the Board of Guardians give full consideration to closing the Skibbereen Union to all further admittances.'

'In my medical opinion, given the level of illness and contagion,' added Dan, 'I agree with the master. This is the only safe and wise thing for the board to do.'

'I also must inform the board that there is not sufficient food in the workhouse to provide meals,' Mr Falvey continued, his voice breaking. 'We will not be able to serve the inmates with breakfast tomorrow morning. I will be obliged to pay in ready cash for any food that I purchase, for nobody will give us credit.'

No food! There was utter shock around the table at such a disastrous state of affairs.

'Why is that?' demanded chairman Thomas Somerville.

'I assume it is because we already have many creditors among the suppliers in the town.'

'I am a creditor,' signalled Daniel Welply, the local linen and woollen supplier. 'For I am owed three hundred pounds.'

'And will you give further credit?'

He nodded. 'Given the dire situation, I suppose that I am prepared to give you more if it is required.'

'But where are we to find money for meal, or milk or firing, or other necessities that are required?' worried wealthy landowner James Redmond Barry, who, of late, had taken on feeding a hundred people from the soup kitchen run from his own home at Glandore House. 'There must be some sort of funds, surely.'

'James, we have exhausted our funds,' the treasurer admitted. 'We have one hundred and sixty-five pounds only in the bank, while the demands we have to meet are one thousand four hundred and twenty-nine pounds.'

'Given the urgency of the situation, these funds must be used today to make such purchases,' insisted the chairman. 'We cannot have it that people who fled to the Union for protection and shelter go hungry. They deserve at least to be fed.'

'To fund the Union we will have to somehow raise the poor rate and more subscriptions,' admitted Daniel McCarthy. 'No easy task!'

'There is another matter,' added Mr Falvey. 'Seven members of the resident staff have been attacked by inmates this past week. One of the nurses has demanded her discharge, the apothecary signified his intention to tender his resignation yesterday, and Dr Donovan is nearly broken down in his bodily powers by his persevering exertions.'

Dismayed, the guardians expressed their deep concern for the staff members and thanked Dan warmly for his dedication to his patients and the inmates.

'I am only doing my duty as a physician,' Dan acknowledged humbly.

'So, Mr Falvey, you are telling us here today that the Union is dangerously full with the sick and dying, there is no food, no money to purchase food, and many of the workhouse staff are ready to give notice and resign.'

'I am sorry, Mr Chairman, but that is the extent of it,' the master said with a sigh of despair, relieved to sit down finally after bearing such calamitous news.

Following the recommendations of both Dan and Mr Falvey, the Board of Guardians voted to agree to the immediate closure of the Skibbereen Union Workhouse to all further admissions. They also agreed to issue an urgent appeal for increased funding to ensure that they could continue to operate the workhouse. A few of the guardians decided generously there and then to make a personal donation, while others offered to advance a temporary loan to the Union in order to rescue the desperate situation in which they found themselves.

They all knew it wasn't a permanent solution to the crisis they faced, but at least for the present the inmates would be fed and the sick would be cared for as best they could.

Chapter 37

HENRIETTA WATCHED DAN AS HE PICKED DISTRACTEDLY WITH HIS FORK at the mutton they were eating. He never complained of tiredness, for he was blessed with a vigour and energy few men possessed. However, of late, she could not help but worry, for her husband looked careworn, with dark shadows under his eyes. He was rarely home any more, gone from early morning to late at night, seemingly at the beck and call of every beggar and sick person in the district. When he did appear, he usually excused himself to attend some committee meeting or other.

The children missed their father and his attention, just as she missed their chats and walks together, or the hours they used to spend sitting reading a book, sharing a story or discussing an item in the newspaper, for Dan was not just her husband but her dearest friend.

Ellen, Fanny and Harriet vied for his attention, waving to see if he noticed they had had their hair cut. Dan remained lost in a world of his own as he ate slowly.

'Dada, you must notice something different about me today,' demanded Fanny, coming over to sit on his lap, waggling her pretty head.

Henrietta laughed to herself and gave Dan a warning kick under the table to attend to Fanny's antics.

'Fanny, you have grown taller!' he ventured, which drew cries of 'no' from his daughter. 'Fanny, you have got heavier since yesterday!'

'No,' she protested.

'You learned to speak French!'

She pouted. 'Dada, you know I can't speak French.'

'I know,' he said. 'You have cut and curled your pretty hair just like your beautiful sisters!'

Fanny jumped up and did a few twirls to show off her new hairstyle. Ellen and Harriet joined in, while young Daniel laughed and their older brother Jerrie threw his eyes to heaven at the antics of his sisters.

'Certain little girls had developed a bit of an aversion to my bristle brush,' Henrietta confided, 'so losing a few inches of hair will make it a lot easier.'

'Of course, my dear,' he said, putting down his napkin and standing up from the table. His eyes showed he had little interest in her simple tittle-tattle about the children.

'Dada, play with us!' pleaded Fanny.

'I'm sorry, children, but I have to work,' Dan said, excusing himself and disappearing to the confines of his small study.

It was late and Dan was still working, no doubt writing his diary again. Passing his study door, Henrietta decided to wish him goodnight as she was about to retire. She found her husband sitting at his desk as usual, but he was not working. Instead, he held his head in his hands, deeply upset over something.

Henrietta flew to him.

'Oh, my dear, what is it?' she asked, fearful that he might be unwell. 'What has upset you so?'

Dan let out a shuddering, heavy sigh.

'Today I lost a patient. A small boy only a year younger than our Daniel, a workhouse boy,' he said, trying to control his emotions. 'He died from dysentery.'

Henrietta had never seen her husband so upset. Every day he saw the most awful sights and endured huge distress dealing with the dead and dying. Often he would discover putrid, rotting corpses and foul-smelling bodies, things she knew well he kept and protected her from.

'But Dan, all the sick you attend,' she ventured gently.

'It is ridiculous of me, but the boy, Will, was a fine little fellow. I helped to deliver him, the day the Liberator came. His young mother abandoned him to the Union's care. Yet the boy had such spirit. Every time he caught sight of me doing my rounds, he just wanted to play or talk to me, even if it was only for a few minutes. He was a bright child and I'm sure he would have made his way in the world when he was older. We were his guardians, responsible for his care, such as it was, and we let him down. I let him down.'

His eyes welled with unshed tears as he slumped in misery.

'You looked after that boy, Dan, and cared for him as best you could,' she assured him, running her hands along his shoulder. 'I know that, for I see it every day – the dedicated way you look after all those who need your help.'

'Instead of any hope of a good life, young Will has ended up buried in the workhouse graveyard.'

'It's not your fault.'

Henrietta held her husband as he gave in to the onslaught of emotion, stroking his hair like a child's. She kissed the top of his head and soothed him until all the hurt and pain that had built up in him was released.

'What must you think of me for being so foolish?' he apologized.

'I do not think it foolish to mourn,' Henrietta said gently. 'Especially when there are so many to mourn and grieve for.'

She took his hand and kissed it, knowing that she loved him more deeply than any other human in the world, and that though Dan may not say he needed her, she would always be there for him . . .

Chapter 38

Creagh

MARY EXAMINED JOHN'S FEET GENTLY AND BATHED THEM IN WARM water and salt. They were blistered and sore, and his big and second toe on one foot were blackened and swollen from where a heavy stone had fallen on them yesterday. She suspected they may even be broken.

'Stay home,' Mary pleaded with her stubborn husband, who had also had a fierce bad cough these past few days and looked ill. 'You are not able for such work tomorrow.'

'I'll be grand,' John insisted, though he could barely walk.

Watching him join Denis Leary and Tom Flynn the next morning, she felt increasingly fearful for him, for he was walking like an old man, limping along beside them.

'Oh, dear God,' she cried on his return home that evening.

Her husband's face was grey, and he could barely talk without provoking a fit of coughing. His body was hot then cold, and although she had piled the turf high on the fire he was unable to get warm. She watched helplessly as he shivered and sweated. Mary worried that he had caught road fever like so many of the men had.

In the morning he made an attempt to rise for work.

149

'You are going nowhere, John Sullivan. You are too sick to work!' she screamed at him like a harridan.

For the next few days he barely stirred, and she dared not leave his side.

'Con, take Nora and Tim and search for anything we can eat!'

She could see the fear in her eldest son's eyes as they set off for the woods and fields.

Despite their best efforts, the children returned empty-handed, so Mary added more water to the remnants of the thin gruel in the pot. She ignored the gnawing hunger pains in her own stomach as she fed her children.

For three days John was lost in a heavy sleep. As he lay wrapped in a blanket, barely waking or drinking, her mind filled with the awful possibility that her already-weak husband might not recover.

If they still had the horse and cart she would be able to take him to the dispensary or ask for a ticket for the doctor to visit him. But she did not dare to leave him, for he was gravely ill. His body and the blanket were soaked in sweat, and as the fever progressed he tossed and turned and wandered in his sleep as if in some kind of nightmare. She feared for him, as the sickness had overtaken him and he had not the strength left to fight it.

The children were scared and watched their father furtively. Nora wept openly at the sight of him in such a state.

'Hush, Nora. We just have to wait and see what will happen,' Mary said, hugging her close.

'I don't want Da to die,' her daughter begged.

'Your father is fighting as hard as he can to get better,' she tried to reassure her, 'but he is in God's hands now.'

All the night long, Mary sat with her husband. She did not know whether to be alarmed or pleased when at last he fell into a deep, heavy sleep. He neither stirred nor made a sound until the early hours of the morning when he opened his eyes slightly and winced at the candlelight before returning to sleep.

Hope flickered inside her. She allowed him to slumber but a few hours later, when she called his name softly, she was rewarded by him opening his eyes again and staring at her.

'Oh, John!' she burst out. 'You are awake again.'

She managed to get him to take a little water, and then a spoon or two of watery gruel. By the end of the week his breathing was easier and his colour had improved, though he was still too weak even to sit up.

Exhausted, Mary curled up like a small girl and slept on the ground near him . . .

Chapter 39

FATHER JOHN WAS FEELING BONE WEARY. HE WAS SPENDING MOST OF HIS days ministering to the sick, giving them the last rites, or praying over those who had already died and trying to console their families. His brother James had written to him of similar conditions in his own parish.

He said prayers over the mass graves in Chapel Lane and in Abbeystrewery, where they had been forced to open deep burial pits to cope with the large numbers of men, women and children losing their lives to hunger and fever.

The parish house was besieged, and the minute he stepped on to the street he was pursued by starving people begging for a penny, a prayer or some bread.

'Father Fitzpatrick, how can you fulfil your duties with so many following you?' ventured his concerned neighbour, Tim McCarthy Downing. 'You can hardly walk a few steps with them. Perhaps you should hire a man to accompany you?'

'Do you really think such a person is necessary?'

'I do, Father, for your own protection and to make it easier for you to walk about and perform your parish duties without being accosted constantly.'

Perhaps Tim was right. He should give it consideration, for

he knew plenty of men who would be glad of a little paid work.

The priest's heart had lifted at the news that Daniel O'Connell, the ageing Liberator, had journeyed across the Irish Sea to London despite his failing health. The purpose of his travels was to raise his voice in Westminster and the newspapers and journals were full of it. So too were the people as all across the nation they read of O'Connell's last desperate plea to Parliament for help on behalf of the starving Irish citizens.

'I go to Parliament as a food man,' O'Connell had said as he stood up in the House of Commons to beg Parliament to give Ireland a loan of thirty to forty million pounds to buy food.

'Ireland is in your hands. She is in your power. If you do not save her she can't save herself. And I solemnly call on you to recollect that I predict with the sincerest conviction that one-quarter of her population will perish unless you come to her relief.'

Bridey had hugged Father Fitzpatrick tearfully as he read O'Connell's words from the *Southern Star* to her twice over.

'God bless the man for his love of the people. They must surely listen to him. Help will soon come, Father.'

In every cottage and cabin in Ireland's villages, towns and cities, expectations were high. They were certain that large-scale official government assistance would now follow quickly. Such hopes were soon dashed, for the British parliament and its members, despite Daniel O'Connell's entreaties, refused to provide any further assistance to Ireland.

Heartbroken O'Connell, whose health remained poor, was advised by his doctors to travel to warmer climes. Father Fitzpatrick had heard that it was the Liberator's intention to journey to Rome to see the Pope, and plead with him on behalf of his people.

God speed his journey.

Chapter 40

Oldcourt

MARY LIFTED THE SHOVEL AND BROUGHT IT DOWN AS HARD AS SHE could to break the stones. She did it once more, watching them crack and split as she hit them again and again. Her shoulders, back and arms ached, for she was still not used to such heavy work, but at least she was getting paid for it.

'A little smaller,' advised Ellen Clancy, the woman working alongside her.

Mary continued to pound the stones with the shovel and was relieved to see that a few had finally broken up to resemble those in the growing pile in the basket beside her.

''Tis the divil of a job but we all need the four pennies,' sighed Ellen.

She went on to explain what was expected of Mary and showed her how to lift the baskets of stones and rocks as needed.

The foreman walked over to where they were working. Mary could tell that he was watching her, but she kept her eyes down, glued to the ground, for she wanted no trouble with him.

'He's gone,' whispered Ellen a few minutes later, and relief washed over her.

With John sick, Mary desperately needed this work. She had

come to the foreman to collect John's pay but, seeing the other women at work with their backs bent, she had begged him to employ her until John was fit to return. He'd been reluctant at first, but she had won him over by telling him how strong and steady she was and that she would not let him down. Flor and Molly had kindly offered to keep a good eye on her husband and the children in her absence.

The jagged stone was rough and hard and heavy, and soon Mary's hands were scraped and cut. Her muscles strained as she went from basket to basket. She shivered against the cold, but was glad of the warmth of John's heavy wool coat; many of the women around had only shawls and rags as scant protection from the elements.

The gang of women and young boys put to work breaking and sorting the stones for the men to use was only small in number. They would only get half pay, but half pay was better than no pay.

'My husband died four months ago,' Ellen told her as together they lifted a basket from the cart. 'It was the saddest day of my life . . . but I have two little girls to look after and I'll not see them follow their father.'

Mary was filled with sympathy and admiration for the other woman, who was prepared to work so hard for her children, in much the same way as she was doing for her own family.

'John, my husband, took sick with road fever three weeks ago,' she confided to Ellen. 'He nearly died on me. For six days I didn't know whether he would live or die, but thank God he survived it. He's still very weak, so if he can't work then I will . . . I'll break every stone on this road if I have to for the money they pay.'

It was so cold that the women's breath formed clouds of steam. Mary watched Denis Leary and the other men work, lifting boulders and rocks and layers of stone. A few looked near to collapse as they laboured on.

John had objected to her working, saying the relief works were no place for a woman. Mary did not want to go against his wishes, but she was still strong and prepared to work . . .

*

At the end of that first day Mary was footsore and weary, her muscles ached all over and she did not know how she would have the strength to walk home. But the four pence she had earned would ensure that tomorrow her family would not go hungry.

Chapter 41

Skibbereen

A FREEZING GALE BLEW UP THE RIVER ILEN AND THE LASHING RAIN pounded on the roofs and windows of the homes of Skibbereen. On such a night, Dan was glad of the comfort and warmth of his own hearth.

He had decided to hand over to Tom Marmion the task of selecting passengers who were suitable to travel on James Swanton's ship. He had so many competing demands on his time that he could no longer dedicate himself to the endeavour, though he still ensured that those chosen were medically fit to sail.

His rest was disturbed by a knock on the door.

He opened it hesitantly to an awful apparition: a poor woman who could barely stand, emaciated beyond belief and soaked to the skin. She was so pale and skeletal that it was as if she had appeared from the grave itself.

'Dr Donovan, you have to help me,' she wept. 'My boy is dead and I have not even a coffin to bury him.'

Shocked by her appearance, Dan racked his brain trying to recognize her, for no doubt she was a patient of the dispensary.

'Mrs . . .'

'It's Mrs Keating. Mary Keating,' she said, taking a shuddering

157

breath. 'My husband died two weeks ago. I had only buried him in Chapel Lane when my little boy was taken from me. I was sick with the fever myself and there was nothing I could do, but now I have to get a coffin for my boy and bury him decently.'

'Where is your son now?' Dan asked.

'I laid him out in the ditch, near my cabin. A coffin is all I want for him,' she begged, trying to control her emotions. 'You are a good man, and I trust that you will help me, because no one else will. Please, Dr Donovan, help me to find a coffin to bury my boy.'

Dan had the pity of his heart for the woman, but he could not invite her inside. His own wife and children were only yards away from her and she clearly had fever.

'Mrs Keating, you should not be on the streets, for you are unwell,' he advised.

'A coffin is all I am asking for,' she repeated, her hollow, near fleshless eyes mad with grief. 'I am fixed in my purpose. I'll not let the dogs in the fields eat him.'

'I'm sorry but I cannot help with your son's coffin,' Dan said regretfully. He desperately wanted the sick woman away from his family and his doorstep. 'My duty is to care for the living. Do you have other children?'

'I have a boy and a girl waiting on me back home,' she admitted.

'Then you must return to them, Mrs Keating, for they are the ones who need you,' he cajoled, hoping that she would take her leave. He simply could not put his family at risk.

He felt in his pocket and found a shilling, which he gave to her.

'Please take this money. Go and purchase meal and some victuals to nourish you and the children.'

'Thank you, doctor,' she said, her claw-like fingers grabbing at the shiny coin.

He sighed with relief that at last she might go.

'What about my boy, Dr Donovan?' she continued. 'What am I to do? I cannot leave him in the ditch. He was the blood of my heart and I am lost without him.'

Immediately Dan felt guilty. Here was a mother, who was ill

herself, standing in the bitter cold before him, showing how desperately she cared for her lost child. What kind of man was he if he ignored her plea for help?

'I will come and visit you later, to see if we can resolve the situation,' he promised as he watched her shuffle away in the darkness.

The rain had eased but it still was near freezing outside by the time Dan and his assistant, apothecary Jerrie Crowley, drove out to Letterlishe and found Mrs Keating. Her cabin was an absolute hovel. The water poured through the rotten thatched roof and on to the muddy floor.

Jerrie had brought his lantern with him and in the darkness they could see the two surviving Keating children lying on the floor like small skeletons, their ribs and other bones protruding under their skin. Outside, in the ditch near the front door, was a small coffin containing the putrid body of a boy of about seven years old, who must have died ten or twelve days ago.

'Where did you manage to get the coffin?' Dan asked Mrs Keating.

'I bought it with the shilling you gave me,' she admitted. 'And I carried it home.'

'Mrs Keating, I gave you that money to buy food for you and your children,' he admonished her gently.

'The children and I do not care about food now,' she replied flatly. 'It is so long since we've had any to eat, we have forgotten the taste of it.'

Jerrie could not hide his upset at such suffering as he looked over at her starving children.

'I want my boy buried decently,' Mary Keating demanded. 'That is the only help I ask of you.'

'Well, that is what we will do then,' Dan promised, as he and Jerrie took up the shovels they had also brought with them.

They carried their lantern to an abandoned patch of ground at the side of her cabin.

'Will some of your neighbours give us a hand with the digging?' he asked.

'The neighbours did not a lift a finger to help us in our time of need,' she pronounced bitterly. 'Not even a sup of water would they bring to us.'

The ground was wet and heavy as they began their sombre task. Dan found it hard to believe that not one of the neighbours made any offer to help while they continued to dig out the sodden earth, making a large hole rather than a deep grave in which to bury the boy.

They worked in the bitter cold and near darkness until both he and Jerrie were exhausted, sweating and unable to dig any more. Prayers were said as they solemnly lowered the coffin into the ground. The boy's mother seemed satisfied as they began to shovel the soil back into the makeshift grave to fill it in.

Back inside, Dan examined the boy and girl.

'Mrs Keating, both you and the children are sick,' he told her. 'I can make a special arrangement to admit you all to the Union's fever ward tomorrow morning. I promise you will be cared for there.'

'I am grateful to you, doctor, and to you, Mr Crowley, for what you have done here tonight, but I'll not go to the Union and have my children taken from me,' she said, shaking her head stubbornly. 'We are better staying here, in our place.'

As he and Jerrie drove the icy road home to town, they both were filled with concern for Mrs Keating and her children.

'I suppose you cannot blame her reluctance, Dan. We all know how bad things are in the workhouse,' Jerrie sighed.

It was nearly eleven o'clock when Dan reached home. The house was asleep except for Henrietta.

'Dan, you are freezing cold,' admonished his wife. 'You will get a chill after being out so late on such a night.'

She pulled up the blankets and piled them around him, before settling her own warm and drowsy body against his. She rubbed her legs and feet up and down his to warm him up.

'I am a fortunate man,' he said as she touched her warm hand to his icy face, 'to have you, my dearest, to come home to.'

Chapter 42

DAN STUDIED THE TORN FLESH . . . AND EXPOSED BONE . . . BITE MARKS were clearly visible on the corpse. One arm had been torn from its socket and chewed. Part of the torso had been gouged out and the dogs had done their worst in trying to feed off the man's putrefying body.

Dan sat on his haunches, holding to his nose the lavender-scented handkerchief Henrietta insisted he carry. It was evident that Mr Leahey's body had been savaged by the starving canines. He had seen the damage a few rats inflicted on the dead, but this was different. He detailed the injuries carefully in his notepad, for he had not seen the like of this before. Judging by the various-sized bite marks all over the body, five or six dogs had been involved. The only saving grace was that poor Mr Leahey had been long dead from fever when the pack of starving mongrels had found him in his cabin.

From the reports Dan had received, Mr Leahey's wife and children had kept his body in the cabin for days. They had no way of burying him, but the stench of his decaying corpse finally drove the family out and they had fled.

Mr Leahey's elderly mother had heard growling and barking inside the cabin. On opening the door she came upon the hungry dogs, chewing and gnawing the flesh from her son's bones. She and some neighbours had managed to beat and drive away the animals but, to Dan's mind, the dogs entering the Leaheys' cabin in the first place was his primary concern.

Dogs were known to dig up corpses buried in shallow graves or to prey on bodies left awaiting burial, but for the animals to enter a dwelling to feast on human flesh wasn't something he had come upon before.

Most of the dogs were crazed, abandoned by owners who had died, fled or could no longer feed them. The starving creatures roamed the fields, roads and lanes of the district. It alarmed Dan to see that they were becoming bolder, packing together unafraid, and likely to attack those who were weak.

The matter was serious and Dan intended to write an urgent report. He would recommend that, for the safety of the public during this crisis, all dogs in Carbery be culled. He found it deeply offensive that those with position and money still fed and kept their pet dogs and hunting hounds while the children of the poor starved.

On his return to the dispensary, he felt someone grab and tug at his coattails. Turning around, he discovered Mrs Keating, who was carrying her young daughter in her arms. Dan immediately went to help her but was shocked to discover that the small girl was already dead.

'She died yesterday,' Mrs Keating explained, caressing her daughter's thin face. 'As no Christian will come near me, I carried her into town myself to lay her alongside her father in the graveyard in Chapel Lane.'

Dan tried not to betray his emotion as he imagined the terrible journey the poor woman must have made along the roads. He ushered her to the dispensary immediately, where he took the girl from her gently and promised the woman that he would look after the burial of her child.

'I am grateful to you, doctor, but it is my poor boy in the grave that you and your friend made the other night that I am worried over,' she explained. 'My neighbours' pigs are scratching and digging at the ground. I fear they will uproot the grave and his coffin if they get a chance!'

'I'm sorry, Mrs Keating, but we did not know there were pigs roaming close by.'

'Doctor, won't you send someone to bury him properly?' she begged. 'Away from the pigs and other animals.'

After seeing what the dogs had done to Mr Leahey, Dan found himself agreeing to help Mrs Keating again. He sent two men to drive out to Letterlishe, exhume the boy's flimsy coffin and have it transported to Skibbereen where it would be buried in consecrated ground. He also agreed to provide a coffin for the little girl's burial.

A few hours later the men returned empty-handed.

'I'm sorry, doctor, but there is no moving that putrefying corpse,' Dinny Burke told him stubbornly. ''Tis in a terrible state and best left buried where it is. Paddy and I will not touch it!'

Mary Keating, however, was made of sterner stuff. She returned home and somehow found the strength and resolve to lift her son's coffin from the earth by herself. The following day she carried it heroically all the way into town, so that her son could be buried properly, with his father and sister.

A week later, Mary Keating accosted Dan once more. Her gaunt face remained pale and worn, her eyes red-rimmed.

'Doctor, I need another coffin to bury my youngest boy. He is the very last of my family,' she pleaded, broken-hearted.

Dan was torn. He had given her the money for two coffins now and she was expecting him to pay for a third. Although he was a doctor and held a good position, he was certainly not a wealthy man!

'In the name of the great God,' she implored him, 'don't let my fine boy, who would be my help and support if he lived, be thrown into the grave like a dog.'

Dan looked at this ghost of a woman, who seemed near death herself. How could he possibly refuse her plea?

Mrs Keating took the money and disappeared to purchase another small coffin. He caught sight of her from the dispensary window as she set off for home with it placed on her head. She was far too weak to be carrying such a load and he ran down the street after her.

'Mrs Keating, you are too sick to go home.' He tried to persuade her to let him help. 'I will endeavour to arrange a bed for you today in the fever ward. Please, I beg you, stay here in town.'

She shook her head firmly, refusing his offer. As he watched her walk away, Dan was overcome with a strange sense of foreboding.

A few days later, Dan heard of Mrs Keating's death. The poor woman had collapsed and was found dead at the door of her cabin, the empty coffin beside her. The neighbours were too terrified of contagion even to come near her.

Dan arranged immediately for both her youngest son's body and hers to be transported to Skibbereen for a proper burial in Chapel Lane with her husband and other child. At least she might sleep in death with those she had loved so much in life.

Her passing affected Dan so deeply that he vowed in time to erect a headstone over her grave.

Mrs Keating's reaction to her children's deaths, and Mr O'Shea's to his son's, demonstrated to Dan that people were fixated on the dead and their need for a coffin. In his opinion, the need for prompt burials before putrefaction set in was the most pressing concern. Proper arrangements needed to be made for a cart and a man – or two – to collect the dead both in the town and the district and bring them for immediate burial in Abbeystrewery to stop the spread of disease.

As a doctor, Dan's focus needed to remain on the living. There was little he could do for the growing numbers of dead, except ensure that their corpses were collected and safely interred, but something had to be done to persuade the people to take action swiftly.

Chapter 43

FATHER JOHN FITZPATRICK WAS BUSY WRITING HIS SUNDAY SERMON when Bridey showed in Dan Donovan. The housekeeper knew well that he did not like to be disturbed when preparing for the following day's service.

'John, I need to talk to you urgently,' Dan said, sitting down across from him. 'As you and I are the ones in this town who give care to the dying and the dead.'

'That is the way, with any physician or priest,' Father Fitzpatrick sighed, putting away his pen.

'It is the dead that are my great concern,' the doctor said with worry, wringing his hands.

It was evident that the priest's friend was upset over some matter.

'The starving and poor are spending every last penny they have on the dead,' Dan continued, exasperated. 'They are set on purchasing coffins in which to bury their loved ones despite not having a scrap of food in the house to feed their children, or a warm coat, a shawl or shoes to wear! They come to me, or to the dispensary, begging for money for one. Even worse, they'll keep a putrefying body in their home with the rest of their family rather than admit they cannot afford to bury them in a coffin.'

'I fully agree with you, Dan. They accost me in the street too, or come here to the presbytery, looking for me to arrange the price of

165

one. Poor people, they have no care for their own misery and misfortune, even though some of them are so weak with hunger they
can barely walk.'

His stomach turned as Dan told him of a man whose corpse had
been attacked by dogs and a poor woman who spent the shillings
given to her by the doctor on coffins for her children instead of
food! He himself had witnessed the dead bodies of children and
parents lying beside the living when there was no money to purchase a coffin.

'The authorities do not seem one bit concerned on the issue,' Dan
railed angrily. 'But the situation is now urgent. I intend on putting
in place arrangements to have a public cart to transport bodies away
from the town and district as swiftly as possible for safe burial in
Abbeystrewery. I have also heard of a new type of coffin being made.
It has a hinged base that can be used for such occasions and then be
reused again and again. It is something to be considered.'

Father John felt a deep despair at the prospect of such necessities.
However, he knew Dan Donovan to be a man of great integrity, who
would only ever act in the best interests of the community.

'Something must be done to stop this repugnance the people have
to bury the dead without proper coffins,' the doctor continued. 'I
have told my patients again and again: it is the living we must care
for and nourish, not the dead. They do not listen to me, Father. I
implore you, speak out about this. You are the only one to whom
they will listen.'

'I'm not sure they will listen to me, Dan, but I promise that I will
try to convince them.'

Father Fitzpatrick looked down from the pulpit at the good people
of Skibbereen. Many of the congregation who sat quietly and respectfully in the pews at Sunday mass, awaiting his sermon, were in rags
and tatters, half-starved. These days, he found it difficult to speak
to them and console them; to promise them that though they may
suffer greatly in this life on earth, they would find their reward in
the next life when they entered the heavenly kingdom.

How could he utter such inane words to a man who had just buried his three children in the pit in Abbeystrewery, or to an old woman left to die at the side of the road!

He knew all too well their hardship. Day after day, he visited cottages and cabins where entire families were sick with fever. Often they lay together on nothing but straw, clad only in rags with not even a blanket to cover them, as he gave them extreme unction.

But they were a simple people, who put their trust in the church. Many who continued to attend mass had lost children, husbands or wives and neighbours to the hunger and fever, yet somehow, despite their distress, they retained their faith and belief in God.

Of late, his own belief was being challenged, and his own faith tested every day as he asked himself, where was God's hand in all this? The hand of the merciful God about whom he preached?

'My dear people,' he began, addressing them from the pulpit.

All raised their eyes to him, and the coughing and nose-blowing ceased.

'We are all possessed of a soul,' he continued. 'Even the tiniest baby in arms. For the glory and majesty of the human soul is the most important part of our creation as divined by God himself. Our soul makes us human; the people we are. We all strive to live the best life we can. Some will enjoy a great age while others will have a life shortened by disease and hunger; others may not even get to enjoy a childhood. But it makes no difference, I tell you, for when the time comes to leave this earth, no matter the circumstances of our death, our soul flies heavenward, returning back to God from whence we came.'

He could see and sense that he had their full attention, from the town's well-to-do citizens to the poor dwellers of Bridgetown and the homeless wanderers who took refuge in the church during mass.

'As the soul flies, we leave our frail and often scarred human body. We must leave the world of human flesh behind. The rituals of burials and funerals must be observed as we place and inter our dead in the ground, but it has come to my attention that many here are deeply worried about this, during this terrible time of rampant hunger and disease among us. Many parishioners believe that they must somehow provide a wooden coffin for the burial of the departed, for this is what is expected by our church.

'Unfortunately, with the times we are in, I know well the difficulties faced by many, and there are few coffin-makers. So I say to you today that the purchase of a coffin for a loved one when you, or your wife or children, are in desperate need of nourishment or shelter is not what the Lord expects.

'Remember, my good people, that the Bible tells us that Jesus himself was taken down from the cross and wrapped in a simple material – a shroud – and laid in a cave as his tomb. There was no coffin, no great funeral, no multitudes, for his was just a simple burial.

'So we can see from the Bible that the dead have no use or care for such earthly forms. I tell you that our Christian duty is to the living. It is paramount that we follow the faith we profess and obey the commandments and, despite all the difficulties we face, continue to love our fellow man,' he concluded, blessing himself.

Father John caught sight of approving nods from some of the relief committee members and their families in the front pews. However, it was to the rear and sides of the large stone cathedral that his missive was directed.

After mass and communion the congregation flocked around him, asking him to clarify what they had heard.

'Neither God nor man expects you to pauper or starve yourself for the sake of a wooden box,' he assured them.

The gratitude, and even tears of relief in some of their eyes, was evident. He prayed that they would accept his words.

Later, as he set about locking up the doors of the magnificent church that stood high over North Street, built to serve the large and growing population of the once prosperous Skibbereen, Father Fitzpatrick reflected on the beggars and destitute, the hungry and the poor of the town. He was tempted to fling open the heavy doors of St Patrick's Cathedral and admit all those who needed comfort and shelter. It is what Jesus Christ would have done. Father John's ideals were in conflict with the bishop's, however, who certainly would not approve of this house of God being used as some kind of shelter for the hungry.

A few members of the congregation still knelt in the pews, their heads bent, praying for help in their time of need.

'The church is closing,' he reminded them gently.

Once they had left, he himself knelt before the cross in the solitude and quiet of the church. He prayed for God to give him the strength and courage to continue to do his work.

Chapter 44

Oldcourt

ON THE STONE ROAD, MARY'S SKIN TOUGHENED WITH THE BACK–BREAKING work. Her feet were swollen and sore, often numb with the cold and the damp. Her hands were cut, her nails broken, and two fingers were hot with chilblains. But she kept her head down every day as she was set to breaking up stones to make them smaller and more usable. She ignored the stiffness in her arms and shoulders, and the weakness that came over her at times. She forced herself to keep working.

The men were like beasts of burden, made to lift and move the heavy baskets. Sometimes the stones fell, injuring some poor fellow, while other men such as Denis Leary were set to dig the heavy, near frozen earth to create the channels and surfaces where the stones would be laid.

She witnessed one poor man break his arm and be sent on his way with only four days' wages, and only two days ago, a grey-haired old woman, Mary Pat O'Donovan, had fainted on the ground beside her.

'Be on your way, grandmother,' the foreman had told her sarcastically. 'You are no use to us.'

'Not a word,' Ellen had warned Mary under her breath, 'or we will all be in trouble with him.'

*

Mary, petrified of losing her job, said little as she worked. She missed being with her children as she shivered in the frost and the freezing wind and rain where she felt chilled to the marrow. The one consolation was that she could at least buy some food, though it angered her that the price of corn and meal had risen substantially, making it even worse for them all.

The only good news the family had had was that John had received a short letter from Pat, who was now living and working on a building site in New York. His sea journey had been long and arduous but her brother-in-law was well and living in a fine house. By all accounts he was enjoying his new life in America.

John read his few words over and over again. They were both glad to hear that Pat was well and had escaped from the hard life they were still enduring. She imagined his life in New York, far from the stone roads, the hungry faces and the weeping land.

When she returned home most evenings, Mary barely had the energy to set the pot over the fire. After serving a hot meal to her family, she would curl up and try to warm herself, relaxing her aching muscles as she let sleep overtake her.

On Monday, Mary and the other women were surprised as there was no sign of Ellen.

'She has the road fever, God help us!' one of her neighbours told them. 'They say she is bad with it.'

As Mary hit the stones, splitting them and mixing them together for the men to use, she cursed the officials that had designated such work for the poor and starving.

On Friday, news of Ellen's death reached the women. It upset everyone deeply and they all said a few prayers in remembrance of her.

As she was paid her wages, Mary considered the pennies in her hand. Her head filled with thoughts of how Ellen's children, now orphans, would survive without their mother.

*

'Mary, you cannot keep on,' warned John when she told him about Ellen. 'I fear you will collapse and get sick, and then what will happen to the children?'

She knew in her heart that he was speaking the truth. The heavy work and hunger were draining the life from her, but there was nothing else for it. She had to work or else they would surely starve.

'I am well again and ready for the work!' her husband insisted, but anyone could see that his eyes were still sunken in his head and he was not the man he used to be. She knew he was still weak and his muscles were gone. There wasn't a chance that he was yet strong enough to swing a heavy shovel or pickaxe.

They argued hotly over it, but Mary refused to give in. As long as she had the strength to work, she would break all the stones in the world if it meant her family would survive the hunger.

'John, I will only do it until you are better,' she conceded. Her back and shoulders ached constantly, but she wrapped herself up in his heavy coat and set off for the works.

Chapter 45

Skibbereen
February 1847

DAN WAS FROZEN TO THE BONE. THERE HAD BEEN A FEW MORE SNOW flurries during the day and he had got damp doing his rounds. Returning home, he was glad of the warmth of the fire and the plate of comforting beef stew with dumplings. Henrietta, with her hair softly curled and pinned up, looked more beautiful than ever as she served him some tea.

'Dada, we have a big surprise for you!' announced Fanny once he had eaten.

Young Daniel grinned. 'We made it all ourselves.'

Henrietta smiled but would give him no clue as to what they were up to.

To tell the truth, Dan was exhausted. After an awful day he would have liked nothing better than to stretch and relax in the armchair undisturbed, but he could see from his young son's eyes that he was bursting with excitement.

'Very well, what is it?' he asked, curious.

'You have to come upstairs to see it,' coaxed Ellen, pulling him by the hand. 'We have been working on it all day.'

'For days,' Daniel added.

'It was a secret,' whispered Harriet as Dan followed them upstairs as they trooped to the nursery.

Henrietta said nothing as she bounced Margaret up and down on her hip.

'You and Mama are to sit in those two chairs where you can watch the show.'

He laughed. 'What is it?'

'You are invited to the amazing, daring and delightful Donovan Puppet Show,' declared Ellen, pulling back a sheet to reveal a large, home-made puppet theatre.

'Henry and Jerrie made most of it,' said Ellen, beaming at her older brothers.

'And we all made the puppets and painted them,' added Harriet proudly. 'The show will start in two minutes, Father, so do please sit down.'

'They have been working on it these past few days,' whispered Henrietta.

Her eyes shone as the young puppeteers disappeared behind the tall, red-and-yellow striped box. The curtains were pulled back to reveal the painted cardboard figures of Cinderella and her two ugly sisters. Ellen did the voice of Cinderella, and Fanny and Harriet used thin sticks to move the ugly sisters.

It was a wondrous show and even young Daniel managed to operate and move a few figures . . . A dog, a cat, and a jiggling glass slipper.

Entranced, Dan watched and listened to the children having fun as the snow fell outside. He, Henrietta and Margaret gave a huge round of applause as Cinderella and her prince took a final bow.

A few minutes later, Dan was roped in with Jerrie to help tell a variation of the story. This time the dog took to barking at the ugly sisters, and was the one who found Cinderella's lost slipper. It was a long time since Dan had laughed quite so much or had such fun, and he chased the children to bed with the promise of a story.

'Only a happy one, Dada,' reminded Fanny as he tucked her into bed.

'Once upon a time . . .' Dan began.

Chapter 46

'MR MAHONY, WELCOME,' SAID DAN AS HE GREETED JAMES MAHONY, the illustrator and journalist from the *Illustrated London News*, at the Becher Arms. 'I trust you had a good journey despite this terrible cold weather.'

'Yes, it was fine, though I saw crowds of hungry walking the icy roads as we passed in the carriage from Cork. At Clonakilty, where we had breakfast, they flocked around us, looking for money and food. One poor woman was carrying the corpse of a fine child in her arms—'

The artist's voice broke off.

'She was begging alms of us passengers to purchase a coffin to bury her dear little baby,' he managed. 'It was an awful sight. One that I will never forget.'

'Unfortunately, you will see many such tragedies in this town, and worse,' warned Dan.

'Dr Donovan, I have avidly read the diary you publish in the *Southern Reporter*, which my own paper then publishes. Your words have reached many,' he explained, his brown eyes serious. 'Each of your reports is both moving and informative. They are why my editor suggested this visit, so that our readers are made aware of the terrible suffering faced by so many.'

Dan nodded. 'Words in a newspaper can do so much.'

Nicholas Cummins's letter published in *The Times* before Christmas had resulted not only in a huge wave of donations but also in the setting up of the British Relief Association, which had already raised substantial funds to aid Ireland. Dan's published diary had been reprinted not only by some English newspapers but in some American ones too, his words helping to raise much-needed donations and subscription for relief from many quarters.

'It is why I allowed them to be published,' the doctor continued. 'Too many people have ignored the plight of the hungry and needy in these terrible times.'

'Then perhaps I can do some good also,' James Mahony offered modestly, 'by my reporting and illustrating the truth of the matter.'

Dan worried that the artist might not be able to cope with the terrible deprivation and human misery he would witness.

'My assistant Mr Crowley and I are more than happy to have you accompany us on our visits to the sick and needy, Mr Mahony. But I have to warn you, it is exceptionally distressing work, even for a medical man.'

'Dr Donovan, I have seen much in Cork City. The hungry and homeless roam the streets and the Cork workhouse is crowded out, but here, judging from your reports, the situation appears much worse.'

Dan had taken an immediate liking to the artist. He had watched him earnestly carrying his leather bag containing his paper and pens, and had decided that he trusted him. He might have slender hands and the long fingers of an artist, but it was clear that this Cork man was determined to do his best for his fellow man in his own fashion.

'Have you been to other towns yet and seen the results of hunger and starvation there?' the doctor asked.

'No,' Mahony admitted. 'This is my first time undertaking such work. My forte is to paint in watercolour – French and Italian, and sometimes Irish landscapes. I endeavour to capture the beauty of such places.'

'I fear there will be nothing like that for you here,' snorted Jerrie

Crowley, who had joined them. 'Believe me, there is nothing beautiful left to see in this poor town of ours.'

'I am fully aware of that, Mr Crowley, and will endeavour to record accurately all that I see.'

'Well then, let us begin with a visit to Bridgetown,' Dan said, 'where there is enormous suffering and many of those weakened by starvation have succumbed to fever.'

'It is a poor area, with nigh on a few hundred cabins and cottages – if you can call them that,' added Jerrie Crowley, turning up the collar of his heavy coat to try to keep out the biting wind as they walked along.

'So many of the people here have no coats or shawls, or clothes,' Mahony remarked as they passed a group of paupers and beggars, and women and children who sat along the street, shivering. 'How do they not perish in this freezing weather?'

'Unfortunately, many do,' Dan admitted. 'In desperation, many sold or pawned every piece of clothing or blanket they possessed months ago to try to feed themselves.'

As they entered the narrow lanes of Bridgetown, Dan could not help but notice the artist wrinkle his nose at the fetid odours of urine and excrement that seemed to envelop the place, where human dunghills abounded.

'Be careful where you walk,' he warned.

'Is it always like this?'

Jerrie grinned. 'It can be worse on a hot summer's day, but you just get used to it.'

The artist stopped and immediately began to sketch. He drew the curving line of low cabins and hovels with their rotting straw roofs and the cluster of barely dressed children and women who moved among the lanes.

'Our first visit is to the Murphys,' Dan said as he led them into the darkness of a low cabin where the sound of moaning filled the air.

In the dim light it was difficult to see, but the family lay on the floor, as near to the dying embers of the fire as they could get. An old woman with streeling white hair lay on the straw in a filthy shift.

'Doctor, my son Paddy died a day – no, maybe two or three days – ago,' she announced. 'The daughter-in-law, Brigid, went not long after him. God be good to them, but I'm weak myself and left with the two young boys here.'

A bout of coughing consumed her as she pointed at the children lying on the rough earth.

'And not even a soul to bring us a bit of food or sup of water.'

Dan caught the look of utter shock and disbelief on Mahony's face as he realized that, with the exception of the old woman, the rest of the family were dead. Their eyes were staring and their bodies were already beginning to decay.

The artist pushed past Dan and rushed outside, gasping for fresh air.

Dan followed him.

'Sit down,' he ordered. 'Put your head between your knees. The faint will pass. Just try to breathe slow and easy.'

He reached for the small bottle of smelling salts he kept in his inside pocket. He opened it and passed it back and forth in front of the man's ghastly pale and clammy face.

'Any better?'

After a few minutes, Mahony nodded.

'Yes. It's just the smell. The cabin and the children. I've never seen such horror. That woman, how did she not know they were dead?'

'She's old with no one to help her . . .' Dan tried to explain.

Dan and Jerrie made their way back inside the cabin to make clear to Mrs Murphy that they would arrange for the bodies of her family to be collected by the death cart in a few hours' time. There was little they could do to comfort her, but Dan promised to return the following day to visit her.

The next stops on Dan's rounds were the Connollys' and the Carews' cabins. Both families had children sick with dysentery. The ominous signs of bloody flux from terrible diarrhoea were spattered all over the mud floor.

'Keep back, Mr Mahony, it is dysentery,' Dan explained. 'There is little I can do about it except tell them to try to keep the children away from the rest of the family. If they don't, they will likely all get it.'

In the Cotters' cabin they were greeted by a skeletal young woman with two small children.

'Have you a biteen of food for us?' she pleaded. 'For the hunger is fierce bad on us.'

'I'm sorry, Mrs Cotter, but we are here on our medical duties.'

Dan examined the middle boy, who was about five years old. The child's belly protruded and his little legs were like gnarled sticks. He was quiet and listless, and his huge eyes simply stared up at Dan.

'Have you been to the soup kitchen today?' he urged the young mother. 'You must go and try to get some nourishment for you and the children.'

'Denis is too weak to walk there, and I do not have the strength to carry him and Peggy together,' she admitted tearfully.

The artist was visibly upset as he began to draw a simple sketch of the cottage and child.

'I will arrange that soup is delivered to you and your family today, and for as long as it is needed,' Dan promised.

With so many too sick or weak to walk to the soup kitchen, Dan and the relief committee had arranged for a number of men to deliver soup to his patients and those in desperate need.

'I will also arrange for fresh straw bedding to be brought here.'

'Thank you, doctor,' Mrs Cotter said, her eyes filled with gratitude.

Over the course of the next few hours, the trio visited cabin after cabin. They saw typhus, dysentery and starvation everywhere. The snowy lanes were quiet, with no sight of a dog nor a cat nor even a bird. The silence was broken only by the scurry of rats darting down the tracks and among the rotting roof thatch of the miserable huts and hovels.

'Rats are the only things thriving in this poor place,' pronounced Jerrie. 'There is not a cat in the place to hunt them.'

One crazed man, Peadar Dempsey, refused to let them take the body of his dead wife.

'She's hungry and tired, but I tell you she's just asleep, Dr Dan.'

James Mahony said little, his skin still pale and his countenance serious as he drew and sketched. He filled his drawing pad with images of the dead and the living; the starving men, women and children of Bridgetown.

After their time in Bridgetown Dan brought Mahony to Old Chapel Lane. There they made their way to a tumbledown house with a window and door missing, which was crowded with destitute people trying to shelter from the cold. Some were already sick with typhus, and two or three were dead, including a big strong country fellow he bent down to examine. The man's body was already cold.

'Doctor, how could he be dead when he was only down here near me a few hours ago?' demanded the man next to him.

Dan sighed.

'I suspect he had typhus. Stay outside, Mr Mahony,' he begged. 'Do not come inside this place, for there is rampant fever here, and I advise you not to engage with those standing around you at the door, for they may also be sick.'

The artist moved down the street quickly, capturing with his pen the house and lane and those waiting admittance. Dan joined him shortly after and showed him the nearby watch hut that overlooked the graveyard in Chapel Lane. A matter of days ago, he and Jerrie had found a family hiding there, amid the decaying bodies.

'They would have died here, among the skeletons and diseased corpses of the graveyard, except for the actions of my friend here,' he said, praising Jerrie Crowley.

'I don't mind telling you that it was a shock to find the living, hidden among the putrefaction of this crowded graveyard, with not even a drop of water to sustain them,' the doctor's man told their companion.

'What happened to them?'

'Fortunately, Mr Mahony, the six of them were removed from

this abode of the dead to the fever hospital, where they are improving. I will write it up in my diary,' Dan affirmed.

'Then certainly I must sketch this hut,' Mahony said, trying to find a good angle from which to draw the structure without miring himself in the sodden, putrid ground around him.

With a few swift swipes and scribbles of his pen, James Mahony captured the watch hut from which the family had been rescued.

'Tomorrow I must attend my duties at the Union workhouse,' Dan explained. 'But Mr Everett is a good man. He will collect you in the morning and take you to Ballydehob and Schull.'

'Thank you for your great kindness today, Dr Donovan,' Mr Mahony said as he took his leave of them. 'I hope to see you when I return to Skibbereen to take the mail coach.'

Dan watched the artist walk down the street, hoping that somehow his sketches and drawings would help convey the terrible situation the starving people of West Cork were enduring.

Chapter 47

ON HIS RETURN TO SKIBBEREEN, MR MAHONY CALLED IN TO THE crowded dispensary. Dan was happy to see him again and accompanied him to the Becher Arms where the coach stop was. The coach wasn't due for a short while, so they went inside to take a cup of tea.

'Tell me, Mr Mahony, how did you fare on the rest of your visit?' Dan asked.

'The people in Ballydehob and Schull are in a terrible state too. I cannot understand how the authorities are allowing such extreme suffering to occur. These past few days I have seen women, children and babies all starving before my very eyes.'

Dan could detect the huge emotion and strain in the man's voice.

'I'm sure that you will do your best to reflect this grave situation in which we find ourselves, Mr Mahony.'

'In Ballydehob, Reverend Triphook told me that anyone who can gather a few pounds is leaving the town to escape the fever and the distress.'

'Aye, Mr Mahony, you cannot blame them!'

'And in Schull, I saw hundreds of women, desperate to buy meal which had been delivered by sloop to the town. Apparently, there are tons of Indian meal on board, but it is being guarded by a government steam ship. I saw only miserable quantities being doled out to those waiting and it was being charged at exorbitant prices.'

'They are saving food for a rainy day,' Dan said, exasperated, 'when it is clear that the full force of the storm is already upon us.'

'I was also introduced to the rector there, Dr Robert Traill. I found him to be a most charitable man. Every day, he and his good wife feed a few hundred people with a warm nourishing soup, from their own door at the rectory in Schull. Such are the numbers that they now employ a number of men to help them make and distribute it. The townspeople are fortunate to have such a dedicated vicar among them.'

'Robert is indeed a good man,' Dan agreed, 'and well respected by all of us.'

'It's strange, Dr Donovan, but in normal circumstances, Skibbereen and these towns and villages are places I would visit to paint or sketch for their great beauty, their inspiring landscapes and views with the sea and river, and the coastline and islands nestling in the shadow of Mount Gabriel. Alas, my work now is of a very different nature.'

'Mr Mahony, your work is of great importance to the people of this town and West Cork,' Dan reminded him.

'As are your reports in the newspaper,' he admitted. 'I perhaps doubted their accuracy somewhat, or suspected they may be highly coloured and exaggerated, but from my visit here I have seen at first hand the terrible truth of the extreme suffering of the people. Neither pen nor pencil could ever portray the misery and horror to be witnessed at this moment in Skibbereen.'

Dan nodded gravely as he sipped his tea.

'If anything, Dr Donovan, you have tried to make the reports less graphic and more palatable for the readers by hiding the hideous reality that you and Mr Crowley have to contend with day after day.'

'That is true,' Dan admitted calmly. 'I have found that the human mind can only deal with so much distress and horror.'

'I have observed that there is little sympathy shown between the living and the dead,' Mahony continued. 'Men driving carts filled with corpses show little respect for them, and foremen and managers on the work schemes show no care for the men they oversee.

183

Men who may have walked miles stand in the mud and cold to break stones and build roads, with not even a scrap of food in their belly. It is a cruelty beyond any belief.'

Their conversation was interrupted by a shout that the coach to Cork would be ready to leave in a few minutes. The artist nodded and stood up to leave.

'I'd better take my seat.'

'Mr Mahony, we are very appreciative of your visit, as distressing as it has been for you. Thank you for coming to Skibbereen.'

'Dr Donovan, I have filled my sketch pads and am as well informed of the situation as I can be. I promise you that I will endeavour with fidelity to portray what I have witnessed in order to make the suffering and afflictions of this famine-stricken people known to the charitable public and readers of the paper.'

'Sir, God bless you and your work.'

Dan caught Mahony by the shoulder and gripped his hand firmly as they bade each other farewell.

A crowd of beggars swarmed around the horses and coach as the artist took his place aboard.

'The hunger is on us,' they called and shouted, over and over, as the remaining passengers climbed inside and sat back in their seats. 'The hunger is on us!'

The driver ignored them as he checked his fares were safely ensconced. He grabbed the reins swiftly and urged on the horses to pass the crowd and leave the hungry town behind them.

Chapter 48

FATHER FITZPATRICK'S HEART HAD GROWN HEAVY. NEARLY HALF THE town had fallen victim to the fever that was raging across the population. The wealthy and powerful had been afflicted just as badly as the beggars in the street.

With his own eyes he had witnessed vermin, dogs and even pigs lay claim to abandoned and poorly buried bodies. On Windmill Lane a pair of dogs had tried to pull apart the body of a small baby but for the quick intervention of two soldiers who killed them.

Anger and rage grew in him that the British authorities, who did so little to sustain the living as the country starved, still permitted food, grain and livestock to be exported to English cities, and made absolutely no provision for the inevitable – the interment of the dead.

It was the town officials who declared that all dogs be culled, though it brought cries of outrage and protest from many who were reluctant to relinquish their animals, even if it was for the common good. Shame on all of them!

Never had he imagined such a terrible end for the innocent people of Skibbereen.

Charles Trevelyan, who controlled the Treasury, considered the failure of the potato crop and the ensuing hunger divine retribution from the Lord on the ever-growing Irish Catholic population for

185

their indolence and laziness. That a man in such a crucial position should entertain such unchristian thoughts grieved and upset the priest deeply.

He sat down to write to Frederic Lucas, editor of the English Catholic journal *Tablet*, which had published some of his letters, to thank him and his readers for their generosity towards the town's starving and sick. He'd been overwhelmed by the post office orders and donations sent to him by congregations, charitable ladies and good men from Aberdeen to East London, and Cardiff to Cornwall. The British people, unlike the government, had shown themselves to be both charitable and most generous. Mr Lucas had kindly opened a bank account in London for such purpose.

Father Fitzpatrick had also appealed for much-needed clothing by asking readers of the journal to send him items care of Thomas Galwey at the Skibbereen coach office in Cork, and this had already borne results.

A British Relief Association had been founded, raising huge sums of money, which the charity intended to be used to give grants of food aid, and Queen Victoria had issued her Queen's Letter, an appeal for money to relieve distress in Ireland, to which many had contributed, including the Queen herself, who had donated one thousand pounds.

The priest's eyes grew heavy and he was suddenly conscious of Bridey trying to rouse him.

'Father, you must away to your bed or you will not be fit for tomorrow,' she warned.

He stood up stiffly. His back and right knee ached.

'You need your rest, Father,' she persisted.

'I am finished here,' he assured her, signing and folding the letter. 'And will be glad to get some sleep.'

Lying in the darkness, his mind was crowded and tormented by the memory of those to whom he had attended during the day. He said a quiet prayer for them all, before rolling on to his side and giving in to the utter exhaustion that he felt.

Chapter 49

'DAN, IS IT TRUE THAT POOR JOHN CLERKE IS VERY ILL?' HENRIETTA asked, for he and the bank manager were close friends.

'I fear his condition is grave,' her husband admitted, his voice breaking. 'The Provincial Bank sent a replacement manager to take over the running of it, but apparently he has already fled the town for fear of contagion. The new official they sent is apparently no better as he too is threatening to leave!'

'You can't blame them, Dan. Anyone with an ounce of good sense would pack up and go,' she said pointedly.

'Unfortunately that is precisely what the matron, the apothecary and some of the staff in the workhouse have done,' he told her, clearly worried. 'And a number of staff there have also fallen ill.'

'Oh, Dan, what will you do?' she asked, shocked at such news.

'We will have to manage with a limited staff.' Her husband sighed, a heavy tiredness in his eyes. 'We must treat the sick, feed the hungry and bury the dead. Fortunately, Mr Mahony's graphic illustrations of the tragedy of our terrible situation have resulted in massive donations to help Ireland and our people. Hundreds of thousands of pounds by all accounts, not just from the readers of his paper but from all around the world.'

'Oh, thank heaven,' she said, relieved.

'Such contributions are badly needed and we have now arranged to have soup brought to the sick in the town and delivered by cart to Kilcoe, Ballydehob, Rath and outlying areas to stop more people flooding into town. We are feeding near eight thousand people, Henrietta, and delivering fresh straw for bedding throughout Bridgetown and the lanes to try to cope with the filth and sickness. Unfortunately, there are even fewer people now to assist us with such work.'

'Dan, you are working too hard. You must rest,' she pleaded with him, 'or you will fall ill yourself.'

'I have a strong constitution, my dear,' he reminded her gently, 'and my duty is to attend to my patients.'

As she made her way to the market that morning, Henrietta was lost in thought. She stopped in her tracks when she bumped into Reverend Townsend, who doffed his black hat to her.

'Good day, Reverend,' she greeted him politely.

He paused, appearing upset by her words.

'I'm afraid that as far as my household is concerned, Mrs Donovan, this is not a very good day. For we have suffered a great loss.'

'Oh, no. Is Mrs Townsend unwell?'

'She is quite well,' he assured her, 'but she is distressed by events. Our two servants were both stricken with fever these past few days. Despite our best efforts, both died during the night.'

Henrietta felt herself grow weak as she thought of the new pretty little maid who had played with her children only a few weeks ago.

'I must call to her,' she blurted out, knowing how deeply affected her friend would be by such loss. 'Is she at home?'

'Yes.' He nodded gravely. 'I need to attend to the arrangements for them. Please convey our gratitude to your husband, for he was most kind and attentive to them during their travails.'

Henrietta watched as he walked away, and decided to call to Glebe House immediately.

Through the long drawing-room window she could see Elizabeth sitting sewing, head bent in concentration. She rang the bell twice and her friend came to answer the door herself. Her eyes were red-rimmed from crying and she looked utterly grief-stricken.

'I met your husband and he told me about what happened to your servants,' Henrietta ventured. 'I wanted to come and offer my condolences on their deaths.'

'I still cannot believe it!' Elizabeth's voice broke with emotion. 'The two of them taken from us like that in a matter of days. Young women with their lives ahead of them, taken by fever. How can such a thing happen?'

'I am so sorry. I know how good you were to them.'

'Kate had worked for us since she was sixteen years of age. She had such a kind heart and helped out with serving in the soup kitchen only last week. And as for young Jane, she was like a little bit of sunshine that came into our lives. They were part of our small family and will for ever be greatly missed,' she sobbed.

Henrietta took hold of her arm gently and led her back into the drawing room, where Elizabeth lowered herself into the velvet armchair.

'Do you need anything?' Henrietta offered. 'Can I help in some way?'

Elizabeth Townsend shook her head and slowly took up her sewing again.

Henrietta realized that the linen she was stitching neatly and carefully was a white shroud.

'This one is for Jane,' Elizabeth explained.

Another shroud lay spread out on a nearby chair.

'Would you like me to make you a cup of tea?' Henrietta offered.

'Thank you, but I just need to finish my sewing so these will be ready for the funeral of my two girls.'

'I am so sorry for your loss,' Henrietta repeated, words escaping her.

Tears ran slowly down Elizabeth's pale face. 'They were like our family. I don't know how people can bear such sadness – children, sons and daughters, husbands and wives, parents all stricken by fever.'

'These are terrible times,' Henrietta consoled her friend.

'Nobody is safe from this disease and torment, no one!' warned Elizabeth.

Distressed, Henrietta hurried home, her head bent low as she avoided meeting or talking to anyone. Skibbereen had become a blighted town and she dearly wished that Dan would give consideration to fleeing as others had done. However, she knew well that, despite her entreaties, her dutiful and steadfast husband would never desert the town and people he loved so much.

Chapter 50

'YOU HAVE VISITORS, FATHER,' INTERRUPTED BRIDEY, AS FATHER Fitzpatrick ate his breakfast and read the newspaper. 'They are gentry,' she reassured him, showing in two well-dressed young gentlemen who were students at Oxford.

'Father Fitzpatrick, we apologize for disturbing you so early in the morning,' explained Frederick Blackwood, as he also introduced his travelling companion, George Boyle. 'Both Reverend Townsend and Dr Donovan told us we should speak to you before we leave Skibbereen later today. We have a great interest in Ireland and are keen to record the effects of this terrible calamity on this good land.'

Father Fitzpatrick sighed, for only a few days ago a wealthy philanthropist – an editor from an American newspaper, Mr Elihu Burrit, who was devoted to helping mankind – had called on him with similar intentions. He had agreed to take Mr Burrit around and had taken him to the soup kitchen and to the hovels and cabins where he ministered to the dying. Shocked by such scenes, Mr Burrit said he had no language to describe the suffering of the people consigned to this battlefield of life. With disease raging, the priest had worried for the health of the American visitor but admired the man's courage and zeal to help the poor and vulnerable.

He smiled at his two young visitors for he could see they displayed a similar zeal!

'We arrived only yesterday,' Mr Blackwood went on, 'but Reverend Townsend has been most generous with his time. He has shown us around the cottages, the town graveyard, and we have met some of his parishioners. Dr Donovan has also told us of the terrible state of affairs and of the people.'

'Then you will have witnessed terrible things,' replied Father Fitzpatrick, feeling pity for the privileged twenty-year-olds and their innocence in coming to visit a place like Skibbereen.

The pair intended to write an account of their journey to inform family and friends of the distress and suffering in Skibbereen and took notes as he endeavoured to answer all their questions.

'It is far worse than we ever could have imagined,' admitted Mr Boyle, trying to control his emotions.

'We visited filthy hovels around the town where people lie dying with no food or furniture.' Mr Blackwood's voice broke as he folded his notes away. 'How could we ever believe the terrible conditions that exist here if we had not travelled and seen them with our own eyes?'

'Now, excuse me, please, gentlemen, for I am afraid that I must finish,' Father John said, shaking their hands. 'I am expected soon at St Patrick's. Perhaps we shall meet and talk again later.'

George Boyle informed him that they were planning to leave on the next coach to Dublin.

'Then I wish you both a good journey and safe return to Oxford.' The priest smiled, sensing their reluctance to stay in the midst of so much disease any longer.

By chance, only a few hours later Father Fitzpatrick met the young men again, outside the Becher Arms.

'The coach to Dublin was full,' explained Mr Boyle, 'but we have managed to hire a jaunting car with an extra horse to transport us to Cork.'

'We have ordered some bread from the bakery to be distributed among the people here before we leave, Father,' added Frederick Blackwood as they said goodbye again.

*

Father Fitzpatrick was heading home when he noticed a huge crowd surging along North Street towards the Becher Arms. What could it be? The noise was deafening. A hundred or more screaming women and children gestured wildly, begging and shouting up to a hotel window above them. Freshly baked loaves of bread were being thrown down from it, cascading into the grasping hands of the crowd below.

Word had spread of the young men's deed and more people joined the fray, gathering outside the hotel as the bread rained down on them like manna from heaven.

Father John grew alarmed as women and small children screamed, fought and scrabbled fiercely over the scraps of bread and loaves that had fallen to the ground. Those who were successful held on tightly to their bounty. His young English friends were well-intentioned, but as the flow of bread from above began to dry up, the cries of the huge crowd intensified.

'Bread! More bread!' they demanded angrily. 'Feed us! More bread for the hungry!'

He watched with dismay as the two students emerged from the hotel in fear. Struggling with their baggage, they had to fight their way through the crush of starving people to get to their waiting jaunting car. The two horses, terrified by the noise of the mob, reared and thrashed as some of the crowd began to run alongside the car, pleading and begging the gentlemen for more.

As the crowd realized their benefactors were well on their way, they dispersed with their precious spoils and the priest returned to his business.

A few weeks later he received a published copy of their journey from Oxford to Skibbereen, with the young Frederick Blackwood promising him that all the proceeds from their work would be donated to Skibbereen.

Chapter 51

THAT MORNING, FANNY WAS STRANGELY QUIET AT BREAKFAST. DESPITE Henrietta's entreaties, she refused to take even a spoonful of porridge.

'I'm not hungry, Mama,' she declared.

By mid-morning Fanny was burning hot and running a fever. Henrietta tried not to give in to the mounting sense of alarm she felt as she tried to cool her daughter with a flannel cloth soaked in water.

'Sally, you must mind the others while I stay with Fanny,' she told her maid.

Children always get fevers, she tried to reassure herself as she wished that Dan was at home rather than being away at the work-house or seeing one of his patients.

During the course of the day Fanny slept fitfully and Henrietta was up and down attending to her.

'Mama, my head hurts,' she cried quietly.

As she helped her back into bed, she noticed a reddish rash developing on her child's stomach, which she had itched.

About half an hour later, Sally called to her. Young Daniel was now sick too.

'He has vomited his lunch, ma'am, and says he has a bad headache.'

'Young man, you are going back to bed too,' Henrietta ordered, plumping his pillow as she settled him and brushed back his fair hair.

She made her way into the bedroom next door to check on Fanny, whose condition had deteriorated rapidly. The poor child was shivering, her teeth chattering with rigors. She would barely open her eyes when Henrietta tried to rouse her.

'Sally! Sally!' she shouted in alarm. 'You must go to the dispensary immediately and fetch Dr Dan. Tell him that the children are sick and he must return home.'

Nearly two hours passed before Dan returned. By that point Fanny was in a deep sleep, her skin burning with fever, while young Daniel tossed and turned in his small bed.

Dan examined each child in turn, talking gently to them as Henrietta looked on.

'It is typhus,' he announced.

'Oh, Dan, don't say such a thing!'

'They both have the symptoms,' he admitted dejectedly. 'Half the town is sick with it.'

'Then you must make them better,' she demanded in fear, her hysteria rising.

'My dear, the fever will run its course. Unfortunately there is little else I can do except ensure the children are kept comfortable and drink some water.'

'What about all the people who have it? What do you say to them?'

'Many who have the fever are severely malnourished and weak, but our children are strong, young and healthy,' he explained quietly.

'You are a doctor and you will make them better,' she insisted. 'I will not have anything happen to our children, Dan. Do you hear me?'

Henrietta broke down when she saw the powerlessness in her husband's eyes and the pain he felt that the disease was now within their own home.

Harriet too soon fell sick with fever. The Donovan family were now in the grip of typhus, as were so many other families in the town. As death lingered at her own door, courting her beloved children, Henrietta was filled with a mother's fear like that of every poor mother in the town.

Dan too was consumed with worry, but he still had to attend to his professional duties. Henrietta knew that her husband blamed himself for their children being ill. She thanked heaven that Henry, Jerrie, Ellen and twenty-month-old Maggie displayed no signs of the fever yet and insisted that Sally tend to them.

Fanny's small body was now covered with a dark spotty rash and her fair hair clung damply to her head in curls. Her fever refused to break and her breath came raspingly in her small chest, like a butterfly trying to escape from a net.

'She is much worse,' Dan sighed as he took her wrist and felt her pulse.

Henrietta had no words for him, for her heart was heavy with anger. How she wished she had packed up the children and fled this place when she was able to. She had condemned them to this. Why had she not acted to protect them!

Chapter 52

DAN HELD FANNY IN HIS ARMS AS SHE SLEPT. SHE WAS STRUGGLING TO breathe, her small life slipping away. His heart was heavy as he looked at his sick daughter, for he knew only too well the path of the disease at this stage, and how little could be done to aid the afflicted.

He slipped her back into the bed gently and dampened her bare skin with a flannel he'd soaked in water, washing her face, brow, neck and chest, and wetting her cracked, dry lips.

'Dada is here with you, Fanny. You must try to get better.'

He wanted her to hear his voice, to cling to it, and to fight to hold on to life.

'Mama and I, and all your brothers and sisters want to see you back up playing and running around, singing your funny little songs for us.'

Fanny exhaled, and fell deeper and deeper into sleep. Dan stretched out in the chair beside the bed and watched over her. She was normally so lively and full of chat. Named after his mother, Frances, his daughter had inherited much of her grandmother's spirit. To see her lie so quietly like this was alarming.

As the week ended, young Daniel seemed a little better.

'Good boy,' Dan praised his son, who, with a little coaxing, took a few spoonfuls of broth. Harriet remained weak and slept a lot, but

197

he was hopeful that she too would recover. Unfortunately Fanny's condition showed little improvement and her breathing was still laboured. His wife was so tired that she felt giddy.

'Henrietta, you must sleep,' he insisted.

'How can I sleep, Dan, when I fear the worst will happen to one of them if I am not there?' she protested.

'I will stay with Fanny, and will wake you if need be.'

All through the night Dan sat with his young daughter as she moaned softly in her sleep. Her skin was clammy to touch and all the colour was gone from her face. Looking at her pretty face and pert little nose, he was overcome with emotion. He held her small fingers to let her know he was there and that she was not alone.

As he watched the sun come up, he breathed a sigh of relief that his little daughter had somehow survived the night and seemed to be sleeping easier.

Hearing Henrietta stir, he went to tell her the news, only to find her slumped by her bedside, saying that the room was spinning all around her.

'Oh, my dear,' he said, rushing to her side and putting her back into bed.

'I must stay with the children,' she protested, trying to get up, but a fresh wave of exhaustion overcame her and she fell back against the pillows.

'Henrietta, you are most unwell. You need to remain here in bed.'

His wife eventually closed her eyes, too weak and sick to move. Her throat and head hurt, she told him, as she was stricken with a sudden bout of coughing.

Dan removed her dressing gown and the warm blanket from the bed, for she was too weak even to move a muscle as she gave in to the waves of fatigue that overpowered her.

Chapter 53

FATHER FITZPATRICK WENT TO CHECK THE ALTAR AND ENSURE THAT the chalice, chasuble and heavy leather-bound Bible were stored away safely for the night.

He said mass every day and these days he presided over funerals mostly. Often they took the form of a simple blessing and prayers over a shrouded corpse, for most of the deceased were penniless. Earlier that morning he had officiated at the funeral of William Crowley, a young man of means, who had been struck down with famine fever and now lay buried in Abbeystrewery with so many others from the town.

He was about to go into the sacristy when he became aware of a man kneeling in a pew to the side of the altar, his head held in his hands, lost deep in prayer. The man's tall black hat sat beside him on the bench. It was Dan Donovan. The priest hesitated but decided not to disturb him and moved on to the room behind the altar.

The people came to the church every day, heads bent in prayer, begging the Lord to help them in this time of need. Father Fitzpatrick ensured that the church door was opened early before mass so at least his congregation could come inside to shelter from the harsh elements and could sit quietly or doze in the pews. He had been warned not to leave the church open all day and night for it would soon become home to the poor and needy, and those who walked the roads.

The bishop had reminded him that the church was a sacred place, the house of God meant for prayer and contemplation and the sacraments. However, Father Fitzpatrick suspected that if Jesus Christ still walked the earth, every Christian church in the country would have flung open their doors to the hungry and sick during this time of calamity.

When Father Fitzpatrick returned from ensuring that his vestments were clean and in good condition for Sunday mass, he was surprised to find Dan still kneeling down, his shoulders hunched, his countenance miserable. Filled with concern for his friend, he went over to him.

'Dan, are you all right?'

The doctor looked up with reddened eyes.

'Father John, it's Henrietta and the children. They are sick, so sick with fever.'

'I'm sorry to hear that.'

'I blame myself, Father, for bringing sickness and contagion to our door. No matter what time of day or night I return home, the sick are there awaiting me. I tell them to go to the dispensary, but they all know well where my home is. We have had to harden our hearts to those who come inside our door, but now illness besets my family. I have been so busy with my medical duties that I did not pay enough attention to my own family and wife. What kind of man am I?'

'Dan, I know you to be a good person, who does his best for his fellow man. The town is filled with fever – not just in the poor lanes and cabins, but in the big houses too. Death, unfortunately, does not discriminate the way we do.'

Dan sighed heavily. 'I know you are right, Father John.'

'Will we say a prayer or two together, for Henrietta and the children?' the priest offered.

Dan nodded, his face filled with misery and despair as they began.

Pater noster, qui es in caelis,
sanctificetur nomen tuum.
Adveniat regnum tuum.
Fiat voluntas tua,
sicut in caelo, et in terra . . .

When they had finished, the priest urged his friend to return home.

'The Lord will understand, Dan. Your place is not here in the church with me, but at home with your family, where you are needed. I promise that I will keep them all in my prayers.'

Chapter 54

THE MORNING SUN STRETCHED ACROSS THE BED AND ITS SILK COUN-
terpane. As Henrietta began to wake, she felt its warming rays on
her face. It was as if she had been in a deep sleep for days, but the
reality was that she had been ill with fever and had little memory of
it, only Dan tending to her, washing her and changing her like a
child, and encouraging her to get well again.

She opened her eyes slowly as she became used to the light. She
took in their bedroom, and the heavy oak wardrobe and chest of
drawers. Dan, his long thin face serious, sat in a chair, watching her,
his writing pad on his lap.

'My dearest, how are you feeling?' he asked with concern.

'Strange,' she replied, her mouth and lips parched.

He filled a glass from the water carafe on the small table.
He helped to prop her up in the bed and held the vessel to her
lips.

'It is good to see you sitting up and able to speak to me,' he said,
overcome with relief.

She was filled with a profound alarm.

'The children?' she asked, dreading his response.

'They are well,' he reassured her. 'All of them, I promise you,
are well.'

*

Hours later she woke again, conscious of someone watching her.

Harriet sat in the chair next to her, sipping from a cup of milk.

'Oh, Harriet, you are well again,' she said with relief, and reached for her daughter's hand. 'I was so fearful. So fearful.'

'Dada said I must drink some milk to help get my strength back.'

Harriet gave her mother a smile and licked at the creamy whisker of milk on her top lip like a little kitten.

'Well, your dada is right, and tomorrow I will take a little milk too. Where are Fanny and Daniel?'

'Daniel is downstairs, playing with Henry and Jerrie, and Ellen is next door reading a story to Fanny. She still has to stay in bed,' she said seriously, 'but Mama, I am much better.'

'I can see that, darling girl.'

Later that evening, Henrietta went and sat beside Fanny's bed. Her daughter's face was pinched and gaunt, but her eyes lit up when she saw her mother.

Dan appeared in the doorway and smiled.

'You are the best medicine for her.'

Chapter 55

DAN'S BREATH FORMED ICY CLOUDS IN THE COLD AIR AS HE DROVE OUT to Lough Hyne. He was thankful for his heavy grey coat and Henrietta's gift of a knitted scarf and gloves to keep him warm, as it was near freezing outside. He was on his way to see Daniel McCarthy's wife after his fellow committee member had stopped him at the end of Monday's meeting and asked him to pay her a visit.

McCarthy's voice had been filled with concern. 'I don't like asking you to come out so far with this bad weather, but she is tired all the time, and her legs and feet these past days are badly swollen.'

Dan knew the worry of having a sick wife and had agreed immediately to see Mary McCarthy.

He turned his horse off the main road and took a small winding track down through the green forest that led down towards Lough Hyne. The ancient saltwater lake was a place of stunning beauty. Shaped like a bowl and surrounded by tall trees and steep rocks, its crystal-clear waters contained fish like you'd never seen before. It was a wondrous place.

The track began to slope suddenly, and grew slippery with ice. Dan soothed his mare as she began to lose her footing on the steep descent. He stopped for a minute, got down from the trap and began to lead the horse instead.

The McCarthys' large house with its magnificent view of the

lough came into view, but he also became aware of a group of men working down at the edge of the water. Surely they were not doing works in this appalling weather?

As the ground levelled off, he climbed back into the trap and continued towards the house. He watched in disbelief as men in rags stood partially immersed in the freezing water, lifting heavy stones, shivering and shaking with the wet and cold. They were building some kind of sea wall in the rapids at the edge of the lough.

'What is going on here?' he demanded, slowing the horse and coming to a halt.

'We are part of the public works scheme,' replied the foreman, a tall fellow in a warm, heavily-lined coat. 'The men are building a wall here.'

'The men cannot work in such conditions,' Dan said, getting down. 'You can see how poorly clad they are. I am the Union physician and I am telling you that these men will meet their end if they continue to stand in the water like that. Tell them to come out. This is no work for such men in this weather.'

'If they want to get paid their eight pennies they will work,' the foreman replied stubbornly.

The men could hear the argument but kept their heads low, not wanting to cause a disturbance.

'I order you to take these men from the water immediately,' Dan countered firmly. 'I will check on them on my way home.'

The uselessness of the situation assailed him, as did the absolute folly of the public works. He had protested about them so much already and this despicable display of lunacy would no doubt cost lives.

He turned into the avenue leading to the McCarthys' home. The maid showed him to the drawing room where McCarthy greeted him and offered him a warm drink.

'Did you see the men working down at the lough?' the doctor demanded of his host.

'Aye, they've been working there these past two months on a public works scheme to improve the lough.'

'Are you telling me that these men have been working that long in this terrible snow and the cold?'

'Yes, I protested to the county supervisor, Mr Treacy, and Major Parker,' McCarthy said angrily, 'but to no avail. Wrixon Becher is the landlord here and owns most of the land around the lough. Even this house of mine is part of Lord Carbery's estate, so there is little I can do. Believe me, Dan, it upsets my wife and me to see them treated so.'

'How is your good lady?'

'To be honest, I am worried for her.'

'Let me see her.'

'She is upstairs. I'll ask Peggy to tell her that you are here.'

'I will see her upstairs if I may.'

'Of course.'

Peggy, the maid, led him up to the enormous bedroom, which was lavishly furnished and had a breathtaking view of Lough Hyne.

Mary McCarthy sat at the window in a loose gown.

'Dr Dan, thank you so much for coming all this way to see me. I feel foolish dragging you out here, but my husband insisted.'

Dan could see immediately that Mary's hands were swollen, as were her feet. She had a slightly puffy look about her, which some women develop in late pregnancy. But Mrs McCarthy was not that far along.

'Will you sit on the bed and let me examine you?' he asked politely. 'Is there any sign of cough or fever?'

'Of course. And no, my husband insists that I stay away from town lest I catch something.'

'He is probably right, Mrs McCarthy. You have a lovely comfortable home here, where I believe you should rest.'

'Rest?'

'Your child is not due for another few months, but I think you should do little until it is time for your confinement, which may be a bit sooner than we expected. The baby is growing fast.'

She sighed. 'I feel like I am very big and heavy.'

'I want you to get as much bed rest as you can, here at home. No gallivanting into town or carriage rides,' he said sternly.

'Yes,' she mumbled. 'I will stay home.'

'Good,' he said, satisfied.

He did not want to say anything more at this stage, but he was concerned by her size. He worried that either there was something amiss with the baby or that there was the possibility that she could be carrying twins.

'I will visit you again in two or three weeks.'

'Thank you for coming, Dan. I know how busy you are with other, far more important things in town,' she said, her blue eyes filled with gratitude.

Back downstairs, over tea, Dr Donovan explained the situation to her worried husband and told him to ensure his wife had bed rest. He was to send for him immediately should there be any sudden change in her condition.

Peggy offered Dan a plate of scones. He was not hungry but asked if she minded if he took one for later.

'Take two,' encouraged McCarthy. 'You won't get the like of them in the workhouse.'

It began to sleet as Dan climbed into the trap and guided the horse slowly back down the avenue towards the lough, where the men were still working in the water. It was unbearable to watch.

One poor fellow looked blue with the cold. Every vein on his skeletal frame stood out. His teeth were chattering and his entire body was overcome with shivers and shakes.

'I told you to stop this work,' Dan bellowed, approaching the foreman. 'I will complain about the inhumane treatment of these men when I get to Skibbereen. Mark my words.'

The foreman shrugged, uncaring.

'These public works schemes are all due to shut down soon,' Dan warned the bully of a man, 'and your role here will be well remembered in the district.'

The fellow grew visibly uncomfortable at Dan's threat.

'Get that man out of the water,' Dan continued. 'I am taking him with me, for he is too unwell to walk home. But first you must pay him for the work he has done.'

Muttering and complaining as the other workers looked on, the foreman reluctantly tossed the man a few pennies.

Dan helped his patient into the trap. He handed him the rough towel he kept for the horse and made him dry himself off with it then wrap the rug around his shivering body.

The climb back towards the main road, away from the lake, was desperately steep and the horse struggled. Dan walked beside her, calmly urging her along the slippery surface. Heaven knew how the weak men managed to make such a trek after working all day down at the lough.

The old man lived alone only a mile away. He neither spoke nor stirred the whole way home. There was not a scrap of clothing left in the small dirty cabin and so Dan left him with the warm rug from the trap, though he knew Henrietta would scold him over it. He also took out the scones and placed them near him.

'Thank you, doctor,' the man said weakly, his eyes welling with tears.

'In a while, when you are warmed through and feel better, eat those, little by little,' Dan ordered gently. 'You must not return to that work. I will call to see you again in a day or two.'

Chapter 56

Oldcourt

SINCE ELLEN CLANCY'S DEATH, MARY KEPT HERSELF TO HERSELF AS SHE worked on the road, and thought only of what she could buy with her hard-earned pennies. She pitied the old widow women who worked alongside her, as they grew weaker and frailer by the day.

One of the men working nearby had collapsed. Denis Leary and a few of the other fellows tried to give him some water and a little bread to revive him, but their efforts came to nothing. The foreman ordered three of the men to lift the man's body carefully on to one of the carts and to cover him with a bit of tarpaulin. He instructed two others to take him into town to the dispensary.

Ten days later the foreman called the workers together to inform them that the public relief works scheme was ending. Come Monday there would be no more work for them.

Mary's heart sank at his words. The implications for her and her family were too terrible to contemplate.

'We are willing to work,' big Tom Corrigan shouted angrily. He was a six-foot-five giant of a man. Although he was lean, he could still swing a pickaxe higher and harder than anyone. 'You cannot just dismiss us when we all have hungry mouths to feed. We have killed ourselves working for you.'

'We need the work,' Denis joined in. 'We have families to feed.'

'Who has decided it?' called another voice from the crowd.

'The British government has issued orders that all public relief schemes across Ireland are to end and I must follow such orders,' the foreman informed them dispassionately.

'Please, sir, let us work,' cried one of the women. 'Our children will starve.'

'I'm sorry to impart such news,' the foreman said, looking embarrassed at the tattered and exhausted motley group of workers before him, 'but this is no decision of mine. I too must follow orders.'

'We are willing to work,' a few shouted. 'Give us work!'

'There is not the money to pay for further works,' the payment clerk interrupted loudly, daring them to challenge him. 'You will receive the wages due to you tomorrow but that is all, for officially this scheme is ended.'

Angry, dissenting voices murmured their disapproval and upset.

'Get back to work,' threatened the foreman, 'if you do not want to be docked a few hours' pay.'

As she walked home across the fields, Mary's upset at such bad news gave way to a strange sense of relief that neither she nor John would have to undertake such terrible work on the roads. Far too many lives had already been lost over those paltry few brass coins. Surely there must be some other means and a better way for their family to survive.

Chapter 57

Creagh

WITH THE RELIEF WORKS CLOSED, MARY WORRIED FOR HER FAMILY, FOR they now had little to eat. Two or three times a week they walked with the children to the small soup kitchen set up only a mile and a half away at the home of Reverend Caulfield, the church rector, and his wife. It made a huge difference to the Sullivans, for the children were far too weak and no longer able for the eight-mile round trip to Skibbereen to take the soup. Flor brought Molly in the rickety cart pulled by Smokey the donkey, as both her legs and feet had become strangely swollen and she could not walk far.

'Little Annie can sit with me,' Molly volunteered. 'Poor Smokey is old like myself and not able for much of a load these days.'

Some days they were fed and others they had to quell their disappointment, when too many families came and the soup ran out.

John took the boys out hunting for any wild thing they might find or catch that could go in their pot. On one occasion he had killed a fat wood pigeon, using a stone in a sling he had fashioned, and she had plucked and cleaned the bird as she would have done one of their old hens.

Each day, they foraged and hunted in the fields. Nearly every bush and hedge was picked clean, and there wasn't a rabbit or hare to be found, or a bird's nest to rob. They collected snails, which she boiled up with some herbs and salt water. Her stomach turned as she swallowed them, but they said nothing to the children who sniffed at them before eating them. All except Annie, who kept her mouth closed stubbornly in refusal.

They dug up roots, which she boiled and mashed, and picked mushrooms and puffballs in the shady woods and young nettles.

'But I want taties to eat,' Annie whined.

'Well, there is not a tatie to be had in the county, so you will have to make do with something else,' she told her firmly. 'Your grandfather Corny used to always say that nature's bounty is there for the like of us.'

Con and Tim had found a hedgehog hidden under a pile of leaves. John cut its throat and covered it in clay before they roasted it over the fire. It was fatty but the meat tasted a bit like rabbit.

In desperation, they also fished in the river for little pinkeens, speckled trout and carp, even though the old heron had long since disappeared. They had little luck. At low tide they searched the rocks and pools for baby crabs, cockles and mussels, limpets and periwinkles, and gathered dulse, kelp and carrageen moss.

Famished, Mary even resorted to digging up earthworms. She watched them wiggle as she washed and cut them, and put them in her pot. She prayed that they were safe to eat.

But still the Sullivans grew hungry . . .

Chapter 58

'AWAY! AWAY!' MARY SHOUTED.

The mangy dog kept watching her as she tried to shoo it away with her broom. She could see it, sense it. A scrawny thing that insisted on hanging around. No doubt the mongrel was hungry, but there was little she could do about it. Every scrapeen of food they had was for them, not some cur of a dog that had appeared out of nowhere.

But it kept showing up. As time went on, Mary hadn't even the strength to chase it away.

The family were growing weaker and weaker by the day. The watery gruel she heated up to feed the children simply passed through them, only filling their small stomachs momentarily.

She kept a careful eye on the dog, making sure it did not come too near the house or the children. She feared it was just biding its time.

The following day she spotted the animal further down the field, chewing on something. A bone. She had no idea where it had found it or from where it had dug it up. It turned and growled at her. The pit of her stomach turned in fear.

'Go! Go! Off with ye!' she screamed, but it continued to gnaw at its filthy bone.

213

There wasn't another creature to be seen – not even a fox, or a rabbit or a hare – and yet this dog was still here . . .

There was nothing to put in the pot. Water, a bare handful of Indian meal, salt, and a few herbs and nettles to cook over the fire. What kind of a meal was that?

Then she saw it. The dog had come nearer to the house than ever before, as bold and brazen as you like.

Suddenly fearful, Mary grabbed the broom to chase it away, but as she did so the animal raised its snout. Growling, it bared its teeth, ready to attack and bite her. As she swung the broom, the beast jumped up and snarled, trying to grab at it with its teeth. She made contact with its head as hard as she could. Again and again, she struck the dog until it was still. Its tongue hung from its mouth in a small pool of blood, its eyes glazed over.

She had killed it. Triumph filled her and a feeling of inexplicable joy took over her.

Close up, it looked to be about two or three years old. Its head and paws were big but its body ill-fed. Still, it was a good size. Mary studied the animal further, wondering where she would bury it or how she would get rid of it before the children and John returned home. She went to lift it and was surprised at how heavy it still was. The weight of a lamb or a piglet . . . And then it came to her . . . She knew what to do.

Mary dragged the animal's lifeless body to the back of the cottage where John often worked, and laid it on a stone slab. She took a sharp knife and quickly began to skin it, removing its short coat deftly. She then opened it up and pulled out its entrails before cutting off its head, for she could not bear to see its sad eyes. She butchered it as she used to prepare their lambs, removing its paws instead of hooves and its long narrow tail.

Meat still sat on its bones. Not a huge amount, but enough. She set about quartering it and then divided it into fleshy segments that she could manage.

*

The smell of meat cooking filled the air as she stirred the boiling water and added a few herbs to the pot.

The children sat around the turf fire, watching and waiting, and John returned with a bucket of water from the well.

'What is it?' he whispered, coming over to investigate.

'A kid goat I found caught in the thorns out back, half dead,' she lied.

'Whose goat is it?' asked Tim, curious.

'I don't know, but it was lucky for us that I found him before someone else came along.'

Nora said nothing and sat staring into the fire.

The meat was strong . . . and tough. It was much like mutton but they ate it slowly, spoonful by spoonful. Mary dared give only a little mouthful to Annie.

'Only a small bit tonight,' she warned the children. 'For fear the taste of meat in your belly after so long will make you sick.'

'It will not make me sick.' Tim grinned, wanting some more.

'You may have more tomorrow,' she promised him.

As she ate, she tried to push thoughts of the animal out of her head, knowing that the meat of the poor creature would somehow help them to survive.

She cooked up more of the dog meat the next day and roasted one of its legs slowly over the fire.

'Eating dog will do us no harm,' John assured her once she had shared her secret with him. 'A sailor once told me that in some far-off countries in the Orient they eat them all the time.'

'God preserve us!'

'We will do what we have to. Anything to keep us from starving,' he said matter-of-factly. 'If I had seen that dog, Mary, I tell you, I'd have killed him myself.'

She had never expected to become so hard, so strong and determined. She may have a woman's light touch with her needlework, but deep inside Mary knew that if the situation demanded it, she would fight like a wolf to protect those she loved.

Chapter 59

THE LAST OF THE DOG MEAT WAS GONE AND THE CHILDREN GREW weaker, whining and complaining of pains in their bellies much of the time. Mary couldn't bear it, so, with an eagle eye, she searched their cottage for anything left to pawn or sell to buy meal.

She bundled up the warm patchwork counterpane she had made for their marriage bed, which left them with only a grey blanket. She gathered up her only good dress, the pin-tucked dresses she had made for Nora and Annie, and John's tweed waistcoat, and folded them up neatly to take into town.

'Near everything we have is gone to that man!' John shouted angrily as he watched her. 'Hegarty and his like are robbing the people blind with the hunger and making money.'

Skibbereen was busy, with beggars, hands outstretched looking for food or money. She pushed past them all and joined the short line outside Hegarty's pawnbrokers. As the young couple ahead of her moved forward and put down their heavy load on the floor in front of the shop counter, Mary kept her eyes low.

'The chair and footstool were made by a craftsman and are in perfect condition,' the young man began.

Mary could tell Hegarty was intrigued, but he feigned disinterest.

'I have a warehouse of furniture. What am I to do with them?'

'We have to sell them, for we are taking passage to America.'

'Sir, we are not looking for a fortune, but we are here to sell them today,' the young woman insisted.

The proprietor shrugged. 'Perhaps you could try somewhere else?'

'I am selling my bridal dress too. It is made of fine lace and embroidery, and is precious to me,' she continued, the desperation in her voice growing.

Mary remembered how bad she had felt when she brought her own wedding dress to the shop last year.

Hegarty fingered the young woman's garment and carefully examined its pearl buttons and delicate stitching. His wife and daughter were known for their fashion and Mary could see at once that he was tempted by the gown.

'For a young couple going to the New World, I will be generous. What do you say if I give you two guineas for the furniture alongside the dress?'

'It is not enough,' blurted the husband. 'They are worth far more.'

'I will take the dress with me,' the woman added defiantly. 'Sell it when I get there.'

The pawnbroker sighed, exasperated. 'Three pounds and not a farthing more.'

The couple stood still, taking stock of the offer. Mary could see that the young wife was ready to argue with Hegarty, but her husband's fingers caught her wrist, warning her to say no more.

'Thank you, sir. We will accept your offer,' he muttered.

Before Mary could step forward, an old woman with a bundle pushed ahead of her. The woman's grey hair fell lank around her shoulders and her dress was soiled and muddy. Mary caught the stale odour of the woman's body as she reached to untie her parcel of scraps of material.

'It's just rags,' the pawnbroker retorted. 'Rags are no good to me.'

'A few pennies are all I want, sir,' the woman argued loudly. ''Tis all I've left to sell.'

Mr Hegarty cut short her pleas and ordered her from his premises.

'I can't have beggars like her in here. This is a place of business,' he said brusquely, beckoning Mary to come forward.

'Mr Hegarty, I have a few more items that I wish to sell,' Mary said, placing them in front of him. 'I made the counterpane and dresses myself. It is good work, for I am a seamstress.'

As the pawnbroker thumbed the coloured patchwork cover, she could sense his greedy brain working and assessing what price the items might fetch. They finally settled on only four shillings and Mary hid her disappointment as she bid him good day. It was little enough to buy what she needed.

As was her habit, Mary paused outside Honora Barry's dress-making shop. Honora was inside and so Mary knocked on the glass, filled with a wild hope that her former employer might have some mending work for her. Miss Barry let her in and enquired politely how she and her family were faring.

'Things have been very hard,' Mary admitted. 'John took ill and could not work, so I had to work breaking stones on the road these past weeks.'

'My poor dear child,' she sympathized. 'Look at your hands and fingers!'

'Just a few bruises and scratches,' Mary said defensively. 'I can still sew.'

Their conversation was interrupted by the arrival of a customer at the door to collect an item. Honora disappeared into the back of the shop for a minute and returned with a white garment, which she rolled up carefully and wrapped in paper as the tearful older woman paid her.

'Thank you, Miss Barry, for your kindness to us in our time of trouble,' the woman said, dabbing her eyes with a handkerchief.

'I'm sorry for your loss,' the dressmaker said, walking her to the door.

'Mrs Callaghan's daughter died two days ago,' she explained to Mary once her customer had left.

She gestured to a roll of creamy white material on the far side of the room.

'All people want me to make these days are shrouds to bury their dead in. For God help us, there are no coffins. This is what keeps me busy. Have you ever made one of them, Mary?'

'No.' She shook her head. 'Never.'

'I didn't ever think that I'd see the day I'd be taking on such work either,' the dressmaker admitted ruefully, 'but it is what is necessary. I promise that they are easy enough to make. That is, if you are interested in helping me?'

Eager for work, Mary agreed without hesitation.

'They are a simple pattern,' she explained, 'and people will pay promptly for them.'

Mary studied the shroud that the dressmaker had been stitching when she came in.

'I can teach you how to make one,' Honora offered, leading her to the workroom.

The dressmaker showed her quickly how to cut out the pattern, wasting as little material as possible, and how to shape it and sew the simple seams.

'No one is going to examine it stitch by stitch,' Honora reminded her, 'but people do expect good work for their dear departed . . . despite the circumstances of their burial.'

It was certainly not the type of work Mary had expected to be offered, but work was work. She promised to return next week with the five shrouds they had agreed upon.

'Do you have a good supply of thread and needles?' the dressmaker asked as she carefully measured out and parcelled up the lengths of material that Mary would need.

Mary blushed. How could she admit that she had come here looking for work and yet had barely a spool of thread at home! The other woman lowered her eyes discreetly and generously added a packet of needles and a few spools of thread to one of the packages.

'If you want, I could let you have an advance of six pennies now and the rest when you are finished,' she offered.

Mary was overcome with gratitude for the kindness of her old employer, who was proving herself a true friend.

'But you must promise to have the shrouds back to me by Tuesday,' she urged. 'And they must be spotlessly clean, with no smudges of turf or dirt on them.'

Mary agreed without question and watched as Honora took some coins from the small drawer and counted them into her hand. It was little enough but it would buy a small bag of oats to take home with her.

'Take this too, for it doesn't agree with me,' insisted the kindly woman, wrapping up a half loaf of rye bread for her.

Mary carried the parcels through the town, deciding to stop at Kathleen's as she hadn't seen her sister for weeks. Sarah and Lizzie were both sick, and her sister looked more tired and thinner than she had ever seen her before.

'We are lucky we can take the soup every day,' she sighed, 'but it runs through me.'

Mary looked around the cottage. The straw underfoot was dirty and foul and in need of changing. The whole place could have done with being swept out and washed down.

'I haven't the energy for cleaning it,' admitted Kathleen, as if reading her sister's mind.

Mary told her about getting work making the shrouds.

'God between us and all harm, but I suppose someone has to do it!'

'I'm happy to have work,' she said defensively.

'If only my Joseph could find some kind of job now the roadworks have closed down,' Kathleen complained, 'we wouldn't always be in the terrible state that we are in.'

Walking home, Mary couldn't wait to tell John the good news of her new job, even if it was as a shroud-maker to the dead.

Chapter 60

Skibbereen

DAN STOOD IN THE GROUNDS OF ABBEYSTREWERY GRAVEYARD. IT WAS A beautiful spot, situated on the Ballydehob side of town on a sloping hill with some shady trees, and overlooked the broad expanse of the river. However, the peace and beauty of the burial place was now destroyed by the large, deep trench that had been dug in the graveyard to receive the large numbers of bodies of those who had died overnight or during the day. With such large numbers of decaying corpses being brought to the graveyard, immediate interment was imperative.

Many of those poor souls who had died in the workhouse during the night and in the early morning would be buried here in the deep pit – the mass grave that had been dug to contain them. It was his duty to ensure that the bodies were disposed of as quickly and safely as possible, and to ensure that once one section of the pit was full, it would be covered with lime and filled in with earth as a new pit was dug and prepared to receive more bodies. There was no time for gravestones or crosses to mark the last resting place of so many.

He watched as the cart arrived and the men made ready the hinged coffin they used to place the remains of the deceased, one at a time, into the burial pit. Dinny Burke and his helper approached the grave and released the coffin base, so that the body of a skeletal middle-aged woman fell on to the decaying corpses below.

No prayers or blessings were uttered for the deceased. Father John and his curate tried to attend some days but often, like himself, they were too busy administering to the sick to come and say a few words of prayer over those who had left this world.

The men returned to refill the coffin and repeated their actions.

The stench from the pit was overpowering. The gravediggers most certainly needed to close this section once these new bodies had filled it. Dan stared down at the young men and women who should have had their lives ahead of them, the innocent children and babies who deserved better than this undignified end in a crowded, unmarked grave. How much longer could this appalling situation continue without some proper form of rescue for the people? Dan sometimes felt like a moth batting against a lantern as he tried to attract attention and aid for his patients and the hungry.

As he walked over to the gravediggers to tell them they must close this pit and begin a new one, a woman arrived at the site. Dressed in nothing but rags, she staggered over to him, her legs bloated with oedema. She was almost too weak to walk but she demanded to know where they were interring her husband, who had been on the cart.

'Where is my Paddy?' she wailed. 'I'll be in the grave with him before too long.'

The man's body was gone from the cart and had been deposited already. For a moment, Dan thought the poor, crazed woman was going to jump into the pit herself to join him.

'Your husband is at peace,' he said, taking her arm gently, 'but you are most unwell and need to be cared for.'

Tears ran down the woman's dirt-creased face.

'Your husband would not want you left here like this. I am a doctor in the Skibbereen Union where I promise you will be cared for.'

'I'll not go to the workhouse,' she spat stubbornly. 'I'll stay here close to him.'

'The men will lock the graveyard soon,' he cautioned. 'So it's far better that you come with me to the Union where you will have, at the least, some nourishment and a place to lie down.'

The woman swayed on her feet, near to collapse. She was starved but when he observed her he could detect no sign of fever. With the help of Dinny, Dan managed to get her to his carriage where she lay down, exhausted. She closed her eyes and said nothing more as Dan drove towards the workhouse and down the avenue leading up to it, passing all those waiting outside in the desperate hope of admission.

'Dr Donovan, you know better than anyone else that we are full,' the newly appointed matron protested sternly as Dan pleaded for the woman to be admitted to the women's section.

'I could not leave this poor woman lying near her husband's grave, waiting to be thrown into it,' he petitioned her.

The matron's cheeks flushed and she acceded reluctantly to his request.

He was all too aware that Skibbereen Union Workhouse was overcrowded, but he was very hopeful of acquiring a warehouse down by the quay that could be used soon as an auxiliary workhouse to accommodate more women during this crisis.

As he turned the carriage for home, Dan felt himself grow weak. He found himself having to stop for a few minutes to get his breath back. He checked his pulse and temperature, aware of the worsening of the headache he had felt since earlier that morning. He had stayed at the dispensary for three hours, but in the end had to refuse to see patients, and made the excuse that he was urgently needed somewhere else.

By the time he arrived at the house on New Street he felt wretched and wanted nothing more than to crawl into bed. His body was already feverish as he made his way upstairs, undressed and lay down on the cool sheets.

As Henrietta followed him, she was unable to hide her concern.

'What is it, Dan?'

'You must fetch Patrick Dore,' he told her. 'Tell him I have the fever . . .'

Chapter 61

HENRIETTA COULD NOT BEAR TO SEE DAN SICK. WATCHING HIM ARRIVE home in a state of near collapse, she had been overwhelmed by fear and panic but composed herself. She knew that her husband would not wish for her to be in such a state. She had asked Sally calmly to go to North Street to fetch his friend and colleague Patrick Dore.

Thoughts crowded her mind as she considered the many diseased hovels her husband attended, as well as the workhouse and grave-yards, but she reminded herself that in the years since they had first met, Dan Donovan had never been sick a day or complained even of being unwell or in pain. He was a strong man and, as he said himself often enough, had the constitution of a horse.

She dispatched the children to play in the back garden and warned them to be quiet as their father was not feeling well.

Meanwhile, Dr Patrick Dore arrived promptly and went upstairs to examine Dan. His face was serious when he told her that Dan had contracted typhus fever, was very poorly and would need good care and nursing.

'I have already had typhus,' Henrietta informed him as she promised to follow all his instructions with regard to Dan's medical care.

'I will call to see him tomorrow,' the doctor promised, 'but if there is any change for the worse during the night, please send for me.'

*

Henrietta slept in the chair at Dan's bedside as his fever raged. A reddish macular rash covered his body and his head was splitting with the pain, causing him to thrash around and moan. She did everything in her power to cool him down with cold compresses and keep him comfortable.

The following day he would not even open his eyes and lay curled in their bed like a small child.

When he made his promised visit, Dr Dore reassured her that even though Dan appeared seriously ill, it was the normal progression of the disease.

'I may consider bleeding him in the next day or two, if it is needed,' he told her. 'But, knowing Dan, I am hopeful that he has the strength to fight this disease.'

Patrick Dore was a fine physician and he and the town's other doctors, Cornelius O'Driscoll and Thomas Tisdall, all assisted by seeing patients at the dispensary, while Patrick temporarily took over Dan's workhouse duties.

Father John was the only visitor Henrietta permitted to see Dan, and both of them prayed for his recovery. The priest told her that their friend Tim McCarthy Downing was, like Dan, very ill. Poor Mary Hegarty from the hotel was bereft as her daughter had died a few days ago. So too had Major Parker.

The next week and a half passed in a blur, and the children remained wide eyed and fearful for their father's health. The older boys and Ellen hovered at the bedroom door, terrified whenever Dr Dore called to see their father.

'What will happen if Father dies?' Jerrie asked with worry.

'I will not have you talk like this,' Henrietta said, hugging him. 'Your father is a man of good health and his body will fight this illness.'

Her reassurances were as much for her own benefit as for her son's and she prayed with all her might for Dan to recover.

One evening, when Henrietta had dozed off in the bedside chair, Dan stirred and sat up. To her amazement, almost in a whisper, he asked her for a sip of water before slumping back on to the pillows and falling into an exhausted sleep again. The following afternoon he asked for fresh sheets on the bed and the morning after that, to her relief, Dan took not only more water but also three small spoons of milky porridge.

Each day, Henrietta watched as her husband, little by little, regained his strength. Ellen would come in to sit and read a story to him that she had written, while young Daniel and Harriet showed him drawings they had made for him: Dan in his tall hat and long coat in a sunny garden, and a family portrait of Dan and Henrietta surrounded by all seven of their children.

'What wonderful artists you are!' he encouraged them. 'I will treasure them always.' Henrietta's heart soared to see Dan gladdened by the short visits of his children.

In no time Dan began to demand that he be allowed to dress and return to work.

'You have been very sick, Dan,' Henrietta pleaded with him. 'Dr Dore says that you must have a period of convalescence.'

'Henrietta, I have had more than enough of lying down and convalescing,' he complained, exasperated. 'It is high time for me to return to work and tend to my patients.'

Two days later she watched as her husband, in his usual long frock coat and black hat, set off for the dispensary, medical bag in hand and a zealous glint in his eyes.

Chapter 62

EVERY WEEK MARY WALKED TO TOWN WITH HER WORK STRAPPED TO her back.

'Let me come with you,' Con begged and pleaded with her, but she refused. Truth to tell, she did not want her son to see the hollow-faced hungry and sick who besieged the town.

The dressmaker inspected each shroud as if it were a pretty dress or fine coat for a customer, meticulously checking the seams and stitching. Happy with Mary's work, she went to the drawer in the back room and, taking out some money, counted the coins for her.

'Would you be able to make another eight shrouds for me for next week?' she asked.

Mary nodded, delighted to have more work.

'Then I will measure out the yards of linen for you.'

'If it is all right with you, Miss Barry, I will return in a while and collect it on my way home?'

'Aye, it's better not to be traipsing it around,' agreed the dress-maker. 'I'll have it ready for you.'

Mary made her way to the soup kitchen, took the broth and was grateful, for it sustained her after her long walk. Then she went to see her sister.

Bridgetown had become a place of sickness and reeked with the

227

smell of human ordure. Brazen rats scurried along the filthy muddy lanes, under the eaves of the thatched roofs and across the filthy floors as there was not a dog nor cat left to hunt them.

'The Murphys and Molloys should have kept their cats,' complained Kathleen, 'for now we are plagued night and day by those stinking, filthy vermin. I heard that one or two have trapped and boiled them, but they can make you fierce sick. That is one thing I would never do.'

Mary's stomach heaved at the thought of it.

The cottage was even dirtier than on her previous visit. The straw had not been replaced and the children were unwashed. Her once pretty sister's face was haggard and grey, her body run to bones, just like her own. Four-year-old Lizzie was weak and listless, her small stomach swollen like a ball. She lay on her sister's lap as pale as a ghost.

'She will not take even a spoon of water and gruel for me,' fretted Kathleen.

Mary gave her sister two of her precious pennies to buy cow's milk for Lizzie in the hope that that would help.

'I shouldn't take it off you, but the milk might give her new strength,' thanked Kathleen. 'We have nothing since the works closed. Every day Joe disappears down to the river for hours, sitting on the bank fishing.'

'Maybe he'll have luck,' Mary encouraged.

'Joe's no fisherman and the river has been near fished out,' her sister said bitterly.

'Are you all right, Kathleen?' Mary asked, suddenly concerned for her.

'I'm tired, Mary. More tired than I have ever been in my life,' she admitted quietly. 'I don't know what will become of us.'

Mary had never seen her sister like this. Kathleen had always been the headstrong, carefree older sister who had gone against her parents' wishes to marry handsome Joseph Casey. She usually shrugged and laughed off all her cares and woes, but now she seemed defeated, done in by her circumstances.

'I'm glad that Mother and Father did not live to see these terrible times,' Kathleen continued despairingly, 'and what has befallen us and our children. And poor James and Denis, and their families at home in Goleen. 'Tis meant to be fierce bad there. I thank God that I have you, my sister.'

'We have each other,' Mary reassured her as she hugged Kathleen goodbye, promising to see her again the following week.

Mary felt like crying as she handed over the meagre pennies she earned to buy some oats, flour and tea in Healy's. The prices had all gone up. As she turned for home, she called in to Honora's shop to collect the material.

'I have already sold two of the shrouds so I have added more material for you to make an extra two for me if you can,' Honora declared.

Mary accepted, but was torn between delight at the fact she would earn more pennies and guilt that so many shrouds were needed.

Her load of material was extra heavy as Mary walked the road to Creagh, and every time she heard a cart, or a pony and trap near her, she looked up hopefully. But no luck. People passed her by and then it began to rain. She wrapped her shawl around her precious bundle of linen and provisions, trying to ignore the pain in her back, shoulders and arms, and kept going.

She was about two miles from home when she spotted Con sheltering under a tree, waiting for her.

'Da sent me to help you.' He grinned and took the wrapped oats and flour from her arms.

With her load lightened, she was glad of her eldest boy's company.

'I worry for your aunt and her family living in Bridgetown,' she confided in him as they walked home, telling him how terrible things were for the people in the town.

*

She cooked a large pot of meal that evening. When they had finished eating, she sent John over the fields to Flor and Molly's with a
bowl of it along with a screw of tea. The old couple barely stirred
from their cottage these days. The Sullivans had little enough to
share, but she and John did their best to visit the pair, for they were
family.

Chapter 63

Creagh

SILENCE . . . EVERYTHING WAS STILL AND HUSHED, FOR THERE WAS NOT a bird in the sky or even a field mouse to be seen. Nests, burrows and lairs had all been pulled apart and searched, robbed in desperation. No spring bird song, mating calls or flurries disturbed this strange empty peace.

The fields about the Sullivans' cottage were quiet too, lying fallow and unplanted. The children said and did little, for the hunger had weakened them so much. They did not have the energy for playing and chasing about the place. It grieved Mary to see them so.

The neighbours kept to themselves, all fearful of sickness and disease. Even Nell Flynn had stopped begging from her, for she knew that Mary had nothing to give her.

Brigid and her family struggled and whenever the women met, they hugged, for there were no words to describe the great sympathy they had for one another, nervously asking, 'Are the children well?'

Truth to tell, all Mary cared for was John and Con, Nora, Tim and Annie. Her husband and family were the world to her. She called in to see Flor and Molly regularly, and it saddened her greatly to watch as her two elderly relatives grew weaker by the day. Their

231

flesh had already melted from their bones and Molly's skin hung loosely from her poor skeletal frame.

'I am too tired for it all,' admitted Flor. 'Molly and I are not able for going to the soup kitchen or to hunt for food any more. We are content to rest easy here.'

Every few days, she and John brought them a little gruel, some oatcakes or a cup of nettle broth. What little they had, they tried to share.

'I don't know how much longer they can manage,' John said, worried. 'We cannot starve ourselves for them.'

'We may be family but they don't expect it of us,' she reassured him.

When she brought them a few spoonfuls of warm, watered-down meal the following morning, she broached the subject of the workhouse.

'Mary, girl, the workhouse is not for us,' Flor said, shaking his head.

'Flor and I would be in different parts,' Molly protested. 'We have never been parted since the day we married and will stay together for the rest of our days.'

Mary understood. They were proud people, only expressing the same love that she and John shared.

Less than a week later, John called up to them with some turnip, but Flor told him not to cross the door or come inside.

'Molly's sick,' he reported to Mary when he arrived home, 'so I left the bowl of food at the door and fetched them some water.'

Over the next few days, Mary and John continued to call up to the cottage, bringing any food they could manage to spare and re-filling the large water jug that was left at the door. Flor had also fallen sick and they could hear him coughing as he begged them to stay away for fear of spreading the fever.

Mary placed the small pot of meal at the door, knocking to let them know that she was outside.

Flor called out from inside to thank her, but his voice had grown weak.

'Mary, promise me that you will bury us together.'

Alarmed, she gave him her word but asked him to let her in to assist them.

'Molly is asleep,' he said quietly.

Mary sobbed as she walked home, deeply upset by the suffering and hardship the old people endured, locked away in their cottage with not a child nor grandchild to help or comfort them.

The following day, on her return, the food and water jug lay untouched, and there was not even a whisper of smoke from the chimney. She called their names again and again, and knocked and rapped on their door, but Flor and Molly were silent.

She rushed home to John.

The couple had died as they lived, asleep together in their pallet bed. Peaceful, eyes closed, tucked in together.

Mary blessed herself.

'What will we do?'

'I'll bury them in the same graveyard as my father,' John said resolutely, 'where the Sullivans are buried. It's the least they deserve.'

There was not a penny for a coffin but John knew his duty. He harnessed their old donkey to the turf cart and, having wrapped his uncle and aunt gently in their blankets, placed them in it.

'I will ride to Creagh with them and find the gravedigger there,' he sighed. 'You stay here with the children.'

The neighbours came out and stood at their doors, blessing themselves as the cart passed. The children were all upset at the loss of their old grand-uncle Flor and kind grand-aunt Molly, who used to make them scones and cook up the best pot of rabbit stew they had ever eaten. Molly, with her endless patience, sitting with a glint in her eye by the fireside, telling them stories of the *sidhe*, and their old uncle Flor, who could not only play the tin whistle but was also

233

blessed with a fine singing voice, often singing as he worked or walked in the fields.

It was late when John got home.

'It's done and they are buried together,' he told her.

'In a pit?' she asked, worried.

'No, thank heaven. The gravedigger laid them together in a shallow grave. The poor donkey was barely up to it, but he got them to Creagh at least.'

They watched the clouds scud across the yellow moon.

'They always loved each other dearly,' John said after a while.

'I know,' she said, reaching for him. 'Like I love you.'

He kissed her softly and she kissed him back, for life and love were more precious than all the gold in the world, once she and John had each other.

Chapter 64

MARY AND JOHN WERE WOKEN IN THE MIDDLE OF THE NIGHT BY THE loud braying of Smokey the donkey. The poor animal sounded very distressed. Alarmed, John jumped out of bed immediately.

'What is wrong with the creature?' Mary fretted, also getting up as her husband pulled on his trousers and jacket.

'He's old and half lame but he seemed fine when I left him. Unless a pack of dogs has found him,' he said, rushing out of the cottage in the darkness.

Con and Nora had both been disturbed by the commotion and were stirring. Mary soothed them gently and told them to stay in bed.

'I'm running out to see if your father needs help,' she explained.

She didn't want him to confront a pack of hungry dogs on his own and so, pulling on her shawl, grabbed a blackthorn stick from by the door before running blindly across the field. The noise from the old donkey had stopped but, in the silence, Mary could hear shouting.

Wary, she kept a firm grip on her stick. The darkness was beginning to lift and ahead of her she could make out John with three other figures. Relief washed over her that there was no sign of any dogs.

As she neared the group, she recognized Nell and Tom Flynn,

and their older boy, Paddy. What were they doing out here at this hour? John was shouting at them angrily, and there was some kind of argument going on.

Then she saw it. The donkey lay dead on the ground, blood seeping from where its neck had been sliced open by Tom, who still held the bloodied axe in his hand.

'Why did you kill him?' she cried, rushing over. 'He was Flor and Molly's animal.'

'They are both in their grave and have no need of him now,' Nell said boldly, 'while others do!'

'Flor Sullivan was my uncle and that animal was his property, Nell,' John said through clenched teeth. 'You and your family had no right to lay a hand on him!'

'There's good eating in a donkey,' snivelled Nell.

'How do you think we felt, watching that yoke wandering the fields and us starving with hunger pains in our stomach?' Tom defended himself. 'I have to think of my wife and the boys.'

'Flor and Molly loved that animal,' Mary countered. 'He used it to take his cart to the bog and the cove. You know well that he let most of us borrow it when we needed to. If he had wanted to kill it for food, he would have done so.'

'He was a fool, then,' Nell muttered sarcastically. 'He should have done it and saved himself and Molly!'

Mary was tempted to raise her stick and belt her neighbour with it but John, as if reading her mind, stayed her arm.

'You have done something you had no right to do,' he said coldly. 'Stealing an animal is a crime.'

Mary saw a dart of fear flash between Nell and her husband.

'They meant no harm to you, Mr Sullivan,' Paddy piped up, shamefaced. 'They thought that old Smokey was there for the taking.'

'Sure, what difference does an old donkey make to anyone?'

'The difference was that he was ours.'

'The beast is dead,' argued Tom. 'There is no bringing him back. We'll skin him and butcher him and share him with you. There is not a lot of meat on him, but enough for two families.'

Mary's stomach turned at the mere thought of it as she remembered Uncle Flor giving the children rides on the back of the gentle animal.

John considered Tom's proposition. He was torn between anger and fury at his neighbours for what they had done, and a grudging acceptance of the situation.

'Mary, you go home and I will return later,' he decided. 'Not a word of this to the children.'

Mary nodded, relieved to escape Nell's smug glances.

John returned as the sun rose, and explained to the children that the old donkey had died.

Mary cooked the meat slowly in the pot. It was lean but stringy, and had a sweetish taste when mixed with wild garlic and the last few wizened turnips. She would make soups and stews from it and use a little grain to eke out every bit of it. However she might regret the beast's death, she knew that it would give them renewed strength and nourishment.

The following day she and John went to check on Flor's cottage. To their dismay they found that there was nothing left in it. Even the old couple's bolster and pallet bed, few pots, cups, jug and Flor's tin whistle had disappeared. Mary noticed that Molly's shawl, which she kept on a hook on the back of the door, had vanished too. Her heart broke as she realized how much she would miss her relative.

'The turf pile, and Flor's spade and few tools are all robbed,' John declared in fury as they looked around them. 'This is the Flynns' business. Nell and Tom have been here. They have always been thieves, with no regard for their neighbours.'

'How could they do such a thing when poor Flor and Molly are barely cold in the grave?' Mary cried in despair.

'I am going over there to tell Tom Flynn what I—'

'Shush,' she said, grabbing hold of him. 'We want no more fighting with the likes of them. They are not worth it.'

'I'll not let them away with it,' he said, enraged, as he pulled away from her.

'No, John, you must promise me not to go near them,' she begged, standing in front of him. 'Flor is at peace now. He wouldn't want you to get in a fight with Tom.'

'He never trusted him.'

'No one trusts them any more. The hunger has changed them, made them worse.'

'They were always like that.'

Somehow, she managed to persuade him to return home with her, and he agreed reluctantly not to set foot near Tom, or his wife or children.

Nell fell sick with the fever first, then their youngest boy got it and then Paddy. There was no donkey and cart to take them to the work-house fever shed, just Tom Flynn and his middle son to push them in a small handcart on the long road to town.

Chapter 65

Skibbereen
April 1847

'THE POOR MAN,' HENRIETTA HAD SIGHED WHEN DAN TOLD HER THAT his friend Reverend Robert Traill of Schull had contracted typhus. Mindful of the terrible effects of the illness, she had prayed for his recovery.

Two days later, as they sat in the drawing room, Dan broke the news gently.

'I'm afraid, my dear, that Reverend Traill has unfortunately died.'

'It's so desperately unfair, Dan,' she said, unable to hide her anger. 'He was such a devoted minister, and he and his wife, Anne, worked tirelessly, feeding hundreds of people in Schull every day. Now, because of his good works and charity, he has been taken.'

'Fair doesn't come into it, my dear! Robert Traill was a dedicated church man with a fine mind, who deserved a better end.'

'I must write to Anne to express my sympathy,' Henrietta said, thinking of the poor widow and her children, now left to cope alone.

'I see here that the government has finally opened a soup kitchen,' Henrietta observed as she read aloud from the newspaper article

239

describing the official opening of the government's first large soup kitchen in Dublin, at the esplanade near Phoenix Park, beside Dublin's Royal Barracks. 'At last, they and the Lord Lieutenant are doing something to address the situation.'

'About time too,' Dan said caustically.

'It was a grand affair, by all accounts, with his Royal Highness Prince George of Cambridge, Lord Bessborough, the Lord Lieutenant and the Lord Mayor of Dublin all in attendance for the gala launch. It was quite a social occasion for Dublin's fashionable young women and gentry. Apparently, Dublin society paid five shillings each to watch the paupers feed, and there is also to be a Government Fever Ball later this month.'

'My dear, opening a soup kitchen for the poor is certainly not what I consider a social occasion, and how rude to treat the hungry as if they were animals from Dublin Zoo!'

Henrietta smiled wryly and carried on, for she could see he was curious.

'A renowned French chef from London's Reform Club, a Mr Alexis Soyer, has developed the nutritious soup recipe himself, and it says that he can make up to one hundred gallons of soup for less than a pound. The soup kitchen has a three-hundred-gallon soup boiler and an oven that can bake one hundredweight of bread at a time.'

'That is bigger than our boilers!' remarked Dan rather enviously. 'But I know well that to make that quantity of soup for less than a pound is near impossible.'

'And more soup kitchens are set to open throughout the country,' Henrietta continued as she passed him the newspaper.

'The more the better,' he agreed, re-reading the article avidly and scratching out notes in the small leather notebook he always carried.

Dan pored over Soyer's recipe assiduously.

'If this is made in the quantities Mr Soyer suggests, it would have little nutritional value,' he insisted, and was delighted when, not long after, an article in *The Lancet* concurred with his findings, declaring Soyer's soup 'quackery'.

Dan's sentiments were further vindicated when Sir Henry Marsh, the Queen's own physician, came out and declared that the soup would pass through the human system too quickly to assuage hunger and nourish the body.

Chapter 66

A STRANGE STILLNESS HAD DESCENDED ON THE TOWN OF SKIBBEREEN. The sick and starved sat listlessly on the ground and in doorways, the streets otherwise quiet.

Honora Barry barely spoke to Mary when she delivered her work. The dressmaker looked ill, with a sickly yellow pallor to her skin.

'I should have moved away, Mary, while I could,' she pronounced as she paid her. 'Death stalks this town, and no lock or key can stop him from entering every door.'

Mary felt a fear rise in her.

'Don't dawdle here,' Miss Barry warned, as she gave her the lengths of calico and linen she needed. 'Away home to your family.'

Mary had intended to take the soup but, seeing so many in such a bad state, decided to ignore her hunger pains. Instead, she made her purchases quickly and decided to call briefly to her sister before returning home.

Her nose wrinkled at the putrid odours that dominated the lanes of Bridgetown. As she neared Kathleen's cottage, she was surprised to see little Sarah and Jude, both sitting on the step.

'Is your mammy gone out?'

'She's inside,' Sarah replied quietly, her head down, barely looking at her aunt.

'She's as cold as stone,' sniffed Jude.

Alarmed that Kathleen had fallen ill, Mary pushed in the door. The room was gloomy and she wondered how Kathleen could be so foolish as to let the turf fire go out. In the poor light, she could make out the form of her sister, lying curled up on the settle bed.

'Kathleen, are you sick?' she asked, trying to keep the fear from her voice.

Kathleen said nothing. Perhaps she was asleep or too ill to talk.

A noise reached Mary's ears and she saw some movement under her sister's filthy blanket.

'Kathleen.'

She bent forward to rouse her, but was greeted with a flash of squirming and screeching. With horror, she saw the eyes and hunched backs and tails of three – no, four – rats that ran over her sister's body, their sharp teeth busy gnawing at her flesh.

'Get off!' she screamed in the near darkness. 'Get out of it!'

Grabbing the nearby broom, she frantically beat the teeming rats away from her sister.

'Get off her!' she cried over and over, belting and chasing them as they scurried and jumped all around her.

'Kitty!' she yelled, agonized. 'For God's sake, Kitty, wake up!'

But Kathleen did not stir or move.

'Wake up!' she sobbed again, stretching out her hand to touch her sister, whose skin was ice cold.

She levelled one last whack at a furtive rat that had burrowed under her sister's skirt. As she gently turned Kathleen over, she discovered little Lizzie, curled up and hidden protectively in her mother's arms. Both dead . . . Both gone from the world.

Shock overcame her as she took in the damaged face and left eye of her beautiful sister, and the myriad bites that covered her neck, torso and left arm.

Bile cascaded from her mouth as she retched on to the earth floor again and again, despite her empty stomach. The only mercy was that Kathleen had been dead when the rats had attacked her.

Wiping her mouth with her handkerchief, she stood, shocked and shaking, as she considered what to do. As she battled to regain her composure, she pushed out the door to the waiting children.

'Is Mammy really sick, Auntie Mary?'

She nodded, not trusting herself to speak for a minute.

'Your mammy is gone to heaven,' she said eventually, hunkering down beside them, 'along with little Lizzie.'

'They've been sick these past few days.' Sarah sobbed quietly. 'Mam told us yesterday that we were to stay outside so we wouldn't get sick too.'

'Your mammy loves you both very much and always wanted the best for you,' she explained. 'She is at peace now.'

The children looked miserable, dirty and half-starved. And now they were motherless.

'Where is your da?'

'He never came home these past five days,' whispered Sarah. 'Mam was fierce worried for him. She searched the town and kept asking for him, but no one has seen him.'

'Maybe Da went looking for work,' argued Jude defensively.

'I must go to the dispensary straight away,' Mary said gently, 'and tell them about your mam and sister's deaths.'

Sarah's scrawny body was racked with crying and Mary took her niece protectively in her arms.

'Hush, pet . . . Hush,' she soothed, realizing that the children were in no state to be left alone. 'We'll go together.'

Mary went as fast as she could to the dispensary, where a kind man dutifully took down Kathleen and Lizzie's names and their address, and details of how they had been sick with fever.

'The cart will collect them in an hour or two,' he told her. 'There are a few stops to be made in Bridgetown before they go to Abbey-strewery for burial.'

'It is better you two stay outside,' she told her niece and nephew on their return to the cottage, for she did not want them to see their mother the way she was.

'That's what Mammy told us to do,' acknowledged Jude, wiping his tears with his raggedy sleeve as he sat back down on the stone step.

Mary swept the room noisily to rid it of any bold vermin that might have returned in her absence, before taking some linen from her pack. Carefully, she wrapped a length of it around Kathleen and Lizzie's bodies, before taking her needle and thread to stitch the shroud, so that they would be buried together.

Finding a little turf, she blew the ashes in the grate and relit the fire. She set the pot to boil before bringing the children inside. She would make a little gruel for them with some of her oats.

'What will happen to us, Auntie Mary?' asked Sarah nervously. 'Will we have to go back to the workhouse again?'

'Jude, what do you mean?' Mary countered.

'Mammy took us there on Sunday to look for my da,' Sarah explained. 'She told them that she and Lizzie were both sick, but they said that the workhouse was full.'

'Mam got angry with them, told them that our da helped build the workhouse, and said they must have space for us,' Jude continued.

'They could see Mam was sick,' Sarah finished bitterly, 'but they told her to go home.'

'There will be no workhouse,' promised Mary.

She made up her mind there and then that somehow she would take on minding her niece and young nephew. It was what Kathleen would have wanted – for her children to be raised with their own.

It was midday by the time the death cart came to collect the bodies. Two men with cloths wrapped around their noses and mouths lifted Kathleen and Lizzie with little gentleness on to the mounting pile. A few neighbours looked on from their doorways and Mary told them that she was taking the children with her, in case Joe reappeared, looking for them.

Along with a few other Bridgetown residents, Mary and the children followed the cart slowly across the river to the nearby graveyard where the large pit lay open to receive the dead. It was hard to believe that it was where her beloved sister would be laid to rest – a crowded grave with other poor souls from the town. Kathleen, with her green eyes that would crinkle with laughter, her red-gold hair and a smile that could charm the hardest heart, buried like a pauper.

They watched from a little way back as the men unloaded the bodies, one at a time, into the hinged coffin, which was carried to the pit and lowered before being lifted up to be used again. She made the children close their eyes, for she did not want them to witness such a terrible thing.

'Your mam and Lizzie's souls have gone straight to heaven,' Mary assured Sarah and Jude once the men had left.

Her niece broke down in sobs while Jude stood silent and red-eyed, staring at his mother and young sister's last resting place. There had been no priest to say a few words so she wrapped her arms around both children and said a few prayers herself.

The breeze blew in from the water and across the Ilen as she did so, and the reeds whispered a lonely song.

The trio walked back to Creagh almost in silence, all lost in their own thoughts. Mary had no idea how John would take the news that there would be two more hungry mouths to feed, but she would not see Jude and Sarah put in the workhouse. As far as she was concerned, they were in her care now until their father returned.

Chapter 67

Creagh

BY THE TIME SHE AND THE CHILDREN ARRIVED HOME, MARY WAS HEART-sore and weary. Never had she been so glad to see their cottage, as she led an exhausted Sarah and Jude inside.

Her own children were full of questions at the arrival of their two cousins, but a stern look from her ensured they said little. John, as if reading her mind, assured Kathleen's children that they were family and welcome to stay with them.

Straight away she busied herself tending to their immediate needs. She made the two siblings strip out of their filthy rags and washed their dirty bodies all over with warm water. Despite their protests, she tended to their hair with the lice comb before putting Sarah into a clean shift, while Jude had to make do with a patched pair of Con's britches and a shirt.

'Let's get you both something to eat and then you need to sleep, for you are all done in and need to rest.'

They managed a few oatcakes but their eyes were heavy with sleep. Con had fixed some fresh straw and a blanket on the side of the room where his sisters normally slept and the exhausted children lay down together, safe and warm.

'They have suffered terribly,' Mary explained to her family, 'and are in need of kindness. They have lost their mother and sister, and their father is nowhere to be found. What little we have we will share with them.'

'Poor things,' said Nora. 'Sarah can share with me.'

Once the rest of the children were asleep, Mary told John of the terrible circumstances in which she had found her sister and her youngest child. His eyes filled with anger.

'Poor Kathleen,' he said, shocked. 'What a terrible way for her to die!'

'I know that taking in the children means we now have two more mouths to feed,' she admitted despairingly, 'but I could not bear to see them end in the workhouse.'

'We will manage,' he vowed, taking her hand in his. 'Like we always have.'

Mary worried for the young Casey children. Sarah often sobbed herself to sleep, while Jude said little of his family and roamed the nearby fields on his own. She did her best to eke out the little food that they had, but Con complained constantly that he was hungrier than ever, as did little Annie.

John had worries of his own, for there was talk of evictions across the district. George Hogan was said to be giving the tenants of Sir William Wrixon Becher orders to leave their holdings.

'There is a new law that has come in,' he told her one day. 'I am going to go over to meet Michael Hayes and a few of the men to find out what it means, but I fear it is not good for the likes of us.'

In the still of the night Mary sat quietly, sewing the linen shrouds and watching the low flames flicker in the grate, wishing that these bad times would soon come to an end.

Chapter 68

Skibbereen
May 1847

'IS IT TRUE, FATHER?' BRIDEY ASKED, RUSHING INTO THE ROOM. 'IS IT true that he is dead?'

Father John nodded solemnly, deeply saddened by the news of Daniel O'Connell's death. He found it hard to believe that Ireland's mighty champion would no longer rise up to defend his people. The great Liberator, who had won Catholic emancipation, fought for repeal of the Act of Union and, only a few short months ago, pleaded to Parliament on behalf of his starving people, had died in Genoa, far from his native land. It was the worst of news.

'They say that he was going to see the Pope, Father?'

'It would appear that he intended to travel from Genoa to the Vatican to appeal to Pope Pius for assistance.'

'Oh, God be good to him!' Bridey broke down. 'To think that he stayed here under this roof and I cooked him his breakfast.'

Although he was well used to death, Father John, like Bridey, felt overcome by a great sense of loss as he thought of the man himself, sitting by his fire and chatting with him less than four years ago.

The great Daniel O'Connell was, at last, reunited in death with his wife, Mary, and much-loved young grandson. It was a sad day for Ireland and her people, for all hope was destroyed. Who would champion their cause now?

Father John resolved that he would arrange to say a special mass in the morning for the remarkable leader.

'The best of men taken from us.' Bridey continued to sob. 'For without him we are lost!'

The reaction to the devastating news was the same everywhere. In every street, lane and cottage in Skibbereen, the people were shocked to hear of the Liberator's death.

The following morning the townspeople crowded into St Patrick's Cathedral and prayed fervently for Daniel O'Connell. They mourned the loss of Ireland's great leader, giving thanks for his long life and his deep love of his country and its people.

'We'll not see his like again,' murmured Tim McCarthy Downing as they gazed across the river and up towards Curragh Hill where the great man had spoken to them all.

A week later, Father John heard that O'Connell's last wish had been for his soul to go to God, his body to be returned to his beloved Ireland for burial, but that his heart be removed and sent in an urn to the Pope in Rome.

He smiled, thinking of O'Connell's huge funeral, one last great massive Monster Meeting to be held in Dublin to welcome their great hero home to his native land.

Chapter 69

SINCE KATHLEEN'S DEATH, MARY HAD SPENT MUCH OF HER TIME CARing for her sister's broken-hearted children.

'You two are my kin,' she assured young Sarah and Jude. 'You are my blood, and I promise you that John and I will take care of you. You have a home here with us.'

John had gone to town in search of Joe Casey twice. He had made enquiries everywhere, but no one had seen sight nor sound of Kathleen's husband. Her brother-in-law seemed to have vanished, unaware of the death of his wife and child.

'Perhaps he's gone away to Dublin or Liverpool for work?' John suggested to Mary.

'Joe would have told Kathleen if he had found work. He would know how happy that would have made her.'

Mary had written a simple letter to Kathleen's eldest boy, Michael, who was still employed in the big house in Clonakilty, telling him of his poor mother and Lizzie's deaths. She assured him that she was caring for his sister and brother.

Her own children found it strange at first to have their two cousins now living with them, but had pity for them and did their best to be kind.

*

Mary had finished making the shrouds for Honora Barry, but worried that the dressmaker would be annoyed with her. She should have returned them nearly two weeks ago and had used some of the material for Kathleen and Lizzie. Truth to tell, she had not been able to face visiting town since finding her sister dead, but she could no longer put off returning her work, for she needed the payment badly.

She rang the shop bell but there was no sign of the dressmaker. She peered through the window and rapped loudly at the door, calling her name. When there was still no answer, Mary decided she would try the back door, and was just about to knock on it when a maid came out of the next-door building with a bucket of ashes for the bin.

'If you are looking for Miss Barry she's not there,' she said matter-of-factly. 'Took sick a few days back. All on her own, she was, when they found her and took her to the fever sheds. Poor woman, she died there the next day.'

Mary stood rooted to the ground, shocked by the news of Honora Barry's death and the loss not just of her employer but of her friend, who had been both generous and supportive to her since she had first started working for her.

'Oh, I'm sorry to hear that,' Mary said, dismayed. 'She was a good woman, and always kind to me.'

'Sad, no husband or child or relation to mourn her by all accounts!' The maid turned her back on Mary and disappeared inside.

A strange instinct made Mary check beneath the loose stone near the back step where the dressmaker used to keep a key. She couldn't believe that it was still there. Taking it, she let herself in to the empty shop.

She walked through the workroom that housed the cutting table and sewing table where she used to work. The wooden shelves that once were laden with bales of satin, silk, velvet, lace and sprigged cotton were now bare. Two or three unfinished garments hung forlornly and forgotten from the work rail.

Miss Barry had been telling her the truth about her business drying up. She thought back to how busy the shop used to be, with plenty of customers. The needle and thread, and measuring tape and scissors were on the go constantly. Poor woman, Mary thought, to have to watch her business all but disappear. She must have struggled to stay open these past awful two years.

Mary put down her packet on one of the tables and wondered what she was meant to do with the shrouds now. It was likely there was no money to pay her for her work.

Curious, she walked around the empty shop and went upstairs to Honora's living quarters. She had never crossed the door of her employer's abode. Its kitchen was small and the dining and drawing room was a simple affair with few luxuries, only a couple of tasselled, pink and green satin cushions on her chairs and a small table with a vase of faded flowers. It certainly was not what she had imagined for the stylish dressmaker. As she continued to look around, she could not help but wonder if some of her employer's finer items had already been sold or pawned.

Opening the bedroom door, Mary was assailed immediately by the smell of sickness and stale air. She reached to unlatch the window in the simple but pretty room. A large bed lay tousled and bare, with only a blanket, some dirty sheets and a rolled-up bolster on it. Folded away neatly on a chair was a beautiful French lace counterpane and two delicately embroidered pillowslips. A few fine dresses, along with a satin wrap, a cloak and a velvet-lined coat hung in the mahogany wardrobe.

As Mary sat on a carved chair in front of a mirror, she thought of Honora. Despite how little she really possessed, the older woman had always shown great kindness towards her. She had not only given her work but also had insisted on several occasions that Mary take some bread, eggs or salted fish back home to share with her family.

A small, nearly empty glass bottle of perfume sat on the neat dressing table. Unthinking, she opened it and the scent reminded her immediately of Miss Barry. She sprinkled a little around the room before replacing the stopper.

A sense of guilt engulfed her. She felt she had let Honora Barry down, just as she had Kathleen. If only she had returned the shrouds

253

when she was meant to, she would have seen her employer was sick. Perhaps she could have fetched the doctor, or helped her in some fashion.

Back downstairs, Mary remembered the money drawer in the back room of the shop from which Miss Barry had paid her once or twice. Bent down, she reached around and found the narrow drawer. Her hand closed in on a few brass and silver coins.

She counted out her wage fairly, unsure of what to do with the rest of the money. Should she just leave it there, where likely the next person to enter the shop – be they beggar or thief – would come upon it? Then her fingers touched some paper, a rent book and an envelope with a sheet of paper, which contained a note in Honora's hand. 'For Mrs Mary Sullivan', it read, and detailed the money due to her.

Tears pricked Mary's eyes as she realized that she had not been forgotten. Across the back of the paper was an additional note, scribbled in larger, looped writing: 'In the event of my demise, I bequeath to my employee, Mrs Mary Sullivan of Creagh, all of my remaining personal possessions to dispose of as she wishes.'

Mary read it and re-read it, over and over again. This good woman in her hour of sickness had made a special point of remembering her.

She took a while to compose herself, considering what she should do. The note made it clear that Honora had left her few possessions to her, but what if a distant relative of the dressmaker appeared, or her landlord made a demand for rent? She wished that she could go home to consult with John, but worried that on her return to the shop she would find the place boarded up and empty, which is what happened to so many vacant buildings in the town to prevent trespassers and beggars from entering the premises.

Honora knew well the desperation of Mary's circumstances and her family, and so Mary decided she would follow the wishes of her employer. Returning to the bedroom, she gathered up the heavy lace counterpane carefully along with the embroidered linen pillowslips. She was torn about selling the dressmaker's personal things but it was what the good woman had wanted, her last wishes. She also took the satin cushions and bundled them all together. She would go to Maguire's pawnbroker, who took furniture and household goods only, to see what they would fetch.

There were only two people ahead of her. Most people in town had sold off their valuables and possessions a long time ago.

Julia Maguire raised her head suspiciously at the likes of Mary having such fine items to sell. She fingered the French lace, admiring its beauty.

'My employer, Miss Barry the dressmaker, sent me with them,' Mary lied, hoping that the news of Honora's death was not yet known through the town.

The other woman smiled. 'I have done business with her previously, but today can only offer her two pounds for the lace and a guinea for all the cushions and bed linen.'

Mary hesitated, for she knew well that they were both worth a lot more. She was, however, in no position to argue the case and accepted the payment.

On her return to the dressmaking shop, Mary searched the shelves and living quarters for any remaining items to sell. The little furniture was likely the landlord's so she dared not touch that. Her heart lifted when she found a teapot and some cutlery, which might fetch a pretty price. There were also a few items of clothing of Honora's which might sell too.

As she continued her search, she found a packet of needles of all sizes and Honora's large fabric scissors, along with a tray of spools of coloured thread and a pincushion. Tears welled in her eyes as she remembered the sight of the dressmaker busy at work, her head bent and concentration on her face. She would keep these items in memory of Honora.

This time she took her collection of items to Hegarty's. Denis Hegarty ran his fingers over the stylish satin dresses, warm woollen coat and fine leather boots.

Mary held her breath and prayed that he would not question her about them, but with two women and well-dressed gentlemen behind her, all pushing and demanding attention, he concluded their business quickly and gave her two pounds for everything.

She returned to the shop one last time to lock it up. Silence hung around her as she replaced the key under the stone and took the shrouds with her.

She called to the dispensary and explained the situation. She asked if they knew anyone who would be willing to buy them from her. The apothecary himself told her immediately that he would happily take all five of them, and paid her generously sixpence for each one. She couldn't quite believe her luck.

Using that money, she purchased a few items of food before setting off home.

On the long walk to Creagh, Mary's heart sat heavy in her chest at the death of her friend. The realization that there would be no more work for her hit her hard. However, the knowledge that she had a few pounds in her purse provided her with a sense of comfort, for which she would always be grateful.

Mary was determined that Honora's gift to her be set aside for a special purpose, used only to protect and save her family.

Chapter 70

Creagh

JOHN HAD SAT AND LISTENED QUIETLY AS MARY TOLD HIM ABOUT THE death of the dressmaker and her unexpected generosity. Upset and nervous, Mary showed him the money she had raised from pawning the woman's few possessions.

'Am I a desperate thief for taking Honora's things and selling them?' she fretted. 'Perhaps I should have left everything as it was.'

John studied the few short words.

'Miss Barry wrote you this note,' he said. 'Obviously the poor woman was all alone and afraid of dying. You were the one who visited her more than most. She helped you as best she could, by giving you some work when she had it.'

'I feel so guilty that I did not get the chance to say goodbye to her or pray over her.'

'She is at peace now,' he soothed, 'but I think it is clear that as she neared her end, she intended for you to get your wages and follow her wishes.'

'I will never forget her for it,' Mary said softly, finally giving in to tears at the loss of her friend.

*

As spring turned to summer and the days grew warmer, the Sullivans' fields lay bare. Like all their neighbours, they had no money for seed potatoes and were still afraid to plant them. Mary had sown half a field of turnips and cabbages because at least they were crops upon which they could rely.

All around them her family saw small farms and holdings empty as starving families were forced either to abandon their holdings or give up their land. The landlord's agents were ruthless and turned out men, women and children on to the roads.

'If they come near us we will use Honora's money to pay the rent,' Mary offered.

'I fear it is too late,' John said. 'The landlords and their gombeen men want to rid the land of people like us. They want to clear small tenants off their holdings and turn the fields to tillage and pasture.'

Fear crawled in Mary's stomach. What would happen if they were put off their land? They had six children to think of now.

'Four families were evicted off their holding up near the Old Hill Road four days ago,' John said, his face serious. 'I am going to the Learys' to meet Denis and a few of the other men to talk about it. There's a rumour that anyone with more than a quarter-acre will get no relief or assistance of any kind unless they give up their holding.'

The sun was dipping in the red sky when he returned home that evening. Anger and dismay were written across his face as he beckoned her to come outside.

'What is it, John?' she urged.

'It's all true. This new quarter-acre law affects tenants like us. Anyone with more than a quarter-acre must give up their holding if they want to get a bowl of soup or a bed in the workhouse. Imagine, a man must renounce the field he has worked for thirty or forty years in order to get any type of assistance – a bite to eat for his child or a bed for his sick wife to lie in. What kind of law is that?'

'It's cruel!'

'Cruelty doesn't come into it!' he spat bitterly. 'All across the Mizzen they are tumbling the cottages, pulling down the thatch and kicking out the doors so people cannot find any shelter there. They're forcing people to move from their home place. All they want is to clear the place of small tenants.'

'Where are people going?' she ventured.

'It's some choice,' he said scornfully. 'The road with nothing, or the workhouse. I've heard that the Union's guardians are making each landlord pay a contribution to the keep of their tenants there. Some are offering to assist with paying their passage to Québec and New York. I'll not give up this place easily.'

Mary could sense her husband's rage and sadness at the prospect that they might be forced to leave Creagh.

'John Sullivan, I tell you, if we are put out of here, this family will not set foot in the workhouse,' she told him firmly. 'Flor and Molly wouldn't go because they would have been separated, and I'll not be separated from you and the children.'

'Then we'll take passage to North America, like Pat did.'

'Leave Cork? Leave Ireland?'

'Aye, what else can a man do if he is left with no roof over his head and no land to work but travel the ocean in search of a new life away from this misery? Pat was the wise man who left when he could.'

Mary tossed and turned all night as John's words ran through her head, over and over. How could they ever leave this, their home place?

Chapter 71

July 1847

'MAMMY!' SCREAMED NORA AND TIM, RUNNING ACROSS THE FIELDS AS fast as their legs would carry them. 'Mammy, the men are coming! The 'viction men are coming!'

Mary could see the upset and fear in their eyes.

'They were up at Learys' cottage,' Nora panted, coming to a stop.

'We saw them batter their door and pull down the thatch roof,' added Sarah.

Mary tried to control the trembling that overcame her body.

'Run and get your father,' she told them. 'As quick as you can. He's up in the woods with the boys.'

It would be only a few minutes before the landlord's eviction gang reached their cottage, and she was sick to her heart at the thought of what to say or do.

Frantic, she began to put things in order. She folded up into a sacking bag whatever food they had left, along with spoons and a knife or two, and a pot with tin mugs and bowls. She hid them in the corner.

Over the past few days, she and John had discussed over and over again how this might come to pass. Despite his misgivings, she had hoped naively that they would not face such disaster.

Quick as a flash she saw them come – ten, maybe twelve of them, in a group, surrounding the cottage and trampling over her young cabbages. Some she recognized: James Murphy, Denis Carmody and his younger brother, Sean, who had the reputation of being a powerful fighter; the others burly strangers bearing sticks and cudgels. George Hogan was at their head.

'Sullivan,' they shouted. 'Sullivan!'

Mary pulled her shawl around her and stood at the door to face them.

'I'm Mary Sullivan,' she said coldly. 'My husband is not here at present but is due back.'

'We have orders to follow, Mrs Sullivan, from your landlord and his agent,' George Hogan boomed, his long and narrow face serious as he gazed around him, taking in the well-cared-for cottage and her vegetable patch. 'Any tenants behind in their rent must leave their dwellings and the holdings that they have occupied.'

Just as he finished speaking, John arrived with the children behind him. Relief flooded over her as he came and stood protectively beside her.

'What is your business here, Mr Hogan?' John asked.

'I have orders to clear these holdings today, Mr Sullivan. My employer has been patient for far too long with unpaid rent monies, but now seeks the return of his property.'

'You know well that not a man in this district could pay his rent with the hunger,' he stated firmly. 'I promise you that when the crops return and the land is fertile again, Sir William will have his full rent. But we can only offer you a part payment this day. The Sullivans have always been good tenants here. You know that well, Mr Hogan.'

The overseer barely acknowledged John's words.

'Give me a chance to pay the rent,' John continued. 'It may take a while but every penny and shilling will be returned to you.'

Mary could see a frown crease the man's brow.

'I'm sorry, Mr Sullivan. The decision has been made that this area is to be cleared and tenants moved off Sir William's estate and properties.'

'We will not give up this place,' John said loudly, his temper rising. 'You cannot put us off these fields and land, for we have earned them with our labour. You have no right to do such a thing.'

'You are wrong, Mr Sullivan. A legal eviction order has been issued for this property and holding.'

'There is no justice when a scrap of legal paper declares this land can be held for eternity by a man who cares not a whit for it or those that work it!' John said contemptuously.

'My advice is for you and your family to go quietly and cause no trouble here. Pack up any of your belongings and leave this place.'

'Leave our home, our land?'

'The land agent, Mr Marmion, is a fair man and arrangements have been agreed with the Union workhouse for payments to be made for tenants agreeing to enter there.'

'You would put my wife and children and me in the workhouse?' John shouted, unable to control his anger any longer. 'We who have done nothing wrong but try to feed our children? With not even a penny of help or as much as a bag of grain from our landlord, I may remind you.'

Mary could see Mr Hogan growing uncomfortable and one or two of the men looked shamefaced, but he continued with the job he had been sent to do.

'Otherwise, for all tenants giving up their holding, there is an offer of paid passage on ships to North America.'

'Leave our home, our land *and* our country? What choice is that?'

Mary swallowed hard, trying to control her impulse to scream and kick at the men.

'Do not cause trouble, Mr Sullivan,' George Hogan warned again.

'What kind of man do you think I am, Hogan? I will not give up our holding.'

With that, John grabbed his wife's arm and beckoned for the children to follow as he stepped back inside the cottage. He closed the door behind them firmly and put on the iron bolt.

'Don't be a fool, man!' Mary could hear the exasperation in Hogan's voice on the other side of the door. 'Step outside.'

John, Con and Tim blocked the window quickly with the wooden pallet and pushed the settle bed against the doorway. The girls stood by, terrified. John and the boys braced themselves, ready to hinder the group of men for as long as they were able.

'We Sullivans will not go from here easy and give up what is ours without a fight,' he told the children as the men began to push and rush against the door, pummelling the wood. 'Do you understand?'

The words had barely left his lips when the wood began to splinter and crack, gaping as sticks and heavy shoulders pushed at it.

'Hold firm!' he urged as Mary and the boys used all their strength to resist the attack, trying to push the settle bed back against the men while Nora, Sarah and Annie stood at the window.

Despite their best efforts, the settle bed was shoved backwards and, with a mighty bang, the cottage door gave way. At the same time, over their heads, men began to strip the thatch from the roof.

Poor Annie began to scream, petrified.

'Shush, shush,' said Nora, taking her little sister in her arms.

Dear God, they were going to pull and tumble the place down around them.

John and the boys pushed hard against what remained of the door, trying to hold back the men, but they were no match for the might of the group. Mary braced herself as five of the men entered the cottage. Part of the roof was already open to the sky as she and the three girls managed to flee outside. John pushed against Sean Carmody, telling him to leave the place for this was no fight of his, and earned a few punches in the stomach and ribs for his trouble.

'Leave my father alone,' Con shouted at them angrily, his eyes blazing.

Hogan entered the cottage and gave a signal to the men to stop.

Annie whimpered like a little puppy as John and the three boys appeared slowly, standing in front of the battered wall and door.

'Former tenants of Sir William Wrixon Becher if not entering the Union,' Hogan announced, 'may avail themselves of fully paid passage to Liverpool or North America. Tickets for those wishing to travel will be issued at the shipping office in either Baltimore, for those who wish to make the long journey, or Queenstown in the coming days and weeks.'

John said nothing and stared blankly out over the fields.

'My employer has generously agreed an amount with the shipping agents, who have a complete list of our tenants,' Hogan continued. 'My advice, Mr Sullivan, is that you and your wife and family avail yourselves of this good offer, for we will not tolerate tenants remaining on this property or attempting to stay on these lands. You and your children cannot remain here. Is that clear?'

Mary's breath caught in her throat, but she would not give Hogan and his men the satisfaction of seeing her break down and cry.

'Is that clear?' the overseer repeated.

'Yes,' John said, meeting his gaze directly. 'This injustice, this act of putting my family from land that we Sullivans have tended all our lives, will be remembered, Mr Hogan. I promise never will it be forgotten.'

Mary could see an angry purple blush blaze against the overseer's cheek.

Behind him, a few of the younger men had pulled every last bit of thatch from the cottage roof and broken the roof supports. They had knocked the chimney so that their home now lay ruined, open to the sky and elements.

'You must leave this place today,' Hogan ordered. 'Are you agreed?'

'There is nothing left for us here,' John replied bitterly. 'You have made sure of that.'

'Is it to be the Union or the road to Cork, or wherever? It is not my concern where you go once you leave this place.'

'Passage,' interrupted John. 'We will take assisted passage for my family to sail to North America.'

'A sensible decision,' pronounced Mr Hogan, relieved that his business was done. 'Passage will be arranged for you and your good wife and children to sail from Baltimore. I believe that I have a list of all your names.'

They watched as he mounted his horse and turned to ride away, the rest of the men following in his wake.

Mary felt like a wet rag as they disappeared. Sarah and Jude looked at her, wide-eyed and scared.

'You are coming to America with us,' she reassured them both. 'You know that we are your family now.'

She ran her eyes over the broken and battered cottage. Her marital home, her children's home; Sullivans' Cottage, where John had spent his boyhood. Soon they would be gone from it and rain and wind, weeds and wildlife would claim it. She was heartbroken at the thought of the children never playing in the surrounding fields again.

Slowly, she went around and gathered up the few things they had. The precious vegetable patch had been trampled, her young cabbages and turnips all but destroyed underfoot. She did her best to salvage what she could, for they still had to eat.

A tearful Brigid and Denis came to say goodbye to them with their children.

'There's nothing left for us here,' proclaimed Denis. 'We are going to my brother's place in Tipperary. He's an old bachelor and we are hoping he would not see us on the roads.'

'God bless you all,' Mary said, embracing her friend for the last time.

'We'd best be leaving too, and get on the road to Baltimore,' John said quietly. 'We cannot stay here.'

Without a word, Con went up to his father and hugged him, burying his head in his chest. Eight-year-old Tim stood in front of the cottage with his feet apart, taking it all in.

'I want to remember every stone and every bit of straw and every blade of grass in this place,' he said solemnly. 'I want to make a picture of it so I will never ever forget it.'

John went and took a few small bits of stone that had come off the fireplace and doorway and handed him one.

'Tim, you will always have this place and the memory of it,' he told him. 'We all will. No one can take that from us.'

Mary reached for John and held him close. She noticed him wince with pain but he assured her that he was fine.

'We'd best get on the road,' he said gently, pushing back a lock of hair that had fallen across her face. 'My darling girl, 'tis time for us to go . . .'

At the end of the road, hand in hand, they turned and looked back, knowing full well that they would never see this place again.

Part Three

Chapter 72

Baltimore, County Cork

THE HUNGER HAD STALKED AND STARVED THE LAND. THE ONLY SOUND to be heard was the forlorn cry of a lonely corncrake as the Sullivans packed up and made ready to leave.

They took only a few possessions with them: two pots, a knife, spoons and bowls and mugs, and the tin bucket, all items needed for their journey. Mary took her precious scissors and dressmaking tools with her while John carried his shovel and fork in the hope that he might sell them, for he had no use for them now.

With heavy hearts they said a final goodbye to their home place, with its unplanted potato patches and empty cottages with not even a curl of turf smoke in the sky. Scraggy thorn trees, leafy ferns and bushes of gorse and bramble lined the stony road, broken by the shimmer of blue as the broad, curving river Ilen flowed out to meet the wide sea.

As the family walked down the curving hill towards the village of Baltimore, they passed the school, a tavern and Dún na Séad, the once grand castle of the O'Driscolls.

'Is that the ship?' Con shouted excitedly, running ahead. They took in the large vessel moored down below in the harbour with its tall mast and rigging, sailors busy scrubbing the deck and checking the thick ropes. 'Can we go and see it?'

'Later,' John promised. 'First, we need to find the shipping office.'

The office was part of a chandler's, overlooking the harbour. A few men stood outside, smoking their pipes. A gaunt-looking man with his wife and three boys was ahead of them in line. They were tenants like themselves, booking passage for a ship that was sailing in three days' time. The wife looked ill and coughed constantly.

Once they were finished, the shipping clerk beckoned the Sullivans forward. John duly gave his full name and the address of their holding, and told him their circumstances and desire to book passage to America for the family.

'It will be to New York if you sail this week. Otherwise you will have to wait until we have one sailing in twelve or fourteen days.'

'As we have left our holding, we have no need to wait.'

The man looked down at the pages of names and record numbers from the Becher estate, running his stubby finger along the list.

'Sullivan, Dan . . . John . . .'

'That's it. John Sullivan, sir.'

'Aye, here it is. John Sullivan and wife, Mary, and four children, I see it noted here.'

'There are six children in our family that will be travelling,' John informed him calmly.

'Six? I have only four listed here,' the clerk looked up, puzzled. 'There is a Cornelius, Nora, Tim and Annie Sullivan. This is what is entered on the estate record. Have you had more children?'

'We have two other children who are our family now. They were orphaned and had to come to live with us,' he explained. 'Their names are Jude and Sarah Casey.'

'That may be, Mr Sullivan, but they are not listed as tenants of the estate. As such, they do not qualify for the estate's assisted passage payment to North America.'

'They are my wife's family and will travel with us,' John told the man firmly. 'We will not leave them behind.'

'I have my orders to follow, sir. I can issue boarding tickets for the

Lady Jane for you, your wife and four children as former tenants, but I have no authority to issue passes for others travelling with you, be they family members or not.'

'There must be some way we can bring the children,' he pleaded, trying to gain the man's sympathy. 'We cannot leave them behind.'

'Free passage does not apply to extra family members or friends,' the clerk responded tetchily. 'Otherwise we would have half the people of the parish wanting to bring relations on board with them. If they want to travel with you, then you must purchase tickets for them.'

'How much is the passage for New York?'

'Seven pounds per passenger is the normal fare.'

'Seven pounds,' John repeated, incredulous. There was no possibility they would be able to pay such a vast sum of money.

Mary felt giddy. After all that had happened that day, she could not believe they were facing such a dilemma.

'Are you telling me that it costs seven pounds to bring a young orphan child across the Atlantic?'

Sarah had begun to sniffle loudly, drawing everyone's attention.

'Seven pounds is the adult fare but for children it is less. Given they are travelling as part of a family situation . . .' The clerk began to tot up figures on a piece of paper with his pencil. 'They can both travel for two pounds and five shillings, if you wish to pay passage for them.'

John's eyes met Mary's. She had given him all the money she had earned, every penny of it, along with what she had got from Honora Barry. He carefully counted out the coins. Jude and Sarah's names were added to theirs on the steerage passenger list, and all of them were issued with official boarding tickets.

The clerk gave them details of their ship, the *Lady Jane*, and its departure time. He also told them what rations of food and water would be provided for passengers.

'We advise people to purchase extra oatcakes and food supplies for the long journey, and a chamber pot or bucket for their personal needs. We offer all of these items in our small provision store here.'

John was tense and worried by the time they stepped outside, and the children were silent and watchful.

'We have all got our tickets,' Mary said, trying to cheer the situation, 'and will set sail in two days' time. Until then, we need to find somewhere sheltered and dry to sleep.'

Baltimore harbour looked out over the water and Sherkin Island in the distance. The sea was a mixture of blue and green, shimmering in the sunshine as the waves rushed against the harbour. Further out, beyond the wide curving bay, lay the blue ocean. There was a fine church in the village, and a scattering of houses and fishermen's cottages dotted along the shore, but few vessels, as many fishermen had sold them in order to feed their families.

It was a place of trade, where boats and ships carrying timber, grain and flax loaded and unloaded their goods to be transported between Cork and Liverpool and Cardiff, and upriver to Skibbereen.

The Sullivans went to look at the large ship that would carry them to the New World. Its mast reached up skywards like a tree, supporting the great folds of heavy white sails, its boom and rigging. Only a few sailors were working on the large wooden deck as the waves lapped gently against the ship's timbers.

'Soon we'll be sailing across the wide Atlantic Ocean in that ship,' declared Con proudly. 'Just look at her sails!'

'I hate big ships,' said Annie stubbornly, 'and I'll not go on one!'

'You will too,' encouraged good-hearted Nora, promising to look after her younger sister.

A curious seal bobbed its head up and down, diving in the foam near by and making the children laugh with its antics.

Down by the cove they found a sheltered spot. John lit a fire and Mary cooked up the ends of the food they had brought with them. They were all tired and exhausted.

Lying in the darkness under the moonlight that night, Mary could hear the waves lap against the shore and felt strangely comforted by the familiar childhood sound.

*

By mid-morning the harbour had come to life rapidly as the sailors began to load the ship and make ready for the long sea voyage. The crew were busy with their preparations, climbing along the rigging, and creeping up the stays and out the yard arm as the heavy sails were readied and raised.

'They say that the *Lady Jane* is not regulated or as well-equipped as the bigger ships that leave from Cork and Queenstown,' John said with worry in his voice.

'This is the ship we have paid passage on,' Mary assured him. 'And for the children's sake, we must try to make the best of it and put our trust in the Lord.'

John finally managed to sell his shovel and fork to a man from Clear Island.

'He got the bargain,' he said ruefully.

Following the advice of the shipping clerk, they purchased two cheap rolled-up ticking mattresses for the hard, slatted wooden bunks, and oatcakes and oats for their journey. Most of their money was gone and they had not even left Cork!

The children played for hours down at the shore, paddling and splashing in the water, and it did Mary's heart good to hear them laughing.

That night Mary slept fretfully, dreaming of towering waves and crashing seas. She tried not to give in to the terrible fear that engulfed her. What would happen if the ship was wrecked or foundered crossing the vast Atlantic Ocean?

'Mam, look! Our ship is nearly ready to sail,' announced Con with delight early on Thursday morning. 'We'll be sailing soon, before the tide turns.'

Mary, John and the children hastened to join the line of passengers waiting to board, many of whom were tenants from their district.

The ruddy-faced captain's mate, Mr Dwyer, examined their tickets and called out names on a passenger roll. Each traveller in turn was checked over to ensure they were well enough to travel before they were directed below deck to the steerage part of the ship.

273

'There is one bunk per three or four people,' Mr Dwyer informed the passengers, which drew groans of protest. 'Everyone must share.'

Stepping across the gangplank, Con and Jude jumped up and down in excitement at the adventure that lay ahead of them. Mary was glad to be escaping the hunger and sickness. Although she was filled with trepidation about the sea journey, relief coursed through her veins that she, John and all the children, including Kathleen's two, had somehow survived and were bound for a new life far from this torn land.

As they made their way down into the murky hold, it took her eyes a few seconds to adjust to the lack of light. As soon as she could make out her surroundings, she rushed to place their belongings on two bunks. There was no separation of men and women so, acting quickly, Mary decided that she would share with Sarah, Annie and Nora while John and the boys would sleep together in the bunk above them.

She felt the narrow rough slats of the bunks and was mighty glad of their two mattresses as she unrolled them. Though there was such little space to sleep, she was relieved, for at least they were together and not forced to have some stranger lie with them. Already, she could hear people around them fighting and arguing about not wanting to share.

It was horrendously crowded down in steerage, the bunks all on top of each other with only a narrow passage running between them. Some bunks were even worse, with wooden posts between them, and the roof was so low that John, and many of the men and taller boys, tipped their heads against it. There was no privacy or ventilation, and already the air below deck was heavy. The bunks she had chosen for them were near the steps, where there was at least a little more light and fresh air, but Mary worried for the modesty of the women on board, for there was no provision to protect themselves from the prying eyes of the men and boys around them.

'We all better get used to this,' a big man called Denis Murphy declared, looking around at them all. 'We'll be living here on top of each other like pigs for the next six or eight weeks, so they say.

There's no point in fighting with each other, for it will do us not a bit of good.'

'Hear, hear,' added two other men.

The ship's bell cut through the chatter, signalling the vessel's departure, and there was a change in mood as everyone pushed and rushed to climb up the steps and back on to deck. The sailors had untied the coiled ropes and hauled in the heavy anchor. The ship was ready to sail as the tide and the wind in her hoisted sails began to lift and move her.

The *Lady Jane* began to tilt and rock, and every man, woman and child was up on deck as she began to move through the waves, leaving the harbour, the wide cove and the headland behind.

Mary felt immense sadness and grief for the land they were leaving but, as the ship began to cut through the waves and John reached for her hand, she felt a strange rush of hope and excitement that this was a new beginning for them.

They drank in the view of the harbour and shoreline, the cottages, green fields and rolling hills, the woods and gorse and bracken. They savoured their last glimpse of the tall headland as the *Lady Jane* caught the waves. Within minutes, they had left Baltimore far behind, as they headed out past the sandy beaches of Sherkin Island and Clear Island towards the open sea.

A few women sobbed, and a young woman holding a baby started to pray out loud. The other passengers joined in with her. Tim and Annie clung to Mary nervously, scared by the strange rocking of the wooden deck under their feet. She caught sight of tears in her husband's eyes and she knew how much leaving their home place grieved him.

'This is a sad day for all of us, but at least we are going to a country that is no longer shackled by British rule and parliament,' declared Denis Murphy loudly, to nods and murmurs of approval.

Con and Jude bounded up and down as the wind caught their breaths.

'America!' they whooped and hollered at the grand adventure that lay ahead. 'We are going to America!'

Standing in the sea spray as the rolling waves around them rose and swelled, they took in every last vestige of the rugged coastline that they would never see again. Every rock, stone, hue, tree and field, the sheer beauty and wildness of their beloved land, they seared into their memory.

Chapter 73

'THE SICKNESS WILL SOON PASS,' MARY PROMISED THE CHILDREN, TRY-ing to comfort them.

No sooner had the voyage begun than they had fallen seasick, like most of the passengers. The rough motion of the ship as it was tossed by the ocean waves left them puking and retching, covered in sour vomit. Their throats burned and they lay curled together in their bunks, clammy and miserable.

'Let me die,' roared an old man, crouched in his bunk like a child.

Their clothes and blankets reeked, for there was not enough fresh water for washing to rid the hold of the pervading stench. Water was strictly rationed, with only one gallon allowed per adult for drink-ing, cooking and washing, no matter how much the passengers begged for more.

Annie got the seasickness worst. She lay beside her mother like a little ghost, whimpering and distressed. Dark circles grew under her eyes as she became ever more listless, unable even to hold down a few sips of water.

John recovered first, followed by Con and Jude, who found their sea legs quickly, running and playing around the steerage accommodation.

'Mr Dwyer showed us four dolphins swimming by the side of the ship this morning, when we went up on deck to empty the piss bucket,' Con declared with excitement. 'Mam, you should see them. They are the biggest fish, and he said they can talk and signal to each other, and jump and swim faster than any horse. The ocean is full of such creatures!'

The rest of them suffered terribly. It was five days before the awful queasiness and retching began to ease. The captain agreed to let the steerage passengers up on deck to take some air while they tried to clean part of the hold.

As she gazed at the vast blue ocean, spread like a field all around them, Mary made the children take in deep breaths of fresh sea air to try to revive them. The wind and salt and spray stung her skin, and though there was no sight of land, only endless blue sea and sky, life coursed through her, for the past and their home place now seemed so far away.

Mary had never imagined such a voyage, cramped together with barely space to walk around or turn in your sleep. The air below deck was heavy and pungent from foul human ordure as people shared buckets and chamber pots or tried to use the water closet that hung over the side of the ship, perilously close to the waves. Most just chose to do their business in corners and hidden parts of the deck with no regard for their neighbours.

Every day the routine was the same. The ship's mate would ring the bell to summon the passengers to line up for their food rations.

'There's barely enough to feed us,' complained John as they each were given only a pound of bread, or meal or hard biscuits. Con, Jude and Nora got half portions, while the younger ones received barely a third. Some days, there were no rations at all, and the mate simply ignored their complaints. The bread and rock-hard biscuits often were green and mouldy, and the meal was not much better.

Up on deck was a caboose, with a grate for cooking over the fire. Crowds gathered around it with their pots and pans, and Mary waited patiently for her turn to use it to cook her family's portion of the meal.

'I've no pot of my own,' wailed a young woman from Coronea

278

who was travelling with her husband and a three-year-old. 'What use is a pound of meal if I cannot cook it?'

Mary took pity on her and generously let her use her pot.

Con and Jude befriended the Murphy and Collins boys, who were about their own ages. The seven youngsters, their heads down, jostled and laughed, whispering and plotting together to pass the time. Nora and Sarah grew to become like sisters. They slept curled up beside each other and walked arm in arm around the crowded hold as if they were strolling down an avenue in New York, both of them full of plans for the future. Tim and Annie stayed close to Mary, frightened by the rough men who played cards and drank and cursed each other, day and night.

'They are just bored like us all,' she tried to reassure them.

In the murky gloom of steerage, the days ran together. Sleep was their greatest friend as it helped to pass the desperate hours. However, even that was usually disturbed by the cries of children who had woken, terrified or sick, and who clung to their mothers as Mary lay awake in the cramped bunk, listening.

Then there was the constant snoring and sounds of the other passengers at night. The loud, rough banter of some men who played cards into the early hours of the morning as they smoked their pipes; while others looked to satisfy themselves with a wife or woman under the cover of darkness. Women, on the other hand, desperately sought some privacy to relieve themselves.

John was quieter than Mary had ever seen him since they had first walked out together. She knew that his heart was broken by the loss of their land and home place. He brooded over it and it was doing him no good.

'John, we have to try to be glad that we and the children have a chance of a new life where we are not beholden to any agent or landlord.'

'It is not that easy to leave the place where I was raised, where I farmed, and where our children were born,' he told her despairingly. 'I think of it night and day.'

'You and I will never forget it, I promise, but America is where our new home will be. Let us talk of New York,' she encouraged. 'Do you think Pat will be able to help you to get a job and help us find a place to stay?'

'My brother will likely suit himself, as he always does.'

She pondered on it.

'He is your flesh and blood and cares for you and the children. I'm sure Pat will do his best for us when we arrive.'

One of their fellow passengers, Johnny Meagher, had a tattered map of New York which he had acquired from one of the sailors in place of a half bottle of *poitín*. He and John and the rest of the men pored over it for hours, sharing information they had, and trying to learn the names of the districts and streets where they might find work or rooms to rent. John's eyes lit up when he recognized his brother's address.

'There are factory and labouring jobs aplenty to be found,' John reported to Mary, 'and up north or out west there are thousands and thousands of acres of government land being sold cheaply to any man who has a few dollars and is prepared to clear the land and farm it.'

'Land that would be our own!' she ventured, seeing the hope in his eyes.

'Aye, all legal and proper like, once a man has the money in his pocket to pay for it. 'Tis not like at home at all. In America work is rewarded and we will be no man's servant.'

Relief flooded her heart. She could see that planning for the future finally was helping her husband to banish the terrible despair that had clung to him since they had boarded the ship.

She too had her own ideas for life in America. Once the family and children were settled, she would try to find work as a seamstress. In a city the size of New York, there would surely be a workroom or dressmaker's or garment factory that would employ her or give her piece work. She had no intention of sitting idle.

Chapter 74

Skibbereen

DAN DONOVAN WAS RETURNING FROM OVERSEEING THE OPENING OF A
fresh pit in Abbeystrewery graveyard. Despite his best medical
efforts, the numbers of those falling ill with fever continued to grow,
and the fever wards and sheds were now full.

The Union had opened a new auxiliary workhouse for women on
Levis Quay, and another, smaller government soup kitchen had been
set up on North Street. They were feeding near eight thousand
people. Two men with a horse and cart brought soup and biscuits to
be distributed to outlying areas such as Kilcoe, Ballydehob and Rath,
and also to the sick and weak. The guardians and the relief committee were doing what they could to cope with the enormous numbers
now being dispossessed who found themselves in need of assistance.
It was disheartening to say the least.

He stopped to gather his thoughts and took in the sight of the
riverbank and the beauty of the Ilen as it wound its way towards the
curving stone arches of the town's bridge. It was a calm spot away
from the misery and deprivation all around him. Scraggy thorn
branches bowed low over the river, and a light breeze rippled through
the rushes that grew along its edge. The sunlight sparkled on the

clear water, where ducks, swans and waterfowl aplenty used to swim and dabble. However, such creatures were long gone.

The river was low that day and Dan's eyes were drawn to something caught among the silt and stones and rushes. He left his horse and walked down to the water's edge to investigate. It soon became apparent to him that what he could see was a body that somehow had fallen into the river and become trapped among the rushes. He surmised that it had been there for a few weeks at least, for nature and the river had done their worst.

He climbed back up the bank, mounted his horse and returned to the graveyard where he ordered the men there to give him a hand in raising the body. Between them, they managed to use their shovels to catch the dead man by his coat and drag him out and up on to the riverbank.

'Putrid,' grumbled Martin, the older gravedigger.

Dan knelt to examine the body, which was clearly emaciated. Most likely the man had drowned either by throwing himself in the river or falling into the fast-flowing water. It was hard to tell, but then he noticed the remnants of a fishing line and two hooks that had wrapped themselves around his torso, which indicated that his fall had probably been accidental. There were no signs of identification on him and the state of the decomposition made recognition impossible.

'What do you want us to do with him, doctor?'

'You can put him in the cart and bury him today.'

There was no need for Dan to do an autopsy on this poor fellow who had been fishing and likely fallen into the river when he lost his footing.

He wondered if the man was from Bridgetown or Windmill Lane. Did he have family there, or was he just another stranger passing through the town? At least whoever the poor man was, he would be buried in Abbeystrewery.

Chapter 75

Atlantic Ocean

THE *LADY JANE* HAD BEEN AT SEA FOR NEARLY THREE WEEKS, WHEN THE Sullivan family noticed people sickening around them, coughing and spitting up and burning with ship fever.

The woman they had seen at the chandler's office, Mrs Cassidy, had died a few days earlier. Her scrawny body had been committed to the ocean by the captain and his men, with a few prayers said by her fellow passengers. Her son, a sickly boy, soon followed his mother to a watery grave, for there was no doctor on board.

One of the Murphy boys, Michael, also had taken bad with the fever. He began to complain that his head was going to burst and then developed pains in his legs and all over his body. Within a day or two, he was covered with spots and awful sores.

'Keep away from him,' Mary scolded Con and her nephew. 'Or else you will get sick too.'

'But we are friends,' her son pleaded.

'Friends doesn't come into it!' she warned, giving him a sharp clip to his head to scare him into obeying her. 'You stay far away from those Murphy boys.'

Fear stalked her that the ship fever would spread to her children and she kept them close to her and John. The boys grew scared when thirteen-year-old Michael Murphy lay quiet and still after drawing his last breath in his bunk. At midnight, his poor mother's wailing at the loss of her once healthy boy woke them all.

'We should never have come on this voyage to hell,' Mrs Murphy lamented as her husband and younger sons tried in vain to comfort her.

Chapter 76

MARY WORRIED FOR ANNIE, WHO WAS FADING AWAY LIKE A LITTLE BROWN bird. She was watchful for any change in her, coaxing her gently to try to eat or drink a little. Con too had grown quiet since his friend had died. He no longer played with the other boys and at night she could hear him cough in the darkness in the bunk above her.

'Mary! Mary, wake up!' John was standing before her. 'It's Con. He's burning up.'

Mary moved Annie off her. Climbing out of her bunk, she could see that Con was curled up tightly on his side, his head and neck wet with sweat. Jude and Tim lay beside him fast asleep. She woke them gently and told them to go down below with the girls as she tried to rouse Con. He moaned and complained that his stomach and head hurt before lapsing back into sleep.

Mary tried not to give in to the panic she felt. John fetched a damp rag with which to cool him down, despite her son's groans of protest. For the rest of the night, she sat on the corner of the bunk, watching over him as John lay beside him. In the morning, he was no better and pulled the blanket over him as the others got up. His cough had worsened, racking his chest, and he had developed a few sores on his body.

'What are we to do?' she pleaded with John. 'There is no physician on the ship.'

John and Nora took over caring for Annie as Mary minded Con. She spent the hours talking and singing to him, as she had done when he was younger. He was drowsy most of the time, retching bile into the bucket a few times before slumping back on to the bunk. Although his body was burning up, his teeth were chattering, and he shivered with rigors as he groaned and mumbled in his sleep, thrashing around on the mattress. With a damp piece of cloth, she desperately tried to keep his fever down.

Kate Connolly, a kindly woman from Sherkin Island, gave her a special poultice she had made of herbs and seaweed from the island to put on his chest.

'It may do your boy some good,' she offered quietly, but Con pushed it off him roughly.

As time went on, her eldest son's condition worsened. Though she tried to make him drink, he refused, saying he was not thirsty. His breath grew laboured and it sounded as if he had a whole bag of water in his chest.

The other children were scared. They tried to talk to him and encourage him to get better, but Con looked away and closed his eyes. It was as if he could no longer see them.

Mary railed against God for allowing her child to fall ill. She had done everything in her power to protect him from the hunger and fever, and still her boy was sick . . . Sicker than she had ever seen him, struggling for his life.

For two full days he thrashed and moaned as she sat with him and stroked his head.

'We will be in America in a few days, Con,' she promised him. 'You will see your uncle Pat and New York. Everything will be grand there for us.'

She rambled on, trying to get him to fight and cling on to life. John told him of the day he was born and how much he loved him from the first second he held him in his arms. Mary's eyes welled with tears at the memory of it.

But all their words and all their prayers and all their love were not enough. Late into the long night, as the ship moved on the ocean waves, Con simply closed his eyes and, with only a few deep, shuddering breaths, was still . . .

With his arms stretched out peacefully on the mattress beside them, Con's young beating heart finally stopped. Mary sat in silence, holding her own breath, for she too felt that she might die, while John sobbed openly, his head in his hands, broken-hearted.

Chapter 77

MARY WASHED HER SON'S BEAUTIFUL LONG BODY AND COMBED HIS light-brown hair. She had taken her scissors and cut a few locks of it, sewing them quickly into a small pouch she had fashioned from a piece of material from his shirt. She kissed his handsome face for the very last time as the first mate, Mr Dwyer, and two of the sailors came to take him from her to bury him at sea.

'I'll carry my boy,' John insisted hoarsely.

Mr Dwyer told the others to step back as he helped John wrap Con's body loosely in a light sheet and carry him up on to the deck.

The sun nearly blinded Mary as she stepped into the light. The sky and the sea were so blue that they made her feel giddy. Nora, Sarah and the boys all cried as the ship's captain appeared. He began to read slowly two passages from the Bible and they all said the 'Our Father'. Annie stared out at the sea, still as a statue, and said nothing.

There were two bodies to bury at sea that morning. The other casualty was a thirty-year-old man who was travelling on his own and planning to journey out west and stake a claim for some government land. Three of the men he had befriended on the ship were the only ones there to pray over him.

'Let us pray for the soul of Peadar O'Malley, who has gone to his rest and is now reunited with the Lord,' said the captain, blessing himself.

The sailors lifted the loosely wrapped body on to a wooden plank, which was tilted and then lowered into the sea, consigning the man to the deep water.

Mary began to shake with disbelief as they took Con's body and moved it on to the plank in the same way. John came and stood beside her, gripping her shoulders.

'May God and his grandparents watch over him!' prayed John.

The captain began to recite the 'Our Father' again and everyone present joined in.

'Let us pray for the soul of this young man, Cornelius Sullivan, nearly thirteen years old and taken before his time, who has this day gone to his rest and is now reunited with the Lord,' the captain intoned.

Mary watched as they began to lower and tilt the plank towards the water. Con's body slipped down into the cold, cold sea, floating there for a few minutes before the ocean's waves knocked and pulled him down below into the dark blue depths that would for ever be his grave.

She wanted to fling herself into the churning water after him, but Nora and Annie had taken a grip of her hands. She began to sob and ran to the side, peering down into the depths to see if she could catch any further glimpse of him.

'Mr and Mrs Sullivan, I am sorry for your loss,' the captain said solemnly as he took his leave of them, gesturing for Mr Dwyer to escort them all back down to steerage.

'Please, I want to stay here with him,' Mary begged. 'Just for a little while longer.'

Two sailors suddenly appeared, carrying the ticking mattress and soiled blanket on which her boy had lain. Despite her protests, they tossed them into the waves.

Mary watched the ship lurch and roll, the wind in her sails, as the vessel skimmed and moved through the waves, carrying them further and further away from her first born. Her eyes raked the rippling field of waves, but she could see no trace or sign of Con.

*

Back below deck, John cared for Annie, for all Mary wanted to do was lie down in the bunk, close her eyes and somehow pretend that Con was still alive. She imagined she would hear him laugh or talk beside her.

For three days, Mary could not eat or drink, though she had no fever. The young woman from Coronea kindly offered to cook meals for their family, while her friend from the island, Kate Connolly, gave her a bitter herb to take at night to dull her terrible pain.

As she lay in the bunk, watching the ship's timbers and feeling the constant rise and fall of the vessel, she knew her heart was broken. She had been fooling herself to think that somehow they could escape fate and the hunger. Like a ghost, it had followed them on to this ship and across the ocean.

'Annie needs you,' said John tentatively. 'I need you.'

She could see the fear in his pleading eyes. She nodded dumbly as he helped her up. Though her legs felt weak, they walked slowly around the narrow rows of steerage.

'We are sorry for your loss,' people murmured.

'He was a fine boy!'

'Thank you.' She nodded, trying not to cry.

The children stared at her as she fetched the cooking pot.

'What is this I hear, Annie Sullivan, about you not taking a sup of food from your father?'

'I don't like it!' the small child said stubbornly, her face the colour of snow.

'Well, there will be none of that kind of talk. I am going up top to make us some gruel and woe betide anyone who doesn't eat it. We all need to keep our strength up.'

Her nephew was quiet and she feared he too might be getting ship fever.

'Are you sick?' she asked him, feeling his brow.

'No!' Jude blurted out tearfully. 'I'm so sorry, Auntie Mary, but Sarah and I are the ones who brought the sickness to your door. It should have been me that died, not Con!'

'Jude, hush with that talk.' She could not believe that he was blaming himself. 'Con's death was not of your doing. He was as right as rain when we all boarded the ship. It was here that he got the fever, the same fever that took that boy Michael and a few others.'

She could see the relief in the young boy's eyes as she hugged him and kissed the top of his head.

'Now, Jude. You stay well, do you hear?' She smiled. 'I made a promise to your mam that I would look after you.'

Chapter 78

SIX WEEKS OUT, THE *LADY JANE* GOT CAUGHT IN A TERRIBLE STORM
and was tossed like a log in the towering Atlantic waves. The wind
roared like a banshee, and thunder and lightning flashed above them.
Sea water poured over the deck and in on the passengers, flooding
the low steerage hold. For once, Mary pitied the crew.

'Hold on to the bunks!' John ordered the terrified children, using
his belt to tie Tim and Annie to the upper one.

All around them people prayed that they would not drown.

As the ship gave a huge creaking lurch, Sarah was flung on to the
soaked floor, howling in pain as Mary and John pulled her back up,
for her arm was badly hurt. One man smashed the bones in his leg
and a woman had her eyes blackened and nose broken as she was
thrown against a wooden beam. Everyone was terrified, for they did
not know how much more the ship could take. Some resorted to
prayers while others sat in silence, watching the water rise, terrified
they would drown.

There were tears of relief when the gales and waves finally abated,
although there were bruises and cuts aplenty among the passengers.
Despite the severity of the storm, Mr Dwyer reassured them that the
ship was undamaged and he gave the orders for the water below to be
bailed out as the *Lady Jane* sailed on across the tall, churning waves.

*

Six, seven weeks, all the days ran together. The family's supply of oatcakes was long gone and the food they received was not fit for a dog. However, they had no choice but to eat the meagre rations and the little water that was allowed. Bored, some passengers played cards, listened to the fiddle, or told stories of their townland to pass the hours on the seemingly endless voyage.

Suddenly there was a change at sea and the sailors gave orders to clean up the bunks and the steerage deck. All the filth, the stinking mouldy mattresses, the straw and the blankets were jettisoned to the churning depths of the Atlantic Ocean. The deck was washed with lime and new bedding straw appeared. The over hatch was left open and fresh air finally filled the fetid, squalid darkness.

'We have entered American waters,' declared Johnny Meagher. 'I tell you, soon we will be landed.'

The excitement was contagious as the passengers roused themselves from the terrible inertia and despondency that had hung over them for the past seven long weeks. Faces were scrubbed and children wailed in protest as mothers combed and tried to clean their hair.

'America! We are nearly there,' John told his family proudly.

However, their hopes of landing any time soon were halted as the captain announced that an inspector was due to board the ship shortly.

'Those who are deemed ill or display any symptoms of fever will be removed from this ship immediately to a nearby quarantine facility for medical care. By law, they must remain there until they have recovered sufficiently.'

Consternation spread among the passengers, for many among them were unwell and incredibly weak.

Mary looked at Annie, who resembled a ghost child. She had kept down little food during the journey and deep circles shadowed her eyes. Her lips were parched and flaking, and she sported a dark bruise on her leg where one night the previous week she had hit it on the bunk.

What would they do if she was removed to this quarantine place? They had all heard terrible tales of what happened to the patients of such hospitals where fever, as in the workhouse, spread quickly. They knew stories of families who had endured the long ocean crossing, only to succumb when they landed there.

'Mammy, what is happening?' Annie asked, fearful.

'It is all right, pet. No need to worry,' she reassured her little daughter. 'The captain said our journey is nearly over. Sit up and let me plait your hair.'

Chapter 79

'THERE IS TO BE A MEDICAL INSPECTION OF PASSENGERS AND CREW before we are allowed to sail into New York harbour,' announced Mr Dwyer as the *Lady Jane* dropped anchor near Staten Island. 'Anyone found with fever or contagion will be removed from the ship to Staten Island's Marine Hospital – a quarantine station. It is the law here.'

The passengers grew nervous and uneasy as a smaller ship docked beside them and an official inspector came on board.

'I heard that if a large number of passengers shows any sign of fever, the ship itself could be quarantined for thirty days,' Johnny Meagher had told them grimly.

'Thirty days!'

Mary's heart sank at the thought of having to spend another month in these conditions. Surely people would not be so cruel to them when their journey's end was so tantalizingly close.

She watched silently as two men, unable to hide their disgust at the foul conditions, moved quickly among the passengers while another sat grim-faced at a long rough table. A sailor stood beside him with the ship's manifesto, as he called people forward.

The medical inspector's expression was serious as he examined each person from head to toe. Eyes, nose, ears and throat. Feeling their neck, looking under their arms, and examining their skin carefully, looking for tell-tale typhus pustules and ship fever spots.

Poor Mrs Murphy, Mary thought. The inspector, who had already been informed of Michael's death, examined her, her husband and two younger sons. He pronounced gravely that they all were infected and were to be taken to the hospital. A young wife, who had lain in her bunk, sweating and tossing and turning since last week, was also lifted off the ship, accompanied by her upset husband.

Mary and John stepped forward slowly when their names were called. She worried for all the children, but mostly for Annie who looked wretched. She gave her daughter's cheeks a quick pinch to try to give her some colour.

'I see you already have lost a son,' the medical officer stated matter-of-factly, as he began to examine the children.

'Yes, sir.' John nodded, trying to disguise the concern on his face as the man began to examine Annie.

The poor child was terrified of him, her eyes welling with tears.

'I am well, sir,' said Tim, standing straight and strong when his turn came.

Nora, Jude and Sarah were all nervous and quiet as the inspector made them cough and stick out their tongues.

Then it was Mary's turn. She blushed at the filth and odour of her skin and clothes as the man ran his fingers over her neck, shoulders and legs, and studied her throat and mouth, examining her as you would an animal at the market. He then called John forward and repeated the exercise all over again.

'Mr and Mrs Sullivan, I have to admit that I have concerns about your youngest child, Annie. She seems very weak.'

'Sir, she's had the seasickness since we left Cork,' Mary tried to explain. 'She has kept little down and has just lain in her bunk the whole journey, only eating like a little mouse.'

'Aye, so that is it,' he said, writing on the list. 'Mrs Sullivan, my advice is that once you land, your child will need good care and nourishment if she is to be well again.'

He gestured for them to move away as another passenger's name was called.

Mary's legs nearly went from under her with relief as she grabbed hold of Annie in her arms and hugged her tightly.

Ten passengers in all were removed to the hospital from the ship, along with a seaman who had been ill and unable to do his duties the past few days. Fortune had smiled on the rest of them and the captain was given permission to continue their journey.

The *Lady Jane* sailed slowly through Upper Bay to the wharfs and piers of New York where the rough Atlantic Ocean met the mouth of the broad Hudson River. A strange mixture of excitement, nervousness and emotion overwhelmed Mary as she, John and the children caught their first glimpse of the country that would be their new home.

'Look, Mam, just look it!' declared Tim, his eyes shining as they took in the city with its tall structures and streets all crowded together, the roads and warehouses, the horses and carriages. 'It's huge.'

New York. The name tripped off their tongues and John gripped Mary's hand tightly as they approached the wharf where they would anchor.

The buildings, people and horses were getting closer and closer. The children began jumping up and down, giddy with excitement as at last they reached land.

Chapter 80

New York City
October 1847

HOLDING HER BUNDLE, MARY STOPPED TO CATCH HER BREATH AS SHE stepped up on to the gangplank. Her thoughts were with Con, who, only two months ago, had crossed it back in Cork, filled with hopes and dreams. Their son should be here with them in New York today, instead of lying buried in the depths of the cold ocean.

'Mam, come on,' Nora called, her eyes shining. 'Mam!'

Mary tried to gather herself, seeing the hope and excitement written on the children's faces.

'I'm coming.'

Taking hold of Annie's hand, she smiled as she, John and the children crossed the narrow gangplank and put the first foot on this new land . . . America.

Crowds milled everywhere. As they stood to take it all in, a group of young boys and men, runners from the various boarding houses near to the wharf, accosted them.

'I know of a clean room, missus. With a large bed for you and the children!'

'Welcome to New York, good sir! Come with me to cheap

boarding in a well-run Catholic establishment. Only a ten-minute walk for you and your family.'

'Rest your head in the cheapest lodgings in the whole of the city.'

The boys and men clustered around the exhausted passengers, trying to grab their bundles and baskets, to lead them towards their employers' boarding houses.

Johnny Meagher had warned them about such a thing happening, so Mary held on to their small bundle tightly, anxious as her legs and body struggled to adjust to the feeling of standing on dry land again after the constant movement of the ship.

A large, red-faced woman in a fashionable blue dress and bonnet approached her as if they already knew each other.

'It will all be strange to you, my dear, but if you are in need of clean lodgings, I am an honest woman.'

'Madam, we are to find my brother's place and hope to lodge with him,' interrupted John. He held Annie in his arms, fearful she would be hurt in the crush of people and carts around them.

'Well, good luck to you all.' She smiled and took a printed card from her large pocket. 'Here is my address should you be in need of somewhere to lay your heads.'

'Thank you,' Mary said, grabbing the card and putting it into her bag.

The boys had started to run around, glad to stretch their legs and enjoy the warm sunshine and salt-scented breeze. Above them, noisy seagulls whirled and dived as goods and passengers were unloaded from the ships all around them. Carts and horses were quickly packed and laden with goods to be taken to nearby ware-houses and businesses.

'Move out of the way!' shouted their impatient drivers.

Mary, jumping aside, had never witnessed such a frenzy of activity. She began to fret about what lay ahead of them in such a large strange city that was so different from their tranquil home place.

'Come, we must make our way to Pat's address,' John insisted. 'Hopefully he will have space for us to rest and stay with him.'

'Your brother is in for a surprise,' she teased as, arm in arm, they set off with the five children in tow.

John had only his brother's letter to guide them but, having gained some knowledge of the streets and layout of the city, he had some idea of the direction they had to take.

The streets were lined with tall wooden buildings and crowded with shops and stores, slaughterhouses, tanneries and breweries. There were all kinds of wares on display, from tin and copper to linen and lace, sides of beef and haunches of bacon.

They passed a long avenue which was home to fancy shops and provision stores. Mary had never seen the like. They were well-stocked with food and bread, clothes, boots and shoes, hats and gloves, furniture and linens to entice the customer inside. Fashionable, well-dressed ladies and gentlemen paraded by, ignoring them. Mary was all too conscious of her family's dishevelled and pitiful state.

'More filthy Irish,' a man in a velvet coat sighed, holding his handkerchief to his nose.

Anger burned inside her and she was tempted to shout back at him. Did he have any idea what they had endured these past eight awful weeks at sea, these past hungry years? Instead, she concentrated her attention on trying to find Pat's address, which they were told was in the Five Points district.

They took a few wrong turns on the way, and Nora and Sarah grumbled about how tired and hungry they were.

'After all that time on the ship, we are not used to walking. That's all it is,' she tried to reassure them.

'We will eat soon,' John promised. 'Once we find where your uncle lives.'

They had turned off the main roads and larger avenues to an area of crowded, narrow streets. Ones where tall houses were cramped together near yards, stables and busy factories. Rubbish was strewn everywhere – outside the factories and the houses, in the yards and dung heaps – and waste food scraps and unwanted goods were piled high. Pigs rooted and scrambled and searched among them, gobbling up the city's rubbish. As they passed through Mulberry Bend and Cross Street, John asked a burly cart-hand who owned the animals.

'They are the city's pigs,' he responded.

A short walk later, a look of concern crossed John's face as he recognized the name of the street from his brother's letter.

Pat Sullivan was living in Little Water Street, a rundown part of the city from what he could tell, in a shabby wooden house with ramshackle windows, a peeling door and broken steps. It was certainly not the fine dwelling he had boasted of to his brother.

'Is this it?' Mary could not hide her disappointment.

'It seems so. I will enquire for him.'

Mary stood by his side as John rang the bell again and again. It took an age before a heavy-set woman in an apron came to the door.

'We are looking for my brother, Patrick Sullivan from Ireland. Does he live here?'

'Pat Sullivan. Aye, he does,' the woman replied, her eyes raking over them as she took in their poor condition. 'But he's not here at the moment. He's at work. You will have to come back later, after six thirty. He should be here by then, for it's dinner time.'

'Ma'am, we hate to trouble you, but could we wait for him?' John pressed. 'We have just arrived in the city and the children are all exhausted. Could we wait in Pat's rooms, do you think?'

' "Rooms", is it? I'll have you know that Mr Sullivan shares a room upstairs with three others. This is a men-only establishment.'

'We've been at sea for nearly eight weeks and the children need to rest a bit,' Mary said quietly. 'I promise you that we will be no trouble and won't be in your way.'

She could see the woman considering their situation.

'My husband and I came over on the ship from Galway, nearly ten years ago,' the landlady said, her tone softening. 'I still remember what it was like. I suppose that I could let you sit awhile in the dining room until Mr Sullivan returns home. But you and the children will have to leave then.'

*

The dreary dining room was home to a long table surrounded by fourteen chairs, and was already set for the evening meal. A sideboard containing bowls, serving platters and cutlery ran along the far side of the room, and a tall window looked out over the street.

Every member of the family was relieved to sit down but John stood at the window, watching the passers-by.

'Well, we can't stay here, so we need to find somewhere else to stay tonight,' Mary reminded him.

They did not want to be wandering the city streets of New York when darkness fell.

'I'm sure Pat will know of somewhere.'

Mary did not share her husband's faith in his brother's ability to procure lodgings for them.

'I think that we should go and look ourselves. We can see Pat later, or tomorrow.'

They were interrupted by the arrival of the landlady, who brought them a pot of soup, some bowls and spoons, and a plate of fresh soda bread.

'I'm sure you are all hungry,' she said kindly, distributing the bowls.

The children rushed around her as she ladled out portions of the thick meaty soup.

'Thank you, Mrs . . .'

Mary blushed with embarrassment, for she did not even know the good woman's name.

'It's Mrs Catherine Ryan.'

Mary could not believe the kindness of this stranger to them.

'Thank you,' she said tearfully, for it had been the longest while since such kindness had been shown to them.

Later, Mrs Ryan returned to remove the dishes and Mary took the opportunity to ask her if she knew of anywhere close by where they might find lodgings.

'Stay away from the Old Brewery,' she warned. 'It's a rookery and no place for children. Try down around Mulberry Bend or Cross

Street. Number forty might have space. Or try the corner building near the tannery.'

Mary thanked her for her generosity and began to organize the children to get ready to leave.

'If you wish, you and Mr Sullivan may leave the children here with me a short while,' she offered. 'It will make it easier for you to go and search for rooms without such a brood.'

Mary was not sure about leaving the children with a stranger, but there was something about Mrs Ryan that made her feel she could trust her. Annie and Tim refused to stay with the landlady but the others remained in Little Water Street while John and Mary set off on their search.

There were no rooms anywhere they went, or if there were, they were not fit for a family.

They walked up and down the streets, knocking on doors. In desperation, Mary took out the card that the well-dressed woman at the wharf had given her. She realized it was for a boarding house on nearby Orange Street.

The owner shrugged. Mary was too late – her best rooms were already let.

'We would be happy with anything,' pleaded Mary.

Mrs Beatty hesitated, before beckoning for them to follow her down a set of steps to the rear of the house. The steps led to a room containing two old beds, a stained mattress stacked against a wall, and a few chairs. It was lit by a small window and, even though the day was warm, it still felt chilly.

'I provide rooms only and no meals,' she told them firmly. 'And this will cost a dollar a week. There is a tap and sink and shared water closet in the yard.'

Mary wrinkled her nose, for the stench from it was overpowering.

She suspected that what they were being shown was more of a storage room, but at least they and the children would fit here.

'Thank you, Mrs Beatty,' John said. 'My wife and I are grateful to you. We will take it.'

*

'It's grim,' he admitted as they walked back to collect the other children, 'but hopefully it will only be for a short time.'

They returned to the boarding house on Little Water Street to find Pat Sullivan deep in conversation with Nora, Sarah and Jude. He and John, the minute they saw each other, embraced tearfully.

'Brother, forgive me, but I never thought that I would see you again in this lifetime, let alone here in New York.'

'Nor I,' admitted John ruefully. 'But we had no choice. Mary and I were evicted from the home place and Wrixon Becher's men offered us paid passage to here.'

'Nora told me about what happened to Con.' Pat's voice broke. 'I asked her where her brother was and it's right cut me up to hear tell of his death on that ship! I'm so sorry for the both of you to lose your boy.'

Mary nodded tearfully as she saw the sympathy in his eyes.

'He was precious to us.'

'He was the finest boy ever,' added John, clasping his brother's shoulder.

John outlined the terrible events and tragedies that had befallen the family and their neighbours since Pat had left Skibbereen.

Pat's eyes filled with anger as John told him about the death of his uncle and aunt.

'I'm sorry, John. I know how much the place and the land meant to you. And poor Flor and Molly.'

Pat looked well, Mary thought. Compared to John, he was healthy, strong and muscular. If possible, he was even more handsome than ever, she decided, as she watched him covertly. He was full of talk of New York and this new land of opportunity, where a man could make his fortune. He explained how he had found work in a slaughterhouse at first.

'All that blood fair turned my stomach, for I had the job to clean it all up. Then I got hard labouring work on a house two blocks away. These days, I am working as a carpenter on a big new house. It's being constructed on a plot of land not half a mile away and will house plenty of families.'

'So there is work!'

'Plenty of it, but they work us hard. The foreman is a decent sort. I'll ask him if there is any work on offer.'

'But I know nothing of building and construction.'

'That's no matter. Like us all, you will soon learn.'

The other boarders had begun to return, so Mary took the children outside.

'We have found somewhere to stay,' she explained to them, as John and Pat joined them on their walk to Orange Street.

Mrs Beatty was not too pleased when she realized they had five children, not two.

'We are well used to sharing beds,' Mary said pleasantly as she led her family down the steps to the large dank room.

At least the landlady had provided them with a few blankets and a lamp. The following day they would go in search of a few more essential items they needed to purchase.

Pat had disappeared and returned shortly with two cans of milk, a few slices of salt beef and a loaf of a strange type of dark rye bread. He handed the items to John and pressed a few dollar bills into his hand.

'I'll pay you back once I start earning,' John promised his brother earnestly.

Annie and Nora were already half asleep, and Mary could barely keep her eyes open as John and Pat said goodnight, agreeing to meet again tomorrow.

As she lay in the darkness, Mary missed the rocking of the ship and the sound of the slapping water. As she listened instead to the strange and unfamiliar noises of New York City, she finally fell asleep.

Chapter 81

MARY OPENED HER EYES AS THE MORNING SUN CREPT INTO THE GLOOMY room. John lay asleep beside her and the children slept too. Tim's arm was flung across his head, while Jude snored lightly. Annie was curled up like a kitten beside Nora and Sarah. They were all tired and dirty, still wearing their soiled clothes from the long voyage.

She felt strangely weary as she stared at the damp-stained walls and grimy woodwork, the mouldy rug and mattresses. She tried not to give in to the disappointment she felt that after such an arduous journey they should end up in such a place, so different from their neat, tidy cottage and green fields. She was tempted to go back to sleep but there was much work to be done if they were to get used to New York and its ways.

She got up and went outside to the empty yard. She was delighted to see a large tin wash basin and that some obliging tenant had left a bar of carbolic soap beneath it. Quickly, Mary slipped back inside and lifted dresses, shirts, britches and jackets from the bodies of her sleeping family for washing and airing. Being poor was no shame, but being dirty was. She would not have her family sneered at or insulted!

She hung the laundered clothes to dry on the rope line that was strung across the narrow yard.

'Where is my shirt?' demanded John when he woke up.

'Mammy, my dress is gone!'

'They are washed and will be dry soon,' she assured them.

Despite the howls of protest, she washed herself and the children in the yard, scrubbing at their skin until it was pink, then combed through their wet hair to get rid of the lice and nits that had plagued everyone on board the *Lady Jane*. Finally satisfied that everyone looked decent and clean, she shared the remainder of the black rye bread and milk between them.

A few hours later, John set off in search of work.

'I hope you find something,' Mary said, kissing him lightly as she saw him on his way.

'Even though Pat put in a good word for me, they say they already have enough men employed at his place,' he sighed in disappointment, but he persisted in walking the district.

He enquired at the livery yards, abattoirs, and even the docks. He was glad to find work eventually at the nearby fish market, cleaning up and sweeping out the place.

'At least it's work, John,' she encouraged him when he told her the news.

The pay was low but Pat insisted on giving them a small loan to tide them over.

'You can give it all back to me when you get a better job,' he reassured his brother.

Mary purchased a bucket and a scrubbing brush, some baking soda and vinegar, and set to cleaning their place from top to bottom. Lord knows how long it had been since anyone had lifted a finger to clean it! She aired the mattresses and beat the rug. She washed away the grime and polished the glass in the small window.

'This place looks much better. If you keep this up, Mrs Beatty will want more rent,' John teased when he came back from work one day.

As she combed the markets and provision stores, she thought of the hunger back home. She could not escape a profound sense of guilt at the abundance of fresh meat and fish, butter, cheese and eggs, potatoes by the sackload, and vegetables, breads, cakes and spices available to buy. She longed to be able to cook a proper meal for her family, spend time preparing and making something John and the children would want to eat that would not sicken them or barely fill their stomachs.

However, Mrs Beatty refused to let her use the kitchen. Instead, they had to make do with cooking on a small fire they lit on an iron grate placed against the stone wall. Mary made the best of it, though. With her pot and a new pan and some cheap vegetables, a little lard, some offcuts of meat and a half-sack of flour and oats she had bought, she began to make more nourishing meals that little Annie and the children would eat.

The children played in the street with the other youngsters who lived in the neighbourhood. It wasn't long before they lost their pasty, gaunt look and began to regain their strength.

Mary found out about schooling from a neighbour. Jude, who had just turned thirteen, was considered too old but the rest of the children were enrolled at the old school building a few streets away. Tim was declared an excellent student, and Nora and Sarah, to her surprise, both took well to reading and began to learn all about the history and geography of this new country of theirs.

'They can teach *us*,' Mary said proudly.

Mary found those first days and weeks in New York a terrible trial. Although Pat was there to guide them as best he could, they remained outsiders, unused to city life. The crowded tenements, noise and pungent smells were overwhelming, for she missed home – the quiet of the fields and the fresh breeze blowing across their land.

Though their lodgings were now clean, the room remained damp and cold, and Catherine Ryan, who had been so kind to them on their arrival, was most helpful to her, warning her that soon the winter would come.

'Mary, I tell you, there is nothing as cold as New York in the winter. We'll soon be covered in snow and ice. 'Tis nothing like home and you'd best be prepared for it!'

'I need to get some material to make us warmer clothes,' she told John urgently.

She'd discovered a haberdashery that sold cheap offcut remnants of the exact material she wanted. With some money John had set aside, she bought what she needed and cut, sewed and made new warm dresses, shirts and coats for them all, to see them through the long winter days ahead.

Chapter 82

Skibbereen

'GOOD MORNING, FATHER,' CHORUSED THE SCHOOL CHILDREN LOUDLY as they welcomed him.

Father Fitzpatrick smiled as he took in the desks packed with young pupils keen to learn and to receive the free meals supplied by the British Relief Association. Since the inception of its charity scheme for feeding children a few weeks ago, attendance at St Fachtna's School had never been so high, the place now crowded out. The Association's schools scheme ensured that nearly every hungry child in the district could not only get an education but also be fed.

A few of the children had protested and objected at first to the conditions that hands and faces had to be scrubbed clean, and hair had to be combed for lice and nits, but if the children wanted to avail themselves of the two free meals provided generously by the British Association every day in the school, they must abide by the rules. The scheme was a good one and though, at first, Father Fitzpatrick had wondered about its efficiency, the promise of a bowl of gruel in the morning and oatcakes later in the day enticed the hungry. Children from all over now flocked to school.

'It's a devil of a job, Father, trying to get them to let their faces and hands be washed every day,' confided the school master. 'And

you should hear the roars from some of them when the poor assistants are trying to use the fine comb to de-louse their hair.'

'But it has made a difference?'

'Most certainly. How can a child be expected to learn when they
have an empty belly?'

'Aye,' he nodded. 'The hope is that feeding and washing and
cleaning the children will help curtail the spread of disease.'

The school and its classrooms had not been built to accommodate
such huge numbers, but if the parents wanted the children to attend,
he was happy for the school to oblige. It meant the burden of feeding
so many mouths in a poor family was somewhat eased. No longer
wan and pale-faced, the boys and girls, he hoped, could concentrate
and learn.

As the priest walked through the town, he wondered how much
longer they would have to endure such conditions. He remained
tired and drained from the constant demands for his services. The
young curate, who assisted him as best he could, looked of late to be
exhausted too.

A few of the young men with whom he had studied and trained
for the priesthood had already succumbed to fever, which they had
caught while performing their religious duties in their parishes. His
friend Father James Coyle had died of typhus only a few weeks ago.
A kind-hearted, gentle man, it had been a great loss.

Some days, he felt as if there must be an angel watching over him
as he attended the sick and dying in the lanes and hovels of the town.
His job was to bless and comfort them in their final hours on this
good earth. He had come to realize that doing the Lord's work here
in Skibbereen was what he had been called for, and that it was a true
testimony of his faith.

'I have your meal ready,' declared Bridey when he returned home
that evening.

The woman fussed over him like a mother hen, making sure that
he ate enough and slept enough, and got a little peace to himself.

'If I don't look out for you, Father, who will?'

'Thank you, Bridey. Without your good care I would be lost,' he said, seeing her flush with pride as she returned to the kitchen.

Taking out his Bible, he began to read, finding great comfort in the familiar words . . .

Chapter 83

New York City
March 1848

THAT LONG, FREEZING FIRST WINTER IN NEW YORK WAS THE WORST, FOR John earned little and they had not even a proper fire or stove to warm them. In early spring, as the snow melted, a lad who worked on Pat's building, hulking bricks and materials, injured himself. He broke his shoulder and arm badly and was no longer fit for work.

'One man's bad luck is another's good luck!' observed Pat as he sent John to talk to the building foreman.

'He offered me the job,' John reported with delight after his brief interview. 'I start tomorrow.'

'I told you that Jerome Daly would change his tune mighty fast.' Pat laughed. 'And he's glad to hire you.'

In his new job, John disappeared early in the morning and returned home exhausted, but was glad to have found a position that paid decent wages.

'At least here we can afford to pay rent, buy food and some of the things we need,' he said proudly.

Pat also found a job for young Jude. The nearby printing factory was looking for an apprentice who was ready to learn and not afraid of hard work. Jude, in his own quiet way, was exactly what they wanted. He was turning into a fine young man and was very like Mary's late sister.

'Your mam would be proud of you,' she said, hugging him close.

Mary had struck up a growing friendship with Catherine Ryan, who would give her honest advice on where to go and what to do.

'I hear there are rooms coming up to rent in a house on Mulberry Street,' she tipped off Mary one day. 'The people renting them are moving out west.'

Immediately, Mary and John arranged to go and see them. The lodgings were on the second floor of a four-storey house and were made up of three rather cramped rooms, one of which was a kitchen with a small stove. In all, there were ten families living in the building.

'Oh, John, it's so much better than where we are,' Mary enthused, noting the way the sun streamed in through the windows, and the neat back yard with a water closet.

'It will cost us more,' John fretted, 'but to be honest, I don't know if I could face another winter where we are.'

The sun was warm in the sky when they packed up their few belongings and, with a small handcart, moved from the dank basement to their new rented home. Mrs Beatty watched from the door with a face like thunder, for she had been most put out when they had told her they were leaving.

'Mrs Sullivan, you might regret leaving this establishment,' she cajoled. 'As I may have two better rooms to let in a month or so.'

Mary certainly didn't have any regrets, though, and was in no way sad to say goodbye to Mrs Beatty's establishment on Orange Street.

'That old rip will soon find two other greenhorns off the ships to take our place!' shrugged John as they moved to Mulberry Street.

Annie, Nora and Sarah ran around their new home, delighted as Mary hung a curtain to divide into two the bedroom they were to share with the boys. There was a bed for them on one side, and a mattress on the other.

'Uncle Pat and I will make bunks for you boys when we can afford it,' promised John.

As she looked around their new home, Mary hoped that they and the children would find happiness there.

Each week, at Sunday mass at the Immigrants' Church, Mary prayed for Con. Not a day went by when she didn't think of and miss him. She asked the Lord to help her family get used to their new life and to look after the hungry and sick who were suffering back in Skibbereen. Afterwards, as the children ran and played and chased each other in the newly opened Madison Square Park, she and John walked arm in arm like two sweethearts.

Chapter 84

MARY STUDIED THE FIGURES SHE HAD WRITTEN DOWN, THEN TOTTED them up again. John worked hard but, with their rent and food purchases, they were barely making ends meet. Putting on her coat, hat and boots, she made her way to Catherine Ryan's boarding house on Little Water Street and consulted with her about the prospect of finding dressmaking work.

'Some folks don't like hiring married women. That is the truth of it, but a family has to eat, I know. There are a few that might take you on, though keep away from Mena Stronge as she is meant to be a right old rip, and difficult to work for.'

Mary had taken out her sewing kit and gone from dressmaker to dressmaker and numerous garment factories in the district to offer her services, but with little luck.

'I'm sorry, Mrs Sullivan,' said dressmaker Betsy Smith, shaking her head, 'but I already have three women working for me.'

'I am a good worker with plenty of experience,' she pressed.

'I'm sorry, my dear. Why don't you try Mena Stronge on Pearl Street?'

Mary thanked Mrs Smith, but was nervous about approaching Mrs Stronge. However, needs must. Putting her pride away, she found herself on Pearl Street looking at the narrow shop window with a dress and a maid's uniform both on display. Taking her courage in hand, she pushed in the door and introduced herself to the tall woman presiding at the counter.

Mena Stronge's wavy hair was pulled back into a tight bun and she wore a neat, high-collared blue dress, which showed off her trim figure. She had enormous limpid, pale-blue eyes, which might lull a person into thinking she was perhaps a quiet type of woman, but once the conversation started, those eyes became wide and searching, for she was a highly intelligent and astute woman.

Mrs Stronge said little as Mary told her about working for Honora Barry.

'You seem to have made everything, from bridal dresses to fashionable styles and children's clothes, and done difficult alterations to patching and mending,' the woman said, somewhat sarcastically.

Mary blushed to hear her work described in such a fashion.

'Have you brought any samples of your work?'

Mary's hopes plummeted for a moment or two, before she thought to pass Mrs Stronge her plum-coloured winter coat and pointed out the finer details of the navy dress that she was wearing.

The woman examined the seams and hems, pin tucks and button holes meticulously.

'This is good work, Mrs Sullivan. Very good work,' she said admiringly.

'Thank you.'

'My business has a definite type of customer. I don't make wedding dresses or fine stylish gowns for women to wear. Mostly I service the needs of people who wish to have uniforms fitted and made for their staff.'

'Uniforms?'

'For house maids, nursery maids and cooks. Of late, I have been fortunate to make the uniforms for all the maids in two new hotels – one in Brooklyn and one over on Lafayette Street. There are big houses, wealthy people employing staff, who want their maids to look neat and tidy but also to have some kind of personal detail on their uniform to distinguish them from their neighbours'. I tell you, it's a growing business. That is, if you are interested in coming to work for me.'

'Mrs Stronge, I would very much like to work with you,' agreed Mary.

The other woman told her what her wages would be and explained that she would work for her for three full days a week at first.

'Then we can see what's what!'

Almost every day, maids came to the small shop on Pearl Street to be fitted for new uniform or to have an existing one repaired.

Every so often, Mary accompanied Mena as they travelled by coach to some grand house, where the maids were lined up to be fitted. Mary carefully wrote down measurements, names and details for Mena.

'Hold up your arms, please?' she asked a pretty girl from Kerry, as she ran the measuring tape over her.

Mary had started off fearful of Mena but, in time, came to respect the Belfast woman.

'My husband and son and I came over here nearly fifteen years ago,' Mena explained. 'He was working in the bank for nearly three years when he suddenly took ill. A week later he died of a bronchial attack, leaving me and my poor boy, Henry, here in New York without a soul to help us. What was I to do, return to Belfast or try to make a life here?'

Mary was filled with admiration for Mena's determination and business acumen. Bit by bit, she had built her business from scratch and, like Honora Barry, was a woman from whom she could learn much.

Chapter 85

MARY GOT TO KNOW THE MAIDS WHO WORKED IN MANY OF THE BIG houses and mansions in St John's Park, Gramercy Park and Washington Square, and she listened to their tittle-tattle good naturedly. They were most happy to have comfortable, well-fitting uniforms, unlike the hand-me-downs and outfits either too tight or too big that were used by the staff in some other grand houses.

'I'm getting married in eight months' time,' confided Kitty O'Kelly one day. 'And that will be the end of my uniform days. What I will be wearing next June is a fine wedding dress that I am saving for. Would you consider making it for me, Mary?'

Mary had checked with her employer and Mena Stronge had made it very plain that she had no interest in such work, but had no objection to Mary taking it on. For Mary it was a chance to sew something beautiful and delicate again, for the pretty young Kerry woman, compared to the functional uniforms she usually spent most of her days making.

Over time, Mary developed quite a reputation in the Five Points for her dressmaking skills. She found herself making summer and winter dresses, outfits for weddings and funerals, and fine dresses for maids, housekeepers or cooks who, upon leaving their employment after long years of service to open boarding houses or eateries, wanted to be suitably attired.

It was good work and reminded her of Miss Barry's shop. Often, she found herself thinking of her friend the dressmaker, who had helped to make their survival and journey to America possible.

She worked hard and saved every dime and dollar she could, week after week, putting it into a savings bank.

Catherine's daughter, Lily, was getting married, and Mary was delighted when she asked her to make her dress. She was a pretty girl with the same thick dark hair and big brown eyes as her mother.

'I'm getting married in a month's time. It is only a simple affair, Mrs Sullivan, and I'm not one for fashion, but my mam told me that you will make me a special dress.'

'I'd be happy and honoured to.'

Mary smiled and did her best to put Lily at ease as she took out her measuring tape. The girl had a good waist and long legs. Taking out some samples of lace, tulle and pretty sprigged cottons, Mary showed them to her, and was not surprised when Lily chose the cotton. She suggested a high cinched waist, and encouraged Lily to consider adding a lace trim to the collar and cuffs.

'I can make them removable for easy washing and dressing the dress up or down.'

'We are to be wed at the Transfiguration Church,' Lily told Mary as they continued to chat. 'Mam is putting on a spread for us afterwards, back in the boarding house. If the day stays fine, she intends on putting two tables outside with summer daisies.'

'That sounds like a lovely day for you all,' Mary enthused.

'Michael Connolly is the man of my heart,' Lily confided, her face lighting up, 'and truth to tell, all I care about is that the two of us are married.'

'I felt the same as you when I was wed many years ago.' Mary smiled, remembering the day that she and John were married back in Cork. 'And it's still the same.'

Chapter 86

THE CITY COULD BE A LONESOME PLACE. EVEN THOUGH MARY WAS surrounded by the constant noise and sounds of the teeming, over-crowded neighbourhood with its packed tenements, abundant stores, back-lane saloons and brothels, and busy streets, she still, at times was heartsore and longed for the peace and quiet of the countryside. She missed their cottage in the sea of green fields and the stillness there. Her homesickness gnawed at her like a pain some days, as she knew that she would never set foot in her native land again.

When she thought of Con, she longed to hold him close and never let him go, to banish the memory of his death. It still grieved her so but she took comfort in the other five children and the joy they brought her, for she now considered Jude and Sarah very much her own children too.

Tim had taken to drawing and sketching. The school master said that he had a talent far beyond his years.

'Ma, I made you this,' he said proudly, handing her a sheet of paper one day with a picture on it. 'It's our cottage. The way I remember it.'

Mary gasped. Although it was simply sketched and coloured, the cottage was exactly as she recalled.

'There's your vegetable patch, and the hen-house.'

Mary couldn't believe how their son had managed to capture with his pencils the place that meant so much to them.

'That's where Da had to fix the hole in the thatch, and there's where Patch used to lie in the sun.'

'Ah, Tim, this is the grandest present I ever got in my life,' she said, hugging him close.

'I wanted to always remember our home place,' he said softly.

John had studied it carefully, tears welling in his eyes.

Mary insisted on getting it framed, and made John hang it up for them all to see.

She and John both worked harder than they had ever expected. John continued to find work in construction, and proving himself a good carpenter he had been promoted quickly. On every street and piece of land, frame or brick building after building was being thrown up to house the city's growing population.

Nora often watched her sewing at home. One day, Mary took out a spare needle and began to show her daughter some simple stitches.

'That's the way, and try to keep the stitches even and the same size,' Mary urged her gently.

Nora chewed her lower lip, her hazel eyes filled with concentration as her fingers worked lightly. Mary could see her satisfaction when the neat square she had sewn was examined.

'Good work!' she said, praising her.

Sarah, on the other hand, like Kathleen, had no instinct for sewing. She pricked her fingers and tangled her threads and stitches terribly.

'I hate sewing, Auntie Mary!' she declared. 'I much prefer baking and cooking.'

A few weeks later, when Nora asked to be allowed to try to make a skirt, it came as no surprise.

Watching the children grow and settle in this new land made Mary accept that New York was their home now, and she must learn to get used to it.

Chapter 87

'BUSINESS IS GROWING IN THE CITY, MARY,' CONFIDED MENA. 'WHAT with all the big new fancy houses with staff, and grand hotels like the St Nicholas that are opening up. There are garment shops springing up all over, but as my work is custom made, I am thinking that I will soon need to find a bigger premises, away from the Five Points in a better area. The customers expect more of me than these two small rooms here in Pearl Street.'

'That is good news.' Mary smiled, pleased that Mrs Stronge was including her in whatever plans she was making.

'To be honest, I'll be sad to say goodbye to this place, but I have built a good business and reputation over the years, and I don't intend to lose either.'

'That wouldn't happen!'

'People can be fickle. They'll flock to whatever new fancy place or dress shop that opens, believe me!' She laughed. 'But I've seen a suitable one on Centre Street, which needs a bit of work. It's got three larger rooms and if I can agree a fair rent with the landlord, I'll take it.'

'Three rooms? Then there will be lots of space!'

'Yes. As you know well, Mary, we are kept busy with so much work, but I was considering hiring a young apprentice. A suitable quiet girl.'

'My Nora is good at sewing and is a steady, honest girl,' she

323

ventured, hoping she hadn't overstepped herself with Mena by mentioning her daughter.

'I intend on interviewing a few girls, so you send your Nora here to meet me. Mind you, I am not making any promises.'

Mary smiled. 'Of course.'

She'd far prefer her daughter to work for Mrs Stronge than one of the nearby garment shops, which employed large groups of women making clothes. Sweatshops – that's what people called them!

Nora was nervous about meeting Mena. Mary remembered how anxious she had been when she had first met the tall Belfast woman, but the one thing she had come to learn from working for her was that she was fair.

'Show her the few pieces you have made,' Mary encouraged her daughter. 'Your skirt and the blouse, and remember to tell Mrs Stronge that you want to learn.'

'I do, Mam. I really do,' said Nora, her pretty face the picture of eagerness as she set off to Pearl Street.

Mena had examined her work thoroughly and then made her sew part of the hem of a dress, Nora told her mother when she returned home.

'I was scared but I did my best.'

Two days later, Nora was offered the apprenticeship, but would not start until they moved into Mena's new premises.

'She's a credit to you, Mary,' Mena told her. 'She is bright and polite, and will no doubt prove a good learner.'

'Thank you, Mrs Stronge. I am grateful to you for giving Nora the opportunity.'

'To tell the truth, Nora was head and shoulders better than the other girls. One, I suspect, had never even sewn a stitch in her life!'

Three weeks later, they moved into the new shop at the better end of Centre Street and, as Mena had predicted, the customers followed. As did many new clients – New York families that had come up in the world and could now afford staff.

Nora, to her delight, since leaving school was proving herself a good and willing worker, and got on well with the dressmaker, learning quickly from her.

A friend of Catherine's, who lived only a block away, had offered Sarah a position. She was in need of a kind, bright girl to help with cooking and caring for two small children.

'Lord knows you have plenty of experience of that,' agreed Mary when Sarah accepted the job gladly.

Jude was happy in his work and, to his delight, his wages as an inker had been increased.

'My poor da never got regular money. He was always full of plans but from what I remember never got a proper wage,' he admitted quietly. 'But I'm not like him, Auntie Mary, I want to stay where I am and work my way up.'

'Your mam and da would both be so proud of you, Jude,' she encouraged, hugging him tightly. 'I know they would.'

Tim and Annie both remained healthy and well, and were good students, thriving in school.

Sometimes when she walked down by the wharf and along the river, Mary would catch sight of the haunted look of fear and hope on the worn faces of weary men, women and children who were disembarking from ships that had crossed the Atlantic, or walking the city streets in their filthy rags. It still reminded her of when they had first arrived and how much their lives had changed.

However, she saw also the hope in the eyes of all those arriving month after month, not just from Ireland but from Germany too, hardworking people who lived near by in the Kleindeutschland neighbourhood. It grieved her to see some of her fellow countrymen fall victim to despair and drink. The hunger had marked and scarred them, and homesickness consumed them as they often struggled to survive in the overcrowded Five Points.

'God help them,' she sighed. 'There is just too much sadness in them.'

Chapter 88

'MARY, PAT WANTS ME TO GO IN WITH HIM TO BUY A RUNDOWN FRAME building on Mott Street,' John told her nervously on his return from work.

'Are you gone cracked? We don't have the money for that,' she told him outright.

'Listen to me. Pat says it is a huge opportunity and that if we don't grab it, someone else will. The place is falling down but we can repair it and fix it up. In a year or two we can either rent it out or sell it.'

'We are paying rent and food. I'm telling you straight, John Sullivan, we have no spare money for such things,' she sighed, exasperated. 'Pat may have the money for it – he has no responsibilities – but we don't!'

'Pat says he'll put up a much larger share, but he wants me to be a part owner with him. We can use our savings and borrow the rest from the Emigrant Industrial Savings Bank.'

He badgered her over the next three days, wearing her down about the house and opportunity that he would miss out on.

'Oh . . . I don't know.' She gave in, exasperated. 'Tell Pat to come here and talk to us about it.'

'The worst that will happen, Mary, is that we improve the old building and sell it at a higher price than we paid for it,' explained Pat, his face serious. 'I promise you that we both will still have our proper jobs. We will do the renovations in the evenings and at weekends when we are free. We'll get a few of the men we know to give us a bit of a hand if need be.'

'But when will you have the time?' she asked with worry. 'You already work so hard.'

'You find time for extra dressmaking work,' John reminded her gently. 'It will be the same for me.'

She smiled. 'God knows we are both hard workers!'

Despite her reservations, Mary agreed reluctantly to John using their meagre savings to go in with his brother on the house. She prayed that he was not being foolish or wasteful.

The two brothers nearly killed themselves fixing up and repairing the house, month after month. John was so tired he would nearly fall asleep standing up.

By September, the work was finished and it was ready to be rented out.

'It's a lot better than Mrs Beatty's,' Mary had to admit when she went to see the finished Mott Street building.

The wood was freshly painted, which was basic, but the place was at least now dry and warm. They rented it quickly to six families, who were glad to find rooms with a stove and proper outside water closet.

'Isn't it a bit crowded?' she asked, worried.

'We could have rented it out ten times over,' Pat reminded her dryly. 'Remember, it's the tenants who help us to repay the loan.'

Chapter 89

AS DAN DROVE FROM BALLYDEHOB INTO TOWN IT GRIEVED HIM TO SEE field after field with tumbled cottages, their stones now used to make low walls, and all the overgrown potato patches covered with weeds and nettles, ferns and gorse, terrible reminders of the hunger. Large areas of land all across the Mizen had been cleared and now lay empty as family after family had been evicted. Those people were now scattered to the winds like birds across the Atlantic to Canada and North America.

From reports he had read, the attrition rate on sea voyages was a disgrace and many died on board. Coffin ships, some called them. Even if they survived the journey, many died in the quarantine hospitals, and for what? The herds of cattle and sheep that now grazed these forlorn grassy fields! What a travesty, he thought as he urged his horse homewards.

He looked into the crib at his newborn daughter, Catherine. A perfect, healthy baby. He prayed that she would stay well.

'She looks like you, Dan,' Henrietta said with a smile. 'See that serious look on her little face, and the way she scrunches her nose?'

'She is a beauty like her mother.' He laughed, noting the pert little upturned nose of his daughter and perfect tiny rosebud lips.

The older children were all delighted with their new sister, especially three-year-old John, while one-and-a-half-year-old William was naturally a little jealous of the baby.

'Now, go run and play, children,' Henrietta urged them with a smile. 'Give your dada and me some peace.'

It did Dan good to see the family happy, and Henrietta was in her element with this latest baby to attend to. It had been a straightforward birth and Catherine seemed a good child so far.

He kissed his wife's head. She seemed surprised by his sudden show of affection.

'You and the children are everything to me,' he declared. 'You do know that?'

'Of course I do. We all do,' she said, reaching gently for his hand.

Dan took her in his arms and held her close. His wife was the one constant in his life. Her love gave him the strength and courage to carry on, even on the darkest of days.

'I love you, Hetty, and I always will.'

'Dan, I've loved you practically from the minute we were first introduced,' she teased, 'and I will love you till I am a very old lady.'

Satisfied, he held her close to his heart, where she always was.

Chapter 90

New York City
April 1853

MARY AND JOHN STROLLED PAST MR BARNUM'S AMERICAN MUSEUM ON the corner of Broadway and Ann Street, with its exotic Siamese twins and strange and terrible wonders of the natural world. A place she longed to visit!

They stopped to admire the recently opened St Nicholas Hotel. It was magnificent and even more decadent than New York's renowned Astor Hotel.

'It cost a million dollars to build,' said John admiringly. 'There are six hundred rooms, but soon it will have one thousand.'

'It's beautiful,' murmured Mary.

She watched a little enviously as the crowds of wealthy women and gentlemen in their fine style passed through its tall, polished brass doors, noting the finer details of the ladies' dresses so that she could endeavour to copy them.

'Some day we will dine there,' promised John.

'We will never afford it,' Mary said with a laugh, as instead they walked on until they stopped at the corner of Broadway to buy oysters from the busy oyster cart.

'This country is different from Ireland, for here one man is as

330

good as the next,' John said seriously, adding a shake of salt to his oysters. 'And one man's money is as good as another's! Once you work long and hard there is an opportunity, even for the likes of us.'

'And heaven knows we both work hard enough,' she said, squeezing his arm.

'Do you recall the narrow brick house down at the very far end of our street, with the broken windows?' asked John.

'Not very well. Is it the derelict one? 'Tis in a terrible state. A piece of shingle fell off it and nearly killed a poor messenger boy. It should be condemned.'

'Aye. Pat heard that the owner is moving away and selling it next month. I was wondering if we should consider trying to buy it.'

'You and Pat want to buy it?'

Mary sighed. She wasn't sure she wanted her husband borrowing more money or undertaking so much work again.

'No, it's nothing to do with Pat,' he protested. 'I was thinking that it might suit us to live in.'

'How can we possibly buy a home of our own?' she argued hotly. 'John Sullivan, you know well we don't have that type of money!'

'I admit it needs a whole heap of work, but Pat and I, and young Tim can do much of it, and Pat says the Emigrant Industrial Savings Bank might consider lending us the money.'

John sighed heavily as they inspected the inside of the ramshackle house on Mulberry Street. Its decrepit condition was far worse than Mary could have imagined.

'The floorboards are rotten and there is a big hole in the roof. The staircase has collapsed and half the windows are broken,' he admitted. 'I suppose that is why it is so cheap.'

Mary's heart sank with disappointment. A strong musty smell pervaded the property and one wall was running with damp. The yard was infested with cockroaches. It was a wreck of a place. No wonder it was lying abandoned and empty. She doubted there was any hope of salvaging such a place.

'However, there is more room than I expected,' declared John.

'I know that it will take months to make the building even habitable, but I believe it could make a decent home for us.'

'I'm not sure,' she admitted, 'that I'd ever want to live here.'

'Pat and Tim will give me a hand. With the right amount of work, I think that it will suit us and our needs. There is even a little room that you could use for your dressmaking.'

Mary could see how excited John was at the prospect of taking the old building and renovating it.

'It's an opportunity for us, Mary,' he pleaded. 'If the savings bank lends us the money, then it's a chance for us that we may not get again – to have a few rooms that we can call our own.'

Three months later, despite her reservations, John had borrowed from the Emigrant Industrial Savings Bank and the broken-down house was theirs.

Chapter 91

September 1854

MARY RAN HER FINGERS OVER THE NEW DRAPES, CUSHIONS AND counterpanes that she and Nora had made for the house on Mulberry Street. She and her daughters had scrubbed every last inch of the place. John, Tim and Jude had done much of the carpentry and repair work themselves. Pat too had helped with the rebuilding work and she was grateful not only for this but for everything he had done for them since they had first arrived in New York.

'Mam, look at our proper bedroom!' eleven-year-old Annie laughed as she jumped on the bed that she and Nora would share, while Tim and Jude were happy to no longer have to share with the girls. Instead, they would have the narrow room that overlooked the street.

The large kitchen was warm, with a fine new stove, and there was a smaller room that looked out on the yard that would serve as her sewing room. The top floor, with its two attic rooms, they would rent out.

She had never imagined that in time they would have a home of their own here in the city.

'I know that it's not in the best of neighbourhoods and still needs some repairs, but at least it is ours,' she said proudly.

'No one will ever take the roof from over the head of a Sullivan again,' pledged John firmly. 'Not while there is still life in us.'

'This place reminds me of a *meitheal* back home,' suggested Pat as he hammered some nails into the last step of the wooden staircase. 'Where everyone helps out, whatever way they can.'

Mary smiled, remembering when neighbours and friends gathered together to help bring in the harvest, mend a thatch roof, or repair a cottage damaged by gales or storms. Or even to give a hand to a young couple to build a simple cabin of their own. A *meitheal* always meant food and drink and hospitality.

Pat was right – so many had helped to turn this place into a home. She and John happily drew up a guest list for a housewarming, surprised by how many new friends they had made since they had first arrived in New York.

Catherine Ryan and her husband, James, insisted on bringing a large maple-glazed ham for the party, while Mena had made her a fine tablecloth and napkins. Lily Connolly and her new husband, Michael, brought along a porter cake, John's boss, Jerome Daly, arrived with a large bottle of *poitín*, and Sarah brought along a friend who worked with her.

'They never get proper home cooking, Auntie Mary,' confided Jude, who had invited two of the other apprentices who worked with him at the printer's.

Pat, much to their surprise, arrived, eyes shining, with a pretty, dark-haired young woman in tow.

'This is Ellen Cleary,' he said, introducing her. 'She works in the haberdashery shop near Broad Street.'

'I sell buttons and bows, mostly,' she said with a laugh.

'Welcome,' Mary said, smiling, delighted to meet the kind, blue-eyed girl who she suspected had stolen Pat's heart finally.

'I bought you this.' Pat laughed as he unwrapped a large slab of cooked corned beef in the kitchen. 'Try as I could, I couldn't find a hare to catch!'

'Mary and I thank you all for coming this evening and for your help in making this old house into a home,' John said to everyone, as all the guests cheered and clapped.

Smiling, they looked around them proudly at their family and friends, and everything this new life and hard work had brought them.

Later, with the house quiet and their friends gone, Mary and John sat out on the narrow back step together. The night was still warm and, as Mary gazed up at the starry sky and moon glowing over the city, she pondered the past. The calamity and sadness they had endured; the terrible hunger and crossing the wild Atlantic Ocean, where they had lost their beloved boy Con. She would never forget the ravaged streets of Skibbereen and all those dear to them who had been taken, and how she and John had been forced to leave their home place for ever.

Life had been so cruel, but somehow they had survived. Fate had surely brought them and their family here to this new life in New York.

Mary laid her face against John's. She still loved her husband as much as the day he had asked her to marry him. She had no idea where time would take them, but as long as they were together that was all that mattered to her.

They spoke little of the past. Instead, they looked to all that life here in this new land, America, would bring them and their children. Their heads and hearts were full of dreams and plans for the future, and the years together ahead of them . . .

ACKNOWLEDGEMENTS

I would like to thank the Skibbereen Heritage Centre where I did much of the research for the book.

Huge thanks are due to Philip O'Reagan of the centre for his invaluable assistance, his patience and kindness, and his insights into the life of Dr Dan Donovan and Skibbereen at the time of the Great Famine.

Thanks also to Margaret Murphy, Skibbereen Heritage Centre's genealogist, who helped me with Dr Donovan's family history.

Thanks to Father Patrick Hickey for meeting me. His book, *Famine in West Cork*, is a huge source of local information.

To the town of Skibbereen. Walking its streets and lanes, and seeing Abbeystrewery graveyard and the Old Steam Mill on Ilen Street where the soup kitchen once was, made it easier to write such a story.

Special thanks also to Professor Christine Kinealy for her absolute dedication to researching the period of the Great Hunger, and to the Great Hunger Institute at Quinnipiac University, Connecticut, US – a wonderful resource.

To Caroilin Callery of Strokestown Park House – the National Famine Museum – in Roscommon, for her huge commitment to creating even more awareness of the Great Irish Famine.

To my cousin Paddy Murphy for a piece of Skibbereen lore he shared with me.

My thanks go to my publishers, Transworld, and the team in both Ireland and London.

Special thanks to my editor, Fiona Murphy, for the enthusiasm and support she gave to me and the book during the long journey from page to print, and also to my London editor, Francesca Best. Huge thanks are also due to my copy-editor, Rebecca Wright, for her insightful suggestions and her patience working on such a big book, and to production editor Viv Thompson, Donna Hillyer, Josh Benn and Orla King.

To Fíodhna Ní Ghríofa in Dublin and Katie Cregg in London for their creative publicity campaigns, and huge thanks to Marianne Issa El-Khoury for her great cover design.

To my agent, Caroline Sheldon, for her constant support and friendship over the years, and to Rosie Buckman, my foreign rights agent.

To all the bookshops and booksellers, your support over the years is very much appreciated.

Thanks to all my writer friends for their encouragement and wisdom, especially Sarah Webb, Martina Devlin and Don Conroy.

My final thanks go to my wonderful family. My kind and patient husband, James, who has been by my side since I started this writing journey.

My children, Mandy, Laura, Fiona and James, and their partners, Michael Hearty, James Hodgins, Mike Fahy and Se Young An, and my grandchildren, Holly, Sam, Ben, Max, Evie, James, Alex and Harry.

ABOUT THE AUTHOR

Marita Conlon-McKenna is one of Ireland's favourite authors. Her books include the award-winning *Under the Hawthorn Tree*, which is set during Ireland's great famine. Widely translated and published, it is now considered an Irish classic. Her other books include bestsellers *The Magdalen* and *Rebel Sisters*.

She is a winner of the International Reading Association Award, USA and a former chairperson of Irish PEN.

Marita lives in Dublin with her husband and family.

MY SISTER, MY LOVE

Also by Joyce Carol Oates

MY SISTER, MY LOVE

Joyce Carol Oates

FOURTH ESTATE • London

First published in Great Britain in 2008 by
Fourth Estate
An imprint of HarperCollins*Publishers*
77–85 Fulham Palace Road
London W6 8JB
www.4thestate.co.uk

Originally published in the United States by Ecco

Visit our authors' blog: www.fifthestate.co.uk

1

A catalogue record for this book is
available from the British Library

ISBN 978-0-00-728509-9

Typeset in Filosofia

Printed in Great Britain by Clays Ltd, St Ives plc

Mixed Sources
Product group from well-managed
forests and other controlled sources
www.fsc.org Cert no. SW-COC-1806
© 1996 Forest Stewardship Council

FSC is a non-profit international organisation established to promote the
responsible management of the world's forests. Products carrying the FSC
label are independently certified to assure consumers that they come
from forests that are managed to meet the social, economic and
ecological needs of present and future generations.

Find out more about HarperCollins and the environment at
www.harpercollins.co.uk/green

IN MEMORY OF MY SISTER BLISS
(1991–1997)

AUTHOR'S NOTE/DISCLAIMER

Though *My Sister, My Love: The Intimate Story of Skyler Rampike* has its genesis in a notorious American "true crime mystery" of the late twentieth century, it is a work of the imagination solely and lays no claim to representing actual persons, places, or historical events. This includes all characters in the Rampike family, their legal counsel, and their friends. Nor is its depiction of "Tabloid Hell" intended to be a literal depiction of media response to the crime.

Despair is a sickness of the spirit, of the self, and accordingly can take three forms: in despair not to be conscious of having a self; in despair not to will to be oneself; in despair to will to be oneself.

SØREN KIERKEGAARD
The Sickness unto Death
(translated by Howard V. and Edna H. Hong)

The death of a beautiful girl-child of no more than ten years of age is, unquestionably, the most poetical topic in the world.

E. A. PYM
"The Aesthetics of Composition," 1846

CONTENTS

I

Red-Ink Heart

You do not belong here

MY SISTER, MY LOVE

SKYLER HELP ME   **SKYLER I AM SO LONELY IN THIS PLACE SKYLER I AM**
so afraid   *I hurt so Skyler*   *you won't leave me in this terrible place*
will you   *Skyler?*
   Nine years, ten months, five days.
   This child-voice in my head.

"SURVIVOR"

DYSFUNCTIONAL FAMILIES ARE ALL ALIKE. DITTO "SURVIVORS."
Me, I'm the "surviving" child of an infamous American family but probably after almost ten years you won't remember me: Skyler.

It *is* a catchy name isn't it? *Skyler: sky.*

A name specifically chosen by my father, who'd expected great things from me, as his firstborn child, and male.

A name, my father Bix Rampike believed, to set its bearer apart from the merely commonplace.

My last name—"Rampike"—has caused your eyelids to flutter, right? *Ram-pike.* Of which, unless you're willfully obtuse, or pretending to be "above it all" (i.e., the ravaged earth of tabloid America), or mentally impaired, or really young, you've certainly heard.

Rampike? That family? The little girl skater, the one who was . . .

And whoever did it, never . . .

The parents, or a sex maniac, or . . .

Somewhere in New Jersey, years ago, has to be at least a decade . . .

Which is why—at last!—I've made myself begin whatever this will be, some kind of personal document—a "unique personal document"—not a mere memoir but (maybe) a confession. (Since in some quarters Skyler Rampike is a *murder suspect* you'd think that I have plenty to confess, wouldn't you?) Fittingly, this document will not be chronological/linear but will follow a pathway of free association organized by an unswerving (if undetectable) interior logic: unliterary, unpretentious, disarmingly crude-amateur, guilt-ridden, appropriate to the "survivor" who abandoned his six-year-old sister to her "fate" sometime in the "wee hours" of

January 29, 1997, in our home in Fair Hills, New Jersey. *Yes I am that Rampike.*

The older brother of the most famous six-year-old in the history of the United States if not all of North America if not all of the world for consider: how many six-year-olds you've ever heard of, girl or boy, American or otherwise, have such name and face "recognition" as Bliss Rampike; how many have more than 500,000 citations on the Internet; and how many are immortalized by more than three hundred Web sites/home pages/blogs maintained by loyal/crazed cultists? These are facts.

Irony is, this celebrity, which the parents of virtually every six-year-old in the country would die for, came to my sister only posthumously.

As for me, Skyler? Anonymous and forgettable as a soap bubble. O.K.: a weird-looking soap bubble. If you've followed the Bliss Rampike case, most likely you've only glimpsed Skyler in passing. The brother has been ignored in your haste to ogle, with prim-disapproving frowns, the prurient documents posted on the Internet, pirated Rampike family photos, illicitly acquired crime-scene photos and morgue photos and autopsy reports in addition to a seemingly inexhaustible supply of video footage of Bliss Rampike at the peak of her brief-but-dazzling career as the "youngest-ever" Little Miss Jersey Ice Princess 1996, skating to triumph on the cold-glittering ice rink of the Newark War Memorial Center. How "like an angel" in a strawberry-colored satin-and-sequin skating costume with a perky tulle skirt and white lace panties peeking out from beneath and tiny sparks—"stardust"—in the beautiful little girl's ringleted blond hair as in her widened moist eyes, you feel your heart clench watching her, the small child alone on the ice, a chill lunar landscape glittering beneath her flashing skate blades, ah! there's a leap that brings a collective gasp from the audience, there's a spin on two skates, and now a spin on a single skate, these are tricky maneuvers even for older, champion skaters, these are precisely timed maneuvers in which the slightest hesitation or faltering or wincing-with-pain would be disastrous, and though you have seen this footage numberless times (if your misfortune is to be me, Skyler Rampike, that is), yet you break out in the proverbial cold sweat staring at the little girl on the ice, praying that she won't slip and fall on the ice . . . But Bliss's score will be posted at 5.9 out of a possible 6.

And all this to the soft-rock disco beat of the 1980s, "Do What Feels Right."

(ANY FELLOW/SISTER SUFFERERS OF R.C.S.* AMONG MY READERS? IF SO, you will sympathize with my helpless need to repeat, re-view, and re-vise certain episodes from my past/my sister's past *ad nauseam*.)

AT THE FRENZIED HEIGHT OF MY FAMILY'S FAME/INFAMY IN THE APPROXI-mate years 1997–1999, you could hardly avoid seeing heartrending pho-tographs of the "prodigy" girl skater who'd been murdered in her own home in an affluent New Jersey community less than eighty miles west of the George Washington Bridge. You could hardly avoid seeing photo-graphs of the little girl with her family, particularly the media favorite taken just before Christmas 1996 of the Rampikes seated before the ten-foot extravagantly decorated fir tree in the living room of their Fair Hills, New Jersey, "part-restored" Colonial: broad-shouldered good-looking Bruce "Bix" Rampike, who is Bliss's daddy; strikingly dressed, eagerly smiling Betsey Rampike, who is Bliss's mummy; little Bliss in a crimson velvet frock trimmed in white (ermine) fur, with the glittery Jersey Ice Princess tiara on her small head, white eyelet stockings and shiny black patent-leather ballerina flats and that famous sweet-shy-angel smile, between Daddy and Mummy and each is clasping Bliss firmly in the crook of an arm;† and, at the edge of the family portrait, in a vulnerable position to be handily cropped from the photo, the older, talentless brother Skyler.

By "older" I mean nine, in December 1996. Three years older than Bliss.

And now, astonishingly, I am thirteen years older than Bliss was

---

* *"Repetitive Compulsion Syndrome." A self-explanatory condition only just recently recognized by the American Association of Mental Health Practitioners.*

† *If you look closely at this much-downloaded photo, with a magnifying glass, and the mono-maniacal scrupulousness required of a Bliss Rampike cultist, you will see that Bix Rampike, "Daddy," has also cupped his left hand beneath Bliss's foot, casually it seems.*

when she died. *Skyler? what has happened to you? Skyler what terrible thing has happened to you   too?*

I don't think I will describe what I look like, just yet. An "invisible narrator" sounds like a good idea to me.

In the Christmas 1996 photograph of the Rampikes *en famille*—which was subsequently printed up as a Christmas card and was to be used by Mummy as the Rampikes' official family photo replacing an earlier, out-dated family photo taken before my sister was crowned Little Miss Jersey Ice Princess 1996—I am a runty little kid with a smile so eager it looks as if it had been sliced by a knife. In response to the photographer's tedious reiterated command *Smile please! And again—smile please!* the runty little kid is smiling as if his jaw has become unhinged. I guess—false modesty aside—I've been told—I was "cute"—"adorable"—even "a little gentleman"— but no one called me "angelic"—still less "magically photogenic" like my sister, nor am I "photogenic" here. No Christmas outfit for me! No silver tiara! God knows what rumpled shirt, clip-on tie, itchy woollen blazer and trousers Mummy threw together for me to wear after having spent an anx-ious hour making up Bliss's face which required making up in order to ex-ude that air of china-doll beauty, fragility, and innocence for which Bliss Rampike had come to be known, and primping Bliss's overly fine, limp hair in a cascade of ringlets to set off the tiara, subsequently dressing, undress-ing, and dressing her, not to mention the yet more anxious minutes Mummy was obliged to spend on herself in order to exude the glamorous/poised/yet warmly maternal look Betsey Rampike desired.* Hastily running a hair-brush through my hair, stooping to peer into my evasive eyes, in a lowered voice begging *Skyler please darling for Mummy's sake try not to twitch and make those awful faces! Try to look happy for Mummy's sake this is Christmas at the Rampikes and Daddy is back with us and we want the world to see how proud we are of Bliss and what a beautiful happy family we are.*

---

* *In this photograph, Betsey Rampike is only thirty-three years old but looks older, not so much in her face (which is a fleshy-Renoir girl's face with flushed cheeks) as in her body. As Mummy con-fided in Skyler in the early years before Bliss came into their lives like a comet, she'd always "bat-tled" a "weight issue." In these years Mummy wore her brunette hair in a sleek hairdressy "bouffant" style out of a fear that her head would be perceived as "too small" for her body. And when her hair began to streak with gray, Mummy had it dyed at once. But this came later.*

I tried, for Mummy's sake. You will see how hard I tried.

You couldn't see that I was crippled, I mean not in a still shot like this, but in such festive family photographs I look as if I might be crippled or deformed, hunched at the edge of the frame as if about to fall out. You feel an impulse to peer closely at me, to see if there might be telltale braces on my legs, or maybe I am cringing in a child-sized wheelchair but *I am not.*

Sure, I had "physical" problems. "Mental" too. And I was "medicated" as a child. (As who in Fair Hills, New Jersey, was not?)

All that you remember of Skyler Rampike, assuming that you remember me at all, is a prime-time television interview in which I didn't appear. This, the notorious interview with high-profile TV personality B____ W____ which was broadcast several months after my sister's death at a time when, following the advice of their lawyers, my parents were "unavailable" for interviews with Fair Hills police. Canny Ms. W____ greeted Bix and Betsey Rampike with a show of warmth and sympathy for "your tragic loss" then proceeded to confront them with the "fact" that no evidence had ever been found at the scene of my sister's death to suggest that anyone outside the Rampike family, any intruder or "abductor," had killed their daughter: "How do you explain this?" Both my parents were said to have reacted with shock at such a question, for indeed B____ W____ had seemed so friendly initially; and before my father could compose himself to speak, my mother Betsey Rampike smiled bravely, saying, "All that we can 'explain' is that God has put our faith to the test, and we will not fail that test. A stranger came into our lives and took our darling Bliss from us—that is all we know, Ms. W____! For I did not murder Bliss, and my husband did not murder Bliss, and"—pausing with a quick sharp frown between her eyebrows, a becoming flush in her cheeks—"our son Skyler did not murder Bliss." And B____ W____ exclaimed, " 'Your son Skyler'—why, the boy is only nine years old, Mrs. Rampike," and my mother said, quickly, "Well, he didn't anyway."

STILL, I LOVED HER. I LOVED THEM BOTH. IT WAS TERRIBLE. IS.

*

*Black hole into which the despairing "memoirist" seems to have disappeared for an unaccountable period of time, approximately forty-eight hours of catatonic paralysis and amnesia irretrievable and forever lost to oblivion.

WHO I AM, AND WHY I AM WHO I AM I

WISH THIS WAS AN "INSPIRATIONAL TEXT"—BUT IT ISN'T.
Americans crave knowledge of *how-to*; all I can offer is a firsthand account of *how-not-to*. (My original title for this document was *Not All Survive: The Unexpurgated Story of Skyler Rampike*. Alternate title: *Down the Drain with Skyler Rampike*.) No uplifting Christian tale of sin—suffering—enlightenment—redemption; the kind of "searing"—"heartrending"—"genuinely transforming" memoir featured on TV talk shows in the fleshy-female torpor of late-afternoon TV before the male-sobriety of Evening News.

WHAT I BELIEVE *IN*:
    sin (original & derivative)
    evil (Holocaust-dimension & petty/crummy/banal)
    crime/criminal acts (as defined by law)
    "depraved indifference to human life" (ditto)

And I believe in redemption/forgiveness. For you others, if not for me.
The only person whose forgiveness can "redeem" me will have been dead, as of midnight tonight, nine years, ten months, and sixteen days.
Skyler   where are you Skyler please   help me
The tenth anniversary of my sister's death is fast approaching. Which is the occasion for this document. I am squatting on the railroad tracks as the locomotive rushes toward me. I am staring into the blinding headlights as into a vision of God hypnotized/paralyzed/unable to move away.

Skyler it's so dark in here
Skyler don't leave me   alone here
Skyler would you die   in my place?
And that is the crucial question, isn't it? *Would you die in my place.*

Reader, ask yourself: is there anyone for whom you would give up your life? Not a (mere) kidney transplant but a heart transplant? To save a *loved one*'s life?

CHECK HERE:

☐ Would give up life unhesitatingly for any *loved one*

☐ Would give up life hesitatingly for any *loved one*

☐ Would give up life for any *loved one* bearing my DNA

☐ Would give up life for—maybe—one or two very special *loved ones* bearing my DNA

☐ Would give up life for only just one very special *loved one* bearing my DNA

☐ Sorry, *loved ones*: my own life is just too precious

(This is a confidential survey, don't be alarmed! You have only to check the appropriate box, tear out the incriminating page and dispose of it and who's to know the sobering truth you've discovered about yourself?)

(What a strange attraction I am feeling, to terminating this document prematurely: dousing myself in kerosene, lighting a match. A sanitizing death with ritual overtones that is also plenty showy/great filler for Tabloid TV.)

(We Rampikes! Veterans of Tabloid Hell who know which buttons to press.)

(Reader, don't worry: I may be a self-centered kid but I am not a cruel kid wishing to set an entire house ablaze and burn up others in my funeral pyre, certainly I would take care to "incinerate"—"immolate"— myself in an outdoor setting. Preferably a bleakly romantic scene beside the moody Raritan River that isn't too far to limp.) (Frankly yes, I would prefer a fiery-death scene on a high bank of the more picturesque Hudson River majestic and awe-inspiring beneath a storm-toss'd wintry sky, but the Hudson River is too damned far away, I'd have to borrow someone's car.) (More practical: behind this rundown residence at the southern edge of the sprawling Rutgers campus there is an alley of trash cans, overflowing Dumpsters, a whirlygig—whirligig?—of litter as in a pastiche of outtakes from a David Lynch film laced with a pungent smell of drains, yet—so wonderfully!—not a quarter-mile away on Livingstone Avenue there looms the bravely gleaming faux-gold cross of the New Canaan Evangelical Church of Christ Risen where each Sunday morning and each Wednesday evening and at other, uncharted times fervent Christians come to worship their elusive God and His Only Begotten Son. In this alley, the faux-gold cross of an unfathomable Christian sect suggestively in view, what more appropriate setting for Skyler Rampike to erase himself from history, as his sister Bliss was erased nearly a decade before?)

LONGTIME SUSPECT IN SISTER'S DEATH IMMOLATES SELF IN NEW BRUNSWICK, BLISS RAMPIKE "COLD CASE" OF 1997 REOPENED?

WHO I AM, AND WHY I AM WHO I AM II

NIGHTS ARE HARD. "EARLY HOURS" OF THE NIGHT BETWEEN 1 A.M AND 4:30
A.M. which was when the medical examiner of Morris County Dr. Virgil
Elyse determined that my six-year-old sister Bliss died of "blunt force
head trauma" though her body would not be found until nearly 8:30 A.M.
and the "cooling" of the body was impeded by the warmth of the place
(furnace room) in which the body was found. And so during those "early
morning" hours at least on unmedicated nights the "longtime suspect"
isn't able to sleep nor do I try to sleep.

Amateurs don't know how to tell stories, even their own life-stories
brimming like tears in their brown-doggy eyes. I acknowledge this, for my
instinct is to spew everything out immediately, and keep nothing back,
except writing is *linear* and *diachronical* meaning that, if you cast down
your first card X, this first card X has displaced all other possible cards—Y,
Z, A, B etcetera. If I reveal that I am nineteen years old—nineteen going on
ninety!—this blocks out the possibly more crucial fact that since my sister's
death in the "early hours" of January 29, 1997, there has never been any
murderer indicted, still less prosecuted and tried; the notorious case remains "open"—"unsolved"—in the trendy parlance of our time, "cold." And
why? Despite more than thirty thousand pages of police (Fair Hills PD,
Morris County Sheriff, New Jersey State Police) and FBI documents, medical reports, and forensics reports? Reader, you will see why.

Not that I have read these reports. Much of the material is classified
but even the available material is off-limits to me. For I intend to approach this subject from the inside purely, as one who lived through it.
Trust me! I swear, I will tell only the truth *as I have lived it.*

• • •

SKYLER?   HELP ME   PLEASE

Too late for already Bliss has been awakened in her bed. Someone has entered her room in stealth. The Mother Goose lamp on the bedside table is on, dim-lit. Just enough light to navigate by. Once this has begun, it cannot be stopped.

Cannot be stopped by Skyler who was sleeping in his bed at this time. Little punk-sized kid but nine years old.

Skyler who remains nine years old.

Already her small protesting mouth has been taped shut so that she can't scream. Already her small wrists and ankles have been bound with duct tape so that she can't struggle. Such a small child weighing forty-three pounds (as Dr. Elyse would inform us) she has been wrapped in a (pink cashmere) blanket removed from her bed, in haste she is being carried along a darkened corridor—past her brother Skyler's room—to a darkened stairway and down this stairway to a yet darker stairs at the rear of the house into the basement as she struggles to free herself, and to breathe, desperate to breathe, a wild struggling animal desperate to breathe, heart beating frantically you could feel like a small fist *Skyler help   help me!* but Skyler will not help because Skyler is sleeping in his bed in his room oblivious of his sister's struggle so deep/dreamless/leaden a sleep you would think (possibly) the nine-year-old had been drugged for his frightened mother will have a difficult time waking him hours later and now it has been nine years, ten months, and twenty days and still the accursèd child has not fully wakened.

"A VERY BRAVE LITTLE GIRL"

. . . AND NOW OUR NEXT LITTLE CONTENDER FOR MISS ATLANTIC CITY ICE *Capades 1995 here at the fan-tas-tic new Trump Hotel & Casino, Atlantic City, New Jersey, ladiez 'n' gentlemen here is a little-girl skater who is truly little no word but exquisite! angelic! fan-tas-tic! there is a gasp from the audience what a luscious sight: platinum-blond cotton-candy hair cascading in curls   she's wearing a black-lace Spanish veil mantilla d'you call it?   qui-ite a dra-matic costume for a five-year-old   one of the most eye-catching of this fan-tas-tic evening   the audience is clearly appreciative!   this little skater is a real pro   left shoulder daringly bared   tight black-sequined bodice   black taffeta skirt very very short   black lace matching panties peeking out beneath   black eyelet stockings and sexy black leather high-top skates like boots   with crimson appliqué roses!   Look at those skate-blades flash   this little girl is skating/ dancing to the pulse-quickening Latin beat "Begin the Beguine"   applause for MISS BLISS RAMPIKE of Fair Hills, New Jersey   Miss Tots-on-Ice Debutante Winner 1994   Tiny Miss StarSkate 1995   runner-up last-month's Miss New England Figure Skating Challenge 1995   what skating form, ladiez 'n' gentlemen!   look at those graceful glides Miss Bliss is pos-itively angelic   the crowd adores her   ah! a near-perfect spin   triple figure eights and is it   a jump spin?   and Miss Bliss Rampike has executed the tricky maneuver   bravely   this might be the highlight so far of our evening here at Trump Hotel & Casi-no   the audience is at the edge of their seats   fierce competition for the gold trophy, $5,000 prize, photo and résumé on all Trump Hotel & Casino*

promotional materials for a solid year   The Don himself is rumored to be
in the audience   in-cog-nit-o   could be, ladiez 'n' gentlemen we
have here a future Olympic gold medalist a future Sonja Henie (winner of ten
world titles: Sonja Henie) ooops spoke too soon did I   just a wee fal-
ter   a moment's hesitation   quickly the skater has recovered from
wobbling now spinning on two skates without   wobbling   now a
traveling spin   hold your breath ladiez 'n' gentlemen this can
be   tricky   judges are taking note   judges are im-
pressed   judges will factor in the difficulty of these maneuvers in their
scoring   now   is it?   a flying spin   such a sweet
smile!   but the mantilla seems to be slipping from Bliss's head   uh-
oh looks like a—jump spin?—executed just a little uncertainly   is Bliss fa-
voring her left ankle?   rumors of a previous injury to that ankle   this
is a brave little girl   listen to that applause   Miss Bliss Rampike
along with incredible Miss Kiki Chang last year's Trump Hotel & Casino Skating
Capades champ (Junior Division) are clearly the audience's favorites so far this
evening   uh-oh!   gosh-darn mantilla is on the ice let's hope Bliss's
skates don't get tangled in the gosh-darn thing   now a flying spin no hes-
itating   wincing when she lands on her left skate   throbbing beat
of "Begin the Beguine" pulses ever higher, louder   a second flying leap,
oops! that was a shame   this is a brave little girl Miss Bliss Rampike has
recovered her poise not a quitter   tears spilling down those doll-cheeks
she is not a quitter   the audience is hushed   the audience is
deeply moved   the audience has erupted into applause   the audi-
ence is on its feet   let's hope The Don is truly among us tonight in-cog-
nit-o or otherwise   a fan-tas-tic performance let's have a final round of
applause for Miss Bliss Rampike five years old of Fair Hills, New Jersey   a
very brave little girl with a very big future

RED-INK HEART

MAKE ME A LITTLE RED HEART   **SKYLER?**   **MAKE ME A LITTLE**
RED HEART *like yours Skyler?*   *please*

In two days Bliss would be seven years old. And I was nine years old. At bedtime of January 28, 1997.

Skyler please   *Mummy won't know*

Mummy frowned at the little red-ink tattoos that were my specialty at this time.* It wasn't unreasonable of Mummy, like any Mummy, especially any Fair Hills, New Jersey (where spotless surfaces, high-glisten polish, "understated" expense were the norm), Mummy to object to ink-tattoos on her children's bodies that were "vulgar" and "messy" and "hard to scrub off." So, inking a tiny red heart on the palm of Bliss's left hand, to match one of my own, had to be done in secret, as in secret I tattooed tiny figures on my own hands, and in other less visible parts of my body (armpits, belly, pinched little belly button).

Secrets! So many.

Daddy was away. Ever more, Daddy was away: Singapore, Tokyo, Bangkok, Sydney—or maybe only just New York City where he had an

---

* *Must've been, already by the age of nine Skyler was in the thrall of "ritualistic"—"obsessive-compulsive"—behavior, especially in regard to his puny little male body. Not just tiny valentine-hearts the budding psychopath inked on his skin but iridescent-purple snakes with bared fangs, shiny black spiders and scorpions, blood-dripping daggers, grinning skulls and even, in shameless imitation of a posse of older boys at Fair Hills Day School, Nazi swastikas. (How tricky it is, to "tattoo" a fingernail-sized swastika in black ballpoint ink, in some hidden part of your kiddie-body! Never could get the swastika right.) How horrified Mummy would have been, and how disgusted Daddy would have been!—but they never knew.*

apartment. Or, so mysteriously, Daddy was somewhere closer, yet Daddy was *away*.

We were not to speak about Daddy at such times, was the message in Mummy's fierce eyes. We were not to ask about Daddy.

And yet: Daddy might suddenly arrive home. As in a Disney movie of fantastic transformations and reversals there might come Daddy bounding up the stairs just in time to "tuck" little Skyler and little Bliss in their beds; there might come rueful-Daddy, beaming-happy-Daddy, teary-eyed-with-love-Daddy, and (maybe! these were the happiest times) Daddy and Mummy clasping hands and Mummy bravely smiling as if Daddy had not ever been away; and Mummy had not ever locked herself in her bathroom sobbing and muttering to herself and refusing to answer the door upon which Skyler shyly knocked: "Mum-*my*?"

Skyler   sometimes I feel so bad

Nobody loves me Skyler   do you love me   Skyler?

In the Rampike household in those crucial years there were two kinds of time: when Bliss was skating, and when Bliss was not-skating. When Bliss was skating there was excitement in the air like static electricity before a storm and when Bliss was not-skating—if she'd "hurt herself" for instance, or had been sidelined by "phantom pain"—there was a feeling of dread in the air like static electricity before a storm.

And so always there was: static electricity before a storm!

The red-ink heart would protect her, Bliss believed.

Sky-ler please? Mummy won't know

Mummy had trained Bliss to open her cobalt-blue eyes wide and to smile in a certain way not to "grin"—not to "grimace"—but to smile shyly, prettily. Smile just enough to show her beautiful pearly teeth. *Make me a little red heart like yours Skyler please?*

In our senior physics class at Basking Ridge we were wittily told by our instructor that Time is

—**finite**; or,

—**infinite**; or,

—**"flowing," and bearing us with it**; or,

—"static": a fourth dimension in which everything that will ever happen has already happened and continues to happen and could not have not happened and how then could any of it have been prevented?

The career began with Tots-on-Ice, Meadowlands, Valentine's Day 1994. The career would end with Hershey's Kisses Girls' Ice-Skating Festival, Hershey, Pennsylvania, January 11, 1997.

Skyler please   *a red-ink heart*   and so I grabbed my sister's moist little hand and inked into her palm a little red heart to match my own

"SEXY"—"SEDUCTIVE"—"MYSTERIOUS"

MORE OF *ME*? YOU'D LIKE TO "SEE" ME?

I suppose I don't blame you. Even the reader who hasn't bought this book but is only skimming it—please, not too rapidly!—in a bookstore aisle has a right to "see" whoever the hell it is who's addressing him/her. For obviously the advantage for most writers is that no one sees them. The writer is invisible, which confers power.

First thing you'd notice about Skyler Rampike, for instance limping along Livingstone Avenue, which intersects with Pitts Street, is he's a freaky kid.

The hair, especially.

After Bliss's death, my wavy "fawn-colored" hair began to fall out in clumps. Soon my hard little head was bald, my zombie-eyes were stark and staring. Cancer victim? Chemo? Kiddie-leukemia? After about a year hair began to grow back but it was the weird metallic-zinc color it is now that looks as if it might be radioactive, and glow in the dark; no longer wavy fine little-boy hair but coarse and thick like that perverse species of weed said to thrive in toxic soil. Often I'm mistaken for an older guy and/or the bearer of a particularly repulsive disease (leprosy, AIDS). Through school it was my teachers' strategy to sort of not-see me in the classroom and more recently, now I'm an "older" adolescent grown scrawny-tall people are wary of me on the street.

This zinc-hair is so stiff and bristly, it's like sprouting quills from my head. Mostly I wear it shaved close to the skull. (A bony, bumpy skull! And my scalp reddened from rashes provoked by scratching.) Sometimes I've worn the hair in a funky little pigtail at the nape of my neck with the sides of my head shaved Nazi-style, and that gets people's attention. So maybe, though I'm humble in spirit, yearning to be as a little child, at the same time I'm an arrogant son of a bitch not unlike my father Bruce "Bix" Rampike except not Daddy's size and lacking Daddy's so-called charisma.

(Do you hate the word "charisma" as much as I do? Yet to find a viable synonym isn't easy.)

The most astonishing thing is, "Skyler Rampike" with his zinc-quill hair in or out of a funky pigtail has proved attractive to certain sicko individuals both female and male. Mummy had begged me to allow her to dye my hair back to its former color—"Skyler, if Bliss saw you now, so changed, so ravaged-looking, she wouldn't recognize you"—but I told her *no*.

For, if you believed in God, you could say that God has sent my zinc-hair to me as a sign.

Mummy stared at me not daring to touch me not daring to ask *A sign of what, Skyler?*—for fear that I would say *A sign that I am damned, Mummy. The mark of Satan on your little man's head.*

Another thing you'd notice is that freaky-Skyler walks with a limp, all that remains of his child-prodigy-gymnast days (of which more later, for those readers with a morbid interest in the just punishments of those who dare to "go for the gold"). Some days this limp is scarcely discernible to the naked eye but at other times there's no disguising the limp, on bone-chilling winter days I walk with a cane dragging my stiff (right) leg throbbing with pain like old childhood memories. For years it was quite a risible sight—"risible" being a fancy word for "hilarious"—to the crude, cruel eyes of prepubescents, when, a runty prepubescent himself, Skyler Rampike limped along with a dwarf-cane, like an antic three-legged insect. (Now, you should see me limp along with a man-sized cane swiftly and belligerently and betraying little awareness of alarmed fellow pedestrians forced to leap out of my way; though, conversely, or perversely, when crossing a street with or against traffic, if I'm walking with my cane I take my own damned sweet time to cross, you bet. *Dare to run me over, you bastards!*)

As anxious Mummy foresaw, by the time I was eleven I'd more or less obliterated the "cute"—"adorable"—little-boy-face of the nine-year-old Skyler, by compulsively grinning/grimacing and making what Mummy called "pain faces." By tenth grade, in prep school, my face had become a boy's face bizarrely overlaid with a mask of snarls like tree roots. Pastor Bob has said *Skyler your soul shines in your eyes, you can never hide your soul* but is this true?

Yet—to my astonishment!—and disgust!—there are plenty of sickos out there in cyberspace who claim to find Skyler Rampike attractive—"sexy"—"seductive"—"mysterious"—and who feature him on lurid Web sites in which images of my ravaged face and Nazi-zinc hair are featured above such captions as

SKYLER RAMPIKE "SURVIVING" OLDER BROTHER OF MURDERED ICE PRINCESS BLISS RAMPIKE

SOMETHING BAD*

SKYLER HELP ME SOMETHING BAD IS   IN MY BED

---

* *This enigmatic little chapter is all that remains of dozens of scribbled pages written over the last seventy-two hours. For I was mistaken the other day, not a "panic attack" but a full-fledged "manic attack" overcame me now that I am permanently off psychotropic drugs.*

FOE PAWS

IN THE INTERESTS OF FULL DISCLOSURE IT MUST BE REVEALED: SKYLER HAS broken his Sobriety Pledge.

That's to say, Skyler's most recent Sobriety Pledge.

After writing the preceding chapter, I caved. Sure it was a measly little chapter and sure, any one of you could have tossed it off in a few hours, yet, for Skyler, it was gut-twisting/nerve-wracking/sick-making and so Skyler caved, on Day 59. Having endured fifty-nine miserable days, in the very early hours of the sixtieth day, Skyler "relapsed" with some suspicious-looking hydrocodone (generic for Vicodin) scored from some hip-hop black guys of my acquaintance.

As Daddy used to say with sheepish-shit-eating-Daddy smile *Forgive me my foe paws as you'd wish to be forgiven yours, hey?*

A VERY LONG TIME SINCE I WAS NINE YEARS OLD. AND THEY SENT ME AWAY when Bliss was found, and I never saw my sister again, and my hair fell out in handfuls, and when it grew back in, it grew in wrong. And something in my brain is wrong.

GURNEY

IN THE BEGINNING—LONG AGO!—THERE WASN'T BLISS.

This is my (proposed) beginning. I have written this sentence numerous times. I have written this sentence on several sheets of paper hoping to "jump-start" a second sentence, and, in time, a third, but so far, so far only this single sentence has emerged. But I am Sober again now, and I will remain Sober. I swear.

Though Pastor Bob has suggested that it might be easier to begin *in medias race** and not at the beginning since there is something terrifying about beginnings as about the numeral (if it is a numeral, strictly speaking) zero.

A child can't comprehend zero. As a child can't comprehend the vast Dumpster of time before he/she was born.

I am Sober again, did I record this fact? Six capsules of hydrocodone ("Warning: May cause dizziness, heart palpitations, liver failure") in a gesture of bravado I flushed down the toilet like a character on TV!

(Except, the damn toilet, shared by several of us up here on the third floor, doesn't truly flush. The capsules swirled 'round and 'round teasingly but did not go down and for all I know, and believe me, dear reader, you don't want to know either, one of my fellow tenants fished them out for his own purposes.)

Just chance, a lone newspaper page blown underfoot, in the damp-gritty

---

**Classy Latin phrase for "in the middle"—"midst"—of action. In medias race is how most of us live our blinkered, stumbling, clueless lives not knowing where the hell we're going, nor even where the hell we've been.*

grass up the block. A vacant lot gone to rubble and weeds and every kind of litter including a section of page twenty-two of the Newark *Star-Ledger*, December 2, 2006, squinting up at me with a ghoulish smile was Dr. Virgil Elyse.

Not that I knew what the longtime medical examiner of Morris County (which is where we lived, in Fair Hills; New Brunswick is in Middlesex County) looked like. I never did.

Dr. Elyse had dissected, as affably he remarked to an interviewer on the occasion of his retirement (at age sixty-eight), "somewhere in the neighborhood of twelve thousand, six hundred corpses" in his forty-three-year career. Quickly I scanned the blurred columns of newsprint to see the name *Rampike* leap out at me as I knew it would, and the name *Bliss*, and quickly I kicked the newspaper away.

But not before seeing *most famous case. Most controversial.*

Though I had not ever seen Dr. Elyse with his glittery pinch-ney (?) eyeglasses before yet it seemed to me in that instant that yes I had seen him. In that confused interlude after my sister's death when little Skyler was heavily medicated and slept much of the day waking only agitatedly at night between the hours of 1 A.M. and 4 A.M. lying paralyzed in his bed seeing Dr. Elyse approach Skyler's bed which had become a gurney as the air in his bedroom had become the chill formaldehyde air of the Morris County Morgue. There came Dr. Elyse (at the elder Rampikes' bidding?) in rubber-soled shoes with a squeak, in soiled white butcher's apron tied over a civilian suit, wearing those rimless pinch-ney glasses that magnified his eyes like a fly's as horribly he lifted lifted a hacksaw to saw open Skyler's skull with the intention of deftly running a soldering iron through his brain (at the elder Rampikes' bidding?). Which is why ever after Skyler has trouble remembering.

And trouble with math! Where previously, though dyslexic as hell, he had not.

In rehab the meth-heads said: Nothing like crystal meth! Crystal meth is the high every other drug is trying to achieve but can't.

So why are you here, Skyler wanted to ask. If the high is that terrific. If the high is worth dying for, why'd anyone want to live?

Skyler has no choice, Skyler has to live. One day, Skyler has to reveal all he knows of his sister Bliss's life/death. It is Skyler Rampike's responsibility.

(Did I note that, when Skyler was busted and sent into rehab, he weighed 139 pounds, five-feet-eleven in his bare feet? His hair was shaved close to his skull and zinc-quills had begun to grow back in rash-like clusters. Even the meth-heads tattooed in flaming skulls and black-widow spiders steered clear of Skyler Rampike.)

Truth is: I'm scared of crystal meth. It's a class thing.

Fair Hills, New Jersey, is a long way from Jersey City, New Jersey.

Mostly, we don't snort, sniff, inject. Needles scare the hell out of us. We "take pills" just like our moms do.

Just "legal" drugs in the suburbs: the brands you can buy in drugstores.

Even if you acquire them on the street, still these are "legal" drugs. Some doctor, somewhere, licensed M.D., he'd have prescribed them for you, or she. It's a higher class of criminal.

Pastor Bob said: Drugs are a crutch, son. You know that.

Told Pastor Bob: Why'd I need a crutch, I use a cane.

Told Pastor Bob none of his business, was it?

Told Pastor Bob you don't know me. Stop looking at me.

Told Pastor Bob go away, man.

Pastor Bob paid no heed. Pastor Bob said: That suffering in your face, son. Immediately I saw. Know what I saw, son? In your face?

Told Pastor Bob noooo. Told Pastor Bob don't want to know.

Pastor Bob said: In your face is Christly suffering, son. In one young as you.

Told Pastor Bob: Bullshit.

Pastor Bob said: Hear your voice, son? The fear in it.

Told Pastor Bob: Fear and trembling? Sickness unto death?

Told Pastor Bob: It's old. It's been done. Nobody believes that bullshit.

Pastor Bob said: You must unburden your soul, son. You must tell your story.

Told Pastor Bob hell I'm dyslexic. Or something.

Pastor Bob said: Dictate your story to me, son. The story of your lost sister Bliss. In your living voice, son. We can begin today.

Told Pastor Bob there is no "your story." Noooo.

Told Pastor Bob he had to be crazy. A religious lunatic like who's it—"Kirky-gard." Bullshit nobody believes except pathetic assholes with I.Q.'s drooping around their ankles. You fat fuck Pastor Bob, I said. Don't touch me.

Calmly Pastor Bob said: Your sister Bliss is in heaven, son. Yet even in heaven our loved ones suffer, sometimes. If we are unhappy, they suffer. You must put your sister's soul at rest, son. You know that.

Told Pastor Bob he wasn't hearing me, nobody can ask such things of me, nobody in all the world has dared ask such things of me, *nobody not ever!*—and Pastor Bob winced at the sick-Christ fury in my face but clasped me in his beefy big arms till I quieted saying: Son, you are mistaken. Trust me.*

---

* *Hell, I know: I'm wincing, too. Such clumsily executed scenes are painful to read, yet more painful to write. And yet more painful to have lived . . . As an amateur writer who has lived a mostly amateur life, I wish that this document contained more elegantly turned passages, as I wish that it contained a more refined* dramatis personie *[sic?] but in confessional documents you must work with what you have.*

WHAT HAVE YOU DONE

SKYLER   WAKE UP

Not his sister but his mother is pulling at him, in the confusion of that long-ago morning that was no morning but inky-black night as at the bottom of the sea.

Mummy with disheveled hair, agitated eyes. Mummy in one of her silky nightgowns and Mummy's large soft swaying breasts straining against the fabric, Skyler has glimpsed through a doorway Daddy gripping and kneading Mummy in playful-Daddy hands and now as then Skyler looks quickly away.

Skyler? where is

Near the floor of the sea such bizarre life-forms all mouth, sharp glittery teeth, fins, spiny backbones. Yet such a sweet-groggy sleep for a child to be wakened from, Skyler understands that something is very wrong for Mummy is not so angry, Mummy is upset and confused and Skyler tries to push Mummy away but Mummy is too strong for him, with a small exasperated-Mummy cry she pulls back the bedsheets where Skyler has been lying hunched in a pretzel-twist on his left side, both hands pressed between his knees and his knees drawn up toward his chest like a creature not yet hatched.

Skyler is she in here   hiding in here?

Frantic Mummy checks the foot of Skyler's bed as if Skyler's six-year-old sister might be hiding there, somehow. With a sob/grunt Mummy kneels to check beneath the bed, stumbles then to Skyler's closet, switches on the light and paws through Skyler's hanging things, kneels and gropes about the floor. Muttering to herself *Where! Where is* and returning then stumbling like a drunken woman to Skyler standing beside his bed, dazed and frightened in pajamas, shivering barefoot, that look in Mummy's eyes, the alarm in Mummy's voice, briskly Mummy pulls Skyler out of the room, across the hall to Bliss's room, obviously Mummy has already been in Bliss's room looking for her, Bliss's bed is empty, Mummy has been tearing at the bedspread and at the sheets and Mummy is murmuring to herself as often when he is alone Skyler murmurs to himself for Mummy's thoughts are spilling out of Mummy's head like skittering bats. Skyler wonders: Where is Daddy? Has Daddy taken Bliss away in the night? Is it Bliss's birthday outing in New York City, where Daddy and Bliss have gone? Skyler is confused, Skyler will remember none of this clearly, the events of this night about which he will be questioned and will question himself though recalling how in Bliss's room (formerly a nursery with a door in the wall like a magic door opening into Mummy and Daddy's big bedroom) there is a lamp on Bliss's bedside table in the shape of Mother Goose which had once been Skyler's lamp when he'd been a baby, this is Bliss's special lamp which has to be turned on at night or Bliss can't sleep or, if she sleeps, she will have nightmares of ugly-shaped things that hide beneath her bed as in the murky penumbra beyond the brightly lit ice rinks where the crowd erupts in spontaneous applause at the mere sight of Miss Tots-on-Ice Debutante, Tiny Miss StarSkate, Little Miss Jersey Ice Princess except it is a different time now, Mummy is not joining in the applause now but gripping Skyler's arm as if somehow Skyler is to blame as Mummy stares at Bliss's small bed with its white satin headboard, beautiful frosted-pink satin spread decorated with white ice-skate appliqués, now tangled on the floor with the bedclothes, and Bliss's pillow looks as if it has been thrown down, hard. And there is the smell.

Bad girl! Not again

On purpose to spite   me

Both Mummy and Skyler see the stained mattress, and smell the sharp ammoniac smell of urine, and worse-than-urine, for there are dark mud-colored star-shaped smears on one of the white linen sheets. And Mummy is furious, or is Mummy frightened?—digging her nails into Skyler's thin shoulders inside his flannel pajama top, Mummy pleads with him *Skyler what have you done to Bliss? Where have you taken your little sister?*

II

"Happiest Little Girl on Earth"

IN THE BEGINNING

IN THE BEGINNING—LONG AGO!—THERE WASN'T BLISS.

There was Skyler, but not Bliss. Not yet Bliss!

No one knows this. No one has recorded this. Of the tens of thousands of Bliss-cultists who have polluted cyberspace with their crazed factoids and perve-rantings not one of them knows this: that in the beginning it was Skyler who'd been meant to be the star. It was Skyler who'd been meant to be the figure-skating prodigy of Fair Hills, New Jersey. Or some sort of prodigy.

"SKYLER! THIS WILL BE OUR SECRET."

A very cold morning in the second week of December 1991. Mummy was breathless, and Mummy was excited, and Mummy was wearing her long red quilted winter coat lined with goose-feather down so it weighed scarcely anything, and on Mummy's head, pulled down snug over Mummy's dark hair, was a knitted cap of vivid rainbow colors, a cap with a floppy eight-inch tassel like something a TV cartoon character or a clown might wear to make you smile. Unless I was mistaken, for Skyler was so frequently mistaken, peering up anxiously at the giant adults who surrounded him looming over him with their cryptic smiles, their frowns, their grimaces, their tics and twitches and mysterious signals you could not ever hope to decode, probably yes, four-year-old Skyler was wrong about Mummy's new cap, the rainbow-knit cap with the floppy tassel was intended to be *stylish*, recently purchased at The Village Arctic Shoppe on Main Street where in the shoppe's show window it was displayed on anorexic-adolescent-girl models with skis or ice-skates slung over their shoulders. Mummy's new tassel-cap with its rainbow stripes was *serious*.

"—our secret, Skyler, which you must never tell Daddy, you know what a cruel tease Daddy can be. Skyler, please?"

Skyler's eager little head nodded *Yes! Yes Mummy.*

"—scolds me for 'wasting gas'! 'Never staying home'! Next thing, he'll be checking the what-is-it on my car—'odormeter.' You know, tells how many miles you've driven? A little gauge, on the dash?"

Skyler nodded, less certain now. Wasn't sure he knew what an "odormeter" was but he knew what's called a "dash."

"This little drive of ours, with a—destination. Which I think you will like, Skyler!"

This little drive was a drive we'd begun to take frequently together, Mummy and me, ostensibly into town on errands of Mummy's but by a leisurely, looping, circuitous route that took us miles into the "scenic" countryside north and east of the Historic Village of Fair Hills, New Jersey (to which we'd come to live only a few months ago, in September) and yes, often there was a destination to which Mummy headed as if helplessly, by these circuitous routes. "Daddy doesn't need to know, Skyler. 'What Daddy doesn't know won't hurt us.'" Mummy laughed, with a shivery shudder.

"Skyler! Shove your stubby little arms into these sleeves."

Damn: I've forgotten to "set the scene."

We were in the garage. We'd "snuck out" into the garage through a back door opening off the kitchen and we were whispering. That is, Mummy was whispering. Often Mummy whispered, it had come to seem natural for Mummy to whisper which meant that you should whisper back or better yet just nod your head *Yes Mummy!* For there was some urgency here. The phone had been ringing much of the morning but not one of the calls was the call Mummy had been waiting for, only just tradesmen, telephone solicitors, Mummy wasn't answering any more calls but would let the calls be picked up by the answering service which Mummy would check later which would be soon enough for Mummy, who didn't want to sabotage this special day. In her cheery-jokey mood already zipped up into the quilted red coat that made Mummy look like—well, a bobbing red balloon, and with her gaily colored tassel flopping over her forehead, Mummy paused to kiss Skyler's cute-kid snub-nose though the nose was probably leaking, as Daddy complained the poor damn kid seems always to have a cold. "Shhh! Don't want Maria to hear us." Hurriedly Mummy was bundling me into a fleece-lined little parka with a hood made tight and snug, almost too tight and too snug, by drawstrings at the neck manipulated by Mummy. And on my stubby four-year-old's legs warm flannel sweatpants, and on my stubby feet waterproof boots. Both the parka and the sweatpants still had tags attached for they were new purchases from The Village Arctic Kids Shoppe.

"Skyler, do you hear—? Is it—"

Mummy's eyes widened in an expression of guilty fear. We listened.

Faintly in the distance, maybe: a wan, wailing sound. Could be a siren. Could be an airplane high overhead. Could be the wind in the 150-year-old brick chimney about which Mrs. Cuttlebone the perky/canny real estate agent who'd sold Mr. and Mrs. Rampike the overpriced house had nervously joked: "Ghosts! All our 'historic' Fair Hills houses have them." But the danger passed, no one opened the door behind us. No one stared at Mummy with dark-quizzical eyes and inquired politely in heavily accented English when did Mrs. Rampike think she would be returning?

"—will be all right. Doesn't need *me*. Nobody needs *me*. *I need me*."

In our three-car garage only two vehicles remained that morning. For Daddy was away at Baddaxe Oil "corporate headquarters" and had taken his shiny black Lincoln Continental, that Mummy was not "encouraged" to drive. Left behind was Daddy's even bigger and heavier steely-gray Land Rover that was so large and so "tricky to maneuver," only Daddy could be trusted to drive it. But there was Mummy's lime-green Chevrolet Impala (a '94 model that Daddy bought for Mummy to "cheer my gal up" when we'd moved from Parsippany to Fair Hills where Mummy had not wanted to move) that Mummy drove into town at least once a day. It was in the backseat of the lime-green Impala that Mummy had placed, with no explanation, a bulky zip-up satchel. Sharp-eyed Skyler asked, "Mummy, what's in there?"

Was it Baby? Baby Sister? Puny little Edna Louise? That Mummy did not want, or anyway did not want so soon after Skyler? That Mummy is tired of, for

crying all the time, for being colicky and keeping Mummy awake, a fretful baby,
a homely baby, a blue-bug-eyed baby, a baldie baby with only a few blond hairs
on her head, a silly girl-baby missing a real pee-pee like Skyler's, an exasperating
baby demanding always to be fed (chalky-milk formula prepared by Maria), de-
manding always to have her diaper changed, needing to be bathed and again
fed, nappy-nap time and diaper changed, bath, towel-dry, new diaper, all babies
do is sleep pee and poop and shriek like a cat being killed and babies try to win
your heart by cooing and "smiling" and reaching their astonishing little baby-
fingers at you but babies are SO BORING unable even to say their names or walk
upright or go potty in the bathroom using the flush. Not like Skyler who is Mum-
my's little man!

Behind the wheel of the '94 lime-green Chevy Impala, Mummy was
humming. Here, you could see that Betsey Rampike was *happy*.

"Let's get buckled in, Skyler. 'Safety first.' "

Since Skyler was still a little too small to sit comfortably in the passenger's seat beside Mummy, Mummy had placed a cushion there for him.
(Was this legal? The seat belt fit Skyler kind of loosely.) So proud to have
graduated from the silly strap-in kiddy-car-seat in the back that, when
homely Edna Louise had to be transported, was used now exclusively for
her.

Surreptitiously Skyler glanced into the backseat at the satchel. Was it
stirring? Was there a living creature inside? *Was* it Baby?

Skyler asked another time what was in the satchel and Mummy said
with a mysterious smile he'd find out, soon.

"Here we go!"

The Chevy Impala emerged out of the garage rear-end-first like an
explosion.

THE WINTER AIR WAS BLINDING-BRIGHT. OVERHEAD THE SKY WAS A
painted-looking robin's-egg blue. On the ground snow lay in sculpted
drifts and swirls vivid-white as detergent or Styrofoam. (Hey forgive me:
this is how the memory is coming to me in a blinding rush like Dexedrine. And my heart is hammering, too: 260 beats a minute!) You had to
conclude that, if there were airborne "toxins" in the idyllic hills of north-

central New Jersey where the wealthy live, said toxins blown by mischievous winds from the "industrial corridor" fifty miles to the east, out of fire-rimmed smokestacks lining the New Jersey Hellpike, these toxins were magically transformed into the most dazzling-white snow. Mummy fumbled to put on stylish oversized gold-plastic-framed dark glasses, and Skyler blinked eager watery eyes. Each little drive with Mummy was an adventure!

Serpentine Ravens Crest Drive! In my fevered brain, where I travel ceaselessly like an astronaut reeling about in space, there's the dreamlike scroll of neighbors' houses ("neighbors" who were utter strangers and their houses barely visible from the road) and the curves, turns and twists of the too-narrow drive where the imminent danger was oncoming traffic: distracted Fair Hills wives like Mummy careening in the middle of the road, as Mummy habitually did, in oversized vehicles like the Chevy Impala. It was Mummy's custom to drive slowly along Pheasant Run, Hawksmoor Lane, Woodsmoke Drive and the Great Road (frequently traveled, in long-ago history books, by General George Washington and his aides in the 1770s), passing roadside mailboxes with such names as "Tyce"—"Hambruck"—"McGreety"—"Stubbe"—"Brugh." This phase of the *little drive* had become so familiar to me, I had memorized the names and pronounced them, as Mummy did, in a tone of admiration, awe, wonderment—"Frass"—"Durkee"—"Bloomgren"—"Hudd." Even as a young child I seemed to know that, hidden among this litany of names, were the names of Mummy's and Daddy's friends-to-be; as the Fair Hills Golf and Country Club (at Cross Tree Road and the Great Road), the Pebble Hill Tennis Club (on hilly Brookside Drive), the Sylvan Glen Golf Club (on labyrinthine Sylvan Glen Pass, heralded with PRIVATE ROAD   NO WAY OUT signs which Mummy, gnawing at her lower lip, daringly ignored), and (in the heart of the cramped little "historic quarter" in the Village of Fair Hills, on Idle Place), the Fair Hills Women's Club in its classy Italianate villa, were destinations-to-come. "The Sylvan Glen Golf Club is much more exclusive than the Fair Hills Golf and Country Club," Mummy confided in Skyler, who was always interested in Mummy's insider knowledge. "—Mrs. Cuttlebone assured us, if you are invited to join 'The Sylvan' as it's called, you can join any other Fair Hills club you wish." Of the

Pebble Hill Tennis Club, Mummy said, "Mrs. Cuttlebone's son is engaged to the daughter of the president of the club, she has promised to introduce your father and me sometime this holiday season. Daddy does play tennis, just as Daddy plays golf, and squash, and raquetball, but we could take tennis lessons together at the club, Skyler! You and me."

Have I said that, behind the wheel of the lime-green Impala, Mummy was eager and hopeful as a young girl?—or, for that matter, a young boy? Her mood was adolescent, yearning: you would not want to thwart such yearning.

Have I said that Mummy had beautiful (anxious, glistening-wet, somewhat close-set) brown eyes that, fixed upon me, Skyler, seemed to penetrate me, to the (modest) depths of my child-soul? That I loved Mummy desperately before even there was desperation in our lives?

Those *little drives*! Naturally, you're a kid, you think *what is* will go on forever. That dreamy spell when Mummy's "little man" was at last old enough to be a companion to Mummy yet not quite old enough for kindergarten. When Daddy was a "rising" young executive at Baddaxe Oil headquarters a mere fifteen miles away and so returned home for dinner most nights by 8 P.M. When Skyler's baby sister was so young—so small— you could pretend she—"it"—did not matter. And Mummy was eager to escape the big white Colonial house in which the phone so often rang and yet: *it was never the call for which Mummy waited.*

"Skyler! Tell me one true thing."

Inside the quilted red coat, Mummy must've been perspiring. As Mummy drove the Chevy Impala in choppy waves—pressing down on the gas pedal and then releasing it, again pressing down, again releasing it— so the engine seemed to be hiccuping, or starting to stall. Skyler's sensitive nostrils picked up a familiar talcumy-briny smell of Mummy's underarms and the shadowy crevice between Mummy's breasts that was a dreamy comfort like a smell of baking bread or his own slept-in bedclothes when he pulled them over his head.*

---

* *God damn: did I really write this? These words? Last night, in what felt like a Dexedrine rush? Maybe this is why the faintest whiff of talcumy-yeasty-sweaty female flesh from any source renders me nauseated/totally impotent.*

Sharply Mummy said, "Skyler? Are you listening? Tell me: why don't people like me?"

Skyler stammered, "Mummy, I l-like you."

"You? You're my son. What do you know."

Mummy laughed to signal this was meant to be funny. But it didn't seem funny. For already at age four—more precisely, four and a half—Skyler was forced to understand that love from such a source just wasn't enough.

Mummy said, sighing, "It's petty, I know. I try to pray each morning *God let me rise above this, Jesus help me for I am not just a sinner but a ridiculous person* and yet: people are crazy for Bix Rampike—why not *me*? I mean, wouldn't some of it spill onto *me*? Wouldn't you expect that? I'm Bix's wife. Of course I don't mean 'crazy for me'—nobody has ever been crazy for me except some sex-crazed boy and that isn't 'liking'—there's no dignity to that. (Excuse me for speaking frankly, Skyler, I realize that you are a boy, and I hope that you will be a normal, healthy boy but not a 'sex-crazed' boy. Not my Skyler! Not my little man!) What torments me is why don't women like me. In Parsippany, I had friends. I had a few friends. Your daddy is 'moving up the corporate ladder' so damn fast, we never stay in one place long enough to 'sink down roots'—you can't count the wives of Bix's business colleagues, those are *not friends*. Here in Fair Hills, all these women I meet, and I give them my telephone number, and I call them, or try to, why don't they call me back? Fair Hills is so hateful, these women are so cruel, we've been here almost four months, men look at me, at least some men look at me, but the women just look through me. Skyler, why?"

Poor stunned Skyler could only repeat, weakly: "But Mummy, I l-like—"

Mummy interrupted, "God damn I try *so damn hard*. Always smiling, always 'good-natured' and 'fun'—and 'nice'—I am sick and tired of being 'nice.' Back in high school I was a popular girl. I had girlfriends not just boys trailing after me. I had nice girlfriends. I was voted second runner-up in the Queen's court at our senior prom, Hagarstown High School '81, of a class of forty-two girls. That is not just nothing, Skyler! Popularity contests like that in high school are sheer hell. When I was fourteen—Skyler, this was the most exciting day of my life!—I qualified for the Tri-County Girls' Figure Skating Challenge. Next year I skated in the Adirondack All-Girls' Regional Tournament and didn't do bad at all considering how scared I was, and practically fainting from starving myself to fit into my skating costume. It's known how judges are prejudiced against 'plump' girls—by 'plump' it's meant a just-normal weight, in a skating costume tight as a swimsuit every bulge and fat-roll *shows*. On the ice you don't want whistles, you want applause. If I'd been encouraged, I would have done better—if I hadn't sprained my ankle—but, Skyler, *I did try.* You believe me, honey, don't you?" Mummy fumbled for me, riskily removing her eyes from the narrow graveled roadway that might have been Charlemagne Pass, or Monument Lane, or Bear Mountain Road. A single tear ran down Mummy's flushed cheek. Mummy's crimson lips were twisted in a bitter-brave smile.

Skyler mumbled *Yes! Yes Mummy.*

(Must've, don't you think? Though I had not a clue what the subject was, or what any of the subjects were, of such crucial significance to the adults looming over me.)

"In Hagarstown, my family had a 'known' name. Your great-grandfather Sculhorne who'd been a 'decorated World War II hero' was mayor while I was in high school and our family owned the largest textile mill on the Champlain River, that made women's and children's knitted clothing, it was like royalty living in such a small town where everyone knows you. In Hagarstown people looked up to us Sculhornes and had expectations of us and, well—that could be kind of, what's it, 'clausta-phobic'—you know, where it's hard to *breathe.* Which was why I had to run away, I mean I almost ran away!—to the State University at Albany, I had part-time jobs to pay my own tuition, you know I majored in 'Communi-cation Arts' and worked at the SUNY Albany TV station, it was my dream to be a TV news 'anchor'—till I met your dad, at the wildest frat-party weekend at Cornell, I pray you will never behave with the recklessness of Bix Rampike and his lunatic Ep Phi Pi brothers, Skyler! Anyway," Mummy sighed, smiling, with a sudden faraway look, "the rest is history. I guess."

Behind us, a horn sounded rudely. Mummy's foot had been easing up on the gas pedal and a pickup truck had come up to within a few inches of the Impala's rear fender. Mummy, the most unaggressive of drivers, the most easily intimidated, quickly swerved off the road and onto the shoulder to let the pickup pass.

I had a glimpse of the jut-jawed driver, a burly man in a carpenter's cap, glaring over at Mummy but then, when he actually saw her, relenting, casting her a sidelong, forgiving smile.

It was true that men seemed to like Mummy. Skyler could understand why.

"SKYLER! YOU WILL REMEMBER THIS DAY FOREVER: YOUR FIRST DAY *ON* the ice."

Mummy's voice quavered with excitement. Skyler stared. Somehow it had happened that we were at Horace C. Slipp Memorial Park, in a part of Fair Hills new to me. Here was a skating rink that must have been, in warm weather, a children's wading and swimming pool. Overhead, loud tinkly music was playing. On the rink, where ice glittered meanly, dozens of people were skating, predominantly children and teenagers. The children appeared to be years older than Skyler. A gaggle of boys were shouting, pushing and shoving one another like ice hockey players. Teenaged girls in jeans, heavy sweatshirts, bareheaded with long gleaming straight hair cascading over their shoulders. Amid these were a scattering of adults including feisty "senior citizens" skating in defiance of stiff joints and breakable bones. There were young mothers and Maria-like nannies urging children on skates out onto the ice and, when they fell, helping them up. Squeals, cries, peals of wild laughter. If there were cries of pain, dismay, fear these cries seemed to be muffled. The general mood was one of gaiety, festivity. Skyler's kiddy-sized heart shrank even smaller. Skyler's mouth had gone dry. "Mummy, I d-don't—"

Mummy was calling, "Is the ice smooth? Is it—safe?" but the girl skaters to whom Mummy dared to speak scarcely glanced at her, a stranger in a balloon-like red coat, with a kooky knit cap on her head. And a tremulous little boy at her side, whose hand she was gripping. Mummy was in too elevated a mood to take notice of the girls' rudeness but urged Skyler onto a bench, tugged his boots off, and replaced them with his "nifty new"

Junior Olympics skates, "exact replicas" of adult-sized skates, made of a dark red fabric with zigzag lightning bolts on the sides. "Aren't they beautiful, Skyler? Your surprise pre-Christmas gift, for being such a good boy. Mummy can't wait to see you perform in them!"

Also in the mysterious satchel with Skyler's skates had been white-leather Lady Champ skates for Mummy, too. *For Mummy was going to skate with Skyler.*

Skyler protested, "Mummy, I'm afraid," wiping his leaky nose on his mitten, "Mummy, I d-don't feel good—" but Mummy paid him no heed saying, "Skyler, you will love the ice. At your age you'll learn fast. Children are natural athletes. My handicap as a skater was that I'd started too late. Not until I was thirteen and 'mature' for my age. I attracted lots of attention but not for my skating. You will start young. It looks like you're the youngest here! And Daddy doesn't need to know anything about it until you're skating well enough to perform for him. Skyler, I promise!"

What was Mummy promising? Skyler had no idea.

Mummy was lacing the Junior Olympics skates up tight. By his feet, Skyler knew himself trapped.

Mummy laced up her beautiful white Lady Champ skates and stood, letting the quilted red coat fall like a negligee onto the bench, revealing herself, to Skyler's astonished eyes, in a costume he had never seen before: a beautiful, clearly brand-new purple cable-knit sweater, a pleated tartan-plaid miniskirt with a large ornamental brass safety pin at the side, and textured purple tights that displayed Mummy's shapely legs, plump knees, and something of her chubby thighs. And there was the knitted cap in vivid rainbow colors with the floppy tassel intended to lift behind the skater as she flies across the ice. Though Skyler was too young to have been yet subjected to the cruelty of school-age barbarians immediately Skyler sensed that his gorgeous Mummy would attract the wrong kind of attention here at Horace C. Slipp Park, Fair Hills, New Jersey, as she'd attracted the wrong kind of attention in Hagarstown, New York, as a girl. But Mummy only clapped her hands with childlike enthusiasm: "Sweetie, come *on*. Look at all these skaters having *fun*."

When Skyler held shyly back, Mummy half-lifted him from the bench and led him hobbling and fearful on his skates—as if you could walk on *skate blades!*—onto the ice. Oh but Skyler didn't want to skate! Skyler didn't want to fall down and hurt himself and be laughed at, which had been the culmination of more than one of his "playdates" on solid ground. The loud tinkly music had become fiercer. "Like this, Skyler! Don't stand so stiff. Move your right foot. Just a few inches, Skyler, c'mon *try*." But Skyler's ankles were weak, as if boneless. The skates were too high, it was natural to fall off them. And Skyler's knees were buckling. And Skyler's damn nose was running like a leaky faucet. "Mummy, my stomach feels funny," Skyler whimpered, "Mummy, my feet are *so cold*." Mummy scolded: "Skyler, are you my little man, or are you some *sniveling baby*?" and at this Skyler felt the terrible insult, that Mummy would speak of him as a baby, as just another sniveling baby, when there was a sniveling baby-girl back at the house Mummy had fled, and Skyler was *four and a half years old and walked upright*.

As Mummy, inching backward on the ice, was trying to tug Skyler forward, a passing skater nearly collided with Mummy, muttering, "Excuse me, ma'am," and Mummy called out apologetically, "Excuse *me*. I haven't skated in twenty years . . ." A second skater, a rail-thin girl with long straight shimmering chestnut hair, in a Fair Hills Day School jacket, swerved to avoid missing Mummy; and Mummy called after her, "Oh *I am sorry*. I haven't skated for twenty years, I've had two babies and these are *new skates*." Skyler would have liked to crawl on hands and knees off the rink, his small face throbbed with embarrassment for Mummy, and for himself. It seemed that a continuous stream of skaters came flying by, some of them ignoring the struggling mother/son duo, some staring rudely. Several noisy twelve-year-old boys lurched by shoving and elbowing one another, someone's swinging arm struck Skyler a blow on the back causing him to stagger on his skates, to lose his precarious balance and fall; in an instant the ice had flown up to strike Skyler's bottom and the sensitive bone Mummy called Skyler's tailbone, hard. Skyler, accustomed to falling on softer surfaces, like a carpet, or grass, was astonished *how hard ice is*. Too surprised to cry, Skyler sat gaping on the ice as Mummy struggled to pull him up. A burly boy came flying by narrowly missing Skyler's bare hand on the ice—Skyler's mitten had come off, somehow—with the terse remark, "Asshole!" If Mummy heard, Mummy gave no sign. By now Mummy's fleshy cheeks were blazing as if they'd been slapped. The silly rainbow-yarn tassel was swinging in Mummy's face. Mummy was pleading for Skyler to get up: "You aren't hurt, honey. A child's bones are made of rubber, practically. Your bones will bend, not break. You just had a little spill. Sweetie, this is only your first day, sweetie this is so much *fun*." How strong Mummy was, lifting Skyler's limp and boneless body up onto his feet, his feet still trapped in those terrible skates, and for a dazed several seconds like a cartoon character who has rushed off a precipice into thin air, not yet aware that it's air and not solid ground he's standing on, doesn't fall, so Skyler managed to remain upright and keep his balance. Mummy instructed: "See how I'm moving my foot, Skyler? You do the same. Just push, this foot, sweetie, your right foot, like you're in your stocking feet sliding along the floor, okay now your left foot, sweetie don't tense up like that, Mummy's got you." Mummy laughed breathlessly. Mummy held Skyler beneath the arms, like a sack of something, and for several amazing seconds Mummy and Skyler "skated"—*it was fun!*—then again, with rude abruptness, the damn ice flew up to strike Skyler's bottom, hard. Also Skyler's right elbow, his right leg, and the right side of his head. Luckily the hood of Skyler's parka was still covering his head. "Skyler, are you *hurt*? Oh, dear. What will I tell Bix if . . ." One of the white-haired old-lady skaters paused to help. In a kindly voice she said: "Your little boy is so little, dear. How old is he?" Quickly Mummy said, "Skyler is four and a half. His birthday is in June. He's precocious for his age. His 'physical coordination skills' are advanced for his age. He loves all sports, and he loves the outdoors. He takes after his daddy. He's doing just fine." The grandmotherly skater provided Skyler with a tissue out of her pocket, for Skyler's nose was running horribly. Mummy thanked her, but you could see that Mummy was annoyed. As the white-haired old old-lady skater moved away, with surprising ease, she shook her head doubtfully. "Your son does seem rather small for ice-skates, dear."

Under her breath Mummy murmured, "Nosy old busybody. Whyn't you mind your own business." To Skyler she said brightly: "You are *not small*, honey. Not for your age. This is just your first ice-skating lesson, for heaven's sake." When Skyler was upright, Mummy brushed at his

clothes, examined the side of his head, frowned and kissed his pug nose.
"Oh wouldn't it be my damn bad luck, that nosy old lady turns out to be
some 'very important person' in Fair Hills, or one of our neighbors, or
she's head of the membership committee at the Sylvan Golf Club, wouldn't
that be *fate*." Shrewd Skyler complained that his leg was hurting, his elbow was hurting, his stomach felt queasy, so Mummy relented all right he
could sit down for a few minutes, and catch his breath; and Mummy could
show him a few simple moves. With Skyler for an audience Mummy skated
in stiff tentative lunges like one fearful that the ice might crack beneath
her. "This is a 'glide'—see? You just kind of—glide." Several times Mummy
nearly slipped and fell, Skyler shut his eyes in dread. But Mummy managed to right herself, laughing. "Oh I am out of shape! Twelve pounds at
least since—last winter. All I need is a little practice . . ." Skyler winced to
see how passing skaters glanced at Mummy, some of them amused, some
of them frankly curious, a few downright rude. Boys sniggered and
nudged one another but the worst were the snotty teenaged girls giggling
at Mummy as they glided effortlessly past her. Skyler was indignant: what
was so funny about Mummy? Mummy was the nicest-looking woman at
the damn old ice rink! Mummy was a sight like a woman in a movie, or on
a giant billboard, with her large "moon-shaped" face and smooth warm-
flushed skin, her prominent crimson lips and her skating costume that
was so much nicer than the drab old boring jeans and dull-colored parkas
the other skaters wore. Mummy's new sweater fitted her ample torso snug
as a glove and Mummy's tartan-plaid miniskirt swirled about her hips
showing her legs in purple tights, her knees and thighs. Skyler wished
though that Mummy would not call out to Skyler so loudly as she did,
laughing and chattering, as if wanting to attract attention, or anyway un-
concerned that she was attracting attention: "Skyler, see? Are you watching? This is your lesson, honey. Mummy is 'gliding'—this is a 'glide'—see
how easy it is? Here is my first 'figure-eight' in twenty years. Ooops!"
Somehow, Mummy seemed to lose her balance. Or one of Mummy's ankles turned. For suddenly, with a cry, Mummy fell, onto her bottom on the
ice, hard. Mummy sat spread-legged on the ice with a look of stunned
hurt and you could see that Mummy was wearing just the purple tights
beneath the miniskirt and that there were rolls of flesh on Mummy's

upper thighs. The rainbow-knit cap was crooked on Mummy's head and Mummy's breath came in harsh steaming pants.

Several skaters stopped at once to help Mummy back up onto her feet. Mummy astonished them by bursting into tears. "My life is over! My body has been taken from me! It isn't fair! I'm still young! *I can't skate anymore.*"

The skaters who'd helped Mummy to her feet and brought her hobbling back to Skyler were two youngish women and a youngish man with rust-colored springy hair, large rubbery lips, a high bony dome of a forehead and a blunt broad knob of a nose. He wore stone-washed jeans and a spiffy fawn-colored faux-suede jacket and his high-top skates had silver lightning bolts on their sides and in his left earlobe was what looked like a silver clamp. He appeared to be just slightly younger than Mummy and no taller than Mummy and smaller-built than Mummy and why am I remembering him?*—because there was something wonderful in the way he took Mummy's arm to steady her, and was very kind to her; and peered at me with his loose rubbery smile, saying to Mummy, "Is this your beautiful little daughter, ma'am, or your beautiful little son?" and Mummy said, wiping tears from her flaming face, "Skyler is my beautiful *little man.*"

* *The canny reader will note that there must be a reason for highlighting this eccentric individual who appears fleetingly in this chapter as both "kindly" and somewhat sinister. Keep the rubbery-lipped young man in mind! (If I were a revered literary writer, I could assume that readers were primed to read my prose with, well—reverence, and care. But I am not, and so I can't. But note that nothing in this document is extraneous.)*

GOD HELP ME

GOD HELP ME RISE ABOVE THIS, JESUS HELP ME FOR I WAS NOT BORN TO BE *this woman not just a sinner but a ridiculous person* so Mummy fiercely prayed and was Mummy's prayer answered?—did something astonishing and wholly unexpected—"undeserved"—happen to Betsey Rampike soon, within a few years though from which direction and in which earthly form, no one, certainly not Betsey Rampike, might have predicted?

So when God's blessing strikes us, like lightning it will strike from an unexpected source. Like lightning it will shatter our mere mortal beings, to make of our souls something molten and pure.

AND DID MUMMY SUCCEED IN HER MORE IMMEDIATE CAMPAIGN TO *MAKE* *friends* in Fair Hills, as so desperately she wished? Was her childlike yearning, so painful to watch at close quarters, rewarded at last? Yes!

Not to keep the reader in suspense: Yes.

Except, as Daddy chided: "Not overnight, Betsey. You won't make the kinds of women friends you'd like to make, and I'd like you to make, overnight. So calm down."

In the interim it should be conceded that Mummy didn't initially *make friends* with the most popular/socially exalted/admired of Fair Hills women, those flawlessly made-up and elegantly attired women whose photographs appeared in the Style section of the *Fair Hills Beacon* after a "whirlwind" weekend of private parties, lavish receptions, gala fund-raisers (the Friends of the Fair Hills Medical Center Christmas Ball, the

Friends of the Fair Hills Public Library Valentine's Day Dinner Dance and Silent Auction, the Fair Hills Planned Parenthood Tulip Luncheon, et al.), women who appeared to be uniformly blond, uniformly size four, uniformly very wealthy and of no discernible age except *not-elderly*. Mostly Mummy "made friends" with wives of other Baddaxe junior executives and with wives of local businessmen and professional men with whom Bix Rampike began to play golf, squash, tennis, and poker frequently as Daddy became increasingly "known" (and "popular") in Fair Hills. Our church was the quaintly eighteenth-century Trinity Episcopal in the heart of the Historic Village, of the genre you've seen countless times: hoary gray stone, tasteful stained glass, calendar-art belfry emitting sonorous chimes like reverberations from the dignified Episcopal deity in the sky. (Though Mummy admitted to have been baptized and brought up in the United Methodist Church and Daddy's ancestors had belonged to a radical Calvinist sect in northern England whose primary tenet was: All of mankind is damned by original sin. Bar none.) Mummy and Daddy were married (not that Skyler was on the scene to observe!) in the First Episcopal Church of Pittsburgh where Daddy's well-to-do family lived for, as Daddy sagely said, Episcopal trumps Methodist in the corporate world, you betcha.

God help us succeed, Skyler can skate if he tries I just know he can was another of Mummy's prayers whispered half-jestingly/half-seriously in Skyler's hearing as, in the lime-green Chevy Impala, we wended our way, you will cringe to hear, back to Horace C. Slapp, excuse me Slipp Memorial Park, to the ice-skating rink. Yes, back to the rink! Back to the ice! Can you believe this? Not once but four times that winter 1991–92 Mummy insisted upon bringing me back to "try" again for Mummy was a fervent believer in the American credo *If at first you don't succeed, try, try again!*—an uplifting imperative that originally appeared, in German, above the entrance at Auschwitz; unless it was engraved, in Dante's Italian, above the entrance of Hell. In a more calculated literary document comprised of "selected dramatic scenes" Skyler's initial ghastly skating lesson would have been his last, but, as luck has it, this document is an unadorned, bluntly truthful account of us Rampikes in the tumultuous years leading to the early morning hours of January 29, 1997, and away from those hours and not mere fiction (which anyone, knowing nothing of my family, could concoct) and so I am obliged to say here that, yes Mummy did take Skyler back for additional humiliations, administered by Mummy, stubbornly and doggedly and often with a bright, brave smile Mummy took Skyler back to Horace C. Slipp Memorial Park in the mad belief that the child had surely—surely!—inherited at least a scattering of genes—DNA chromosomes—or whatever—from his big strapping (six-foot-three, 210 pounds of mostly solid flesh) ex-athlete (fullback, Cornell varsity football 1981–82) Daddy if not a passionate yearning for public success/recognition of some kind inherited from Mummy. Strangely—sadly!— Mummy never again laced on her spiffy new Lady Champ skates but only just strode out onto the ice in her boots with poor tremulous Skyler, gripping his shoulders through the parka, aiming and nudging him into a "glide," picking him up when, inevitably, he fell. Nor did Mummy (so far as Skyler knew) ever again wear the dazzling purple cable-knit sweater or the pleated tartan-plaid miniskirt or the rainbow-knit cap with the funny, floppy tassel. On the ice with Skyler, like other Mummys-with-children, Mummy wore just woollen slacks and jacket, or the quilted red coat that made her look like a balloon. Probably, for Mummy remained at heart a frugal upstate—New York girl, Mummy returned, or tried to return, her expensive skates to Winter Wonderland! at the Fair Hills Valley Mall but Mummy refused to return Skyler's Junior Olympics skates for Mummy did not believe in giving up, not without a struggle. But to Mummy's disappointment, and what seemed to be genuine surprise, subsequent ice-skating lessons for Skyler were no more successful than the first; and by the fourth lesson the usually malleable child was becoming sulky/rebellious/brattish, and ever more physically uncoordinated, so deeply had he come to fear, dread, and loathe anything to do with ice-skating. Anything to do with ice! With cheery tinkly music! Soon, Skyler began to whimper and tremble at the very sight of the lime-green Impala in which he'd once been so privileged and joyous a passenger. And Mummy sighed, and Mummy said finally, "All right, Skyler. You win. Your stubborn little wizened-raisin willful heart *has won*. I can donate these damn old skates to Goodwill, some other grateful little boy will appreciate them."

TWO MUMMIES

Vivid memories but jumpy, jerky and disjointed like a low-budget film made with a handheld camera.

Skyler! came the cry but faint and fading and possibly in fact he'd heard no cry *Skyler!* out of the tremulous air *Mummy's little man, Mummy loves for all her life.* Though possibly this was confused in the child's thoughts with Baby's crying, for Baby was often crying, Baby was fretting in her high chair in the kitchen kicking and flailing her little baby-fists, oh oh oh! what a shrieking, though Maria was trying to feed Baby, red-faced Baby with a mouth like a tiny bird's beak, dribbling a watery-clotted whitish unnameable baby food down her chin, onto her already stained bib, Baby was a tiny girl-Baby and yet astonishingly strong, if Baby kicked you, you felt it, and if Baby seized your pudgy finger in Baby's tight little fist, you felt it, and if Baby cooed and "smiled" and drew you close to her tiny flushed face, those cobalt-blue eyes making their claim on you, Baby might suddenly take fright, and begin to shriek, and oh oh oh! what did you do to upset Baby, *bad Skyler what have you done to make Baby cry?*

Baby was a hot quivering little bundle in Maria-from-Guatemala's arms. Maria-from-Guatemala knew to calm Baby by cooing, kissing, murmuring a magical incantation in what you had to surmise was her own language incomprehensible to Skyler as it was incomprehensible to Mummy and excluded them both.

But where was Mummy?

Frightened Maria-from-Guatemala wringing her sturdy-peasant hands appealing to Skyler in breathy, heavily accented English, where is

Mrs. Rampike? Skyler where is your mother? but Skyler had no idea where Mummy was, Skyler had himself been calling Mummy? Mum-*my*? in a whiny-kid voice, in another room Baby was shrieking, or Baby was "running a fever," or Baby had "thrown up all her breakfast," and where was Daddy?—"away." In fact, Daddy had flown to Burbank, California, and would not return to Fair Hills until, vaguely, the "end of the week"—which week, Skyler wondered—and the damned phone was ringing/ringing/ringing and went unanswered since Mummy did not want Maria to answer the phone, just let the messages go onto the answering service, Mummy will play back the messages in the evening (maybe) with a good stiff drink (Daddy's Scotch, no ice), except Maria is appealing to Skyler, what to tell the ladies?—for it seems that Mrs. Higley and two other women have just arrived to take Betsey Rampike to one of the Trinity Episcopal Women's Altar Society luncheons at the Fair Hills Golf and Country Club, for Mrs. Higley is the lavishly perfumed/big-bosomed wife of Reverend Archibald ("Archie") Higley, snowy-white-haired head pastor of Trinity Episcopal Church, dear sweet "Mattie" Higley who'd recently been so kind to Betsey Rampike, "taken Betsey Rampike under her wing," but where is Betsey Rampike, *where the hell is Mummy hiding?* Or, more alarming still, a gang of swarthy-skinned Mexican laborers (carpenters? painters? roofers? lawn crew?) speaking no English has just arrived for what precise purpose only Bix Rampike might know, but Daddy is away, when Mummy tries to call Daddy "at work" Daddy is frequently "not at his desk," Daddy is so popular and so much in demand Daddy seems scarcely to have a desk at Baddaxe Oil, Inc. though Daddy has not one but several assistants/secretaries with cooing mellifluous voices to placate the hysterical wife-Mummy, promising to tell Mr. Rampike please call home as soon as possible. *But where is Mummy?*

POSSIBLE MUMMY-HIDING-PLACES:

- **Bathroom.** In the hot steamy full-blast shower where Mummy can't hear Baby crying. In theory.

- **Bedroom.** Blinds shut tight against the morning glare and in the massive "king-sized" bed beneath a mound of bedclothes in black

silk glamour nightgown with plunging neckline barely containing Mummy's white blue-veined big-nippled breasts, Mummy is
snappish cursing whoever this is, has to be Skyler, rousing her from
the most delicious sleep when poor Mummy has only just managed
to fall asleep after a hellish insomniac night of Baby crying in the
adjoining nursery *Skyler go away damn you leave me alone what time is
it don't tell Daddy shut the door on your way out* clamping a pillow over
her head to muffle Baby's crying.

- **Various rooms** in the house including guest rooms, guest bathrooms, the attic, in the basement the preferred hiding place is the
furnace room where, in cold weather, not one but two large furnaces
exude an airless warmth humming, thrumming, rattling and vibrating and where you can't possibly hear Baby crying even a floor above.

- **Garage.** In the lime-green Chevy Impala in the (shadowy, unlighted)
space, only once did Skyler find Mummy here but it remains a
memorable memory, a stink of auto exhaust in the chill air and the
car hood feels warm to Skyler's fingertips as if the engine, though not
running now, has been running until just now, for Mummy has just
switched off the ignition, Mummy sprawled behind the steering
wheel in a nightgown beneath the haphazardly zipped quilted red
coat, now sitting up quickly, wiping her pale, doughy, unmade-up
Mummy face and peeking at Skyler through her fingers: "Surprise!
Fooled you."

MUMMY WHY ARE YOU CRYING ASKS SKYLER AND MUMMY SAYS *DON'T BE
ridiculous I am not crying* and Skyler asks *Mummy does Baby make you cry*
and Mummy says hotly *I am not crying, Baby is not to blame* and Skyler says
Mummy don't you like Baby and Mummy says more hotly *I love Baby! What
a thing to say* and Skyler says *Do you hate Baby, Mummy* and Mummy says
again *I love Baby, I love Baby and I love Skyler and I love Daddy and I love my
life here, each day I thank God on my knees for my life here, what a terrible thing
to say, bad Skyler!* and Skyler in a torment of child-anguish, anxiety says

Mummy should we give Baby away? Maybe somebody else would want Baby, like my ice-skates? and Mummy laughs harshly, Mummy wipes at her eyes with the palms of her hands and laughs harshly scolding *Skyler! You know very well that Baby is your sister Edna Louise, she is named for Grandmother Rampike and she is here with us to stay.*

YET: THERE WAS THE OTHER, ALTERED MUMMY, SPLENDIDLY DRESSED IN A new champagne-beige cashmere suit from The English Shoppe, or a new cranberry-crinkle silk frock from Renée's Fashion Boutique, or a svelte black "slimming" cocktail dress from Saks, brunette hair gaily "bouffant" from Evita's Beauty Emporium where Mummy's nails, too, that inclined to be small, bitten, broken had been boldly re-imagined as glamorous crimson talons to match Mummy's smiling mouth; here was a Mummy not barefoot stumbling about the house, or in bedroom slippers clumping about the house, but in high-heeled shoes that gave her sudden height, dignity, and purpose. Here was a Mummy adored by her son Skyler: "Mum-*my*! You look nice." Here was a Mummy not feared, pitied, and despised by Maria-from-Guatemala (to be followed in jerky time-stop sequence by Maria-from-Mexico, Maria-from-Paraguay, and, in time, Lila-from-the-Philippines) but respected and admired: "Mrs. Rampike! I like very much, the new 'outfit.'" Here was a beaming Mummy warmly greeting luncheon guests at the door: "Come in! So wonderful to see you! Julia, and Francine, and—is it Henrietta?—and Mattie! Come *in*." Here is Mummy in a snuggly-warm white angora sweater and silk-wool white slacks, and gold slippers with heels like small clattering hooves, hurrying to embrace Daddy who has just returned from Burbank, or Dallas, or Atlanta; Mummy being hugged by Daddy: "My gorgeous gal! Missed you." And there is Baby newly bathed and smelling of Baby talcum instead of Baby-poo, Baby Edna Louise who isn't fretful or shrieking but happily flailing miniature Baby-fists, flashing miniature Baby-eyes, gurgling, smiling, cooing what sounds like "Da-*da*! Da-*da*!" proudly displayed in Mummy's arms. (Where is Maria-from-Guatemala? Nowhere in sight.) Looming over

Mummy and Baby Edna Louise Daddy is deeply moved, saying, "My two gorgeous gals! I'd say things are pretty good here at 93 Ravens Crest Drive." For a terrible moment it looks as if Daddy has forgotten Skyler who has been sort-of-shyly hanging back, and Daddy sees him, of course Daddy sees him, grabs Skyler and lifts him in the crook of his arm so that Daddy is hugging Mummy, Baby Edna Louise, and Skyler: "My little family. Missed y'all."

And there is Mummy in peach-colored chiffon stooping over Skyler in his bed careful not to smudge her lipstick on Skyler's cheek, for it's New Year's Eve and Daddy and Mummy are on their way to a party, or parties. "Happy New Year, darling! This new year will be much, much nicer than the old year, I promise." But Skyler has no idea what year it is.*

THESE TWO MUMMYS EXISTED AT MORE OR LESS THE SAME TIME, IN THE same household. Like small carved figures in a weather clock—"good" weather, "bad" weather—when one Mummy appeared, the other Mummy remained in hiding. But only in hiding.

* Poor dumb kid! He'd have been dazed/dazzled by Mummy's perfume and Mummy's creamy breasts in danger of spilling out of the tight peach-chiffon bodice. And maybe there was Daddy, or a tall hulking Terminator-figure in a "tux," looming in the doorway behind Mummy. By my calculation the new year Mummy promised had to be 1992. Fact: it wouldn't be much different from the old.

"FILTHY"—"ODIOUS"—"ABOMINABLE"*

IT WAS NOTED, A FEW PAGES BACK, THAT MY RAMPIKE ANCESTORS HAD ORIG-
inally lived in the north of England, and belonged to a "radical Calvinist
sect"; in fact, my father's most—sole?—distinguished ancestor was the cel-
ebrated/notorious Reverend Joshua Rampike who'd brought his small but
fanatically devoted flock of believers ("flock"—sadly, a cliché!—is invariably
the most appropriate word for such Calvinist/Christian ancestors of mine)
to the newly established settlement at Philadelphia, in 1688; their hope was
to escape religious persecution in the unfathomably dreary hills of Hum-
berside, on the North Sea, and to establish a theocracy, under the thunderous leadership of Reverend Rampike, in which they might persecute other
Christians. Of more than forty pilgrims in my great-ancestor's flock, less
than half survived the hellish Atlantic crossing of several weeks; the cruel-
est fate was to have endured weeks of seasickness, dysentery, and despair
only to die near the end of the crossing; lucky pilgrims died early on, the
coast of England yet in sight. Within a few months of settling in Philadelphia, yet more of Reverend Rampike's flock died, including his wife and
several of his eight children; yet Reverend Rampike seemed weirdly to have
flourished in the New World, remarrying, siring more children (nineteen
in all), and cutting a fiery swath through this region mostly settled by paci-
fist Quakers with his hair-raising sermons of original sin, predestination,
total-depravity-of-humankind, and infant damnation.

---

* *This chapter is for Puritan history buffs among my readers, possibly a very small fraction. All
others may skim and skip to the paragraph beginning "Quakers—so much more sane, like
ourselves!"*

Like other Christian settlers to the New World, Reverend Rampike believed passionately that child-bearing, child-rearing, and the "bringing of children to salvation" was the primary task; unlike most other Christians of his era or any other, Reverend Rampike believed that children were "but miniature beasts in a crude semblance of human form" who had to be "continuously and severely disciplined" by both their parents and by the community; mothers were warned not to allow their babies to crawl "beyond what was necessary" for the resemblance between the "crawling, bestial baby" and the "serpent on its belly" was "filthy" to behold. The souls of infants luckless enough to die before being baptized went directly to Hell; the souls of those who managed to live longer had a slightly better, though not much better, chance of salvation; for most of mankind was doomed, no matter the effort made for salvation. Adult life was a matter of work, except on the Sabbath; children were to be pressed into work by the age of three, or even two. It must have been that my stern Calvinist ancestor, father of nineteen squawling babies, had reason to know firsthand that babies were "defiled with the stain of original sin, filthy, odious and abominable." Reverend Rampike did allow for the possibility that there existed, in the most bestial of babies, a divine spark that original sin could not wholly extinguish. This was a spark, Joshua Rampike preached, that "only Jesus Christ Our Savior could breathe upon to fan into the flame of Salvation."

Rampike family history! Maybe I am just slightly impressed.

Quakers—so much more sane, like ourselves!—tended to believe that small children were "pure"—"innocent"—"moist wax to be molded" by caring adult hands.

Skyler wasn't sure what he believed. Observing Baby close-up.

Once Baby was able to totter about upright, Skyler had to concede that Baby was to be an actual person, though Baby would never be a very important actual person, like Skyler himself.

For Baby would always be a *girl*. And Skyler was Mummy's *little man*.

As a toddler of two, Edna Louise began to lurch and stumble about "getting into everything like some kind of demon" (as Mummy said). It seemed that Edna Louise was "very pretty" except sometimes you could see that Edna Louise was "downright homely, like me" (as Mummy said).

Visitors remarked on Edna Louise's "beautiful" cobalt-blue eyes but these were also unnerving eyes that stared so hard, sometimes they seemed about to bulge out of their sockets. (Ugh! Secretly Skyler pried both blank blue glass eyes out of the rubber head of Edna Louise's favorite doll and was frightened by the eyeless sockets and tossed away all the incriminating evidence in the trash where no one, not even Maria-from-Mexico, could find it.) "Such an angel!" visitors to the house were always cooing, especially female visitors; yet Edna Louise could certainly be, after visitors disappeared, a "very bad girl" (as Mummy said).

Poor Edna Louise! Mummy shook her head, "Edna Louise" was such an ugly name.

(Anxiously Skyler asked: was "Skyler" an ugly name, too? And Mummy said quickly No! "Skyler" was a beautiful name.)

Edna Louise had been named for Grandmother Rampike who was Daddy's mother from Pittsburgh. The reason for this, Skyler gathered, was to make Grandmother Rampike "like" Edna Louise, and Mummy, more than Grandmother Rampike might otherwise have liked either of them; for Grandmother Rampike was, as Daddy conceded, an "icy-hearted old gal" with a smile that was the "exact way" a pike would smile "if a pike could smile."

(Skyler erupted into peals of laughter when Daddy said such funny things for often Daddy did not himself smile but spoke gravely, which made Daddy all the funnier. And if Mummy did not laugh, but looked uncomfortable, or blushed, somehow it was even funnier. Especially Skyler laughed when Daddy said how Grandmother Rampike and certain relatives of Daddy's lived in "Piggsburgh" which was the "gruntiest, stinkiest" city in the United States.)

Daddy adored Edna Louise, mostly. Skyler felt a stab of jealousy when Daddy lunged at Edna Louise to swoop her up in his arms calling her "my bestest prettiest little gal." But Daddy was not home much of the time. Mummy was home.

Skyler observed Mummy with Edna Louise and was not jealous, for Skyler sensed how Mummy did not love Edna Louise. Not as Mummy loved Skyler. For Mummy enrolled Edna Louise in the Montessori school when Edna Louise was just two, where Mummy had not wanted to enroll

Skyler at that age because Skyler had been Mummy's *little man* and Mummy's companion on lonely days.

Maria-from-Mexico was in charge of Edna Louise most of the time. Skyler overheard Mummy giving Maria instructions in a rapid distracted voice as if her mind was on other, more important things. Each school-day morning, Maria got Edna Louise ready for school and walked her to the end of the driveway to be picked up by the Montessori minivan; but Mummy got Skyler ready for school and often drove him to Fair Hills Day herself, in the lime-green Chevy Impala, and picked him up after school.

Sometimes, Edna Louise was so lonely!—though she could see that Mummy wasn't in the mood, Edna Louise hung about her, whining, whimpering, wanting a hug from Mummy; so that Mummy had to say, in an exasperated voice, "You make me weary, Edna Louise. I feel as if the two of us have been together a long, long time. Go away."

Skyler felt a mean thrill of satisfaction, hearing this. When Mummy told Skyler to go away it was clear that Mummy did not mean it.

When Mummy relented and told Edna Louise that she was a very good girl, and Mummy loved her, Skyler heard the false brightness in Mummy's voice and thought *No! Mummy loves me.*

One wintry day Skyler saw his little blond sister sprawled on the family room floor amid a scattering of dolls like dead things. He had heard Mummy's sharp voice, and he had heard Mummy on the stairs. (Of course Mummy had not slapped or struck Edna Louise no matter how impatient she became with the strange, willful child, as Mummy did not slap or strike Skyler. That was not Mummy's way!) And Skyler came to Edna Louise, and Skyler asked Edna Louise what was wrong, why was she crying, and Edna Louise sniffed, and wiped her runny little nose on her hand, as Mummy would have been disgusted to see Edna Louise do; and Edna Louise lifted her teary cobalt-blue eyes to Skyler who was so much bigger than Edna Louise, and older, and mattered more, and Edna Louise said in a plaintive voice: "Why doesn't Mummy like me, Skyler, the way Mummy likes you?"

And that was the day Skyler began to love his younger sister. Just a little.

GOLD MEDAL GYM & HEALTH CLUB I

"WHO'S COMPLAINING?" WAS A FAVORED DADDY-SAYING IN THE RAMPIKE household. Also "What's the deal?"—"What's the problem?"—"What's the bottom line?" With cheery vehemence Daddy pronounced "No problem!"—"Case closed!"—*"Fin-it-to"* and *"Batta!"* and "Mission accomplished!"—*"Homo homin lupus!"* Childish fears and tears and terrors were handily banished by a snap of Daddy's fingers for Daddy had a saying, or a snappy comeback, for any situation: "Stay the course!" (Daddy had been a cadet at Bleak Mountain Military Academy in Gallowsville, Pennsylvania, as a boy)—"Cut your losses!" (Daddy had quit Bleak Mountain after two years)—"Never say never!" (Daddy had been a much-lauded athlete through high school and college)—"Don't pour money down a rat hole!" (the essence of financial wisdom, acquired by Daddy from his manufacturer-financier father). For a youngish guy Bix Rampike had already acquired enough world-wisdom to stuff a Grand Canyon of Chinese fortune cookies.

I loved him. I was in terror of him.

Like Mummy. (Too much like Mummy!) For even as you recoiled in hurt, indignation, utter disgust, you could not help but love Bix Rampike, like a kicked, craven puppy, and want Bix Rampike to love *you*.

Daddy was one of those tall seemingly clumsy/alert and "competitive" alpha males with a shaggy-bison head, battered-handsome face, soulful brown eyes that exuded sympathy, sincerity. Big, breezy, affable, and shrewd, he was immensely attractive to both men and women. (Are you thinking of Bill Clinton? Bix Rampike was Slick Willy with a soupçon of Ronald Reagan. Politically, Daddy was all-Reagan.) His skin was ruddy as if pumped with blood and his teeth were large and chunky and frequently bared in a happy carnivore smile. The soulful eyes were "empathetic"—think of that fat juicy water spider that fixes his gaze upon the paralyzed pond frog as by slow inexorable "utterly natural" degrees he sucks the life out of the pond frog: "empathetic." You could feel, no matter who you were, Bix's height or shorter, dazzling beauty or frump, Fair Hills (male) VIP, chic caterer's assistant in black miniskirt or just another of the sturdy-bosomed Marias everyone in Fair Hills employed/complained about; you could feel, even if you were Bix Rampike's runt-son, that Bix Rampike peered into your very soul, and "engaged with" *you*. Only you.

Except that, let's be frank: in a crowded room, as in the vast spaces of life, there are so very many *yous* to be acknowledged, how could Bix Rampike be expected to remember you all?

Way I see it, son: buck up.

Stay the course, never say never, recall that Daddy loves you and that is the bottom line, Amen.

Your mother has shown me, son. The videotape.

It has been destroyed, son. For your protection. Only know: God will forgive.

NO. THIS IS NOT WHAT I WANT. READER, DELETE THIS. READER DELETE this. Emergency *tabbouleh rasa** here!

FAST-FORWARD AND FREEZE AT: BRUCE "BIX" RAMPIKE AS A YOUNGISH suburban dad of thirty-three. The year is 1993. Skyler is six years old and walks (my God, look!) without the slightest suggestion of a limp nor does he wince with pain, or, as he walks, stoically suppress a

---

*Tabbouleh rasa. *Damn "foreign phrase" isn't in my dictionary which is an ominous sign maybe I've misspelled it. No matter: for those of us haphazardly (if expensively) educated and pretentious as hell, dropouts eager to be mistaken as O current, O fate, and O fund, of the cognozenti, polylingual and polymorphous and non plus ultra, it means, possibly in Latin, "a smooth or erased tablet": that's to say "the mind in its hypothetical primary blank or empty state." (Sounds good!)*

wince of pain. Here is a naively happy little boy, you would reasonably think: but you are wrong.

"Sky-boy? Son?"—here comes Daddy striding into the family room with a big-toothy-Daddy smile, slapping his khaki pants with the flats of his hands, in excess-Daddy-exuberance; unless maybe it's Skyler's room, upstairs; must be a Saturday since there seems to be no school and Daddy isn't at work or away for the weekend, as Daddy so frequently is; and Skyler is furtively hunched on the edge of his bed (on the pale blue bedspread with the nautical figures: sailboats, frigates, man-o'-wars, harpoons and anchors); lost in thought Skyler is frowning over one of the Junior Science Series books he has brought home from the school library—*Space Shuttle Heroes?*—*Adventures of a Microbe Hunter?*—*So You Want to Make an A-Bomb: Home Chemistry Fun?*—*Our Venomous Friends: Beware?*—except no, none of these admirable titles, instead Skyler is frowning over one of Mummy's (forbidden) glossy magazines, those glamorous magazines Mummy brings home in her sumptuous Prada handbag; six-year-old Skyler isn't drawn to the pale, gaunt, eerily young-looking girl-models draped near-naked on the magazine covers, and not by the seductive scents released when you scratch a patch of special paper on a perfume advertisement; Skyler isn't even drawn by the garish cover headlines HOW TO ENTICE, ENTRAP, AND PLEASURE THE JADED HUBBY: SIX NO-FAIL STEPS—ALONE OR WITH OTHERS? NINETEEN NO-FAIL STEPS TO ORGASM-PLUS—HOT TIPS FROM TOP DIVORCE LAWYERS—BEYOND PROZAC: BOTOX?—CONFESSIONS OF A (HOT) (MALE) PERSONAL TRAINER—IS LIPOSUCTION THE "PERSONAL TRAINER" OF THE FUTURE?—but by the wish, pathetic in a six-year-old with the halting, fevered reading skills of a budding dyslexic, to understand why Mummy is so unhappy even now that Edna Louise no longer cries through the night and Skyler, Mummy's *little man*, has managed to perform so well in the first grade at (exclusive, expensive) Fair Hills Day School that he is being "seriously considered for promotion" into the "highly competitive" H.I.P. track at the school (of which more later, unfortunately); and before Skyler can steel himself, or protect himself, there's a cuff—playful!—but hard—to Skyler's head, for a dazed instant Skyler sees tiny suns, meteors of neurological sparks as Daddy snatches the magazine out of Skyler's sweaty fingers without glancing at it, tosses it aside with a fierce

Daddy-chuckle: "Son, enough of ruining your eyes with that 'print' crap. We're going out. There's a surprise in store. *Pear und feese*, eh? *Veeta!*"

JESUS. MAYBE I CAN'T DO THIS ONE, EITHER. FOR THIS IS TURNING OUT TO be the dread Gold Medal Gym & Health Club Memory I. (Years of psychologists, therapists, grimly "empathetic" adults raking through, with Skyler, the maggoty rotted flesh of Skyler Rampike's All-American Late-Twentieth-Century Childhood, have reduced my most traumatic memories to such shorthand designations; and the original events themselves, especially horrific in their seeming ordinariness, in the way (as above) they so innocently begin, have been reduced to something resembling stale TV sitcom plots.)

Pear und feese. What does that mean? From time to time Daddy would utter these words in my direction, with a Daddy-chuckle, and if Mummy was close by Daddy would cast me a sly sidelong wink as of male-conspirators, but what's it mean? (Mummy had no idea, either. "One of Daddy's foreign 'sayings,'" Mummy said vaguely.) *Veeta!* was uttered only at the conclusion of a statement, and was usually accompanied by finger-snapping, so you got the point to get moving, hustle fast; years later Grandmother Rampike explained that *Veeta!* was an Italian command, unless it was a French command, favored by my late grandfather Winston Rampike, Daddy's father, invariably accompanied by an impatient snap of his fingers. Loose translation: "Move your ass!"

Maybe for now, since I'm not feeling so great about this, I can back-track a little, away from Gold Medal etcetera to an earlier time. Maybe Daddy from a kiddy-perspective will remind you of your own special Daddy, the Daddy that was just-for-you. Or maybe (lucky you!) if you've never had a Daddy like this, you will feel a perverse sting of envy.

Well! Daddy was big. (Have I said that?) Daddy loomed, Daddy towered. Sometimes, as if playfully (but how could you know for certain?), or threateningly, Daddy teetered above you. Daddy pinched, Daddy poked, Daddy tickled. (Daddy's "spider fingers"!) Daddy was always hurrying in from somewhere (where?) to hug ("Big Bear Hug"—made you swoon!) and to kiss ("Turkey-Gobbler Kiss"—"Boa Constrictor Kiss"—made you giggle!). Because Daddy was so tall, Daddy did a lot of stooping, and swooping, and scooping-up in powerful Daddy-arms, and Daddy lifted you above his head so your own head brushed against the ceiling, Daddy twirled and swirled and tossed and "flipped" you. Daddy had "pet" names as he called them for you: Little Guy, Little Toot, Little Smelly ('way back when Skyler was just emerging from diapers to potty, we can skip this), Junior Peepee (let's skip this). Later came Big Guy, Hotshot, Skye-boy, Son. Also Kid. Also Buddy. Daddy had not nearly so many pet names for Skyler's little sister and only just a few names for Mummy whom he called Gorgeous—My Gorgeous Gal—My Gorgeous-Luscious-Big-Busty Gal—My Sweet-ass Pumkin—My Good-Girl-Scout-Girly-Gal—My Pussy Galore etcetera. (Certain of these Mummy-names were growled in Daddy's throat as Mummy laughingly, or flush-faced with embarrassment, or annoyance, tried to push Daddy away; Skyler was probably not supposed to overhear. So we'll skip these, too.) (As I intend to skip an inventory of Bix Rampike's sex toys, too. Don't expect it.)

In our household, we were very proud of Daddy. Grandmother Rampike, the icy-hearted old gal with a pike's smile, was, it was hoped, proud of Daddy. (And would remember Daddy more generously in her will than she would remember Daddy's conniving, mendacious, deceitful loser-siblings who were, in other guises, Skyler's "uncles" and "aunts.") For Daddy was likely to be, in any gathering, the tallest man in the room; and for a long time, Daddy was likely to be the youngest. It was said of Bix Rampike that he was "up-and-coming" and it was said that "headhunters" were in constant pursuit of him. When the subject came up one day in the Rampike household, and Skyler happened to overhear, the silly kid piped up fearfully, " 'Headhunters'? After Daddy's h-head?" and Mummy and Daddy laughed at Skyler, and filed away little Skyler's query to be repeated, for laughs, in subsequent years; explaining to Skyler that it was "corporate" headhunters who were in pursuit of Daddy, ever tempting him with offers from Baddaxe Oil competitors, and such "corporate" interest was a very desirable thing, and made Daddy "more valuable" as it put Daddy in a "very good bargaining position." Mummy laughed nervously saying, "Darling, we can't move again. We've only just moved here." And Daddy said, "Never say never, darling." And Mummy laughed again, though Mummy's eyes were frightened, and Mummy said, "I still miss Parsippany, we were happy there, I thought," and Daddy chuckled saying, "You said the exact same thing, gorgeous, when we lived in Parsippany: you missed Whippany. And before Whippany, you missed New Axis." (Whippany, New Jersey, and New Axis, a Philadelphia suburb, were before Skyler's time and were not places that meant anything to Skyler, could've disappeared into enormous sinkholes or tar pits, who cares? Except Mummy seemed to care.) (Skyler did not like to think of a time in Mummy's life *before-Skyler* still less that Mummy was claiming now tearfully to have been "happy" then.) Daddy spoke pleasantly, but with an edge to his voice; and Mummy spoke falteringly, as if not knowing what she was saying; and Daddy said, "In such matters, it's wisest to cultivate a strategy of *sand-feud*. Like on the football field. Or poker. That way the sons-abitches can't figure you out." Mummy asked, doubtfully, "Isn't it— *sand-freud*?" Daddy laughed. " 'Freud' is the Jew shrink. What's he got to do with this?" and Mummy said, "Bix, 'Jew' sounds crude. In Fair Hills, people don't talk like that," and Daddy said, "Jews call themselves 'Jews' all the time. What's crude about it?" and Mummy said, "The way you say it sounds different, Bix," and Daddy said, still pleasantly, "Different from what?" and Mummy said, "There are many Jewish people in Fair Hills. Just down the street—" and Daddy said, "Not in the Sylvan Glen Golf Club. I don't think so," and Mummy said, excitedly, "The Sylvan Glen? Did you say *Sylvan Glen*? Were you playing golf there, Bix? That's where you were today?"

They were moving away, out of Skyler's earshot.

IN THOSE YEARS *PEAR UND FEESE* EMERGED AS A RAMPIKE HOUSEHOLD theme at irregular intervals. Skyler understood that it had to do with Daddy spending "quality time" with him, and not (for instance) with Skyler's baby sister, or with Mummy. (Mummy said, "You don't want Skyler to grow up 'gay,' you know a boy needs a 'male model' to emulate," and Daddy said, with a grim Daddy-chuckle, "No way any kid of mine is growing up 'gay.' That's like an obscenity for you to utter, darling.") (Did Skyler really overhear such exchanges? Often!) In the family room in the sprawling white Colonial on Ravens Crest Drive Daddy had installed not one but two gigantic "state-of-the-art" TV screens so that, when crucial sports events occurred simultaneously, Daddy could watch both at the same time, wielding remote controls in both hands. Sometimes a few of Daddy's close buddies joined him to watch "the Stags wash out the Bruins"—"the Pythons crush the Elks"—"the Stingrays destroy the Condors"—"Crampas clobbers McSween"—and all these occasions, which roused Bix, Jim, Dan, Wade, Russ and Rich* to a pitch of noisy enthusiasm, and made them very thirsty, and very hungry, Skyler was pressed by Daddy to attend. "Skyler! Say hi to my friends," was Daddy's genial command, "and run tell your Mummy we'd like some curb service here." (Daddy was just joking! Of course.) Hurriedly Mummy came in Cuban-heeled slippers, a cashmere sweater the hue of crushed strawberries, designer jeans and Mummy's hair perfumy-bouffant-bouncy, and Mummy was blushing with pleasure, Mummy knew herself much-admired by Daddy's buddies, and consequently by Daddy himself, bringing the men ice-cold beers, imported ales, overflowing bowls of pretzels, potato chips and Daddy's favorite salsa dip, and Daddy's favorite cashews; and, after a few minutes' banter, flirtatious, just slightly risqué, Mummy tripped back to another part of the house, and Bix and his friends returned avidly to the giant TV screens where, in football season, mega-men, humanoid figures in bizarrely padded costumes and helmets shiny as the glistening shells of beetles plummeted at one another mercilessly, tirelessly, in pursuit of an object that, at a distance, resembled a giant peanut. "Jesus! Fucking Jesus you see *that*?"—the men's reiterated cries erupted around Skyler leaving him dazed, disoriented. He knew better than to yawn for (as Mummy often observed, fondly) Daddy had "piranha eyes on

* *Do we give a damn about Bix's blurred boozy sports-buddies? Do we care to know their last names, what they looked like, where they lived and whether their wives were friendly/not-so-friendly to Mummy? We do not. For Jim, Dan, Wade, Russ and Rich will be dropped within a few months by Bix Rampike as the "up-and-coming" junior exec is promoted above and beyond their income range/social status with naught but a mildly abashed-boyish backward glance of regret.*

the sides of his head" and Skyler did not wish to be scolded by Daddy in front of Daddy's friends but Skyler could not prevent tears of boredom from sliding down his cheeks.

(In the kitchen, Mummy was laughing. Why was Mummy laughing? And was this sad Mummy-laughter, or happy Mummy-laughter? And was Edna Louise with Mummy? Skyler wanted to be with Mummy and Edna Louise where Skyler was the *little man* and the center of both Mummy's and Edna Louise's attention.)

(Skyler was not jealous of Edna Louise for Edna Louise was not happy at the Montessori school, described by the director as "weepy" and "listless"; while Skyler, in first grade at Fair Hills Day, was one of the top students in his class and already reading "at least at third grade level.")

Stupefyingly dull as TV sports were, halftimes and breaks were more hellish for it was then that Daddy tried to spark "sports-talk" between Skyler and the men, each of whom was equipped with at least one husky strapping athlete-son named Mikey, or Dickie, or Kevin, or Charles and the question pitched to Skyler was which sport was his sport and Skyler had no sport, especially Skyler disliked rough rowdy running-and-yelling sports (football, soccer) where the sole object was jeering triumph: WE WIN, YOU LOSE. Yet Skyler was expected to reply, had not better shrug, or mumble, Daddy had a fierce dislike of mumblers for "only losers mumble," or was it "only assholes," Skyler had sensed that *frisson* of pride when Bix Rampike had introduced Skyler to his friends *This is my son. This is my DNA* and did not want to disappoint Daddy and so said, vaguely, haphazardly, having seen a few minutes of TV Olympics gymnasts, astonishingly agile young athletes from China, Russia, Ukraine: "Gymnastics." The men regarded Skyler with inscrutable expressions and Bix, wielding both remote controls, cursed to himself for what reason Skyler did not know.

The game was over! One of the games, at least.

Must've been halftime. The men were talking. Like Bix Rampike these were affable, breezy, good-humored men who laughed often, and loudly. There was a kind of contest among them: who could make the others laugh most. Or the contest was: who laughed the most. Yet there was Daddy saying, "God, I miss the team. My Cornell teammates, I miss. I miss being young. Y'know, that young. Double-practice days, in the heat. I mean serious heat. Then, in the season, like a locomotive it goes so fast, we'd play in the mud, starts to snow we'd play in the snow, get knocked around, in the head and in the gut and stay up all night drinking, and screwing, and get smashed, and fucked-out, and next day by early afternoon you're ready to go again, Jesus that's a life." Daddy sighed, roughly wiping his mouth on the edge of his hand. "That's a life that is gone from us now."

Daddy's buddies were still smiling but looks of doubt and uncertainty had come into their faces. One of the men, Rich, or maybe Russ, made a snorting sound to signal mild derision, good common sense: "Sure, shit, but there's compensation, isn't there? You can't be twenty all your life."

Another said cheerfully: "There's—well, getting married. Having kids."

A long silence.

"There's making money."

The men laughed, loudly. There was a merry clicking of beer/ale bottles against teeth.

But Daddy persisted, in a pensive mood: "Those things are what you get for losing the other. Future generations of *Homo sapiens* will engineer themselves not to age. 'Genetic engineering.' Way I see it, the bottom line is *Homo sapiens* will be extinct in a century, the old species I mean, like we are not our puny ancestors, y'know?—we are taller, and smarter, and live longer if maybe not long enough. 'Humankind is something that must be overcome.'"

"CLIMB IN, SKYLER. I TOLD YOU, WE'RE RUNNING LATE."

Daddy was in a hurry. Daddy did not like to be delayed. Impatiently Daddy jammed the key into the ignition of his new Jeep Crusher XL as Skyler struggled to crawl up into the cab that rode as high from the ground as Skyler was tall. Daddy took no notice of Skyler panting and puffing nor did he check, as Mummy always did, to see if Skyler had buckled himself into the seat-harness.

With one hand Daddy steered the new steel-blue vehicle along serpentine Ravens Crest Drive at twice the speed limit—no burly guy in a carpenter's cap was likely to tailgate Daddy and honk at him to speed up, you betcha!—while with the other Daddy fussed with the dashboard's vents, air temperature control, tape deck. Daddy was wearing a (faded) Cornell sweatshirt and rumpled khaki trousers and size thirteen Nike running shoes and Daddy's hair had been recently trimmed and stood straight from his head like dense grass. His profile looked like something hacked out of a coarse kind of rock (soapstone?) but his expression was intended to be upbeat, optimistic. (One of Daddy's more recent favorite sayings was *If you're not an optimist you're dead meat.*) The previous week had been a time of more than usual confusion in the household since Daddy had been away for several nights in succession and Mummy had not seemed to know where Daddy was, or when Daddy would be home. At the Great Road, Daddy swore under his breath having to swerve around a crew of dispirited-looking Hispanic laborers waiting in the rain (it seemed to be raining here) to be picked up by a foreman. Daddy said, "That's something no white man need ever do, if he's educated."

Shyly Skyler asked where were they going but Daddy took no notice for Daddy was waiting for a light to change and eyeing a fellow in a Road Warrior on the other side of the intersection, whose red-blinking turn light signaled *left-turn.* Softly Daddy murmured, "Don't even think of it, chum." In the very instant the light turned from red to green, Daddy floored the gas pedal and the Jeep Crusher XL charged forward and through the intersection and Daddy had only to chuckle deep in his throat at the other driver's expression. The Jeep's sudden acceleration had caused Skyler to become tangled in the safety harness but Skyler was able to extricate himself without drawing Daddy's attention. In his brooding/visionary voice Daddy was saying, "Way I see it, son: your generation of Americans, born in the late 1980s, is about to burst out of the starting gates. You may be just a kid—what are you, seven?—*six?*—but already at six, in other parts of the world, the new generation is being primed for combat. The bottom line is, civilization is 'worlds in collision.' Civilization is 'survival of the fittest.' The United States is the sole remaining superpower now the Commies have been crushed which means that every lesser power has got us in their gun sights, to overcome. Here's the deal, Skyler: your grandmother Rampike put plenty of pressure on your Mummy and me, to name you after my father Winston Rampike but guess what?—though your Mummy gave in, I demeered. I said, 'Momma, I loved Dad but my son is my son to name and the name I have chosen for my firstborn son is 'Sky-ler.' 'Sky-ler Ram-pike.' That is a beautiful name. When they gave me you to hold, Skyler, in the hospital, Jesus! Still get tears in my eyes at the memory. 'Skyler' is to rise above the merely commonplace, son. 'Sky's the limit!'—that is your secret destiny. Mummy believes so, too. Mummy has the identical hopes for you that I do. Which is why we went that extra mile, son, to get you into Fair Hills Day School, to set you apart from those children who attend public schools. But Mummy has told me that the head-master at your school has told her 'Skyler is going to need special instruction in physical fitness'—so the athletics director has reported to him. Sure, you're only in first grade, but like I said 'survival of the fittest' starts young. Most animal life doesn't survive the first few days; hell, the first few minutes." Daddy laughed exuberantly, as if this was amusing, or served most animal life right. "See, to get you into the H.P.I. track at the school—"

Skyler said: " 'H.I.P.,' Daddy." What Daddy had been saying was diffi-cult to follow and what he could follow was upsetting to him but this Sky-ler knew: "H.I.P." (Though he hadn't any idea what the initials might mean.)

" 'H.I.P.,' 'H.P.I.'—whatever. The bottom line is, it's the fast track at that expensive God-damn school and we're not going to fuck up our kid's chances for the rest of his life because he needs 'special instruction' in athletics. Now, team sports were my thing. Little League I was playing when I could barely hold up the bat. And playing pretty God-damn good, too. Sure, these days I play golf, tennis, squash, but when I was a kid and through college it was running with the guys, mixing it up with the guys, nothing like it. Happiest time of a man's life, he'll tell you if he's being honest. On the football field, with your buddies, you know life for what it is and the rest is bullshit. Gymnastics is a whole other thing. Gymnastics is for another kind of athlete and another kind of body. I have to admit, Skyler, I was kind of—well, hurt—when—"

Gymnastics? Was this the surprise? Was Daddy taking him

to—gymnastics? A *gym*? Skyler felt the safety harness strap tight against his throat like a gripping hand.

"—but put aside personal feelings, that's what a father learns to do. The deal is, we have to start you really young, to keep up with the competition. In the Free World which is where we live, we don't wallow in state-supported athletic programs. Individuals have to pay. This is over and above property taxes. 'No free lunch in the universe'—know who said that, Skyler?—Einstein. Also, 'God does not play dice with the universe.' The father of the A-bomb. Einstein was a Jew and you don't fuck with Jews, Skyler. My father used to say, 'I may be a bit of a Jew,' with a wink, meaning he had the Jewish brain for making money and I like to think that I've inherited some of that and have passed a little of it on to you, too, Skyler. Why I transferred from Rensselaer Polytech to Cornell and switched from chemical engineering to business administration, and sure have never regretted the switch. You're an engineer, you do what people tell you, for hire; you're an executive, you do the telling and the hiring and you don't need to break your head over God-damn fucking 'higher math.' Spring of my senior year there were pro football teams recruiting me and there were top companies wanting to hire me and the point is, Skyler, to get anywhere, start young, and *stay the course*. Who d'you think will be the Olympic gold medalists of your generation, Skyler, but those who—"

As Daddy turned the Jeep Crusher XL onto Cross Tree Road, the car phone rang, and Daddy cursed under his breath and fumbled to answer it, "Rampike here," as Skyler stared numbly at him. Skyler had been able to follow only snatches of all that Daddy had seemed to be confiding in him but understood that something crucial was imminent, and that he must not disappoint Daddy again.

On the phone Daddy was speaking in a lowered voice. Murmuring, "No. Can't. Tomorrow. Right!" Daddy listened briefly, grunted something monosyllabic, and hung up.

"Son, did I ever tell you how I played fullback in high school? And how we'd play these redneck bastards from country high schools who were really built, I mean *built*—and no fucking steroids in those days?" Daddy shook his head in grudging admiration. "They kicked my ass plenty, but I learned from them. I learned that a boy does not take the easy course, as a man must not take the easy course. I learned that a boy's teammates are his closest brothers, he can depend upon. My best friend was Spit Hotchkiss—fearless player, and smart. But the redneck bastards ganged up on him. Our first game away, senior year, Spit was tackled, fell hard, half the opponents' team jumped on him, his neck is broke and his 'upper vertebrae' and Spit is carried off the field on a stretcher and—" A muffled sob escaped from Daddy's throat as skillfully he negotiated the Jeep Crusher XL into traffic on Cross Tree Road. "—the point of this is, Skyler, on this crucial morning in both our lives, my buddy Spit was confined to a wheelchair ever after that night, and the rest of that season, at our games, Spit's teammates would carry Spit out onto the field before a game, and our North Hills cheerleaders had a special 'Spit cheer' the crowd went crazy for. Skyler, son, I am warning you: any point in your life, ask yourself the way your life is going, who the hell's gonna carry you out on the field in your wheelchair and cheer *you*?"

And suddenly, they'd arrived at the Gold Medal Gym & Health Club.

IN SKYLER'S QUAVERING MEMORY THE STUCCO BUILDING DOMINATING AN entire corner of the Cross Tree Shopping Center was enormous, surrounded by a sea of gleaming vehicles. On the windowless facade were "mosaics" of gigantic humanoid athletes intent upon arduous physical activities: diving! swimming! running! tennis! weight lifting! pole-vaulting! Happily Daddy said, "Here we are, kid! 'First day of Skyler's new life.'" Daddy took no notice of how Skyler was struggling to disentangle himself from the damned safety harness, how Skyler managed to climb/fall down from the high cab of the Jeep and in the process discovering that something seemed to be stuck to the sole of one of his sneakers—a wad of gum, and a dried, stiff tissue smeared with something like ketchup, or blood. "Scrape that shit off your foot, Skyler," Daddy said irritably, as if what was stuck on Skyler's shoe was Skyler's doing, "before we go inside." Skyler stared at what appeared to be a small, soggy, deflated rubber balloon stuck to his sneaker sole: what was a small, soggy, deflated rubber balloon doing on the floor of Daddy's shiny new Jeep Crusher XL?* And the stained tissue. Quickly Daddy herded Skyler into the Gold Medal Gym & Health Club complaining that they were late for their appointment, Mummy had slowed them down. Yet Daddy appeared to be in good spirits as if just stepping into the special atmosphere of the Gold Medal was cheering to him. In the (faded) Cornell sweatshirt and rumpled khaki pants Bix Rampike moved like an affable upright bear, scenting prey.

A young woman receptionist in a cherry-red jumpsuit with outsized brass zippers, frizzed streaked-blond hair and three-inch polished nails, greeted this father/son duo warmly. Took Daddy's name and made a quick call to "Vassily" in another part of the building. Saying to Daddy, her eyelashes lowered, "Know who you remind me of, Mr. Rampike? Arnold Schwarzenegger." Daddy shifted his shoulders in a gesture of boyish modesty though the resemblance had been pointed out to Bix Rampike in the past. "Wish it was so, Chérie." (For there was CHÉRIE in gold satin script on the receptionist's cherry-red left breast.) Seeing that it was Mr. Rampike's first visit to the gym, Chérie volunteered to take him and his son to their destination: "Wouldn't want you to get lost, would we?" Only vaguely Skyler took note of Daddy and the receptionist striding ahead as, like a puppy fearful of being left behind, Skyler had to trot to keep up with the adults who seemed to have forgotten him. How quick Daddy was to "make friends"! Anywhere they went, especially when Mummy wasn't with them, Daddy struck up conversations with complete strangers. Especially women.

It was good that Chérie was escorting Daddy and Skyler to their destination, for the interior of the Gold Medal Gym & Health Club was vast and labyrinthine. There were brightly lit courts marked RACQUETBALL, BASKETBALL, VOLLEYBALL. There were areas marked ACUPUNCTURE, CHIROPRACTIC, VITAMIN & HORMONE THERAPY. There was SAUNA, there was MASSAGE,

---

* *What the hell is this? A used condom? A condom? In Daddy's new Jeep Crusher? That bastard! That deceitful son of a bitch! Only now it dawns on me, Daddy must've been screwing one of his girl assistants, or, who knows, some hooker he'd picked up somewhere. Skyler, poor dumb kid, wouldn't have had a glimmering of a clue what any of this meant for all Skyler knew of "sex" was that it involved doing desperate things to "keep your hubby from wandering."*

there was STRENGTH TRAINING and there was FITNESS CENTER: a large, brightly lit space into which jaunty rock music was being piped, where individuals of various sizes were struggling with machines (Skyler recognized NordicTrack, Nautilus, treadmills and stationary bicycles, but there were more sinister machines trussed with leather straps like torture-chairs, he shuddered to see), their frantic efforts doubled in mirrors as if in mockery. There was an enormous swimming pool, bright aqua water in which individuals swam in lap lanes like demented seals and next was WEIGHT ROOM where individuals, mostly men, were perceived struggling to lift weights, grimacing, grunting, sweating as covertly they eyed their reflections in floor-to-ceiling mirrors that seemed to shimmer with inaudible laughter. A cruel punishment it seemed to Skyler, that adults had not only to struggle so, but were made to watch themselves in mirrors.

At the farthest corner of the building, as in an anteroom of hell, was GYMNASTICS LAB. Here the jaunty rock music had been supplanted by somber electronic music, a slow, wan pulse barely discernible above the vibrating hum of air-conditioning. "Vassily! Here is Mr. Rampike and his son Skyler," Chérie called gaily to a gnome-like little man who was overseeing the predicament of a lanky boy who seemed to have gotten one foot caught inside a leather ring hanging from the ceiling, while the other foot had come free, so that the boy dangled helplessly upside down a few inches above a floor mat, like a mangled worm on a hook. Skyler tasted panic: Was Daddy going to make him do *that*?

Before departing Chérie wished Skyler "the best of luck" and gave Daddy her "personal card" which Daddy pocketed in his khaki pants in a fluid, intimate gesture.

Deftly Daddy guided Skyler forward, his fingers lightly gripping the nape of Skyler's neck. Skyler's frightened eyes observed that he was by far the youngest, and the smallest, individual in the Gymnastics Lab. There appeared to be about twenty or twenty-five gymnasts—boys, girls?— difficult to tell for all were painfully thin. The most energetic were those swinging on rings, kicking their feet high, arms and shoulders straining and in their faces looks of pinched concentration. Others were working out on parallel bars, and on horizontal bars, and on fearsome-looking ropes that hung from the ceiling high above. There was a large trampoline upon which several individuals were noisily jumping, flailing their arms, somersaulting forward, somersaulting backward, in wayward leaps and lunges as if at the mercy of fierce gusts of wind. (Weren't trampolines supposed to be dangerous? Didn't children break their necks, their backs in falls from trampolines? Skyler took comfort knowing that Mummy would never let him climb up on any damn old trampoline, ever!) On long mats laid on the hardwood floor a number of gymnasts were "tumbling": multiple somersaults, handstands and cartwheels, straining back-bends, terrifying "splits." A lone young gymnast (evidently male, adolescent, with puny, grape-sized genitals outlined in spandex tights, upside-down) balanced himself on his head and forearms, motionless as a stalagmite.

In "Phs. Ed." class at Fair Hills Day, Skyler had been made, with other first-grade boys, to "tumble" on similar shinily-gray mats laid on the floor, mostly somersaults, frantically rolling to the end of the mat where if he wasn't careful, or even if he was, Skyler invariably struck a knee against the floor and winced with pain.

It was the mats he hated: the sight of them, and the smell.

Like flattened snakes, they were. Or worse, those flat-bodied seemingly eyeless undersea creatures called rays. The distinctive smell—rubbery-plastic, moist and sweaty—made his nostrils pinch.

Skyler tugged at Daddy's arm whispering, "Daddy, I don't w-want to be here," but Daddy was already addressing the gnome-like Vassily: "Hi! I'm Bix Rampike and this is my son Skyler who wants to be the best God-damned gymnast you can make him."

Vassily smiled, startled. His smile exposed damp gums and oddly spaced tea-colored teeth. He seemed in awe of this American Daddy who loomed over him, extending a hand to shake his hand, vigorously. The gymnastics instructor was perhaps five-feet-five, to Daddy's six-feet-three, and at least seventy pounds lighter than Daddy. He was of any age between thirty-five and fifty-five, with a tight, compact body covered in ropey muscles like scar tissue. His face was creased and shrewd, his thumbnail eyes wary, watchful. In exotically accented English he said, " 'Ram-pick.' 'Skeel-er.' Yes he*llo*. I am instructor here: 'trainer.' I am Vassily Andreevich Volokhomsky. I am 'White Russian.' I am winner silver medal, gymnastics, World Olympics Japan 1972, when I am eighteen. I am departed Soviet Union, 1973. I am U.S. citizen now. Frankly said, I am the best trainer of young athletes, for hundred miles." Daddy said, impressed, "First time I've shaken hands with an actual Olympic medal winner. This is great, Vassily! And 'White Russian'—we're 'White American.' Mostly this part of New Jersey is except in some fields, like for instance computers, and engineering, and medical technology, and 'research' . . ." Daddy's voice trailed off, it was time to nudge Skyler forward, to shake Vassily Andreevich Volokhomsky's hand, too.

"'Skeel-er'? Is not usual name, eh?" Quickly Vassily released Skyler's limp little hand as if fearful of breaking it. "He is very very young, Mr. Rampike. There are preschool classes for gymnasts, but not here. 'Every gymnast a star'—that is their boast. But not here, we are more serious as you can see."

Daddy said, "*I'm* serious. My wife and I are eager to support our son who has a dream of being a gymnast and can't get the right kind of professional training at his school, for sure. We don't have time to dawdle, frankly. Skyler is almost eight."

"Eight?" Vassily regarded Skyler doubtfully. "Very young for eight, and his muscles are soft tissue, you can see."

Daddy laughed heartily, Vassily was so mistaken. Deftly Daddy flexed Skyler's right bicep for him, and squeezed the minuscule flesh between his massive thumb and forefinger. "See? The kid's got muscle. Budding-muscle. And these leg muscles"—Daddy gripped Skyler's right calf, hard—"are even more impressive. Not bad for a suburban kid who sits on his ass doing homework and perusing his Mummy's sex magazines, eh?" (Daddy winked at Skyler who stared at him open-mouthed. Just kidding!) "Sure, Vassily, I'm aware: there are gymnastics classes for younger kids. But Skyler is not like other kids his age. This 'peer-group' bullshit, marching in lockstep like socialist robots, is not for us. (Sorry: you might be a 'Marxist,' eh? Except if you're one of us U.S. citizens now, could be capitalism is looking more attractive?) Like I said, we don't have time to dawdle. I've paid for one hour's instruction today and we're wasting time talking. Start the kid out with 'tumbling' like those kids are doing, that doesn't look too hard. Small kid like Skyler, he'll be great on the mats and at those kinds of showy routines the Olympic gymnasts do on the bars.

Skyler can work his way up to rings and ropes, I'm assuming those are more challenging. Me," Daddy laughed, shifting his shoulders in an abashed gesture, "I'd be lousy at gymnastics. Already in grade school I was playing football and I went on to play fullback at Cornell and had a few pro offers, now I'm a decent golfer, I play tennis, squash with guys like myself, but gymnastics?—hell, I'd break my neck on the mats, or pull down the ceiling on the rings. So I'm going to entrust you with my son's athletic future, Vassily, because you're not just a pro who comes highly recommended, you're an Olympic winner and obviously you know the ropes of amateur sports and whatever progress Skyler makes in the next few months, if it's what I hope for, the bottom line is there's a bonus for you, comrade! 'Sky's the limit,' see?"

During this impassioned outburst, the gnome-like White Russian gaped upward at Bix Rampike towering over him: this fervent American with his frank, boyishly open face and intense soulful eyes, something shrewd and carnivorous about the mouth. "I will try, Mr. Ram-pike. 'Skeel-er' and I, we will try very hard."

ALL THIS WHILE, SKYLER HAD BEEN STARING AT A YOUNG GYMNAST CLOSE by—bony-chested, prominent pelvic bones inside a tight blue-black spandex doublet, a fixed, fanatic expression in the angular face— possibly a girl, of about fifteen—hair scraped back into a meager ponytail—who was lifting herself with excruciating slowness onto a horizontal bar and then, somehow, by sheer tremulous strength, above the bar, the tendons in her neck taut and her arms quivering with strain. The girl's glassy eyes locked with Skyler's *Run away! Run out of here! It isn't too late for you, run away!*

Instead, Skyler shut his eyes.

GOLD MEDAL GYM & HEALTH CLUB II

YOU, THE CANNY/PERCEPTIVE READER, INFUSED WITH A (SECRET, SUBTLE) streak of sadism, are pretty sure you know where this is headed, aren't you? Poor hapless Skyler left in the Gymnastics Lab with Vassily Andree-vich Volokhomsky while Daddy ambles off elsewhere in the Gold Medal Gym & Health Club with the admirable intention of, as he says, lifting weights, maybe run on a treadmill, whatever daddys do, restless and randy daddys like Bix Rampike who are frequently told by adoring young women like Chérie that they resemble the Terminator Schwarzenegger himself; poor Skyler whose fate careens toward him like a tractor-trailer truck with failed brakes plunging down a steep mountain road. You steel your-self for the inevitable crash. You might even shut your eyes as Skyler did, back in whenever this was, an unnamed season in 1993 when Skyler walked without the slightest suggestion of a limp and "Bliss Rampike" had not yet been invented.

A happier time, it must have been. A more innocent time.

For *What if* Skyler had thrived as a young gymnast? *What if* that day at the Gold Medal Gym & Health Club, Skyler had unexpectedly revealed athletic promise, hitherto unguessed-at? *What if* the Rampike son and not the Rampike daughter had become the child-prodigy celebrity of Fair Hills, New Jersey?

What if. These tattered and corroded memories are being presented in this document as if only just unfolding, which gives to the document a cinematic sort of "present-action" that is misleading, for of course all this is over. Skyler in the Gymnastics Lab where, that first day, he is made to exhaust himself in repetitive "stretching exercises" on a rubbery-plastic mat, with only a few clumsy somersaults overseen by the disdainful White Russian, *and no injuries*; Skyler's Daddy mysteriously elsewhere, who knows where, or with whom, so that Daddy is forty minutes late returning to the Gymnastics Lab to call out with a large, lopsided, abashed-but-unapologetic grin, "So, comrade, how'd the kid do?"*; the Gold Medal Gym & Health Club dominating an entire corner of the Cross Tree Shopping Center with its stucco fortress and "mosaic" humanoid athletes long since bankrupt, the very building razed, gutted to the ground and replaced with a steel-and-aluminum high-rise office building. (For the Cross Tree Shopping Center, dazzling-upscale in its era, could not compete with the far more dazzling-upscale, gigantic Mall of Liberty only three miles away near a handy exit of Interstate 80.) *Sick transit gloria* or whatever the (Latin) expression is, maybe my editor will know.

Jesus! These vertiginous fast-forwards into what's called the future, they scare me, too.

Let me return to that first Saturday. And slow-motion forward as in a dreamy cinematic montage: as Daddy led me, fingers at the nape of my neck firmly guiding me in a reverse course through the labyrinthine corridors of the Gold Medal Gym & Health Club on that first occasion of my gymnastics training, and back outside into daylight, as we headed back to the Jeep Crusher XL amid a sea of similarly shiny, expensive, American S.U.V./military-style vehicles, Daddy asked how I felt about my "workout"

---

* *"Never apologize, never explain!" was one of the cheerier cornerstones of Bix Rampike's personal ethic. So in the Rampike household you'd never know where Daddy was, particularly at any time when, you'd thought, Daddy was supposed to be with you. (So Mummy had come to realize. Not very happily.) In this case, in the Gymnastics Lab, to be replicated on each subsequent Saturday there, four in all, Daddy was somewhat short of breath, flushed in the cheeks and seemingly distracted but in very good spirits as if, possibly, he and the glamorous streaky-blond Chérie had crept off somewhere for a romantic/erotic tussle (there was a wheelchair-access lavatory in the corridor beyond the receptionist's counter, a sizable space and totally private; there was a soiled-towel laundry room; there was the domain of the masseuse K. Chee, currently unoccupied); or, less intriguing, and a disappointment (sorry!) to the voyeur-reader, Daddy had actually been lifting weights ("pumping iron") or panting away on the treadmill or another of the dread cardiovascular machines; or, who knows, Daddy had slipped away from the Gold Medal Gym & Health Club entirely, to have a beer or two at the Cross Tree Bistro close by. Maybe Daddy called back whoever it was who'd dared to call him, on a suburban Saturday morning, on his car phone. Hey: didn't I tell you? Never call me on my home turf.*

with my "personal trainer" and, in typical eager-Skyler manner (despite a dazed dizziness in my head from somersaulting on the mat and sharp pains in both knees from striking the gym floor, I did truly feel a glimmer of—was it hope?), I said, "Good, Daddy! I l-loved it," and Daddy gave a little *Whoop!* of pleasure, grabbed me in the crook of his strong arm and kissed me wetly on the mouth, saying, in a choked-Daddy voice, "Son, I'm damned proud of you. Hell, I'm *impressed*."

Daddy! I guess I adored the son of a bitch, like everyone else.

(MUMMY AND EDNA LOUISE ASKED WHAT HAD SKYLER LEARNED AT THE GYM and so, on the thick-piled rug of the family room, clumsily Skyler replicated somersaults, a handstand or two, or attempts at handstands, culminating in a collision with a chair, an overturned lamp. Mummy laughed, and Mummy scolded. And Edna Louise who was just a little girl, so much smaller than Skyler, and more nimble, imitated her big brother by somersaulting across the floor in an almost-fluid motion of her wiry little body. Her handstands were less certain, at first. Said Skyler, "Not bad for a girl.")

SUBSEQUENT VISITS TO THE GYMNASTICS LAB, AS THE CANNY/PERCEPTIVE reader with the sadistic streak might suspect, were not always so festive, nor did they end with Daddy hugging-and-kissing his son. Not invariably!

Though, to give him credit, Vassily tried valiantly and without evident irony (excepting, at times, an upward roll of his inscrutable eyes, a look of clenching about his jaws) in the rigors and rewards of "elementary" matwork; and to instill in him, in grave, heavily accented English, the gymnast's catechism: "Strength. Flexibility. Control. These are our goals. To which we add: grace, harmony of movement, and control. To which we add: to overcome uncertainty, and to overcome the fear of pain. 'In gymnastics, each pupil is a potential star.' *That* is Vassily Andreevich Volokhomsky's belief, Skeel-er. Who fails, does so for lack of will."

Skyler smiled faintly. Was that a good thing, to overcome a fear of pain? Wouldn't it be better, the shrewd six-year-old reasoned, to overcome pain? Better yet, to avoid pain?

Who fails, does so for lack of will.

This, grimmest of Russian folk-proverbs, causes a shiver to ripple up my spine, to this very day.

Yet: you'd be wrong to think that, despite how things turned out, I have no happy memories of the Gymnastics Lab and the hours of "training" under the tutelage of the gnome-like White Russian, because I do. Truly, I do!

- The heart-stopping occasion when, aided by Vassily's practiced, patient hands, I managed to balance myself on my head and forearms on the mat, quivering legs stretched aloft, and feet together, for enough seconds to warrant a spontaneous round of applause from several observing young gymnasts ("Great work, Skyler!"—"That is so cool, Skyler!") and gushing insincere praise from Vassily ("Skeel-er! You are seeing it is not so hard is it?")

- A dazzling demonstration of gymnastics by Vassily's star tumbler Kevin, at Vassily's request, that involved a running leap onto the mat, a sequence of flawlessly executed cartwheels the length of the mat, and back; yet more remarkable body-flips, front-, back-, courageously performed and seemingly effortless; coaxing a rare smile from Kevin at the sight of my astonished face, and the mumbled prediction that, if I "kept at it," I'd be "just as good, someday."

- A murmured query from the usually reticent Vassily, shortly after Daddy breezed out of the gym one morning: "Your papa, Skeel-er, must be VIP, I think? 'Ram-pike'—a politician?"

- Vassily's kind encouragement when, gripping the horizontal bar, I finally succeeded in pulling myself up to—nearly!—the level of my chin, not once but several times; and even, trembling with the strain, holding myself for several suspenseful seconds until my grip weakened, and I fell onto the mat: "Very good, Skeel-er! Each small step is a step to success."

(Please don't sneer: these casual words in Vassily's exotic English yet reverberate in the murky air of this squalid room on Pitts Street, New Brunswick, more than thirteen years later. Sure I know Vassily didn't mean it, not for a nanosecond, and yet! for those of us so rarely praised, even insincerity can touch the heart.)

AND THEN.

Unexpectedly.

So strangely . . .

Grimly smiling/carelessly shaved Bix Rampike jet-lagged and cranky from a trip to Saudi Arabia (which Skyler misheard as Sandy Arabia) on oil business, was late driving Skyler to the Gymnastics Lab on that final Saturday in some dismal New Jersey season (winter? overcast sky like the interior of a soiled canvas tent) with his big beefy shoulders hunched over the steering wheel of the Jeep Crusher XL and his fleshy lower lip outthrust. Where on previous Saturdays, Daddy had been cheery and talkative and in a good-Daddy mood, today it seemed that Daddy was not good-Daddy, and scarcely glanced at Skyler trussed in the safety harness beside him. Earlier that day, Skyler had overheard muffled voices in Daddy and Mummy's bedroom and (unless he'd dreamt it) from time to time during the night. Outside their parents' bedroom, sitting on the top step of the stairs, her Colonial American Girl Doll in her arms, was little Edna Louise in pajamas, barefoot and shivering. Skyler scolded, as Mummy would have done: "Edna Louise, you shouldn't be barefoot. It's *cold.*" Skyler liked to scold his little sister, for Edna Louise looked at him so pleadingly, as if begging to be forgiven; and Skyler liked to forgive. Skyler took his sister's limp chill little hand and led Edna Louise back into the nursery, as Edna Louise's room was still called, and found fuzzy yellow slippers for her to put on. It was 7:50 A.M. and Edna Louise's Mother Goose lamp that was the size of an actual goose had been burning through the night. Skyler, so much bigger, older, and smarter than Edna Louise, and now training to be a gymnast, did not require a "night-light" in his room in order to sleep. No longer!

Wide-eyed Edna Louise said, "Skyler, where does Daddy go when

Daddy goes away?" and Skyler said importantly, "Sandy Arabia. On oil business."

Aren't kids cute? At least, before the age of ten.

IN THE GYMNASTICS LAB, DADDY FAILED TO GREET VASSILY ANDREEVICH Volokhomsky with his usual beaming-Daddy smile, and failed to thrust out his mammoth-Daddy hand for a bone-crushing hand-shake between macho males, if of contrasting sizes, body types. In-stead, Daddy greeted the diminutive Vassily coolly: "H'lo." And Daddy lingered longer than usual—ominously longer, Skyler could have told Vassily—observing his son being instructed on the mats; at last interrupting Vassily in a lowered voice, yet not so lowered a voice that others in the gym might not overhear: " 'Scuse me, Vas'ly Andervitch—Kolonoskopi—whatever—I'm not seeing much progress here. I know you're a pro, you're a *bonafid* Olympic medal winner, I know because, comrade, I did a little background check, but at these prices, I have to admit that I am just a little disappointed, *verstayen*? My son isn't a 'natural-born' athlete, I grant you. His gifts are more what you'd call 'intellectual'—'cerebral.' I can accept that. But you, Vas'ly, are not challenging him sufficiently. Damn kid is as clumsy today as he was last week and the week before and that's the bottom line. Either you are making progress or you are not. Either you are improving or you're screwing up. See, watching Skyler this morning, I'm thinking that he isn't 'improving' at any reasonable pace. Kids younger than him are already world-class gymnasts and look at him—panting like a dog. At these prices, comrade, I want better for my son than a *turd farce*,* see? I was an athlete all through school. I had a succession of damned good coaches, and they worked us like hell. Kicked our asses, we didn't put out for them. Bottom line is, Vas'ly, I'm not impressed with what's going on here. I'll be checking back in a while and I will expect to see some visible 'progress' in this

---

* Turd farce? *This one has me stumped.*

kid's performance, Vas'ly. And no panting like a dog, *ver-shstayzen-zie?*"

Daddy departed. You could feel the air cleaving as Daddy passed through. Poor Vassily stood as if stunned, unmoving like one who has been penetrated by a bolt of lightning that has fixed him in place even as he's been gutted. Skyler did not need to look at the gnome-like trainer to know that a hot blush had come into his creased face suffusing upward into his scalp even as the little man's posture remained ramrod straight.

On the flattened-snake mat with its faint sickening smell frantic Skyler began somersaulting fast, fast, FAST.

FUCK IT: LET'S FAST-FORWARD. TERMINATE THIS SORRY EPISODE IN SKY-ler's childhood some twenty minutes later: the (mouth-panting) kid has fallen, hard. Like a sack of damp sand he lies stunned beneath gaily swinging rings, beginning now to whimper, and to writhe on the hardwood floor where the momentum of his reckless flight has propelled him—fatally—beyond the mat. Most stupid of mistakes for a gymnast, you don't land on the mat. A scant few seconds before the kid had seemed not to hear his trainer telling him to stop, wild careening swinging *Hey this is fun! I can do this! Look at me I can do this* until as one might expect his left hand lost its grip and Skyler fell, fell hard, harder than you'd expect such a puny body to fall, in an instant his right wrist is sprained, right side of his skull slams against the floor, right leg twice-broken (femur, fibula), this kid will be a medical novelty at the Fair Hills Medical Center. And there comes tragic Vassily Andreevitch Volokhomsky stumbling to his fallen charge, seeing, in the child's writhing figure, the dream of the Bonus fading like a mirage in hot sunshine, poor Vassily screaming in an incomprehensible tongue for someone to dial 911.

CRIPPLE?*

JESUS KID I'M SORRY

    Skyler darling? this is Mummy   Mummy loves you so

       swear to you, son   never meant push you   son

    pray for you darling both of us Mummy and

          God-damn very best orthopetric   pediatic

    good as new, darling!   Mummy and Daddy promise

         damn Vas'ly   can't trust Commie bastard

     Edna Louise is here honey   can you open your eyes honey?

    million-dollar lawsuit that Commie bastard and Gold Medal Gym

       (got to be Jews: "Gold")

    we are all praying for you to be well again Skyler

    love you so honey

       hadn't been so reckless, showing off on the rings

    love you so honey

      very best medical care or somebody's ass will be kicked

      Mummy's little man

* *This is an artful rendition of disembodied voices that floated to me in my hospital bed in the Maimed Children's Wing—or was it just the Children's Wing—of the Robert Wood Johnson Medical Center in New Brunswick, N.J. These quasi-recognizable voices barely penetrated a haze of weirdly throbbing pain (think neon/strobe lights) spun to airy thinness/foamy & frothy through the pharmaceutical magic of the codeine painkiller Nixil. There were numerous other voices (doctors, nurses, orderlies, visitors, etcetera) which I won't trouble to record. A few days after I was admitted to the hospital there came, unexpectedly (when you are floating in gauzy white cumulus clouds high above your mangled little body most things are "unexpected") a steely-haired old woman with a wide pike's mouth to stare at me stricken with a hitherto unsuspected ungrandma concern/ anxiety: "Is my beautiful grandson going to be a cripple? Is this child going to limp, for life?"*

THE BIRTH OF BLISS RAMPIKE I

FOR READERS WHO'VE BEEN IMPATIENTLY MUTTERING *WHERE THE HELL IS Bliss Rampike, why's it taking so long to get to our little ice princess* this chapter will introduce Bliss, at last: within five months of the *little man's* demise, "Bliss" is born.

OUT OF THE ASHES OF THE BROKEN SON, THE PHOENIX OF THE SHINING DAUGHTER.

(I'd thought maybe this catchy phrase might be used on the dust jacket of my book, on the lurid paperback cover at least, but nobody in marketing much liked it. I concede that it's not only overblown and pretentious but illogical. Yet it is "poetic speech" and most of my writing so far has been flat-footed reportorial speech hardly adequate to convey the more subtle/paradoxical ambiguities of our psychic lives.)

It is a fact, though, that while Skyler was still in rehab, an "outpatient" hobbling gamely if often sulkily/brattishly about on runt-sized crutches dragging a massive white mummy-leg in a cast, like some portion of Skyler's grave marker-to-come, it happened, as in a fairy tale, one of the crueller tales of the Brothers Grimm, that Skyler's little sister Edna Louise, scarcely four years old, first put on a pair of ice skates and—

"The rest is history." (Imagine a sonorous male voice-over.)

Except not poor Skyler's history: for Skyler, firstborn, long-cherished and favored *little man* of the Rampike family, fades now as rapidly and as irrevocably as poor Vassily's mirage-dream of the Bonus so tantalizingly promised by Daddy. As we say in American-youth-vernacular *Skyler is dead meat.*

. . .

"MUM-MY! LOOK."

On the enormous TV screen that appears to hang suspended on a wall of our family room a young girl figure skater is gliding, leaping, pirouetting to lush romantic music. A very graceful and very pretty young skater in a beautiful short-skirted glittery costume now lifting her slender arms, bowing her head, smiling with becoming modesty as the large audience in the arena bursts into applause.

"Mum-my, can I skate, too? Mum-my *plea-se*."

You have to imagine—that is, I have to imagine, since Skyler wasn't in the family room at that time—the child's voice quivering with hope and yearning; and her smile plaintive, cast at Mummy who seems scarcely aware of Edna Louise, staring at the TV screen on the wall.

Edna Louise is uncertain if she is seeing the warm-Mummy face or the other-Mummy face.

Warm-Mummy is Mummy-who-loves-Edna-Louise. Other-Mummy is Mummy-who-does-not-love-Edna-Louise.

(But why? Why is this? On the brink of four years of age, Edna Louise has discovered that most mummys love their little girls all the time. You can see this in their eyes, you can hear it in their voices, even when they are scolding their daughters, you just know. Edna Louise would ask *Why don't you love me all the time Mummy* except she does not dare for fear of Mummy's answer.)

Still Edna Louise can't help persisting: "Mummy? Can I skate, too? I know I can, Mummy. I promise, I *can*."

Was it the U.S. Olympic Festival 1993 that both mother and daughter were watching that evening? The nationally televised event that marked the dazzling emergence of thirteen-year-old Michelle Kwan, who placed first? Or was it Skate America 1993, where Michelle Kwan was one of the stars?

"Mum-my! Mum-my! Mum-my! *Plea-se*."

It's a fact: Mummy says *no*.

In how many "frank"—"confiding"—"intimate" interviews in the course of how many years including even those years following her prodigy-daughter's tragic death, would Betsey Rampike laugh incredulously, press a row of red-manicured fingernails on her breasts shaking her head in disbelief *Only imagine: I said no. No! to Bliss Rampike. In my ignorance.*

For Mummy could hardly bear to watch the astonishing young girl-skaters on TV. For Mummy—hunched in her chair, hugging herself in a way to suggest how badly she wished she might make herself smaller, again a girl—was made to recall how, long ago, she'd had such hopes for an ice-skating career until she'd sprained her ankle: "And that was the end of the dream."

Wistfully, and frequently, Mummy spoke of her "lost dream" to Skyler and Edna Louise who were made to feel, perhaps mistakenly, that they were somehow to blame, for making Mummy into a "Mummy" and depriving her of a career. Mummy had learned not to allude to her lost dream-career or to any alternative life of Betsey Rampike to Daddy, whose reaction was likely to be a booming laugh and a wet smacking kiss for his "big busty gorgeous gal" and say, with a downturn of his lips to indicate profundity, "Got to cut your losses, honey. 'Don't pour money down a rat hole.'"

Bix was right of course! Bix was always right.

Yet: Betsey had had a vague hope—"Oh I knew it was naive, I think I knew even at the time"—that little Skyler might have had some talent for ice-skating.

Wanting to think that the talent-gene might run in the family. Mother to son?

(Now Skyler is thumping around upstairs on his crutches. Even when Skyler is trying not to make noise, keeping to carpets, his Mummy can hear him.)

So when Skyler's little sister Edna Louise asks about ice-skating, Mummy bites her lower lip not to speak sharply at the child who stands before her eager and exasperating, jamming half the fingers of a hand into her mouth, a nervous habit Edna Louise's instructors at the Montessori school have noted, like Edna Louise's habit of pulling at her hair, and scratching herself inside her clothes, just pure nerves, or maybe the child does it to annoy, make Mummy want to grab her by her small shoulders and *shake! shake! shake!* some manners into her as manners had been shaken into Betsey years ago by her exasperated mother except shaking children, especially small children like Edna Louise, is not a practice condoned in Fair Hills, New Jersey. Absolutely not.

Mummy smiles at Edna Louise to soften the harshness of what she has to say: "Sweetie, I don't think so. You're too little and you're not very graceful. Look how you're always colliding with things, and you still make messes eating, and forget to flush the toilet. Those girl-skaters are years older than you. And very special girls, you can see."

On the TV screen the girl-skaters continue to glide without seeming effort, several of them now, first-, second-, third-place winners, astonishingly graceful as they glide, leap and turn, spin, skate backward lifting their slender arms, smiling with becoming modesty as the crowd applauds another time. You can see how such applause is life to the girl-skaters and without such applause there can be no life.

This blunt wisdom the child Edna Louise grasps by instinct, who could not have formulated it in words.

This task has fallen to me, the "survivor." As Pastor Bob has said *Put into words Skyler what can't be spoken because there are not adequate words and so you must create these words out of your own guts.*

That day, years ago, before there was Bliss Rampike, or even the thought of Bliss Rampike, only just Edna Louise gazing at Mummy with a look of commingled hurt and hope, Mummy says, with the air of one obliged to speak the truth for her daughter's own good, "And you have to be pretty, Edna Louise. Look at those girl-skaters, their lovely faces. Every one of them. Your face is bony and your eyes are too small and so strange, and *stark*. You seem always to be staring, and it makes people uneasy. Best to learn this before your heart is broken."

"But Mummy, you could make me pretty, couldn't you? Like you make yourself, Mummy. *Ple-ase.*"

Mummy laughs, startled. Mummy has not expected Edna Louise to protest. And not in such terms.

"Well! Maybe. Someday."

In the meantime Mummy switches off the TV and the giant screen that appears to be floating on the wall goes black.

. . .

ONLY IMAGINE! I SAID NO.

In my ignorance.

BUT—DIDN'T I TELL YOU, THIS IS A FAIRY TALE OUT OF GRIMM?—IT HAP-
pened nonetheless that one of Edna Louise's little friends at the
Montessori school, Carrie Chaplin, was, at the age of five, a novice
ice-skater; and that the Chaplins, a well-to-do Fair Hills family, had
two older daughters, both "promising" figure skaters, taking lessons
with a 1980 Winter Olympics bronze medalist at the Halcyon Hills
Ice Rink.

Now when Edna Louise excitedly told Mummy that she'd been invited by her little friend Carrie to go skating with her, how could Mummy
say *no*? For Betsey Rampike was eager to accept such (relatively rare)
invitations from the mothers of Edna Louise's classmates at the Montessori school, as Betsey Rampike was eager to accept (yet more rare)
invitations from the mothers of Skyler's classmates at Fair Hills Day
School. "Edna Louise, did you say 'Chaplin'? The Chaplins who live on
Charlemagne Drive?" Mummy's voice quavered for Mummy knew of
Henry and Patricia Chaplin from the *Fair Hills Beacon* where photographs of these prominent local residents often appeared on both the
front page and in the Style section. "Why yes, Edna Louise. Of course
you can go skating with Carrie Chaplin. And I'll come with you, to see
you don't get hurt."

Edna Louise blinked away tears. Edna Louise loved Mummy *so*.

(So sentimental! And so awkwardly rendered in prose. Yet Skyler remembers how his little sister would dissolve into childish tears when
overcome with childish happiness; how she would hug Mummy, or try to
hug Mummy; how she would cry, "Mum-my I love you." There is just no
way to render this in respectable adult-literary prose, is there? Yet I must
try.)

Taking preschool girls to the Halcyon Hills Ice Rink twelve miles east of Fair Hills required any number of telephone calls of course for nothing in Fair Hills was ever easily accomplished, especially where children were involved. ("Children: Our Most Precious Commodity" was the watchword of more than one Fair Hills school, private and public.) Mrs. Chaplin called Mummy, and Mummy called Mrs. Chaplin. Here was a call for Betsey Rampike that Betsey Rampike prized! How astonishing it was, Mrs. Chaplin (whose name was Patricia, "Trix" to her friends) turned out to be so warmly friendly with Betsey Rampike, it seemed to Mummy that, overnight, her homely exasperating little Edna Louise became easier to love.

It was arranged that Mummy would drive to the Chaplins', and Trix Chaplin would drive everyone to the ice rink in her eight-seater Road Warrior S.U.V. Hesitantly Mummy asked if she could rent skates for Edna Louise at the rink, and there was a pause of just a moment before Trix Chaplin said, "Well, no. I wouldn't think so. But I'll bring a pair of Carrie's last-year's skates for Edna Louise, Carrie has outgrown. I'm sure that they will fit her."

Mummy bit her lower lip! Had Mummy made, as Bix would say, a *foe paw*?

(How reluctant Mummy was to purchase ice skates for a four-year-old, especially expensive ice skates of the kind you'd naturally expect to see at the Halcyon Hills Ice Rink; after Mummy had paid so much for little Skyler's skates, that had come to nothing.)

Charlemagne Drive was less than two miles from Ravens Crest Drive yet on the far side of a social abyss, as Betsey Rampike knew well. The meandering private drive crested the northern ridge of the Village of Fair Hills and the Chaplins' house was a custom-built multi-level structure by the architect Shubishi, that descended a small mountain looking across Sylvan Lake (*not* man-made) to ex-Senator Mack Steadley's horse farm/estate on three hundred acres of prime New Jersey land; their house, as Trix Chaplin ruefully complained, had become "out-grown"—"crowded"—for the family, with only six bedrooms (the Chaplins had four children of whom Carrie was the youngest) and Mr. Chaplin's elderly mother living with them; an indoor swimming pool, a guesthouse, a gazebo, tennis courts and a pond (too small for the girls to skate seriously on, and anyway the ice was rippled and not smooth enough for skating). All this, on just five acres! Mr. Chaplin, Bud to his friends, was an investment officer at Fiduciary Trust of New Jersey and Trix Chaplin, with a law degree from Fordham, was a "full-time mom"—"or do I mean an 'over-time' mom?"—just like Betsey Rampike.

It was so, on her wistful *little drives* in the lime-green Chevy Impala Betsey Rampike had several times cruised along Charlemagne Drive undeterred by signs warning PRIVATE ROAD NO WAY OUT but she'd never seen the Chaplin house set back from the road and teasingly hidden by evergreens. Now when Mummy turned into the Chaplins' gravelled driveway and approached the multi-level glass-and-stucco house on a hill overlooking Sylvan Lake, Mummy stared and seemed about to speak but did not speak; and in the passenger's seat beside her Edna Louise said, fearfully, "Is that where Carrie lives, Mummy? Is that a *house*?"

AT THE HALCYON HILLS ICE RINK, WHICH WAS SO MUCH LARGER AND NICER than the outdoor rink at Horace C. Slipp Park, Mummy tried not to be intimidated by the other mothers and their skater-daughters, all of whom were older than Edna Louise; she tried not to expect too much of Edna Louise, as foolishly she'd expected too much of Skyler. There were girl-skaters at the rink of middle-school and high-school age who were skating as well as, or better than, Betsey Sckulhorne had skated as a girl, among them Carrie Chaplin's older sister Michelle who was seventeen and a senior at Fair Hills Day. Edna Louise seemed nearly feverish with anticipation as Mummy laced up Carrie Chaplin's outgrown skates (white kidskin, high ankle supports, exquisite stitching) on the girl's tiny feet and walked her hand in hand out onto the ice where other younger children, both boys and girls, were skidding, staggering, losing their balance and falling onto the ice, and being hoisted up to try again amid a good deal of noise; and there was Edna Louise frowning in concentration, her strange stark cobalt-blue eyes narrowed, at first wobbling on the new, unfamiliar skates, but by degrees as tightly she gripped Mummy's hand and followed Mummy's instructions—"Go slowly, honey: Mummy has you"—"Right foot forward, sweetie: 'glide' "—it seemed that Edna Louise already knew how to skate, by instinct.

The other girls were so encouraging! Trix Chaplin laughed in delight: "Edna Louise is doing so well, Betsey! Are you sure she has never skated before?"

It was during this first skating session, while watching Edna Louise on her borrowed skates, on the ice, now in the company of eleven-year-old June Chaplin who'd taken the little girl by the hand, to give her instructions, that Betsey Rampike was made to realize for the first time *My daughter is special! my daughter is blessed by God! my daughter will be the way God will reward me for my faith in Him and God will elevate my daughter above all rivals.**

AND SO IT HAPPENED, ALMOST BY CHANCE, THAT, IN THE FALL OF 1994 while Skyler Rampike was still made to endure the rigor/pain of rehab three times a week, his little sister Edna Louise began taking skating lessons at the Halcyon rink, along with the Chaplin girls; and that Betsey Rampike who'd so yearned to be, one day, among those Montessori mothers invited to the Chaplins' house for their annual Christmas party, was invited that year, with her husband Bix Rampike. Of the girl-skaters who regularly practiced at the Halcyon rink, it was Edna Louise who captivated the attention of onlookers with her diminutive size and her skating talent that seemed so disproportionate to that size. "Why, what a little angel!" began to be heard, by Betsey Rampike whose heart beat hard in anticipation, and in apprehension.

Noted, too, was the fact that while other child-skaters frequently fell on the ice and cried, the "little angel" did not often fall and, when she did,

---

* *Wonder how I know this? How Skyler Rampike, who wasn't even at the Halcyon rink that afternoon, could be privy to his mother's innermost thoughts at this moment? The explanation is simple: Betsey Rampike spoke of this "moment of revelation" numerous times in her numerous interviews. Possessed by the certitude of her Christian faith, Betsey never wavered, or doubted that God had designated her, as well as her daughter, for a special destiny.*

only just laughed to show that she wasn't hurt, and quickly scrambled to her feet and continued skating.

So too Edna Louise was likely to be the last child to leave the rink. The last child to unlace her skates. *As if her life depended on skating* more than one observer noted. *As if, even so young, she could see into the future and understood her destiny.**

Four-year-old Edna Louise Rampike was one of thirty-plus child-skaters in the annual Halcyon Winter Carnival, a gala event attended mostly by adoring families and relatives, and on the ice that evening, to amplified, antic Tchaikovsky ("Dance of the Sugar Plum Fairies"), Edna Louise was an appealing, diminutive figure in a pink satin fairy costume with bobbing fairy-wings attached to her small shoulders, matching ribbons in her hair and wide frightened eyes. (Glancing into the audience for Mummy? for Daddy?—but of course, Daddy hadn't been able to come, Daddy was away on business and "damned sorry.") Skyler who'd never seen his little sister in such public circumstances, shyly skating with a troupe of small, very novice child-skaters in fairy attire, winced at the sight, steeled himself for the inevitable fall, shut his eyes—and when he opened them, there was Edna Louise completing her brief, somewhat shaky performance, clearly the most skilled of the little troupe, and still on her feet. Applause was immediate and lavish for all the skaters: "Bravo!"—"Terrific!" With other mothers, Mummy hurried to hug her darling little skater, as Skyler remained seated and staring, bewildered. For hadn't Edna Louise fallen on the ice? Hadn't Skyler clearly seen her fall? As Skyler himself had fallen on the ice, and from the rings in the gym, and injured himself?

Tears sparkling in her warm brown eyes, Mummy was hugging a dazed-looking Edna Louise. As Skyler limped to them he overheard Mummy's ecstatic voice, "If only Daddy could have seen you, darling. He'd have been so proud of us both. Next time!"

---

* *See the ABC documentary* The Making and Unmaking of a Child Prodigy: The Bliss Rampike Story, *February 1999. These cryptic/prophetic remarks were made by skating instructor Ivana Zuev, the Olympic bronze medalist who'd been my sister's first teacher, at the Halcyon Hills rink. I'm quoting Ivana Zuev here though elsewhere in her interview the spiteful woman said cruel things about Betsey Rampike, of doubtful veracity.*

WAS SKYLER JEALOUS OF HIS LITTLE SISTER, NOOOO SKYLER WAS *NOT*.

Did Skyler hope for a mishap on the ice, an injury to his brave little sister, noooo Skyler did *not*.

(REALLY, THIS IS SO! I SWEAR.)

AS ALL BLISS-CULTISTS KNOW, IT WASN'T AT THE HALCYON WINTER CAR- nival in 1994 that Bliss Rampike made her official debut on the ice but at the "Tots-on-Ice Capades" at the Meadowlands, New Jersey, on Valentine's Day 1994.

"Tots-on-Ice" was a popular annual New Jersey event open to any aspiring young skater whose parents were willing to pay the $200 entry fee in exchange for the possibility of winning glittery fake-silver tiaras and fake-brass trophies plus a few seconds of local TV news footage and a few photographs in the back pages of newspapers. For ambitious/deluded parents thinking to launch their children into Olympic-team status "Tots-on-Ice" was ideal. As Mary Baker Eddy so famously said *You can't go broke underestimating the taste of the American people.*

Or was it *A sucker is born every minute* the canny seer Mrs. Eddy said. Whichever.

At the Halcyon Hills Rink, where Edna Louise Rampike had become a fond, familiar sight, one of the most dedicated, as she was one of the most talented, of young skaters, it was suggested to Betsey Rampike that she enter her daughter in "Tots-on-Ice" though Edna Louise was very young and inexperienced. (There were just two divisions in Tots-on-Ice for both sexes: skaters to age eight, and skaters to age eleven.) The older Chaplin daughters had both skated in previous "Tots-on-Ice Capades" and the elder, Michelle, had placed second in her age category as a ten-year-old. But Trix Chaplin believed that, at age five, Carrie wasn't yet ready for the competition; and that it might be "unwise"—"premature"—for Betsey to enter Edna Louise. "She's obviously a gifted skater but she hasn't had experience with such a large, noisy audience. Think how much stronger Edna Louise will be next year."

Mummy, who'd come to adore Trix Chaplin,* even as she was intimidated by Trix Chaplin, and, in a way, resented and disliked Trix Chaplin, felt the sting of the woman's jealousy. *Unwise! Premature!* For weeks, Mummy had felt the near-palpable jealousy, envy, and covert spite of the other skaters' mothers at the Halcyon rink, even as Mummy was reminded of the jealousy, envy, and not so-covert spite of her high school girlfriends in Hagarstown when Betsey Sckulhorne, daughter of a renowned local family, had won beauty competitions and skated in regional challenges.

And there were Fair Hills women who envied Betsey Rampike her attractive, gregarious, frankly sexy husband, murmuring behind her back *What can that man possibly see in her* and, yet more ominously, *There's a marriage that can't last.*

Politely Mummy explained to Trix Chaplin: "I will do whatever my daughter wishes. And whatever is best for my daughter's career."

A DREAM OF SUCH INTENSITY! THREE NIGHTS BEFORE VALENTINE'S DAY.

It was as if my eyes were open, there was blinding light in the room, at first I was terrified it must be the Angel Gabriel who comes in blinding light but more wondrous yet it was my own daughter who came to me transfigured in light in the guise of a blond angel touching my face with both her gentle hands saying Mummy I am not Edna Louise, you must not call me by that wrongful name I am BLISS, I am your daughter BLISS bearing a vision from God that you are blessed as I am blessed, with God's blessing we will realize our destiny on the ice in the face of all our enemies, we will not be defeated.

---

* Hey sorry: I haven't described Mrs. Chaplin—"Trix" to her friends—for the benefit of (female) readers with an unhealthy interest in affluent American suburban lifestyles. In fact, Skyler only glimpsed Mrs. Chaplin a few times and like most young kids he scarcely registered adults. Let's just say that Trix Chaplin was one of those ageless blondes celebrated in the society pages of suburban newspapers everywhere: rich, stylish, smiling, svelte and perennially size two. Beside Trix Chaplin, poor Betsey Rampike (size ten) looked and felt short, dumpy, fat-faced, unstylish and, as Daddy would say with a grim downturn of his lips, goosh.

THE BIRTH OF BLISS RAMPIKE II

BIX WAS ASTOUNDED. CHANGE THEIR DAUGHTER'S *NAME*?

From *Edna Louise* to—*Bliss*?

"Sweetie, my mother won't understand. She'll be damned hurt."

Betsey murmured she would try to explain. She would write a letter to her mother-in-law. She would argue that the vision had come to her with such clarity, and such power, it could not have been an ordinary dream but a divine message from God.

From God? Divine message? Bix smiled uncertainly. He was one who believed unquestioningly in God—the Christian/biblical/Caucasian God—but he was not one who wished to discuss God for such subjects embarrassed him. As uttering such clinical terms as *sexual intercourse, masturbation*, would have terribly embarrassed him, who spoke without hesitation among male companions such words as *fuck, screw, jack off*. A hot sullen blush came into his face. Only just returned home from Newark Airport, his flight delayed three and a half hours from Frankfurt where he'd been sent on urgent business by his supervisor at Scor Chemicals, Inc., a new job for Bix Rampike and a very well-paying job it was, except it did involve travel, and would involve travel, and a fiercely competitive young assistant-manager of project development requires from his wife and family one primary thing: that they not surprise him.

Surprises in the Rampike household would be Daddy's, exclusively. That was the bottom line.

Yet Bix was smiling. Though the pupils of his eyes had narrowed to ice pick points.

Yet Bix was caressing his wife's arm, above the elbow. Though his big thumb and forefinger were squeezing the fleshy-soft muscle.

"You know my mother, Betsey. If her pride is wounded, we'll be the ones to pay."

Unspoken between husband and wife was the prospect of the elder Mrs. Rampike punishing them by cutting Bix out of her will. Or, nearly as cruelly, leaving her favorite son Bix only a fraction of what she left Bix's endlessly conniving/loser siblings.

"Mother doesn't seem to especially like her little granddaughter as it is, even named 'Edna Louise.' D'you think she's going to like her better, named 'Bliss' like some sexpot pop star or some Indian-mystic asshole-charlatan?"

Betsey winced. "Bliss" was a beautiful name!

"Bix, it was 'Bliss' herself—our daughter—who appeared to me, in my dream. The room was flooded with light and there came Bliss like an angel to explain to me that we'd wrongly named her, it was her destiny to be named—"

"What's that damn drug you're on—'Elixil'—'Nixil'? Is that what precipitated your 'vision'?"

Betsey wrenched away from Bix. In her upper arm there were reddened imprints of a man's fingers. Her face, like Bix's, was flushed and warm and there was an excited quaver in her voice. "My vision came from God. You are not going to deprive me of my vision. Always we do things your way, 'the bottom line' is Bix's way, but in this, I know that I am right, and that history will prove me right. Since I've started taking Edna Louise—that is, Bliss—to the skating rink, the scales have fallen from my eyes. Our daughter is a born skater, no one else at the rink remotely resembles her, and so young! The instructor Ivana Zuev—an Olympic bronze medal winner—says that our daughter has an 'old soul'—she has 'lived many lives before this life'—and has come to ice-skating in this new life with a memory of the old. Don't look so skeptical, Bix: I am convinced that Ivana is right. Our daughter is fated for—something grand! I am not imagining any of this. In fact, I am taking fewer capsules of Elixil than Dr. Tyde has prescribed. In my dream Bliss came to me to tell me how urgent it was, we rectify our mistake in naming her. Our daughter is 'Bliss'—not 'Edna Louise.'"

"Betsey, hey—for Christ's sake—"

"It is for Christ's sake, and for ours. Bliss Rampike will be skating under her true name tomorrow evening at the Meadowlands, and 'Edna Louise' is no more."

How fiercely Betsey spoke! Her eyes appeared dilated, glazed. When Bix made a gesture to calm her, or to restrain her, Betsey airily threw off his hand as she'd never dared do in the past and Bix stared at her in astonishment. Was this Bix Rampike's big-busty gorgeous gal, who stammered when she was excited, and became stricken with shyness at social occasions? Was this *Mummy*? In the shadowy corridor outside the bedroom little Skyler had limped near attracted by his parents' urgent voices, he'd seen that the door to the room wasn't completely shut and so he might listen unnoticed, it was the most innocent of childish maneuvers, poor Skyler had taken to listening to his parents' exchanges when they had no idea anyone else was listening. *Will they talk about me?* is the child's hope. *What will they say about me?* For Daddy had just returned home from a business trip and had not seen his son in several days and yet: would you have guessed that the Rampikes had any other child, apart from the new, mysterious "Bliss"?

(JESUS! THAT WAS AWKWARD. THESE PRECEDING PAGES. WHAT I OVER-heard in my parents' bedroom was more or less what I've recorded here but somehow it doesn't sound right. (Does it?) I don't think that I did a very good job of imagining what Bix Rampike was thinking, and feeling; and what Betsey was thinking, and feeling. Not easy! There is something forbidden about such imaginings, where our parents are involved; a taboo, maybe. In deciding to call my parents Bix and Betsey, not Daddy and Mummy, my logic was that much of the time our parents aren't thinking of themselves as parents per se, not Daddy/Mummy but the distinct individuals they are, apart from us. Yet the paradox is: I can know them only as Daddy, Mummy. I can know them only as *my* parents.)

" 'BLISS'! THIS IS YOUR NEW NAME NOW, HONEY. 'EDNA LOUISE' HAS BEEN changed to 'Bliss'—isn't that wonderful?"

The puzzled little girl smiled at Mummy. Was this good news? Was this a nice surprise? From Mummy's expression, you would definitely think so. "Your new name 'Bliss'—how do you pronounce it?"

" 'Bli-zz'?"

" 'Bliss.' 'Bliss Rampike.' "

Names were so strange! Why is any name what it is, and why is any name attached to any person, or thing? Little Edna Louise, now little Bliss, smiled uncertainly as if she'd been presented with a gift—as often, when you are a child, you are presented with gifts from beaming adults who have been very good to you and wish to be acknowledged as very good—she didn't comprehend but understood that it was a very special gift, and she must be grateful for it.

"And so, darling, when people ask your name, especially at the skating rink, you will tell them 'Bliss.' Spelled '*B-L-I-S-S.*' It is a vision from God. Do you understand?"

Vehemently Edna Louise nodded. *Yes Mummy!*

FOR HADN'T SHE BEEN PRACTICING HER "FIGURES" UNDER THE FROWNING tutelage of Miss Zuev, whose face, though not old, was crisscrossed with lines of impatience; hadn't she and Miss Zuev been skating together at the Halcyon rink, days in succession as the buoyant melody "Over the Rainbow"—chosen by Mummy!—was played; and hadn't everyone at the rink who noticed them lingered to stare, and to praise the remarkable little skater? Now the reason had been revealed: on the ice Edna Louise hadn't been "Edna Louise" at all but "Bliss."

Yes Mummy!

BRISKLY MUMMY CAME INTO SKYLER'S ROOM, WHERE MARIA WAS HELPING him dress for school on this chill February morning. "Skyler? Maria? There will be a change in the Rampike family from now on: 'Edna Louise' has a new name, 'Bliss.' "

Bliss? Skyler scowled. Though it can't be said that Skyler was exactly surprised.

"From now on, Skyler, Maria—you will call Skyler's little sister 'Bliss' and not 'Edna Louise.' Not ever again, 'Edna Louise.'" Mummy shuddered, and laughed, as if they'd all narrowly escaped something very unpleasant.

Accustomed to Fair Hills *gringa* whims and edicts which were never pronounced in tones other than profound, Maria-from-Ecuador politely murmured *Yes ma'am.* While Skyler in brattish-boy mode, for his broken-in-two-pieces-slow-to-heal leg was hurting like hell, and his knee, too, and his morning Nixil dose hadn't yet kicked in, had to ask *Why*?

"'Why'? Because Mummy says so, dear. Mummy has explained: your little sister is no longer 'Edna Louise' but 'Bliss.' You will call her 'Bliss' from now on."

"'Bliss.'" Skyler swiped at his runny nose with the edge of his hand as street urchins do, in crude documentary films. Not as Fair Hills boys do just shrugging into their Fair Hills Day School navy-blue blazers embossed with the Fair Hills Day School heraldic shield involving a lion rampant, crossed staves or maces, a sacred book out of which flames sprung, in miniature. "'Bliss' is a goofy name, Mummy. People will laugh at 'Bliss.'" Skyler laughed, not very mirthlessly, as if to demonstrate, but Mummy wasn't in a mood to be amused by her little man, not right now. "No one will laugh at your sister, Skyler, I assure you. The name change will be legal as soon as our lawyer can file papers at the courthouse and in the meantime just call your sister 'Bliss'—a much prettier and more special name than 'Edna Louise.' And don't make silly baby faces."

Silly baby faces! Skyler was shocked, his mother would so insult him in the presence of the nanny.

Skyler saw that Mummy was anxious to leave, yet Skyler plucked at Mummy's arm to ask: "Do I have a new name, too?" though knowing damned well that he did not; and Mummy laughed and said, "Honey, no. Why would Daddy and I want to change your name?—'Skyler' is a beautiful special name, a 'questing' name of which you should be proud."

But shrewd-sullen Skyler knew, there would be nothing of which Skyler should be proud.

"MISS TOTS-ON-ICE DEBUTANTE 1994"

"THE HAPPIEST DAY OF MY LIFE."

Or was it a nightmare? Take your choice!

NOT PLAIN/UGLY EDNA LOUISE RAMPIKE BUT BEAUTIFUL/TRANSFIGURED
Bliss Rampike made her skating debut, aged four, at the Meadowlands ice rink on the windblown snowy evening of Valentine's Day 1994. Mummy wept with gratitude that Tots-on-Ice officials were willing to make the last-minute change of names for a penalty fee of just fifty dollars.

There were no printed programs at the rink. There were no pre-assigned seats. Tickets were twelve dollars for adults, six dollars for children, you pushed your way into the bleachers. The air was chill yet stale-smelling: in a corridor outside the rink, Skyler had seen stacks of grim wire cages, kennel cages, to the ceiling. (Must've been a dog show the day before. A stink of dog-hair, dog-excrement, dog-panic prevailed.) Underfoot, the stained concrete floor was sticky from spilled drinks and food. There were vendors noisily hawking drinks, food, skaters' gear. Overhead were blinding fluorescent lights. Out of booming loudspeakers, sugary-deafening Tchaikovsky: "Dance of the Sugar Plum Fairies." The doors to the rink had opened by 6 P.M., by 6:45 P.M. a considerable crowd had pushed inside. Few ushers were visible and these were shapely young girls in skating costumes, pink satin high heels and pink satin caps with TOTS-ON-ICE 1994 in white. There appeared to be few security guards and these were elderly black men. The atmosphere was shrill, festive. There were numerous children running and shouting unsupervised. Photographers milled restlessly about, individuals with videocameras, a bemused three-man TV crew from New Jersey Network filming some of the older and more glamorous girl-skaters in their short skirts and snug-fitting bodices like swimsuits. Mummy had arrived at the Meadowlands early driving the Chevy Impala at cautious, halting speeds on the Turnpike, whispering fervent prayers as traffic crept along in windblown snow; Mummy had organized us—Bliss, Skyler, and Maria—to leave home by 4 P.M. and so we'd arrived early and secured front-row seats but these choice seats were in constant danger of being claimed by aggressive strangers: "You sittin' here? All these seats, here?" Apart from a scattering of men and boys the skating crowd was female, mothers and relatives of young skaters: not Fair Hills—type females but what Mummy called, with a look of disdain, "a coarse New Jersey element." The heft of these females was considerable. Even the younger women, even girls and children were heavyset. In such a melee Betsey Rampike in her dark mohair coat with a mink collar, in expensive Italian boots and with her brunette hair shinily styled, appeared relatively slender, youthful. Mummy's lips were very red, and Mummy's eyes were damp with excitement. Repeatedly Mummy dialed a number on her cell phone that failed to go through. To Bliss she said, "Daddy will make it here, I'm sure. He'll drive directly from his office. 'Can't miss my bestest little gal's ice-debut!' Daddy has said. He knows where the Meadowlands is, I've given him directions to the rink. All those banners for TOTS-ON-ICE, you can't miss it. Daddy is anxious to see you skate, Bliss! He is. But his new office isn't close to the Turnpike like the old office. 'Scor Chemicals'—it's almost in Paramus—so big, it has its own zip code!" Mummy was chattering nervously, Bliss seemed unaware, hunched in her seat, in her coat, glassy-eyed and shivering. So much noise! So many people! The Tots-on-Ice Capades was nothing like the family-oriented Halcyon Winter Carnival. Why was there no one here Mummy knew? None of the other young skaters, who took lessons with Bliss? It seemed that Trix Chaplin was snubbing Tots-on-Ice this year for little Carrie wasn't good enough to make her debut. (Had Mummy hoped that her friend Trix would bring her daughters to Tots-on-Ice to watch Bliss skate? To provide moral support for Betsey and Bliss?)

Mummy was excited, anxious. Mummy kept standing, to peer into the crowd. Mummy could not keep from primping Bliss's hair, which was fine, somewhat limp, and of no distinct color; Mummy combed and fluffed out Bliss's bangs, and adjusted pink satin butterfly-barrettes. Beneath her coat, Bliss was wearing a little-girl skater's costume which Mummy had ordered from Junior Miss Lady Champ: pink satin, a short pleated skirt and pink panties beneath, a tiny red heart above Bliss's left breast, or what would have been a left breast in an older girl, and transparent wings. Mummy had not made up Bliss's face for Bliss was only four years old and Trix Chaplin had remarked to Betsey how "vulgar" it was, how "unacceptable," that certain mothers made up their child-skaters to look "luridly glamorous" but now, at Tots-on-Ice, Mummy saw to her alarm that the other debut girl-skaters, who would be competing with Bliss, seemed to have been made up with lipstick, rouge, even eyeliner. (Maybe then, hurriedly, just a touch of Mummy's cherry-red lipstick? And, so that Bliss didn't look so ghastly pale, as if she were suffering from some dreadful wasting-away child disease like leukemia, a discreet touch of blush to both cheeks? Bliss feebly pushed at Mummy's hands, but soon gave in.) Skyler too had been noticing the other little-girl skaters and their hefty mummys who were crowding the Rampikes and Maria on their bleacher seats. And Skyler had been noticing a scattering of lone men, of varying ages but mostly middle-aged, in the audience, with cameras. Skyler was becoming frightened for his baby sister who was going to skate before such a rowdy audience. It was so, Skyler hadn't liked his sister so much lately since she'd acquired her new, special name but seeing her now so tiny in her seat, her feet in skates not touching the floor, wan and resigned like one of his fellow outpatients at the children's rehab center, Skyler reached over to take her cold, limp hands to comfort her: but Bliss only shivered in response. Her strange, stark, glassy eyes were fixed on the ice, she seemed scarcely aware of her surroundings. Skyler saw that Mummy seemed unaware that Bliss was so frightened for Mummy was distracted by the other girl-skaters (polished fingernails! pierced earrings! such garish costumes! what were their mothers thinking!) and by her need to continually stand, and peer toward the back of the arena hoping to see a familiar face. (But Skyler knew: Daddy wasn't coming. If Daddy couldn't make it back home for dinner much of the time, Daddy wasn't likely to drive to the Meadowlands; nor would Daddy set foot in such a "lowlife"—"cruddy"—atmosphere.) "Mummy? Maybe we should go home? Before the program starts?" Skyler tugged at Mummy's coat sleeve, but Mummy paid Skyler not the slightest heed for Mummy had finally sighted someone she knew—a woman?—a few rows back in the bleachers, Mummy was on her feet waving and calling and yet: no one waved back.

Abruptly in mid-note the high-decibel Tchaikovsky ceased. Deafening announcements regarding emergency exits, evacuation in case of fire were made over the speaker system. A mammoth lizard-faced individual in a shiny black tuxedo with a broad cummerbund of valentine hearts stood in a spotlight at the edge of the rink, smiling broadly, microphone in hand. His eyelids looked inflamed, his manner with the crowd was jocular, familiar. His shoulder-length dyed-jet-black hair had been parted in the center of his large head. Simply the sight of this striking individual provoked applause in the audience, cheers and good-natured catcalls. The lizard-faced man acknowledged such attention with a show of mock-modesty. His voice—gravelly baritone, subtly mocking—scraped against the microphone like fingernails: "*Hel*-lo ladiez 'n' gentz 'n' all the rest of you"—pause for laughs, titters—"I am your 'umble 'ost for this perspercarious non-puerile Tots-on-Ice Capades 1994—Jeremiah Jericho!" A louder wave of applause, laughter, and whistles washed through the arena like sudsy water, before which, with some discomfort because of his girth, the lizard-faced Mr. Jericho bowed. "And our esteemed judges—world-renowned VIPs of the skate world—returned to the glorious Meadowlands for another momentous evening—" At Jericho's bidding, three individuals of indeterminte sex and age, each solidly built, attired in black with gaudy red roses in their lapels, rose from their front-row seats to smile and wave at the crowd. Skyler wasn't sure he'd heard the judges' names clearly: Krunk, Snicks, D'Ambrosia?

While Mummy and the other debut-skater mothers nervously prepared their daughters for the first competition, the lizard-faced master of ceremonies introduced Miss Hot-Tot-on-Ice 1993, the "Grand Prix" winner of the previous year's competition Tiffany Pirro of Jersey City who began the program with a flashy presentation of skating/dancing to a strong sulky-sexy disco beat—"I Will Survive"—and explosive applause. Tiffany was a short, curvy, busty girl presumably no more than twelve years old but very mature for her age, with brass-colored hair, a shiny royal blue spandex leotard and rhinestone-studded cowgirl vest, teasingly short flared skirt over leopard-skin spotted panties, numerous pierced earrings, pouty cherry-red lips. In dramatic lunges Tiffany executed figure eights, glided backward lifting one sinewy leg behind her, abrupt turns and spins and a sudden somersault that left her panting and spread-eagled on the ice, intentionally or unintentionally it seemed not to matter. As the lizard-faced Jeremiah Jericho urged the crowd: "Go crazy for Tiff! Let's hear it!"

There was a Jerscy City contingent that went especially crazy for Tiffany and seemed reluctant to let her go, to be replaced by far less showy/ sexy girl-skaters between the ages of four and eight, in the competition for Miss Tots-on-Ice Debutante 1994. There were nine very young girls competing among whom Bliss Rampike came seventh alphabetically. The first six skaters were older than Bliss but shaky and frightened and drew sympathetic murmurs and mild laughter from the crowd. Two fell down almost immediately. One plump little Hispanic girl, seven years old, an olive-skinned little beauty with shiny black plaited hair, managed to skate through her routine to the beat of "I Wanna Be Loved by You" without falling or stumbling and was greeted with an enthusiastic response. Then, in Jeremiah Jericho's grating, intimate voice, " 'Miss Bliss Rampike'—four years old—of Fair Hills, New Jersey! Wel-come, Bliss! And isn't Bliss—oh *my*!—isn't this little gal *lit-tle*! And *beau-ti-ful*!" Though Fair Hills had no contingent at the rink, and may even have drawn some titters of disdain, as soon as Skyler's little sister skated out onto the ice, shakily at first and then with more confidence, in a frilly pink satin costume with a lacy bodice, a pleated skirt, white eyelet stockings, and translucent butterfly wings, or fairy wings, attached to her shoulder blades, the crowd was wildly enthusiastic. So young! Four years old! So *small*. The shock of it was, as the crowd registered by quick degrees, that this tiny tot skater could actually skate, with the grace and skill of a much older child; it soon became evident, to the buoyant beat of "Over the Rainbow," that she could skate better than Tiffany Pirro, in long steady glides, turns and slow spins executed with the precision of a mechanical doll. Bliss's eyes were somber beneath fluffy blond bangs, and the rosebud mouth Mummy had painted over her pale little mouth was fixed in a small shyly-sweet smile that never wavered. It was Bliss's backward skating, a graceful if somewhat studied backward figure eight, that most astonished the crowd and provoked bursts of applause. So many times at the Halcyon rink had Bliss practiced her six-minute "Over the Rainbow" performance under the sharp-eyed tutelage of Ivana Zuev and Mummy, so fiercely had she concentrated on each required movement, by the end of the six minutes Bliss seemed to have forgotten her surroundings entirely and was startled by the applause, which endeared her yet more to the enthusiastic audience. Skyler who'd been watching through narrowed eyes waiting for the inevitable slip, stumble, fall, *Ohhh!* of the crowd, blinked in astonishment, as surprised as his sister, when the applause washed through the arena, and numerous spectators rose to their feet.

Even Jeremiah Jericho seemed startled: "Ladiez 'n' gents that was a truly perspercacious *day-beyoo!* New Jersey's answer to Sonja Henie! Right here at Tots-on-Ice Capades 1994! My oh *my.*"

Was Bliss's performance over? So quickly? Those photographers who'd taken little interest in the previous child-skaters now pushed forward to take Bliss's picture, frightening her with their flashes. The NJN TV crew was galvanized into action, filming the dazed-looking little girl and her beaming mother who declared, into a microphone thrust at her, "Thank you, thank you for your applause, my daughter is a born skater, my daughter *will be* the next Sonja Henie, we are so grateful for this wonderful opportunity, this is the happiest day of our lives, and most of all thanks to—" but the NJN microphone was withdrawn before Mummy could say *God.*

Returned to their seats beside Skyler and Maria, as the crowd gradually quieted down and lizard-faced Jeremiah Jericho announced the name of the next little-girl skater, Mummy continued to hug Bliss and drew her clumsily onto her lap, skates and all. Tears streaked Mummy's cheeks, Mummy was so happy. "Bliss, Mummy is so proud of you. And Daddy!— wait till Daddy hears. You were so much better than those other little girls, *you must win.* But whether you win or not, honey, Mummy loves you. And God loves you, tonight has been proof." Close beside them Skyler tried to insinuate himself into Mummy's embrace, too. Tried to feel happy and proud and excited, too.

And yet: hadn't Bliss fallen on the ice? Skating backward, showing off for the crowd? Hadn't Skyler seen his brazen little sister stumble, start to fall?—quickly then he'd shut his eyes, to be spared seeing. Hadn't that happened?

THE REMAINDER OF THE EVENING PASSED IN A DELIRIUM OF CONFUSION, excitement, mounting anticipation. Several times Mummy tried to call Daddy on her cell phone, but could leave only a message: "Bix darling! Bliss has just skated, and she did so well. Darling, the crowd went wild for her! Our daughter! If you can get here by ten, Bix, please come. You still have time, the winners won't be announced until the end of the evening, and if Bliss wins her competition—"

Ravenous with hunger they bought food from vendors—the kind of food Mummy never allowed at home: hot dogs, French fries, slices of gummy pizza, giant Cokes. Bliss stared at the glittering ice without seeming to see it, Skyler became very restless in his seat. In a pretense of needing to use the men's room he prowled the arena looking for—was it Daddy, whom he knew he wouldn't see? (Yet: we must look.) In the dingy men's room a youngish man with rust-red hair and an eager smile approached Skyler who was scowling into the grimy sink wondering should he wash his hands or return to his seat with contaminated hands asking, "Little boy? Are you lost? Or—looking for your dad?"

Rudely Skyler fled the men's room and back to his seat.

AT LAST, THE PROGRAM WAS ENDING. IN A BLAZE OF AMPLIFIED MUSIC— not tortured Tchaikovsky but a rock-and-roll rendition of "Adagio from *Spartacus*"—mammoth Jeremiah Jericho took the spotlight to announce the evening's winners. As Mummy gripped both Bliss's and Skyler's hands tight, her lips moving in a silent prayer, the gratingly intimate voice proclaimed: "Our 1994 Tots-on-Ice Debutante is—none other, and the crowd's favorite, Miss Bliss Ranpick of Fair Hills, New Jersey! Ladiez 'n' gents, let's go crazy for this fan-tas-tic li'l gal on the start of a fan-tas-tic career!" Mummy screamed, and

Mummy and Maria hugged, and Mummy led Bliss in a daze of exhaustion, stricken with shyness, fingers jammed into her mouth, out onto the ice another time to accept from the leering master of ceremonies a bouquet of waxy-looking red roses, a lightweight "silver" tiara, a lightweight "silver" trophy and a pink satin sash proclaiming tots-on-ice debutante 1994. Jeremiah Jericho helped Mummy display the glamorous satin sash slantwise across little Bliss's meager chest, all the while engaging Mummy in jocose banter: "Mrs. Rampick! Where were you when li'l Jerry Jericho was a gec whiz champion skater from Jersey City in the bad ol' days of rock-and-roll?" Mummy blushed in confusion provoking laughter and a roar of approval from the audience that seemed to have decided, seeing how deeply moved Mummy was, how her girlish face glistened with tears, that they liked Fair Hills after all. As Mummy led Bliss back to their seats, photographers swooped upon them aiming their flash-cameras into their faces and the NJN TV crew followed in their wake. "Smile for us, Bliss! Over here, sweetheart! Smile!" Well-wishers crowded about them like old friends, the mood was one of drunken revelry as the dazed-looking little blond girl was asked for her autograph but since she was too young to write even her signature, her laughing mother had to sign it for her: BLISS RAMPIKE. Among the more eagerly aggressive individuals in the crowd were several men with video cameras and most eager of all was a lanky youngish man with loose rubbery lips in a besotted smile and kinky rust-colored hair and an orangish-red silk scarf tied about his neck, who stooped over Mummy and Bliss to record Mummy's stammered words: "This—is—the happiest day of my life."

Beautiful Mummy seized Skyler's hand, too. So hard, the bones felt as if they'd cracked. But it was a happy feeling. Warmth flooded Skyler's heart: *Mummy loves me, too.*

POSTSCRIPT

DO YOU RECOGNIZE THIS PERSON? *LANKY YOUNGISH MAN WITH LOOSE rubbery lips in a besotted smile* . . . In fact, I did not. And probably, Mummy did not. Yet we know from subsequent developments that Gunther Ruscha, at this time thirty-one years old, had to have been at the Meadowlands ice rink that evening, sitting front-row center (alone? or with a like-minded companion?) since videotapes confiscated from Ruscha's house by Fair Hills police officers would show all of the young girl-skaters on the Tots-on-Ice program that evening, including Bliss Rampike; and, as Mummy half-carried Bliss back to her seat, through a buzzing swarm of well-wishers, Ruscha was holding the camera only a few inches from them. On this blurred and grainy tape, Bliss's small, pale face had gone slack with exhaustion and her glamorous pink satin sash proclaiming TOTS-ON-ICE DEBUTANTE 1994 was askew across the bodice of her costume, and Mummy's flushed moon-shaped face gleamed with perspiration. It seems clear from the tape that Gunther Ruscha was speaking to Mummy, and that Mummy was listening; and that Skyler, close by, might well have heard these exact words: "Mrs. Rampike, congratulations! Your daughter is beautiful! A born skater! A born champion! Do you remember me from Horace Slipp Park? That day, you had a beautiful little boy-skater with you, and now—you have a beautiful little girl."

"WATERY SOULS"

AND WHAT IS THE HAPPIEST DAY OF YOUR LIFE, SKYLER?
  I'm still waiting.

FIJI ISLANDERS,* AMONG THOSE LUCKY ABORIGINALS FAVORED BY ANTHRO-
pologists, speak of very young children as having "watery souls"—
meaning that they are undefined, indistinct, incomplete until at a
certain age they are drawn into the web of reciprocal human relations. To be human means to be, not "watery" but defined in a kinship system meaning you have duties to perform, you take on
responsibilities and you will be punished/rewarded accordingly.
  Punished, anyway! For sure.
  So I'm wondering: did Bliss, who died so young, ever acquire a human
soul? Did Skyler, who died so young—excuse me, who didn't die so young
but "survived"—ever acquire a human soul?
  Or, maybe: was Bliss the only one of us, to acquire a human soul?
  Make me a little red heart Skyler   *like yours?*

---

* *Impressed with my erudition? Maybe not. But this nugget of scientific information is impressive
to me. The proposition is a mind-blower: Apart from human culture there is no human nature. Can this be? That I, Skyler Rampike, to acquire more than a merely watery, unformed soul,
must somehow re-connect with the rest of you, or some of you? Somehow?*
  The information is taken from The Interpretation of Cultures *by the noted anthropologist
Clifford Geertz which I was reading, well to be truthful skimming, in a local bookstore yesterday;
might as well confess, I'm one of you, the worst of you, rarely buy a book even a paperback (can't
afford it), slouched in the aisle of bookstores blocking the way of serious customers.*

Mummy won't know

And the realization comes to me: if only Bliss had lost that first competition, at the Meadowlands! If only (as envious Skyler had halfway wished) the darling little four-year-old hadn't executed her skating routine like a wind-up doll but had slipped and fallen cutely on her little rump! Very likely, my sister would be alive today. She would be approaching her seventeenth birthday. Maybe we'd be together at this very minute. Or maybe we'd be apart, but each alive. Maybe her name would have reverted back to Edna Louise.

BUMPED

"SKYLER, TRY NOT TO LIMP. YOU CAN WALK PERFECTLY NORMALLY, IF YOU make an effort. And please don't twitch, and squirm, and make those 'pain faces'—people will only be depressed, and want to avoid you." Mummy's manner with Skyler had come to be one of gently chiding, scolding. But always Mummy stooped to kiss Skyler, and give him a quick hug, to show that he was still Mummy's *little man.* He was!

Please don't think that Skyler was neglected by his parents, as his sister's star so rapidly rose in the frantic years 1994 to 1997. (Do stars rise? Maybe I mean meteors.) Detractors of Betsey Rampike knowing nothing of our family would claim that both she and Daddy ignored me, to concentrate on Bliss, but that wasn't true, exactly. Let's just say that Skyler got bumped to second place.

Second of two. How shameful is that?

Though it was true, Mummy no longer took Skyler on their little drives together, for Mummy was busy with Bliss. It was Maria who helped Skyler get ready for school in the mornings and saw that he took his meds and it was Maria who prepared many of Skyler's meals when no one else seemed to be home; it was Maria who took Skyler to his dreaded therapy sessions at the Fair Hills Rehabilitation Center, held his hand and comforted him insisting in heavily accented English that *Yes!* Skyler was getting better, soon he would be walking normally again; and gravely Skyler would say, with one of his wizened pain faces, "You must think I'm a really dumb little kid, to believe you," causing Maria to blush to the roots of her thick dark hair. Mummy now prepared Bliss for school, and drove her there; of course, Mummy oversaw Bliss's skating lessons (after frowning Ivana Zuev came morbidly cheerful Olga Zych, another Olympic medalist) and Mummy drove Bliss to skating competitions initially in New Jersey though in time, as Bliss's star continued to rise, farther afield. *As high as her wings will bear her, Jesus! In your name, Amen.*

Daddy's complicated new position at Scor Chemicals, Inc. took him away from home (to Tokyo, to São Paulo, to Stuttgart, to Singapore) even more than his old position at Baddaxe Oil, but when Daddy was home in our house on Ravens Crest Drive, as Daddy exclaimed *he was home.* "Where's my bestest li'l gal Bliss?—where's my Big-Boy Sky-Boy? Loveya, kids!" Daddy's shaggy-bison head swooped downward for a kiss, Daddy's soulful eyes brimmed with sentimental tears, Daddy lurched through doorways rubbing his hands briskly together staring at Skyler and Bliss as if trying to recall who we were, and why he loved us. Hurriedly crammed into weekends were Rampike family holidays, and Rampike family outings; if Daddy was in a playful mood there were wild games of hide-and-seek in the maze of the large house vexing Mummy nearly to tears: "Bix, what if Bliss hurts herself playing that silly game? She isn't just an ordinary girl, our daughter is Bliss Rampike." Sincerely Daddy regretted he hadn't yet found time to see Bliss skate, except on videotape, on one of the giant TV screens in the family room; the first time he saw his little girl skating with such unexpected skill, Daddy stared in astonishment, ran his hands through his stiff springy hair, and smiled stupidly: "Jesus. That's my daughter?" With a sharp smile of rebuke Mummy said: "Our daughter."

Daddy spent quality time with Skyler, too. Daddy sure did!

Watching TV sports together weekend afternoons though the kid annoyed his dad by never seeming to know what the hell was going on in the game, restless and squirmy; driving the kid to his physical therapy appointment, or to the most recent pediatric-orthopedic surgeon; or to the lavishly appointed law offices of Kruk, Burr, Crampf & Rosenblatt where in a halting mumble exasperating to Bix Rampike his son gave a "deposition" to be whipped up by canny Morris Kruk as the dramatic centerpiece of Bix Rampike's six-million-dollar lawsuit against the Gold Medal Gym & Health Club and its (former) employee Vassily Andreevich

Volokhomsky.* Returning home from Kruk's office one blustery day Daddy confided in Skyler as if impulsively, let's have a close-up of Big Daddy Bix warmly confiding in runt-sized Son Skyler strapped in beside him in the passenger's seat of Daddy's Jeep Crusher: "Way I see it, Sky-boy, a man can't start too young knowing the rules of engagement of the playing field. You're what—nine? ten?—only eight?"—the warm-Daddy eyes muddied for a moment, then cleared, "—still it isn't too early for us to sit down one of these days, maybe with Mummy, too, with your 'career strategist' at that posh school we are sending you to, and see what prog-ress you're making, this HPI thing or whatever the hell it is: the 'fast track.' Mummy has said, 'Skyler doesn't seem to like school'—'Skyler's teachers say he isn't living up to his potential'—'Skyler's leg doesn't seem to be healing the way it should be'—'Skyler doesn't seem to have many friends'—and I'm not going to dignify all that neurotic-Mummy-angst by asking you point-blank, son, if there's truth to it, I'm going to assume that Mummy is exaggerating for dramatic effect as Mummy sometimes does. Bottom line is, 'Tomorrow is the first God-damned day of your new life so don't fuck it.' Say you want to follow your dad into the challenging corpo-rate world, or you might wish to strike out on your own in law, or medi-cine, or biotech pharmaceuticals—you're going to need a top education for these fields, and a strong network of contacts to help smooth the way. Your generation, man!—you are going to need to be smarter than your parents. *Homo homin lupus.* My father used to quote, know what it means? Greek for 'wolf is friend to man.' Meaning you got to be man enough to harness the wolf, son, the wolf-blood coursing through your 'civilized' Rampike veins—" at that tense moment, to Skyler's relief, interrupted by a ringing car phone.

And, most Sundays, we Rampikes went to church together.

In Englishy-quaint Trinity Episcopal Church, beneath the benevolent

*This personal-injury suit, much contested by legal counsel in the hire of Gold Medal Gym & Health Club, Inc. was to be settled out of court for an undisclosed sum of money, in some quarters rumored to be between $350,000 and $1,000,000, of which the "permanently afflicted" minor Skyler, most minor of minors, would not see a penny. (D'you think Daddy Bix set it aside for Sky-ler's Ivy League college fund? Nice thought.) And soon afterward the Gold Medal Gym & Health Club vanished from our local mall, to pass into the oblivion of local memory.

smiling gaze of Father Archibald Higley, the Rampikes became, over the course of my sister's "meteoric" career, a luminous presence in their third-row, near-to-center pew. As I've said earlier, Mummy and Daddy were Christians of the most American kind: unquestioning, and adamant. Mummy rarely spoke of her family but of course, Mummy had been raised as a Christian, like Daddy. Worldly success is certainly a sign of divine grace in the eyes of most Christians—no matter what priggish old theologians like Daddy's Puritan ancestor Joshua Rampike preached— and because Bliss Rampike began to be perceived as special, so the Rampike family was perceived as special; because the Rampikes were members of the Trinity Episcopal congregation, the Trinity Episcopal congregation was perceived as special. Especially Reverend Higley, our spiritual pastor, was perceived as special. God bless all, Amen.

What a mystery! At the age of eight Skyler was made to see the supreme illogic of the adult world: his younger sister had the power to confer "specialness" upon others, even strangers, who came into her orbit though Bliss herself was shy, uncertain, self-doubting and fearful of falling on the ice, like all skaters.

If I fall down, Skyler, no one will love me!

And cruel Skyler said *Better not fall then, Bliss.*

PAINFUL CLOSE-UP: IN MUMMY'S CAR EXITING THE NEW JERSEY TURNPIKE at Camden, headed south to Cumberland County and Mummy is speaking on her cell phone in the new-Mummy voice that quavers now not with hesitation, apprehension, dread but with entrepreneurial zest and confidence, and Bliss is seated beside her unmoving as a rag doll in snug-fitting skating costume beneath her winter coat.

Bliss's newly crimped hair shimmers a startlingly pale blond, and Bliss's face is made up in artful mimicry of a ceramic doll-face with a small pink "kissable" rosebud mouth. Bliss is staring out the car window at the sepia haze of urban New Jersey passing in a blur of used dreams in rapid and disjointed sequence and Skyler thinks with cruel satisfaction *She is frightened now, she knows she will fall tonight* and Bliss shudders pressing her forehead against the window as if something in that broken and fading landscape is of crucial meaning, and Skyler (who has been brought along both as brotherly support for little Bliss and as map navigator for Mummy who becomes hopelessly lost on such massive interstate highways as the New Jersey Turnpike) is prompted to ask in a tone of calm to disguise the unease he feels, where are they going? and Mummy who has just completed her cell phone conversation says in the new bright Mummy-voice, "The War Memorial on Fort Street, Pennsauken, that is where tonight's Garden State Jersey Girls' Challenge is being held," and Skyler squinting in the fading light, holding the map close to his watery eyes locates the Fort Street exit, Skyler directs Mummy off the Turnpike in quest of that shimmering crown, or title, or silver-plate trophy: "Little Miss Jersey Girl Skater Debut of the Year"—"Little Royale Miss New Jersey 1994"—"Miss Junior Ice Princess 1994."

These honors Bliss Rampike would win, in time. And more!

ADVENTURES IN PLAYDATES I

Playdate.(n) A date arranged by adults in which young children are brought together, usually at the home of one of them, for the premeditated purpose of "playing." A feature of contemporary American upscale suburban life in which "neighborhoods" have ceased to exist, and children no longer trail in and out of "neighbor children's" houses or play in "backyards." In the absence of sidewalks in newer "gated" communities, children cannot "walk" to playdates but must be driven by adults, usually mothers. A "playdate" is never initiated by the players (i.e., children), but only by their mothers.

FOR THOSE READERS—POTENTIALLY, MILLIONS!—WITH AN AVID INTEREST in American-suburban social climbing through playdating, this is the chapter you've been awaiting. For in one of the upstairs rooms in our house where Mummy had established a "private space" for herself, there was a stylish desk that gleamed with what looked like laminated plastic, lipstick-red, and in a center drawer of this desk was a large sheet of kindergarten-pink construction paper containing an elaborately hand-printed pyramid of names, some of them boxed, some distinguished by *, **, or ***, with mysterious codes and crisscrossing arrows, bewildering to the eye at first glance, yet, like any cryptic puzzle, yielding by degrees to the obsessive scrutiny of one, like eight-year-old Skyler Rampike, who focuses his attention on it, as if his life depended upon cracking the code. Out of loneliness/precocious morbid curiosity, Skyler often found himself in Mummy's colorfully decorated, perfumy room when Mummy was absent, and Skyler had no more shame than to search through Mummy's things, discovering this document in the center drawer to which

Mummy had given the title *FHFF* in tall letters, meaning, maybe, "Fair Hills Future Friends" (?), the poignant significance of which even an eight-year-old lately diagnosed with incipient dyslexia could discern. A meticulously constructed pyramid of names, as in

STEADLEY WHITTAKER WHITTIER McGREETY

KRUK HAMBRUCK FRASS STUBBE DURKEE O'STRYKER

FENN McCONE HOVER GRUBB MARROW KLAUS BURR KLEINHAUS

—and so forth, to the very bottom of the sheet of pink construction paper where names were more plentiful and (you had to think) less distinctive, exalted. I have made no attempt to replicate here the numerous codes attached to these names, for instance CH (church?), BX (Bix? contacts of Bix's), SK (skating?), HOS (Fair Hills Hospital Auxiliary, one of the more accessible local "service" organizations comprised primarily by well-to-do, somewhat idle Fair Hills matrons), FHCC (Fair Hills Country Club?), PHTAC (Pebble Hill Tennis Club?), SGGC (Sylvan Glen Golf Club?), VWC (Fair Hills Village Women's Club?), FHD (Fair Hills Day School?). To some of these, notably to the high-ranking McGREETY, the cryptic code PD was affixed: *playdate*.

"SKYLER! PLEASE TRY NOT TO LIMP, AND TWITCH, AND MAKE THOSE frightening 'pain faces.' A playdate is a *fun occasion*."

Must've been March 1995 this happened. When Skyler was only just eight years old and in third grade at Fair Hills Day and his twice-broken right leg had not yet entirely healed but the settlement out of court from the Gold Medal Gym & Health Club had come through. (As the *Fair Hills Beacon* discreetly noted, for an "undisclosed" sum.) When Daddy was traveling weekly on business missions for Scor Chemicals, which aggressive American-owned company had entered, in Daddy's words, "our global phase." This harried season when Bliss was beginning to skate in regional competitions in which, if she didn't place first, she placed second, or third, though her rivals were likely to be several years older than she; a season when Bliss no longer attended school with her little class-mates but was being "home-tutored" by a succession of tutors under Mummy's supervision. (Bliss: "I miss school, Mummy! I miss my teachers and I miss my f-friends." Mummy: "Don't be silly, sweetheart: you will make lots of skater-friends—you will make professional contacts for life. Darling, you are one very lucky little girl.")

Devoted as Betsey Rampike was to her daughter's "burgeoning" career, Mummy was determined to provide "social contacts" for her problematic son Skyler, who seemed to be virtually friendless; or, in any case, lacking the kinds of valuable contacts Mummy wished for him, whose surnames Mummy had hand-printed on the pink construction paper charts. Zoom into a TV-type scene between Mummy and Skyler:

" 'McGreety.' I've heard that there is a McGreety boy in your class, Skyler, is this so?"—a canny light coming into Mummy's liquidy brown eyes, though Skyler mumbled a snuffle-reply intended to discourage. But shrewd-Mummy persisted: "What is this boy's first name, Skyler?" and Skyler, squirming, foreseeing where this exchange must end, had no choice but to reveal: "T-Tyler." And eagerly Mummy said, " 'Tyler Mc-Greety.' He must be the son of Tyler McGreety the 'wizard financier'—his mother must be Thea?—Theodora?—whose picture is always in the Style section of the paper. I'm sure that I've met Mrs. McGreety at least once."

Tyler, Skyler. The very rhyme was ominous.

Cut now, as in stylish fast-forward, to Mummy driving Skyler to his playdate at the McGreety French Normandy manor house on East Camelot Drive; close-up on Mummy's disappointed face, her stunned-blinking wounded-brown eyes, when she is greeted at the massive front door not by socially prominent Theodora McGreety but by an olive-skinned housekeeper who says, in a forced simulation of her *gringa* employer's insincere-gracious smile, "Mz. Ranpick? Mz. McGreety so 'regrets' she is not here to 'say hello.' She asks will you please return by five P.M. to take home your son, thank you."

Mummy smiles bravely. Mummy nudges Skyler inside the house, to be greeted by a smirking sallow-faced boy lurking in a doorway, Tyler McGreety who mumbles, barely audible, "H'lo."

Tyler, Skyler. Glumly the two eight-year-olds stare at each other. Mummy kisses Skyler good-bye: "Have fun, boys!"

ONCE UPSTAIRS IN HIS BEDROOM, WHICH IS TWICE AS LARGE AS ANY CHILD'S room that Skyler has ever seen, with an adjoining bathroom and Jacuzzi, Tyler relents somewhat, inviting Skyler to "look around anywhere, see anything you'd like to do, do it." Tyler sprawls on his bed, observing Skyler with those small close-set smudged eyes that Skyler finds disconcerting. (As with Tyler's bed, most of the available surfaces are covered with objects with the look of being both expensive and tossed-aside: battery-operated motorized toys, electronic games, model rocket ships and missiles, Robo-Boy, Terminator-Boy, Star-Boy, alarmingly realistic rat-sized models of dinosaurs and prehistoric reptile birds. Some of this is on shelves, some on windowsills and some of it is underfoot. Skyler stumbles on—can it be?—a headless doll-baby of the approximate size of an actual baby, cut open as if with a sharp knife, of amazingly lifelike flesh-toned rubber. Smirking Tyler on his bed says: "Just kick Dolly out of the way, Sky. No sweat."

Skyler shudders, backing away. Skyler means to occupy himself with one of the motorized vehicle-toys, U.S. DEATH SQUAD, isn't this what a normal playdate-guest might do? As Tyler informs Skyler he's an "only" child: "My mom and dad are kind of old, see. 'Specially my dad the 'wizard financier' people call him. They had me, see, and decided to call it quits." Tyler chuckles, vastly amused. Skyler laughs, politely. "You?"

" 'M-Me'?—what?"

"Sky, are you kind of, y'know, 'mentally challenged'? You keep asking 'What'?"

"No. I just don't know what you're asking."

"I was asking if you have 'siblings'—or if you are a 'singleton' like me."

Skyler isn't sure. These words sound unpleasantly clinical, like something you overhear the orthopedic surgeon telling your parents and then wish you hadn't.

With exaggerated patience as if speaking to a moron, Tyler asks Skyler if Skyler has any brothers or sisters. Quickly Skyler says yes: "My sister is Bliss Rampike."

Tyler makes a rude noise with his lips: "So? Who's 'Bliz Rampuke'?"

Skyler is shocked. For one wearing an H.I.P. pin in his lapel, and the son of rich parents, Tyler McGreety is unexpectedly crude. And how is it possible, he's never heard of Bliss Rampike? Mummy would be astounded. Mummy would be disbelieving. In the Rampike household it has come to be believed that virtually everyone in Fair Hills, if not in all of New Jersey, knows of Bliss Rampike the four-year-old skating prodigy . . .

Tyler is saying, philosophically: "See, Sky: it's a better deal, to be one. 'Singleton.' Your parents focus on *you.* Or if they don't, 'cause they're too busy, they know they should, and you can work that to your advantage. Like, all this"—Tyler makes a negligent gesture, taking in the hundreds—thousands?—of dollars of expensive toys scattered about his room—"not to mention cash. Mommy is always whining, 'Tyler, why don't you invite your little friends from school here, the way normal children do,' but my impression is, at Fair Hills Day, nobody's got that much spare time. Not in the H.I.P. track, for sure." Tyler chews at his lower lip, smirking; then, with childlike bluntness, "How'd you get crippled?"

Skyler is taken wholly by surprise. Stammering, "I—I'm not. Crippled."

"Hell you're not! Everybody at school knows you limp."

"I don't *limp.* I'm not *crippled.*"

"You stutter, too."

"I d-d-do *not.*"

"Is your right leg shorter than the other leg? It sort of looks like that might be the problem."

Tyler is peering at Skyler pensively now. Not smirking.

Skyler protests: "It is *not.* There isn't any *problem.*"

"C'n I examine the leg? I'm pre-med."

Skyler shrinks away. "N-No."

"Hey man, I wouldn't hurt you. What I'd do is, like, measure both legs. How's that going to hurt?"

"I said no. Stay away."

"There's this 'way cool test, Sky: the neurologist pokes pins in you, in 'extremities' like your toes, to see if you feel 'sensation.' It's a game, like, if you feel the pin, to act like you don't. C'n we try that?"

"No."

Skyler is hurt, indignant. All these months he'd believed he had disguised his limp . . . Like the normal kids, he had been taking P.E.—dreaded Physical Education.

Like an eager young doctor-in-training Tyler persists, asking Skyler if his leg problem is "congenital" or "accident-related" and Skyler hears himself admit, yes: his leg was broken in two places when he was six, his knee was "messed up" also, but he has had surgery to fix it, his leg is "almost healed," he never uses crutches any longer and almost never needs a cane . . .

Tyler asks how'd this happen and Skyler says, embarrassed, "I was t-training to be a gymnast. I fell."

Tyler laughs. " 'Gymnast.' You?"

"My dad wanted me to. It was his idea."

This Tyler can respect. The ideas of dads, that go wrong.

"Hell, Sky: I'm a cripple, too. C'n you keep a secret?"

Sure.

"Since pre-school, I've been G.C.S.S." Tyler confesses this with scarcely concealed pride, but Skyler has no idea what G.C.S.S. means.

"*You're* not?" Tyler sounds disappointed. "I thought maybe, the way you act at school, kind of weird, twitchy and nervous and sulky, you'd be one of us: 'Gifted Child Syndrome Sufferer.' "

Gifted Child! Skyler has to wonder: maybe he *is*? For there are facts about himself known only to Fair Hills administrators and to Mummy, who rarely tells Skyler the results of the many tests he has had to take since kindergarten, both "cognitive" and "psychological"; only those tests Mummy arranges for him to take over, sometimes more than once, in a general, never-ceasing effort to *raise his score*.

The effort of *raising one's score*! Fair Hills children understand that a lifetime is required.

Skyler asks what "syndrome" means and Tyler tells him, with clinical precision: " 'Syndrome' is a congeries of 'symptoms,' seemingly related but possibly not, in a cluster. The more symptoms, the higher the 'pathology quotient' of the subject. Some G.C.S.S. kids in our class are only just D-level; I'm A-level." Tyler pauses to allow this fact to sink in. Skyler says apologetically that he has just been classified "I.D." and "I.A.D.D." (though to be precise Skyler has been ranked infinitesimally below the "I.A.D.D." diagnosis). Tyler doesn't seem very impressed: "'Incipient Dyslexia'—'Incipient Attention Deficit Disorder.' Sure. But in high-quotient G.C.S.S. you have these disorders plus a minimum one-fifty-five I.Q. (It isn't cool to reveal what your I.Q. is, Sky. So don't!) I have so many symptoms in clusters, both 'intermittent' and 'chronic,' my pediatric neurologist at Columbia Presbyterian and my pediatric psychiatrist at Robert Wood Johnson are both writing papers on me. Maybe you've noticed, Sky, my left eye isn't in a line with my right eye? It's as if I'm looking in two places at the same time, except my brain can process only one vision-field at a time. 'Uncanny child'—Headmaster Hannity remarked of me to my mother; you can be sure that Mommy has repeated it all over town. (Mommy suffers from 'R.C.S.'—'Repetitive Compulsive Syndrome.' Especially if it's something Mommy knows she shouldn't be repeating. The poor woman can't help herself, so I try not to blame her.) I've been diagnosed with an 'impairment of the cerebellum' which results in 'poor motor coordination' so I have a permanent medical excuse for P.E. while the rest of you chumps have to trudge around outdoors in the cold kicking a stupid soccer ball. (Did you know that the original 'balls' in field sports were human heads? Decapitated heads of enemies? How cool is that?) If you tried you could get 'P.M.E.' status at school—'Permanent Medical Excuse.' Have your mother put some pressure on Hannity, after all you are a cripple."

Skyler winces: he is not a cripple.

Skyler protests: he wants to take gym class like the other guys, he wants to be normal . . .

"Freaky kids like us can't ever be 'normal,'" Tyler says smugly. "Our generation is some new kind of 'evolutionary development,' my shrink says. 'Normal' is just 'average'—not cool. My latest diagnosis is 'A.P.M.'—'Acute Premature Melancholia,' usually an affliction of late middle age, they think is genetic since Ty Senior has had it all his life, too. You look as if you might be A.P.M. too, Sky: that kind of pissed-off mopey look in your face like you swallowed something really gross and can't spit it out. Want to try some of my meds? They're 'way cool."

Feebly Skyler protests he hadn't better, he has meds of his own he takes three times a day, and you aren't supposed to mix them. For the first time Tyler fixes Skyler a look of genuine interest: "*You* have meds? What kind?" When Skyler tells him Nixil, but his doctor has been cutting back his prescription, Tyler says, "Nixil is cool. But have you tried Excelsia?—this new anti-depressant, the F.D.A. has just approved. My mom and me are both into Excelsia." With sudden energy Tyler rouses himself from his sprawl on the rumpled bed, clumps into his bathroom and returns with a handful of plastic pill containers which he arranges reverently on top of his bed, shaking out sample pills. Also, with a grunt Tyler rummages beneath his mattress to bring out his "stash": a dozen or more "psychotropics" he has pilfered from other people's medicine cabinets, including his parents'. Also, Tyler trades meds with kids at school. How like an avid little boy chunky Tyler is, showing a friend his prize marble collection: except, in Fair Hills, children don't collect marbles any longer. " 'Tranks,' uppers, 'muscle relaxant,' Ritalin. An old classic: Dexedrine. These weird-colored tabs are from Mommy's prescription." Skyler stares at shiny green pills, dull-green capsules, chalky white pills, chunky yellow pills, tiny beige pills and lethal-looking tablets the hue of faded blood. One or two of these look familiar to Skyler, painkillers/sedatives from the nightmare months following his fall in the gym. Why not? Maybe Tyler McGreety will like him better and want to be friends with him and Mummy will be happy with him, as Mummy hasn't been happy with Skyler in some time. Skyler swallows down one shiny green pill, one chunky yellow pill, and one of the lethal-blood capsules. Tyler, observing, whistles thinly through his teeth, seems about to stop Skyler but does not stop Skyler. "Sky: cool. Way cool." Tyler scoops up one of the faded-blood capsules and swallows it dry.

There follows then, with the rapid skids, lurches, and leaps of an accelerated film, an indeterminate period of time during which Skyler's talkative playdate confides in him, breathing moistly from his opened mouth, ". . . obsessed with me 'following in his footsteps' which is why I'm taking algebra this year and started Mandarin Chinese, the only third-grader H.I.P. in a class of asshole fifth- and sixth-graders . . ." as Skyler begins to feel a very strange buzzing/humming/vibrating sensation at the base of his skull, very likely in his cerebellum, and an erratic beating of his frantic heart like a moth trapped in a cobweb, ". . . Dad has his 'heart set' on me being a 'wizard financier' like himself, Yale B.A. like the old man, Skull and Bones like the old man, then to the Wharton School and beyond that—'McGreety Père et Fils, Inc.'—delusions of grandeur! Except Ty Junior has his own plans for what he's going to do with his freaky G.C.S.S. life, see—" Skyler's mouth has gone dry as chalk. Skyler's moth-heart is fluttering inside his rib cage. Weirder yet, the familiar pain-tinges in Skyler's legs seem to have vanished—in fact, both Skyler's legs seem to have vanished—even as Skyler is smiling a goofy-kid smile and blinking rapidly to keep his vision in focus. *Don't disappoint Mummy— again!* Mummy had kissed/murmured into Skyler's shamed ear for (as Skyler would prefer not to remember) several recent playdates arranged by Mummy with such hope were not what you'd call successes; for the mothers of Skyler's playdate friends did not call Mummy back nor even, a matter of painful concern in Fair Hills, return Mummy's repeated calls. And so Skyler is determined not to disappoint/annoy/offend/bore his strangely excited classmate who has pulled Skyler over to his bed to show him the opened pages of oversized medical books containing color plates of—Skyler squints, tries to see—moist-pink flesh, flesh veined terribly with red, eerily lard colored flesh and sallow-grayish skin, a lattice-work of stark-white bones—Skyler gapes having seen nothing like these photographs in his life. ". . . pathology is way cool, see, Sky: you get to use surgeon skills but there's no bullshit from your 'patients'—they're dead. Don't need to talk to them, or to anybody mostly; you set your own hours and work on your own and nobody's going to complain about you or sue for 'malpractice' "—Tyler giggles, quivering and wiping at his mouth as he slowly, reverently turns pages of the medical book for Skyler to stare at— "Mommy is always raiding my room and taking these books from me, like there is something sicko about my chosen profession. Dad tells her, 'Ty Junior will grow out of it, it's just his age'—like they know the first thing about *me*! See, Sky?—this is 'steps of an autopsy'—you get to use an actual saw on the skull and rib cage, and the actual heart you kind of pull out in your hand and place in jars like these. If you want any of these pictures to take home I can photocopy them for you in Dad's study, he's got a color copier. On the Internet you can order 'Junior Pathology Kits' which I have tried to do—but somebody, has to be my damn mother, intercepts them. Three times I've tried but I'm not giving up, I was thinking, Sky, maybe I could use your address?—the kit could come to you?—and we could have a playdate here, you could bring it over, would that be cool? Here: this is my favorite. How she's been opened up, they don't show the faces but you can see it's a girl, our age or a little younger. I mean, is this cool?" as Skyler is blinking in horror at what he sees, and Skyler's little fists are raised, Skyler's fists are pounding at the other's astonished face in the fleeting moments before something like a slot—a slash?—opens up blackly to suck Skyler through.

PROMPTLY AT 5 P.M. AS BIDDEN, NOT DARING TO BE EVEN A FEW MINUTES late, Skyler's mother in her peach-colored cashmere coat that gives her a festive-girlish appearance at odds with her strained smile arrives at the oaken front door of the McGreetys' faux-Normandy manor, to pick up her son: hoping that the Fair Hills *mover and shaker* Theodora McGreety will open the door even as with another, more somber part of her mind, Mummy knows that Theodora will not be greeting her. And when the door is opened, even as Mummy is still depressing the doorbell, as if someone inside has been watching urgently for her arrival, there stands the olive-skinned housekeeper in the (now somewhat soiled) white uniform, not snooty-aloof as before but frankly alarmed, shaken; and in a jumble of heavily accented words informing "Mz. Ranpick" that "your son" had be-come "sick"—"some kind of flu"—he'd been "throwing up"—"seizing"—"like with ep-lepsy"—and Mrs. Ranpick should take him away right now, before Mrs. McGreety comes home, for Mrs. McGreety is going to be "very upset" at the "nasty smell" from "him being sick all over"—clearly the housekeeper is far more frightened of her wealthy *gringa* employer than she is of the *gringa* playdate mother staring at her astonished.

And there is—can it be Skyler?—on a dwarf settee in the foyer, hunched like a fetus, shivering in a blanket that would seem to have been wrapped hastily and carelessly around him, Mummy's *little man* shivering and whimpering, deathly-pale; he is dazed and incoherent and, so strangely, his clothes and hair are soaking wet. (It will turn out that his playdate host Ty, panicked at what appeared to be a lethal reaction to the meds-mix he'd taken, dragged the convulsing eight-year-old into the bathroom adjoining Ty's room, and into the shower where Ty turned on "full blast" the cold water in an effort to "calm" Skyler.) At this time, when Betsey Rampike arrives to take her stricken son away, Tyler, Jr. is nowhere in view.

"Oh my God! Oh Skyler! Oh what have you *done.*"

Fortunately, Skyler does seem to revive in Mummy's car, on the way to the Fair Hills Medical Center, vomiting up a yellow gruel-like liquid onto the floor and Skyler insists to Mummy that he's all right, he is feeling much better, so Mummy decides against the ER as she will decide against recounting any of this unfortunate episode to Skyler's dad when he returns home from Toyko, or Singapore, could be Bangkok. At home Skyler overhears her speaking agitatedly on the phone, in the stilted voice in which Mummy leaves voice mail messages she suspects will be futile, "Theodora? This is Betsey Ranpick—Rampike!—may we speak? Please will you call me as soon as you get this message? I'm a little upset about what happened at your house—what my son has told me happened at your house this afternoon—I don't mean that I am terribly upset but yes, I am upset—so will you call me, please? Skyler is much, much better now—you will be relieved to hear—please tell your son—and he is hoping—and I am hoping—that the boys can t-try again—we can plan another p-playdate—soon?"

Though Mummy telephones Mrs. McGreety several times, her calls are never returned; and when the women encounter each other in Fair Hills, which is not frequent, and always in the presence of others, Mrs. McGreety will seem not to know who Mrs. Rampike is.

Wiping a tear from Skyler's eye he hasn't known he has shed, Mummy whispers fiercely, "Skyler! Don't cry. Next time, we will try *harder.*"

ADVENTURES IN PLAYDATES II

SKYLER! WE ARE NOT GOING TO GIVE UP ON A SOCIAL LIFE FOR YOU, I promise. And so there were others. Numerous others. Playdates with other Fair Hills children, mostly boys, and mostly classmates of Skyler's at Fair Hills Day School or the yet more prestigious Drumthwrack Academy for Boys, or children of families belonging to Trinity Episcopal Church, these dates arranged by Mummy at her most exacting, ambitious, and hopeful in the interstices of Mummy's ever-more busy life as the mother-manager of Bliss Rampike in those frantic years 1995 through December 1996 for after January 1997 there would be no more playdates for Skyler Rampike, no indeed.

Ah, but memories! What is childhood but a giddy repository of memories! Quick cut to: fat-faced/sullen-giggly Albert Kruk who was a year older than Skyler, in fourth grade at Fair Hills, not H.I.P. track, not G.C.S.S., whose father was Morris Kruk the "highly regarded" criminal attorney and whose mother Biffy Kruk was membership chair of the Village Women's Club and one of Fair Hills's "movers and shakers," whose photographs appeared frequently in the Style section of the *Fair Hills Beacon*: Albert Kruk who clearly had not wanted a playdate with Skyler Rampike but took him "fishing"—as he called it—on the immense flagstone terrace at the rear of the Kruk house on Hawksmoor Lane, stomping on luckless worms marooned on the terrace after a recent rainstorm but Skyler hadn't much enthusiasm for "fishing" and the playdate with Albert Kruk was not a success, and would not be repeated. And there was Elyot Grubbe, fourth grader at the Drumthwrack Academy with whose heiress-mother Mummy was acquainted through Reverend and Mrs. Higley: Elyot was a boy of precocious mental gifts (it was claimed) yet strangely slow in speech, slow in movement and sinuous as a sloth, prone to staring off into space, as if mildly sedated; a playdate friend with whom Skyler could sit quietly for an entire playdate, in fact mutely, at either Elyot's home or Skyler's, each boy deeply absorbed in his own homework with no need for the usual phony small talk: "D'you like school?"—"It's okay. You?"—"It's okay." Of Skyler's playdate friends, Elyot Grubbe was his favorite; if Skyler had had a brother, Elyot Grubbe was his brother; perhaps because, unknown to Skyler at the time, of course, Elyot Grubbe was one day to become a child of media scandal (in April 1999, Elyot's heiress-mother Imogene would be "brutally bludgeoned to death" by an intruder in the Grubbes' Neo-Edwardian mansion on the Great Road at the exact time when Elyot's father A. J. Grubbe was deep-sea fishing in the Caribbean off the coast of St. Bart's with friends on his thirty-foot sailboat) as if anticipating that his life, like Skyler Rampike's, would be but a footnote ever after.* And there was Billy Durkee, a Fair Hills classmate of canny mathematical skills who taught Skyler to play poker ("This game is five-card stud, son: you in?") in order to win from the naive boy his meager allowance (meager by Fair Hills Day standards, just twelve dollars weekly) and meds (by this time Skyler was taking Ritalin for his now-active A.D.D. in addition to the new F.D.A.-approved-for-children painkiller Balmil much touted for its minimal side effects); and there was fifth-grader Denton "Fox" Hambruck whose father was an older Scor Chemicals associate/squash partner of Bix Rampike and whose mother had befriended Betsey Rampike, to a degree. Fox Hambruck was famous at school for bringing with him, inside his loose-fitting clothes, small screw-top bottles filled with his father's blended-Scotch whiskey, which he shared with a very few select

---

* Though the "career criminal" who confessed in May 1999 to having killed Mrs. Grubbe for $75,000 ($25,000 up front, remainder to come) allegedly paid to him by Mr. Grubbe, was tried in Morris County, found guilty and sentenced to 260 years in prison, somehow it happened that the wily Mr. Grubbe, very capably defended by the equally wily criminal defense attorney Morris Kruk, was acquitted of all charges by a jury of his peers and shortly afterward moved from Fair Hills to "divide his time" between Manhattan, Palm Beach, Florida, and Jackson Hole, Wyoming. Quickly remarried and quickly again a father, Mr. Grubbe chose not to take his son Elyot with him into his new life; and what became of Skyler's playdate friend and shadow-brother, Skyler would not learn until September 5, 2003.

fifth- and sixth-graders. At school, Fox would not have been caught dead in the company of a third-grade runt/cripple like Skyler Rampike but, cajoled into a playdate with Skyler by his mother, Fox seemed friendly enough, offering to show to Skyler, on the occasion of their first and only playdate, what he called his father's home movies: "These are tapes of my dad's special friends, that nobody knows about but me"—adding with a wink—"and Dad doesn't know about me." A dozen videos were kept locked in a small safe in Mr. Hambruck's office (to which, by what sleight-of-hand Skyler could not guess, foxy Fox had the combination) in somber black cases identified only by initials and dates. "Know what X-rated is, Rampike?" Fox teased the younger boy, "—well, this is XXX. Hang on!" As soon as Fox began the first tape, and starkly black-and-white images leapt onto the large TV wall screen, Skyler was unnerved: no mood-music? no voice-over? only just a crudely photographed scene of—was that an adult woman? an adult naked woman? a fleshy woman like Mummy with large softly sagging breasts cupped in both her hands, dark eye-like nipples, an alarming swath of something dark and bristly as a beard, but in the wrong place for a beard. As Skyler stared slack-jawed the naked woman lurched toward the camera opening her arms as if to embrace him, as Mummy used to do when Skyler was younger, and Mummy's *little man*; the woman made kissing/sucking gestures with her thick lipsticked lips and a wave of panic washed over Skyler—Was this Mummy? Even as Skyler could see clearly that the woman was heavier than Mummy, not nearly so pretty as Mummy with a bumpy nose not a snub nose like Mummy's, and yet—Was this Mummy? What if this was somehow Mummy? Jerkily the camera moved to show a second female figure, much younger, a girl?—of about eleven?—a girl with long straight hair and pouty lips who resembled a sixth-grader at Fair Hills Day School yet could not be that girl of course, for this girl was naked, and you never saw naked girls, this was a girl made up glamorously as the woman, in fact made up to resemble the woman, Skyler thought, who was she?—the girl's mother, as Mummy was lately making up Bliss to resemble her when Bliss was performing on the ice and the lights, as Mummy said, bleached all color from a child's face, and made a child's eyes disappear so you had no choice really except to put on makeup including eye shadow, eyeliner, mascara; and now the

camera swung drunkenly around to show a pot-bellied middle-aged man
who appeared also to be naked, though wearing black socks like Daddy's,
that came halfway to his knees, and a watch of the kind Skyler had learned
to identify as Rolex, for Daddy wore a Rolex watch, and the man in the film
was not Daddy because the man in the film was older and his body slack
and sagging and the man's face was blurred, for the camera was unsteady,
and Fox was saying, snickering, "That's Dad! That's Dad!" and "watch
what Dad does," giggling and wiping at his mouth; and Skyler pushed
desperately away from Fox, as Fox laughed crudely and grabbed at Skyler
saying he had to stay! had to watch! and Skyler shielded his eyes from the
screen as often watching TV in the family room when neither Mummy nor
Daddy was with them Bliss would shield her eyes with her fingers—yet
peeking through her fingers?—even when, by Skyler's standards, nothing
was happening on the screen that was scary or upsetting, but Bliss was
just a little girl, easily made anxious by loud noises, jarring intrusions
and swift changes of scene and of mood-music and huddled on the sofa
blinking and staring at so much that seemed to be rushing at her—from
where? from the Adult World?—a whirlwind of sights, sounds, sensations
you could not hope to make sense of, not when you were four years old, or
scarcely five, the only remedy was to shield your eyes, better yet shut your
eyes *Is it over, Skyler? Is it gone now?* in a faint quivery voice to make Skyler
jeer *What a baby! There's nothing there, silly baby* but now Skyler wasn't jeering and Skyler wasn't laughing for Skyler had had a glimpse of someone,
another man, a blurred and mirthful face?—* beyond the fattish figure of
the naked man said to be Fox Hambruck's father and so broke away from
Fox's clutching hands and ran from Fox's room (as large and as cluttered
with expensive boy-things as Tyler McGreety's room) to hide frightened
and panting in a bathroom of perfumed soaps and gleaming white walls,
the door locked to protect him until sometime later there was a sharp rap
on the door and a female voice called to Skyler: "Your momma is downstairs, Sk'ler. It is time for you to go home."

* *Repeatedly I have read this passage, brooded upon it, and frankly don't know: did Skyler catch
a glimpse of his father in the background of the video; or did Skyler panic, imagining that he might
catch a glimpse of his father in the video? What do you think?*

What nice people! Skyler you know your father works with Mr. Hambruck who is a senior executive at Scor Chemicals! Oh I hope I hope that you and that fascinating little Denton got along well and he will want to see you again and that you did not disappoint Mummy again, darling!

SORRY TO GIVE THE IMPRESSION THAT MOST OF SKYLER'S PLAYDATES WERE disasters,* or took place at others' houses. In fact there were plenty of playdates in which nothing happened—"forgettable" interludes, you could say—which is why I've forgotten them. And there were plenty of playdates at our house under the eye of the current Maria, when Mummy was out; and sometimes, when Mummy was home, Mummy hovered over Skyler and his little visitor like an anxious hostess asking would they like something to drink? Would they like some fresh-baked (by Maria) chocolate-chip cookies? Some banana-nut bread? One of Skyler's visitors said politely, "Thank you, Mrs. Rampike. But I am on the Atkins diet." Another was innocent freckle-faced Calvin Klaus, Jr. the ten-year-old son of scrawny-sexy-blond Morgan Klaus who would one day soon give Bix and Betsey Rampike's shaky marriage a final nudge into ruins, of which more later. I guess.

"WISH YOU WERE MY BROTHER, SKYLER." BREATHY MILDRED MARROW paused, wiping at her damp eyes. "Wish I had a brother, and he was you."

Mildred Marrow was one of Skyler's very few girl playdates. (Why was this? Did our mothers anxiously fear pre-pubescent sexual gropings, "experimentation"? Even among the walking-wounded of the up-coming generation?) A moony fifth grader a year older than Skyler, Mildred was famous for her high—"off-the-radar"—I.Q. at Fair Hills Day, and was generally disliked. How could you tolerate a smirky girl who'd not only been tapped for the H.I.P. track (in pre-school!) but was ranked in the "highest one-percentile" of all H.I.P. students at the school,

---

* *Exactly like most "great works" of art, culture. Why?*

K through twelfth grade? Mildred was the daughter of a New Jersey state senator of independent means and his socialite wife: a lanky girl with brooding damp eyes, a quivery mouth and rounded shoulders who'd been designated both G.C.S.S. and R.A. ("recovering anorexic") by fourth grade. Mildred's schedule was as crammed and purposeful as Bliss's, though more varied: a special nanny-driver transported Mildred to and from school, to and from her Mandarin Chinese tutorial; to and from equestrian lessons, tennis lessons, dance lessons; sessions with her acupuncturist, and with her (Jungian) therapist; and, at least once a week, a playdate with a child like Skyler Rampike who was deemed to pose no threat, intellectual or otherwise, to Mildred's delicate sensibility. To Skyler's surprise, Mildred seemed actually to like him, perhaps out of pity?—for Skyler was known not to be H.I.P. nor even G.C.S.S. and though he tried hard to disguise it, one of Skyler's legs was obviously shorter than the other, causing him to limp, occasionally even to walk with a cane ("Sprained my Akills tendon in the gym, this is just temporary") thereby endearing him to his girl-classmates even as it roused to scorn most of the boys.

High-strung at school, Mildred relaxed in Skyler's presence. Her "favorite thing" was helping him with his homework, especially arithmetic which Mildred said was "restful" to her: "To slow my mind down, to keep pace with you, Skyler. I love that!" Once in a thoughtful moment Mildred confessed that she wished that Skyler could be her brother, and live at her house: "My neurotic parents would then have someone else to obsess over, not just me." Mildred was Skyler's sole playdate to speak of his sister, with frank admiration and envy. "Bliss is just a little girl, and she has a career. In a few years, she can live *by herself*."

Skyler laughed uneasily. "Live by herself? Bliss is five years old."

Mildred, who hadn't actually seen Bliss in person, only just photographs of her in local publications, seemed not to hear. She was showing Skyler a clipping from the *Fair Hills Beacon* with the headline FAIR HILLS "PRODIGY" WINS GIRLS SKATING TITLE. The article included a photograph of both Bliss and her mother: the occasion was the Junior Miss Girls' Skate Challenge 1995 held in Roanoke, Virginia, a few months before. Wistfully Mildred said: "Your sister is so pretty, and so little. I wish that I was pretty like her and not ugly like I am; I wish that I could skate like her, and get my picture in the paper. She is *so lucky.*"

Skyler wondered if Mildred was joking. Mildred Marrow, a rich-girl famous for her I.Q., the highest one-percentile of H.I.P students, both G.C.S.S. and R.A., was envious of Skyler's little sister?

"I hate who I am!" Mildred said. "Of course I am superior to just about everyone at school, at damn old tests anyway, but who cares? I don't care! I'd rather be a champion ice-skater with blond hair."

Skyler, staring at Bliss and Mummy in the newspaper photo, had to suppose that, if he hadn't known that the beautiful little doll-girl in the photo was Bliss, he wouldn't have recognized her. For her performance, Bliss had been transformed into a fairy princess in white tulle, white satin, white feathers, with a glimpse of white lace panties beneath the little skirt; in her plaited hair was a sprinkling of what Mummy called "stardust," and on top of this plaited hair a small silver—or silver-plate—tiara had been placed. It was so, Bliss looked beautiful. And behind her, embracing Bliss with her chin resting lightly on Bliss's shoulder, Betsey Rampike looked beautiful, too.

Skyler had attended the Roanoke competition. Skyler had seen his sister win an "upset victory" over exquisite little ten-year-old Chinese-American prodigies, as she'd won over all other girl-skaters in the junior competition. Skyler had frankly doubted that Bliss would win, skating to a slightly syncopated "Sleeping Beauty Waltz"; more than once, Skyler had shut his eyes, and clenched his fists; thinking *Now she will fall! now it will end* but somehow God had protected Bliss on her hissing skate-blades, as Mummy had prayed He would do. The little girl with the "fairy sparkle" had won the audience's fickle heart away from the Chinese-American twins, and she'd won the judges' hearts: out of a perfect score of 6, Bliss was awarded 5.88 and the title Miss Girls' Skate Challenge 1995 (Junior Division). And now Mildred Marrow, brainiest of brainy Fair Hills children, feared by her classmates and even by some of her teachers for her sarcastic tongue, was saying, sighing, "Skyler, your parents must be *so proud* of your sister. 'Bliss Rampike' must be the happiest little girl on earth. Gosh!"

HAPPIEST LITTLE GIRL ON EARTH

IF I FALL, WILL PEOPLE STILL LOVE ME?
   If I fall, will you still love me?

FOR SOMETIMES, YES SHE FELL. FELL SUDDENLY, AND FELL HARD. NOT (yet) while performing publicly (though that would come, inevitably) but in practice. In practice, falling happens often. For when you practice each day, as many as two hours each day, and when you are attempting new, ever more difficult maneuvers, naturally you will falter sometimes, and you will slip sometimes, and you will fall sometimes, and fall hard. And you will lie unmoving on the freezing-cold ice that is not your friend but your enemy, unyielding as the hardest of concrete floors; and you will feel every pulse in your small body beat in shock and mortification and shame and the terror that when you try to get up, you will not be able to get up; when you try to stand, you will not be able to stand; when you try to skate, the most elementary right-foot-forward glide, you will not be able to skate. And yet the taped music continues, that Mummy has selected, as if in mockery of you, that you have fallen, and are blinking tears from your eyes, biting your lower lip trying not to cry. And they are crouched over you, they are tugging at your arms, Mummy, and Olga Zych who is your trainer, they are frightened, and they are crying into your face *Bliss! Bliss are you hurt!*—nowhere to hide, for everyone at the rink is staring now, and Bliss is *you*.

.   .   .

TAPE THE ANKLE! WE CAN TAPE THE ANKLE! SHE DIDN'T SPRAIN HER AN-
kle, you can see it isn't a sprain, it's just a little sore where she turned it.
Bliss is not hurt! Bliss's left ankle is her major weakness. We can give her
painkillers. Listen to the poor child *Mummy I'm not hurt, Mummy I want to
skate, Mummy I want to skate!* Bliss will be devastated if after all our work
we pull out of the competition on Saturday. We have been praying so hard.
All of our supporters have been praying so hard. And her daddy is planning to see her skate, this time. Bliss will be devastated if she lets her
daddy down. She will be devastated if she lets her Mummy down, and her
trainer. We can tape the ankle so she won't turn it again, and we can give
her painkillers. And her left elbow, where she banged it on the ice, that
isn't a sprain or a break, just a bruise and a bump and nothing that can't
be disguised by makeup. It's this pancake makeup, like putty. Exactly
Bliss's skin-tone. What a brave girl Bliss is, hardly crying! But she didn't
hurt herself really, like the other time. This will heal by Saturday, and a
little pancake makeup will hide the bruises on her leg, and on her knees.
She's just a little girl, small children are clumsy, small children fall all
the time, and they have less distance to fall than we do, and their bones
are so supple. Their bones are like elastic. And after Wilmington, Bliss
can rest for a while. After Baltimore, and after the Tri-State Regionals,
and after StarSkate Ice Capades, and after Little Miss Royale New Jersey.
And after the Lady Champ Juniors. And after Atlantic City. She can rest.
She can take pressure off the ankle. We can give her painkillers. Dr. Brea
has said, Balmil is perfect for children and is not habit-forming. Balmil—
unlike that damned Nixil—that's been taken off the market, did you
hear?—has no side effects. Balmil is state-of-the-art for young athletes.
Like Hi-Con Vitamin. Like SuperGrow. Over the holidays, Bliss can rest.
Until January, and the Hershey Kisses Festival, when she'll be good as
new.

. . . WATCHING BLISS SKATE. WHEN BLISS WAS ALONE, AND NO ONE ELSE
was watching. At the practice rink after the other girl-skaters were gone,
and their trainers. And Olga Zych was gone. And Mummy was gone somewhere making phone calls. (Mummy is always making phone calls, girl-

ish and excited. Laughing Mummy says how'd we ever exist without the cell phone!) Late afternoon at the Halcyon rink and just Bliss skating, not showily, not straining herself, not risking injury but only just skating, using the entire rink, long slow glides and dreamy turns, in silence. No sound but the sound of the skate blades on the ice. Such days when impulsively Mummy would invite Skyler to come with them to the rink: "Bliss needs you, to watch!" And Skyler felt a pang of gratitude, and anticipation for the peaceful interlude when the other girl-skaters, their sharp-voiced trainers and mothers, had departed. When the music has ceased. When Bliss is free, and alone, while Mummy makes her numerous cell phone calls, and Bliss skates in silence, no adults observing, or judging. Only Skyler watches, at rink-side. Only Skyler who is Bliss's big brother—eight years old—and Bliss's friend. Bliss's only friend. (For somehow it has happened that Bliss no longer sees her little-girl friends/classmates since she no longer goes to school, but is "home-schooled" by tutors, under Mummy's supervision.)

"Skyler? Put on skates—skate with me?"

Lonely Bliss calls to Skyler, waving to him as she glides across the ice, but Skyler quickly shakes his head, *no*.

SKYLER LOVES HIS LONELY LITTLE SISTER, SURE. YET SKYLER GLOATS that there are secrets in their family that Skyler knows, that Bliss will not ever know.

For instance, what Daddy says, sometimes. What Daddy says and what Mummy says in the late-night in Daddy and Mummy's bedroom with the door shut and only a faint crescent of light showing beneath.

How the hell much is this costing us, Betsey?—Daddy's voice just audible through the door, and Mummy laughs as if this is a cheeky interview question she isn't really expected to answer so Daddy asks, *How much, Betsey?* And quickly Mummy says as if reciting prepared words, *Our daughter is a skating prodigy! Our daughter is a—potential world champion! Bliss could be the next Sonja Henie, Bix!* and Daddy persists in firm-Daddy voice, don't-bullshit-me-Daddy voice, *How much, Betsey?* And Mummy says, in mild protest, as if still this is a cheeky/flirty interview, *Bix! You've seen our*

*daughter skate, you've heard the applause, at least on video. You know that Bliss
has won titles, already! How can you doubt us, Bix, you must know how hard
we've both been working.* And Daddy says, *Honey, I know. I know, and I am
impressed as hell. My two beautiful gals, in the newspapers! But: how much?*
and Mummy is hurt-sounding now, and Mummy is trying to argue, and
(Skyler seems to know this, through the door) Mummy is backing away
from Daddy, or, yet more audaciously, turning away, as if to walk away, which
(Skyler knows) Mummy should not do for such an action is "insulting"—
"provoking"—to Daddy as, if Skyler is being (mildly, lightly) scolded by
Daddy, and yet Skyler squirms, twists, makes one of his pain-faces and
tries to shrug out of Daddy's grip, this is "insulting" and "provoking" to
Daddy and not a very good idea for Skyler, for mild-Daddy can shift
abruptly to angry-Daddy; yet Mummy continues to edge away from Daddy,
evasively Mummy says *I don't know how much, Bix!—not exactly, can't we talk
about this in the morning?* And Daddy says, an edge now to Daddy's voice,
Skyler is frightened for Mummy seeming to see through the shut door
Daddy's soulful brown eyes narrowed now and hard-fixed as a pit bull's
eyes on its prey: *These bills, these credit card receipts, cancelled checks—did
you think I wouldn't discover them? That lesbo 'Zych' and her 'fee'—fees at the
rinks—hotel bills, restaurant bills—fucking doctor bills—more fucking doctor
bills—insurance policy premiums—this 'publicist' you've hired—I'm estimating a
minimum sixty thousand for this year, Betsey.* And Mummy cries, *Sixty thousand! That's ridiculous,* and Daddy says, *Are you saying that I am wrong,
Betsey?—that I am ridiculous, Betsey?—is that what you are saying, Betsey?* and
Mummy says quickly, *No but I—I don't think—Bix, I'm sure that—* and Daddy
says, *Sixty thousand this year, and next year will be higher, obviously. If you
keep on as you are. I've looked into the amateur-skating scene, girls' figure skating, I understand that Bliss has promise, Bliss is doing very well for such a little
girl, she's won a few trophies and might win more but it will be years before she
makes any real money, and if she hurts herself, what then?* And Mummy says,
Bliss will not hurt herself, Bix! I promise you. And Daddy says, *How the hell can
you promise me that, Betsey? Can you see into the future?* And Mummy says,
pleading now, on the other side of the bedroom door where he stands rapt
and unmoving Skyler can envision Mummy sinking to her knees in front
of Daddy, Mummy in her silky nightgown, a strap slipping off her bare,

fleshy shoulder, and Mummy's hair is in her face, and Mummy's cheeks are flushed, and Mummy's warm brown beautiful eyes are damp with tears, Mummy plucks at Daddy's hands, Mummy is like a blind woman groping at Daddy who looms up before her, Mummy is begging, *Trust me, Bix. Darling, have faith in me and trust me, our daughter is our destiny.*

DADDY LOVES YOU BUT DADDY DOESN'T LOVE YOU ALL THAT MUCH. AND *maybe Mummy doesn't, either.*

DESTINY:
1. **Something to which a person or a thing is destined: FORTUNE.**
2. **A predetermined course of events often held to be an irresistible power or agency.**

(Sure, Skyler looked up the word in the dictionary. Skyler-with-one-leg-shorter-than-the-other, destined to be nobody's destiny.)

"SKY-LER! I LOVE YOU."

Sweet little Bliss, lonely little Bliss, so often hugging her big brother around the neck, and kissing him wetly, which was embarrassing to Skyler for what eight-year-old boy wants to be hugged/kissed by his little sister so often? And Bliss's thin arms are surprisingly strong, tugging at Skyler, making him wince. Skyler knows that boys don't hug/kiss their little sisters unless forced to, which sometimes happens when photographers are present and Mummy urges her two adorable children to hug/kiss for the camera. And there is Skyler Rampike in a kiddy-tux, clip-on black bow tie, dazzling-white shirt with French cuffs, in his lapel a crimson carnation matching the crimson satin ribbons in Bliss's plaited-crown hair as Skyler escorts his sister to the edge of the ice rink where a swooping spotlight awaits her provoking the packed arena (where was this? might've been Baltimore) to burst into applause; or, in the festive StarSkate Winners' Circle reception following, Ballroom B of the Marriott, under

Mummy's guidance ("Sweetie, don't limp! And don't make faces!") escorting the newly crowned Tiny Miss StarSkate 1995 in her frothy pink-and-white finery, through a gauntlet of blinding flashbulbs, TV cameras, and gawking well-wishers.*

INTERESTED IN A FOLLOW-UP TO THE PRECEDING CUTESY SCENE? WHEN Mummy saw the glossy photos of Bliss and Skyler at the StarSkate reception, Mummy almost fainted. For StarSkate Winter Sports, Inc. had intended to use pictures of their several 1995 winners in national advertisements for their skating products, and much had been riding on these photos of the adorable Rampike children, but: "Ohhh my God. Oh what is this. *Oh.*" For it seemed that, though Bliss was smiling sweetly, if wanly, into the camera, and was looking exquisite as a porcelain doll, little Skyler in his kiddy-tux resembled a child-gargoyle, oddly hunched, his face contorted into a scowl, and his teeth bared in a predatory grin. "Why, this isn't possible! How is this possible! Skyler was not making faces when these pictures were taken. I saw him. Skyler was smiling, I swear. And he wasn't hunched! I watched him every second, and he looked absolutely adorable, and everyone said so, nothing like this—*freak.*" On this relatively rare occasion when Daddy was home with his little family, on a Saturday morning, and making an effort to spend quality time with them, Daddy laughed at Mummy's alarm saying, "Now darling, you exag-

---

* *Probably some of you, skeptically inclined, are wondering where such "news" photos appear? Such TV footage of such minor events in the cultural history of our great nation? Frankly, I'm not sure. I do remember Mummy avidly clipping stories from such publications as the* Netcong Valley Bee, *the* Ashbury Park Weekly, East Orange Sentinel, Delaware Valley Beacon *and, of course, our own* Fair Hills Beacon, *which never failed to feature, often on its front page, New Jersey's "newest, youngest" figure-skating prodigy; one day soon there would be a feature on page three of the* New York Times *New Jersey Sunday section, and a five-page feature in glossy upscale* New Jersey Lives; *if we were lucky, there might be a fleeting clip of beautiful little blond Bliss Rampike skating and/or smiling shyly into the camera, at the tail-end of a New Jersey Network program. It was Mummy's belief, strengthened by her energetic new publicist/friend Samantha Sullivan whom she'd hired to "aggressively" promote Bliss's career, that fame can be, for some, a matter of a steady accumulation of publicity; suddenly there is a "tipping point" and, overnight it seems, everyone knows your name, and your face. "Of course," as Samantha cautioned, "Bliss does have to win."*

gerate. You hyperventilate. Such over-reactions can be contagious for the children, you should know better." But when Daddy took the glossy photos from Mummy to examine, Daddy whistled through his teeth: "Jez-zuz. Sky-boy, your mummy is right. You look like 'America's Most Wanted' here—what kind of asshole face is that, to make into a camera? At such a time? In public? With your little sister beside you? Is this some kind of joke?"

Frightened, Skyler protested: "Daddy, I d-didn't. I didn't make f-faces . . ."

"Don't try to bullshit me, kid. Here's the evidence!"

Skyler stared, astonished. It was as Mummy had said: in the photographs, he was grimacing, making his "pain face" with a look of demented hilarity; it was a look that resembled the expression on Tyler McGreety's face when, from time to time, wholly by chance, and against each boy's intention, Skyler and Tyler confronted each other at school, suddenly close up, and face-to-face. (For after their single playdate, the boys did all they could to avoid each other.)

But Skyler knew that he hadn't made his "pain face" while being photographed with Bliss at the StarSkate event, as he'd taken care not to limp that evening, either, when so many people were watching him. Damn, he *knew.*

Mummy wiped at her eyes, furious: "So—ugly! So nasty! Skyler, how could you betray me, and your sister? In her very hour of triumph! You know that StarSkate is interested in having Bliss endorse their products, if she wins the Miss Jersey Ice Princess title next year—are you trying to sabotage our effort? For shame!"

Mummy cuffed at Skyler, who continued, indignantly, to protest; as Daddy intervened, "Betsey, maybe Skyler can't help it. Maybe it's some sort of prepubescent male hormone. *Homo homin lupus.* Our Rampike wolf-blood, kicking in."

Mummy dealt with the hideous photos by carefully scissoring Skyler out of them so that only beautiful little Bliss remained, looking dazed and dazzled, and very small, in the camera flashes. And though these glossies obviously couldn't be used in StarSkate's upcoming advertising campaign, Mummy was assured by a company representative that StarSkate was still "very interested" in Bliss, should she win the coveted Miss Jersey Ice Princess 1996 title.

(God damn: I remember this utterly baffling and inexplicable incident, and I can assure the skeptical reader that, that evening, in my kiddytux, which Mummy insisted upon, as Mummy insisted upon having my hair, then a very ordinary normal-boy fair brown, "moussed" and "blown-dry" at the Fair Hills Beauty Salon, I *had not* made faces during the photography shoot but had SMILED SMILED SMILED as the damned photographers insisted. "Beau-ti-ful!"—"Ador-able!"—"Now kiss your little sister! Yesss." I did exactly as I'd been told to do by Mummy yet still— somehow!—the prints turned out ugly; and when I think back to this incident, I can see that it was the beginning of Mummy ceasing to love me, or in any case not-loving me as much as she had; and maybe, it was the onset of what Daddy called the *Rampike lupus-blood*, kicking in.)

NOVEMBER 1995. AFTER THE MISS NEW ENGLAND FIGURE SKATING CHAL-lenge where Bliss was runner-up for the junior division (to age ten) title having wowed the crowd as a pert little cowgirl with rouged cheeks and flying pigtails beneath a cowgirl hat set at a rakish angle, gliding/leaping/twisting/spinning in a tiny suede fringed skirt with shiny-pearl panties beneath, in a tiny fringed vest glittering with rhinestones, skating to a syncopated rendition of "Streets of Laredo," there in the rear of Mummy's Buick Lady Toro she lay waiting for Mummy while inside the arena Mummy was heatedly contesting the judges' decision, and Skyler, stunned with exhaustion now that the strain of the competition was over, now that it was time to drive to the Sheraton Inn Brunswick to spend the night (where they were, somewhere in the State of Massachusetts or possibly the State of Maine, Skyler had to know since he'd been the navigator with the road map, but now he was too sleepy to remember), Skyler was touched to hear Bliss speaking earnestly to her favorite doll, a battered old Raggedy Ann nearly her size with a soft little smile, shiny button eyes and a soiled gingham pinafore, that Mummy tried numerous times to take from Bliss who had a dozen beautiful, expensive dolls, Skyler heard Bliss addressing this doll in an eerie mimicry of Mummy's voice: "Next time we will work harder, and we will pray harder, and Jesus will see to it that *we are number one*."

Skyler asked Bliss what was the name of her doll, for no one seemed to know the name of this battered old doll; and Bliss shook her head vehemently saying it was a "sec-ret." But Skyler, leaning over the backseat of the car, persisted, promising he wouldn't tell, until at last Bliss admitted, hugging the doll to her flat little chest, "Her name is Edna Louise."

SKYLER KEPT BLISS'S SECRET. SKYLER NEVER TOLD.

THE MARRIAGE OF MISS FINCH AND COCK ROBIN

WE LOVE YOU BLISS!

YOU ARE OUR DARLING BLISS!

OUR PRAYERS ARE WITH YOU BLISS!

GOD BLES YOU BLISS!

BY DEGREES, THOUGH PERVERSELY ACCELERATING IN THE FINAL WEEKS OF 1995 in the wake of Bliss's heroic performance at Atlantic City in December,* there began to arrive, at the Rampike house at 93 Ravens Crest Drive, Fair Hills, New Jersey, flower deliveries for MISS BLISS RAMPIKE. (How was our private address "leaked" to the public? Daddy was furi-

---

* *Sorry! See Part I, "A Very Brave Little Girl," where I've already recorded this painful episode. Anyway, a "poetic" dream/nightmare version of what happened: nearing the end of her routine, Bliss turned her ankle suddenly, lost her balance and nearly fell, but managed bravely to skate (wobblingly) to the end of hot-throbbing "Begin the Beguine" even as the showy black-lace mantilla slipped from her hair, tangled in her legs and nearly tripped her . . . Yet Bliss had been skating so beautifully before these mishaps, the crowd at the Trump Tower & Casino applauded her wildly; and her performance was to become famous/notorious, frequently played on TV, on countless cable channels, especially after her death. Along with her prize-winning performance at the Miss Jersey Ice Princess competition in 1996, the "Begin the Beguine" routine with five-year-old Bliss Rampike dressed in sexy black lace and taffeta, and glamorously made up like a much older girl, is the video clip you are most likely to see of her, if for instance you click onto one or another of the numerous Bliss Rampike Web sites for somewhere in cyberspace the clip is being played, replayed. Is this our immortality? Not Heaven, if there ever was Heaven, but the possibility that somewhere, someone, who knows who, who knows with what motives, sympathetic, lurid, "just curious," will download our most heroic/tragic/humiliating moments to ponder as if they might mean something?*

ous. Mummy insisted she "had no idea.") Not only fresh-cut flowers of every variety, quantity, and price were brought to our house via florists' delivery vans, but potted plants of all species from sherbert-colored orchids to blooming cacti and stunted little bonsai trees. So strangely!— after each of Bliss's performances, whether Bliss placed first, second, merely third or, as at disastrous/triumphant Atlantic City, fifth among contenders in her age division, yet there came cards bearing joyous messages:

CONGRATULATIONS WE LOVE YOU BLISS RAMPIKE

YOU ARE A BRAVE BEAUTIFUL LITTLE GIRL BLISS

REMAIN TRUE TO YOUR VISION BLISS

WE LOVE YOU AND PRAYE FOR YOU

Such messages from strangers!—at first, New Jersey neighbors (not snooty Fair Hills, but "the other" Jersey), but eventually people in many states including remote-improbable Idaho, Alaska, Hawaii and nations distant as Denmark, Germany, Japan and Australia. Most of these "fans" had never seen my sister skate, you had to assume they'd seen TV clips, in who knows what contexts: "girls' figure skating"—"American winter sports"— "cute-kid routines"—"exploited-American-kid routines." Mummy examined each of the cards carefully, making sure that there were no alarming or mysterious messages, or cryptic symbols or signals, before passing the card on to Bliss to see, and taking it back then to file away, in Bliss's ever-growing album of photos, clippings, promotional material and such cards from fans.

And there were gifts as well: little-girl gifts of dolls and stuffed animals; hand-knitted wool caps with tassels, hand-knitted mufflers, mittens, leg-warmers; handmade little skating skirts and vests in unusual fabrics like felt, taffeta, corduroy. There were handmade little tinsel tiaras. Often there were photographs of Bliss skating beneath bright lights and, at times, alarmingly up close, taken by fans who'd gotten within a few feet or inches of her, for Bliss to inscribe in her childish hand—

—to be returned in stamped self-addressed envelopes.

Wistfully Bliss asked, "Do all these people love me, Mummy?" and Mummy said proudly, "Darling, yes! They love 'Bliss Rampike,' they are our 'fans.'"

The most beautiful gifts were likely to be entire skating costumes, some of them in expensive fabrics, crushed velvet, pleated Fortuny silk, shimmering gold lamé, with tiny bodices covered in seed-pearls, aurora borealis crystals, gold-dust. *My beloved Crista wore this when she was crowned Miss Royale Ice Princess at the Miss Royale Ice Capades in Bangor, Maine, 1957 when she was ten years old, please wear this in Crista's memory. God bless you dear Bliss we love you.*

"OH, SKYLER! IS THAT FOR—ME?"

It was. Of course it was. On January 30, 1996, which was Bliss's sixth birthday there were many cards and gifts from fans but one singular gift was the strangest and most wonderful of all.

The Marriage of Miss Finch and Cock Robin was a tableau of life-sized birds with "real" feathers, all of the birds dressed in old-fashioned finery. The birds were stiffly arranged inside a Plexiglas cube each side of which measured approximately ten inches so that the viewer could look into the box from any angle and, if you gently lifted the lid, you could touch the birds. Miss Finch the demure little bride, was a small bird with a delicate snub-beak, sparrow-like wings and a rosy head and breast, in a lace wedding gown with a long skirt, a trailing train, and a veil; Cock Robin was a suave bridegroom, considerably larger than Miss Finch, with an uplifted grayish head and sparkly eyes you might almost think were real and a splendid russet-orange breast, in a gentleman's frock coat and tails. The bride and groom were being married by a black-feathered bird with a chunky beak and a benign if somewhat unfocussed look and in attendance were a dozen smallish birds in exquisite replicas of old-fashioned human attire: sparrows, chickadees, warblers. And how realistic the birds' feathers, though the birds themselves, their little bodies, were stiffly/awkwardly posed.

This unprecedented gift had been brought to the house by special delivery, according to Maria, who took it from the "delivery man" who'd offered to carry it into the house for her, which was not necessary since the package wasn't that heavy. Maria brought it inside to place beside the day's more ordinary mail on a table in the small room opening off the foyer, that Mummy called the den; and when Skyler returned from school that afternoon, Skyler wanted to open it, as he opened most of Bliss's packages for her, while Bliss looked on, but had to wait until Mummy and Bliss returned. (For Mummy and Bliss were always away, somewhere: each day at the rink, for Bliss's lesson and skating practice, but also at one or another of Bliss's appointments: hair salon, where Bliss's "naturally dingy" hair, as Mummy called it, had to be "lightened"; pediatric orthodontist, for Bliss had "an overbite, that has to be corrected"; pediatric nutritionist, for Bliss required weekly injections of vitamins and "growth stimulants" to enable her to "keep up with the competition.") And when at last the elaborately wrapped package was opened by Skyler, and *The Marriage of Miss Finch and Cock Robin* was revealed, both children and both adults, Mummy and Maria, were astonished.

With widened eyes Bliss stared into the Plexiglas box. Skyler saw an expression almost of dread, or fear, pass over his sister's wan little face, *The Marriage of Miss Finch and Cock Robin* was too wonderful to be borne. "Oh Skyler! Is that for . . . me?"

Skyler had to resist the wisecrack *Who else is it for? You know damned well it isn't for me.*

How enchanting, a wedding of birds! And such exquisitely attired birds! Little Miss Finch in her wedding dress, in the bashful pose of a real-life girl-bride; and swaggering Cock Robin in frock coat and tails, head set at a rakish angle, chunky beak just perceptibly open. Mummy laughed: " 'Cock Robin'—he looks just like Daddy, doesn't he?" Mummy searched for the card which Skyler, typical careless child, had crumpled with the wrapping paper, and discovered it to be an old-fashioned Valentine, with a red satin heart on its cover. Mummy read aloud:

HAPPY BIRTHDAY CONGATULATIONS BLISS

LOVE & KISSES FOREVER

YOU NUMBER ONE DEVOUT FAN WHO WOULD DIE FOR YOU

G. R.

Neither Bliss nor Skyler was very interested in the identity of the mysterious *G.R.* but Mummy was curious, Mummy was suspicious searching in the torn wrapping paper for a return address: but there seemed to be none. By this time, Mummy's sensitive nostrils were picking up a very strange yet somehow familiar smell, a sickish smell, still faint, remote, yet alarming, so Mummy, ever-resourceful *gringa* employer, enlisted Maria to lift the lid to the box and to "put your head inside, and tell me what it smells like." And so it turned out, to Bliss's and Skyler's surprise, that the utterly wonderful *Marriage of Miss Finch and Cock Robin* was hastily bundled up in torn wrapping paper and carried away by a grave-faced Maria, even as Bliss protested: "Mummy, that's mine. Where is Maria taking it? That came to me—'Miss Bliss Rampike.' I saw it. That is mine."

Mummy said: "That thing is not for you, Bliss. That 'gift' should never have been allowed into this house, it has come by mistake."

"It has not. It is not a 'mistake.'"

Bliss's voice was rising dangerously. A bright frantic look came into her face, her eyes were narrowed. It was the look that sometimes came into Bliss's face for just a moment, fleetingly, like a struck match, when she skated badly, or fell. Skyler, too, was demanding, "Mummy, *why*?"

Both children would have rushed after Maria, but Mummy blocked the way. Sharp lines in her forehead, that stern bulldog set to Mummy's jaws, she said: "Nooo you don't! Both of you. Go up to your rooms and do your homework and enough of this. Bliss, you will be celebrating your birthday with your family, tonight—Daddy is going to be home for the occasion. And we have gifts for you, ever so much nicer than—"

"I want that gift! I want *Miss Finch and Cock Robin*—it came for *me*."

"Bliss, you're making Mummy angry. Mummy has told you to go upstairs to your room. You are not going to play with that repulsive 'gift' so just pretend it never arrived. Maria used very bad judgment to have brought it into this house, and—"

"Mummy, it is *mine*. It is *mine*. Those are my birds, Mummy! They came for 'Miss Bliss Rampike' and that is *me*, that is *not you* Mummy! That is *me*! You know that is *me*. That is *not you*, Mummy!" Bliss began to scream, white-faced and furious as Mummy struggled with her. Skyler looked on astonished for it was rare that his little sister became emotional; Bliss never raised her voice, even when others were shouting and clamoring, and Bliss did her best to stoically stifle sobs when she was in pain. Now she cried, furious: "I want my birds! I want my pre-sent! That came to me from a special friend! Somebody who likes me! I own that, that is mine, my friend sent it to me! You can't take that from me, Mummy! He meant it for *me*! He likes *me*, Mum-my, and not *you*. He's my friend! I want to be with him! I own my birds, Mum-my, you can't take my birds from me, I'll tell Daddy on you! Daddy said to me once, Tell me if Mum-my hurts you, if Mum-my makes you do anything you don't want to do, and I will tell Daddy that you *do*! I will tell Daddy that you *do*! Lots of things, that you *do*! I will tell Daddy you stole my birds! I hate you, I will tell Daddy what the doctor does! I don't want to be 'injected'! My bottom hurts, where I sit, from being 'injected.' And I don't want that thing in my mouth! I don't want that nasty 'bite' in my mouth! I will tell Daddy! I want my birds! My birds came to *me*! My birds—"

Hurriedly Mummy called for Maria to take Bliss away: "The child is hysterical. She's being ridiculous. Take her up to her room, Maria, and calm her down. It's the least you can do, you've caused this by being so careless, take her upstairs *now*."

And so it was done, though not without resistance on Bliss's part, and Skyler, who'd been astonished by his little sister's outburst, asked Mummy what was wrong? why couldn't they keep Bliss's gift? and Mummy said, crinkling her nose, "The thing is—what d'you call it—'taxidermy.' Real birds! Those were real birds! You could tell, they looked so strange, not like manufactured birds would look, and I could smell through the glass that something was wrong. They've been treated with something like formaldehyde, and stuffed, and their eyes are glass, but their bodies are real, their feathers are real, and they smell of rot. Ugh! Don't tell your father, Skyler. Not a word about any of this."

Little suck-up Skyler quickly assured Mummy he would not ever tell Daddy: "I promise, Mummy."

Poor Mummy was agitated, trembling, as she hadn't been in some time, gripping her little man's shoulder so it hurt, but Mummy's little man stood unflinching. How like the old days it was, for just this interlude: a frenzied infantile wailing somewhere upstairs, and Skyler with Mummy, at a distance from it, just the two of them.

THE MARRIAGE OF MISS FINCH AND COCK ROBIN IN ITS PLEXIGLAS BOX disappeared at once from the Rampike house, as if it had never been; and was never sighted again; yet in the room off the foyer called by Mummy the den, a faint, sickening odor of decay/rot would linger for a very long time.

"G.R."

HE MEANT IT FOR ME! HE LIKES ME, MUM-MY, AND NOT YOU. HE'S MY FRIEND. I want to be with him!

The alert reader has picked up on these mysterious and riddlesome words flung out in the midst of my sister's unexpected tantrum. But what to make of it? What do you, the alert and "objective" reader, think?

Wish I knew what the hell to think! My skin is crawling with these riddles, like lice swarming over me, as with lice it's futile to try to pick them off with your fingers, the lice-swarm continues undiminished, new generations of lice are being hatched even as you claw frantically at them, so too with obsessive/repetitive thoughts *Did Bliss really know G.R. as she claims, was G.R. somehow Bliss's friend, or was Bliss simply taunting our mother as young children sometimes do, even "good" children, in the temporary madness of a tantrum?*

Or, yet more upsetting possibility: that little Skyler was so stunned by his sister's behavior that he misheard what she said or, trying to recall it afterward, he simply got it wrong?

By the end of *My Sister, My Love* the reader will know why such details are significant. Why, if Bliss had actually "known" G.R., meaning that G.R. had (somehow) contacted her, spoken with her, established a rapport with her, such a fact—if it is a fact—would be crucial to the (yet-unsolved) mystery of who murdered Bliss Rampike.

POPULAR!

THOSE YEARS! GIDDY-HAPPY YEARS! AND NOT MANY YEARS FOR WHAT BEGAN
with Tots-on-Ice 1994 would be finished in late January 1997 and so is
scarcely a fraction of a lifetime, yet in a way a very American lifetime:
obscurity, fame, end.

In those years of the ascendency of Bliss Rampike it happened that Bix
and Betsey Rampike were pulled in their daughter's wake, as scraps of
paper are pulled in the vortex-wake of a rushing tractor-trailer truck. For
wonderfully it was happening, as Mummy could scarcely have dared to
hope on her long-ago *little drives* with Skyler past the splendid homes of
certain of her Fair Hills neighbors, that the Rampikes were becoming
popular among their snooty Fair Hills neighbors.

Even Skyler was becoming sought-after for playdates among his Fair
Hills Day classmates, or anyway their mothers. Even the prune-face runt
with one leg shorter than the other.

Popular! In America, what else matters?

Local newspapers had carried flattering little "human interest" pieces
on Bliss since Tots-on-Ice and in the giddy spring of 1995 glossy upscale
New Jersey Lives published a five-page spread including photographs on
"the 5-year-old skating prodigy some are comparing to Sonja Henie." In
the fall of that year the *New York Times* New Jersey section published a
feature on Bliss and her "devoted manager-mom Betsey Rampike," soon
then followed a cover story in glossy upscale *Garden State Galleria*, a new
publication in the showy faux-aristocrat mode of *Vanity Fair*. In *Galleria*,
there appeared eight pages of crisply fawning prose—"Skating experts
are predicting that before her 10th birthday this gifted and very pretty

little blond ice-skating prodigy from Fair Hills will win the Trifecta of girls' figure skating with a triple crown . . ."—and theatrically posed photographs of little Bliss in one of her sequined skating costumes, on the ice highlighted by a halo of heavenly light; Bliss in the same skating costume, with Mummy behind her, hugging her and partly swathing her in a cashmere wool cape like folding wings, Mummy's chin lightly resting on top of Bliss's small blond head; Bliss in little-girl dress-up clothes, jumper, blouse, tiny white shoe-boots, with her family—Mummy, Daddy, eight-year-old Skyler smilingly posed* in the family room of the Rampikes' "beautiful part-restored 18th-century Colonial nestled in a cul-de-sac in one of Fair Hills's most prestigious neighborhoods." (Prestigious? Was this so? Mummy must've been thrilled, if uneasy. Ravens Crest Drive was only just O.K., in Fair Hills real estate terms.) Most of the feature was an interview with Mummy: "'Family comes first with us! Bliss's career is not our primary concern, only Bliss's happiness'—'We Rampikes are a very close-knit family, we never miss Sunday church services at Trinity Episcopal'—'Oh yes: we are shielding our daughter from the glare of publicity'—'Practice and prayer, prayer and practice—that is our formula for success so far!'" Bix Rampike too was quoted: "'Crucial to keep perspective, as Betsey says 'Family comes first!'—'The bottom line is our love for our daughter, not our ambition'—'Never say never: it runs in the family, a Rampike never gives up.'" The interviewer, a woman with the byline Adriana Fyce, seemed taken with Daddy whom she described as "tall, athletic-built, with a handshake to crush your fingers"—"could pass for a Pittsburgh-born cousin of one of the Boston-born Kennedys"—"a handsome up-and-coming junior executive in that hottest of corporate sectors, project development, at Scor Chemicals, Inc. with a sharp sense of humor and a touching doting-dad devotion to his daughter." Though little was stated of Betsey Rampike's background except that she'd been born in "remote" upstate New York and had "skated competitively, briefly" in high school, it was noted admiringly that Bix Rampike had been a "star

---

* *Well, Mummy, Daddy, and Bliss are "smilingly posed" while little Skyler at the edge of the photo stares at the camera with frown lines in his eight-year-old forehead and the twisted smile of a stroke victim.*

athlete" through school; he'd played varsity football at Cornell University and in his senior year he'd been "aggressively recruited" by several pro football teams, among them the Pythons of Indianapolis and the Stingrays of St. Petersburg.

The *Galleria* feature concluded, in a final paroxysm of a paragraph of quivering-female prose: "Asked what he most wished for his talented but very young daughter, Bix Rampike paused for a long moment, as a look of brooding tenderness came into his warm brown eyes, and the strong-boned features of his face softened. 'May she be granted beauty and yet not beauty to make a stranger's eye distraught.' It's what some Irish poet said, and I say, Amen.' "*

POPULAR! FOR NOW THE PHONES AT 93 RAVENS CREST DRIVE THAT HAD for so long tormented Betsey Rampike by not-ringing, seemed to be *ringing-all-the-time.* And the calls that Mummy placed so strategically, following the logic of the elaborately hand-printed pyramid of names of those residents of Fair Hills and vicinity whom Mummy understood to be Very Important People, were now *being returned.* And nearly each day's mail delivery brought, in addition to cards and packages painstakingly addressed to MISS BLISS RAMPIKE, invitations to dinner parties, luncheons, receptions and gala open houses, for MR. AND MRS. BIX RAMPIKE. "It's like Christmas every day," Mummy told Skyler, with a dazed-Mummy smile, hand pressed against her heart, "—I can feel the love from our neighbors, I could just cry."

In fact, Mummy felt the need to hire another female assistant (Ardis Huddle, real estate/PR background) to help manage Bliss's increasingly complicated career, with a special emphasis upon exploring tie-ins with child-modeling agencies, advertising agencies, and fund-raiser appearances; and since Maria could not be expected to handle so many calls and so much mail, nor could Maria be expected to clean the house, cook for

* *Will you listen to this! Big-Daddy-bullshit! It would take me years to track down this quote, only just discovered by accident in a poetry anthology at the Basking Ridge Academy: the lines are from "A Prayer for My Daughter" by William Butler Yeats.*

the family, shop for, prepare for, cook and clean up after the elaborate dinner parties Mummy began to schedule on the average of one every two weeks, a second Maria, from Peru, younger than the first Maria, with a darker skin, startlingly beautiful dark eyes, and yet more exotically accented English, came to work for us.

Little Maria, Big Maria. By purest chance Skyler happened to observe the initial encounter, in the upstairs hall, between Daddy (only just returned, jet-lagged and sour-smelling, not in the greatest of Daddy-moods, from Bangkok, or Singapore) and Little Maria (carrying the orange plastic laundry basket heaped with laundry just out of the drier): Daddy stared, and Daddy blinked, and Daddy stopped dead in his tracks, and a smile broke over Daddy's chunky front teeth as Daddy shifted his suitcase to his left hand to free Daddy's large strong bonecrusher hand for a handshake, which poor Little Maria, struggling with the laundry basket, could barely manage. In a warm-welcoming deep-baritone voice Daddy murmured: "Bu-ena vis-ta, senorita! Or—what the fuck time is it?—nach-a? I am Bix 'Gringo Honcho' Rampike and who might you be, très-bella senorita?"*

What choice had Little Maria but to surrender her brown-skinned hand to the *gringo* honcho's Caucasian hand?—what choice but to smile shyly, as her new employer loomed above her smiling and licking his lips? And what choice had little Skyler but to duck quickly back into his room before Big Daddy sighted him, and walloped the breath out of him in a Big Daddy greeting . . .

"IT IS LIKE CHRISTMAS, DARLING, ISN'T IT? THREE PARTIES THIS WEEK-end! And Imogene Stubbe has invited me to 'co-chair' the Volunteers of Fair

---

* *Anyway, something like that. Among the bitter dregs of memory, Big-Daddy-bullshit can be recalled only in quick takes. In a woman's romance novel of the kind that sell, in both hardcover and paperback, millions of copies annually, it would be observed* A fateful glance passed unmistakably between them, the tall handsome *gringo* homeowner and the dark-eyed exotic Little Maria *or some hopeful crap of that kind but, to be utterly truthful, as I've vowed to be, if a glance did pass between my father and the young Maria, Skyler missed it, Skyler had not a clue, Skyler hid in his clothes closet waiting for the quake of Daddy's footsteps to fade.*

Hills Spring Madness luncheon with her, and Gwendolyn Burr has just called to invite 'your darling little boy' over for a playdate with her son Baxter . . ."

Of course, Bix Rampike had been well-liked in Fair Hills from the start, but it was unmistakable how, in spring 1995, and yet more conspicuously in the fall/winter social season, the Rampikes were suddenly on everyone's guest list; and Betsey Rampike, yet uneasy and hesitant among her more glamorous Fair Hills neighbors, was made to feel welcome: as if it were as much Betsey Rampike, as the handsome charismatic brisk-hand-shaking Bix Rampike, whom hostesses were vying for, and wished to befriend. Skyler had no need to sneak into Mummy's desk to understand that certain of the asterisked names making up the magical pyramid of names on the pink construction paper had been recently circled in triumph: STUBBE, BURR, MARROW, McCONE, HAMBRUCK, KRUK. And there were EDSON, ROMNEY, BLOOMGREN, FRASS, HULTS. And even WHITTAKER. And KLEINHAUS! (Though not McGREETY. And, to Betsey's continued chagrin, not CHAPLIN.) For a surreal period during the gay, giddy, protracted holiday season that in Fair Hills extended from pre-Christmas through New Year's Eve and New Year's Day to Twelfth Night (January 6), it seemed that several very wealthy and usually remote residents of the large country estates/horse farms in the lush rolling countryside north of Fair Hills, including such fabled old-money New Jerseyans as ex-Senator Mack Steadley and his wife Irma, and the media baron Si Solomon and his wife Mimi, and billionaire Fritz Vizor and wife Fanny, were eager to befriend Bix and Betsey Rampike, or at any rate to invite the young couple to their homes. On such lavish occasions even Bix was uneasy, and prone to drinking too much, for Bix understood that these were individuals who rarely mingled with multi-millionaires like Bix's superiors at Scor Chemicals; these were individuals who knew nothing of the crucial distinctions in Fair Hills among the Fair Hills Golf and Country Club, and the Pebble Hill Tennis Club, and the Village Women's Club, and the Sylvan Glen Golf Club, because these were people who would not have wished to join these clubs no matter how "exclusive" and "prestigious."

Daddy understood, but Mummy did not. Mummy agonized: How could they invite "Mack" Steadley and his wife Irma (Forbes heiress!) to a dinner party at the Rampikes' so unoriginal Colonial, with such "ordinary" furnishings—and on a mere two-acre lot!—when the Steadleys owned hundreds of acres of New Jersey countryside above Lake Hopatcong; how could they invite the Vizors who lived in a baronial "Country French" house the size of a castle, and raised pedigree Black Angus cattle; how could they invite the fabled Solomons who owned newspapers, magazines, television stations and lived in a four-level "classic contemporary" on a private mountain, though Mimi was "so much fun, eager to tell me about her 'amateur skating career' when she was a girl—" and Daddy interrupted, "Get real, Bets. Grow a brain. If your I.Q. caught up with your bra size, you'd be the Einstein of Ravens Crest Drive. These people were just checking us out. No more. They'd seen some of the media about us Rampikes—'Parents of'—'Skating prodigy.' 'Next Sonja Henie.' They won't be inviting us back. That was clinched even before you opened your mouth for the first time and raved on about 'what a beautiful house.' Just the look of you, sweetheart. And maybe me, too. They won't be inviting us back and sure as hell none of them would accept an invitation to dine on Ravens Crest Drive. Comprehendez, sweetheart?"

Comprehendez.

(ADMIT IT, SKY: CAN'T END THIS SCENE. CAN'T STAY WITH IT A MOMENT longer but can't end it, either. Need to cut away quickly but then the suspicious reader would know that the amateur author can't handle his own material when it gets too painful. Surely the scene between my parents came to an end, eventually; but not for several more minutes, as they were undressing for bed; what I'd overheard came through the (shut) door of my parents' bedroom and I wasn't present to register Mummy's shocked eyes, Mummy's stricken face; nor did I see Daddy waving her away, backing off in that way that Daddy had, in this case stomping into his bathroom. Must've been late-night, a weekend, Daddy and Mummy had been out, drinking for hours at one or another of the dazzling Fair Hills parties they were always going to, and giving.)

. . .

QUICK CUT TO: "IT SEEMS SO LONG AGO, SKYLER, DOESN'T IT? ANOTHER lifetime! When Mummy wasn't very happy, and we went on our little drives in Fair Hills, and nobody ever called me, and I was so lonely, and the—what was that baby's name—was always crying, crying, *crying*. If I could have seen ahead to now, Skyler! I might have saved myself some tears."

In Mummy's triumphant hand, an engraved invitation to New Year's Eve at the Whittiers.

ABSENCE OF FURNITURE. SORRY ABOUT THIS!

When Mummy complained that her house was "unoriginal"—"ordinary" the reader should have been provided with a "visual setting" (as in a movie) so that the words registered as ironic. For in fact, the Rampike house was expensively/obsessively furnished in "period furniture" in most of the downstairs rooms which were for show, as in a museum. Readers, likely to be female, with a morbid interest in furniture and home decorating should consult photographs in *Stately Homes of New Jersey: A Guided Tour* by Jacqueline Bigelow, where pages 48–53 contain furniture that resembles some of the furniture in our home.

IN WINTER 1995 TO 1996 IN THE WAKE OF BLISS RAMPIKE'S AMAZING NEW triumphs, titles, and trophies (most publicized: Atlantic States Regional Girls' Ice Figure Skating Challenge in which, in Division One, Bliss Rampike placed first with a score of 5.7 out of a possible 6) there came in rapid succession like fulfilled wishes in a Grimm's fairy tale of ambiguous import yet more invitations, letters bearing the heraldic coats of arms of such Fair Hills bastions of privilege as the Fair Hills Golf and Country Club, the Pebble Hill Tennis Club, and the Fair Hills Village Women's Club; and Mummy was thrilled, and gave a cry of girlish joy, on her knees thanking Jesus—"You had faith in me, when I had no faith in myself." Eagerly Mummy would have joined each of these clubs—immediately!—except Daddy advised "holding out" for the more prestigious Sylvan Glen Golf Club which, as everyone knew, had among its "very select" membership each of Fair Hills's most revered mega-millionaires, and trumped all other clubs. Mummy pleaded, "But what if the Sylvan Glen doesn't ask us to join, and the others withdraw their invitations?" and Daddy said, "O.K.: accept the women's club. That's just women. But don't screw this up for me, sweetheart. Let me play this right."

(SO: D'YOU THINK BIX "PLAYED IT RIGHT"? D'YOU THINK THAT BIX *WAS*** right? Are you on Bix's side? Do you sneer at the Fair Hills Golf and Country Club with its sizable membership, that includes, since the late 1980s, a discreet scattering of "ethnic minority" members, and do you favor, as Bix does, the smaller, more elite, less conspicuously "integrated" Sylvan Glen Golf Club?* What pisses me is: no matter how dramatically, with what closely observed moral indignation, I present a character like Bix Rampike who is intended to be an unmitigated/unredeemed son of a bitch, a "charismatic" bully and an asshole and a predator and (who knows?) the brutal assailant of his own six-year-old daughter,[†] some of you, a reliable fraction of the female readership, will admire Bix anyway; and will imagine, as women who are drawn to such men invariably imagine, that such men would never hurt them but love them dearly.)

QUICK CUT TO: "OH ISN'T SHE DARLING! *ISN'T* SHE! AND SO BLOND. AND SO *small*." For little Bliss Rampike—and little Skyler, too—are helping pass appetizers (stuffed mushrooms, yummy little spicy sausages, crab-puff-pastries) at Mummy and Daddy's gala big party which is the largest party

---

* Are there any readers who will admit to an interest in country clubs? "Exclusive"—"prestigious"— private clubs like these? If so, this melancholy crap is for you. (To learn whether Bix played his cards shrewdly, or unwisely, and won, or lost, a bid to join the Sylvan Glen Golf Club, you'll have to keep plowing on here, into the next chapter or so.)

† Brutal assailant of his own six-year-old daughter. *Can this be? Did I really write these terrible words? Obviously, I wrote them in a burst of rage, and should remove them now, and yet—I think that I will leave these words in. And if Daddy wants to sue his estranged son, let him sue. The tabloids await new Rampike scandal.*

that Mummy and Daddy have ever given in Fair Hills, a spare-no-expenses party Daddy has declared, a truly classy party with valet parking—a small platoon of eager high-school-age boys hired by Daddy: "You can't expect guests like ours to park on the street, and *walk*." From the street, the spacious old Colonial at 93 Ravens Crest is ablaze with lights like a Christmas tree. Inside the house are lavish floral displays, not one but two "full-service" bars manned by professional bartenders, making their way through the crowd are attractive young servers in white uniforms. Amid the babel of high-pitched voices and laughter, the wistful Gaelic strumming of a harp from the first-floor staircase landing where an ethereal-looking female harpist is playing with long slender fingers. So much excitement! So many people! For when you are popular like Bix and Betsey Rampike, and invited out often, naturally you must invite back: "reciprocate." You must "entertain." Skyler has been hearing this, frequently. A party is like many playdates simultaneously, involving as many names on Mummy's pink-construction-paper pyramid as possible. Daddy is too busy to be involved in party plans of course though Daddy loves parties, returning sometimes from the very airport, from "abroad," to hurriedly shower and shave and rush back downstairs even as the first guests arrive, shoving a big-friendly-Bix Rampike hand out for a bone-crushing handshake. And Daddy has the "final veto" on the guest list, of course: No one is to be invited to the Rampikes' just because Mummy likes them, or feels sorry for them, or because they've been "nice." First rule of social life! When Mummy protests weakly, "Oh but gosh, Bix, can't we make an exception for—" Daddy wags his big-Daddy forefinger with comical menace like Jack Nicholson in *The Shining*: "Batta, sweetie. Bat-*ta*."

Bat-ta? Seems to mean case closed, Skyler has learned.

"Oh! Are you—'Bliss'? I saw your picture in the paper, I think! Bessie, or, no—Betsey!—you must be *so proud* of this child."

Within the hour, now that it's dark outside the gala-reflecting windows of the house, little Bliss and little Skyler are to be scooped up by one of the Marias, taken away upstairs to be bathed and put to bed, just now there is a feverish thrum in Skyler's blood, a pained smile on

Skyler's little-boy face, for Skyler has got it into his hardball-head that Mummy, who is Betsey Rampike in this gathering, Betsey who is Bix's wife, and Bliss's mother, must be protected against harm, or hurt: from what source, Skyler has no idea. For a party is a happy time, isn't it?—a gay giddy roller-coaster occasion, where adults drink because they are happy and want to be even happier, a magical occasion, fraught with mystery like a ship embarked upon unknown waters, choppy, turbulent, its prow pitching, its decks tilting, impossible to know if such excitement is a good thing, or not-so-good. Skyler, bearing a tray of appetizers, is drawing some attention, too: at least, his parents' guests pause to snatch up the delicious tidbits, and to thank him. What an adorable little man! Is this—Scooter? Bix and Betsey's son? Skyler's wavy-fawn hair has been damply combed, Skyler has been fitted out by Little Maria in his hunter-green Fair Hills Day School blazer with school insignia on the breast pocket, his shirt is white cotton in emulation of Daddy's white shirt, his clip-on tie is a dark-green school necktie, his trousers are little-boy corduroy from Junior Gap. Entrusted by Mummy with the responsibility of "helping out"—bearing a tray of appetizers among the guests—Skyler is anxiously aware that both Mummy and Daddy might be watching him and has vowed not to limp!—nor even to shift his weight to one leg, to make an inadvertent laughable sight (for, at Fair Hills Day School, Skyler has been mortified to see certain of his mean-boy classmates mocking him by lurching about as if one of their legs was shorter than the other, to the amusement of observers), as adult strangers with drinks in hands loom above him, jostling him and his sister holding her appetizer tray at dangerous slant, for Bliss is such a clumsy ill-coordinated girl on land, however graceful and determined on the ice, and stricken with shyness like measles, though eager to help Mummy on this crucial occasion for Mummy has been planning this party for weeks, Mummy is celebrating the triumph of Bliss's career and yet more triumph to come—there are "deals" pending, of which no one knows except Mummy!—and Mummy has dressed Bliss as a doll-like replica of Betsey Rampike: both mother and daughter are wearing glamorous zebra-stripe dance dresses of crinkly, clingy velvet with provocatively tight bodices and flaring skirts, diamond-patterned black stockings and shiny black patent leather dance shoes adorned with red cloth roses. Quite a sight! Might've been painted by Velázquez, or by Goya in a benign mood! (Renoir? Whistler? Otto Dix?) Mummy's helmet of glossy dark-brown hair sparkles with "stardust"—Bliss's blond, ringleted hair sparkles with "stardust." Expertly, with a very light touch, for Betsey Rampike is strongly disapproving of those figure-skating mothers who "make up" their daughters like "little painted harlots"—Mummy has transformed Bliss's plain-little-girl face into a beautiful-little-girl face by penciling in Bliss's pale, almost nonexistent eyebrows with a light brown pencil and by "dabbing"—"just a touch"—of coral-pink lipstick on Bliss's pale lips. And maybe a little liquid makeup, and an artful "dabbing" of powder. (For the irony is, as few persons know, certainly not Bliss Rampike's adoring fans, that Bliss isn't especially pretty, not even what you'd call cute; but a child-face is far easier to beautify than an adult face, if you know how. And Betsey Rampike has learned!) Mummy herself is very beautiful tonight, Skyler thinks, for Mummy's eyes glow like gems, dramatically outlined in inky-black mascara; and Mummy's lips are full, fleshy, shinily crimson, and the lines and "crow's feet" in Mummy's face that have made her so vexed and sulky in recent months—complaining what is more unfair, more unjust, than lines caused by *smiling*?—by being nice, and *smiling*?—have mysteriously vanished after appointments with Dr. Screed, the Fair Hills dermatologist/otolaryngologist much recommended by Mummy's new friends. Especially, Mummy is thrilled to lead eager new arrivals to her daughter who has been positioned like a fairy-tale princess in a corner of the living room, how thrilled Betsey is when her friends marvel at Bliss with the widened eyes of awe/envy: "Ohhh. Is this child adorable! And that matching mother-and-daughter outfit—*amazing*."

Beaming Mummy is yet sharp-eyed Mummy observing that her daughter isn't lifting her angel-face to Mrs. Frass (judge's wife) nor making eye-contact with Mrs. Muddick (mega-millionaire's wife) but staring fixedly into space like a mechanical doll. With a part of her hyper-vigilant mind (where *is* Bix? where has Bix crept off to, and *why*?) Mummy is aware of much that is happening at her party out of her field of vision, even as Mummy is unobtrusively pinching the soft flesh of Bliss's forearm and lightly chiding Bliss to give Mrs. Fenn a kiss, please! (Mrs. Fenn, another mega-millionaire-developer's wife who only a few months before had snubbed poor Betsey Rampike at the Fair Hills Literacy Volunteers gala fund-raiser.) Bliss consents, but with a shivery little wince detectable only by sharp-Mummy eyes; as Bliss consents to being hugged, cuddled, lifted in arms, "smooched" by Harry Fenn himself. Yet Mummy senses how reluctant Bliss is to please Mummy's guests, Mummy does not like this (secret, surreptitious) little core of her daughter's resistance (like bone-marrow cancer, invisible to the unsuspecting eye) as Mummy *does not like* Bliss removing the plastic "bite" from her mouth during the night and hiding it beneath her pillow or worse yet—as if Mummy wouldn't know, for Mummy has continuous access to her daughter through the nursery door-in-the-wall opening into Mummy and Daddy's bedroom—tossed beneath her bed. "Bliss: take care, sweetie. Hmmm?" (Just a light warning, disguised by a Mummy-kiss, and a Mummy-adjusting of the zebra-stripe bodice.)

But Mummy is in a good mood tonight! Mummy *is*! Drinking the most delicious red wine, expensive French wine Daddy has purchased by the case through his mentor-friend at Scor Chemicals, Mel Hambruck. Mummy has vowed, she will not become vexed/upset/agitated because of Bliss's insubordination, *she will not*. Skyler is feeling protective of Mummy, and Skyler is pained to see that Mummy is drinking too much, and has unknowingly splashed red wine onto the swelling bosom of her zebra-stripe dress; Skyler is determined not to be jealous of poor little Bliss tonight, though Bliss is the child whom guests want to see, or anyway some guests, mostly women, exclaiming over the "angel-child" who reminds them of their own daughters no longer now so young, and not nearly so like doll-angels. Mostly these exclamatory females are women like Mattie size-fourteen wife of Reverend "Archie" Higley, and Mrs. Cuttlebone the real estate agent who'd sold the Rampikes their house and Mrs. Whittier (Mummy's mentor-friend who'd nominated her for membership in the coveted Village Women's Club), and Mrs. Stubbe, and Mrs. Burr, so powerfully do these women smell of perfume that Skyler feels a sneeze imminent, a tingling-ticklish sensation in his nose, or maybe this is the result of naughty little Skyler surreptitiously sipping from left-behind glasses, red wine, white wine, Scotch diluted by melted ice cubes, quick before Mummy sees! quick before Daddy sees! A pair of (male) legs collides with Skyler—"Oh hey, sorry—is it Scooter?—sorry, son, din't mean to spill my drink on you, don't blame you for making an ugly face at me son, but I am sorry, Scoot. I *am*." Not far away on the other side of a coffee table heaped with dirtied glasses and plates Mummy takes no heed of Skyler's distress for Mummy is showing off Bliss to several new arrivals, must be VIP guests judging from Mummy's quavering voice as she introduces Bliss to Mrs. Klaus (one of the lockjawed size-two wealthy-patrician Fair Hills blondes, of whom more later), and to Mrs. Kruk ("Biffy"—an officer of the Village Women's Club and mother of the fat-faced budding-psychopath Albert Kruk, a notable ex-playdate), and to stylish Mrs. O'Stryker (a neighbor on Woodsmoke Drive, wife of "Howie" O'Stryker, Morris County D.A. and squash partner of Bix), urging Bliss to look up and say hello, honey? and smile? as a woman with bright lipstick looms over Bliss—Mrs. Marrow?—thrusting a cocktail napkin at her: "Will you autograph this for my daughter, dear? It would mean so much to my Mildred, the poor child has her heart set on 'figure ice-skating' though she lacks all physical coordination, I'm afraid." Mummy assists Bliss by flattening the wrinkled napkin on a table so that Bliss is able to print on it, in the shaky hand of a child much younger than six—

—even as Skyler dazed and dizzied and queasy from the dregs of whatever left-behind drinks he's been swilling on the sly is made to realize *The*

party will never end, we are trapped here forever, I can't protect Mummy from hurt and I can't protect Bliss, I can't even protect myself.*

QUICK CUT TO: DADDY.

Must've been just a few minutes later, as Skyler lurches/limps in frantic haste into one of two downstairs guest bathrooms (ordinarily off-limits to Skyler, as it is off-limits to Bliss, for Mummy does not want her expensive, specially scented miniature soaps in the shapes of seashells, turtles, and tiny birds and her delicate Irish linen hand-towels to be despoiled by her children's grubby hands), and pukes up a disgusting mixture of acid-liquids and pulpy-masticated puffy pastries, spicy sausages, and stuffed mushrooms he hadn't known he had devoured in such quantity, emerging then shaky but clear-eyed and "sober" and drawn by braying male voices to observe Daddy in a corner of the dining room near one of the full-service bars, in the company of several men among whom Bix Rampike is the youngest and what a presence he is, Bix Rampike! Big-shouldered, craggy-faced, blunt-good-looking American guy, quick to smile, quick to take offense, give you the shirt off his back, punch you in the gut if you insult his kids, his wife, his flag, his corporate employer, his God. An earnest crinkle to Bix's brow, flash of "brown-soulful" eyes, he's wearing an expensive camel's hair blazer that's endearingly rumpled. On all the men's wrists are what appear to be Rolex watches but Bix's Rolex is the least showy, as Bix is the youngest of these burly men, head cocked at a respectful angle as he listens to the indignant rant of his Scor Chemicals mentor-friend Mel Hambruck as flush-faced Morris Kruk, six-foot-three "Howie" O'Stryker and an unidentified other (Caucasian, youngish middle-aged) man emit those grunts and vehement head-nods that mean *Yes! Right! I am listening.* Sneering Mel Hambruck says, "—'global warning'—biggest damn hoax since the Holocaust but know what?—you say so, you

---

* *The skeptical reader recoils in disbelief: "What the hell? A kid of nine, medicated, half-drunk, isn't capable of such a profound 'epiphany,' this is bullshit." But I assure you, dear reader, skeptic as you are, that this is exactly how Skyler Rampike felt watching his little sister sign a wrinkled cocktail napkin.*

get crucified by the left-wing Jew press. So, mum's the word! We know what we know, eh?" There's a pause as the men lift their glasses to drink, possibly to brood, or possibly in the festive party-din there is no need to brood, comes Bix Rampike to the rescue saying, " 'Global warming'—I think you mean 'warming,' Mel—actually there is something to it, Mel. I'm reading all these science texts, I subscribe to *Scientific American*, you can see the charts. 'Polar ice caps'—'Caspian Sea.' Except what they leave out is: global warming is a fact of geology. Remember the Ice Age—it preceded *Homo sapiens* by millions of years. *Homo sapiens* has only been around about fifty thousand years and the big deal with us is, we have 'opposable thumbs'—plus we walk upright—and we learned to grow our own damn food, not chase it bare-ass naked through the jungle as they are still doing, 'ab-originals,' in parts of the world. Now, fifty thousand years is but an eye blink in Time! In the galaxy, Time is relative. It's like half-cooked spaghetti twisting back on itself, coiled and tangled. There's no forward, or backward. It's both. So, if things had not warmed up after the Ice Age, where'd we be? *Homo sapiens* wouldn't have fucking hatched. Is that a profound fact, or not? Sometimes I think, waking in the middle of the night and I think Jesus! We might've not made it, our very civilization is hanging by a thread. So 'global warming' is just the way things work, in nature. It's what Darwin meant by 'evolution.' And we are what Darwin meant by 'evolution'—I mean us, in Fair Hills, New Jersey—'the fruits of natural selection.' " Young Bix Rampike has spoken so convincingly, and so eloquently, his companions have only to grunt in vehement agreement, for what is there to add to Bix's remarkable speech except, as Howie O'Stryker says, impressed: "Just what I was going to say, friend. I'll drink to that."*

And they did.

Quick cut to: solarium, rear of house. Mummy's favorite room she has

---

* *Bix Rampike should've run for political office, you're thinking? State senator, eventually U.S. senator on the Republican ticket? In fact, Morris County Republicans did approach my father, more than once, in the waning years of the Clinton administration, sensing a seismic change to come, but Daddy demurred: there was far more money in the corporate world and you didn't have to get elected to any office, you just took office.*

decorated with white wicker furniture, cushions and pillows in bright parrot colors, rubber plants and orange trees in ceramic tubs. For the party, the solarium is candle-lit but most of the candles have burned low and a few have gone out and no one is here except Skyler who has drifted away from the now-waning party, way past Skyler's bedtime but the wily child has managed to escape attention. Skyler has an uneasy feeling that Bliss is waiting for him upstairs in bed, Bliss sleeps with the Mother Goose lamp burning through the night for Bliss is afraid of the dark though her room is still the nursery with a door opening into Mummy and Daddy's room, Bliss is feeling sad and lonely and her ankle has been hurting but Skyler isn't going to think guiltily of his little sister, not right now. Swallowing down a mouthful of red wine out of one of the glasses—a mouthful of white wine—Skyler coughs, chokes—keeps swallowing— Skyler seems not to have learned his lesson about scavenging alcoholic party drinks—he has heard boys at school boasting of getting drunk on party leftovers like this—damn! Skyler wishes he was friends with Fox Hambruck, good old Foxie would appreciate Skyler's boastful tale of how he got drunk not once but twice undetected by his parents—hearing someone approaching outside the room, awkwardly he crouches behind a wicker rocking chair, at the doorway there's a couple whispering and laughing together, Skyler has a glimpse of a tall man, a woman with blond crimped hair and a throaty chuckle, the man's hands are kneading the woman's mostly bare back and even an asexual runt of nine understands that these two are not married to each other—

> Jesus are you beautiful   when can I see you
> damn you   didn't call back last week
> honey   I've been traveling
> Bix come on   if someone sees
> Say your   car has broken down   I'll drive you home
> Are you crazy?   what about Cal
> Fuck Cal   he's here?   didn't see Cal
> Of course Cal is here   he's drunk
> Can't drive you home if he's drunk can he
> Can't leave him here for heaven's sake Bix

Crazy for you honey
And what about   your wife
What about her?

QUICK CUT.   ANYWHERE OUT OF HERE!

The Skater. In the nursery in the night floating in the little-girl bed
with the white satin headboard decorated with pink and gold satin tiny
girl-skaters, Bliss is sleeping. Not a quiet sleep but a twitchy sweaty
moaning sleep for Bliss is skating in a place that is unfamiliar and inhos-
pitable and a harsh spotlight is following her, if Bliss swerves suddenly on
the ice, cuts her blades into the ice to turn in an unexpected direction yet
the spotlight leaps after her, in fact the spotlight leaps ahead of her, uncanny and rapacious as a living creature. Bliss's eyes are blinded, Bliss's
eyes fill with moisture, Mummy has been noticing lately, others have noticed, Bliss's eyes seem to be filled with moisture much of the time, tears
spill from her eyes and streak her face though she isn't crying. *Bliss what
is wrong with you?* Mummy pleads and there is no answer, Bliss has no answer turning to skate away, shutting her eyes to avoid the blinding spotlight. Though Bliss is six years old and no longer a really little girl yet
Mummy has insisted that Bliss remain in the nursery close beside
Mummy and Daddy's bedroom with the door in the wall between the
rooms that can be locked on one side (on Mummy and Daddy's side) but
not on the other. Mummy has had the nursery repainted and refurnished
so that it has become a very pretty young-girl's room with pink ruffled
organdy curtains and white wicker-framed mirrors and on the pink and
cream walls are framed photographs of Bliss's skating triumphs, in
chronological sequence beginning with now-historic Tots-on-Ice 1994
where the little-girl skater is a tiny figure between Mummy beaming with
happiness and massive lizard-faced Jeremiah Jericho in his gaudy tux. In
sleep Bliss has a habit of grinding her back teeth, breathing harshly
through her mouth as if panting, for there is something wrong with the
ice beneath her skate blades, the ice isn't smooth but coarse and rippled
and the glaring spotlight makes her eyes hurt. She has been zipped into a
skating costume tight as a swimsuit, is it the white-sequined-swan cos-

tume with the fluttery white feathers, is it the red-sequined-*Boléro* costume with the (just slightly) padded bodice and slit-skirt, peek-a-boo
black-lace panties beneath?—Bliss is beginning to sweat inside the costume Mummy has zipped her into so tightly, Bliss has begun to sweat inside the cosmetic-mask Mummy has applied to her face like putty, or
maybe it's bedclothes that have become twisted beneath Bliss, her pink
flannel nightie that has become twisted between her legs. There is a
twitch in Bliss's left eyelid, a sudden stab of pain in Bliss's left ankle, that
familiar pain, it is Bliss Rampike's left ankle that will betray her. Mummy
has said *We must keep this a secret! Our rivals would gloat.* Except for sweet
cherry pop and a few appetizers from the tray she'd been carrying, Bliss
has gone to bed hungry, the more frantically she skates the less hungry
she will be, turning on her skate blade, turning too sharply, the audience
is murmuring somewhere in the shadows, or is the sound coming from
the other side of the wall, voices through the shut door, it is very late, even
in her sleep Bliss understands that it is very late now, her parents' guests
have gone home at last, car doors have been slamming, cars have departed, the loud gay laughing voices have departed, the uniformed servers are gone, the Marias are gone, Daddy has been away somewhere in his
car and Daddy has returned stumbling on the stairs muttering to himself
and in the big bedroom Mummy is awaiting him *How could you! humiliate
me! at such a time! in front of our friends! I hate you!* even as Bliss skates to
the very rear of the ice rink, trying not to hear the voices on the other side
of the door, determined not to hear, skating/gliding/turning/though her
left ankle has been throbbing with pain, and her head is throbbing with
pain, and her cheeks are damp with tears, and her mouth is very dry, and,
oh! that sensation in the pit of her belly that means danger, her bladder is
pinching, but she can't stop skating, must complete her routine, *Boléro* is
accelerating its rhythm, ever faster, faster, as the audience begins to applaud, like a deafening waterfall the audience begins to applaud, Bliss
feels her bladder burst, can't wake from sleep in time to stop the first hot
spurt of pee soiling her pink flannel nightie, soiling her pink-and-cream
bedsheets, and the mattress beneath, this is the bad thing Bliss has been
taught not to do, not since she was a little little girl being potty-trained
bad girl! bad Edna Louise! you are bad on purpose aren't you, you are not trying

are you, what a dirty child, whose dirty child are you, Oh! look at the bad girl shame on the bad girl Edna Louise nobody wanted you in this house, Mummy and Daddy will send you back dirty ugly Edna Louise! but she is Bliss now, she is Bliss and not Edna Louise, waking confused in her bed, frightened and guilty in her bed, for the wet is rapidly becoming cold, and smelly, and her mattress is soaked, and her bedclothes and nightie, and there will be nowhere to hide, that Mummy will not find her.

BAD GIRL! I

WETTING HER BED.

Trying to hide the evidence.*

SLEEPWALKING.

Rising from her little-girl bed in the nursery, in the night.

Open-eyed yet sleeping—not seeming to know where she was, what she was doing—as she'd claim afterward—"like a dream"—"something was making me, not *me*"—prowling in the darkened house colliding with things, recklessly descending the stairs, falling on the (carpeted) stairs to lie stunned and whimpering on the first-floor landing mistaken then for her bed—"where I was meant to sleep."

Were the sleepwalking episodes more prevalent when Bliss was preparing for a skating competition?—when Bliss was practicing at the ice rink for more than three hours a day?—so it was asked, by one or another of the child psychologists/neurologists/therapists to whom Bliss was brought, in that final year of her life.

---

* *Poor Skyler! When Bliss had her bed-wetting/bed-fouling "accidents" to whom did she come but him?—pushing open his bedroom door (which, door to a mere child's room, had no lock), waking him rudely and pleading with him—"Skyler help!"—"Skyler something happened in my bed!"— "Skyler there is something bad in my bed"—wanting Skyler to remove the wet/smelly/disgusting sheet for her and replace it with a clean sheet; and Skyler was cranky being wakened but usually agreed to help because his sister was so agitated, and repentant, though the mattress of Bliss's bed was still damp, and stained, and smelly, and Maria, whose never-ending task was to make up all the Rampike beds, would probably report this fact to Mummy.*

. . .

DISAPPEARING.

Skyler where is your sister? Oh where has that bad girl got herself to now?

Mummy laughed, though Mummy was agitated: for Mummy had to know that, though Bliss wasn't in her bed, wasn't in her room, wasn't in her bathroom or in any of the rooms in which Mummy had looked, nor beneath beds in those rooms, or sofas, or behind drapes, yet Bliss had to be somewhere in the house, for no one had broken in to kidnap her, Mummy had to know.

To worry me! To spite me! To make me upset! She does it on purpose that bad girl!

Yet sometimes Bliss was in (almost) plain sight, for instance curled up asleep like a little animal in a children's storybook, in the shadowy alcove beneath the front staircase. And sometimes curled up on the homely nubby-fabric sofa in the basement family room never used by the Rampikes, like a room belonging to a ghost family that shared the house with us, whom we never saw: open the door and there's Bliss sleeping, her wan little face upturned, disheveled hair, she's breathing raspily through her part-opened mouth, barefoot and twitchy and her pretty pink embroidered nightie disfigured by stains.

Bliss's strangest hiding place: the smutty floor of the furnace room where twin furnaces like great beasts throbbed and vibrated in cold weather.

Except Bliss protested she wasn't *hiding*. She'd just been *dreaming*. And the dream took her to wherever it was, *she was meant to sleep*.

SUCKING HER THUMB!

Sucking her fingers!

A nervous habit of course. An infantile habit a child of six should have outgrown years ago. (Like bed-wetting.) (Like worse-than-bed-wetting, which also happened, too, sometimes.) Such bad habits were annoying enough at home, when only Mummy and Skyler were witnesses, but totally unacceptable in public, where others could see, at the rink for instance, worse yet when Bliss was being interviewed!—interviewed on TV in bright-glaring lights!

Bliss how could you! Right on TV! Haven't you been told, and told: keep your hands away from your mouth! Only babies suck their fingers! There are disgusting germs all over your hands! And it looks—oh honey, it looks terrible.

TWITCHY, FIDGETY! RESTLESS! WORST OF ALL WAS CHURCH, SUNDAY mornings in the Rampike family pew almost directly in front of Reverend Higley's pulpit, when Reverend Higley delivered his sermon, when the choir of Trinity Episcopal Church sang hymns in loud joyous voices that got inside your head like buzzing bees, then Bliss was most fidgety, prey to her "jumpy leg"—no matter how she tried to sit still, quietly like a good girl, invariably there came a tingling sensation in her left leg which Bliss tried to "keep back" as it became stronger and stronger until finally it "jumped out"—even if Bliss tried to hold her leg down with both hands, and pressing her foot hard against the floor, yet the rebellious leg would kick loose and cause people nearby to glance over at Bliss wondering what was wrong with her. And poor Mummy trying to smile, biting her lip to keep from crying, for nothing so upset Betsey Rampike than being embarrassed in public, in this upscale place of worship in Fair Hills, than bad behavior on the part of her children!

You can control that twitching if you try, Bliss. I learned to—we all did!—and so can you, if you try.

. . .

EVEN AT THE ICE RINK, BLISS SOMETIMES BEHAVED BADLY.
Suddenly breaking away, skating off to the farthest edge of the ice oblivious of the other girl-skaters staring at her and of Mummy and her (new) trainer Masha Kurylek calling after her.

She'd been practicing her routine for the upcoming 1996 Royale Ice

Capades (in which Bliss would perform to *The Firebird*), or maybe she'd been practicing her routine for the 1996 Little Miss Jersey Ice Princess Skate Challenge (in which Bliss would skate-dance to the sultry disco song "Do What Feels Right") and suddenly with no warning or explanation she simply skated away, as if Masha Kurylek wasn't out on the ice with her giving instructions, and Mummy wasn't sitting in the first row of seats talking on her cell phone which immediately Mummy dropped, to run to the edge of the rink calling *Bliss where are you going? Bliss come back here at once!*

Mummy in stylish tight knee-high leather boots dared not venture out onto the ice for fear of slipping, and falling. So Masha Kurylek (Olympic silver medalist, women's figure skating 1992) had to skate hurriedly after Bliss to bring her back, gripping her pupil's little hand tight. "Why did you skate away like that?" Mummy demanded in a quavering voice, and Bliss seemed at first not to know how to answer, shyly smiling, or defiantly smiling, mumbling, ". . . was my jumpy leg made me do it, Mummy. Not *me*."

LYING!

Saying terrible untrue things!

And in the most matter-of-fact little-girl voice, you'd swear such lies had to be true.

On a rare playdate, for instance, with a girl classmate she'd known at the Montessori school, whose surname—"Hover"—figured prominently in Mummy's pyramid of magical Fair Hills names, while watching a video of Disney's *Cinderella*, saying suddenly: "I was adopted. I was found somewhere."

"Oh! You were? Where?"

"They don't tell you where. Nobody will tell you."

Bliss giggled. Then Bliss began to cry.

Little Miranda naturally passed on this shocking news to her own mummy and naturally Mrs. Hover spread the tale through Fair Hills by way of the Village Women's Club where members met frequently for lunch, and so the tale naturally found its way to Betsey Rampike who was livid—"That is not, not true! There is not an ounce of truth in such a lie!"—and felt the need, though knowing it was probably not a prudent idea to betray such emotion in a place like Fair Hills, to make numerous frantic telephone calls assuring her women friends/acquaintances that her little Bliss was certainly not adopted but had a naughty habit of inventing, making things up—" 'Confabulating' is what Bliss's neurologist calls it, Dr. Vandeman says that all children fantasize, it isn't abnormal, or unusual, it's the sign of a healthy imagination but in Bliss's case there is not an ounce of truth in what she has said: I am Bliss's biological mother, and Bix is Bliss's biological father. We *are.*"*

DISOBEDIENT. SNEAKY-SLY.

Couldn't be trusted to eat the special-dietary foods Mummy had Maria prepare for her (high-protein/high-fiber/low-carb/low-sugar) for Mummy dreaded her little girl gaining weight, becoming "plump" as she herself had been as a girl, to the detriment of her skating career: "If Bliss could remain a tiny child forever, no more than forty-five pounds, how wonderful that would be!" Nor could Bliss be entrusted to take the numerous pills, tablets, and "dietary supplements" prescribed for her by the Fair Hills sports-pediatrician Dr. Muddick, which Maria—usually, Little Maria—gave her, or tried to give her, having to be especially vigilant that the cunning six-year-old didn't just pretend to swallow her (expensive) meds and spit them out when she was alone, later. How frequently Skyler (who had his own battery of meds to swallow, or to

---

* *Yet to this day, despite Mummy's efforts, scattered through the cesspool of cyberspace you will find the misinformation that Bliss Rampike was adopted as an infant by Bix and Betsey Rampike who could not have children of their own. In some quarters it is believed that our parents adopted both Bliss and me in order to "exploit"—"abuse"—us. Naturally, there have been a number of "biological mothers" who have come forward boldly to claim us, and if any of you "biological mothers"—or, as the case may be, "biological fathers"—are thinking to approach Skyler Rampike following the publication of this memoir, PLEASE DO NOT. I am no one's son any longer, I swear!*

pretend to swallow, three times daily) overheard this domestic-Beckett playlet:

> **Maria:** Bliss, did you swallow those pills?
>
> **Bliss** mumbles a reply, vaguely *Yes Maria.*
>
> **Maria:** Bliss, did you really swallow those pills?
>
> **Bliss** mumbles a reply, vaguely *Yes Maria.*
>
> **Maria:** Then what is this messy white stuff under your plate?
>
> **Bliss** mumbles a reply, vaguely *Don't know Maria.*
>
> **Maria** (losing patience, pronounced Hispanic accent): Unless you take every one of your pills, Bliss, I will have to tell your mother.
>
> **Bliss** with a muffled sob gives in.

Taken to Dr. Muddick's office each Friday morning for her shots— SuperGrow, Hi-Con Vit-C, CAGHC (Child Athlete Growth Hormone Concentrate)*—Bliss was ever more sulky and resistant, as she was, in Mummy's exasperated words, "self-destructive"—"irrational"—in the matter of the dental bite she was supposed to wear whenever she was home, to correct her "minor but disfiguring" overbite, that would prevent her, Mummy had been told by more than one figure-skating consultant, from achieving the very highest goals in women's competitive skating: Olympic medals, World Skating and Grand Prix championships, the most lucrative product endorsements (Elite Sporting Goods, StarSkate Sportswear, Flawless Cosmetics).

When Daddy objected, as sometimes Daddy did, to what he called

---

* *What do you think: was this some kind of sinister steroid? Was Mummy colluding with Dr. Muddick to inject steroids into a six-year-old, to "enhance" her performance on the ice? In my half-assed amateur way I've tried to find out more about the controversial performance-drug CAGHC but it was taken off the market in 1999 and the trail seems to have gone cold.*

Mummy's "super-micro-managing" of Bliss's career, Mummy said quickly, "Bix, you don't know the first thing about girls' skating and I *do*. No one wants to acknowledge that the competitions are basically beauty contests, but of course, take one look at the next big competition on TV, those camera close-ups, you will see it *is*."

"So? If it is? Our daughter doesn't have to compete, does she?"

For a moment Mummy simply stared at Daddy, who loomed (threateningly?) above her, too confused to speak.

Saying then, a hand to her breast, in a breathy-choked laughing voice, "Ohhh Bix! Damn you had me fooled, for a second I thought you were *serious*."

OR SOMETIMES AT SUCH MOMENTS MUMMY WOULD SAY TO DADDY, DRAWING a hand along his arm, sexy-pleading-vehement Mummy: "Darling, I've told you to trust me. Our daughter is our destiny."

(OKAY, YOU'VE HEARD THIS BEFORE. BELIEVE ME, IF YOU'D LIVED IN THE Rampike house on curvy Ravens Crest Drive, at the throbbing white-heat center of R.C.S disorder, you'd have heard it many, many more times.)

SULKY, SULLEN. STUBBORN.

In those devious cobalt-blue eyes, *not-there*.

Mummy impatiently brushed aside the tutors' excuses: "If you can't teach my daughter basic skills, let alone a foreign language, I'm afraid that I can't keep you on. And please don't ask me for a recommendation, I am unable to *lie*."

. . .

(AND THIS WAS TRUE, I THINK. BETSEY RAMPIKE WAS UNABLE TO CON-sciously and deliberately and with premeditation *lie*. Such untruths as

Betsey told, and retold, were but variants of truth, as Mummy perceived it. Don't judge her harshly!)

AT GRANDMOTHER RAMPIKE'S SPANISH-VILLA MANSION FRONTING THE UNRULY ATLAN-tic Ocean at Palm Beach, March 1996. Where Mummy, Skyler and Bliss were spending five days, to be joined by busy-Daddy for the weekend, damned if Bix is going to miss such a special occasion. Mummy wished for a "change of pace" for Bliss—and for her!—away from the ice rink for a few days at least so that Bliss could "relax"—"play"—"like an ordinary six-year-old." But at Grandmother Rampike's house that was showy-formal like a small hotel, to Mummy's annoyance Bliss was both insomniac and prone to that damned habit of hers, sleepwalking; she was twitchy/anxious like one who is missing a limb without quite knowing which limb it is, unable to "rest"—"relax"—"sunbathe" on the terrace or the beach—"swim in Grandmother's pool, or splash in the surf" with her brother—"play with her dolls, watch videos, read"—whatever it is ordinary six-year-old girls do: for Bliss missed the ice rink, that was obvious. *Bliss was miserable away from the ice rink* even in sunny Palm Beach amid such luxury where she'd been meant to bask also in Grandmother Rampike's (revised) estimate of her as pike-mouthed old Edna Louise's favorite grandchild. (Which elevated Mummy, too: though poor nervous Mummy had a very long way to go before becoming Edna Louise's favorite daughter-in-law.) (And what of Skyler? The kid had to concede, his rich grandma scarcely took notice of him any longer, spoke to him only briefly and then about Bliss—"Oh aren't you proud of your sister, Skyler! Your mother has been sending me the most amazing videos of that child's skating performances! And one of these days soon, I hope to see her compete! I hope to see her crowned—what is it?—your mother has been telling me—'Little Miss Jersey Ice Princess'—and on TV!—the most beautiful amazing prodity in the Rampike family, at last"—so emphasizing *prodity* with an excited clack of her formidable gleaming-white dentures, Skyler had to wonder if the mispronunciation was deliberate, as it often seemed her son Bix's mispronouncements/malapropisms must be deliberate.*

"Well, Skyler? Why are you sneering like that? Aren't you proud? You must be."

Skyler blinked nearsightedly at the annoyed old woman. He'd been recalling how shocked and appalled his grandmother had been at his bedside in the Maimed Children's Wing of the Robert Wood Johnson Medical Center in New Brunswick seeing her six-year-old grandson so frail and sickly and his badly broken leg in traction, moved to wonder if he would be a cripple for life . . . Now what was the subject? Who was the subject?

Had to be Bliss, he supposed.

"Yes, Grandmother. That is all that I am: proud of Bliss."

(Skyler hadn't been sneering! He was certain.)

(In the new/rapidly accelerating grip of R.C.S. [remember? Repetitive Compulsion Syndrome, said to be spreading like the bubonic plague of old among middle- and upper-middle-class Americans of all ethnic types, especially afflicting adolescents and "precocious" juveniles] Skyler peered at his reflection in mirrors and in mirroring surfaces a dozen times a day, more likely two dozen times a day, to see if he was making what his exasperated mother called *your damned pain-faces* and it seemed to Skyler that he was not. *He was not.*)

Yet Grandmother Rampike had to be disappointed with Bliss who never exhibited, in the several days of her visit to Palm Beach, any

---

* *D'you wonder how old Edna Louise reacted when Bix revealed to her, reluctantly/apologetically we have to suppose, that her four-year-old namesake-granddaughter Edna Louise was no longer "Edna Louise"—no longer named after her—but was, from that time forward, legally, "Bliss"—a name for which, in the patrician Rampike family, there could be no precedent? D'you wonder if the vain old woman was so shocked that for a long moment she could not speak, then snorted in derision, and hung up the phone? (For Bix had called her, soon after he'd given in to Betsey's demands.) D'you wonder if, for some uncertain time, prospects of winning back the old woman looked grim? worse than grim? Until at last, "Bliss Rampike" began to win skating competitions, and began to be "known," and old Edna Louise changed her mind. And, as Bix explained, in any number of apologetic-son calls, renaming their daughter, making the change legal, was after all a fate accomply.*

personality you'd call special: at Mummy's urging, Bliss was never less than sweetly/shyly polite with her grandmother, though stiffening in the old woman's embrace as if she were being hurt; smiling the most wan, wistful smiles in response to persistent if well-intentioned questions, and mumbling near-inaudible replies meant to be *Yes Grandmother. No Grandmother. Thank you Grandmother.* Skyler overheard some of these exchanges and smiled meanly: the *prodity* on ice wasn't a *prodity* on land, was she? The most painful of these scenes occurred when Edna Louise invited over a dozen of her rich-widow Palm Beach neighbors to meet her son's family, in the absence of her actual son (Daddy was expected to arrive the next morning, at last): the Palm Beach ladies were meant to feast their eyes upon Edna Louise's prized granddaughter, and to ply Bliss with questions, but, despite Mummy's encouragement, the six-year-old was stricken with shyness when asked "what is it like" to skate so beautifully, and to be applauded by so many people, and to see her picture everywhere?

Quietly Bliss sat, sucking at her thumb, or several fingers.

The next morning, there came Grandmother Rampike to lead Bliss away after breakfast, gripping her hand. On the oceanside veranda of Grandmother Rampike's house she instructed Bliss to please call her "Grandma"—not "Grandmother Rampike"—for it would mean so much to her, far more than she'd ever expected it might mean.

"Just 'Grand-ma,' dear. Please?"

What was this? The steely-eyed pike-mouthed old woman who'd insisted upon being called Grandmother Rampike by all her grandchildren, and Mother Rampike by her terrorized daughter-in-law Betsey, was begging now, in a clumsy-coquettish voice, her skating prodity granddaughter to call her Grandma? A muscular spasm passed over Skyler's face, transforming it (Skyler had to suppose) into an ugly-gargoyle face.

"'Grand-ma.' Please try, dear: 'Grand-ma.' When you win that 'Ice Princess' title and you are interviewed on TV, you can wave and smile and say 'Hi Grandma!' and I will be watching, dear—I promise. No one has ever called me 'Grandma,' I have no idea why, I am eighty-two years old and so very *lonely*."*

WETTING HER BED. (EVEN AT GRANDMOTHER RAMPIKE'S.)
    Trying to hide the evidence.

BAD GIRL! AT YOUR AGE! YOU MUST BE DOING IT TO SPITE ME.

Simultaneous with this awkward scene overlooking the unruly Atlantic Ocean, an equally awkward scene is taking shape at gate nine of the West Palm Beach Airport. For Mummy has insisted upon driving to the airport to pick up Daddy. But the 11:08 A.M. flight from J.F.K. has just landed, and by 11:19 A.M. all the passengers have left the plane, and where is Daddy? Where is Bix Rampike? Mummy is trying not to panic, Mummy fumbles to make a call on her cell phone but on the luminous little blue screen emerge the cryptic words CALL WAITING.

BAD GIRL! II

"IT IS A CURSE, IN A YOUNG ATHLETE. I HAVE SEEN IT MANY TIMES, IN THE best young skaters for they are frightened of their gift. We must fight, fight, fight to prevent it!" So Masha Kurylek spoke passionately, the small gold cross at her throat glittering like fire. And Mummy grimly amended: "We must *pray*."

How she exasperated them, in the midst of a near-perfected routine, suddenly wobbling on her skate blades, flailing her thin arms, falling. Masha Kurylek stared in disbelief. Mummy could not bear it, a red mist passed over Mummy's brain *Jesus why? To spite me but why? When I am the only one who knows that child's wicked heart, and loves her anyway? Why?* As Bliss tried to scramble to her feet, up on her skate blades as quickly as possible as if she hadn't fallen though white-faced, biting her lower lip to keep from whimpering in pain.

Exchanging a look with Mummy, in Bliss's eyes a look of guilty shame, unmistakable.

Such a bad careless girl: why?

To hurt yourself, to hurt me? Why?

No one could understand. At the practice rink, often the other skaters paused in their routines to watch Bliss Rampike under the tutelage of the demanding Masha Kurylek, skating with such precision, such grace, such courage, and yet—sudden as a sneeze it might come, ugly and ungainly as a sneeze, a moment's loss of concentration, a misstep, a fall.

Eagerly the child stammered: "M-Mummy, I'm not h-hurt. I'm *not*."

And "Mummy, I don't want to stop, I'm not hurt. Please, Mummy, I can keep skating."

How the child's thin wavering voice pleaded, Skyler will recall through his life Please Mummy I can keep skating.

Depending upon Masha Kurylek's advice, Mummy sometimes allowed Bliss to continue. At other times, when the child was too obviously limping, or wincing with pain, Mummy murmured in exasperation what sounded like *Jesus give me patience!*, bundled Bliss up in her soft-down red coat (that was a birthday present from Daddy, or from Daddy's "personal assistant" at work) and drove her to the Fair Hills Medical Center emergency room for X-rays; if the fall seemed to warrant such a measure, Mummy would arrange for an MRI at the Robert Wood Johnson Medical Center in New Brunswick, where Betsey Rampike had begun to be known. Mummy's great fear was that Bliss's careless skating would result in serious injuries to her spinal column, her neck. What of a head concussion? Broken ribs? If Bliss turned an ankle and broke it, that might be the end of the skating prodigy Bliss Rampike.

"Cost doesn't matter! We're insured for 'personal injury.' And where the insurance doesn't cover everything, my wonderful mother-in-law Edna Louise has said she will 'help out.' "*

After Bliss had a skating mishap practicing her routine for the 1996 Royale Ice Capades, stricken in the midst of executing a "butterfly gyre" to the frenetic rhythms of the crowd-pleaser *The Firebird*, and having to be taken (via ambulance) to New Brunswick, it began to be whispered at the Halcyon rink that Bliss Rampike of all girl-skaters was becoming accident-prone.

Accident-prone! As Masha Kurylek noted, the curse of the gifted skater.

And yet: Bliss loved to skate. This was no exaggeration, no false claim by her manager-mother. You could see, quite simply Bliss loved to skate. Never mind the shy, withdrawn, seemingly-not-so-bright-nor-so-pretty

---

* *It was so: to Daddy's astonishment, old Edna Louise had taken an unexpected interest in her youngest granddaughter, at last. Must've been the publicity in the* New York Times New Jersey *section, or the five-page spread in* New Jersey Lives. *Shrewd-Daddy understood that this bode— boded?—well for him, too: the favorite son who'd pissed off his mother by marrying, as Edna Louise persisted, no matter the banality of the cliché, "beneath" the Rampike family. For maybe it was so, as Mummy had so extravagantly predicted,* Our daughter is our destiny.

little girl with the maddening habit of sucking at her fingers, here was a girl transformed on the ice, eager and fearless and flying on her hissing skate blades, a delight to observe. Even seasoned veterans of the girls'-figure-skating circuit smiled at the spectacle of Bliss Rampike. Even the older brother Skyler who had seen Bliss skate almost as often as their mother had seen her, could be capable still of being enchanted by her. And so very proud of her.

She is what I would be. If God had loved me instead.

Both Skyler and his sister were vastly relieved to be back home, after the sun-glaring strain of Palm Beach. Skyler understood that something was amiss between Mummy and Daddy, had been amiss for some time but was (maybe) worsening, though Mummy would not speak of it except to say with her bright-lipstick-Mummy smile *You know how Daddy is: bizz-zee!* nor would Daddy, when Daddy was home, speak of it except to take Skyler aside man to man, press a beefy forefinger against his (Skyler's) lips, and murmur in enigmatic-Daddy tone: *Sky-boy! Hell of it is* Homo sapiens' *troubles began when we started to walk on our damn hind legs and the female buttocks became repositioned vis-à-vis the male olfactory organs. It's a bitch!*

After Palm Beach, Bliss was VERY HAPPY to be back in the cold climate of New Jersey. (The time: late March 1996.) VERY HAPPY to be back on the ice. (As Bliss said: "The ice can hurt you but the ice is your friend, Skyler.") SO VERY HAPPY to be back in her size-two little-girl skates and no longer in exile in Grandmother Rampike's Spanish villa on the Atlantic Ocean where there seemed to be no ice rinks and no interest in ice-skating and nothing to do all day long but *be*.

Truly Palm Beach for all its beauty was a hateful place for Daddy had not joined them after all for a few days "R & R" as he'd promised. There were phone calls, there was a "private" discussion between Mummy and Grandmother Rampike (which Skyler could not manage to overhear), at last red-blinking-eye'd Mummy had explained to her children that Daddy had had to fly suddenly to Singapore, or was it Sydney, on emergency-business matters, Daddy was so very sorry to be missing his family and his mother but hoped to "make it up tenfold" to everyone when he returned.

And Daddy promised to watch "my bestest-best gal" skate in her next competition, and *win*.

"'PHANTOM PAIN.' IT IS THAT CURSE, MRS. RAMPIKE. I HOPE THAT MASHA is mistaken!"

(It was a charming character trait, or an alarming character trait, that Bliss's new trainer Masha Kurylek, fierce pale skin, fierce hyperthyroid eyes, fierce-palpitating nostrils, sometimes spoke of herself in the third person: "Masha.")

Executing the tricky "butterfly gyre" to the fiery pounding music of *The Firebird* in preparation for the high-profile televised 1996 Royale Ice Capades in Wilmington, Delaware, Bliss had suffered one of her more serious falls, she'd been x-rayed and MRI'd and no "visible" injuries had been detected in her backbone, her neck, her skull, her right wrist; her injuries were mostly just bruises, bumps and minor abrasions which Dr. Muddick, Fair Hills's most admired sports-pediatrician, treated with discreet doses of the handy painkiller Codeine 7. Bliss insisted that she wasn't in pain, she was eager to resume skating, yet it soon became clear at practice that something was wrong with her: after about forty minutes on the ice Bliss began to tire, to breathe through her mouth, to favor her right leg. (Where previously she'd been favoring her left leg.) In even the simplest routines—figure eights, double-skate-turns, single-skate spirals—Bliss's coordination was conspicuously off, the "fairy sparkle" that had elevated Bliss to the title of Tiny Miss StarSkate 1995 was sadly dimmed. Observing the child-skater closely, Masha decided that Bliss was "secretly" in pain though she denied it, for fear of disappointing Mummy; Masha believed that this "phantom" pain was very like the elusive "cervical spine strain" which she herself had suffered at the age of sixteen— "That had almost destroyed Masha's career, there at the bud." Masha insisted upon outfitting Bliss with a flesh-colored foam-rubber collar which would support her head, lessen the strain on her neck and upper spine, yet not interfere with her skating.

Mummy fretted: "But Bliss looks so piteous out there on the ice, like an invalid. What if she's photographed! What if a camera crew from New Jersey Network hears of this!"

Masha advised: "It is only just for now, Mrs. Rampike. So the child's 'cervical spine' regains its strength, and she resumes her old confidence again, and we can remove the collar a few days before the Royale Ice Capades."

Trussed up in her foam-rubber collar, Bliss skated dispiritedly and insisted she wasn't in pain. She was *not*! The nasty pills Dr. Muddick prescribed for her made her "head heavy," that was all. And her stomach "queasy." She hated to take Codeine 7—slimy clam-colored capsules—as she hated all her other "meds" and the nasty weekly injections in her "bottom" and the nasty plastic-and-wire "bite" that made her mouth hurt and having to go to the beauty salon with Mummy to have her hair lightened with harsh-smelling chemicals that made her eyes sting and her nose run and at this point Mummy interrupted Bliss's litany of hated-things uttered in a rising voice, that dangerously rising tantrum-voice Mummy could not risk allowing to erupt anywhere outside the privacy of the Rampike household, especially not in such a public place like the Halcyon rink where others would hear, other skaters and their trainers and mothers, how shocked they would be, how scandalized and delighted to witness angelic little Bliss Rampike fly into a temper tantrum like any other spoiled girl-skater: "Bliss, darling! I have you. And Jesus has you."

Instinctively Mummy knew to embrace the quivering child. To contain the convulsive fury that made the child's muscles twitch, and her jaws clench tight. No one had known to embrace Betsey Sckulhorne as a child of six, no one had loved her in such a way. No one had known her heart. For Betsey, who was now thirty-three years old, all that was over. But for Bliss who was Betsey Sckulhorne in this new far more beautiful and blessed form, it would be her destiny.

Mummy stroked Bliss's hair that was so fine, and luminous-blond, smelling of chemical bleach. Mummy kissed Bliss's forehead that was clammy, yet sweaty. Mummy spoke chidingly in Bliss's ear, as one might speak to a small child.

"Jesus loves you, Bliss! Jesus loves us both. We know that, there is nothing else to know."

AND WAS SKYLER JEALOUS, LOOKING ON? WAS SKYLER JEALOUS, SEEING how everyone at the rink watched Bliss both on the ice and off, murmured *Hello, Bliss!* and *Good night, Bliss!* as if the very utterance of that magical monosyllable *Bliss* gave them pleasure, as a lover takes pleasure in speaking the beloved's name? Was he jealous seeing how strangers smiled after Bliss, looking through Skyler as if his body were transparent and of no more substance than his soul, that's to say as if he did not exist? Was Skyler jealous on the drive home to Fair Hills, in the cluttered backseat of Mummy's Buick while Bliss slumped beside Mummy in the passenger's seat, her small luminous-blond head against Mummy's shoulder.

Plunging south into the rapidly growing dusk on New Jersey route 15. Headlights of oncoming cars rushing at them. And the windshield of the Buick splotched with rain and each rain-splotch shining like an eye.

Bliss is what Skyler would be if God had loved Skyler instead.

If there was Skyler. If there was God.

Skyler asked Mummy what is "phantom pain" he'd heard Masha speak of and Mummy frowned into the rear-view mirror above the windshield seeking out Skyler's eyes. Often it seemed to Skyler that his mother forgot his presence and his voice was to her a kind of nudge waking her from private thoughts. "Why, Skyler. I didn't think you were listening, I thought you were doing your homework . . . 'Phantom pain' is when you only imagine pain, as Bliss seems to be imagining it. When the pain isn't really there."

" 'When the pain isn't really'—where, Mummy?"

"Isn't *there*. In your neck, or ankle. In a joint, or in a muscle." Mummy paused, looking at Skyler in the little rectangular mirror. In the shifting glare of oncoming headlights her face appeared strangely shaped as a moon that has been flattened and her eyes that normally seemed to Skyler so beautiful were bulgy and wetly shiny like the rain-splotches. Carefully Mummy said, "It is only in your head."

With nine-year-old pedantry Skyler said: "Pain *is* in the head, Mummy.

It's in the brain. Bliss's tutor was telling me—he showed me a science article, about the human brain."

"Bliss's tutor? You mean Rob? What is that young man doing with you, it's Bliss he's supposed to be tutoring, and a poor job he seems to be doing of it." Mummy was incensed, suddenly. Mummy pursed her lips in the way Daddy teased was Mummy's pit-bull look. "Bliss's pain—if she has pain, which she denies—you know how devious that child is!—is in her head only, meaning that she is imagining it, as Dr. Vandeman says: it isn't real."

Yet Skyler persisted, leaning close behind Mummy as Mummy drove through the splotching rain: "But the only pain we feel is in our heads, Mummy. Pain is registered only in our brains and if we feel it, it is 'real.' "

Mummy laughed irritably. Skyler should have known this was a warning laugh.

"Jesus can take our pain from us, if He wishes. If we are worthy. I know you don't believe, Skyler, I've seen you squinching up your little gargoyle face during church services, you are a budding little skeptic like your father, and Jesus could no more burrow into your heart than He could burrow into a wizened old raisin, nonetheless it is *true*. Bliss's pain is not 'real' and if it is 'real'—Jesus will take it from her. And Bliss Rampike will be crowned Little Miss Royale Ice Princess 1996, and Daddy will be with us at the rink to see her crowned, and that evening we will have a special celebration, and Daddy will come home with us. That is our destiny, Skyler: what is yours?"*

* *Wow! Jesus! That's telling off the annoying little bastard, isn't it? In such sudden flare-ups, in such unexpected shifts from soft-pop-rock to Puccini, you had a sense that the Mummy/Betsey Rampike everyone took for granted wasn't, actually, the individual we all thought she was.*

QUERY

AND WAS BLISS RAMPIKE CROWNED LITTLE MISS ROYALE PRINCESS 1996, and was Daddy present to see his bestest-best little gal wildly applauded by an arena of admiring strangers, and was there a celebration afterward at Wilmington, Delaware's "most prestigious/historic" downtown hotel; and did Daddy come home with his little family the next morning?

Read on.

GOOD MEMORY?*

"HOMO SAPIENS WILL DEVASTATE THIS PLANET WITHIN THE NEXT FIFTY years but an 'evolved' *Homo sapiens*—enhanced by genetic engineering— may relocate to other planets. That's our only hope."

How like Skyler's father Rob Feldman sounded at such mordant/upbeat moments! Though Rob was a lanky twenty-two-year-old molecular biology graduate student (formerly of Columbia U., now back in Fair Hills boarding temporarily with his family) and Bix Rampike was surely one of those *Homo sapiens* specimens who has already evolved and would be "relocated" to another planet, to begin again the effort of capitalism's terrestial despoilation.

Rob Feldman, one of Skyler's first loves. Or maybe this is an exaggeration, in a weak moment. For it is time for a Good Memory—isn't it? In my wizened-raisin heart, I'm still that nine-year-old stunted-runt dreamer Skyler Rampike.

Remembering how, returning home from school, lonely Skyler would attach himself to his sister's homeschooling sessions in the solarium at the rear of the Rampike house. Innocently appearing in the doorway to murmur *Okay if I sit with you?* and the tutor seated across the table from little Bliss would glance up with a hopeful smile and murmur in turn *Why of course!*

---

* *This brief, unabashedly sentimental interlude is not strategically placed to generate what sneering critics call "cheap suspense"—I swear! Nor do I wish in glib postmodernist style to fuck up the already fatally fucked-up chronology of this document. Just wanted, amid so much that is dark, gnarled, blighted and sinister-sorrowful, before plunging into a "harrowing" account of the final months of my sister's life, to acknowledge that there were, now and then, in Skyler's young life, what greeting-card companies call Good Memories.*

Relief that the unexpected visitor was little Skyler and not Mrs. Rampike coming to "check up on" the lesson. Relief that the visitor was Bliss's older brother Skyler who was eager as a puppy for attention, conversation, "eye contact."

Since I'd mentioned Rob a few pages back, Rob Feldman who'd been the penultimate—classy word for "last-but-one"—in the sequence of young tutors hired/fired by Mummy—it seems fitting for me to say a few more words about him. The other night in this squalid room sweatily immersed in the "intensely felt"—"unsparingly intimate"—chapter titled "Bad Girl! I" suddenly I found myself remembering Bliss's tutors, of whom I have not thought in nearly ten years: "Tiffy"—"Brooke"—"Sam"—"Lindsay"—but also "Jennifer"—"Jason"—and "Rob" who'd seemed to like me best.

That is, Skyler. Not me—"me" is a nineteen-year-old junkie in self-imposed exile in a rooming house on Pitts Street, New Brunswick, grimily barefoot in grungy underwear embarked upon a quixotic—"hopeless"—mission to write the only true account of his sister's life/murder/aftermath of/etcetera. "Me" would be a surprise/shock to Rob Feldman who would be in his late thirties by now and maybe married, gainfully employed, one of the admirable adults of the world. What to make of this freaky misfit/murder suspect tugging at his sleeve: *Rob, hello! Remember me? Skyler Rampike who adored you as an older brother?*

(Idea for another project: a "wildly original"- "boldly postmodernist"—ingeniously spliced-together sequence of vignettes focusing upon individuals who'd "adored" a minor media figure like Bliss Rampike. Some of these individuals would be total strangers to the object of their adoration, others would be closer to her, still others—members of her own family!—would know her intimately, and perhaps not wholly adore her. And the figure at the center of the narrative, ideally a variant of "the most poetical topic in the world"—that is, a beautiful young girl-child of no more than ten years of age—would be inaccessible to the reader: a total mystery.)

Rob Feldman: did you sense something "terribly wrong" in the all-American Rampike household, at 93 Ravens Crest Drive? Was that why, alone among the succession of attractive young tutors, you were the only one to quit before Betsey Rampike fired you?

What did you perceive: bruises on Bliss's exposed arms? bruises on Bliss's neck? A slight limp, favoring her left leg? Explained away—so very convincingly!—as casualties of the "accident-prone" young athlete?

Each of Bliss's tutors quickly realized that trying to teach the six-year-old skating prodigy a minimal first-grade curriculum would not be an easy task. For when Bliss Rampike wasn't laced up in her white kid-skin Baby Champ skates flashing and flying across the glittery surface of the ice, or being photographed/filmed/hugged/kissed/fussed-over and lavishly praised by adults, her very spirit seemed to retreat somewhere behind her moist cobalt-blue eyes; a melancholia more acute than the A.P.M. (Acute Premature Melancholia) of Skyler's precocious classmate Tyler McGreety, Jr. overtook her. What a puzzle it was, for Bliss seemed, initially, to be alert, lively, intelligent, and a "good girl" who unaccountably could not seem to concentrate on her lessons, became "distracted"—"confused"—"easily discouraged"—"anxious/lethargic." How many times did Skyler overhear Bliss telling her tutor in a shamed little-girl voice *Can't do it, can't remember . . . I will only get it wrong.*

Repeatedly Bliss was taught the alphabet, memorized the sequence of letters in clusters, recited it slowly and with painful concentration; then, next time, scrambled the order of the letters or forgot them entirely. As repeatedly Bliss memorized the single-digit multiplication tables which subsequently she scrambled, or forgot. If for a week or so Bliss could "read"—in the way of a blind child making her halting way across the floor—mysteriously over a weekend she lost the ability, to the bewilderment of her tutors and to Mummy's disgust.

"My daughter is not 'dyslexic.' She has been tested many times, she has had MRIs, her brain is 'perfectly normal'—as her neurologist has said. There is no reason why she can't learn to read at least as well as her brother, who *is* dyslexic."

(If Skyler were present, the pedantic little brat might pipe up: "Mummy, I am also A.D.D. You know that.")

Some of the tutors had better luck with Bliss than others, at least initially. You could see—at least, Skyler could see—that Bliss was trying very hard. Yet somehow it happened, after a few embarrassing setbacks, tears, a temper tantrum, Bliss seemed to give up, sat unresponsive at the table in the solarium with her arms folded tight across her chest. In her glassy blue eyes as in the tragic set of her mouth was the declaration *Can't do it, can't remember. I will only get it wrong.*

Most memorably, Rob passed on to his little friend Skyler copies of "speculative sci-fi" comic books and the "underground" comics of R. Crumb* after extracting from Skyler the promise that he wouldn't show his parents these items which of course Skyler would not. R. Crumb made a profound impression on Skyler at the vulnerable age of nine and soon the savage sagas of R. Crumb became Skyler's favorite after-bedtime reading; Skyler even tried to draw comics in the inimitable style of R. Crumb. In all of Fair Hills there was no one who resembled R. Crumb's freaky people and yet, how familiar they seemed to Skyler! Slutty big-breasted females with massive buttocks and legs, teetering on ridiculous high heels, pinhead cretin males with enormous floppy feet . . . And runty gargoyle figures like Skyler looking on with leering-demonic grins.

"Rob? What is 'Keep on trucking'?" Skyler asked, and the tutor said, "It means—'Just keep on.'"

"Yes, but—why? 'Keep on'—why?"

"Ask your dad, Skyler. He'd be the one to know."

Skyler was naive but not so naive as to ask Daddy any question to which he hadn't a good idea what the answer might be.

Subversive R. Crumb was Rob Feldman's parting gift to Skyler. Abruptly then the tutor was gone. This was spring 1996. From his mother's indignant reaction, Skyler guessed that Rob had quit just before Mummy could fire him: "That deceitful Feldman! And I trusted him with my daughter! And my son! If he imagines that I will be a 'character reference' for him . . ."

But when Mummy complained to Daddy about the tutor's "betrayal" Daddy was unpersuaded: "A Jewish person, with his tragic sense of progoms through the millennia, he will instinctively jump a sinking ship, can you blame him? That's why at Scor we make them sign legal contracts, so they can't walk away with our secrets and sell them to our enemies."

These were early Zap comics, Rob Feldman must have bought in a secondhand comics store. Long missing, destroyed. See the subsequent chapter in this document "Post-Mortem"—hundreds of pages distant.

Was Daddy kidding? Was this tricky-Daddy speech? Catching his son's eye and winking man-to-man while poor Mummy fumed and fussed biting her lip to keep from crying.

Soon Bliss wanted to see what the comic book was Skyler was trying to copy from but Skyler told her no.

Bliss asked why.

"Because this comic book isn't for girls."

Bliss asked why.

"Because R. Crumb is ugly, and funny. And you're not supposed to laugh at ugly things."

Bliss asked why.

"Because you're not. Because I say so."

Yes said Bliss, but *why*?

Just inside the doorway of Skyler's bedroom his six-year-old sister stood staring at him with a peculiar wistful/insolent smile. Her voice was both pleading and demanding. Here was both the angel-child and the devious little brat. For much of that day Bliss had been practicing at the Halcyon rink under the tutelage of Masha Kurylek for there was an interregnum during which the dread homeschooling sessions were suspended while Mummy searched for a new tutor. Bliss's skin was mottled as if she'd been picking at it with her nails, her nostrils looked inflamed. She had not been given a bath and was wearing her skating-practice jumpsuit of soiled pink wool-flannel embossed across the chest with white satin letters *B L I S S*. Evidently she had not been made to take her several afternoon meds and so was skittish and irritable and could not possibly lie down for a nap before the evening meal for Mummy was out somewhere, and had been gone for hours, and the younger of the Marias had recently been fired for "insubordination"—"incompetence"—"moral laxity" as Mummy had charged.

Bliss ran at Skyler giggling, intending to snatch the R. Crumb comic from him, but Skyler scrambled to his knees on his bed holding the magazine at arm's length. "I promise, Skyler, I won't laugh. Please," and Skyler said again, in a tone of nine-year-old prudery, "I told you: this comic book isn't for little girls."

"I'm not a 'little girl.' I'm a thousand years old."

Wildly Bliss rushed at Skyler trying to wrest the magazine from him, tearing the pages. Each time Bliss attacked him like this Skyler was surprised by her strength and agility and he recalled Daddy's admonition: *Never hit a girl!* In self-defense Skyler tossed R. Crumb across the room, and Bliss ran to snatch up the comic book, peering as if nearsightedly at the crudely drawn humanoid figures. Skyler said, "I told you, it isn't for girls. Now give it back."

Skyler was listening uneasily for Mummy to come home. The sound of Mummy's car in the driveway, the sound of the downstairs rear door opening. When neither Mummy nor Daddy was home there was in the Rampike household an air of excitable tension like the air before an electrical storm which the arrival of one or another of the adults, nearly always Mummy, for Daddy was away "on business," would exacerbate.

On her heels on the floor, Bliss was turning the pages of the lurid comic book. Such ugly figures! Such "nasty"—"dirty"—things, very wrong for a young girl to see. Skyler could hear Bliss breathing through her mouth. Certainly she did not appear to be laughing, nor even smiling. Nor had Skyler laughed much at the comic book. With the look of pained concentration she brought to certain of her lessons before disillusion set in, Bliss continued to peer at the pages, and finally, after perhaps five minutes, she handed it back to Skyler without a word.

Skyler said, "What'd I tell you! R. Crumb isn't for girls. If you tell Mummy, I'll wring your neck."*

Quickly Bliss fled the room.

Soon afterward, Mummy arrived home. By then, Bliss was being bathed by the elder Maria and had taken her meds and Skyler had hidden away his torn copy of R. Crumb in a corner of his closet beneath pairs of smelly old sneakers, where Mummy would never think of looking, not ever.

---

* *My God, did I really say this?* Did I really threaten to wring my six-year-old sister's neck? *I hadn't remembered any of this in ten years and now it is all flooding back and maybe it is a mistake to be doing what I am doing and in the grip of R.C.S. I am fearful that I will be propelled onward to reveal worse . . .*

ANSWERS TO QUERIES OF PREVIOUS CHAPTER "QUERY"

NO, NO, AND NO.

OW!

"HAVE YOU NOTICED, CHILDREN?—YOUR FATHER HAS DEPARTED."

Skyler stared at Mummy: wasn't sure what Mummy had said.

Bliss stared at Mummy: wasn't sure what Mummy had said.

In the doorway of the family room Mummy stood. A glaring light like raging flames behind Mummy, the startled children could not bear to look at head-on and so Skyler who'd been jotting down cheat-notes for a "cognitive-skills" test he was scheduled to take the next day at school looked to the side and Bliss who'd been raptly absorbed in *The Ring of Kerry Irish Skate-Dance Troupe* which was Bliss's favorite-of-all-times skating videos shut her eyes. And Mummy said, "Why are you smiling, Bliss? Is this news amusing?"

Bliss's eyes blinked open. Had Bliss been smiling? A twitch and a tremor in Bliss's left cheek, easy to mistake for an insolent smile. Seated beside Skyler on the sofa Bliss cast her brother a sidelong glance for support, but Skyler was looking away.

Telling himself *Sure Daddy is departed! I knew it.*

In fact, Skyler hadn't known. Or if he'd known with a part of his mind he hadn't *known.* For to even a shrewd child who eavesdrops with the nervous concentration of a sparrow picking in the dirt very little is *known* unless an adult has confirmed it.

It was so, Daddy hadn't joined his family at Palm Beach the month before. Poor Mummy had driven to the airport to bring him home to Grandmother Rampike's house where they waited for Daddy eagerly, Grandmother Rampike's Cuban cook had prepared a lavish late-lunch to be served on the wide white veranda overlooking the sweep of beach and the ocean, but an hour passed, and another hour passed, and finally Mummy returned with reddened eyes, her breath smelling of something very sweet and fumey like gasoline and Mummy told Grandmother Rampike that Daddy had not been on the plane he'd been scheduled to take from J.F.K. and so Mummy had waited at the airport for the next flight, from Newark, thinking that Daddy had missed the first flight and would catch the later flight without having time to call and explain but Daddy had not been on the later flight either and so Mummy who wasn't feeling very well was going upstairs and did not want to be disturbed and when Grandmother Rampike tried to restrain her Mummy threw off Grandmother Rampike's talon-fingers with a sharp little cry *No! Don't touch me.*

(Had Skyler witnessed this? Maybe.)

Later it would be revealed that for weeks Daddy had been caught up in "crucial negotiations" with Scor Chemicals lawyers who were determined not to lose Bix Rampike to the aggressive hiring campaign of mega-global Univers Bio-Tech, Inc. which negotiations in what had promised to be the final hour were dramatically interrupted by the sudden emergence of a similar campaign to hire Bix Rampike at mega-global Vortex Pharmaceuticals, Inc. and so a three-way tug-of-war had been raging the object of which was Skyler's and Bliss's Daddy: "Very flattering, sure. But God-damned exhausting."

Since then, Daddy had been more and more away from home and even when he hadn't been away "on business" he returned home late for dinner, rarely home in time to kiss Skyler and Bliss good night in their beds. Mummy had said with her brave-Mummy smile that it was "a time of transition" and that Daddy was "very, very popular" in the corporate world; from Singapore, from Toyko, from Sydney and from Rio and from Scor Chemicals headquarters in Paramus, New Jersey, came phone messages for Skyler and for Bliss in earnest-Daddy tones *Hey you kids your Daddy is missing you, y'know your Daddy loves you two kids to death don't you?*

Skyler had always known that Daddy was very special—of course!—but this sentiment had been corroborated just recently at Fair Hills Day when not only smirky Tyler McGreety but snooty Fox Hambruck who usually ignored Skyler went out of their ways to speak to him in the school dining room, even to smile at him, and to ask how "Mr. Rampike" was?—a question so baffling to Skyler at the time he could only stammer: "D-Daddy is okay, I think."

But this appeared to be something different. *Your father has departed* had the ominous sound of something not related to the corporate world.

"Skyler, stop scowling! It breaks your mother's heart to see you looking so tragic. And Bliss, *why* are you smiling? Is there something you know, that your father has told you, he hasn't told Skyler and me? Is that why you are smiling?—to mock us?"

Mummy spoke as one might speak with stones in her mouth and Mummy stood with her elbows pressing against her sides as if to keep herself upright. Mummy's crimson lipstick was partly eaten away which meant that Mummy had not glimpsed herself in a mirror for some time and Mummy's hair was springy on one side of her head and flattened on the other as if Mummy had been sleeping on her side, in rumpled clothes. In recent days Skyler had heard Mummy speaking sharply on the telephone and that afternoon, when he'd returned home from school, there was Mattie Higley, Reverend Higley's wife, just driving away in the Higleys' station wagon, with a bright *be brave!* smile for Skyler he hadn't wished to interpret. Skyler saw that the polish on Mummy's fingernails was chipped and Skyler saw that Mummy's hands were loose and quivery and quickly Skyler said, in defense of his trembling little sister, "Bliss isn't smiling, Mummy. She doesn't mean anything by it, she can't help it."

Mummy's dilated eyes swerved upon Skyler. For a moment, Skyler worried that he might be smiling, too. But Mummy only just staggered forward, colliding with the back of Daddy's massive taffy-colored leather chair as if she hadn't seen it, sighing, and saying: "Your daddy has another life, it seems. Which he prefers to his life with us. 'I will always love my little family,' Daddy has said. 'But I can't breathe in that house.'"

Instinctively Skyler and Bliss drew in short panting breaths.

"'Can't breathe'? Daddy? Is he *sick*?"

Bliss gave a convulsive little cry, as if struck by phantom pain in her lungs.

"'Can't breathe.' That's what your father has declared. After you fell and hurt yourself at Atlantic City—that was the first time. Daddy saw the video, you know. Daddy insisted upon seeing. I tried to prevent him but he insisted. And last week at Wilmington, when you cancelled your performance, I think it was too much. Your father was planning to attend, Bliss! He was planning to be with us at the hotel. He'd rearranged his schedule, to be with us. 'To see my bestest-best little gal skate, and to see her win.' But it didn't happen that way. Your father isn't a man of faith, children. He isn't like me! Oh, he says he is: 'I believe in a Supreme Being'—'I believe in a Personal Savior.' But things must be proven to that man, repeatedly. Like all American men—at least, 'alpha-plus' males!—his heart is fickle. That his family is worthy of his love must be proven to him again, and again. He says he loves us—but does he? He knew how hard we've all been working for the Royale Ice Capades competition—how we've been living, breathing, dreaming *The Firebird* for months!—and when Bliss was rejected, it was a rebuke to your father, to his male way of thinking." Mummy paused, her mouth twisted in a bitter smile. "But it isn't your fault, Bliss, and no one blames you. Masha is very disappointed, of course—but doesn't blame you. And I don't blame you. 'Phantom pain'—whatever that is!—can strike any of us, at any time. If we are weak in our faith. If we succumb."

The previous week, Bliss had failed to qualify for the Royale Ice Capades competition. For somehow it had happened that, contrary to Mummy's expectation, Jesus had failed to take Bliss's phantom pain from her, and so, during her qualifying performance, Bliss had been in such conspicuous pain that the Royale Ice Capades officials refused to allow her to compete, and threatened to formally register a complaint against Mummy with the United States Figure Skating Association, for violating one or another of the bylaws of their official *Rulebook*. And so Bliss Rampike wasn't crowned Little Miss Royale Ice Capades Princess 1996 as many had predicted she would be. And so Daddy hadn't been with his little family in Wilmington that evening, and Daddy didn't seem to be anywhere in the vicinity of 93 Ravens Crest Drive now.

Calmly Mummy said: "No one blames you, Bliss. Skating accidents happen all the time. The most promising careers end abruptly if we lack faith. 'Many are called but few are chosen'—Jesus has warned. And, 'From him that hath not shall be taken away even that which he hath.'"

Mummy may have had more to say on the subject but a phone ringing impatiently in the next room distracted her. Skyler's eyes were shut tight and when he opened them, Mummy was gone. And Bliss was still cringing on the sofa beside him, taut and unmoving and her knees drawn up to her chest. Skyler pushed at her—

"*Your* fault, Daddy isn't here! Damn you."

OW! THIS IS A PAINFUL MEMORY.

(Yet *Ow!* is a comical sound, isn't it? *Ow!* you see exclusively in cartoons and comic strips. *Ow! ow! owwww!* the freaky humanoids in R. Crumb cry. But their pain is laughable, contemptible. Anthropologists might tell us that we can laugh at another's pain only if the *other* is sufficiently other and in no way us.)

"BLISS? HEY C'MON. I'M SORRY, I DIDN'T MEAN IT . . . MUMMY ISN'T here. Bliss?"

Later that evening searching for his stricken little sister upstairs in her bedroom and downstairs and again upstairs—had he missed her the first time?—hiding beneath her bed. Barely visible in the dim light of the Mother Goose lamp there was Bliss lying unmoving on her side, knees drawn up to her chest and thumb in her mouth, the raggedy old doll Edna Louise clutched in her arms. Skyler reached for her but his arms were too short. "Bliss, don't feel bad, okay? Mummy didn't mean it." In the dim light Bliss's small moist eyes were barely discernible and Edna Louise's eyes were empty sockets. How many times had Mummy in exasperation taken the old doll from Bliss and disposed of it yet somehow Bliss managed to retrieve it—"like a pack rat"—unless maybe Bliss had found a similar battered old doll abandoned in one of the skating rinks, appropriated it as her own and brought it home with her inside her coat and whispered to it in secret as if to taunt her mother who laughingly admitted to being "at my wit's end" over her six-year-old daughter who was both the most wonderful thing in Betsey Rampike's life and the most vexing. As if God, or Jesus, had sent Bliss to Betsey: *Here! Your salvation, or your damnation.* For so Mummy complained to Skyler, with a brave-Mummy laugh. For it was so, the Royale Ice Capades officials had threatened to register a complaint against Betsey Rampike, mother/manager of Bliss Rampike. It was so, Bliss was under orders to "rest"—"stay off the ice"—for at least two weeks. Dr. Vandeman was prescribing daily doses of the new "wonder drug" F.D.A.-approved for children, the anti-convulsive Serenex, and Dr. Muddick was prescribing daily doses of the anti-depressant Excelsia and the painkiller Codeine 7, and Dr. Bohr-Mandrake (female, M.D. in abnormal child psychopharmacology) was prescribing high-concentrate doses of Zomix for Bliss's C.A.A.D. which, in the past year, clearly seemed to be worsening.* "Bliss? Please. I'm sorry, and I bet Mummy is sorry, too." Yet Bliss remained unresponsive and unmoving beneath the bed. Skyler could hear her quick shallow panting. The trapped air beneath the bed was overwarm, stale, smelly. Skyler's nostrils pinched at the familiar ammoniac-smell of Bliss's mattress and bedding. Dr. Bohr-Mandrake believed that Zomix would "minimize" Bliss's nighttime "accidents" and Skyler dearly hoped that this was so. "Bliss, Daddy loves you. Daddy loves us both, he says so all the time. It's just Daddy is 'busy'—Daddy might be changing jobs. But Daddy is going to see us next week—he promised. When I hurt myself at the gym, it was a stupid mistake but Daddy didn't stop loving me." Skyler paused, wondering if this was true. As a bright (if dyslexic/A.D.D.-afflicted) child of nine he could figure that any kid's father might love him just a little more if he'd turned out to be a prodigy-gymnast and not a runt-cripple whom other boys scorned. Yet urgently Skyler reasoned: "If Daddy says he 'can't breathe' here why is it our fault? In Mummy's magazines you can read about what adults do all the time: 'adult'ry.' It's something nasty called 'adult'ry' because that is what adults *do*."

Yet, closely perusing such fat glossy Mummy-magazines as *Self, Moi!, Cosmopolitan, Chic, Glamour* etc., for many months, Skyler hadn't been able to comprehend what "adult'ry" was and what adults, apparently most husbands, did to so upset their spouses.

---

* *C.A.A.D.: Compulsive Anti-Authority Disorder. Only just recently recognized by the American Association of Child Psychologists, Clinical Psychiatrists and Mental Health Practitioners yet noted in the* New York Times *as "a virtual epidemic in American pre-pubescents."*

After ten or more minutes of futile pleading with his exasperating little sister hiding beneath her bed, Skyler gave up. His own neck was throbbing with pain from his awkward posture and if the pain was real, or only just phantom pain, Skyler didn't like it.

"Damn you, Bliss! Everything in this damn house has to do with *you*."

B.D.B.S.*

BRISKLY RUBBING HIS BIG-DADDY HANDS DADDY LEANS HIS ELBOWS ON THE
table and hunches down to eye-level: "You kids! You know your Daddy
loves you, don't you?"

Eager-beaver Skyler nods.

Sucking at a finger, Bliss stares at Daddy in silence.

"—just that, damn this is hard to articulate!—there comes a time"—
Daddy's eyes fill with moisture and seem to be losing focus, roughly he
swipes at them with the edge of his hand—"in a marriage of—longevity—in
a family"—pausing as if unable to continue, Daddy's throat closing up as
Daddy fixes his gaze on his children's rapt still faces, like mesmerized
little rodents they are, mesmerized by—is it a cobra?—swaying, flicking
its mercury-red tongue, staring with liquidy basilisk eyes—"a family in
which the daddy is very close to his children emotionally and spiritually
and yet, a victim of his own 'corporate success' "—Daddy pauses, laughing
sadly, an edge of bitterness in his soft-Daddy-laughter—"and the mother,
too, is devoted—a super-mom you could say—a remarkable woman of such
verve, imagination, ambition—it has been a privilege and a joy to know—
and to love. Except . . ." Daddy's halting voice ceases. Daddy drains his
glass of Johnnie Walker Scotch on the rocks and with a near-imperceptible
shift of dense-Daddy-eyebrows signals to the waiter who has been discreetly orbiting Daddy's table and in that instant the Rampike children
are jarred out of their Daddy-trance to find themselves—where is this?—

---

* *By the end of this piteous chapter you will know what this title means. And if you don't, sorry.*

in the elegantly chilly upstairs dining room of the Sylvan Glen Golf Club?

Must've been, Bix and Betsey Rampike were voted *in*.

We know how "exclusive"—"prestigious"—the Sylvan Glen is, and we are impressed.

Daddy has insisted upon a window table overlooking the gently hilly eighteen-hole golf course said to be modeled after a famous golf coure in Inverness, Scotland. You would never imagine, gazing at the vista outside the plate glass window, that you were so very close to the residential neighborhoods of the Village of Fair Hills. In Skyler's (mildewed) memory this scene takes place in a wintry season for the sculpted hills of the golf course appear to be covered in something whitely-crinkly like Styrofoam and there is not a golfer in sight. Skyler squints seeing in the distance a tall Daddy-figure brandishing a golf club, a small son-figure uncertainly gripping a child-sized golf club, on the ground there is a small white pellet-like ball that must be struck so that it will fly into the air and roll across the ground and disappear into a hole . . . *You and me, Sky-boy! Out on the links, soon as it's spring* Daddy has promised, though not recently.

(Unless this is literary "unreliable narrator" stuff? Heavily medicated/emotionally unstable nine-year-old confusing his memory of that very special luncheon-with-Daddy with an actual wintry scene in the world outside the window?)

What a very special Saturday-with-Daddy this is for the Rampike children who've been so anxious lately: not only is their handsome Daddy treating them to lunch in this classy place—"Just the three of us! Like old times"—but afterward Daddy has promised to drive out to the fabled Vast-Valley Shopping Mall, one of the architectural wonders of North Central New Jersey, second-largest luxury mall in the state, to take in a matinee of the new family-comedy hit *Benji Goes Ballistic!* Though Daddy has done his discreet-Daddy best to downplay the less-than-festive aspects of this Saturday, it isn't a secret that after today Daddy will not be living in the house on Ravens Crest Drive with Skyler, Bliss, and Mummy. How long Daddy will be gone isn't clear to Skyler and Bliss—"temporarily, I promise!"— "until things get worked out between your mother and me"—nor where exactly Daddy will be living except "not far!"—"close by!"—"commuting distance!" All that agitated morning Daddy was packing his things at the house, hastily, carelessly, thumping up and down the stairs carrying suitcases and duffel bags out to the dull-gleaming Road Warrior XXL parked squat and triumphant in the driveway like a conquering tank. Ah!—Skyler's breath caught seeing Daddy's giant-clothes borne aloft on mere coat hangers, Daddy's silk neckties slithering off like snakes to twist underfoot. In cardboard boxes, Daddy carried away a selection of books.

(A hopeful note: among the books Daddy is taking with him is *A Daddy's Guide.* And the fact that Daddy isn't taking most of his books but leaving them behind for the family "library"—where Skyler will help Maria shelve them—suggests that Daddy will be back, doesn't it?)

By 7:50 A.M. that morning Mummy was gone from the house. For overnight Mummy seemed to have summoned special—spiritual?—strength to withstand this "marital crisis"—"stunning blow to our family"—and seemed almost cheerful, in dressy-Mummy clothes, high-heeled Italian boots, stooping to kiss Skyler good-bye, with a fierce little hug: "If I'm not home by the time your father brings you and your sister back after that ridiculous movie, Maria will be here of course, and will fix you an early supper. Be brave, sweetie! Be good."

For days—weeks?—Mummy had been "upset"—"agitated"—"deeply despondent"—"mad as hell." But now?

Skyler supposed that Mummy had scheduled this fateful Saturday to include a merry-go-round of appointments: a session at the Fair Hills Beauty Salon with Mummy's special hairstylist/colorist Ricki, luncheon with such loyal/supportive/Christian ladies as Mattie Higley, Frances Squires, and "Bibi" Metz at (maybe) the patrician Village Women's Club; a festive afternoon of shopping to follow in Fair Hills's "Fashion Square" or/and a "revivifying" session with Dr. Screed ("To remove creases from the soul, begin by removing creases from the face"), or a "revelatory" session with the Berlin-trained analyst/therapist/"trauma specialist" Dr. Helene Stadtskruller, whom many of Betsey Rampike's women acquaintances have recommended to her in this time of "crisis."

(Skyler has overheard his mother declaring bravely on the phone to one or another of her women friends that her "crisis" with her husband—

and her "trauma crisis therapy" with Dr. Stadtskruller—may turn out to be the "defining moment" of her entire life: "For which I will thank my deceitful husband, someday.")

Daddy had slept in a downstairs guest room the previous night and by the time Daddy stumbled into the kitchen in the morning Mummy had departed in the canary-yellow Buick without a backward glance or a message for Daddy, humming loudly to herself the militant hymn "Come, My Redeemer!" like a TV woman with a secret life.

Now in the Sylvan Glen dining room Daddy is looking slightly dazed, disoriented. Though this is a festive occasion for which Daddy is obliged to smile, repeatedly. Spiky-haired, bleary-eyed, with shadowy indentations beneath his eyes and a look you might interpret as regretful/remorseful—in a "state of nerves" Daddy nicked himself shaving that morning, and tiny coagulated blood-droplets are just visible on the underside of Daddy's jaw. But Daddy isn't wearing his comfortable Saturday-at-home clothes, rumpled khakis, sweatshirts and running shoes, in honor of the occasion Daddy has taken time to dress for "luncheon" at the Sylvan Glen Golf Club, in a navy blue blazer with brass buttons, a pale blue shirt unbuttoned at the throat (brown/graying crinkly chest hair showing), dark trousers with a reasonably sharp crease. Though Daddy is by nature a "warm"—"gregarious"—"charismatic" guy, like an ex-athlete, or a politician, yet Daddy is making an effort to focus his attention exclusively upon little Skyler and little Bliss, not allowing himself to glance up at other diners in the room, many of whom obviously know Bix Rampike and have been casting friendly/inquisitive glances in his direction. (Why is Bix alone with those adorable children? Where is the children's mother? What truth is there to the exciting rumor that the Rampikes are separating? *Is there another woman involved and if so—anyone we know?*)

Sucking on a finger, Bliss murmurs something Daddy can't comprehend. Skyler hesitantly translates: "Bliss is asking—don't you want to be our Daddy any longer?"

"Bliss! What a thing to say." Daddy stares at the child, appalled. Covertly Daddy glances up, to see if anyone has overheard. Daddy is shocked as if the little blond girl in a cherry-red mohair jumper and white blouse, hair prettily plaited (by Maria), a child-sized foam-rubber collar around her neck, has uttered something obscene. "Nothing could be further from the truth. My life as your father is my true life. What have I been trying to explain to you, honey? To you and your brother? Of course Daddy loves you—and Skyler—and Mummy, too. That's the whole point of this, that I *do*."

Flush-faced, trying not to become upset, Daddy spreads his fingers wide above the table like a magician whose magic trick isn't turning out quite as he'd expected and he's wondering has his audience noticed?

Skyler says, "Bliss feels bad, you don't want to live with us any more. Mummy said—"

"Never mind what Mummy said. I don't give a damn what Mummy said. Mummy's words—Mummy's thoughts—are 'atoms in the void'—* sheer whimsy, illogic. I wish I could shield you two impressionable kids from her! Sure I want to live with you and I hope that you will live with me—I mean, visit with me—weekends—'school recess'—when I'm not traveling so God-damned much. I hope your mother made it clear that this new arrangement of ours is temporary—what's called a 'temporary separation'—no way a 'divorce'—I'll be living less than an hour away in Paramus—that is, temporarily in Paramus—until things are settled with Scor, if I will be remaining at Scor—'Deputy Chief of Project Development/Domestic' is the promotion I've been offered—it's been a crazed few months, kids!—as I guess you've gathered: Scor, Univers, Vortex competing for your daddy. 'My kids come first with me,' is what I have told the negotiators. The thing is, Skyler, Bliss, sometimes, in a household, in a house, no matter how terrific the house is, and how much he loves the people in it, a man—a person—a daddy finds it hard to breathe." During this lengthy speech Daddy does seem to be breathing with effort, as if his head is stopped up.

"But Daddy," Skyler protests, "what does that mean? 'Can't breathe.'"

---

* *"Atoms in the void": Roman philosopher/poet Lucretius (98–55 B.C.). Bullshit-Bix couldn't have spent much quality time perusing Lucretius's* On the Nature of Things—*could he?—but must've picked up this catchphrase from one of the popular-science books scattered about the base of the brute taffy-colored leather chair in which, to Skyler's appalled fascination, you could discern the smooth-worn shallows of the man's buttocks if you so wished.*

"What does what mean, Skyler?" Daddy asks patiently. "'Can't breathe'—it means what it says."

Shrewd/brattish Skyler points out: "If you couldn't breathe, Daddy, you'd be dead."

"Well, Sky-boy. There you've said it."

Daddy laughs. Not a happy-Daddy laugh but a pained-Daddy laugh. And maybe, just perceptibly, Daddy's bleary-lidded eyes shift sidelong, to check out Rolex time.

(What time does laff-riot *Benji Goes Ballistic!* begin? Daddy has to keep tabs.)

Hesitantly Skyler asks, "Can we come with you, Daddy? To Para-mus?"

"Skyler, of course not! Your mother would be heartbroken, she'd never allow it. You're in school, and Bliss has her skating, and children remain in the custody of their mothers, mostly. Like puppies. You don't see puppies trailing after their daddies, do you?"

Skyler persists, "Some kids in my class, they live with their fathers. Or there's 'joint custody.' When people get divorced and then married again—"

"Whoa, Skyler! *Bat-ta.* We Rampikes are nowhere near 'joint custody' and for sure we are nowhere near 'married again.' Please don't speak of such things in front of your sister, look how you're upsetting her."

For most of the lunch, Bliss has been fidgeting with the clumsy foam-rubber collar around her neck, which chafes her sensitive skin. And Bliss has scarcely eaten her lunch. In a plaintive voice she asks, "Daddy? We could come to Para-mus with you now, couldn't we? I'm not skating now, until my fantim pain goes away, Mummy says."

Alarmed-Daddy swallows a mouthful of his drink and his big chunky teeth click against the glass. A quick glance out into the dining room, in dread of being closely observed, monitored. (For Fair Hills is a petri dish of rumor, Skyler knows from overhearing Mummy on the phone with her women friends.) "Sweetie, haven't I explained that my living quarters in Paramus will be temporary? It's a 'bachelor condo' in a sleek sterile high-rise just off the thunderous Garden State Parkway. No space for kids! No playgrounds! Plus, I'm still traveling most weekends. If I decide to leave Scor, I won't be staying in that condo; and if I remain with Scor, I won't be staying in that condo. If I'm promoted to 'Deputy Chief of Project Development' I will want a much larger residence, at least twice the size of our current house, kiddies! How'd you like to invite your little chums to visit a 'custom-built New Jersey country estate' with its own 'family rec center'—swimming pool (outdoor and in), gym, ice rink? For Bliss Rampike, her own custom-built ice rink."

How serious is Daddy? Is Daddy serious at all? Skyler recalls the hearty-mock-macho exuberance of mammoth Jeremiah Jericho in his tux, and Skyler feels a tinge of pain in his "weak" leg. Bliss is scratching at already-reddened skin beneath the foam-rubber collar that forces her small chin up at an awkward angle.

Bliss smiles uncertainly and in the hoarse little voice says, "When I'm strong enough to s-skate again, Daddy, will you come see me? Even if I don't win?"

"Why, honey! What a thing to ask. You know I will." Daddy reaches across the table to stroke his little daughter's cheek—a gesture meant to be tender, that causes Bliss to flinch. "Sweetie, I was on my way to watch you skate at Philadelphia, wasn't it?—Wilmington?—the deal that fell through, and the people from *People* cancelled the interview."

Daddy takes care not to sound reproachful, still Bliss feels the rebuke, and even Skyler, who has to be blameless, feels a new tinge of pain.

Unlike other girls her age—unlike boys her age, too—Bliss rarely cries. As Mummy says, there is something *perverse* and *unnerving* about Bliss as if she isn't a flesh-and-blood girl really but an ingeniously lifelike animated doll, the kind that, as soon as you glance away from it, casts you a look of sheer insolence. In public places, Bliss has learned to keep her expression little-girl-softly-rapt, shy-semi-smiling, and she has learned to be very still, for at any time someone is likely to be observing her (certainly true here in the Sylvan Glen dining room where easily half the female diners have been glancing wistfully/curiously in the direction of our table, at both big-shouldered spiky-haired Bix Rampike in his navy blue blazer and angelic little Bliss in her cherry-red mohair jumper and foam-rubber collar, though no one has been gauche enough yet to sidle over to the table to inquire in a sexy lilt *Where's Bethie?—or do I mean Betsey?*) Yet Bliss's mouth is twitching and so Skyler quickly intervenes, to deflect Daddy's attention. "You never took me deep-sea fishing in Palm Beach, Daddy! When we were at Grandmother Rampike's house waiting for you. We were just waiting and waiting, Daddy, you'd promised you would come stay with us, you'd rent a boat and take me marlin fishing, Daddy, and you never came, and nobody ever took me, Daddy. You promised."

"I did? Jesus."

Daddy seems genuinely surprised. Guilty-Daddy has obviously forgotten this extravagant promise entirely, made to his son, if made at all, in a casual aside, possibly when Daddy had been drinking, and not to be taken seriously; but Skyler seizes upon it, indignant as a criminal defense attorney whose case isn't going well. (Is it possible, Daddy has forgotten the notorious Palm Beach episode, acid-etched in stone in the memories of Skyler, Mummy, and Bliss?) Daddy stammers in confusion, "—maybe not 'deep-sea fishing,' Skyler—'marlin fishing'—but, this summer, if you and Bliss come visit me at the Jersey shore—or, no—" Daddy pauses, gnawing at his lower lip. What is Daddy saying? What the hell has Daddy acknowledged? Skyler knows beforehand that Mummy will want to interrogate her little-man spy about Daddy's offhand remarks, the more offhand, the more Mummy will wish to know, so Skyler is resolved not to listen too closely, but to fix flush-faced Daddy with a look of childish resentment shading into childish credulousness as Daddy plunges on, "—or, at my mother's place on Nantucket, we could go fishing for—what?—bluefish, bass? How's that sound, Skyler? And Bliss, you're welcome on board too, sweetie. You can bait our hooks."

With his mauled-at napkin, Daddy wipes at his mouth. Jesus, Daddy-bullshit is hard work, almost you forget.

"Dessert, kiddies? Or"—a frank glance at Daddy's Rolex—"maybe not."

This historic luncheon at the Sylvan Glen—the first time, as it will be the last time, Daddy has taken his children here—is nearly over. However arduous it has been for Bix Rampike, to have a sense of what it felt like to Skyler, and to Bliss, we must multiply the time-expended by two or three, or four, for young children experience time far more slowly than adults. (Let me confess: I can remember only in wayward patches what Skyler endured, and am at a loss trying to imagine how the ordeal felt to Bliss. In this document of loss and yearning, even Skyler's past is elusive to me as a moth battering itself against a high window: *all is guesswork.*) Despite his unease, signaled by a film of perspiration at his hairline, and a hint that he's sweated through his oxford-cloth shirt inside the blazer, Daddy has managed to devour nearly every crumb of his Sylvan Glen Ground-Round Special, gourmet French fries and avocado-cranberry garnish, and to drain two, or has it been three? fist-sized glasses of Johnnie Walker.

As Daddy frowns over the check, Skyler summons up his cocky-little-boy courage to ask something he has rehearsed asking Daddy for weeks: "Daddy? What is 'adult'ry'?" and Daddy glares up at him, blinking, an ox pecked by a sparrow, " 'Adult'ry'—did you say 'adultr'y,' Skyler? Jesus!" Skyler repeats his dumb-kid question and Daddy regains his Daddy-composure managing to smile: " 'Adult'ry' is for adults, Sky-boy. One day you'll know."

On this cryptic note the Rampikes might leave the Sylvan Glen dining room except out of nowhere a woman appears suddenly at their table, prompting Daddy to leap gallantly to his feet and exchange animated greetings that include, from the woman, a flirty-friendly kiss grazing Daddy's strong-boned jaw; effusive greetings to the adorable little Rampike children, wasting no time on the geeky boy but gushing over Bliss: "Oh! You are such a darling, Bliss! Look at this plaited hair! And your eyes!—so blue. We are all so terribly sorry that you injured your neck, we've read about it in *New Jersey Monthly* and we hope hope hope you will be completely recovered in time for the Little Miss Jersey Ice Princess competition, that is the biggie, isn't it! I've taken my daughter Tracey to see you skate, Bliss, and win, at the StarSkate competition, and we've seen film clips of you on NJN. Tracey is ten and has her heart set on 'competitive ice-skating'—just like you—you and Bei-Bei Chang are her idols—or do I mean, she is your idol?—Tracey will be *so thrilled* to learn that I've met you. If it isn't too much trouble, Bliss, and if your Daddy doesn't mind, if you could sign this for Tracey, we would all be *so grateful.*" With a grimly sweet little smile, as Mummy has trained her, Bliss unhesitatingly acquiesces, takes the slightly rumpled SYLVAN GLEN cocktail napkin from Mrs. Hennepin, and a sleek silver Univers Bio-Tech ballpoint pen from Daddy, and, clumsily, as the foam-rubber collar chafes against her tender neck, manages to print—

Bliss

as Skyler gazing on bemused feels a sudden rush of nausea, the sodden mass of undigested turkey club sandwich, greasy French fries, MoonGlo Kiddie Cocktail he'd sucked in its entirety through his straw lurching in his stomach *This will never end, we are trapped here forever, I can't protect her and I can't protect myself** as he rises from his chair with a stammered apology to Daddy he has to use the restroom, fast.

WISH I COULD END THIS EXCRUCIATINGLY PROTRACTED SCENE WITH THE RAMPIKES— big-shouldered Daddy, limping Skyler, limping-Bliss-with-foam-rubber-collar—gaily clambering into Daddy's Road Warrior in the Sylvan Glen parking lot, a chuff of whitish exhaust, enormous black-rubber tires bearing the vehicle and occupants off into the melee of Saturday afternoon traffic on the Great Road, there to Route 15, there to I-80 eastbound to the Garden State Parkway and soon, as in a dreamy film, there appears the faery-alabaster-white of the VastValley Mall, and laff-riot *Benji Goes Ballistic!*—all three Rampikes, big-père und little-kinder, devouring a tub of "hot buttery" popcorn and laughing their heads off like normal Americans who find themselves in "multiplex cinemas"—but, unluckily for Skyler and Bliss, the scene doesn't move in this direction at all. Wouldn't you think that there was a reliable script here: (Stricken-With-Guilt) Daddy Takes Kids to Lunch, Asshole Movie?—but in fact even as Skyler shakily

---

* Déjà vu *all over again, right? The alert reader shares with Skyler the sickening sensation that he's been here before? Well, yes. We have. For in the life of even a minor celebrity like my sister, events repeat themselves endlessly; even people—especially people—are endlessly recycled, say the same things, request the same things, thank you in exactly the same way. How much more nauseating, in the life of a major celebrity! (No one tells the truth about Major Celebrities: their lives are Major Bores.) This could not be what the German philosopher/precursor of Freud, existentialism, deconstruction Friedrich Nietzsche meant by Eternal Return, could it?—The Same God-Damned Things Happening Over Again.*

emerged from the first-floor men's room at the Sylvan Glen Golf Club surreptitiously wiping something chalky-acrid from his mouth, which mouth
he'd rinsed at a sink in the men's room, or tried to rinse, not very thoroughly because there wasn't time, and so smelling/tasting of vomit and
hoping (desperately) that no one would notice, as glowering Daddy tossed
Skyler's jacket at him—"What the hell took you so long in there, kid? Vita-
vita, pronto-*fast*," snapping big Daddy-fingers at the humiliated little boy;
to add to the air of confusion, so frequent in scenes in which Bix Rampike
looms large in the foreground, at this dramatic moment a woman suddenly
appeared in the club foyer, a familiar-looking dark-haired woman in a
sumptuous fox-fur "fun coat" with suede belt, suede trim, and stylish
high-heeled Italian boots very like Mummy's boots except more slender
and, on this woman, more stylish; a woman of about Mummy's age but with
a more sculpted, thinner face, charmingly breathless as if she'd been running to get to them: "Oh Bix! Did you think I'd be late?—*am* I late?"

Gallant-chiding Daddy, sexy-swaggering Bix Rampike said, teasing:
"Glenna, you're exactly on time. I asked you to arrive by one-thirty P.M.
assuming you'd get here by two P.M. and so you have."

Breathless Glenna in the sumptuous fun-fox-fur laughed in delight
like one who has been exposed, a fleeting-naked glimpse, both guilty and
guiltless: "Bix, you didn't! You *did*. Well, Bix. Then I don't need to apologize for being late, do I?"

As Skyler and Bliss looked on utterly confused by the adults' banter, in
the way that one who'd never seen a swiftly-played Ping-Pong game might
gape at the little white balls flying from right to left, left to right, the
woman greeted Daddy in a variant of the Fair Hills ritual: brushing her
lipsticked lips lightly against his cheek, quick little just-friends hug,
quick squeezing of hands. How clear it was to both Rampike children,
Daddy welcomed this ritual greeting more than he'd welcomed the greeting from (dowdy, mid-fortyish) Mrs. Hennepin a few minutes before.
"Kids, this is Mrs. O'Stryker, Mummy's friend. You know Mrs. O'Stryker,
don't you?" Skyler nodded vaguely, for he was sure he'd seen the showily
dressed dark-haired woman before; Bliss stared rudely, sucking at a finger. For in essence, Fair Hills women tended to resemble one another to
an uncanny degree. Amid the bustle of putting on coats, stepping out into

the mineral chill of late-winter New Jersey, rapid-fire exchange of ritual adult queries—"How is Betsey?"—"How is Howie?"—"How are *you*?"—"How are *you*?"—it seemed to be emerging, to the children's astonishment, that they were being led not to Daddy's Road Warrior but to Mrs. O'Stryker's Suburban Charger: they were going to be driven back to the house on Ravens Crest Drive by the glamorous Mrs. O'Stryker and not taken to the VastValley Cinemax by Daddy to see *Benji Goes Ballistic!* after all. Skyler protested, "Daddy, you promised! You promised you'd take us to see *Benji Goes Ballistic!*" and Daddy said, as if genuinely surprised, "*Benji* who? What's this?" and Skyler persisted, fierce as a Pomeranian snapping at a Saint Bernard's feet, "You promised, Daddy! You promised!" and Daddy said, edging toward the Road Warrior, keys in hand, "I'm sure I didn't, Skyler. The plan is that you and your sister are going to be driven home by Mrs. O'Stryker, as a favor to us, so that I can get in my Road Warrior here that's packed with my things and I can drive straight from here to the Parkway and to Paramus in just enough time before the company limo arrives to pick me up for my six-forty-eight P.M. flight from Newark to New Delhi." As Bliss numbly allowed herself to be led by one small mittened hand in the direction of Mrs. O'Stryker's vehicle, Skyler continued to protest, daring to wave a little fist at Daddy: "Daddy! Daddy! You promised! You can't break your promise—again!"

Precisely what happened next is not clear: in one version, red-faced Daddy swerved back in Skyler's direction, with an immense Daddy-fist thumped the brash kid on the side of his head WHONK! sending vibrations deep into the kid's cerebellum that are felt even to this very moment; in another version, the more probable version, red-faced Daddy merely brandished the Daddy-fist as if to thump the brash kid on the side of his head, grimly muttering: "We will discuss this matter at another time, Skyler. Man-to-man." In the meantime, Bliss had yanked her hand away from Mrs. O'Stryker's to run limping to Daddy crying, in a hoarse, piteous voice, "Daddy! Don't go away and leave us! Something bad will happen to us!" and Daddy, exasperated, but trying, for Bliss's sake, to speak tenderly, said, "Honey, I'm not going away and leaving you, I am only going away—temporarily. You will stay with Mummy, you love Mummy and soon you will be skating again and winning all sorts of prizes and on

TV and in *People* and when things are settled a little more sanely, and our interim of 'atoms in the void' has been resolved, you can come visit Daddy in Paramus, or—wherever. Bye now, kids! Love ya."

As Daddy clambered into the Road Warrior, gunned the motor and prepared to make a quick Daddy-getaway, in a sudden frenzy Bliss began clawing at the foam-rubber collar around her neck, kicking at Mrs. O'Stryker who tried to restrain her. "I want to come with you, Daddy! I don't want to be with Mummy all the time, I'm afraid of Mummy!" In the Road Warrior, Daddy was edging toward the exit, as Bliss teetered in front of the vehicle, but Daddy was able to steer the Road Warrior around Bliss, calling out his window: "Kids! Your Daddy loves you more than ever!— that's the bottom line."*

---

* *Jesus! Can you believe this utter bastard? (The melancholy answer is, yes. Somehow, the Rampike children did.)*

III

Little Miss
Ice Princess

You do not belong here

THREAT!

"HEY RAMPIKE."

In grade school, is anything more terrifying than being addressed by your surname, in a jeering-hostile boy-voice?

In the splattered mirror above a sink in the second-floor/east wing boys' restroom at Fair Hills Day School, there loomed a bony-faced yet cutely freckled fifth grader, taller than Skyler by several inches, his icy-blue eyes fixed upon Skyler's alarmed moist-brown eyes; his chin, triangular like a cobra's, thrust aggressively forward.

"I said—'Hey Rampike.' You deaf, asshole?"

Bravely Skyler smiled and, in the spirit of boy-surname-exchange, stammered what sounded like, "Hey, K-Klaus."

This response, far from provoking a smile in the other boy's stern face, or placating him, seemed to offend him. With both hands, Calvin Klaus, Jr. shoved against Skyler's back and pushed him against the rim of the sink, hard.

"'Ram-puke.' 'Sky-ler Ram-puke.' You and me, 'Ram-puke,' what're we s'posed to be, brothers?—*not*!" Like a riddle these reproachful words leapt from Calvin Klaus, Jr.'s mouth that was twisted in an oddly adult fury, and before Skyler could defend himself, or duck and scuttle away as he'd learned to do in grade-school scuffles over the years, Calvin grabbed him by a sleeve of his hunter-green Fair Hills Day school sweater, and slammed him against the tile wall as other boys looked on, startled, alarmed, or smiling in excited expectation of a fight.

A fight? At "prestigious"—"exclusive"—Fair Hills Day? Where expulsion was likely to be quick, and non-negotiable, and would adversely affect the expelled student's admission to one of the Higher Ivies, and by extension his entire life?

Skyler wasn't going to fight back, for Skyler knew when he was outmatched. (Skyler was invariably outmatched.) In the confusion of the moment Skyler was yet able to register that, just visible on his angry assailant's right wrist, beneath his shirt cuff, was a red-inked tattoo of some cryptic kind.

Might've been a skull. Or a dagger dripping blood.

Or a swastika.

Was this a gang attack? Was ten-year-old Calvin Klaus, Jr. a "gangsta" initiate, put up to attacking nine-year-old Skyler Rampike, a "target selected at random," by one of the school's (secret) gangs/fraternities?*

Skyler wanted to protest, wasn't Calvin his playdate friend?

Skyler wanted to protest *But I always liked you.*

There came Billy Durkee pushing his way through the ring of staring boys, to grab Calvin by the shoulder and haul him away from Skyler now cowering on the floor.

"Let him alone, Klaus—the kid's a cripple, for Christ's sake."[†]

S'POSED TO BE BROTHERS?—NOT!

At Fair Hills Day there'd come to be, among other short-lived juvenile slang, buzzwords, and profanities/obscenities culled from the cesspool of

---

[*] *Though all Fair Hills Day School students had to sign a contract binding them to the school's traditional honor code and to a promise not to enter into "any and all secret societies" at the school, yet there were rumored to be two predominant gangs/fraternities there: the Krippes (secret tattoos made with black ink) and the Bloods (secret tattoos made with red ink). In emulation of black-youth drug-dealing gangsta culture, purveyed to them largely through video games and TV, Skyler's Caucasian/upper-middle-class classmates sometimes tied nylon rags around their heads as well, when not on school property.*

[†] *Only the most abnormally retentive of readers will recall Billy Durkee of many pages back. This canny, math-minded, manipulative playdate of Skyler's who'd taught Skyler to play poker, to a degree, so that he could win from the naive kid somewhere in the range of thirty dollars over a period of months. At school, Billy greeted Skyler with a friendly-insincere smile but never invited Skyler to join him and his friends for lunch. Skyler had no idea whether Mummy had "given up on" Mrs. Durkee, who'd ceased answering Mummy's calls, or whether it was, in fact, Mummy who'd ceased calling Mrs. Durkee. The intense social lives of our parents!—mysterious, snarled, as taboo to contemplate as their sex lives.*

popular-TV culture, a clumsy sort of irony involving statements with *not!* attached. As in, I think you're really cool, Skyler?—*not!* Or, How'd you like a kiss, Skyler?—*not!*

Yet, recalling the attack in the restroom, and Calvin's mysterious remark, Skyler fixated on the word *brothers*.

S'posed to be brothers?

Brothers?

"Maybe Calvin likes me? Maybe Calvin wants to be 'brothers' with me?" It didn't seem likely. (Or did it?)

Hadn't Mildred Marrow spoken wistfully of having Skyler for a brother? So that, by a magical way of logic, clumsy unattractive Mildred might've been ice-skating prodigy Bliss Rampike?

So Skyler brooded for days following the attack, as Calvin Klaus stonily avoided him, and Skyler had not the courage to approach Calvin to ask what he'd meant. Nor did Skyler mention the attack to any adult. (Hide your bruises, as you hide your broken heart! Kids learn young. During this interim, when Daddy was no longer living with his family on Ravens Crest Drive but in a "condominium" that Skyler had yet to visit, Skyler was anxious to protect Mummy from further upset of any kind; and when Daddy called, as Daddy made a point of calling his family at least once a week, he certainly didn't want to upset/annoy Daddy by confessing he'd been jumped, thrown against a wall, utterly overcome in a boys' restroom at school, and before witnesses.)

In a previous chapter titled "Adventures in Playdates II," ten-year-old Calvin Klaus, Jr. appeared only briefly and was yanked away at once by the anxious author afflicted with a neurological variant of J.L.S. (Jumpy Leg Syndrome), who could not bear to dwell upon the impending crisis in the Rampike family. In fact, Skyler and Calvin had been brought to each other's homes upon several occasions, to watch popular boy-videos (*Chucky I, Chucky II, Chucky III, Terminator I, Terminator II, Robo-Boy Goes Ballistic! Revenge of Robo-Boy*, etc.) and to be overseen by one or another Maria. Skyler, the younger and less assertive of the two boys, had no idea if Calvin Klaus enjoyed these visits or merely tolerated them, as Fair Hills children tolerated so much for the sakes of their anxious mothers. All that I can recall of the numerous words these boys must've exchanged is *How're things at school with you* and the shrug-reply *Okay, I guess. You?*

For days following the unprovoked attack Skyler unobtrusively (he hoped) trailed Calvin Klaus at a discreet distance like a lovesick/kicked dog, when their class schedules allowed. In the school "dining room"—not a "cafeteria," for this was Fair Hills Day School where tuition rivaled tuition at the Higher Ivies—Skyler sat in a strategic position where he could unobtrusively (he hoped) observe the older boy with his fifth- and sixth-grade friends. How attractive Calvin seemed to Skyler, with his lean, angular, sharp-boned face, his "innocently" freckled skin like the skin of a boy in a Norman Rockwell illustration of bygone times in America, and his wolfish habit of lowering his head as he ate, or laughed. If from time to time Calvin glanced in Skyler's direction and saw Skyler watching him, quickly Calvin looked away. *The stalked has become the stalker.*

Wish I had time to pursue this theme. How we are drawn to and come to adore and will recall through decades of our lives teeming with a Milky Way of other individuals those very persons who, when we were children, terrorized us.

Sly Skyler arranged for Maria to pick him up after school an hour later so that he could linger at the rear of the school, and observe Calvin Klaus being picked up—usually by a Hispanic housekeeper though occasionally by his mother; Skyler's reward was to catch a glimpse, and more than a glimpse, of Morgan Klaus, a glamorous woman with prominent cheekbones, bemused icy-blue eyes, a throaty, lockjawed way of speaking, chic understated clothes and stylish crimped blond hair: the woman in the solarium!

Skyler shut his eyes. Heart pounding seeing Bix Rampike's outspread grasping fingers—Daddy's big fingers, that could grab, and squeeze, and shake if they wished—on the woman's back where the creamy-pale skin was bare—naked!—above the silky black dress.

Jesus are you beautiful
when can I see you
crazy for you   honey

Poor Mummy! Where Mummy was insecure, smiled too much, over-made-up and over-dressed, with her glossy helmet of "tinted" hair even a nine-year-old could see was unfashionable, Calvin Klaus's mother was so assured, so striking in her demeanor, you would scarcely notice that she wasn't beautiful. Some days, Mrs. Klaus showed up at the rear entrance of Fair Hills Day in a low-slung gleaming-avocado Porsche, other days, in suburban-soccer-mom style, for Calvin Klaus did play soccer after school, in a gleaming black Reaper S.U.V. large enough to accommodate half the soccer team though it was only Calvin who climbed into the S.U.V., sulky-faced. Once, Skyler overheard Mrs. Klaus call out to her son in that throaty-sexy drawl: "Come *on*. None of that passive-aggressive shit with *me*. I'm your damn mother, not your damn chauffeur."

There was a mother! *Crazy about you.*

Many times Skyler hoped that Morgan Klaus would take notice of him waiting alone by the curb, stoically bearing the weight of a book-crammed backpack on his narrow frame, still a "cute" kid by most maternal standards; but the bemused icy-blue eyes merely glided over him as if he were invisible; and Calvin Klaus, having caught on that Skyler was hoping to be seen, stonily ignored him. Only once, when Skyler was alone shivering in the rain when Mrs. Klaus pulled up in her massive Reaper, did his classmate's mother take notice of him, with a startled little smile: "Is that—Scooter? Rampike?" As Skyler stepped forward eager to be offered a ride home, and the hell with whoever was coming to pick him up in a few minutes, rudely Calvin elbowed him aside saying in a loud raw voice: "No, Mom. This isn't him."

The threat in Calvin Klaus's voice, Skyler wasn't about to dispute the issue of his identity.

"YOUR DAD AND MY MOM, THEY'RE 'SCREWING' EACH OTHER—KNOW WHAT that is?"

Screwing? A giant—screw? Skyler winced not wanting to think what this might mean.

Not sure, but Skyler mumbled yes.

"You *do*?"

Skyler mumbled yes sort of.

"It's like 'fucking'—know what that is?"

Fuck/fucking were words Bix Rampike sometimes muttered beneath his breath or, if really exasperated, out loud. *Fuck/fucking* had to be something that disgusted you, made you angry and impatient. Less certainly, Skyler mumbled yes maybe.

"Hell you know, punk. You don't know, I bet." Calvin Klaus laughed derisively. "*I* know. I've seen pictures."

Pictures of Bix Rampike and Morgan Klaus? Or—pictures of strangers? Gamely Skyler tried to recall the blocked-out images of Fox Hambruck's lurid "home movies." In Skyler's memory these had become confused with blocked-out images from Tyler McGreety's lurid autopsy photographs.

It was nineteen days after the assault in the boys' restroom. Finally, Calvin Klaus had cornered Skyler Rampike another time, in a deserted corridor at school. Though Skyler was frightened, expecting to be pummelled and slammed against a row of lockers, he had not tried to run from Calvin; he'd decided *I will be brave. Daddy would want this.* But Calvin seemed less angry with Skyler now as if in the intervening days he'd become burnt-out with anger. Or, having seen Skyler Rampike trailing him about with a wistful-doggy look, he'd decided to have mercy on him.

Skyler said impulsively, " 'Adult'ry.' That's what it is."

" 'Adult'ry.' What's that?"

"What they do." Skyler paused importantly. His voice quavered speaking of such matters. " 'Adults' not married to each other."

Calvin regarded Skyler quizzically. Among his classmates, Skyler was acquiring a reputation for being weird in an intriguing way: a freaky kid, given to odd mannerisms, gnomic outbursts, and brooding silences, but not only just a freak. It had become known that Skyler's father was a VIP in corporate business of some kind and that his younger sister, who was too special to attend school, was rapidly becoming a famous ice-skater to be seen on TV, her picture in the media. Vaguely it was rumored that Skyler had been a prodigy-gymnast who'd injured himself irrevocably in an accident. Vaguely it was rumored that the Rampikes were rich and had powerful political connections.

Who knew?—maybe Skyler Rampike himself was a genius? One of those legendary Fair Hills pupils whose I.Q.'s were said to be "off the charts" though their class work, for neurological/psychological/patho-psychopharmaceutological reasons, might seem but ordinary.

Sneering Calvin said, with the belligerence of a humanoid figure in a video game: "Yo smart-ass: what do adults *do*? You tell me."

Desperately Skyler tried to think: what *do* adults do? And *why*? As Calvin poked him in the chest with a bony forefinger, Skyler could see the boy's red-inked tattoos (a heart dripping blood, a dagger dripping blood) on the underside of his wrist.

If Calvin was a new initiate of the (secret, forbidden) Fair Hills Bloods, his issue with Skyler didn't appear to be gangsta-related, but personal.

"Okay, asshole. I'll explain. It's with"—Calvin said, gesturing at the crotch of his neat-pressed corduroy trousers, with a look both lewd and revulsed—"they 'screw' them together. The woman has a hole between her legs, the man's cock fits in. Sometimes, they make a baby. That white stuff out of your little punk cock—that's 'sea-man.' It gets shot up inside the woman like a spray can and can snag in there and turn into a baby, like a tapeworm that gets huge." Calvin paused, swallowing hard; you could see a fleeting nausea in his pale freckled face. "Sometimes, like with my mom I overheard talking once, on the phone with one of her women friends, they 'get rid of' this baby-thing, and it's flushed down the toilet like shit. Could've been you, or me—like, we could've been brothers—twins—see? If your dad and my mom had been screwing, a long time ago. And if they get married, we will be."

Calvin spoke excitedly, not very coherently. Skyler stared at him in dismay. A sudden roaring in his ears, he wasn't hearing this. Brothers?—twins? *Married?*

"You little punk, why're you looking at me like that?" Calvin said, flaring up. "Like you don't believe me? My mom wants to get a divorce from my poor asshole-dad, who's essentially clueless in all this, and marry your dad, except your dad is moved away from Fair Hills, I guess? 'Bix Rampike'—used to be some kind of big-deal football player? My dad's got guns, see. And my mom gets drunk, and mean, and tells him all kinds of things to make him mad at her, your dad better watch out somebody doesn't blow off his head." Now Calvin did shove Skyler back against the row of lockers, though not hard: you might say, companionably. His breath was warm and anguished in Skyler's face. "If my dad doesn't, maybe I will."*

---

* *Wow! Sounds like ten-year-old Calvin Klaus is threatening to blow off Bix Rampike's head, doesn't it? And by telling Skyler beforehand, he's making Skyler complicit in the act; maybe even, in moral terms, a co-conspirator. In a work of fiction, such an utterance would presage violence to come, or at least attempted violence; in this document, though Calvin Klaus blurted out exactly these words, nothing will come of the distraught boy's threat. Skyler went away shaken, with a premonition that something very bad was to happen to someone in his family, and that it would be his father's fault; and that there was nothing to be done about it for it lay in the province of "adults"—"adult'ry"—and was beyond his control.*

MUMMY'S MAN FRIENDS?

. . . WOMAN HAS A HOLE BETWEEN HER LEGS, THE MAN'S COCK FITS IN.
So this is what adults *do*?
There was a crude simplicity about it. A kind of geometry.
Yet Skyler brooded, unconvinced.
For *why*?

"WHY, BETSEY RAMPIKE. DARLIN', HOW ARE *YOU*?"
In Fair Hills, New Jersey, as in every upscale American-suburban community, there is a distinctive male type: hearty, bluff, jovial, with cold blue eyes and a bone-crushing handshake. Short-legged, barrel-chested. One of those men whose skin pinkens as their hair—crew cut, to disguise its thinness—whitens. Bix Rampike moved easily with such men with whom he felt some kinship yet knew himself to be superior (taller and better-fit, good-looking, younger) but Betsey Rampike did not for Betsey Rampike was inclined to believe such men when they swooped upon her gallantly at social gatherings to which (bravely, defiantly) she'd come alone in the wake of her husband's departure, seizing her soft pliable hand, saying, "Betsey. You are looking damn beautiful. Where the hell have you been keeping yourself?"

In the Rampikes' vast and ever-shifting circle of social acquaintances, it was Tigger Burr who fit this profile. So far as brooding Skyler knew, the burly white-haired Mr. Burr was married and had high-school-age children of whom one was Jimbo Burr, a senior at Fair Hills Day whom younger boys knew to avoid for his playful custom of grinding his knuckles against their heads, or shoving them into walls, so why was Mr. Burr so frequently "dropping by" the house to see Mummy, why was Mummy eager to go out with Mr. Burr "for drinks"—"maybe an early, light supper" at the Fair Hills Inn; why was Mummy so often on the phone, laughing shrilly as if being tickled: "Tigger, I can't. Not tonight. I've got the children. I've been with Bliss all day at the rink and seeing doctors and—there's Skyler—my son, I've told you: Sky-ler—he's nine and very needy and so I can't—I shouldn't—Well, just for a little while, I guess. But I shouldn't."

Needy! Skyler was *not*.

Skyler made inquiries at school and learned that Jimbo Burr's dad owned Burr Real Estate & Home Insurance and was in the condition of *being separated* from his wife; which condition resembled Bix Rampike's so was that the connection? Skyler stayed up late to watch for Mummy returning from her "early evenings" with Mr. Burr ascending the stairs of the mostly darkened house with exacting care, in her stocking feet and carrying her high-heeled shoes, murmuring to herself, laughing under her breath, or making a harsh *tsking!* sound as if in disapproval, pausing to sway at the top of the stairs and press a hand against her forehead as if overcome by a spell of dizziness. "Skyler! What on earth are you doing up? I told Maria to put you to bed by nine and give you your medication and make sure that you stayed in bed."

"Mummy, are you drunk?"

"Skyler! What! That's a terrible thing to say to your own mother."

"Are you?"

Mummy slapped at Skyler, lurched and would have fallen except Skyler bravely took the brunt of his mother's warmly soft startled weight, and held her upright and tremulous with indignation. It was very late for a weekday night: past midnight. In the nursery Bliss was whimpering in her sleep and downstairs in the cave-like housekeeper's room off the kitchen Maria had fallen asleep watching the midget TV that came with the room. A sweet pungent scent of Mummy's breath, Mummy's special perfume, and Mummy's special Mummy-smell wafted to Skyler's nostrils. "Yesss I am drunk. I am drunk with hope, and I am drunk with happiness. I am drunk with the freedom of being a woman, at last."

Skyler helped Mummy to bed. Mummy leaned heavily on Skyler as they stumbled along. Skyler was barefoot, and in pajamas. A terrifying thought came to Skyler as Mummy pushed open the door to the bedroom *What if Daddy is back? What if Daddy sees Mummy like this?* but the bedroom was empty.

"Mummy, Mr. Burr is married."

"And so am I, smarty."

"You aren't going to marry Mr. Burr, Mummy, are you?"

"And what if I was? What has Mummy's 'love-life' to do with *you*?"

" 'Cause I don't want to be Jimbo Burr's twin brother, Mummy. I'll run away if I have to be."

Mummy was sitting on the edge of the massive four-poster bed trying to catch her breath. Mummy's hair was in her face and her lipstick was smeared. Mummy stared at Skyler with a look of commingled guilt and defiance. " 'Jimbo Burr's twin brother'—? What on earth are you talking about, Skyler?"

"I hate him, Mummy. I hate him so much. Please say you won't marry Mr. Burr, Mummy, *please.*"

Skyler began to cry, and Mummy's heart melted, and Mummy allowed her *little man* to sleep with her in the enormous king-sized bed for the first time in a very long time; and ever after this night, Tigger Burr never "dropped by" the Rampikes' house again.*

And there was Roddy McDermid.

One of those wonderful bearded fathers other children have, big, blustery and rough but affectionate, like a bear: except not the real kind which would more resemble Bix Rampike, that would tear off your face with his teeth, but the cuddly kind. Mr. McDermid had a bushy beard streaked with gray that looked as if small birds might nest in it, and Mr. McDermid wore leather sandals with wool socks in the coldest weather, and Mr. McDermid was a research ecologist for the State of New Jersey as

---

*Though not because of this maudlin if heartfelt scene! In a work of fiction, her little man's tearful pleading would have been the precipitating factor in Mummy breaking off her friendship with barrel-chested Tigger Burr; in this case, to Mummy's disappointment, Tigger Burr seemed simply to lose interest in her, never called her again or returned her calls. (Maybe because, from Tigger Burr's canny perspective, Bix Rampike's abandoned wife was too needy.)

well as a member of the Fair Hills Chamber Orchestra whose instrument was the oboe. Mr. McDermid's daughter Priscilla was in Skyler's fifth-grade class at Fair Hills Day School and so it was, Mummy and Mr. McDermid met at Open House, and soon thereafter it happened that Mummy arranged for Priscilla McDermid to come to the Rampikes' house for a playdate with Skyler, soon afterward followed by a reciprocal playdate visit at the McDermids' house which was a smallish brick residence on an undistinguished street in the Village of Fair Hills where Betsey Rampike knew no one; yet, to Skyler's surprise, Mummy seemed to like the McDermids, both Mr. McDermid and Mrs. McDermid, who seemed to like Mummy in return; unless the McDermids felt sorry for Mummy who lived in so expensive a house in such a prestigious neighborhood of Fair Hills yet seemed to have no one to call but Mr. McDermid at his office, in a plaintive voice asking could Roddy please drop by the house on his way home from work to check out a "strange beeping thing" in one of the guest rooms: a faulty carbon monoxide detector, its battery dead, emitting a high-pitched squeak like a bat. In September, Mummy took Skyler and Bliss to a performance of the Fair Hills Chamber Orchestra in the public school, to watch Mr. McDermid blow away at his oboe and to talk and laugh with him at the punch-bowl reception afterward. How jealous Skyler was of his classmate Priscilla who seemed unaware that her big bear-like bewhiskered father was so wonderful! Skyler came close to fainting when Mr. McDermid stooped to give him a bear-hug—"Good night, son!"—after the McDermids invited Mummy, Bliss, and Skyler over for a Chinese take-out supper in their kitchen. Next day Skyler said wistfully to Bliss, "Maybe Mr. McDermid could be Mummy's new husband, and our new daddy," but Bliss said, not so much as glancing away from the giant wall TV screen where the Ring of Kerry Irish Dance Troupe in their scoop-necked velvet skating dresses and identical glittering tiaras were performing yet another time, "No. Daddy is our daddy forever."

REDEEMED!

> . . . as if a light had shone upon me out of the darkness. And a light is shining within me, where there had been but darkness. And wherever I go whether I am recognized as the mother of Bliss Rampike or whether I am but anonymous, I am bathed in this radiance which is the gift of God. *I am redeemed.*
>
> —Betsey Rampike, quoted in "Child-Prodigy Figure Ice Skater Bliss Rampike and Mother-Manager," *People*, October 14, 1996.

> . . . so grateful! The past several months, as those of you know, who follow my daughter's career, a shadow lay upon us, for Bliss was stricken with a mysterious ailment, a "phantom pain" that threatened to destroy her career. Since we had to cancel the Little Miss Royale competition last spring, when I realized that Bliss was skating with pain, not a day passed without Bliss pleading with me to allow her back on the ice: "The pain is all gone, Mummy! I promise." Of course, this brave little girl was not allowed anywhere near the ice, for these months were to be a time of "healing" and now, through the grace of God, the pain has been taken from us, and Bliss has resumed her career. *We are so grateful.*
>
> —Betsey Rampike, from "Up Close & Personal in New Jersey," interview, New Jersey Network TV, October 22, 1996.

KNOW WHAT I WISH? THAT *MY SISTER, MY LOVE: THE INTIMATE STORY OF Skyler Rampike* wasn't a (linear) document agonizingly comprised of words, but a film, or a film-collage, or a "video installation" so that at this point I could unleash a torrent of images, film clips, TV footage to speed up the (gut-twisting) narrative. *Something very bad is going to happen to someone in the Rampike family and there is nothing Skyler can do about it.*

Which is why the narrative is gut-twisting, and obsessively slow-paced: Skyler (nineteen years old) can't bear to return to ever-more traumatic scenes in the life of Skyler (nine years old) *and yet he/I must.*

In a visual document, all the author has to do is assemble, or reassemble, visual documents: he doesn't have to create a God-damned thing, except a few captions here and there. Or maybe a voice-over, to be spoken by a professional. As in the (unauthorized/unconscionable) ABC documentary *The Making and Unmaking of a Child Prodigy: The Bliss Rampike Story* of February 1999, ninety-eight percent of the material was taken from pre-existing sources, film clips, photographs etc. in the public domain. In my version, only a few selected—"symbolic"—images would be used, and only a few of the most "revealing" interviews with my mother like those in *People* and on NJN-TV excerpted at the start of this chapter.

The coveted *People* interview finally came through, to Mummy's delight, after Bliss returned in triumph to competitive skating in October 1996 and won the Tiny Miss Princess title at the Golden Skate Challenge in Hartford, Connecticut. The interview/feature covered nearly four pages in the obscenely popular (millions of readers? billions?) weekly magazine, including breathtaking photos of Bliss skating—in mid-leap, and in mid-spin—and a highly flattering portrait of Mother-Manager Betsey Rampike in a "prayerful mood" at rink-side. When the interview appeared, Mummy received countless telephone calls: "You'd think that 'Betsey Rampike' had scarcely existed, before *People*." Mummy spoke wryly, yet wiped away a tear for Mummy was deeply moved.

Celebrity! Attention! At Fair Hills Day where previously Skyler Rampike moved invisibly amid his more ontologically defined classmates and, in general, passed beneath the radar of genial Headmaster Pearce Hannity III, suddenly Skyler was being singled out for attention: why? Even older boys rumored to belong to (secret, forbidden) "gangs" who sported (secret, forbidden) inked tattoos on the insides of their wrists singled him out in the corridors: "Yo Rampike! Lookin' cool." Even the prettiest, most popular girls sought him out, in the cafeteria for instance: "Skyler? That's your name, isn't it?—'Skyler'? Would you and your sister Bliss like to come over to my house sometime, to visit? Say yes!" Yet more alarmingly, there came Headmaster Hannity swooping at Skyler to shake his startled hand: "Son, you and your parents have a standing invitation to 'tea with Headmaster'—'high tea'—'sherry provided as well'—in my residence on campus—five P.M., Sundays. A small—select!—circle of senior faculty, parents and students, trustees, donors. Our office will send out invitations but in the meantime, son, please inform your parents. 'Tea with Headmaster' will celebrate its one-hundred-fiftieth anniversary next Sunday."

Should be ashamed to admit it, and I am, but the fact is: Skyler felt a glow of pride, so singled out. As he'd felt when he'd struggled on the snaky-skinned gym mat and wiry little Vassily had said with forced enthusiasm Ver-ry good, Skeel-er! Each small step is a step to success, yes?

Couldn't wait to tell Mummy his good news and, when Daddy next called, and asked to speak to Sky-boy, to tell Daddy; though knowing that the elder Rampikes were probably too busy for "tea with Headmaster."

(And where was Daddy living now? No longer in Paramus, for Daddy had accepted the "fantastic" offer from Univers Bio-Tech, Inc., whose lavish sprawling corporate headquarters were in Univers, New Jersey, eleven miles north and east of Fair Hills.)

(And did Daddy want to divorce Mummy, and marry Calvin Klaus, Jr.'s crimped-blond mother, in this way providing Skyler with a slightly older, sexy gangsta-brother?—Skyler had not a clue.)

(For Mummy, taken up with "professional duties" regarding Bliss's career, away from the house much of the time and, when home, usually on the telephone, refused to discuss the children's father with them.)

Not long after the *People* interview, Mummy received a call from Sckulhorne relatives in Hagarstown, New York. Skyler overheard Mummy break off the conversation saying calmly and quietly and with such dignity, Daddy would surely have been impressed: "Visit *us*? But why? My daughter doesn't know any of you and, after so long, I don't either."

And calmly then Mummy replaced the phone receiver, and smiled.

The thrill of revenge! Like an electric current the delicious sensation passed through Skyler, too.*

SKYLER? WILL DADDY EVER COME BACK TO LIVE WITH US AGAIN?

Maybe. If you start skating again, and win.

MUST'VE BEEN THE PRESCRIPTION ZOMIX, OR THE SUPERGROW/HI-CON Vit-C/CAGHC shots each Friday morning in Dr. Muddick's office, unless it was the anti-convulsant Serenex, or the anti-depressant Excelsia, or Bliss's new psychotherapist Dr. Rapp whose specialty was child-prodigy athletes, or Bliss's new acupuncturist/nutritionist Kai Kui whom Mummy's women friends so highly recommended, or maybe it was the prospect of working with her new trainer Anastasia Kovitski (Olympic silver medalist 1992, U.S. Women's Figure Skating Champion 1992–93) and, for the first time, a choreographer, the Uzbekistan-born Pytor Skakalov, or some magical combination of all of these, for by September 1996 it seemed that Bliss's debilitating phantom pain had

---

*The thrill of revenge! *Skyler had no idea why his mother who believed herself to be the warmest, most generous and "Christian" of women, and who in interviews spoke of her "devotion to her family," seemed to be estranged from her "well-to-do"—"socially prominent"—relatives living in remote Hagarstown, New York, on the Canadian border which Skyler imagined as a landscape heaped with snow and essentially uninhabitable. Wouldn't you think that this allegedly precocious kid might've been curious, as a normal kid would have been, why he had only one grandmother (chill-eyed and pike-mouthed) and not two, like other children; and no grandfathers at all; and, on Mummy's side of the family, no aunts, uncles, cousins. Among the Rampikes, who were Daddy's family, there were too many relatives to keep track of and for these, Daddy was guarded in his affections: "A family shares DNA. That is a biological fact. But there is 'sibling rivalry'—you could argue, the greatest force in* Homo sapiens. *As our Muslim brethren say, 'My brother, my cousin, and me against you—my brother and me against my cousin—and me against my brother.' That's the bottom line, son."*

lifted from her, or nearly; she'd regained the weight she'd lost, through "finicky" eating; and even the frequency of her nighttime "accidents" had lessened.

HIGHLIGHTS OF THAT DAZZLING *COMEBACK SEASON*:

- The Great Lakes Girls Skate Festival in Buffalo, New York, where, in October, in a red-sequined, abbreviated skating dress that reflected the spotlight like flame, Bliss Rampike skated to the tempestuous notes of Stravinsky's *The Firebird* and placed second in the Girls' Novice Division with a score of 5.6 out of 6.

- The Golden Skate Girls' Challenge in Hartford, Connecticut, where in late October in a gingham "Gretel" costume with a tight-laced bodice, white milkmaid cap on her plaited blond hair and a peep of white-lace panties flashing beneath, Bliss Rampike skated to the thumping melody of Humperdinck's *Hansel and Gretel* winning the hearts of the judges as she won the hearts of the audience with her exquisite glides and spins (flying spin/jump spin/traveling spin) to win the coveted title Tiny Miss Golden Skate Princess 1996 with a score of 5.8 out of 6.

- The All-American-Girl Ice Jubilee in Bangor, Maine, in early November where in a "Vegas showgirl" costume of glittering white sequins and filmy white feathers, long tight sleeves with ermine-trimmed wrists, stardust in her "upswept" hair and on her eyelids, and crimson-lace panties teasingly visible beneath, Bliss Rampike ravished both judges and audience with a skate-dance performance of that sultry-tango pop-American classic "Kiss of Fire,"* another time placing first in the "Little Miss" Division with a score of 5.9 out of 6.

---

* *"Kiss of Fire": the meretricious but crowd-pleasing influence of the suave Uzbekistan choreographer whom Mummy hired in the summer of 1996 to work with Bliss's new trainer Anastasia*

JESUS THANK YOU!

Thank you Jesus for taking Bliss's pain from her!

If Bliss's pain should come again, Jesus give Bliss's pain to me, to spare Bliss. For I am Bliss Rampike's mother, and that is my blessing. For all the days of our lives to come AMEN.

Kovitski and with whom for a brief while during the longer, so very devasttating period when Daddy was living away from us, Mummy seemed to be "taken with." In a more lewd, gossipy memoir the obviously jealous/spiteful Skyler would speak of oily Pytor Skakalov in withering terms; there would be at least one painful scene in which Skyler, having glimpsed Mummy and Skakalov together in a private moment, appeals to her: "What if Daddy comes back and sees you with him? What if Daddy comes to the ice rink to surprise us, and sees you with him, and goes away again? Mum-my!"

ON ICE MOUNTAIN

NOT *WILL SOMETHING BAD HAPPEN?* BUT *WHEN WILL IT HAPPEN?* HAD BE-
come fixed inside Skyler's head like something rattling in the wind.

For so Calvin Klaus* had promised. Or someone had promised.

Though the fall of 1996 was a season of surprises and these were mostly
good surprises and "More to come!—maybe" as Mummy said mysteriously. Upcoming on Bliss's skating schedule was the most coveted of
northeastern skating competitions for girls, for the winners of the Miss
Jersey Ice Challenge—Miss Jersey Ice Princess and Little Miss Jersey Ice
Princess—would be awarded with modeling contracts with Junior Elite
Skates and Skating Equipment, Inc., which meant glossy advertisements
in high-circulation magazines like *Teen People*, *Teen World*, *Teen Life* and on
selected cable channels.

"Not that we are skating for money. Or fame."

So Mummy insisted, and so Mummy seemed to believe.

"But if we begin to make a little money—at last!—to help defray expenses, we can plan for the future: Skate America, Grand Prix America,

---

*Calvin Klaus! To this very hour, the name, classy-chic, sexy-haughty, makes me shiver with
excitement, apprehension, or—is it dread? In November 1996, at the approximate time of the
events transcribed in this chapter, Skyler was (secretly) devastated to learn that his older classmate had been either expelled from Fair Hills Day for being a member of a "secret society" or had
been taken out of school by his concerned parents, following an attempt to (1) run away from
home, taking one of his father's handguns with him, or (2) "do injury" to himself with one of his
father's handguns. Abruptly then this troubled brother of Skyler's disappeared from Skyler's life
as Skyler's rapt stolen glimpses of the crimped-blond Morgan Klaus disappeared from his life
later to reappear, in erotic scenes involving an adult man resembling Bix Rampike, in Skyler's
pubescent dreams.*

U.S. Girls' Skating Championships, U.S. Olympics. 'Follow your dream'—is our belief—'wherever it will lead.' "

Mummy had been speaking to Bliss in the way in which Mummy often spoke to Bliss in a murmurous stream of words as if thinking out loud to which Bliss scarcely seemed to listen, or had no need to listen, while Skyler, if he happened to wander into earshot, couldn't help asking: " 'Follow your dream'—how, Mummy? Can you see a dream? Is it like a butterfly or something, you can see flying, and you can follow it?"

Such questions were posed by Skyler in utter seriousness though masked by a smart-alecky drawl acquired at Fair Hills Day from gangsta classmates.

(In fall 1996, Skyler was now in fifth grade. Though his tenth birthday would not be until March 1997. And Bliss, not enrolled in any school, and at this time "between tutors," was six years, ten months old.)

Patiently Mummy said, "A dream is a 'vision,' Skyler. A dream is within the soul, where God speaks to us." Mummy paused. Mummy took care not to betray her irritation at Skyler's question. Mummy amended, "—to some of us."

To some of us. Skyler caught this.

"Will God speak to me, Mummy?"

"Ask Him!"

Gaily Mummy laughed. On the sofa beside Mummy, sleepy from skating practice that afternoon and struggling to read a children's picture book, Bliss did not glance up.

Bliss's way of reading involved such physical effort, you could feel the strain as she moved her forefinger beneath lines of type and moved her lips to shape phantom letters.

Cagey Skyler backtracked: "What is 'defray expenses,' Mummy?"

A frown line appeared between Mummy's eyebrows. Carefully Mummy said, " 'Defray' means to 'lessen'—'lessen expenses.' When we win the Little Miss Jersey Ice Princess title, and Bliss begins to model for Elite Skates, and acquires 'national exposure,' we will be able to make money at last, and when we do, your father can't continue to object."

Your father. This was a rare utterance. Not frequently did Mummy speak such painful words as *your father* and not in months had Mummy spoken the words *Daddy*, *Bix*, or *my husband*.

At least, not that Skyler had heard. What Mummy spoke of in private phone conversations, shut away in her private room with the door locked, Skyler had no idea.

"What about Daddy, Mummy? Why does he 'object'?"

"Ask him."

This was cruel! How ask *your father* when Skyler hadn't glimpsed his father in weeks and when Daddy called to speak to "Sky-boy" and "my bestest-best li'l Bliss," you could not interrupt the tumult of earnest-Daddy words to ask such a question.

"Because Bliss's skating is expensive? *Is* it expensive? How much does it cost a year? A thousand dollars? A million?"*

"Your sister's skating is an investment, Skyler! An investment is something that will pay off in the future and will repay the initial cost many, many times." Mummy paused, pressing a row of red-polished nails to her breast, for Mummy had begun to speak excitedly as if being interviewed by an unfriendly or obtuse interviewer. "But, as I've said—we don't skate for money, and we don't skate for fame."

Quizzically Bliss looked up from *Three Little Bears on Ice Mountain* to say, "My skating doesn't cost anything, Skyler. It's what God wants me to do. It isn't like other things that cost money, Skyler. It's special."

Seeing the warning look in Mummy's warm moist brown eyes, smart-alecky Skyler smartly backed off.

---

* *And what do you think it might have cost ten years ago to launch a "child-prodigy" athlete into the shark-infested sea of so-called amateur sports? ("Amateur" being a handy euphemism for pre-professional.) By my estimate, considering salaries paid to Bliss's ever-growing/ever-shifting "staff" (trainer, choreographer, Mummy's personal assistants and PR persons et al.), the ever-growing/ever-shifting roster of expensive health-care professionals (Muddick, Bohr-Mandrake, Rapp et al.), fees to the Halcyon rink and entry fees to numerous skating competitions, plus expenses for costumes, makeup, hairstyling, travel and hotels, and health insurance and life insurance premiums (by fall/winter 1996, Bliss Rampike was insured for $3 million), the sum is approximately $200,000.*

THE GOOD SURPRISE I

FROM OVERHEAD, SUGARY-DEAFENING TCHAIKOVSKY: "SLEEPING BEAUTY Waltz." The large ice rink glitters reflecting myriad shifting lights. It's the evening of November 30, 1996. The long-awaited Miss Jersey Ice Challenge at the Newark War Memorial rink, Newark, New Jersey.

Déjà vu! Like a smell of ammonia.

Yet: Skyler is as anxious this time as he'd been the first time. As he is each time his younger sister skates competitively in such arenas, before such crowds. For that is the curse of *déjà vu*: though you've lived it before, you can't remember how it turned out. Not even whether you survived.

"SKYLER? SIT WITH YOUR SISTER, DARLING. MUMMY WILL BE *RIGHT* *back."*

Gaily kissing Skyler on his puppy-dog nose. Leaving the faintest smear of lipstick so (unbeknownst to him) Bliss Rampike's big brother will resemble a dwarf clown.

This beautiful rink! Dazzling rink! No expense has been spared by ELITE SKATES & SKATING, thriving subsidiary of ELITE SPORTS EQUIPMENT INTERNATIONAL. Festooning the rink are banks of waxy white lilies and bloodred roses intricately folded as female genitals in bud; and, inside the rink, clearly visible across the bluish ice, are posters advertising ELITE SKATES & SKATING ELITE SKATES & SKATING ELITE SKATES & SKATING in massive bloodred letters circling the rink like a snake swallowing its own tail.

This long-awaited evening, twenty-two girls aged six to eighteen representing the crème de la crème of girls' amateur figure skating in New

Jersey will be energetically competing for two titles: Miss Jersey Ice Princess 1996 (the older category), and Little Miss Jersey Ice Princess 1996 (the younger category). Since the competition of older girl-skaters is more eagerly awaited, the younger competition comes first. Such excitement! Anticipation! Tension in the air like the tension before an electrical storm! What would America be, without such breathless moments? Such urgent moments? Such almost-can't-bear-it moments? Everywhere in the arena the audience is becoming ever more restless, excited. If you had the prurient cast of mind—as Skyler, prepubescent dwarf-clown certainly does not, to detect such undercurrents—you might sense a sexual urgency here in the flushed cheeks of the females, the shifty eyes of the males. Enormous families—"extended" it seems—of swarthy-skinned ethnic identities are sprawled in rows of seats and are occupied in passing refreshments avidly among themselves. The audience appears to be mostly female—all ages, all sizes, all skin-tones—though you might see, scattered about the arena, men of varying ages as well, though predominantly middle-aged. Some of these men are clearly relatives of the girl-skaters, seated with the sprawling families, while others, hoping to be inconspicuous, even as they cradle cameras, camcorders, and binoculars in their laps, appear to be alone. For invariably at such young-innocent-girl skating competitions there are such male spectators.

Is he here? Gunther Ruscha? Has to be here at the Newark ice rink on the evening of November 30, 1996, but where?

Don't expect me to scan the seething crowd like a TV camera, my guts are too twisted. I am too anxious though this "historic" evening is long past and the terrifying sensation of *déjà vu* like a whiff of ammonia shouldn't incapacitate me now. We can assume, radish-haired pasty-skinned Gunther Ruscha was in the audience that evening, in one of the front-row seats, eager to cheer on his adored Bliss Rampike but if Skyler chanced to see him, Skyler will not remember.

Gripping his sister's hand. Thinking *Something bad will happen. When?*

Maybe Skyler can prevent it. Skyler is Mummy's *little man*—Bliss's *big brother*—isn't he?

Sitting protectively close to Bliss in their second-row seats in the reserved section of the arena where their mother settled them before hurrying off. Noise in the vast arena is increasing exponentially,* rebounding from the domed ceiling high overhead. In the crowded aisles vendors are hawking the usual neon-bright beverages and sleek-turd sausages, fuchsia-colored MISS JERSEY ICE PRINCESS 1996 velour T-shirts, tank tops, and caps, and glossy "picture" programs selling for three dollars. Skyler is holding Bliss's cold little hand to comfort her but Bliss, lost in unfathomable thought, barely responds. Unlike her rivals, the other girl-skaters, who thrive upon the attention of the crowd, Bliss is stricken with shyness in public places; in a kind of panicked catatonia when not in her skates, and on the ice. Through this long day, Bliss has been quiet. On the drive to Newark in Mummy's flashy new lipstick-red Renegade XXL minivan, Bliss was very quiet while Mummy spoke to her in a crooning murmur, as Mummy did at such times, assuring her *You will skate perfectly, you will perform perfectly, Jesus has decreed it, Jesus has taken our earthly pain from us and replaced it with His grace.* (And what does Skyler think of these statements of Mummy's, that seem to have increased exponentially in the weeks/months since Daddy moved out of the house? Is Skyler a Christian boy, does Skyler "believe"? In the Rampike household in which, in times of crisis, such sister-Christians as Mattie Higley are likely to be comforting Mummy, it is difficult not to "believe"—in something. Though canny Skyler has decided that praying is mostly talking to yourself, preferably under your breath, and not expecting God to answer.)

Skyler leafs through the glossy program to page eleven where there's an eye-catching publicity photo of his sister, above the caption

BLISS RAMPIKE, 6

TOTS-ON-ICE DEBUTANTE 1994–MISS GOLDEN SKATE PRINCESS 1996

Because Bliss would have difficulty reading the bracketed quote attributed to her, Skyler reads it aloud:

* *"Exponentially." Classy word, eh? You will find "exponentially" selectively employed in only the very best prose, by individuals who have not a glimmer of its actual meaning, or whether this meaning applies to the situation at hand. (God, I hate writing! One damned poly after another, to make the reader think* Hey! this is real; this really happened; glad it didn't happen to me.)

I love ice-skating! I am SO HAPPY ice-skating! My mommy bought me my first white kidskin Junior Miss Elite skates (size one!) when I was four years old and took me to the ice rink and said, "There you go!"

Skyler wonders: Is this so? He's sure he has never heard his sister say anything resembling these words.

Bliss is staring at the glossy publicity photo of BLISS RAMPIKE in the program. A shyly/coyly smiling little girl who looks more like four years old than six, with wide dark-blue eyes and thick eyelashes, a rosebud smile, platinum blond hair falling in a wavy cascade to her narrow shoulders. The girl is posing on the ice, in beautiful white kidskin Junior Miss Elite ice skates and in the new strawberry satin-and-sequin skating dress with its perky ballerina tulle skirt, a snug bodice, flesh-colored fishnet stockings and just a peek of white-lace panties beneath. This is the "designer" costume in which Bliss will be skating in just a few minutes, to the sexy-peppy disco beat "Do What Feels Right" (an old favorite of Mummy's) which she has been practicing for hours every day—day following day—under the rigorous tutelage of her new trainer Anastasia Kovitski and her new exacting choreographer Pytor Skakalov. *Again!* the adults urge. *Again, again! You can do better, you must do better, you must win.* Wistfully Bliss touches the photograph of BLISS RAMPIKE and whispers in Skyler's ear, "Is that meant to be me? It is *not*," and Skyler says with blustery big-brother authority, as Mummy would wish him to, "Don't say silly things, that some stranger might hear and repeat. *It's you.*"

Since early that morning Mummy has been hinting at a "surprise"—"a good surprise"—beyond the victory that Mummy expects this evening and so Skyler has been thinking *Does that mean Daddy is here? Is Daddy here?* though this is a thought so familiar it has acquired a taste as of something rancid and so Skyler doesn't crane his neck to look back into the arena, at the rows of seats.

Bliss doesn't look. Bliss never looks. If Bliss is (secretly) thinking *Is Daddy here?* Bliss has become experienced at giving no sign.

"Bliss? Smile for us, honey!"

Photographers hover in the aisle amid flashes of light. A brassy-haired interviewer for NJN-TV, who has interviewed Mummy and Bliss in the past, cajoles Bliss into smiling. Mummy returns, flush-faced and indignant. In northeast U.S. girls' amateur skating circles Betsey Rampike has acquired a reputation for being one of the more aggressive mother-managers. Just now she has been protesting Bliss's placement on the skating roster: Bliss is skating too soon in the "little miss" competition, unless Bliss is skating too late. Mummy is determined that Bliss will win the coveted Little Miss Jersey Ice Princess title this evening—"This is the victory we've been working for, for two and a half years." And: "Miss Jersey Ice Princess will be Bliss Rampike's 'springboard' into the nationals." Mummy is hugging Bliss, whispering into her ear what must be a hurried prayer, and then again Mummy is on her feet conferring with Bliss's trainer Anastasia Kovitski and with Bliss's choreographer Pytor Skakalov as Skyler a few feet away tries not to see how the oily-eyed Uzbekistani with the bushy black mustache and shoulder-length shaggy hair stands disagreeably close to Mummy and brings his mouth close to Mummy's ear. Worse yet, Skakalov's hand falls onto Mummy's shoulder, and does not move away.

Skyler squirms in his seat. *If Daddy is here! If Daddy sees!*

Yet: the last Skyler heard from Daddy, Daddy was on his way to a "business summit" meeting somewhere far away: Moscow?

Skyler thinks that his mother has never looked so—intense?—determined?—as she looks tonight. Skyler knows that Mummy has been dieting in recent weeks and has lost weight and Mummy has had "work" done on her face in Dr. Screed's office—nothing so drastic as a face-lift or liposuction—whatever "liposuction" is, Skyler isn't sure—but "miracle injections" to smooth away wrinkles in Mummy's forehead. For this occasion, Mummy had a new dress made for her of shimmery strawberry-colored satin, with a plunging neckline to show the tops of Mummy's creamy-pale breasts; the dress emulates Bliss's skating costume, with a flaring skirt. No wonder photographers and TV crews are drawn to Betsey Rampike of all mother-managers in girls' amateur skating, as they are drawn to "angelic" Bliss Rampike of all girl-skaters.

Oily-eyed Pytor Skakalov must have told Mummy something very encouraging for Mummy impulsively thanks him with a quick kiss grazing an edge of the bushy mustache.

If Daddy sees!

"Hel-lo ladiez 'n' gentz 'n' all the rest of you—"

Abruptly in mid-note the high-decibel Tchaikovsky ceases. A mammoth lizard-faced man in a shiny black tuxedo—can this be Jeremiah Jericho?—appears in a spotlight at the edge of the ice. His intimate drawl stirs a chorus of whistles and friendly catcalls: "*Wel*-come! *Wel*-come to New-ark! Jersey's answer to Athens-of-old! Our largest city and culture-hive bar none! Tonight—" Skyler listens numbed feeling the alarming sensation of *déjà vu* rising in him like nausea. Can there be a nausea of the soul? For Skyler has lived this before as Bliss has lived this before for there is no way out, time is a Möbius strip languidly turning in chill stale air though Master of Ceremonies Jeremiah Jericho does look slightly older and more bloated than he'd looked two years before at the Meadowlands. His genial/jeering face is conspicuously made up with an orangish-tan foundation base and his sleek black hair appears freshly dyed. Skyler feels a stab of revulsion for the man but has to concede, there is something comforting about Jeremiah Jericho. *As if an old stupid thing is more comforting than anything new, you know that you have survived it.*

"—and now, ladiez 'n' gentz letz rise—up on our feet!—for our most sacred of songs—'national anthem'—go crazy, folks, for 'O! Say Can You See'—" like a puppet-master misty-eyed Jeremiah Jericho causes the crowd to lurch to its feet, leading them in a fierce-bawling rendition of the anthem followed by deafening self-applause. Then, Jeremiah Jericho gives a hilariously risqué lewd-grandpappy introduction of that "stellar"—"non-puerile"—"kick-ass Jersey girl" Miss Jersey Ice Princess 1995 eighteen-year-old Courtney Studd of Hackensack who skates/undulates to a panting disco version of Ravel's dogged old classic *Boléro* in a sparkly Vegas-showgirl costume, to deafening applause.

"And now, ladiez 'n' gentz," Jeremiah Jericho rubs his meaty hands lewdly together, "—the first competition of the evening—eleven lusz-ous li'l gifted gals competing for the coveted title Little Miss Jersey Ice Princess! These fan-tas-tic li'l dolls are aged six to twelve and the first to skate for us is—"

When Bliss Rampike is announced, the fifth to compete, there is a heartwarming outburst of applause, whistles and cries *We love you, Bliss!*

that makes Skyler uneasy for it might be bad luck, if Bliss is the crowd's favorite at the moment; for skating crowds are notoriously fickle. " 'Miss Bliss Rampike'—six years old—Fair Hills, New Jersey—here's our brave li'l gal—1994 Miss Tot-on-Ice Debutante—your own Jeremiah Jericho was m.c. on that momentous occasion. Wel-come, Bliss! Wel-come to New-ark! Go crazy, folks, for—" as the arena is filled with the hot thumping rhythms of that disco hit of bygone days "Do What Feels Right." Skyler watches dry-mouthed and transfixed as Bliss seems to fly out onto the ice, skate blades hissing. And what a sight in her strawberry satin-and-sequin costume with the perky tulle skirt and peek-a-boo panties. *And now she will turn her ankle, she will fall*—but when Skyler opens his tight-shut eyes Bliss has not fallen but is performing a dazzling backward glide, Bliss is spinning on a single skate, Bliss is executing a spiral—a gyre—a "floating butterfly"—a "double toe loop"—as the crowd erupts in spontaneous ap-plause. So small-boned is this blond child, seemingly so much younger than her rivals, and so angelic in demeanor, audiences adore her. For breathtaking minutes Bliss performs flawlessly to the quick-tempo beat of "Do What Feels Right," small fixed smile on her face, wavy blond hair cascading to her (narrow, bare) shoulders, a final spin, a final "butterfly," and a gliding bow to the wildly applauding audience as Jeremiah Jericho pants into the microphone: "*Mag*-nifi-co, Blizz! *Fan*-tas-ti-co! Here's a li'l angel skates like a demon! Where wuz you, li'l sweetheart, when Jerry Jericho was eight years old, and hot to trot! Folks, you heard it straight from the old horsey's mouth: Blizz Rampick will one day win an Olympic gold medal! One day, Women's World Figure-Skating Champ! Folks, go crazy for our own Blizz Rampick of Far Hills, New Jersey—"

And so the crowd at the Newark War Memorial on the historic evening of November 30, 1996, goes crazy for Bliss Rampike *one more time.*

THE GOOD SURPRISE II*

"AND THERE MAY BE ANOTHER SURPRISE FOR US, TONIGHT."

Skyler's heart thumped in his chest. *Daddy?*

Bliss sucked at a finger, not daring to ask.

"—it isn't certain but it may be. 'Our cup runneth over'—it may be." Mummy laughed gaily swiping at her tear-splotched eyes.

Skyler asked hesitantly, "Is it a good surprise, Mummy?"

Mummy laughed again. Despite Dr. Screed's effort a sharp line like one made by a knife blade had appeared between her eyebrows. "Of course it's a 'good surprise,' Skyler. All Mummy's surprises are good."

Was this so? Skyler gnawed at his lower lip and made no reply but the thought passed between him and his little sister in the front seat of the minivan: *No! Not all Mummy's surprises are good.*

". . . happiest day of my life. At last!"

Mummy wasn't speaking to Bliss slumped in the passenger's seat beside her or to Skyler in the seat behind her but to herself as if she'd forgotten that her children were with her. And her words were murmured as much in wonderment as in triumph for here is the mystery of Betsey Rampike's life: *a small cup quickly runs over.*

---

* *My original title for these linked chapters transcribing the events of November 30, 1996, was "Cheap Suspense" but my editor insisted that I change it. And I have to concede, when is suspense not cheap? Is there a "costly"—"expensive"—"classy" suspense? Also, the outcome of Bliss's competition at Newark is a matter of public record so, technically speaking, there can be no suspense: you know that Bliss won the coveted title Little Miss Jersey Ice Princess 1996 which was the "high point" and the "end point" of her career.*

In the morning they would be returning to Fair Hills, in triumph. A celebration was planned there in honor of Fair Hills's celebrity-child Bliss Rampike who had just been crowned Little Miss Jersey Ice Princess 1996. There would be gala events in town, there would be more interviews. Photographers, TV camera crews. But tonight Mummy had booked a suite for them in the Garden State Marriott at an exit off I-80 twelve miles north of Newark for Mummy was giddy with happiness and with exhaustion and could not risk driving another hour to Fair Hills, at night. After the delirium of her daughter's victory Mummy had limited herself to one or two—no more than three!—small plastic glasses of cheap red wine in the drafty foyer of the war memorial and though Mummy was far from intoxicated it did appear that the minivan was giving her difficulty for the damned steering wheel seemed to be teasing her with a predilection for easing to the left; and her foot on the gas pedal was too heavy, or too light. "*Mum*-my. Watch *out*." Peering over Mummy's right shoulder at the rushing roadway splotched with rain-on-the-verge-of-sleet Skyler thought with grim satisfaction that if he had to, he'd grab the wheel. If Mummy skidded the minivan. If Mummy lost control. Nine-year-old Skyler would save them and no one would know, not even Daddy.

And if they died, Skyler thought, it would be Daddy's fault.

In the shifting glare of oncoming headlights shimmering with rain Skyler's mother's face was damp with tears of gratitude and seemed to glow from inside with a strange lunar beauty.

". . . happiest day. *My life*."

SO HAPPY! *HAPPY HAPPY HAPPY* SKYLER'S THROAT WAS RAW WITH HAPPI-ness, for the judges had scored his sister 5.9 out of 6 and no other skater in the six-to-twelve-year-old division had received a score higher than 5.7. So happy! Mummy had screamed and wept and would have fallen to her knees to pray to thank Jesus except her assistant Dale McKee (female, young) dissuaded her. Delirium of deafening applause. Cheers, whistles, cries *We love you Bliss!* Mammoth lizard-faced Jeremiah Jericho was moved by Bliss Rampike, you could see. Even that lewd-winking old-grandpappy in the sleek black tux straining at his belly. Even *he*! Predicting that the li'l blond gal from Far Hills—excuse me, Mr. Jericho: *Fair Hills*—would one day win an Olympic gold medal and become a World Champion and (Mummy knew: Mummy would see to it) one of the Disney-on-Ice superstar performers, a multi-million-dollar talent. Betsey Rampike stirred the crowd's sentimental-Jersey heart, for Betsey Rampike wept with such gratitude, her inky mascara ran down her fleshy face, tear-rivulets corroded her heavy makeup. Here was a mother so sincere. Here was a mother so vulnerable. Here was a mother so deserving of her daughter's victory. " 'Little Miss Jersey Ice Princess 1996—may God bless you." For this instant, Jeremiah Jericho's mocking voice quavered as with reverent hands he set the child-sized "silver" tiara on the child's head. A fuchsia-bright satin sash LITTLE MISS JERSEY ICE PRINCESS 1996 was positioned—carefully!—slantwise across the child's flat little chest. Still weeping, Betsey Rampike accepted from Jeremiah Jericho a large bouquet of bloodred plasticine roses and a framed certificate commemorating her daughter's title and an envelope containing a "token of our esteem" (how much? Skyler would one day discover it was only $500) and to the delight of the crowd Betsey Rampike blushed becomingly as Jeremiah Jericho planted a smacking wet kiss on her flaming cheek— "Meet me tonight in dreamland, Mz. Ranpick!"—as deftly the lizard-faced M.C. ushered mother and daughter off the ice and out of the spotlight to make way for the more important crowning of Miss Jersey Ice Princess 1996.

"NOW FOR YOUR SURPRISE, CHILDREN! IF THERE IS A SURPRISE."

Mummy seemed less certain now. Mummy was clutching the plastic key-card to suite 1822 of the Garden State Marriott to her breast as if she feared losing it. Ascending the glass-sided elevator to the eighteenth floor of the hotel Skyler was both light-headed with fatigue and apprehensive of what might happen next; he and Mummy were holding up Bliss between them. In the foyer downstairs Little Miss Jersey Ice Princess 1996 with her silver tiara still on her head, at a rakish angle, in her red mohair coat and darling little white kidskin boots, had drawn curious glances and smiles from strangers, but Mummy had urged her and

Skyler along without wishing to linger. At another time, Mummy would have been thrilled to introduce herself and Bliss and to explain who Bliss was, if necessary; it often happened that Mummy exchanged names and addresses with friendly strangers. But not tonight for it was very late: 10:50 P.M.

"Skyler? You have the magic touch."

Gaily Mummy handed Skyler the plastic key-card to suite 1822. It had long been established between them, and a matter of some small pride to the *little man*, that he rarely had trouble unlocking hotel doors that confounded Mummy.

And so Skyler inserted the card now. But without luck: only tiny red lights flashed by the lock, and not green.

Again, Skyler inserted the card, and withdrew it. Not too fast, and not too slow. Damn, his hand was shaking!

Tiny red lights, not green.

Skyler was about to protest, the lock had to be broken, when suddenly the door opened, and—*there stood Daddy!*

Sheepish-Daddy. Guilty-faced/boyish-Daddy.

Daddy's voice cracked, with emotion. Stooping to hug his astonished children, tears spilling from Daddy's eyes.

"You kids! Jesus! Your Daddy loves you, your Daddy made a very bad mistake, d'you forgive your Daddy?"—sweeping Bliss into the crook of one arm, and Skyler into the crook of the other arm, as Mummy looked on smiling as one might smile on the deck of a drunkenly tilting ship in a "storm-tossed sea"—until Daddy managed to include Mummy in his embrace as well, four Rampikes staggering and stumbling together inside the hotel room. Like a desperate man, Daddy kissed and hugged his children; kissed and hugged them harder; covered their stunned faces with hot smacking-wet Daddy kisses; tried to lift both children in his arms but had to settle for just Bliss, who stared at him with slow blinking dilated eyes, the "silver" tiara slipping from her head. Daddy was moaning like a wounded animal—"You kids! Look at you! Beautiful sweet innocent kids, Daddy doesn't deserve. And my beautiful wife, I don't deserve. None of you, my precious family, do I deserve. Can you ever forgive me?"

Yes yes yes! *Yes.*

"D'you hate me? You should hate me! God damn, I deserve to be hated, d'you hate me? Loathe me? Bliss?—Skyler?—Betsey?"

No no no! *No.*

The room into which they'd stumbled was a lavishly decorated parlor where Mummy had left suitcases earlier that day, before driving into the city to the War Memorial. Now this room was filled with balloons of every color, some of the balloons twisted into tortured-animal shapes; glittering confetti hung from lampshades, and from the chandelier overhead; a room-service trolley draped with a white tablecloth was crowded with food: cheeses, fruit, shrimp, a large (boxed) pizza, a slab of ham with fresh-cut bread and "gourmet" mustard, chocolate-covered strawberries, chocolate mints, bottles of sparkling water and a bottle of red wine and a large bottle of Dom Pérignon. Mummy laughed at Daddy: "Bix! Aren't you ridiculous! You look as if you've bought out the store," in a voice of reproach, and Daddy said, "Damn right I bought out the store, darling. And damn more to come." Clumsily Daddy hugged Mummy who pushed at him, as you'd push at an overgrown child, but Daddy persisted, Daddy kissed Mummy's mouth fiercely, as Skyler and Bliss had never seen Daddy kiss Mummy before.

Though they'd been staggering with exhaustion only a few minutes before, now both children were alert, aroused. Skyler's eyes felt as if he'd been staring into flame. Skyler's little fist-heart beat hard and rapid in his chest and Bliss was breathing through her mouth as she'd never breathed while exerting herself in such extraordinary maneuvers on the ice. By slow degrees it was registering on the children that Daddy was *back*, and Daddy was *here.*

Sucking a finger, shyly Bliss asked if Daddy was going to stay with them all night here?—and Daddy kissed Bliss wetly again on the mouth saying, "Hell yes. Yes yes *yes.* All night tonight and every night to come, darling, forever. With God as Daddy's witness." Skyler was feeling jealous of the attention Bliss was receiving from Daddy and so Skyler crowded against Daddy's legs as a much younger child might, tugging at Daddy's arm, yet for a long frustrating moment Skyler could not seem to dislodge Daddy's gaze for Daddy was staring intently at his little girl whom he hadn't seen in—how long?—several weeks, or months?—as if she were a stranger's child, her small-boned face deathly pale and spittle gleaming on her parted lips. "Bliss darling, I tried my damndest to get to Newark in time to see you skate, God damn I *tried*. The f—ing* plane was five hours late leaving f—ing Frankfurt, there was nothing to be done. And forty f—ing minutes circling f—ing Newark Airport! But I saw you on TV, honey. Switched on the TV in here just in time, it's as if God was guiding my hand, these months Bix Rampike has been forsaken by God, suddenly restored to sanity by God, and I saw my li'l gal skate like an angel, and I could not believe my eyes!— and I heard that crowd go wild for my angel; I saw close-ups of my beautiful li'l angel skating as no one at the actual rink could have seen her, and, Jesus!—when the judges gave 'Bliss Rampike' five-point-nine points out of six, I knew you would win; I didn't have to wait for the announcement, I *knew*. And I bawled like a baby. And when Bliss was crowned 'Little Miss Jersey Ice Princess'—I bawled all over again."

It was so: Daddy's eyes looked raw and reddened.

Slowly Mummy removed her coat, that was red mohair (to match Bliss's little coat) with a mink collar. Mummy smoothed her shimmery-strawberry dress down over her shapely hips, and you could see that Daddy was staring at Mummy, too: for Mummy had lost weight and was now "size ten" and Mummy had carefully repaired the damage to her makeup after her fit of weeping earlier that evening and so Mummy was looking very attractive, Skyler thought. Briskly Mummy said, "Well! Your father is back, children, and we love him; and, as we are Christians, we forgive him of course." Mummy laughed in a throaty-sexy way that reminded Skyler of—who?—Calvin Klaus's mother?—and Mummy kissed Daddy lightly on his mashed-looking mouth: you could see that a mysterious strength resided now in Mummy, that the children had not seen before.

Daddy too was swaying on his feet as if very tired-yet-happy. And it might have been, Daddy's breath smelled of something fumey-sweet: Johnnie Walker Scotch? Daddy's stiff hair was disheveled and his skin had that coarse-gray look Skyler associated with Daddy returning home

---

* *"F—ing": pronounced "f"-"ing" to spare the tender ears of Bix Rampike's children. A linguistic circumlocution sometimes employed by crude assholes like Bix Rampike.*

from a trans-Atlantic flight; Daddy's heavy jaws were dark with stubble. Daddy wore dark pressed trousers badly wrinkled in the seat and Daddy's long-sleeved white cotton shirt was badly wrinkled and stained. "Did you miss your old daddy, kids? I hope to hell you didn't, but—did you?" Daddy was staring at them with such a weird hungry look, Skyler was fearful he might burst into laughter.

"The children missed you, Bix, a bit. And I missed you, a bit. Especially at first." Mummy spoke with that air of teasing reproach, stroking Daddy's arm as you might stroke an uneasy dog, to comfort him. "Now everything is perfect again, Jesus has taken our pain from us and replaced it with His grace and you saw the fruits of that grace tonight: our daughter is Little Miss Jersey Ice Princess 1996. Our daughter is *launched.*"

"Our daughter is *launched.* Amen."

Daddy uncorked the bottle of Dom Pérignon, with funny-Daddy clumsiness. Mummy lifted the pizza (pepperoni and cheese, Skyler's mouth watered) out of its box and Mummy opened a bottle of sparkling water for Skyler and for Bliss. It was very late—long past bedtime!—but Skyler was very hungry, and began eating pizza; Bliss, who'd eaten virtually nothing all day except yogurt, raisins, and "seven-grain" crispbreads that Anastasia Kovitski fed to her, devoured several chocolate-covered strawberries before ceasing, with a stricken expression. Giddy Daddy poured sparkling bubbly champagne into long-stemmed glasses for Mummy and for himself and Daddy lifted his glass to click against Mummy's glass as champagne ran down his fingers: "As God is my witness, Betsey. I stand before you abased, and abashed. And I am home."

Yet more! Daddy had presents for his little family: for Sky-boy, a thrillingly lifelike eighteen-inch-tall Terminator Boy XXL with "laser-eye" features; for "Daddy's bestest-best li'l gal" Bliss a child-sized ermine cape, with crimson silk lining; and, for Mummy, a beautiful bracelet of shiny, shimmering-green stones—"Indonesian emeralds."

Mummy stared in astonishment. Mummy's lips parted, and Mummy's eyes brimmed with tears. Barely audible Mummy spoke: "Oh. Oh Bix. This bracelet is—too beautiful. Jesus has heard my prayers, and He has answered them. My husband is returned. Today has been the happiest day of my life—'My cup runneth over.'"

Mummy's tears were not the wrathful acid-tears of the past several months, that had so frightened Skyler and Bliss, but joyous scintillant tears of the kind usually reserved for the dazzling lights of an ice-skating arena, when Bliss Rampike was being crowned. And Daddy, hugging Mummy hard in clumsy-Daddy humility, Daddy-seeking-forgiveness, hid his large heated face in Mummy's blushing neck and began to cry, too.

Deep-chested wracking sobs provoking Skyler to think *But this hasn't happened before and so it can't be happening again. Can it?** (Editor†: Do we need to know that this is "a deep, exhausted sleep"—"a stuporous open-mouthed sleep"—"an uncanny sleep in which the glassy cobalt eyes were partly open, yet unseeing"?)

Yet another ending, required for a graceful segue into the next chapter (*is* "segue" a word?—a kind of cheaply trendy word, but often helpful):

> That night waking abruptly not knowing at first where he was, in an unfamiliar bed, in an unfamiliar room, and his sister Bliss sleeping in the twin bed beside his, Skyler heard a sudden sound, a sound of protest, a sound of struggle, a thudding/thumping sound and—was it laughter?—Mummy's sharp/startled/involuntary laughter, a moaning laughter, and what had to be Daddy's

---

* *Poor Skyler! As guts can become fatally twisted, and thus suppurating, in the abdominal cavity, so an overtaxed child's brains can become twisted, and suppurating. And yet, I think we know what Skyler means here, at the end of this particularly overwrought scene of "domestic realism."*

Not that the scene ended here. No scenes in literature, as in movies, end as indicated, but trail on and on like broken-backed snakes. Here is the fuller, original ending:

> *And what of Skyler, shoving a slice of clammy-cheese-clotted pizza into his mouth, wildly ravenous as if he had not eaten in days?—Skyler staring at his demon-parents thinking helplessly But this hasn't happened before and so it can't happen again. Can it?*

Beyond this, a "poignant" ending:

> *On a sofa in the hotel suite, wrapped in the snowy-white ermine cape as in a child's blanket, sucking her thumb and several fingers Little Miss Jersey Ice Princess had fallen asleep.*

† *(No editor responded to this query! Which means, I guess, that no editor actually read it. So I think I will let it remain, out of spite.)*

deep-baritone response, poor Skyler had no idea what he was hearing, should he be frightened, should he knock on the door between the rooms, or is it just Mummy laughing, Mummy laughing at one of Daddy's silly jokes?—so Skyler presses a pillow over his head, if Mummy is happy, and Daddy is back to live with them again, then Skyler would be happy, Skyler would be very happy, and Bliss would be happy, too.

You can see why I excised this ending: it's overwrought, and communicates its meaning too clearly. We prefer indirection.

SEX TOYS?

IN THE LOWERMOST DRAWER OF THE HEAVY CARVED MAHOGANY BUREAU IN THE Rampikes' "master bedroom" beneath Daddy's (ironed, folded) boxer shorts, astonished little Skyler discovered, one day when Mummy and Bliss were gone for the afternoon, and the new housekeeper Lila-from-the-Philippines was occupied far away downstairs in the laundry room, these baffling items:

- a rumpled crimson silk scarf about thirty inches long, less than six inches wide, faintly stained

- ladies' lingerie, black silk, lacy crimson, near-transparent champagne-colored: panties large enough to be Mummy's but—so strangely!—lacking crotches; "brassieres" large enough to be Mummy's but made of an impracticably flimsy material that could never support Mummy's heavy breasts, with strategically placed holes

- a black silk garter belt, black silk stockings twisted together

- two masks: a black silk half-mask, and a crimson silk half-mask

- several chains of a lightweight metal meant to resemble gold, with heart-shaped links

- a flesh-colored replica of what looked, to Skyler's astonished eyes, like a monstrously enlarged boy's "thing" with a mysterious leather strap attached to its base

- *Gaspard de la Nuit "Oil of Eros"* in a six-ounce bottle that looked as if it had never been opened

- *Gaspard de la Nuit "Chocolate Licker"* in a similar bottle, that looked as if it had been opened, since less than half of the "chocolate licker" remained

Entranced, Skyler dared to lift one of the black silk half-masks, to peer through the eyes; and Skyler dared to sniff (but did not taste) the *Gaspard de la Nuit "Chocolate Licker"*; and Skyler dared to loop the crimson silk scarf around his neck, and wipe his warm face with it, and inhale its fruity/perfumy scent. Tyler McGreety would know what to make of such things! But not Skyler Rampike whose small heart beat so rapidly, he felt he might faint.

"Sky-ler?"—away downstairs a female voice lifted.

Mesmerized by what he'd discovered, knowing only that these items were, like the *master bedroom* itself, forbidden to him, quickly Skyler shoved the things back beneath Daddy's underwear, and fled.*

---

* *Was Skyler's intrusion ever discovered, you might wonder? No. But then, yes.*
  "Sex Toys?" as a chapter title is provided by the nineteen-year-old S.R., not the nine-year-old who hadn't a clue what he was looking at.

CONFABULATING KIDS

IF SKYLER IMAGINED WHAT *WAS*, BLISS IMAGINED WHAT *WAS NOT*.

Nothing so upset Mummy as those occasions when Bliss "made things up"—"confabulated"—in the presence of outsiders. Especially, Mummy had to be vigilant in public places: if, for instance, an aggressive interviewer prodded Bliss into saying "wrong things" on live television which Mummy could not censure, or even edit, as in this remarkable interview with a slyly malicious female interviewer following Bliss's Newark triumph:

> **Interviewer:** You are such a natural on the ice, Bliss! How old were you when you learned to skate?
>
> **Bliss (long pause, shy):** . . . before I was here, in that other place.
>
> **Interviewer:** And where was that "other place," Bliss?
>
> **Bliss (long pause, finger in mouth):** . . . it was dark. I wasn't there yet.
>
> **Interviewer:** I don't quite understand, dear. You weren't "there yet"—?
>
> (Seated close beside Bliss, an arm around Bliss's small shoulders, Mummy registers unease, though Mummy continues to smile happily.)
>
> **Bliss:** . . . before I was born.

Interviewer: Why, Bliss! Do you remember before you were born?

Bliss (nodding, so vehemently the silver tiara on her head nearly falls off): It was a quiet time, no one was mad at me. No one yelled at me. There was ice, everywhere it was ice where the Turnpike is, you could skate and skate and . . .

Mummy (laughing nervously, adjusts the tiara on Bliss's head, gently tugs Bliss's finger from her mouth): What Bliss is trying to say is "a long time ago"—when she was four. And that very first year Bliss Rampike was crowned Miss Tots-on-Ice Debutante 1994—the youngest ever!

Funny? Chagrined Betsey Rampike didn't think so.

Another time, earlier in Bliss's career, and quite a surprise to Skyler (watching the telecast at home, alone with one of the Marias), following Bliss's victory at the StarSkate competition, another female interviewer was complimenting Betsey Rampike on how "angelic"—"radiantly beautiful"—her daughter was, and Bliss suddenly became agitated, shook her head vehemently from side to side and, before Mummy could stop her, managed to pry off something small and pearly-white from one of her front teeth, to reveal, in glaring TV close-up, a tiny chip in the tooth.

Giggly/stricken Bliss stammered into the TV camera: "I was bad, I fell. I broke my tooth. I am not *how I look.*"

Poor Betsey Rampike! Roused on camera to the most fumbling and shame-faced intervention, trying to smile while profusely apologizing to the interviewer, gripping squirmy Bliss in a firm-Mummy embrace, and trying to extricate the small white dental cap from Bliss's fingers before it fell to the floor.

Now, this *was* funny. Skyler laughed, and laughed.

HONEYMOON I

AS IN ADULT (SEXUAL/MARITAL) LIFE THERE ARE PROVERBIAL "HONEYMOONS"—
interludes of peace, idyllic calm, the highest and most naive of romantic
expectations—so, too, in the lives of families there are honeymoon interludes, precious (if heartrending!) in retrospect. I am thinking of
those several weeks in December 1996 and early January 1997 when
like an old-fashioned schooner blown by balmy winds into seemingly
tranquil tropical waters, the Rampikes entered such a phase, when
Daddy returned, vowing to be a "God-damned good" husband and
father.

Where once Daddy had stayed late at work, or traveled much of the
time, mysteriously, now Daddy was home for dinner with his family every
weekday night, or nearly. Daddy was home most weekends. If Daddy was
to be even a half-hour late, Daddy called! Eager Daddy hugged, and Daddy
kissed, and Daddy brought home surprise presents from the mammoth
VastValley Mall which was on Daddy's commute home from Univers Bio-
Tech—"Just 'cause Daddy loves you." Grinning Daddy spent "quality time"
with his family at every opportunity and planned to spend more: "How's
the lush tropical island of St. Bart's sound, for winter break in February?
The Rampikes are booked for a guesthouse on the water." And: "Next July,
it's the Grand Tetons!" It was a season of Daddy-plans. For Bix Rampike
was the most American of daddies, seething with plans like maggots in a
festering corpse.

The most exciting of Daddy's plans was for a new house!

"Even a terrific house like ours, in a terrific setting, can be outgrown.
It's the nature of *Homo sapiens* to *move on.*"

Briskly Daddy rubbed big-Daddy hands together. A sharp laser light came into Daddy's soulful eyes at the prospect of *moving on*.

First weekend of Daddy's return, following church services on Sunday Daddy spread out oversized sheets of architectural drawings on the dining room table, for his amazed family to admire. "The architect is none other than H.H. Stuart of New York City, who built the Steadley house out here. And I have the dream location for the Rampike Dream House: five acres of prime 'verdant rolling hills' in East Quaker Heights, New Jersey."

Mummy stammered, "But Bix—you can't be serious! You can't want us to move from Fair Hills! Where we know such wonderful people, and have been made to feel so welcome! Quaker Heights must be twenty miles away, we wouldn't know a soul. Oh!" Mummy winced as if she'd been struck to the heart.

During Sunday morning services at Trinity Episcopal, Mummy often became emotional, even tearful; Skyler was embarrassed of his dressy, glamorously made-up mother who listened so intently to Reverend Higley's affable droning sermons and, when bidden, rose eagerly from the pew to "take communion" with an expression of joyous gratitude. Now Mummy was becoming so agitated, Daddy felt the need to wink at Skyler and Bliss to signal *silly-Mummy isn't she*? but Daddy spoke respectfully to Mummy explaining that, yes, he was serious: "Might be, darlin', I've made preliminary negotiations to buy the property. Quaker Heights is *très* up-scale, Bets. If you're worried about the neighbors. And don't fret about not knowing anyone there, it's because your enterprising hubby already knows certain key players in Quaker Heights, my new associates at Univers, who are strongly urging this move for us. *Verstayeh?*"

Even Skyler had heard of the Village of Quaker Heights. It was one of those "quaint"—"historic"—eighteenth-century New Jersey communities where General George Washington and his men had been "billeted" and which was now wholly owned and governed by wealthy Caucasians.

A sliver of unease pierced Skyler's heart: new playdates? He would run away from home.

Mummy was trying to speak calmly, "Bix, I realize that Quaker Heights is a few miles closer to Univers headquarters than Fair Hills, but—think of our dear friends here! The wonderful clubs we belong to, our very special circle of Episcopal friends, how everyone here is aware of Bliss, and proud of her for bringing such renown to the community. And, Bix, you're so popular! Every hostess in Fair Hills will be heartbroken if Bix Rampike moves away! I have worked so hard, Bix. I have worked like a dog, Bix. You can't just destroy this again, Bix. You can't revert me to zero again. And Bliss's career is 'going national'—soon!—and will consume even more of my time. You know what a trauma it was for me to move to Fair Hills, Bix. How no one liked me, how 'existentially isolated' I was, Dr. Stadtskruller thinks that my migraines are caused partly by 'unassimilated trauma' from that move when I'd just had a—a baby." Mummy squinted at Skyler, and at Bliss, as if to determine which of them had been that troublesome baby. "And Skyler has his school, he's devoted to! And Bliss has so many friends and well-wishers here! Why can't we build a new house in Fair Hills, Bix? Lots are for sale in that new development off Woodsmoke Drive where the Frasses have just built a spectacular French Normandy house on at least four acres, and Glenna O'Stryker was telling me—"

Patiently Daddy said, "We can discuss the location another time, darlin'. When we are not so emotional." A flicker of something like fury came into Daddy's smiling face and faded almost too quickly to be detected.

Skyler glared at Mummy. Did she want Daddy to leave them again?

Quickly Skyler said, "This house looks really cool, Daddy. Must be a 'McMansion.'"

But this was a goosh thing to say, Skyler realized. For Daddy laughed sharply and corrected him: "This is not a 'McMansion,' son. The architectural firm I have engaged does not commit 'McMansions.' This will be a custom-made wholly original split-level 'Chesterfield contemporary' not one of those cookie-cutter boxes the size of a Wal-Mart. This is Bix Rampike's 'dream house'—Daddy's gift to his family."

Mummy said uncertainly, "This is certainly a—a wonderful—surprise— but, Bix—don't you think that you should have consulted me? I mean—maybe I could have discussed these plans with you, and with the architect?"

"You'll be 'discussing' plenty with the architect, Betsey. And with his assistants, there's a platoon of assistants at H.H. Stuart. Only just beware: architects bill by the hour. So when one of the team calls you, says 'hello' and asks how you are, remember he's on the clock and if you gab away, you pay." Daddy chuckled deep in his throat, but there was a warning edge to his voice.

"And can we afford a house this size, Bix? And so much land, in Quaker Heights? I realize that you are making more money at Univers than you'd been at Scor, but—"

" 'More money'? Darlin', you have to be kidding."

"But—why? I thought—"

"Of course I'm making 'more money' at Univers, Betsey. Why the hell d'you think I left Scor, where I had a fantastic deal, for a salary cut? The bottom line is, and Skyler needs to hear this, too, for future information, 'salary' is just a fraction of corporate income. The deal Bix Rampike has at Univers, I wouldn't need a salary. It's the bonuses, stock options, restricted stock and 'benefits' that are the big draw, and I mean *B-I-G*. And with tax-deferred investments in a cutting edge field like bio-tech, we are not talking *S-M-A-L-L*. As the youngest member of the Univers executive team, Bix Rampike is, like, the most popular jock in the school, and while I am not claiming to merit such esteem, I intend to fulfill the expectations of my elders, and more. Damn more! 'My family comes first with me' is what I made clear when I was being considered for the job, and *'Homo homin lupus'*—my father's wisdom—Greek for: 'Man is friend to wolf.' Meaning a man must be 'man enough' to acknowledge the wolf-blood in his soul, and to harness it. Harness that blood! And let me tell you, they were impressed. Now look here." Daddy shuffled about the large, elaborate drawings, that covered sheet after sheet of tissue-fine paper; only on one sheet were actual drawings of a house, and an enormous house it appeared to be, producing in the viewer that frisson of vertigo you feel staring into the labyrinthine drawings of M. C. Escher.* As Mummy peered nervously at the house plans, and Bliss stared with a finger stuck in her mouth, and Skyler leaned close beside Daddy to see where Daddy was pointing with his big-Daddy forefinger, Daddy said proudly, "—custom-design seventy-five hundred square feet, six bedrooms plus a 'guest suite' with private sauna. And the 'master suite'—that's

---

*Yes, Skyler knows who M. C. Escher is, having gone through a phase of Escher in middle school as he'd gone through a phase of R. Crumb. Smart-ass readers/editors who doubt Skyler's wide knowledge are hereby refuted.

Mummy and Daddy, kids!—with a private entrance and short-cut corridor to the swimming pool that is indoor/outdoor—state-of-the-art. We are not talking *S-M-A-L-L*. We are not talking *F-R-U-G-A-L*. We are talking 'Olympian'— 'epic.' Forty-foot 'sunken' living room. Two dining rooms: formal, informal. Plus 'breakfast nook' overlooking the terrace. Here's the family room: our 'entertainment center.' State-of-the-art TV, CD and DVD and whatever the hell gets invented in the New Millennium. Next door is the 'family fitness center' where Daddy can beef up his pecs and Mummy can sweat out this spongey-crepey stuff"— playfully pinching Mummy's thigh, as Mummy laughed/winced—"and if Skyler feels the urge to revamp his gymnast leanings, at a more mature age, that would be fantastic. And, not least"—drawing Bliss into a crook of an arm, brushing his lips against the delicate blue vein at Bliss's temple—"for Daddy's bestest-best li'l gal: an ice rink."

An ice rink! Bliss stared, and blinked.

Since returning home, Daddy had been unusually aware of Bliss, as if taking notice of her for the first time. Murmuring now in Bliss's ear, as if Mummy and Skyler were not present, "It came to me in a brainstorm the other night, sweetie, when I saw my daughter—my daughter!—skating like a demon on TV and being applauded by all those strangers, and winning big: Little Miss Ice Jersey. Had to be like a vision, tears just ran from my eyes, God damn I was so moved. Right away—first thing—I called my architect and left a message to add an ice rink to the Rampike home plan. And so he has done. Looks good, eh?"

Skyler, peering over his sister's shoulder, feeling his mother close beside him, registered the faintest glimmer of a secret thought passing in an instant between Mummy and Bliss though neither so much as glanced at the other *The rink is too small! Too small for Bliss Rampike! A silly little-kid ice rink, for Bliss Rampike!* Yet after a pause Bliss said in a whisper, "Thank you, Daddy!" and beaming Daddy hugged his little girl and kissed her with a fierce hot Daddy-kiss.

"Thought you'd like it, honey."

SKYLER WENT AWAY LIMPING, SICK WITH JEALOUSY. AS SKYLER HAD NEVER— well, rarely—been jealous of his little sister before.

Afterward thinking calmly *Because of Bliss he will stay with us longer. He will love us all more.*

"SMILE PLEASE."

Smile smile smile *please*.

En famille the Rampikes are being photographed seated on a sofa in front of their ten-foot gorgeously decorated Christmas tree: Daddy, Mummy, Bliss, and Skyler. It is Christmas 1996 and it will be the Rampikes' final family Christmas photo, to be used on their Christmas card as on promotional materials distributed by Bliss Rampike, Inc. Except that this photo of my family is the one replicated *ad nauseam*, like certain video clips of Bliss Rampike skating, being crowned a winner, smiling into daz- zling lights with that sweet little-girl smile to break the heart, the most "downloaded" of all Rampike family photographs, you can bet that I would avoid it altogether, for the miserable memory of this photo session, stretching beyond ninety minutes, and endured by poor Skyler in itchy trousers and Fair Hills blazer, sappy clip-on school tie, is as pleasant to recall as an attack of diarrhea. (Yes, which Skyler suffered from, too, after such stressful sessions as the photo-shoot, but never mind.)

This is the photograph in which both Rampike parents have managed to clasp little blond Bliss in the crooks of their arms, like awkwardly con- joined Siamese twins with a large stiff doll-child wedged between; with seeming casualness, Daddy has cupped his big left hand beneath Bliss's small right foot in her gleaming-black patent leather shoe.

Gravely it has been noted that all photographs are posthumous.*

Gravely it has been noted that we who have been photographed will be outlived one day by our "photograph-selves."

The special horror of this 1996 Christmas photo of my family is that it is the final Christmas photo and that *no one of us could have guessed it at the time.*

---

* Tout les photographies sont posthumous. *Quotation attributed to the esteemed French phi- losopher Jacques Lacan in some quarters much revered and in others, in New Jersey, little-known and/or dismissed as a bullshit artist.*

Even scowling Skyler at the edge of the cozy family unit could not have guessed. Fidgety little brat clasped and grasped by neither parent. And now a decade later recalling with—is it nostalgia?*—that most asinine of emotions!—the wonderful smell of the pine needles, the beauty of the freshly cut tree and the exciting ritual (yes it was exciting, and yes sulky Skyler did participate) of trimming the tree; how, as the photographer and his assistant were preparing for the shoot there came Mummy looking very glamorous but anxious as well, hairbrush in hand to run through Skyler's matted hair, deftly Mummy's fingers adjusted the crooked clip-on tie and Mummy stooped to peer into Skyler's evasive eyes and out of earshot of the others pleaded, "Skyler, please darling for Mummy's sake try not to twitch and make those awful faces! Try to look happy for Mummy's sake, though Bliss is the family 'star' remember always, Mummy loves you best, for Mummy loved her little man first; this is our happiest Christmas yet for Daddy is back with us and we want the world to see how proud we are of Bliss and what an exacting trainer, she wasn't scheduled to skate again, in public, in competition, until the Hershey's Kisses Girls' Ice-Skating Festival on January 11, 1997, in Hershey, Pennsylvania. For in America this season is decreed *family season.* (Eat your hearts out, you pitiable loners who don't have families! Melancholy as Thanksgiving is, the Christmas—New Year's season is far worse and lasts far longer, providing a rich fund of opportunities for self-medicating, mental collapse, suicide and public mayhem with firearms. In fact it might be argued that the Christmas—New Year's season which begins abruptly after Thanksgiving is now the core-season of American life itself, the meaning of American life, the brute existential point of it. How you without families must envy us who bask in parental love, in the glow of yule-logs burning in fireplaces stoked by our daddies' robust pokers, we who are stuffed to bursting with our mummies' frantic holiday cooking; how you wish you could be us, pampered/protected kids tearing expensive foil wrappings off too many packages to count, gathered about the Christmas tree on Christmas morning as Mummy gently chided: "Skyler! Bliss! Show Daddy

* *Nostalgia: homesickness. You can die of it.*

and Mummy what you've just opened, please! And save the little cards, so you know who gave such nice things to you.")

It was a season of Daddy-arranged outings: family brunches at the Fair Hills Golf and Country Club, the Pebble Hill Tennis Club, the Sylvan Glen Golf Club, and the Charity Hill Club (which the elder Rampikes were recently invited to join); family trips to New York City to stay in family-sized suites at the Carlyle, the Four Seasons, and the New York Palace and to see such lavish entertainments as the Radio City Christmas Pageant, blockbuster Broadway shows so aggressively loud and cheery both Rampike children fell asleep in their seats like soldiers in the trenches of World War I, and the lavish spectacular *Stars on Ice Capades 1996* at Madison Square Garden at which, for two full hours, Mummy and Bliss stared mesmerized. (Teary-eyed Mummy: "One day, Bliss Rampike will be up there with that troupe! On that ice! Those very 'stars,' Bliss Rampike will be among them.")

MUMMY I'M AFRAID   I AM SO AFRAID   SOMETIMES
  Yes but it is a good fear Bliss   God has singled us out for our destiny   not fear but His fiery love is what we feel

HONEYMOON II: "GUY STUFF"

"JUST YOU AND ME, SON. SEEMS LIKE WE'VE BEEN OUT OF TOUCH, EH? *NON-communicado?* Time for some serious guy stuff."

For even in January the Daddy-honeymoon continued, like a tidal wave that has passed its crest but is still frothy, furious, lethal. Though Daddy had returned to work—"Sixty hours minimum per week, it's the least Bix Rampike can do for the company"—and Skyler had returned (reluctantly? relieved?) to the inflexible rigors of Fair Hills Day School, yet Daddy made an effort to spend "quality time" with his son, mostly on weekends and mostly in Daddy's new-model '97 Road Warrior S.U.V., driving. For Mummy and Bliss were often away at the Halcyon rink, or driving to and from Bliss's numerous appointments, preparing for the upcoming Hershey's Kisses Girls' Ice-Skating Festival: "Bliss's most challenging competition yet."

Which left the two Rampike guys free to see guy-movies at the Cine-Max, or to check out the latest in what Daddy admiringly called "electronic gizmos" at the Cross Tree Best Bargain, the VastValley Whiz, Crazy Andy's on Route 33. In the tank-like Rogue Warrior Daddy so exulted in driving, handling the mega-ton vehicle with the zest of a seasoned rodeo rider grappling the horns of a bucking steer, Skyler felt a wave of wary happiness wash over him. Natural to think *Someday, me too!*

"As I've said, son, we need to talk. Damn I'd been hoping that over the holidays you and me could, y'know, hang out more together, but your mummy had 'events' planned non-stop, which were terrific, don't misunderstand me, and what families need to do at Christmas, but, Sky-boy, kind of fucks up opportunities for father-son *raport.* Now your mummy and me, we've been re-opening the lines of communication that'd become kind of encrusted with disuse, and I am feeling good about that. Your mother is a damn fine woman." Daddy paused as if expecting Skyler to concur but, buckled into the passenger's seat beside Daddy, as the S.U.V. plunged into Saturday-morning traffic on Cross Tree Road, Skyler could think of no appropriate reply. *Was* Mummy a damn fine woman?

"But your mother is a woman, and they are born with these extra chromosomes—'sensitivity'—'intuition'—'nesting instinct.' The bottom line is, it makes them prone to monogramy, as the male of the species is naturally prone to polygramy, and we have to understand this distinction. 'In family life as in the palace of the Emperor, sand fraud is the wisest counsel'—that's the ancient wisdom of Confucius, son. When it comes to hoary wisdom, the ancient Chinese have it all over us barbaric Yanks. We are a damn immature civilization, in North America. But the father-son bond is universal. Your mother says, 'Skyler has missed you so! More even than Bliss who has her skating, for Skyler has only—us. A boy requires a male role model if he is to mature into a healthy heterosexual man.'"

Heterosexual! Sexual! Skyler squirmed inside the safety harness like a small trapped rodent.

There followed then at Daddy's urging several awkward minutes as Skyler spoke falteringly of his courses at school, his teachers and "activities" in response to which Daddy smilingly grunted *Uh-huh! yeh? right on!* without further inquiry; when Skyler said he missed a boy who'd been transferred to another school—"Calvin Klaus"—"he was real nice to me"—Daddy made no reply at all, swinging with calculated zest onto a ramp of eastbound I-80. Skyler persisted, "Calvin was my friend. I m-miss him pretty bad, I guess."

Was this true? Days in succession Skyler didn't even think of Calvin Klaus. Yet, now, Skyler missed him badly.

Daddy asked, " 'Calvin'—who?"

"Calvin Klaus. Maybe Mummy knows Mrs. Klaus."

"Could be."

Skyler watched his father closely noting that his father had not betrayed the slightest glimmer of awareness of who Calvin Klaus was, or whose son he might be; not the slightest glimmer of unease, or guilt. You'd never have thought that Bix Rampike had ever heard the name "Klaus."

"Sorry you miss your friend, Sky-boy. But—let's be realistic!—there's plenty of other boys at your school to be friends with, right?"

With relief Skyler thought *It never was true! Daddy and Mrs. Klaus.*

At the mall Skyler's father was drawn to electronics stores where he interrogated salesclerks about their highest-priced computers, laser printers, television sets and CD equipment and camcorders. Clearly Daddy enjoyed these zestful exchanges that allowed him to reveal, in a sequence of questions of escalating shrewdness, what an electronics expert he was; and what pride Skyler took in his father when a salesclerk, impressed with Bix Rampike, asked him what his profession was?—computers? electrical engineering? and Daddy laughed saying, "Hell, no. But I read *Scientific American.*" Often it appeared that Daddy was about to make a purchase, nothing less than the most expensive computer on the floor, abruptly then Daddy would say, "Hey. Great talking with you, Tod. Give me your card, eh?—I'll get back to you." Skyler hurried after his father noting the looks of surprise and disappointment in the salesclerks' faces.

At the VastValley Mall, emerging from The Whiz one Saturday afternoon with his father, Skyler saw a large shambling figure ahead moving in their direction: a ruddy-faced man with fierce eyebrows and untrimmed whiskers, in a disreputable sheepskin parka and shapeless work-pants and, Skyler winced to see, leather sandals with coarse gray woollen socks.

"Skyler, hello!" Mr. McDermid smiled warmly and would have stopped to speak with Skyler, and to introduce himself to Skyler's father, except without missing a beat, as a skilled quarterback passes the ball undetected by confused opponents, Skyler's father steered Skyler past, with a curt nod to Mr. McDermid.

"Who's the kook?"

Skyler was stricken with chagrin. Skyler could not bear to look back at Mr. McDermid who must have been staring after him in perplexity.

"One of your mummy's friends? Looks like a high school math teacher." Daddy laughed in derision.

Skyler mumbled he didn't know, he didn't think that man was a friend of Mummy's. For Mummy had not once spoken of the McDermids and surely had not called them since Daddy had returned home.

Another time, as Skyler and his father were leaving the Fair Hills Sports Injuries Rehabilitation & Physical Therapy Center,* a woman on her way in, stylishly dressed though wearing a foam rubber collar, cried, "Bix!" and advanced upon Skyler's father to brush her lips against his cheek, and seize both his hands in hers: "I'm so happy for you and Betsey, together again." It was Mrs. Frass the judge's wife, unless it was Mrs. Fenn the mega-millionaire developer's wife; a woman of youthful middle age who was clearly a close friend of the Rampikes, though Bix was smiling quizzically at her saying he didn't know what she meant: "Betsey and I have never been apart."

Seeing a look of disbelief in the woman's eyes, Daddy amended: "Except I'd been traveling a lot, last year. But now I'm at Univers, that isn't going to happen. How's Hayden?"

Skyler saw: not the slightest glimmer of chagrin, or guilt, in Daddy's face.

IN FACT, IT'S TOO DEPRESSING TO RECALL SKYLER'S LAST SEVERAL OUT-ings with his father—*Red Alert III* at the Cross Tree CineMax (when Daddy excused himself halfway through the "action-packed" movie and was gone for the remainder who knows where, or for what purpose, though waiting outside for Skyler when the movie ended, with a warm-Daddy smile, and smoking a cigarette); hasty drive-through meals at Jack in the

---

* *Damn! I haven't wanted to allude to the depressing subject of Skyler's ongoing medical maladies. To his parents' dismay, three years after his gym accident Skyler was still suffering "intermittent chronic" pain in his twice-broken right leg: femur, fibula. Also, knee. Also, neck pain. And "crawly numbness" on the right side of his scalp, occasionally "drilling into" his brain. These various pains were treated with an ever-shifting battery of painkillers and (Skyler had reason to suspect) placebos. (How many children of nine are fully aware of what "placebos" are? In Fair Hills, quite a few.) Bix Rampike was especially upset by his son's physical condition and can you blame him? How does a father feel, in the company of a limping son? A limping son with a midget-cane? No wonder, by the time gabby Mrs. Fenn, or Mrs. Frass, enters the scene, the "guy-stuff" interlude was rapidly approaching its end.*

Box, Taco Bell, Cap'n Chili, Wendy's (where Daddy provided, for himself, red wine in small plastic cups); a "golf lesson" at the (indoor) miniature golf range out on Route 33 (where, provided with a child-sized golf club, Skyler flailed away gamely at the silly little white ball until with a warm-Daddy smile, Daddy decreed the lesson *fin-it-to* and a success); a yet more humiliating "swim lesson" in the (indoor) heated pool of the Fair Hills Country Club (where Daddy swam laps like a large frenzied seal and struck up a conversation with a boy-swimmer of about eleven who moved swift and supple as a fish in the brightly aqua/eye-stinging water, another man's son of whom Skyler, doggedly "dog-paddling" in the shallow end of the pool, tried not to be jealous)—and end with Skyler's visit to Daddy's office at Univers Bio-Tech, Inc.

On this windy-sunny Sunday in early January, whatever the plan was for Daddy and Skyler that afternoon, Daddy suggested, "How'd you like to see your dad's 'place of work,' Sky-boy?" The lift in Daddy's voice, Skyler was made to realize how, until now, Daddy had been plain damn bored.

Secret guy-stuff! For Mummy was not to know.

So Daddy and Skyler sped along I-80 to exit 14B UNIVERS—"The company has its own exit and its own zip code, Sky-boy: we are 'incorporated' like you've never seen before"—and immediately there appeared, amid the wintry semi-rural landscape, the vast grounds—"Three hundred acres designated as 'Green Space'—meaning property tax exemption big-time"—and clustered, connected glass-and-steel buildings—"Our architectural model is the Pentagon, son. The 'mystic'—'impregnable'—arch-shape of all geometrical figures as the ancient Greek Pythagoras revealed, centuries before Christ."

"Way cool, Dad. This place." Skyler spoke in the eager-kid squeak of his more popular classmates.

Though it was Sunday, a number of vehicles were scattered amid parking lots. Must be, daddies became restless over the long family-weekends, and felt the need to "sneak back," like Bix Rampike, for "just a quick check-in."

At the rear of one of the impressive mineral-glinting buildings, Daddy provided Skyler with the numerals to punch them into Project Development. How proud Skyler was, when the massive door clicked open. "Remember not to breathe a word of this to your mother," Daddy said, with a warm-Daddy chuckle, "she'd be upset if she knew I brought you here. And Bliss would feel left out, see? That's the bottom line."

"Yes, Daddy. I promise."

So solemnly Skyler spoke, Daddy ran a playful knuckle across his head and nudged him inside.

Daddy's office was on the fifth, top floor of the building: BRUCE RAMPIKE DEPUTY CHIEF OF RESEARCH DEVELOPMENT. You could see that Bruce Rampike's office was a very important office because it could be reached only through an outer office and took up an entire corner of the fifth floor, with enormous windows overlooking a picturesque pond and hillside covered in something feathered and ripply—Canada geese? These were plump stuffed-looking waterfowl that looked as if they hadn't propelled themselves through the air for a long time.

"Sky-boy! Welcome to the future, for the future is *here*."

Briskly Daddy rubbed his hands together. Stepping into his "workplace" as he called it seemed to have energized Bix Rampike considerably.

"Daddy? Can I watch what you do?"

"You'd be bored, Sky-boy. Whyn't you go play somewhere . . ."

Already Daddy was distracted as he sat behind his massive glass-topped desk in a polished swivel chair that creaked comfortingly beneath his weight. Skyler stood irresolutely, watching. In an offhand voice Daddy said: "Remember, son: there are but two sub-species of *Homo sapiens*: those who act decisively, and those who are acted upon. Those who believe 'my first act of freedom is to believe in freedom' and those who are slaves to atavistic instincts, customs and habits of thought that preclude 'free will.' Univers, Inc. is about the 'free will'—'free enterprise'—shaping of the future, son. And your daddy's task is to assist our Chief of Research Development in locating the 'cutting-edge' science geniuses of our time, hiring them away from wherever the hell they are, and set them to work for us . . ."

Daddy's ebullient words trailed off as Daddy squinted at his computer screen. Skyler knew that Daddy was checking e-mail and would not wish to be disturbed. To Skyler's surprise, Daddy had put on a pair of wire-rimmed glasses that gave him a prim frowning look.

"Daddy? What does 'Univers' *do*?"

"What does 'Univers' *do*!" Daddy continued to peer at the computer screen, typing and clicking rapidly. As if repeating familiar words Daddy said, "Univers, Inc. is in the service of the future, son. Much of our bio-tech experimentation is 'classified' and not to be casually disclosed even to loved ones but, bottom line is, 'Where the future beckons, Univers goes.'"

Skyler leafed through a glossy UNIVERS, INC. brochure on a glass-topped coffee table. Columns of print swirled in his eyes and here and there a word or words leapt out *genetic modification, DNA molecules, chimera, human genome project, molecular genetics, "enhanced" embryos, posthuman being.* "Like 'cloning,' Daddy? I know what that is."

"Could be, son, you 'know what that is'—and could be, you don't 'know what that is.' Hell, Daddy doesn't know what cloning *is*, just how to profit from it. Whyn't you go play somewhere until Daddy is ready to leave? There's a fitness center on the third floor that might be open."

Stubborn Skyler thrust out his lower lip and intoned:

"'Human beings will devastate this planet within the next fifty years. But an "evolved" *Homo sapiens* enhanced by genetic engineering may relocate to other planets. That is our only hope.'"

This got Daddy's attention. Through the wire-rimmed eyeglasses Bix Rampike's widened brown eyes blinked.

"What's that, Skyler? What you just said?"

Skyler wasn't sure. Skyler grinned, stupidly. Truly not knowing whether he should be shyly pleased that Bruce Rampike behind the massive glass-topped desk was staring at him with something resembling— was it startled interest? respect? alarm?—or whether he should be frightened, in repeating the much-maligned Rob Feldman's words he'd said the wrong thing; and in another moment the furious-Daddy look he so dreaded would come into Daddy's eyes.

"How old are you, son?"

"N-Nine."

"Nine! Are you sure? You've been nine a hell of a long time."

Was this an accusation? Or just a fact? Skyler felt as if he'd been nine for most of his very long life. "I'll be t-ten on my next birthday, Daddy. In March."

"Might be, Skyler, you're a brainy kid—brainy and neurotic as hell, unlike us Bus. Ad. majors—and you will go into science, and take the 'high road' others can only envy. I'm thinking that you might be lacking the Rampike blood-lust, more like you'll be going for a brainy solution than for the jugular like your daddy. So one day, Univers, Inc. might be seeking you for one of our projects. This I can reveal to you, Skyler: Univers, Inc. is at the very forefront of the technology. Those windowless buildings on the far side of the geese, see?—those are some of our research laboratories. And we have others. And we fund others. For reasons not needing to be divulged, we have research labs in many outposts of the globe, China for instance, where pure science can flourish unfettered by 'ethical issues'—that is the vision of the future! Mostly our scientists are foreign-born, and even those born here are non-Caucasians: Indians, Koreans. Jews." Daddy paused as if expecting Skyler to reply but Skyler was stumped how to reply. Was he "Caucasian"?—he thought so.

"So, now. Whyn't you go play, Skyler, until Daddy is through here."

Daddy returned to his computer. Skyler felt a pang of loneliness. The plan had been, for this Sunday afternoon, that Daddy would take Skyler to the Thomas A. Edison Laboratory Museum in West Orange ("Many original inventions are displayed") but somehow, Daddy had changed his mind. Now Daddy rose from his swivel chair and disappeared into an adjoining room, must've been a lavatory since he left the door ajar and Skyler began to hear the loud-sizzling sound of an adult man urinating, at length. If Mummy was here, Mummy would be offended: *Bix damn you shut that door! You are not living with your Ep Phi Pi brothers any longer!*

Impulsively Skyler slipped behind Daddy's massive desk to peer at his computer screen: nothing but long columns of numbers, symbols. Skyler struck the return key, daringly: yet more columns of numbers, symbols. Rashly then Skyler struck the key that took you backward, as if back in time, several times Skyler struck this key but the screen showed nothing but numbers, symbols, "percentiles" and "projections." A chill came over him *This is Daddy's true soul, unfathomable.* Skyler pulled open a desk drawer: computer printouts. Another drawer—computer printouts. The lowermost drawer—computer printouts.

Skyler's sparrow-heart was pounding in his narrow chest: what had he expected to find in that lowermost drawer?

Rumpled silk scarf. Handcuffs, masks. Chocolate Licker?

"Skyler! Don't mess with Daddy's work."

Skyler steeled himself for a quick cuff to the side of the head—not hard! "instructive"—of the kind the Lion King gives to favorite/feisty male cub, but Daddy was only frowning at Skyler as if, in Daddy's large opulently furnished office, Daddy wasn't sure who he was.

"Daddy has said, *go play.*"

There was a door in the wall beside Daddy's desk that led directly out into the corridor and so Skyler wandered about in the corridor limping past the locked doors of offices with frosted-glass windows and name-plates much smaller than the smart brass plate identifying BRUCE RAMPIKE DEPUTY CHIEF OF RESEARCH DEVELOPMENT; with but a vague concern that he might get lost, Skyler descended a flight of stairs, and another flight; carpeted corridors led off in all directions, as in an ant colony; here and there, lounge-areas beckoned to Skyler, flooded with late-afternoon sunshine. Through floor-to-ceiling plate-glass windows you could see other buildings on hillsides and a portion of the pond and the flock of stuffed-looking Canada geese visible from Daddy's office on the higher floor. " 'Daddy has said, *go play.*' " Skyler paused, smiling strangely. " 'Daddy has said, *go kill yourself.*' "

Kids did sometime! Though you could never find out how.

With the intention of locating the fitness center, so that he could report to Daddy that he had, Skyler found himself limping along a corridor of smaller offices of which one appeared to be occupied for the door was open. A startled-looking young woman came to the doorway: "Excuse me? Little boy? Are you—real?"

Skyler blushed, and mumbled *yes.*

Behind the young woman on a desk much smaller than Daddy's was a computer. On the screen, what appeared to be columns of numbers, symbols. What a sinking sensation in Skyler's stomach, to realize that this was the true adult-world, truer than the playful items in Daddy's underwear drawer at home! Computer screens, columns of numbers, symbols.

"I thought you were a ghost, little boy. You look almost—well, like a ghost."

The young woman laughed. Though the young woman appeared to be nervous. She wore a pullover sweatshirt with faded letters BRANDEIS and rumpled jeans, her dark hair tied back in a scarf. Except she was a few years older, the young woman reminded Skyler of one of Bliss's girl tutors.

"Are you lost? What are you doing here? Where are your parents?"

Skyler mumbled his daddy was in his office working.

"And who is your daddy?"

Skyler mumbled his daddy's name was Rampike.

"Rampike! Oh."

The effect was immediate. A look of wary respect came into the young woman's face. "Your father is Mr. Rampike? Up on the fifth floor?"

"Do you know Daddy?"

The young woman bit at a thumbnail. Her eyes flashed like zinc. She was younger than Skyler's mother but, Skyler thought, not nearly so pretty as Skyler's mother, her angular, intelligent face plain without makeup. "I know your 'daddy'—of course. Mr. Rampike is my supervisor."

Skyler was too shy to ask the young woman where the fitness center was and so mumbled 'bye! and turned away. For the length of the corridor he felt the young woman watching him and at last she called after him: "Tell your daddy that 'Alison' is here—working hard on Sunday afternoon."

There was a tremor in the young woman's voice which Skyler did not wish to interpret: flirtatious reproach? angry reproach? yearning? hope? He hurried away without glancing back.

Abruptly the gray carpeting underfoot had changed to dark green. Without leaving the building Skyler had entered another wing: DEPT. OF PERSONNEL MANAGEMENT. Yet it was the third floor he was on—wasn't it? The words *Alison is here—working hard on Sunday afternoon* echoed inside his head with a tone now mocking, accusatory. He was meant to be the bearer of a coded message but he would not cooperate. As when Mummy questioned Skyler about what he and his father did on their outings together *Are you with Daddy every minute? Does Daddy slip away? Does Daddy "run into" anyone? Does Daddy talk about me?* He'd begun to feel the sensation of crawly numbness in his scalp, which made him want to dig his fingernails into his scalp and scratch, hard. As sometimes Bliss scratched with her nails in a similar way. These were very bad habits. Mummy despaired of such bad habits in her children. Skyler felt a tinge of pain in his left leg—which was his "good" leg—meaning that the pain wasn't real but what Mummy called fantim pain; like Bliss's fantim pain in her left ankle that had returned since she'd begun double practice sessions at the Halcyon rink in early January, in preparation for the Hershey's Kisses competition which was to be televised on ABC-TV. Bliss's fantim pain was a secret from Daddy for Mummy was afraid that, if Daddy knew, he would not want Bliss to be practicing so much; worse yet, he might not want Bliss to skate in the competition.

It doesn't hurt! My ankle doesn't hurt! Bliss insisted wiping tears from her clenched little face.

Skyler understood that something bad had happened between Daddy and Mummy on New Year's Eve. It was meant to be a happy time, for Daddy and Mummy had been invited to three New Year's Eve parties including a party at the home of Si and Mimi Solomon which was a very special party to which other friends of the Rampikes had not been invited. In their glamorous "dress-up" clothes—Daddy in his tux, Mummy in a dazzling gold lamé gown with a very low, tight neckline—the elder Rampikes had been very happy kissing Skyler and Bliss good night but sometime past midnight Mummy had returned home alone stumbling and cursing and when Daddy returned, Skyler wasn't sure for he'd fallen asleep, and was wakened groggy and confused hearing Mummy's fierce voice *You are not starting this again, Bix. Please you are not, for Bliss's sake you know what pressure we are under.* And Daddy's voice pleaded *Betsey I am not. You have the wrong idea. Sweetheart I swear.*

By accident Skyler found the Fitness Center! He was too short to peer through the window in the door to see if anyone was inside but when he pushed the door open, the cavernous space, only partly lighted, appeared to be empty.

Against the farther wall were several treadmill machines. There were stacked weights and the usual machines with leather seats and straps and the air was both chill and stale-smelling. Skyler smiled uncertainly. Daddy would be pleased that he'd managed to find the Fitness Center . . . As he stepped farther into the room he saw, floating in a long horizontal wall-mirror, a child's small pale face floating as if cut off at the shoulders.

Skyler fled.

With a mounting sense of panic Skyler tried to retrace his steps back to his father's office. Which floor was Daddy on?—the fifth floor? But Daddy's office had been on the top floor of the building and now the fifth floor did not seem to be the top floor. And views from windows did not look familiar. And the sun was slanting in the sky. After ten, fifteen, twenty frantic minutes Skyler was drawn to a man's voice and found himself at the end of an unfamiliar corridor staring into an office at a man, seen from the rear, leaning far back in a swivel chair cupping one hand to the nape of his neck and speaking in a low intimate incensed voice into a phone, "—can't risk leaving—right now—she's obsessed with our daughter—she's made a *ding-'n'-such* out of this skating, and out of Bliss, no telling what the woman might do, if—"

The man was Daddy! Skyler backed away stricken to the heart.

Our daughter! And not a word of *our son.*

. . . NOT A WORD OF *OUR SON**

* *Moment at which nine-year-old Skyler Rampike realized irrevocably that in the lives of his parents whom he loved so desperately as in the vast world beyond the Rampike household Skyler Rampike was, at the most, but a footnote.*

FOOTNOTE!*

* In a text that more accurately reflects its subject, the remainder of this narrative would consist exclusively of footnotes. For it's down here, IN FOOTNOTES, that Skyler Rampike actually lived. (And what about you, the skeptical reader? Is it painful to realize that you, too, are but a footnote in others' lives, when you had wished to imagine you were the text?)

H.I.P.!

"THEY DON'T LOVE *ME*. NEITHER OF THEM."

In this dazed/sulky-resentful/muttering-to-himself state at times approaching a kind of ambulatory catatonia, Skyler would make his way like a somnambulist (classy word for "sleepwalker") through what remained of his life.

Wait. Not *his* life. His sister's life.

"SKYLER! CONGRATULATIONS, SON."

Was this a cruel joke? Headmaster Hannity's moist meaty adult hand gripping Skyler's moist-midget-hand in a *handshake*?

For—so strangely!—in these quick weeks leading to his sister's brutal death in the early hours of January 29, 1997, at Fair Hills Day School Skyler Rampike evidently managed to appear no different than usual; no more "stressed"—"agitated"—"unstable"—than ever, among his high-strung classmates: it was in fact a sixth-grader who "went ballistic" in his homeroom, attacking another boy with a sharp-pointed geometry compass and, when their instructor tried to intervene, attacking him as well, and having to be overpowered and carried away. Another boy, and not Skyler Rampike!*

Somehow—don't ask me how!—Skyler managed stoically to disguise from his classmates as from the inscrutable adults surrounding that he

---

* *The boy was Albert Kruk, son of Fair Hills's high-powered criminal defense attorney Morris Kruk, a one-time "playdate" of Skyler's and amateur pathologist.*

was *but a footnote*; managing, through sheer compulsive concentration, to score so high in the battery of tests known as "fifth-form sweeps" that he was designated H.I.P.—at last.

"Skyler, this is very good news. Clearly you have made a determined effort to improve your academic performance in a highly competitive series of tests. Your instructor has informed me that you are currently prescribed for several 'meds'—and these 'meds' are working very well. So, it seems, diligent student, devoted instructor, and canny pediatric-neurologist are to be congratulated! We are sending an official letter to your parents to inform them of the good news that, next semester, you will be moved up into our advanced-placement curriculum. 'Higher Ivy Potential' is a designation you will carry with you through your school years, Skyler. For the Ivy League is itself a 'hierarchy'—a 'hegemony'—not a mere democracy. Not just any 'Ivy League' college should be our goal, but only the very highest: Harvard, Princeton, Yale. In the American meritocracy, Fair Hills Day is betting on students like you, Skyler, to go the distance for us."

In the headmaster's large meaty-moist hand was a small box embossed with the school's coat of arms.

"Take it, son. You've earned it."

In wonderment Skyler took the little box and opened it and—inside was a gold-gleaming little H.I.P. lapel pin for his Fair Hills Day School blazer!

THINKING *NOW WILL THEY LOVE ME BETTER? A LITTLE?*

QUICK CUTS

"WHY, SKYLER! WHAT A NICE SURPRISE."
Distractedly, Mummy kissed her *little man* on the side of his flushed forehead just as, unfortunately for the *little man*, a much-awaited call from StarBright Modeling Agency came in on Mummy's cell phone.

"SKY-BOY! CONGRATS! 'H.P.I.'—IS IT? AND A TERRIFIC LITTLE GOLD DAGGER for your lapel, eh? This is some sort of 'secret society' at that school of yours, I guess? I'd thought those were forbidden at Fair Hills Day but what the hell, good for you, son. A little pin in your lapel, years from now, it's like Daddy's Ep Pi pin who knows what doors might swing open for you."
Distractedly Daddy ran playful-Daddy knuckles over Skyler's head on his way to pour himself a much-needed drink.

AND THERE WAS BLISS, MADE TO BLINK NEAR-SIGHTEDLY AT THE TINY GOLD upright-flame lapel pin her brother held out to her. "Is it for me, Skyler?"
Skyler laughed harshly. "No! For once, it's something for me."
This was unfair. This was cruel. Bliss adored Skyler. Skyler knew better.
"It's pretty, Skyler. Is it like—a pin? To wear?"
Skyler explained: "H.I.P."—"Higher Ivy Potential"—what the headmaster had said to him and how the headmaster had shaken his hand. How

special it was to wear an H.I.P. pin if you were a student at Fair Hills Day for it meant that you were in the highest percentile.

" 'Per-cen-tile'—what's that?"

"The highest of the high."

Even as Skyler boasted he felt the hollowness of his boast. For there was his little sister gazing at him with wistful admiring eyes, sucking her finger.

Poor Bliss! Much of that day she'd been practicing at the rink. Hour upon hour, practicing her routine for the Hershey's Kisses competition which was only five days away. In the late afternoon, Mummy had taken her to Dr. Bohr-Mandrake for a therapy session and to Dr. Muddick for injections. From the gingerly way in which Bliss was sitting on the edge of her bed, Skyler surmised that her bottom was hurting.

From what Skyler had been overhearing lately, Bliss's skating was not going so well as Mummy wished. Skyler supposed it was that damn fantim pain in Bliss's left ankle again, that leapt from Skyler's right leg to Bliss's ankle, and from Bliss's ankle to Skyler's leg, like a flu passed back and forth between siblings.

Skyler said, relenting: "The smart kids at school would all rather be you, Bliss! A champion skater."

Faintly Bliss smiled. "They would? Why?"

"Because then they'd get attention! Their pictures would be in the paper and they'd be on TV."

Still Bliss smiled, faintly. (Sometimes Skyler felt a rush of impatience: you'd think Bliss was a *retard*.)

In one of those gestures of big-brother magnanimity that reverberates to this very hour, as a sign that bratty/envious Skyler could be nice, sometimes, Skyler pinned the H.I.P. flame to Bliss's collar. "This will protect you, Bliss! Next Saturday."

Bliss thanked Skyler! Blinking back tears.

"Will you make me a red-ink heart, too? Like yours?"

(Scattered in secret places on Skyler's body, including the palm of his left hand, were silly little red-ink "tattoos" of the kind Skyler's gangsta classmates sported. But no one was supposed to know about Skyler Rampike's "tattoos" because Skyler belonged to no gang; and

Skyler believed that, if the other boys knew, they'd have been angry at him.)*

"No! Mummy would find out, and Mummy would be mad."

For Mummy knew every inch of Bliss's body. All that had to do with Bliss, Mummy knew.

"For when I skate, Skyler! A red-ink heart."

But Skyler shook his head, noooo.

As Bliss was between tutors, Skyler had volunteered to help her with the same first-grade material her tutors had tried to teach her without success: ABC's and primer reading and (very) primer writing, numerals and the most basic arithmetic. But Bliss made very little progress and was easily discouraged. Skyler perceived a fundamental, you might say a metaphysical rejection of the very concept of Objective Reality, on the part of his sweetly stubborn little sister: for Bliss could not comprehend why, for instance, six times six "must be" thirty-six, and not sixty-six; and how is it possible, if you subtract ("take away") twelve from ten, the answer "must be" minus-two. (And how to explain "minus-two" to a skeptical child? Bliss smiled as if suspecting a joke, a kind of sly-Daddy joke, to make her believe something silly and then laugh at her. And often Bliss asked Skyler, "Would Daddy believe this?" with a doubtful look. Or, "Does Mummy believe this?") How frustrating to Skyler, whatever he managed to teach her, a few days later she'd have forgotten: "It's like my head is a glass bowl of slippery things, Skyler, and if you push new things in, the old things will fall out."

It was so. Bliss's head seemed very crowded. When Mummy was not with Bliss and Bliss was allowed to be alone, and quiet, Skyler perceived that his sister was deeply involved in her thoughts and he knew, from little twitches and tics in her limbs, and the stiff little doll-smile that Mummy insisted upon for Bliss's skating performances, that Bliss was *practice-skating* in her head; and that such *practice-skating* could be as exhausting as the real thing.

As in his own fevered thoughts Skyler often found himself reenacting

* *Damn! This is banal kiddie-stuff, and I am stuck with it. The alert reader will perceive some logic in its clumsy placement here, however. As in a formal mystery, both "clues" and "red herrings" must be planted beforehand.*

again, again, and yet again those catastrophic moments in which his young life was irrevocably altered in the Gymnastics Lab under the tutelage of the Russian Vassily Andreevich Volokhomsky as Skyler bravely/brashly/desperately grasped the rings and leapt into the air ▬▬▬▬▬▬ .

But no: that was over. Long over.

Bix Rampike had received an "undisclosed" sum of money from the beleaguered Gold Medal Gym & Health Club and as Daddy would say with sly-Daddy-smirk: *Fin-it-o*.

Today's lesson with Bliss was a very simple one: Bliss was to spell out, in block-letters, words that Skyler pronounced ("horse"—"dog"—"girl"—"house" etc.), that Bliss was supposed to be able to spell; but Skyler decided to experiment by printing out their last name R A M P I K E and asking Bliss to copy it "exactly as you see it"; and so, gripping a crayon tightly in her right hand, painstakingly Bliss reproduced

R M I P E R

"WELL. WHAT DO YOU THINK?"

As Daddy had spread out his Rampike Dream House plans on the dining room table with a flourish some weeks ago, now breathless Mummy spread out Bliss's "contact sheets" from the StarBright Agency. These were dozens of color photos of Bliss Rampike in modeling poses, in an assortment of Junior Miss Elite Skates Fashions: practice sweatpants and fuzzy pullovers, turtleneck sweaters and little pleated skirts, leotards with colorful sashes, knitted caps with tassels, tartan kilts, tulle tutus, satin-and-sequin "showgirl" costumes. In the most dramatic of the photographs Bliss was posed on a bluish-glittering ice surface, in her beautiful little white kidskin Junior Miss Elite Skates. Yet, though Bliss was in skates, and on the ice, where ordinarily Bliss Rampike felt most comfortable, here she seemed stiff, almost awkward, and her sweet-shy little doll-smile was unconvincing.

"Looks good, sweetie! My bestest-best li'l gal." Daddy had but given the contact sheets a cursory glance, for Daddy had a drink in his hand,

and somewhere (Daddy's "home office"?) to get to, but Daddy took time now to kiss Bliss lightly on the top of her head.

"Bix, wait! These pictures are good, don't you think? Bliss is very—winning, isn't she?"

Brightly Mummy spoke but keen-eyed Skyler could see how, like Bliss whom so often Mummy scolded, Mummy was digging nervously at her thumbnail.

"Sure! Bliss always is. What's the problem, Betsey?"

Daddy spoke in the most affable/patient of domestic-Daddy tones. With a wink to Sky-boy, signaling *These women!*

"Well, they are saying, at the Agency, that Bliss is 'stiff' and 'looks older than her age.' That she might need modeling lessons before we can expect a contract from Elite Skates."

" 'Modeling lessons.' Models have got to be taught, to stand there and have their pictures taken? Chri-ist!" Daddy laughed to suggest that (1) he was being funny, but (2) he was not being funny.

Mummy protested, "Bix, don't be silly! Modeling is a—profession. Not just anyone can 'model.' "

"Like not just anyone can be an astrophysizist, or palyontologist or brain surgeon, eh? Or an alpha-mummy like *you*." Daddy laughed, pleasantly. A dull flush was rising into Daddy's big-boned big-boy face.

"Oh, Bix! Your sarcasm *hurts*."

Now Daddy protested, "Who's being sarcastic? This is just Daddy asking: what will 'modeling lessons' set me back, on top of 'skate lessons' etcetera?"

Mummy's cheeks reddened. Mummy was standing close behind Bliss, loosely embracing her as Mummy pushed the contact sheets about to be better viewed. "Bix, everything in life is not the damned 'bottom line.' There is beauty, and there is—art. For art, people have sacrificed over the centuries! After the Hershey's Kisses Festival next week, where our daughter is favored to win the junior-miss crown, and the Hudson Valley All-Girl Challenge in two weeks in Newburgh, Bliss should have plenty of time for what's called a 'total-immersion' course taught by StarBright, and the Agency will allow us a discount."

Daddy laughed ruefully. "Well! That's good news. For a moment I was worried, I might have to shell out the full price."

As Daddy was about to turn away, Mummy tugged at his sleeve.

Skyler saw Daddy's jaws tighten. *Now Daddy will shake off Mummy's arm*, Skyler thought; but, as if to refute Skyler, and Mummy herself, who may have expected this, Daddy did not.

"Bix, you do think these photographs are good, don't you? I mean—beautiful? We worked so hard to make Bliss up, and to pose her . . ."

"I said, sure. Daddy's bestest-best li'l girl always looks gorgeous."

"But, Bix—"

"Yes, Betsey?"

"They are saying—some of them—at the Agency—that Bliss's hairline is just a 'centimeter of a centimeter' too low."

"Like hell! Our daughter's hairline is just fine."

"They're suggesting electrolysis, to raise it just slightly. The effect would be magical, I think: Bliss's forehead would be higher, and her eyes larger. Electrolysis is a simple procedure in a doctor's office with a very mild sedative and virtually no recovery required."

Now Bliss, who'd been staring at the showy likenesses of herself spread on top of the table, wriggled inside Mummy's embrace and touched her forehead at the hairline. "I don't want 'lectrolysis, Mummy. No."

"Sweetie, we've gone over this. It doesn't hurt at all, it just tickles."

"I don't want 'lectrolysis! Please, Mummy."

"Honey, we can have it together. My forehead has always been too low, too! It's too late for me to be a model—or a skater—but I can have my hairline raised anyway. All right, sweetie? We can have the procedure done together, in New York City, and have such fun—"

Daddy intervened: "No. I don't think that fucking 'electrolysis' is a good idea for our daughter."

"Bix! Your language. Please."

"Betsey! Your language. Pl-ease."

"The Agency wouldn't recommend electrolysis—or modeling lessons—if they didn't think that Bliss has genuine potential as a child model, or even a child actress. They have seen her on ice and they are wild about her—I mean, literally. And electrolysis isn't expensive, and it isn't dangerous, and—"

"I said no, Betsey. Can you spell? *N-O*."

"Bix, you are not the dictator of this household. Damn you Bix, you are not the despot."

"No, I am not. I am that child's father, and I pay the fucking bills around here, and I say *no.*"

"Bix, you make so much money! Your Christmas bonus, alone—"

"Okay, I'm a millionaire. Multi-millionaire. And I intend to be a billionaire. So what? I say *N-O*, and *N-O* it is."

Clumsily Mummy gathered up the contact sheets as if Daddy had befouled them, biting her lip to keep from whimpering. In disgust Daddy stormed out of the room but returned almost immediately to continue the quarrel, as Bliss backed off jamming several fingers into her mouth, and Skyler looked on in ▬▬▬▬▬▬▬▬

(OKAY: I CAN'T END THIS SCENE. BELIEVE ME, I HAVE TRIED, AND I HAVE tried, and I am exhausted trying, and I give up. It is rare for an author to concede to the reader that he has *given up*—probably it is unknown in the annals of literature, or whatever sub-category this is. But Skyler Rampike, nineteen years old going on fucking* ninety-nine, *gives up here.*)

---

* Don't blame me for Bix Rampike's foul mouth! Every crude fucking word that has ever issued from my mouth can be traced back to Rampike père, you can be sure.

WIN BIG (I)

DOORBELL!

The Rampikes' housekeeper Lila Laong hurried to the door. How peculiar this incident was, Lila Laong would recall only in retrospect.

It was mid-morning of January 8, 1997: a bright cold winter morning just three days before Bliss Rampike was to compete with nine other hopeful young-girl skaters for the coveted title Hershey's Kisses Girls' Ice-Skating Princess 1997 and less than twenty-four hours since Bix Rampike left the house at 93 Ravens Crest Drive (but only temporarily, it was believed, since Mr. Rampike had packed only a single suitcase and had but one pair of shoes, which he was wearing). Another time the doorbell was rung, impatiently it seemed, and Lila opened the door, to her surprise seeing on the front step a tensely smiling delivery man "not dressed right for a delivery man"—"a youngish man, very pale"—"redhaired, with no hat"—"smiling so hard, his mouth looked stretched"—with a large bouquet of spring flowers (tulips, daffodils, jonquils, richly scented paperwhites and hyacinth) which he presented "for Miss Bliss Rampike" and which Lila took from his slightly tremulous hands, put in one of Mrs. Rampike's largest vases and placed on a marble-topped table in the foyer, beside it a card neatly hand-printed as if by a scrupulous child:

> DEAREST BLISS I KNOW THAT YOU WILL WIN
>
> ON SATURDAY AND YOU WILL WIN BIG
>
> FOR YOU ARE ANGEL ON EARTH MY DARLING

G.R.'S PRAYYERS ARE WITH YOU FORVER BLISS

LOVE G.R.

What was strangest about this incident was that the "youngish man"—
"not dressed right for a delivery man"—had not brought the flowers for
Bliss Rampike in a delivery van but, cradled in the crook of one arm as he
pedaled, on a bicycle.

WIN BIG (II)

ANGEL ON EARTH MY DARLING.

By bicycle he came! And the winter morning so brightly cold, and the distant sky so purely blue, and an arctic taste to the air! A lone romantic figure on a decades-old English racing bike amid, on the thunderous Great Road, dull suburban traffic, yet ingeniously managing (for he was double-jointed, and something of an acrobat, if fatally clumsy in what is called actual life) to cradle the unwieldy bouquet of spring flowers in the crook of an arm; traversing Woodsmoke Drive, and Hawksmoor Lane, and Pheasant Run, now turning onto serpentine Ravens Crest Drive, and pedaling to the very end of this narrow, curving, bumpy road passing only a single vehicle, a FedEx van; maintaining a steady speed on the bicycle, in a fawn-colored faux-suede jacket snugly fitting his slender body, a gaily-striped muffler around his neck, bareheaded despite the cold so that his coppery-red hair, like Percy Shelley's, is a patch of flame in that drab Dürer winterscape.* What a striking figure he is, if anyone on Ravens Crest Drive is watching (as on a TV monitor in his head always *he* is observing for he never lets himself out of *his* sight), asked by an invisible interviewer why he has made his task so difficult, if not treacherous, bringing this bouquet of flowers to his little angel Bliss Rampike via bicycle from his mother's house at 29 Piper's Lane in the modest "working-class" section of Fair Hills two miles away, he'd have said with a toss of the flamey-red hair, and a disarming smile, "A bicycle is more personal. I bicycle everywhere I can, even in winter."

---

* *Shelley, Dürer: impressive, eh? Just the tip of the iceberg of Skyler Rampike's haphazard but classy prep school education of which, lucky reader, you will be spared 99%.*

And is it true, the invisible interviewer inquires, that he has made this perilous journey more than once in the past, more than several times along serpentine Ravens Crest Drive, often at dusk, undetected, bringing with him his small lightweight Japanese-made video camera to record what fleeting glimpses of his little angel might be available through the downstairs windows of the sprawling Colonial house at 93 Ravens Crest Drive, asked so thrilling a question point-blank, what reply except a wordless toss of the flamey-red hair, and the disarming smile?*

---

* *Ugh! So abruptly inside the mind of a sicko where for sure I do not wish to be any more than you do, reader.*

CHOCOLATE KISSES

"NEXT TIME, WE WILL ALL PRAY HARDER."

For in her chic dark-chocolate velvet costume with tight-fitted sleeves and "tinsel" bodice, Bliss didn't make it. In her short, airy, flirty tulle skirt with a teasing glimmer of white-lace panties peekaboo beneath, Bliss didn't make it. Despite the small gold cross around her neck on a slender gold chain, and tiny gold earrings to match, Bliss didn't make it. Despite the very blond hair (bleached, just perceptibly brittle) charmingly plaited with tinsel ribbons (to suggest Hershey's Kisses wrappers) and her small face meticulously made up like the face of an old-fashioned and very expensive ceramic doll, Bliss didn't make it. Despite her white eyelet stockings, and her white kidskin Junior Miss Elite Skates, and the tense smile frozen on her perfect little rosebud lips, she didn't make it.

So many hours!—days, weeks!—of figure-skating practice at the drafty Halcyon rink, with Mummy scrupulously videotaping so that Bliss's performances might be analyzed by her trainer Anastasia Kovitski and her choreographer Pytor Skakalov; so many hours of skate-dancing to the sultry thumping of *Boléro*, that kitsch-classic of girls' competitive ice-skating; so many sessions with Dr. Muddick, and Dr. Vandeman, and Dr. Bohr-Mandrake, and Dr. Rapp, and Kai Kui (acupuncturist/nutritionist, in case the reader has forgotten); so many injections of SuperGrow, Hi-Con Vit-C, CAGHC and HTT et al. in Bliss's most tender places, and so many milligrams of Nixil, Nilix, Serenex, Excelsia, Zomix et al; so many hours of the hateful "dental bite" and so many hateful sessions at the Fair Hills Beauty Salon (where Bliss's hair was "lightened" and where Bliss was fitted with ten perfect faux-nails to hide the broken and tattered nails beneath); so many ardent prayers beginning "Heavenly Father" and "Dear Jesus"; and yet—*she didn't make it.*

From the start, Skyler knew.

Even before Bliss skate-glided out onto the ice, as the crowd erupted in applause, and the spotlight fastened greedily upon her, Skyler knew.

Though in fact Bliss began her skate-dancing performance with what appeared to be her usual agility and speed, within sixty seconds you could see that something was wrong. Bliss's long looping glides, both forward and back, usually flawless, became hesitant and erratic, as if Bliss's left ankle was giving her pain. A turn, a spin, a leaping spin—Bliss's glossy-pink lips parted with the effort, she was breathless, panting. Her small hands flailed like stricken birds. Her eyes shone with surprise, fear. The audience that had so warmly greeted MISS BLISS RAMPIKE, FAIR HILLS, NEW JERSEY, only a few minutes before became subdued, silent. As the recorded *Boléro* thumped to its climax like a convulsing boa constrictor Bliss suddenly tripped, and fell; fell hard; yet managed to scramble back up onto her skate-blades, clumsily, with a look of shock and chagrin. How pitilessly the spotlight held her, to expose her to strangers' staring eyes! How hushed the arena had become, as at an execution! At last the ordeal was over, the humiliated girl-skater limped off the ice amid a scattering of hollow-sounding applause, and there came Betsey Rampike to seize her daughter and bear her out of the spotlight, hugging the little girl hard as if to shield her with her own body and saying, with a bright, brave, undaunted smile, loud enough to be picked up by the ABC-TV camera crew: "Next time, we will all pray harder."

BLUNT FORCE TRAUMA

THIS BLUNT FACT: EIGHTEEN DAYS AFTER BLISS RAMPIKE PLACED SEVENTH at the Hershey, Pennsylvania, competition, she was dead.

RED-INK HEART

MAKE ME A LITTLE RED HEART SKYLER? WITH CHILDISH PERSISTENCE
begging *Make me a little red heart like yours Skyler? please* and so Skyler did:
a small red-ink heart-"tattoo" on the palm of Bliss's left hand. For it was
the night before the night before Bliss's seventh birthday when Daddy
would be returning for Daddy had promised and there was the wish that
Bliss's birthday would be a happy one since the terrible thing that had
happened at the skating competition in Pennsylvania of which no one in
the Rampike household would speak, not Mummy, not Skyler, not Lila
and not Bliss, for it was so shameful, you could not think of it without a
sick-sinking-sensation in the pit of the stomach, Mummy herself would
not speak of it except to say in her bright-Mummy voice *Next time we will
all pray harder! And we will have greater faith.*

Since what-had-happened in Pennsylvania, Bliss had begun to behave
like a much younger child. A fretful child, a willful child, a sulky child,
an anxious child, a thumb-sucking bed-wetting child who exasperated
her older brother by hanging onto him, following him around the house
and even into his room though he tried to shut the door against her—
"Bliss, go away." Yet Skyler felt sorry for her too: as Skyler felt sorry for the
hapless squirrels run over so frequently on Ravens Crest Drive. (If Daddy
ran over a squirrel, Daddy winced and shrugged: "Sorry, pal. Nothing
personal." Mummy cried: "Oh no not again, God damn.") So Skyler "tattooed" a little red heart on his sister's soft moist palm to match the little
red heart on his own left palm and Bliss shivered and giggled (for "tattooing" in such a soft place tickled) and hugged him tight around the neck:
"Thank you, Skyler!" Her kisses were breathy and sticky, Skyler felt as if

his own breath was being sucked from him. Obsessively Bliss peered at the little red heart on her palm opening and closing her fist and the expression on her pale, thin face was one of such intense concentration you would think *That child is in pain.*

You would think *There is nothing that can be done for that child.*

Guiltily Skyler wondered: if he had inked a little red heart on his sister's palm, or somewhere else secret on her body, as she'd begged him, would Bliss have been protected from harm at the skating competition? Would the shameful thing-that-had-happened, broadcast on network TV, not have happened? But cowardly Skyler hadn't dared for Mummy would have seen and Mummy would have been furious with him and Mummy would have scrubbed off the red-ink heart immediately, in any case. When Mummy was angry at her little man Mummy had a way of speaking sharply to him as if he'd hurt her—"Skyler, there must be a devil in you! A very big devil for such a small boy"—that made Skyler feel terrible.*

Since what-had-happened-in-Pennsylvania Mummy was often away when Skyler returned home from school (where? Lila had only Mummy's cell phone number, to call in an emergency) and when Mummy was home, Mummy was likely to be in her private room on the second floor speaking urgently on the telephone in no mood to be disturbed by her children: "Go away! Keep each other company! That's why there are two of you."

Mummy was just joking—of course! Mummy loved her little man and Mummy loved her little daughter more than ever.

For there was a quarrel with Daddy: Daddy wanted Bliss "never to skate again—not ever" but Mummy was determined that Bliss's career would continue (immediately after the defeat in Pennsylvania, Mummy had fired both Anastasia Kovitski and Pytor Skakalov both of whom were suing her for breach of contract as Mummy herself was suing the StarBright

---

Yet not repentant. For the tattoos were good-luck talismans that Skyler needed for survival at Fair Hills Day School and maybe at home, too. In his classes, in the boys' lavatory, in his room at home compulsively inking daggers, skulls, spiders, snakes and the secret initial C.K. on the insides of his forearms and elbows, on his thighs and flat little stomach, in both red ink and black and mostly hidden beneath his clothes. The task of scrubbing them off fell to Lila who never asked what the ink-tattoos meant and never reported Skyler to his mother as if the Rampikes' housekeeper-from-the-Philippines understood the desperate magic of tattooing.

Agency for breach of contract following their abrupt lack of interest in representing Bliss Rampike's modeling career) and Skyler overheard them quarreling in the master bedroom at the far end of the second-floor corridor *You will not take her from me, damn you! She is my daughter, she is mine, and Skyler is mine, please don't destroy us!* Mummy's uplifted voice like the shriek of a stricken bird and Daddy's voice was lower, muffled so that Skyler could distinguish only isolated words *Hey look I love you, I love all of you, but this is non-negotiable, got it?*

Non-negotiable. Skyler liked the heft of these syllables.

At this time Daddy was sometimes "away" and sometimes "home" and you could not always tell the distinction. Impossible to track Bix Rampike during these crucial weeks of January 1997 except to note that when Skyler's father did return home after work, and had dinner with his family, often he and Mummy seemed to be on very good terms with each other as if nothing was wrong between them but only imagined by their children; at other times, there was such strain, Bliss was too agitated to eat and Skyler had to excuse himself to scuttle away from the table like a wounded crustacean and hide away upstairs in his room overseeing battles to the death between platoons of Robo-Army Warriors.

"What does it mean, Skyler?—Daddy is 'dad'?"

Skyler shrugged. "He just is."

"And Mummy?"

"Mummy—what?"

Bliss peered searchingly at Skyler as if trying to decode his meaning. Now Bliss wasn't practice-skating for hours every day, and was still between tutors, her days at home were very lonely. Grandmother Rampike had sent her a children's picture book called *The Floating Dirigible* which was a book for a much younger child but Bliss studied it with fascination, ran her fingers beneath the spare text and shaped her lips to the words. By now, Bliss must have memorized the simple story of a little girl in old-fashioned white attire who (unwisely, out of curiosity) steps into the basket of a huge black dirigible and is carried off into the sky as her overbearing aristocratic parents run shouting after her, yet still she insisted that Skyler read it to her, repeatedly.

As she'd insisted that Skyler draw the little red-ink heart on the palm of her hand, as if she couldn't have drawn it there herself.

Bliss asked, sucking at a finger, "Skyler? Why are we with them?"

"With who?—Mummy and Daddy?"

"Why are we *theirs*?"

Skyler shrugged again, stumped. If Mummy had been here, Mummy would have slapped Bliss's finger out of her mouth. Not hard, but forcibly. Skyler was tempted.

"Because Mummy and Daddy are our parents. That's why we're theirs. Don't be stupid."

"But, Skyler—why? Why are they our *parents*?"

"Because they just are. Everybody knows this."

"Yes, but—why? Skyler? Why are they?"

"Because—they *had us.* That's why."

"Did they buy us?"

Skyler was beginning to feel disoriented, as if the floor was tilting beneath his feet. Bliss was peering at him with such yearning, her watery cobalt-blue eyes fixed so intensely on his face, he wanted badly to run from the room.

In the kitchen close by, Lila was preparing dinner. It was early evening but dark as midnight outside the family room windows. Mummy hadn't yet returned from her Thursday appointment with Dr. Stadtskruller, unless it was Dr. Screed, or Dr. Eustis, and whether Daddy would be home in time for dinner or was working late at the office or forced to spend the night at the company-owned condo in New York City, Skyler had no idea. Luckily, neither Mummy nor Daddy could overhear this exchange: Mummy did not like such "prying" questions of Bliss's and did not like Skyler to "indulge" her; Daddy thought such questions "morbid" no matter who asked them.

"People don't 'buy' their children, Bliss! Don't be so"—Skyler hesitated, not wanting to say *stupid* a second time, for he'd seen how the jeering word made his sister wince—"silly. Everybody knows where babies come from."

Bliss squirmed so on the sofa, the opened *Floating Dirigible* slipped from her lap to the floor. "They do? Where?"

Evasively Skyler said, " 'Having a baby' is what a man and a woman do together, when they get married. That's how they know the baby is theirs. They make it."

" 'Make it'? Did Mummy and Daddy 'make' us? How?"

Skyler had to concede, this was implausible, and alarming. He tried to remember what Calvin Klaus had told him so vehemently: *screw together, hole between legs, cock fits in.* Something gets shot up inside the woman that turns into a baby inside her belly—how? Skyler could not imagine. His brain flickered like a light bulb about to go out.

Bliss said, in a lowered voice like one imparting a secret, "Mummy says that Jesus will love us again if we have faith, but Mummy says that maybe we *are* bad, and should die. Mummy and me, I mean." Bliss was scratching at her scalp in the way that Mummy hated. The pretty *faux-nails* were gone, Bliss's own nails were bitten and brittle and broke easily. A twitch had gotten into her cheek that made her look as if she was smiling and winking naughtily. "It would be a special place, for Mummy and me. And Jesus would be there. 'Going home,' Mummy says. And Daddy would not be there."

Skyler said hotly, "Where would I be?"

"Not with us. It would be just Mummy and me."

"Yeah? Where's this special place?"

"Mummy knows. Jesus knows."

Skyler felt a shiver of dread. His sister's words were both utterly clear and yet confounding as their mother's words were so frequently since the terrible thing that had happened in Pennsylvania.

Bliss added, in a wistful voice, "Know what, Skyler? Mummy and Daddy don't love me anymore. Since I fell on the ice, nobody loves me," and Skyler said quickly, "Yes they do. I do," and Bliss said doubtfully, "You do, Skyler? Why?" and Skyler said, "Because you're my sister," even as he wondered if that was why; if that was a legitimate reason; and if, if this twitchy little sad-eyed girl wasn't his sister, if Bliss had had no brother named Skyler, would anyone have loved her? (And why did anyone love anyone else?— Skyler wondered.)

In the kitchen, Lila was singing one of her sad-happy songs, she'd told them was a song from when she'd been a girl in a faraway place. They had asked Lila if she was lonely for that place and Lila said no because she carried that place inside her. But Skyler could see, the soft sad look in the housekeeper's eyes, that this wasn't so. Bliss was saying, "I was thinking about the time before I was born, and who was there, and did they miss me," and Skyler said thoughtlessly, "*I* was there. Before you were born. Just Mummy and Daddy and me and we didn't miss you." Bliss blinked slowly, taking in this fact. She seemed about to speak but could not speak. Quickly Skyler amended, "But if you went away now, Bliss, I would miss you."

WHAT HAVE YOU DONE?

"SKYLER, WAKE UP!"

Mummy was shaking him, for Skyler could not wake up.

Mummy was agitated, and seemed to be blaming him, and Skyler tried to wake up but could not for his head was heavy and leaden and his eyelashes were stuck together like glue.

"Skyler, please! I can't find Bliss."

In the night, Bliss had pushed open Skyler's door. This was the third time that Bliss had wakened Skyler that week and Skyler resented his sister and pulled a pillow over his head pretending not to hear her stricken voice *Skyler! Something happened in my bed   a bad accident   in my bed* but peevish Skyler refused to respond this time, in disgust muttering *Go away Bliss! I'm not getting up clean your bed yourself* afterward unable to recall if this had truly happened or if it had been a dream for earlier that night when Skyler had just gone to bed (at about 9 P.M.) Mummy came into his room bringing Skyler his bedtime pills which (Skyler was sure) he'd already taken from Lila as he did every night, with warm milk and cookies or Lila's special warm applesauce sprinkled with cinnamon which both Skyler and Bliss loved. Yet there came Mummy teasing: "Skyler, I know your tricks! You and your sister both, you hide your pills in the side of your mouth and when no one is watching you spit them out, you and your devious sister both, you must be watched." Mummy laughed, Mummy's eyes were lustrous as reflections in glass. "But you can't help it, you're his children. And you are his son. *He* named you." And so Skyler had taken the pills (again) except it seemed to him that there was one extra pill, a large white capsule he didn't recognize for it was easier to take these pills than to rouse Mummy's anger at this time of night. And later wakened by a sharp pressure on his bladder, a terrible need to pee, he'd managed to stumble from bed and into the hall and into the bathroom and on the way back to his room he saw a light beneath the door of Mummy's private room and like a boy in a dream not wholly his own he went to the door that was ajar pushing it open hesitantly seeing Mummy in her silky champagne-colored nightgown and over it the warm white terry cloth bathrobe Mummy wore when Daddy was not home for this bathrobe made Mummy look fat and Mummy did not want Daddy to see her in it. Mummy was at her desk leaning on her elbows frowning and muttering to herself, bent over a sheet of paper, gripping a pen as Bliss gripped a pen in her right fist printing in block letters Skyler glimpsed upside down from several feet away. Mummy glanced up with a startled smile: "Why, Skyler! What are you doing up? What time is it? You little—owl." Mummy spoke playfully though Skyler could see that she was annoyed by the interruption; and Mummy did not like to be spied upon by her children, not ever. On the desk beside Mummy's sprawled arms was a dark amber bottle with a bright green parrot label and a small container of white pills. "As long as you're up, sweetie—how d'you spell 'theaten'?"

" 'Theaten'?"

"Yes. 'Theaten.' "

"Do you mean 'threaten,' Mummy?"

Slowly Mummy blinked as if confused then said, shrugging: "Oh, never mind! You male Rampikes are so smart, aren't you. 'Y' chromosome up your ass." Mummy splashed amber liquid into a glass, and drank, and laughed, and waved Skyler with a negligent gesture.

Next morning Daddy was coming to take Bliss away—"A special birthday outing, just Daddy and his bestest-best li'l gal"—to which Mummy had reluctantly agreed, since Mummy had a "real birthday party" planned for Bliss on the actual date of her birthday to which Daddy had not been invited. Bliss had been speaking of nothing else for days: Daddy would be taking her to New York City to the Plaza Hotel for lunch and then to see a matinee of the Broadway musical *The Princess Bride*; and afterward, Daddy would show Bliss the new apartment where Daddy stayed when Daddy "had business" in the city: not the company-owned condominium but, it seemed, Daddy's own apartment on Central Park South overlooking the park. Skyler had no reason to be jealous of Bliss for (1) It was Bliss's birthday, not Skyler's; and (2) Daddy had promised to take Skyler to see the Knicks play in the city, at which time Daddy would show Skyler the new apartment, too. Now Mummy was shaking Skyler to wake him, for Skyler was so very sleepy, and Mummy was pulling up his pajama sleeves saying, "Skyler, let me see your arms," before Skyler could stop her forcing him into the light so that smudged little rows of black daggers/red hearts were revealed on the inside of Skyler's left elbow. "There must be a devil in you! This is ugly. This is pagan. Hasn't Mummy warned you."

Ashamed, guilty, Skyler wished he could hide. But where?

Mummy pulled back the bedclothes on Skyler's bed—as if somehow Bliss might be hiding beneath them, curled up at the foot of the bed. "Where is she? Where is Bliss!"—Mummy had become frantic, unreasonable, kneeling to peer beneath the bed, stumbling then to Skyler's closet where she pawed through Skyler's hanging things, knelt and groped about on the floor amid Skyler's shoes like a blind woman. As if Bliss might be hiding in Skyler's closet, on the floor. Skyler asked Mummy if she'd looked downstairs and Mummy said Yes! of course she'd looked downstairs, she had looked everywhere but Bliss was gone. Mummy pulled Skyler with her across the hall and into the nursery where the Mother Goose lamp beside Bliss's torn-apart bed gave off a warm soft mild glow lost in the brighter light of the ceiling fixture, Skyler saw that Bliss's sheets and mattress were stained, an unmistakable sour smell made his nostrils pinch. Mummy was striking her thighs with her fists half-sobbing, "Bad girl! Again! On purpose to spite me!" as Skyler stood irresolute as if he was to blame and yes he will be blamed for Mummy turned upon him as if seeing him suddenly in a new, terrible light staring at him pleading, "Skyler? What have you done with Bliss? You've taken her, haven't you?—where?"*

* *This painful account of Skyler's recollection of the night of his sister's death differs in small but (possibly?) significant ways from the account in Part I. How to explain this? I'm stumped.*

RIGOR MORTIS

THESE CONFUSED EVENTS OCCURRED BETWEEN APPROXIMATELY 6:20 A.M.
and 6:37 A.M. of January 29, 1997. I have tried to be faithful—the impatient reader might complain, only too faithful—to nine-year-old Skyler's impressionistic experience. Not for another three hours would his sister's body be discovered, by their* distraught father Bix Rampike, in a shadowy corner of the furnace room of the Rampikes' house, already stiff with rigor mortis.

The scrupulous reader has discovered an error of usage here, which editor and copy editor let slip past: their should be his. For a body is (not) (no longer) a human agent, capable of possessing a father. Reader, you are correct. But I refuse to change what I have written, know why? Even in death, in the throes of rigor mortis, to me my sister Bliss is still alive.

IV

POSThumous

EVER AFTER

AND THEY ALL LIVED HORRIBLY EVER AFTER.

"NINE-YEAR-OLD SUSPECT IN SISTER'S DEATH"

NOT A TEAR DID HE SHED.
Cried continuously!

Traces of his DNA would one day be identified on the crimson silk scarf used to bind his sister's wrists together above her head, in a "seductive" pose on the smutty floor of the furnace room.

HAIR FELL OUT. BOY'S WAVY "FAWN-COLORED" HAIR, IN CLUMPS.
Within weeks of the sister's death, the brother's bumpy/scaly/scratched-at scalp resembled that of a child cancer patient undergoing chemotherapy.

And the eyes: "haunted" "zombie" "ghost" eyes.

MUTE. (EXCEPT WHEN ALONE, OR IMAGINING HIMSELF ALONE: WHINING/ whimpering/sobbing/laughing/muttering/"conversing")

BECAUSE HE IS A NERVOUS CHILD.

Because he is a dyslexic child.

Because he is afflicted with Attention Deficit Disorder.

Because his neurologist believes that he may have an impairment of the hippocampus.

(Hippocampus? "Higher brain," in which memory is stored.)

Because he is but nine years old.

Because he has been nine years old for a very long time.

Because, though soon to be ten years old, forever yet he will remain nine years old.

Because he knows nothing about what happened to his sister.

Because he has told us, his parents, all that he knows. He knows nothing.

Because what he may have known, he cannot remember.

Because we know our rights as parents.

Because our attorneys have advised us.

Because we are a devout Christian family.

Because we place our faith in God.

Because he loved his little sister very much.

Because he is innocent. We know that he is innocent.

Because our daughter has been sacrificed, we will not lose our son, too.

NECROPOLIS

IN ANCIENT EGYPTIAN TOMBS OF THE KIND PATRONIZED BY RICH AMERICAN tourists there are said to be "unfinished murals" on the walls. And hieroglyphs thousands of years old telling fragments of histories of long-ago pharaohs and gods.* Must've been a belief of their religion that such murals/histories should be left unfinished as the ancient dead are not dead exactly but in a suspended state; and so I'm thinking that this

---

*How do I know this? Not from personal experience! In the months following my sister's death it seemed that Daddy's squash partner friend Morris Kruk was often visiting with us, for my parents had hired Mr. Kruk (and, in time, Mr. Crampf, of the prestigious Fair Hills law firm Kruk, Crampf, Burr & Rosenblatt) to "protect the rights, privacy, and reputation of the Rampike family"; and Mr. Kruk had recently taken his family on a Nile cruise and a guided tour of the Great Pyramids. And though Skyler was not meant to hear Mr. Kruk discussing the Rampikes' legal situation yet Skyler was allowed to hear Mr. Kruk speaking in his affable yet bellicose voice on neutral subjects. (Morris Kruk! And Josh Crampf, who came to be much admired as well. The Rampikes' high-priced attorneys who would brilliantly block any and all attempts by the Fair Hills police to interview my parents, or me, on the subject of my sister's death. After a preliminary interview at police headquarters, no Rampikes ever returned to be questioned further. Since sufficient evidence would never be gathered by detectives to convince the district attorney that warrants, summonses, or subpoenas should be served to any of the Rampikes, delivering them into police custody to be interviewed at length, weeks, months, and eventually years would pass in what some observers have called a legal coma.†

   †Sorry to be footnoting a footnote! But I need to acknowledge here that when the reader was first introduced to the criminal defense lawyer Morris Kruk in the chapter "Adventures in Playdates II," the author (i.e., me) gave no hint of the fact that one day soon Morris Kruk would be the Rampikes' attorney, retained within a few hours of the discovery of Bliss's body in the furnace room of our house. Asked by television interviewer B___ W___ why the Rampikes had so quickly retained an attorney at the time of their daughter's death, Bix Rampike said: "To prevent a rush to judgment. Shock and grief didn't blind us to the legal thicket that surely lay ahead."

damned document/"confession" of mine sucking at my soul like a vampire bat fixed to my carotid artery is going to be unfinished—"tantalizingly incomplete"—"unconscionably fragmented"—no matter how hard, how long, how obsessively and with what anguish I work at it. *Forgive me reader I can't help it.*

PROMISE!

MUMMY PROMISED. MUMMY PROTECTED. MUMMY LIED FOR HER LITTLE MAN'S sake *That little red heart on the palm of our daughter's left hand?—Bliss drew it on, herself. It was meant to be a good-luck charm.*

BLACK DIRIGIBLE 2007

"JESUS! CAN'T BREATHE."

Sixteen hours. Without a break. The room smelled gassy like bowels, organic rot.

Panic came over me, *had to get out.*

The day after Bliss's birthday. An eerie January twilight. Something felt wrong. Not just she was dead—she'd been dead for ten years, and I knew this—but 8 P.M. should be dark, dark-as-night, not daylight.

Maybe the Turnpike had caught fire? Reflections of lurid flames in the massed clouds overhead, I could see by kneeling on the floor of my room and peering up anxiously slantwise through the fissures in the blind. A fiery sun was wrong for 8 P.M. in late January, in New Jersey.

Grabbed the jacket with the drawstring hood and stumbled down the stairs. The look in my face, you'd have to know that I was crazy and you'd want to keep your distance and yet: "Hey there, bro'. How's it goin'?"

Evasively I mumbled okay. Goin' okay.

A fellow tenant to avoid, since I'd run into him last month at the Middlesex County Probation Dept.

"You in 3C, eh? Looks like you got mail."

It was so. In the row of dented tarnished-brass mailboxes in the vestibule, in the dented mailbox 3C, there was a single envelope just visible, amid anonymous junk mail.

"Jesus! Not now."

Fortunately no one is tracking Skyler Rampike who seems to have been transformed into a sweaty mouth-breather muttering *Jesus!* every few minutes and clawing at his scratchy unshaven face.

Mail addressed to Skyler Rampike was rare. He'd had friends, a few, in school, of which more later, but none of these friends knew where he was and he'd been estranged from his family for some time. The only mail that came to him at regular intervals like clockwork, every four weeks on the first Monday of the month, came in business envelopes from the Pittsburgh law firm Crunk, Swidell, Hamm & Silverstein* but the size, shape, color (smallish, squarish, pale-apricot) of the envelope just visible inside the dented box was a kick in the gut signaling that this letter wasn't from the single person from his old/former life who knew where he lived now.

"Hey bro': something wrong?"

"No! Nothing is wrong."

Had to escape. Running/limping along Pitts Street not knowing where the hell I was headed.

Bro'! Whose *bro'* is Skyler Rampike!

Damn knee is hurting. Forgot my cane.

Sixteen hours! And all I'd managed to write were those terse—enigmatically terse?—chapters "Ever After" (will someone out there take note of this precisely honed single declarative sentence?)—"Nine-Year-Old Suspect in Sister's Death" (originally, this was twenty-seven pages of halting prose)—"Necropolis" (Morris Kruk's abrasive voice ringing in my ears)—"Promise!" (Mummy's terrifying voice that has burrowed into the marrow of my bones) and—beyond this—utter mental/spiritual collapse.

What you are trying to speak, is unspeakable.

---

* *Suspicious reader! By now you've been wondering how the hell Skyler Rampike, unemployed/unemployable nineteen-year-old high school dropout, can afford to live even in the squalid rented room on Pitts Street, New Brunswick. Right? Fact is, Skyler has been the beneficiary of a trust fund established by his grandmother Edna Louise Rampike at the time of her death in March 2003 after a lengthy illness exacerbated by C.A.E.M. ("Chronic Acute Elderly Melancholia") which first struck the seemingly indomitable old woman in the late winter of 1997 in the whirlpool-aftermath of her granddaughter's (yet unsolved, luridly publicized) murder. Poor Grandma Rampike! Not just the loss of her prized grandchild but the ceaseless "sullying"—"trampling"—of the proud Rampike name seemed to have destroyed Edna Louise utterly. Yet she took time to set aside, in her will, a small trust in her grandson Skyler's name, "as partial recompense for the pain and anguish this boy has endured" which paid out to Skyler, by way of checks made out to him by Edna Louise Rampike's executor G. Gordon Swidell, a modest sum of $500 a month. Not much, you're thinking, and you are right, but on such a sum Skyler could "scrape by." Usually.*

To look upon Death. The very face of Death. Unspeakable.

Through hundreds—thousands?—of pages I'd believed that the sheer rush of writing, the momentum of language would bring me to Bliss's death which this time I would see. Unflinching, unshrinking and courageous I would see whose hands seized the sleeping child in her bed and taped her mouth before she could scream and taped together her wrists and her ankles and bore her downstairs to the basement and into the furnace room, and what happened there, what was caused to happen, by someone known to Bliss and to me or by an outsider who'd entered the house in the night with the intention of abducting (?)/raping (?)/murdering (?) my sister; I would see at last how over the tightly wrapped duct tape the (badly wrinkled) crimson silk scarf was tied, binding Bliss's wrists above her head as in a "seductive" pose; I would see whose hands struggled with Bliss to force her down onto the smutty floor behind the furnace (to be precise, behind the furnace to the left as you entered the furnace room: for two furnaces were required to heat the Rampikes' large, sprawling house and it was behind the farther of the two that Bliss's body would be discovered); I would see whose hands seized Bliss's unprotected head, struck her head against the concrete wall, once, twice, three times heedless of the child's terror, and yet another time, and another (as Dr. Elyse would estimate, Bliss's head had been struck against the concrete wall no less than five times and perhaps as many as seven times) though almost at once the child's fragile skull had been fractured, the very bone shattered, bloody clumps of brain leaking into her hair. All this I was meant to see, and so I would know. But I didn't know.

Skyler! what have you done to your sister

Where have you taken Bliss? Skyler you must tell Mummy

Crossing Pitts at Livingstone, and onto Livingstone where in the excavation pit men in hard hats were working, how strange was this? Past 8 P.M.? And when had it snowed? Blinding-white snow phony-looking as Styrofoam.

Something was wrong. Must've been in Skyler's head.

No one must know   Skyler

Mummy and Daddy will protect you

HUBCAP-SIZED GLOWING DISC OF A CLOCK ON THE WALL ABOVE THE FRONT
entrance of the 7-Eleven store. I was staring trying to comprehend the
time: long black hand poised at one, short stubby hand at eight.

This was a neighborhood store where the Indian clerk had come to recognize me. He was a youngish gentlemanly India-born individual wary-
eyed, prim-mouthed, unfailingly courteous. He had no idea of my name
but he had some idea of my face. For it is not possible to totally hide your
face in public, in the United States. And seeing something more than usually gnarled and frantic in my face had made the clerk alert, though still
smiling.

"Is it—night? Or morning?"

My question was too urgent to be playful. The Indian clerk smiled uncertainly.

"Morning."

Morning! Somehow I'd lost a day. (Or, I'd lost a night.)

This 7-Eleven store had been hit by young guys with weapons, kids as
young as fourteen. Another clerk, very likely a relative of this man, had been
assaulted a few weeks ago, hospitalized. Now came Skyler Rampike limping
into the store, panting and agitated-seeming in a grungy jacket with its hood
hiding much of his freaky Caucasian face. And his hands are shaky.

No way for this Indian gentleman (should've been a dentist, doctor,
engineer but instead he managed a 7-Eleven in a run-down neighborhood
of New Brunswick working twelve-hour shifts to assure that his children
will graduate from Princeton summa cum laude) to know if this shaky
Caucasian kid is high on drugs (has to be crystal meth) or more generally a
mental case confusing morning for night, night for morning. Or maybe
I'm an eccentric individual, could be a grad student, dropout, or genius, of
the kind that exist at the margins of a university like lone rogue elephants
at a distance from the elephant herd.

Meaning to be friendly here's Skyler embarked upon a nervous riff:
"Excuse me but I hope, sir, you are more protected than you appear to be, I
see the surveillance camera aimed at me but I hope you've got a baseball
bat—at least!—hidden beneath the counter. Like, if somebody tries to rob

you again. And it will probably happen, the hours you keep, late-night or morning, and the drug users out there, of which please don't think that I am one, I am not. You—I assume this is a family-owned business?—or are these 7-Elevens 'franchises'?—you people deserve better than . . . A hell of a lot better than . . ." But Skyler isn't sure what he is saying. Or why he has become so emotional suddenly. Embarrassing and upsetting the gentlemanly Indian clerk who has no idea how to reply.

And then, I wasn't sure if I had actually spoken these words aloud or whether like a text-message the words had come into my head in silence and had passed out of my head in silence.

And you must never speak of this   Skyler
Not even to Jesus

By this time, I'd located what I had come into the store to buy. Brought the items to the counter where the clerk waited with his wary polite smile. "Anything else, sir? Cigarettes?"

Sir! Yet the clerk meant no mockery, it seemed.

"Thanks, no."

It has to be registered as strange: the twitchy-freaky Caucasian kid with insomniac eyes and charmless beard-stubble wasn't purchasing his usual bargain junk food and six-pack of diet soda laced with caffeine like strychnine but a five-ounce can of Hercules Lighter Fluid and a single (small-sized) box of Five Star Kitchen Matches.

WHICH PURCHASES BY THE YOUNG MAN TO BE IDENTIFIED AS SKYLER RAMPIKE, nineteen, of Pitts Street, New Brunswick, would acquire what a philosopher defines as *significant meaning* only if said young man uses them to some significant purpose, that very morning.

THIS SCRUBBY PARK WHERE THE PREVIOUS SPRING SKYLER RAMPIKE WAS taken rudely, by force, into New Brunswick police custody in what the media call a "drug sweep." Junkies (scruffy-Caucasian, black), dealers (black), hookers (mixed-race), pimps (black). And Skyler Rampike formerly of Fair Hills, New Jersey.

Yet Raritan Park was my park. Had to be. And now that I understood that it wasn't twilight but morning, I was feeling much more hopeful. The episode in the 7-Eleven had been a good thing.

If your life is a movie—or even if it isn't—you can "deconstruct" it into episodes: "scenes." And you can analyze these "scenes" in retrospect, deriving *meaning* from them that was not apparent when you lived them; *meaning* that, a philosopher of mind might contend, does not exist until you analyze it, in coherent language.

"Hey man: you lookin' to scorc?"

No! Not me.

A few yards farther on the muddy path: "Man you lookin' to score?"—more belligerent this time.

No! Not right now.

Has to be a sick-yearning look in my eyes, my clenched mouth, anyone can see that I've come to this place desperate to score. But *no*.

"I'll kill myself first. That's a promise."

Walking/limping away. Damned hard to retreat with dignity when you fucking *limp*. On the cracked-concrete walkway beside the Raritan River in this somber New Jersey light, looking like molten lead. Snow has begun to fall, soft damp clots like miniature blossoms. Snow melting on the concrete, and in the river. The wind is raw and gusty and tastes of metal and yet "rot"—can't escape "rot," this is northern New Jersey.

In Skyler's most recent school—"private"—"prep"—"high-security"—in Basking Ridge, New Jersey, the taboo subject, the most thrilling subject, darker/deeper/more delicious than sex, was suicide.

Killing your*self*. Taking *your own* life.

A challenge! Any loser can play.

For casual browsers leafing through these pages, is your attention fleetingly captured by *The Suicide's Handbook: 22 Tips for a Safe Way Out*? Or, better yet *How to Die Without Fucking up Yet Again: A Handbook for the Burnt-Out Generation*.

Reasoning in Skyler's case it might not "hurt" too much: as soon as the match is struck, assuming the (wooden, clumsy) match doesn't break, as soon as the tiny flame leaps onto the lighter-fluid-soaked clothing you'll be in shock, right? Shock means plummeting blood pressure, oxygen cut off from the brain, mind gone, no turning back. As Dad would say *Fin-it-o.*

Or as Mummy would say *No one will know Skyler   not ever*

Walking/limping above the ravine of enormous misshapen rocks glistening with melting snow, melting ice, litter of broken glass, junkies' discarded needles. There, the graffiti-covered rock-ledge from which a few months ago a sixteen-year-old girl (Caucasian, runaway from Summit, New Jersey) smoking crystal meth with her boyfriend somehow—"accidentally"—slipped and fell and died on the rocks thirty feet below. The ravine, a place of sordid romance by night when young and still good-looking junkies hang out together and so, an appropriate site for "self-incineration"—"immolation."

Overhead, a gigantic cumulus cloud. Massive, misshapen. In earth science at Hodge Hill, Skyler had learned the names of clouds. Skyler had drawn and labeled cloud-shapes, and Skyler had earned a grade of A. At mid-term.

What you don't usually notice, the beauty of clouds. Even ugly-beauty. All that you fail to see. Yet, it's there. Not the litter or the graffiti or the overturned/mangled park benches but the trees. Damn tall beautiful trees. Might be oaks, with thick trunks. Skeletal branches in this cold season, no leaves but clumps of damp snow like blossoms. The cruelty in such beauty: it stands outside and beyond you.

My right leg was throbbing with pain. But it was the old comfort-pain. Fantim pain Mummy called it. Yet Skyler Rampike's pain has always made him special. As Bliss's pain made her special.

"Bliss had to die. Because she was special."

I was walking now with a makeshift crutch, a broken tree limb. If you are "challenged" by pain often all you require is a slight correction in your walk, a redistributation of your weight. We'd passed the fantim pain back and forth between us and now Bliss is gone, the fantim pain remains with Skyler.

Loud voices, shouts. "Hey man!"—"Fuck man!"—boys playing basketball in the lightly falling snow. Only a backboard and a rim lacking a net but the high-school-age boys (black, big) were managing to sink baskets, leaping and shouting with feverish intensity, Skyler couldn't help watching, and admiring. Skyler has never been, as the reader knows, an athlete; nor even an admirer of athletes; what's the physical body but something to, essentially, *let you down when you need it*, is Skyler's belief.

Also close by, approaching Skyler on the path was a stock-bodied young black woman pushing a baby in a stroller and beside her a little girl of three or four, chattering and laughing and so alive and as I passed the little family couldn't help smiling at the young mother, at the baby in the stroller, and at the little girl whose shiny dark eyes lifted to mine guardedly, the little girl's forefinger was in her mouth, a beautiful child with widened eyes of alarm and interest and the thought came to me Maybe this isn't the time to punish yourself, maybe this isn't the place. More audacity is required to live. I felt a thrill of elation: I could return to my squalid rented room, I could return to my task, no hope of "completing" it for the story of Bliss Rampike must be a story that will never be completed. I smiled to think if I hadn't seen the face of my sister's murderer at least I had not seen my own face.

> *Did I hurt Bliss, Mummy?*   *was it me*
> *No!*   *not you Skyler*   *not ever you*

"Excuse *me*."

On the walk a few feet in front of me the young light-skinned black woman stood, agitated. Out of nowhere she'd emerged. And the baby fretting in the stroller, and the dark-eyed little girl sucking at her forefinger, half-hiding behind her mother's sturdy legs.

"You been followin' us? Why so?"

"I—have? I haven't."

Somehow, I'd returned the way I'd come. Just ahead was a small bleak playground of swings, teeter-totter, littered sandbox and children's wading pool in which snow lay in mysterious clumps and patches in mimicry of child-swimmers long since departed. Falling snow was melting on the pavement and on the heated skin of my face. Without knowing what I'd been doing I seemed to have doubled back on myself once, twice?—three times?

The woman spoke loudly. Her young face was sharp-boned as the edge of a shovel, her eyes bulged and glared with a kind of savage thrilled merriment. "My daughter is asking, 'Why's that man looking at me?'—she's scared, mister. And I don't like it."

Quickly I apologized. I hadn't meant to scare anyone.

"You don't stop following us, mister, know what?—I'm gonna summon the police."

There was logic here. I wasn't going to contest it. Hunched in my hooded jacket, I backed off.

Limping away using the tree limb as a cane, Skyler fled.*

---

* *In fact, it was far worse than this. What I'd hoped to evoke in "Black Dirigible"—keen-eyed readers will note the subtle poetic trope!—was Skyler's poignant epiphany of death-in-life/life-in-death and his (courageous, quixotic?) decision to return to the writing of this exhausting manuscript; what actually happened was less poignant than brutally comic, or maybe just brutal, for as Skyler limped away from the angry young mother he was suddenly set upon by the boys who'd been playing basketball nearby, punched, pummelled, knocked to the ground and kicked repeatedly. For these were indignant black boys, who could blame them? Grungy jacket and trousers torn, pockets turned inside out, loose bills and change taken, as much as twenty-five dollars, plus the new purchases from the 7-Eleven, and a final kick in the face, there Skyler lay wheezing, whimpering, bleeding (nose, mouth), writhing like a giant worm on the cold, very hard and ungiving pavement of some urban park he had no idea where, why he'd come here, what had happened to him, or would happen when he dared to open his swollen eyes.†*

> † *Is this a dramatic way to end a scene? The hapless hero of the narrative afraid to open his eyes? In fact, Skyler soon opened his eyes. And when he did, his assailants were gone. The angry young mother and her children were gone. Even the massive dark cloud had moved on. Skyler had to make his way back limping and wincing with pain to the rotting Victorian house at 111 Pitts Street with the humility of a minor character in a movie who has been shoved out of the movie-frame and has been immediately forgotten by the viewers as by the swaggering principal characters who've moved on to their next scene. All that awaited luckless Skyler was, on the second-floor landing of the rooming house where just possibly he'd been lingering, in wait for Skyler, was his friend from the Middlesex Probation office: "Jesus, bro': was it niggers?"*

"RECOVERED MEMORY"!

. . . LOVED MUMMY DESPERATELY BEFORE EVEN THERE WAS DESPERATION IN our lives . . .

PRICELESS VIDEOTAPE!*

SKYLER WHAT DID YOU DO   HONEY WILL YOU TELL MUMMY

A very poor quality tape. Grainy, murky as if the scene is underwater. The recording device—an old camcorder, apparently—is handheld and the hand is shaky and whoever the hand belongs to, the viewer will not see.

The tape is but a fragment. All that remains is seventy-two seconds long.

The off-camera voice is muffled, distraught, unmistakably female *Skyler tell   where sister   did you*

The child! Seems to be a boy though his facial features are not very "masculine." Blurred and wavy as if in fact he's underwater. Or one of those elusive figures who drift through our dreams, sometimes even relatives of ours, who, so perversely, lack fleshed-out faces. What the viewer can see of this child's face is that his skin is unnaturally pale as if drained of blood, and appears to be sweaty; small, and triangular in shape, like a cobra-face (or do I mean "cobra-head"—do cobras have "faces" *persay*?) and the deep-set eyes are droopy-lidded (exhaustion? evasion? guilt?) and

---

* *What the* National Enquirer *would pay for this lost video! Tabloid TV! Network TV! Leaked to the magisterial* New York Times, *the skeletal transcript would be replicated verbatim and the shadowy figure of nine-year-old Skyler Rampike would be emblazoned on the very front page of the paper, if but below the fold. For this video, which Skyler can only vaguely recall having seen in the tense and suspenseful interlude before his father was summoned to come home, and his sister's body was found in the furnace room of the house, would seem to have been viewed by only Daddy and Skyler and Mummy, who recorded it. Soon afterward, it disappeared. No Fair Hills police officers nor even the Rampikes' zealous attorneys Kruk and Crampf and eventually Rosenblatt would glimpse it. What happened to this incriminating tape, do you think? My feeling is that quick-acting/decisive Daddy destroyed it before any outsiders were summoned to the house.*

eerily glassy (like marbles?). The child's light-colored hair is disheveled as if he's been wakened from sleep. His flannel pajama-top hangs oddly on his narrow chest as if already at his young age (you'd never guess more than seven) he has learned the protective strategy of hunching/scrunching himself to appear smaller than he is, younger than he is, more helpless/innocent than he is.

In theory, the tape is in color. In fact its color is so faded it resembles an old black-and-white film of the kind seen almost exclusively on late-night TV.

Skyler?   tell me what   did you do
Where have   sister
please?   Mummy is

The handheld camera approaches the fearful child who seems to be murmuring a response. Whatever the child says, his words are so muffled you can't hear. To make matters worse, he wipes at his nose, and mouth, with both hands.

Skyler?   Please tell me   in this house?   have looked and looked   playing one of your games?   hide-and-seek?   tell Mummy neither of you will be punished Mummy promises

The child stares blankly as if he hasn't heard or, having heard, doesn't know what the words mean. His lips part but no sound emerges.

Wipes at his leaky nose, begins to cry.

(NOT ON VIDEO)

HASTENED SKYLER INTO HER BATHROOM. REMOVED THE DAZED CHILD'S DAMP
pajamas and her own silky nightgown. Pulled him into the shower with
her murmuring *Skyler it will be all right   Mummy loves you and Jesus
loves you   never lose faith we will protect you.* Shampooed his hair, and
her own. Soaped and scrubbed at his skinny little body on baby-giraffe
legs near to collapsing. Soaped and scrubbed at her fleshy Mummy-body
that was flushed and heated from the steaming-hot shower. When he
slipped, seized his skinny shoulders to bear him upright. And afterward,
he was conscious of her gripping his hands, left and then right, with her
metal nail file cleaning beneath his fingernails and toenails and roughly
then with the fond impatience of a mother bear toweling him dry, and
dressed him in clean clothes and dressed herself and by this time it was
7:48 A.M. Now she would call Daddy.

 *

* *Indicates an additional lost block of time. Might've been two days, or three. After the preceding
chapters. Wiped out.*

HEAVEN SCENT

SKYLER YOU MUST NEVER   **NEVER TELL NOT EVER**

Not even Jesus, Skyler   *He will forgive you anyway*

This is a fact: I'd intended to end the chapter "Black Dirigible" with Skyler bravely opening the mysterious letter and reading it; but, as Skyler stumbled through his unexpected misadventure in the park, and crept on home in defeat, it became evident that the poor kid couldn't cope with the letter at that time, both his eyes swollen, leaking blood from numerous orifices and cuts, nerves so jangled he felt like something shaken in a tin can. And so hauling himself up the stairs by the railing, wincing and whimpering to himself, once inside his room he collapsed on his bed and so for days* the mailbox in the vestibule went unopened until at last it was so stuffed with junk mail that the irate mailman had to jam advertising flyers into the cracks of the mailbox door and at last someone (fellow tenant? building superintendent?) climbed the stairs to the third floor to strike his fist on the door of 3C loudly inquiring if anybody was inside? alive or dead? and so finally, roused from my stupor, I replied that yes, I was still alive; and shortly afterward made my way downstairs, with shaky hands unlocking the mailbox, having no other choice, removed the letter and stared at it trying to think coherently, must've been Swidell's secretary who had for-

---

* *In fact, Skyler stumbled out of his room during this groggy interlude to check himself into the Livingstone Community Medical Center ER to have his deeper wounds, that wouldn't stop bleeding, cleaned and stitched up: left eyelid, upper lip and skin-flap beneath his left nostril. What gratitude Skyler feels for the Medical Center where even indigent Caucasian junkies were not turned away for lack of medical insurance! Maybe the stitches were crudely executed and maybe my face is scarred for life, yet, who's complaining?*

warded this letter to SKYLER RAMPIKE at this address though I had asked Swidell not to forward any mail to me, not ever. Yet, here it was.

Knowing at once who the letter was from and knowing that I would read it though I had vowed several years before not to read any further letters from my mother Betsey Rampike whom I feared as you would fear the cobra's mother and there was the return address on the envelope:

HEAVEN SCENT, INC.
9 Magnolia Terrace
Spring Hollow, New York 10590

And inside, on a single sheet of sweetly perfumed pale-apricot stationery, in lavender ink, in the familiar handwriting like a stealthy caress—

January 25 2007.
Dear Skyler—
Please come to see me!
So long I have prayed that
we would be reconcilled.
Darling your father and your
loving Mother meant well.
I have prayed for you dear.
I am soon to undergoe surgery
and pray to see you before.
Your loving Mother
"Mummy"

RANSOM!

Dear Mr Rampik

We have takn your dagher & will releese here to you if you obey our instrucions. But if you do not you will not see your beatiful daghter again & it will be your blame.

We are awar of your transgresions in this family blessed by God, now we are Gods wrath to punish for transgresions of the Father of this house. You have not lived a decent life but drifted into Sin. We have taken your daghter for her own good. This is not an idle theat but God has theatened you in the name of His Only Begoten Son. Your daghter will be returned safe to you when your heart is deserving. We do not crave $.

Where is your daghter Mr Rampik, you are asking. The answer is, not in this house polluted by Sin. Your daghter is a precious gem to be kept in a Safe House approx. 20 miles away. DO NOT CALL POLICE. DO NOT CALL F.B.I. You may summon your pastor. He will serve for you, in this time of trial. You have not lived a good decent family life as Christ has bid us, Mr Rampik this is the price of evill spilling into the world. Your daghter is in danger of Hell. Yet we will return her to you if you repent. If you return to your Martial Vows to have & to hold until death part. DO NOT CALL HELP. DO NOT THROW ON LIGHTS THROU THE HOUSE. DO NOT DIAL 911 this is a Death Sentence to your daghter. Mr Rampik we are watching you

We will contact you by phone this A.M. We will conssent to speak with your Pastor solely. WE ARE SERIOUS IN THE NAME OF THE FATHER. Here is your daghter to "sign" to you that she is with us & she is praying for you.

DO NOT CONTACT POLICE MR RAMPIK YOUR BEATIFUL DAGHTER WILL REJOIN THE BOSOM OF JESUS IN HEAVEN, TO ESCAPE THE EVILL OF THIS HOUSHOLD. YOU WILL NEVER SEE HERE AGAIN.

X

THE EYE THAT "SEES"*

---

* *This curious—notorious—document! The key to who killed my sister, and why, would seem to be in this alleged "ransom note"—unless maybe it isn't.*

"IMPERFECT PLOTS"

> Of imperfect plots and actions the episodic are the worst. By an episodic plot I mean one in which the episodes do not have to each other the relation of either probability or necessity.
>
> (Aristotle, *Poetics*, Chap. IX)*

AND YET: IF THE PLOT OF ONE'S LIFE IS AN "IMPERFECT"—"EPISODIC"—PLOT? If there is a true dearth of "probability" and "necessity" in one's life? *Terror incognita* of a kind haughty Aristotle had not a clue.

The ransom note, for instance.

This bizarre document attributed to "The Eye That 'Sees'" is not, of course, the original, but the author's typed version of a stiffly hand-printed document; an attempt to reproduce what Skyler saw at the age of nine, under extreme mental duress; though Skyler at the age of nineteen would testify that he recalls the document as vividly as if he'd seen it only yesterday. The original was clumsily hand-printed as if by a young child, on a single long sheet of construction paper; the "sign" of Bliss's misspelled name has been determined by some handwriting experts to be genuine, but discredited by others who believe that it was forged. Very likely the reader knows that "The Eye That 'Sees'" was never identified.

---

* *Yesterday, pilfering through some trash cans behind a rooming house near the Rutgers campus, I discovered a much-thumbed and annotated paperback copy of the* Poetics. *Truly, it is not to impress the impressionable reader that I am quoting Aristotle here, but to make my plea for understanding: this is a cry of* echt *angst to reach beyond the sleazy tabloid tragedy of my poor sister's death, to something approaching Transcendence.*

According to Betsey Rampike's sworn statement, this ransom note was discovered by her at approximately 8:10 A.M. of January 29, 1997, at which time Bliss seemed still to be "missing"; the note had been positioned on a small table in the front foyer of the Rampike house, folded once, like a greeting card, in a way to capture the eye of anyone entering the foyer.

Over the years, this "ransom note" has come to be analyzed more than any ransom note in history. Yet, it was never formally "entered into evidence" in any court trial, nor even in any court hearing, for there were to be no indictments in the case, no arrests and no "defendants."

Reader, you are shaking your head in disbelief. You, like Aristotle, react with aesthetic displeasure to such an unlikely plot. And yet, *all that I am disclosing here is true.*

For it does no good to guess who "The Eye That 'Sees'" is: in United States criminal law, you must mobilize an argument to prove it.

POLLUTER*

"BIX! DARLING! GOD HELP US—BLISS IS MISSING."

The call came shortly after 8 A.M., January 29, 1997. Ringing in suite 729 of the Regency SuperLuxe Hotel north of Fair Hills at an exit off I-80 where, for reasons unclear to his children if ominously clear to his wife, Daddy had been staying for the past several days and commuting to Univers, Inc. nine miles to the east. This was a Saturday: Daddy was expected to arrive at the Rampike house at about 10:30 A.M. to take Bliss with him to New York City to "celebrate—just the two of us" Bliss's seventh birthday which was the following day. It could not be said that Bix Rampike had "moved out" of the family home on Ravens Crest Drive since clearly he had not, for he'd taken very few clothes and personal items with him to the Regency; it could not be said that Bix was "separated from" his wife of nearly eleven years, Betsey; nor could it be stated that the Rampikes' marriage was "shaky"—"troubled"—"storm-toss'd"—except by devious sources insisting upon anonymity, presumed (by the indignant Rampikes, who could not bear gossip about them) to be friends/social acquaintances/fellow members of the exclusive clubs to which the Rampikes belonged.

Damned ringing phone Bix only barely managed to hear over the thunderous sound of the shower. Cursing, leaning out of the shower stall to fumble for the wall phone believing he knew who the caller was, and what she would tell him in her throaty smoker's voice he so yearned to hear, and

---

* *As they say in TV documentaries, this is a "re-enactment."*

    Of necessity, most of this chapter is imagined. But when Daddy arrives home, and is handed the ransom note by Mummy, Skyler is in the kitchen close by, and hurries to the door, to overhear.

how his body, flushed and tingling from the shower, would respond; and so Bix was smiling, in the steamy mirror his teeth flashed white: "Hey. *Hi*."

Except: who the hell was this? Not the woman he'd expected but—his wife?

Yes it was Betsey, and Betsey was agitated about something, impossible to follow what she was saying, abashed and resentful Bix had to ask her please to slow down, repeat what she'd said. A wave of weariness swept over him, his elation of just a few seconds ago had diminished at once, swirling at his feet in sudsy water down the shower drain, telling himself certainly he loved Betsey, certainly Bix loved his wife of—was it nearly eleven years? *eleven?*—for Betsey was the mother of his children, and you know how Bix Rampike feels about his children: "The most sacred trust a man can be—entrusted with." Must've been crazy for her when he'd married her, a fatal weakness he had for submissive/soft-fleshed females gazing up at him in undisguised adoration. Even when one of them reviled Bix as a selfish prick he found such women irresistible, the *sin qua none* bottom line is such females adored his prick, and him. Sure there's a downside, such females are hyper-susceptible to hurt feelings, hysteria; susceptible to despair, and to rage; and so very, so very God-damned fucking *needy*. Betsey fixing those limpid brown cow-eyes on him, that pissed him even though (he had to concede, he's a connoisseur of such matters) the eyes were beautiful; calling him at the office so often, he'd had to instruct his assistant to "keep Mrs. Rampike at bay"—with a wink for the sexy young streaked-blond assistant, Bix Rampike understands adores him. Bix was sure now that whoever had called him in the early hours of this morning, soon after he'd returned to the room (at 2:12 A.M.), and again waking him from a stuporous sleep (at 4:06 A.M.) had to have been Betsey; but when he'd answered the phone both times, quickly she hung up without identifying herself. It wasn't the first time in their marriage of—*eleven years?*—that Betsey, stirred by jealousy, irrational and anxious and convinced (not wrongly, but how'd she know that?) that Bix was "with" another woman, had made such calls to determine if Bix was alone in his hotel room, as if, naively, she believed Bix's woman friend might pick up the phone and reveal herself. And now, what was Betsey trying to tell him?—her voice fierce in his ear, yet desperate, like a woman trying to attract the attention of a spouse who is reading a newspaper at breakfast, for instance. "Betsey, slow down: what?"

"—s-searched the h-house! Can't f-find her. Oh Bix, come home now."

"Betsey, what? Something about—Bliss?"

"—told you can't find her: missing from her room oh Bix—"

" 'Missing'? What d'you mean? 'Missing' how?"

"M-Missing *gone*. Oh Bix come help us, I am w-worried that—something terrible has h-happened—"

Fumbling, Bix managed to turn off the shower. His large broad-shouldered just-slightly-going-to-fat torso, midriff. Hot-skinned Bix Rampike naked and dripping, glistening. Handsome head sleek as a seal's, hair flattened, and the thick wiry pelt-hair of his chest, belly, groin glistening with moisture. Had to concede, he'd put on a few extra pounds since the Cornell days, but still Bix looked good, at least frontally. Squinting at himself in a mirror, cocking his head to the side: just so. Women adored him, how was that Bix's fault? It was like Betsey to call him at such a time. Exactly like Betsey to call him when he was in the shower, and when he was naked. The woman had an instinct for calling him at such times. If she'd been able to call him the previous night when he'd been with ████ of whom Betsey could not possibly know but of whom she had paranoid suspicions, she'd have called him. Now in his ear speaking in a steely-calm-Mummy voice and no longer the hysterical-Betsey voice. This was upsetting. This was worrisome. For when Betsey was emotional, you knew that the emotions were authentic. Now, must've been the Nixil kicking in, to revert her to "calm"—"serenity"—some nights, when she'd been drinking, she'd been near-comatose—or maybe it was Percodan?—Excelsia?—since Bliss's defeat on the ice in where was it, somewhere in Pennsylvania. Poor Betsey! Bix Rampike was so much the master of his moods, as of the moods of others in his vicinity, he had no more need for "mood-elevating"/"mood-stabilizing" medication than he'd have had for testosterone shots in the ass, or steroids. Hard not to feel contempt for such female weakness.

But Betsey didn't sound weak now so much as grim, determined.

Had to wonder, had he ever heard Betsey speak in such a way?

Fumbling to dry himself with a massive towel Bix said, " 'Can't find her'—our daughter? Are you serious?" and Betsey retorted, "Of course I'm serious! Would I be calling you like this if I wasn't?" and Bix asked, trying to maintain control, "Look: are the doors all locked? The windows? All the windows? Could someone have broken in?" and Betsey said, a glimmer of contempt in her voice, "Don't be ridiculous, Bix: that's the first thing I checked. The doors, all the doors to the outside. And the windows. The garage door, you never remember to lock," and Bix felt his face flush, thinking now *Is this a trick, a game she's cooked up with the kids? To make Daddy feel guilty and to get his ass over there fast*, asking if she'd asked Skyler, Skyler might know if Bliss was hiding somewhere, and Betsey said, in a fusillade of words, "The children play hide-and-seek with Daddy, not Mummy. Big Daddy they adore, not Mummy they take for granted. You know that, Bix. Anyway Bliss has never hidden away in one of her secret places for so long. And I've been calling and calling for her and she would never be so willful, not to come out. Last night she was feverish, refused to go to bed at her bedtime, and Lila isn't here to help, Lila has the weekend off, both the children were very demanding, and exhausting. All Bliss could chatter about was 'Daddy this'—'Daddy that'—Daddy coming to take her to New York for her birthday—though Bliss's actual birthday isn't until tomorrow, and we are having a real party here. Wouldn't you think that, after that terrible loss in Pennsylvania, for all the world to see, Bliss would want to hide away for a while, and not run off to New York with her precious Daddy—I know, I would. Bliss was counting the very hours until Daddy came to get her so it makes no sense she'd be playing a prank on us now, does it?" and before Bix could respond, forging on in aggrieved-Mummy voice, "Bliss is a secretive child, nothing at all like her fans imagine her. And Skyler, who has taken to 'tattooing' himself with little skulls, daggers—signs of Satan, I told him—wash those ugly things off, I told him—and d'you know, Skyler not only disobeyed me about that, but Skyler drew a little red heart on the palm of Bliss's hand, too—in *indelible ink*. And so when I woke in the night from a disturbing dream and went to check Bliss's bed, it was empty; and I know, I just know—she's hiding from me, and will emerge for her precious Daddy, and the two of you will laugh at Mummy, won't you! And Skyler is in on it, isn't he? I woke him this morning—to help me look for Bliss—and there was something so secretive about him, his eyes—" and Bix managed at last to interrupt, "What the hell are you saying, Betsey? Skyler is 'in on it'—what?" and Betsey said sharply, "You! The children's father! And you've neglected them, and me, for months. You have defiled our marriage bed—you have polluted our sacred marriage vows—I live in dread of what will sweep upon us, what evil, and whatever it is, we don't dare call the p-police until we know—if—Skyler has—" Betsey broke off as if a hand had been clamped over her mouth; and Bix said, frightened, "Honey, I haven't 'polluted' our marriage, I swear. I love you, and I love our children. I'll make it up to you, darling. You know that, don't you—"

The line had gone dead.

PHONE RECORDS? WE KNOW THAT THEY ARE IRREVOCABLE, IRREMEDIABLE. Just as it would be revealed shortly that the mysterious calls to Bix Rampike at the Regency SuperLuxe at 2:12 A.M. and again at 4:06 A.M. had been made, in fact, from the Rampikes' home number, calls of less than two seconds each, so it would be revealed that, having received an urgent call from that number, i.e. from Mrs. Rampike, Bix Rampike took time to call another Fair Hills number before leaving the hotel and hurrying home. Why?

. . . TRANSGRESIONS IN THIS FAMILY BLESSED BY GOD, NOW WE ARE GOD'S *wrath to punish for transgresions of the Father of this house.*

WITHIN TWENTY MINUTES HE WAS HOME. WITHIN TWENTY MINUTES OF hanging up the phone in his hotel room for the fourth and final time. He hadn't checked out of the Regency SuperLuxe. He'd had to get home. Had to get home! Though a part of his mind assured him *It's a trick, poor Betsey the last trick she will play on me.* He turned into the blacktop driveway at 93 Ravens Crest Drive. No sign, from the outside, of any disturbance. There were no disturbances on Ravens Crest Drive. A disturbance in all of Fair Hills was rare. The sprawling old white clapboard and aged-brick Colonial was a beautiful house, and an impressive house, but on Bix Rampike's new salary at Univers, he'd outgrown it. And it bored him, like the small lives within. And yet: all this was his.

Since he'd bought this property, its worth had tripled in value. Fantastic real estate boom in Fair Hills and vicinity: up, up, *up*. Bix Rampike, one day to be Chief of Research Development (Domestic) at Univers, Inc., was going up, up, *up*.

A man's possessions, which he has earned with the sweat and blood of his brow, God damn a man will defend to the death.

"It's in the species. In the genes. 'Anatomy is destiny.' "

Especially, a man's children: his DNA. His future. Immortality.

If something should happen to Bliss, Daddy's bestest-best li'l gal, Daddy could not bear it.

He did love his daughter! Bawled like a baby, watching her win that title on TV. Astonishing figure skater. *His* athletic talent, in that small body. Astonishing.

Bliss he adored, Bliss was his angel.

Climbing into Daddy's lap, shy-kissing, shy-hugging Daddy who with big-Daddy fingers hugged/tickled in return.

Oh Daddy! Oh!—that tickles!

It would not matter to him, to Daddy, if Bliss ever skated again. Only to her, the mother: Mummy. Only to Mummy did it matter, too much.

In the divorce, Mrs. Rampike would be awarded the house. Two million, bottom line. There'd be a custody suit. He'd demand joint custody. But not too strenuously.

The other one, Skyler—"Poor kid!" It was easy to forget him. Daddy loved the little runt but being a pragmatist Daddy wouldn't have been surprised, whatever befell Skyler: crippled leg, kiddie-cancer, sistic—sistric?—fibrosis, drowning in the shallow end of a swimming pool while other kids are diving, splashing, horsing around: you name it.

Parked the sexy new car—Jaguar XXL, avocado-green coupe, taupe leather interior—in front of the garage, and entered the house on the run, through the garage and into the back hall beside the kitchen, Bix Rampike's usual mode of entry into his house, and there came Betsey rushing at him breathless, thrusting something at him—"Bix! She's been kidnapped!

Here is the ransom note"—* stunned and disbelieving taking it from her, his wife's trembling hand, skimmed the strange hand-printed message, what the hell was this?—" 'Dear Mr Rampik We have takn your dagher & will releese here to you if' " as Betsey explained where she'd found it, only a minute ago she'd found it, in the front foyer, close by Bliss's "trophy room," she had no idea how long it had been on the table there but it must be hours, the kidnappers must have taken Bliss during the night, and all this time—Betsey was speaking almost calmly, biting her lower lip—"Our daughter has been gone, they have taken her," and Bix said, "Betsey, you wrote this, didn't you? Is this some kind of joke?" and Betsey stared at him, and for a moment Betsey could not speak, so stricken, so appalled, her adulterer-husband's ignorance, furious with him denying she'd written it—"How can you say such a thing! Are you crazy! Are you hungover, drunk?"—their daughter's life was in danger, fanatics had taken her, broken into the house in the night, why hadn't the security alarm sounded, why hadn't Bix made certain it was working, Betsey had no idea how to activate it, if only Bix had been home, it had to be one or more of Bliss's "fans" who'd kidnapped her, some of Bliss's fans were "crazy-obsessed"—Oh! Betsey had known that something terrible would happen if Bix remained away, if the children had no father in the household, the world can sense weakness, the world will rush in, like vultures, like hyenas, emissaries of Satan; a ringing in Bix's ears as if, on the football field, in the very arena of a man's strength, expertise, *quidditas*, an invisible opponent has flown at him, has tackled and defeated him, a whack! to his skull he'd believed to be thick as concrete, a whack! to his gut, and another whack! to his groin, staggering and stunned Bix was trying to read the ransom note a second time, trying to make sense of whatever it was, what twisted logic, The Eye That "Sees" was demanding, only then thinking to ask—was Skyler safe? Their son Skyler, was *he* safe?—and Betsey seemed almost to be laughing at him, laughing at such a question, scornful, squeezing Bix's thick wrist, of course Skyler was safe, why would kidnappers want *him*? And Bix said, "Betsey, wait: this doesn't make sense. 'The Eye That "Sees" '—isn't asking

---

* *From this point onward, Skyler overheard; and what is reproduced here of the exchange between Bix and Betsey Rampike is* verbatim.

for money. Whoever this is, they aren't asking for money. You told me that Bliss was hiding somewhere—is she? Is this a game? Bliss and Skyler are—hiding somewhere?" Staring at his wife who was crowding uncomfortably close to him, a smell of something sour in her breath, a glisten of something fierce in her eyes, her smile was charged with God's wrath, Bix Rampike saw and was frightened and his heart clenched, his bowels clenched as not for many years had the conviction come to him, visceral, of the gut, an outmatched athlete's epiphany in mid-stride, breathing through his mouth running pounding on the field with something throbbing in his ankle, lifts his arms to intercept—what?—as *whack! whack! whack!* he's brought down for the final time knowing *This, I can't do. This is beyond me* seeing that his wife's so-familiar face was not so familiar to him now, a girl's face, a girl's angry face, a girl's puffy-pale skin beneath swaths of pancake makeup so haphazardly applied, or in poor light, that the makeup mask ended abruptly at Betsey's jawline, and her bright cherry-red lipstick was both freshly applied and thick-caked as if smeared without a mirror and now partially eaten away. The dark hair that had been "lightened"—"rinsed"—"permed"—was now shapeless and frizzy as if Betsey had shampooed her hair hastily and had not taken time to "condition" it. Strangest of all, though it was early morning and Betsey had been awake, as she'd said, for most of the night, yet she was wearing a striking outfit suitable for lunch at the Village Women's Club, a cream-colored cashmere sweater set, the cardigan with a ribbed bodice, sprinkling of seed pearls, had not Bix Rampike's secretary arranged for the purchase of this high-quality apparel at the VastValley Neiman Marcus, for a price beyond six hundred dollars?—and Betsey was wearing chic new charcoal-gray wool slacks and, around her neck, on a delicate gold chain, a beautiful little gold cross that closely resembled the beautiful little gold cross from Tiffany that Bix had given their daughter for Christmas . . . "You! You are to blame!" Betsey was accusing, her voice not raised and yet, in Bix's ears, piercing, deafening, "You should have been here to protect us! You are the father, you have allowed Satan into this household, and our daughter is the sacrifice." Bix stood rooted to the spot. The final *whack!* had concussed his brain. He could not think, his brain had gone dead. Only with his eyes could he look again at the ransom note: " 'The Eye That "Sees" '—where?"

It did not appear to be a trick. It was not a game. He knew now, it was not hide-and-seek. His daughter was gone. He knew. And yet: The Eye That "Sees" was offering hope. *We will return her to you if you repent. If return to Martial Vows. Until death part. Contact you by phone.* Now it was clear: his daughter would be returned to him. He would be given another chance. Whoever had taken her would have mercy on him. Whoever had taken her would not harm a six-year-old child. There was no logic in harming a six-year-old child. These were Christian people, obviously. The Eye That "Sees" was a Christian. Twenty miles away! Bliss was twenty miles away! But they would bring her back. There was the promise. Wasn't this a promise? His wife's livid body was in his arms. Pressing into his arms. Almost, there was sex-hunger here, a sudden terrible yearning. Bix was hugging Betsey, burying his heated face in her neck. Betsey was clutching at Bix, as if they were struggling together at the edge of a precipice, she alone could save him. Bix could not see Betsey's face but he could hear Betsey's sobs and these were a mother's true sobs, from the womb. He could not hear what Betsey was saying, her words were unintelligible. O God I am so sorry, Jesus forgive me, I am to blame. And then: a doorbell ringing? But who? In desperate hope thinking Bliss is back, they have brought her back, but when Bix hurried to the front door, on the stoop were Reverend Higley and Mrs. Higley ashen-faced, in the next instant clutching Bix's hands: "Betsey called us, Betsey has told us this terrible thing that has happened, the kidnappers have called for your 'pastor'—and I am here."*

---

* *Surprised at this ending? It happened exactly in this way.*

For a "re-enactment" I hope this isn't too amateurish. The canny reader has probably sensed how uncomfortable Rampike fils is at attempting to "inhabit" Rampike père. Probably Sigmund Freud has written impenetrably on this taboo. Though we may think that we know our "loved ones" well, if we try to inhabit them to re-enact an actual event, we discover that, bottom line is, it can't be done.

MORNING AFTER: AUTHOR WISHES TO RETRACT (?)

ERASE THE PRECEDING CHAPTER—"POLLUTER"—FROM YOUR MEMORY, READER!
If you can.

I am thinking it was a mistake. I am thinking that, if I can, I should retract it.

Though it was anguish to compose, and provoked a siege of panic-tachycardia midway (see the offensive paragraph beginning *The other one, Skyler—*), and in my cringing-minor-footnote way I am actually somewhat proud of it, yet the realization came to me just now, the following morning, with the impact of jet-screeches from Newark Airport passing about forty feet above my bed, that earlier in this document, in the chapter "Popular!", it was rashly suggested in a footnote that my father Bix Rampike might be responsible for my sister's death; and that this suggestion—wild, reckless, unsubstantiated, slanderous, weird—may well be true.*

---

* *"Spiteful"—"irresponsible"—"Oedipal ravings"—"plain crazy": readers, I won't contest your responses to this theory. (Though I'm disgusted, that the crude asshole Bix Rampike has so many admirers. What have I been doing wrong?) And yet: it would not have required so very much ingenuity for Bix Rampike to have slipped out a rear exit of the Regency SuperLuxe, sometime after 2:12 A.M., when Mummy first called him, and driven to our house, letting himself in, stealthily making his way to my sister's bedroom, and (for what reason, I don't want to think), bearing her off downstairs and into the furnace room, with terrible results. Daddy then hand-printed the "ransom note" one day to achieve the distinction of being listed in Ripley's Believe It or Not as the "most frequently reprinted" ransom note in the history of kidnappings and abductions—"The War and Peace of ransom notes," as a skeptical FBI agent has noted; this, Daddy left on a table in the front foyer; letting himself out of the house to return to the Regency SuperLuxe in time to receive Betsey's (unidentified) call at 4 A.M.; and again, at 8 A.M. Reader, what about this scenario strikes you as implausible?*

What a blunder on my part, then, to have so effectively "re-enacted" the preceding scene in which the brute Rampike *père* seems to be utterly innocent!

POSTMORTEM I

DADDY WOULD DISCOVER BLISS IN THE FURNACE ROOM.

Not Bliss but Bliss's body. In the furnace room.

Bliss is gone, Skyler. Jesus has taken Bliss to Heaven. What is left behind is Bliss's earthly remains.

Skyler would not attend the funeral. Skyler would not be told when exactly the funeral was.

Skyler would not see his sister's body in the furnace room.

Skyler did not see his sister's body in the furnace room.

Never would Skyler so much as glimpse, through his fingers, or through half-shut eyes, his sister's (stiffened, lifeless) forty-three-pound body with her arms above her head and her wrists bound together by a crimson silk scarf in the shadowy corner of the furnace room where in her desperate search of the house Mummy had several times looked. As Mummy would later lead Reverend and Mrs. Higley on a search of the house and yet no one ventured far enough into the windowless dimly lighted furnace room throbbing with heat like the interior of a lung.

She's been taken, kidnapped. She's been taken from us. She is gone. She isn't in this house. We have looked, we have looked, we have looked everywhere in this house and she is gone from this house, the kidnappers have taken her.

When the cry—cries—went up, Skyler was—where?—upstairs in his room.

At once Skyler had known. The adults' cries. Downstairs.

His sister had been found: Skyler knew.

He ran to the door. Lila clutched at him: "Skyler, no! You must stay up here, with me. Your mother has said . . ."

No! Skyler would not! Squirming out of the housekeeper's fingers that clutched at him as you'd clutch at a reckless child about to fall from a precipice to his death.

On the floor, the ugly *Zap* comics* and crude cartoon sketches Skyler had been drawing, in jerky, jagged lines, clumsy cross-hatching figures (Daddy/Mummy/Brother/Sister) which, in the confusion of that morning would never be seen again *Such filth! In that innocent child's heart! We must protect him.*

Briskly Lila had been changing sheets on Skyler's bed as Lila had changed the (soiled, stained) sheets on Bliss's bed and taken away the (soiled, stained) mattress cover to be soaked in bleach before being laundered as Mrs. Rampike instructed. That morning Lila would run two full loads of laundry (including Skyler's pajamas and Mrs. Rampike's nightgown and terry cloth bathrobe and all the towels from Mrs. Rampike's bathroom) and the shocking fact was, which Lila would recall through her life and never cease to speak of in wonder, dread, awe, while working in the laundry room (such a familiar room to her) Lila had unknowingly been no more than twenty feet away from the furnace room (a room she'd had little occasion to enter, at any time) in which the Rampikes' little daughter was lying lifeless, stiffened in death.

Oh if I had found her! That poor little girl.

This January weekend was to have been Lila's weekend off. And yet the call had come early that morning from Mrs. Rampike sounding "excited"—"upset"—summoning Lila to come to the house at once, to "help out"—"take care of Skyler"—in this "terrible" time.

---

* *Sicko aficionados (there are no other kind) of R. Crumb will want to know exactly which Zaps these were, that had been given to Skyler by Bliss's tutor Rob Feldman who was to cannily quit the Rampikes employ before being fired. These Zaps were early publications, must've been 1970s, in fact one of the comics wasn't a Zap but something called* Dirty Laundry, *typical early Crumb in which there was a weird-goofy Crumb family with a foul-mouthed little kid, possibly named Adam. You would want to know what happened to these cherished comics of Skyler's and what became of Skyler's crude but impassioned attempts at drawing cartoons. Well, what do you think happened to such sicko "evidence"? In the aftermath of my sister's death—i.e., my sister's murder— it was in the best interests of the Rampikes to take away any and all "incriminating" materials in the household, before the first of the Fair Hills police officers were summoned.*

Always such emotion in the Rampike household! Like lightning flashing, and deafening thunder-claps to follow.

Yet: the Rampikes were good people. In Fair Hills, you were not likely to have employers superior to the Rampikes with all their problems and special demands.

Even Mrs. Rampike who was frequently excitable, and exacting, was a good-hearted woman, Lila believed. Sometimes exclaiming to Lila, tears shining in her warm brown eyes, "Lila, you are the only one I trust. God bless you!" (Which was embarrassing, but far better than being scolded, or spoken to sarcastically.) And there was tall good-looking Mr. Rampike like a tornado in the house, clothes and towels strewn in his wake, making Lila's cheeks burn with his teasing ways, and habit of secretly pressing twenty- and fifty-dollar bills into Lila's hand: "Hardship pay, *señora*, for putting up with Big Betsey and Big Bix. I know we're *gringo* pains-in-the-ass." Winking at Lila, sometimes pinching her plump upper arm, what a good man Mr. Rampike was in his heart! And there were the Rampike children, Lila had come to love. Not like the children of other employers for whom Lila had worked who were mean, brattish, cruel but sweet little children: the little girl who was so famous and so sad and the little boy with the "ghost eyes" whom at this terrible time Lila must protect.

Twitchy little Skyler! Lila was surprised to see that, at this early hour, Skyler was wearing one of his white cotton school shirts and over the shirt a cable-knit hunter-green vest sweater and clean corduroy trousers and the newest of his several pairs of sneakers. And Skyler's fawn-colored hair was flyaway-clean as if it had only just been washed. And Skyler was unusually *clean*: so far as Lila could see, the smudged little tattoos that so upset and annoyed his mother had been scrubbed away. It wasn't like Skyler to be so unresponsive to Lila, unsmiling, dazed-looking and seemingly exhausted as if he'd been up through the night. When Lila spoke to him, Skyler only just blinked slowly, and wiped at his pug nose, and twitched in two general ways: shiveringly from the feet up, or tremorously from the head down.

Skyler's dry lips moved. Skyler was asking if there was a party downstairs.

Downstairs was the prayer vigil. Waiting for the kidnapper to call. Lila had been told just the rudiments of the situation. Whoever had taken Bliss away would speak only to the Rampikes' pastor who was Reverend Higley, an Episcopal priest. Mrs. Higley was there also, and several other ladies Mrs. Rampike knew from church: Mrs. Squires, Mrs. Poindexter, and Mrs. Hind. And there was Dale McKee who was Mrs. Rampike's assistant and there was Dr. Helene Stadtskruller who was Mrs. Rampike's therapist with whom Mrs. Rampike had "forged" an intimate bond—"close as sisters!"—and all these individuals, in addition to Mrs. Rampike, and Mr. Rampike (surprising to Lila, how dazed and distracted Mr. Rampike seemed! not his usual smiling bossy self), were gathered in the family room, close by a telephone.

Waiting for the kidnappers' call. Waiting waiting!

And praying: on their knees, even the stiff-jointed elderly Mrs. Poindexter and Mrs. Hind, even Dr. Stadtskruller who'd confessed in a blurting apology to Reverend Higley and the Rampikes that she wasn't a "believer"—"more of a rationalist-agnostic actually"—on their knees, on the Bolivian goatskin rug, and gripping hands tightly as "Archie" Higley led the earnest childlike chanting prayer *Our Father Who art in Heaven hallowed be Thy name Thy Kingdom come Thy will be done on earth as it is in Heaven bring Bliss back safely to us hear us in our appeal Heavenly Father and Jesus His Only Begotten Son have mercy!*

Overhearing, Lila whispered *Amen!* and quickly crossed herself.

In secret offering a prayer to the Virgin Mary: in Whom, so far as Lila knew, Protestants did not believe.

Imagine! What folly! Not to "believe" in the Mother of God who was the true worker of miracles amid mankind if you but prayed in the simplest of ways as you are taught as a child before you learn to read *Hail Mary full of grace the Lord is with Thee, blessed art Thou amongst women and blessed is the fruit of Thy womb Jesus.* Now repeat ten times.

Edgy and anxious staring at the clock—9:48 A.M.—10:07 A.M.—(there had been calls in fact, from Evita's Beauty Emporium confirming Mrs. Rampike's 10 A.M. appointment on Monday, which was to be cancelled, and from Penelope Dressler who was chair of the Gala Spring Frolick [fundraiser for Charity Hill Volunteers of which Betsey Rampike was a member], a somewhat mysterious call from a shrill-sounding female inviting "both Rampikes" to a Valentine's Day cocktail party at "the Klaffs" of whom neither Betsey nor Bix seemed to have heard)—and now 10:29 A.M. and Betsey "too restless" to remain in the family room led Mattie Higley, and Frannie Squires, and Dale McKee, and Dr. Stadtskruller on yet another search through the house—a search not for Bliss (who'd been kidnapped) but for "signs"—"clues"—that Betsey might have overlooked previously: these women climbing to the second floor, and into the attic, and again downstairs to the second floor and into all of the rooms (excluding Skyler's room, where Skyler had been sequestered with the housekeeper to spare him as much trauma as possible); and returning to the first floor, where Archie Higley yet waited for the phone to ring, and Bix was hovering nearby sweaty and ashen-faced opening and closing his fists like a man under sentence of death yet uncertain from which direction death will sweep upon him, or what face death will wear; and as the nervously chattering women made their way as in a procession of pilgrims through the first-floor rooms Betsey called to Bix almost gaily saying please would he join them?—it would be best for at least one man to accompany them; and so like a large clumsy dog roused from sleep, yet still groggy, with slow-blinking-stunned eyes, Bix joined the women, following in their wake unnaturally still, stumbling at times as if losing his balance, as Betsey eagerly led her friends through the kitchen—and such a well-kept kitchen, the women would be impressed—and, again, outside and into the garage, where there was nothing to see, though you expected to see something, as in a suspense film; and beyond the garage, into the cold, still air, to circle the Rampike house that was so sprawling and attractive, alert as watch-dogs the women made their way, and Bix stumbling behind them, on the lookout for "strange footprints" in the snow; except, unfortunately, the snow had been trampled from previous searches. This time, however, as Betsey led the little search party around the back of the house, sharp-eyed Dale McKee cried, "Oh! Oh *look*."

A broken basement window, partly hidden by a dense evergreen shrub. How had this window been overlooked, previously?

Quickly now, the searchers returned to the house, and hurried down-stairs to the basement, and into the storage room which was the room with the broken window. "The most hidden-away room in the house," Betsey said breathlessly.

Here, someone might have entered the house. Slivers of glass lay glittering underfoot.

Excitedly the women conferred: had someone crawled through the broken window, that was partly hidden by stacked cartons? (Which would explain why the Rampikes hadn't seen the broken window earlier.) You could see how, beneath the window, which was large enough for a "smallish man" to crawl through, there was a carton positioned like a step. (Which the intruder would have used, when he left.)

In a flurry of excitement, alarm, commingled dread and elation the women pressed near. If there were cobwebs, quickly the women brushed them away. Betsey was saying, "This is it! Oh God, this is how the kidnapper entered our house! And the security alarm wasn't on—Bix kept promising to have it repaired, so it wouldn't go off for no reason, and it never got repaired . . . And whoever this was, this kidnapper, somehow he knew where Bliss's room was, and he overpowered her in her sleep, and took her away. And I never knew. I was sleeping, I was so trusting, Jesus have mercy on me, I never knew." Betsey was weeping now, and trembling violently, as the women comforted her. Bix neither looked at her nor seemed to be listening to her but was examining the broken window, and the area around the window; grunting with the effort of hoisting himself up, elbows and forearms on the windowsill, panting now, gasping: "So it's here! Here! The son of a bitch! Here's where he came in."

Quickly Betsey chided, "Bix, please. Don't be profane."

QUICK CUT TO: TWO FLOORS UP WHERE SKYLER WAS ASKING LILA WAS IT HIS fault? what happened to Bliss, his fault? for Mummy seemed to be angry with him now. Mummy did not seem to love him now.

Lila assured him no. Mummy could not be angry with him. Mummy loved him.

"Lila, *did I do it?*"

Lila would have hugged Skyler except, needing badly to pee, Skyler pushed away from her, hurried into the bathroom and shut the door and tried to pee, tried very hard to pee, but only a pathetic little dribble emerged from his bruised little pecker. And Skyler began to cry, and Lila entered the bathroom and led him back into his room, brushed his damp hair from his feverish forehead, Lila would have kissed the anxious child except Skyler was not her son to kiss; Skyler was another woman's son; and Lila knew her place, by instinct Lila understood that Betsey Rampike would not want the Filipina housekeeper Lila Laong kissing and coddling her son.

Earnestly Lila assured Skyler one more time that his mother loved him. His father loved him. Everyone who knew him loved him. Soon they would find his sister, and the terrible time would be over. "Why don't you sit here and read your comic books, Skyler? Or—would you like to draw? I promise, I will stay with you."

In the confusion of that morning Skyler would not later recall the sequence of events. For possibly it had been earlier, that Lila had brought him breakfast on a tray, as if he was sick and staying home from school in his room: Count Chocula (chocolate-coated cereal) with sliced bananas, raisin bread toast with grape jelly, a tall glass of hyper-sweetened orange juice, a tall glass of vitamin-enriched milk. How Skyler loved Count Chocula cereal!—yet, lifting a spoonful to his mouth, he chewed but couldn't swallow, spat out the mouthful into the cereal bowl which had to be, as anyone in Skyler's class at Fair Hills Day would say with a sneer, *gross*.

That morning seeming to know how he would never again return to the "prestigious"—"exclusive"—private school where among his classmates Skyler Rampike had acquired—at last!—a reputation for being, if not "normal," no longer hopelessly "weird": for the lustre of Skyler's local-celebrity sister had cast upon him a flattering lunar glow, and it had become common for Skyler to be approached by the most popular girls, including sixth-grade girls, with eager questions about Bliss. And there was the additional lustre of the H.I.P. designation, now to be surrendered forever.

In fact, Skyler Rampike would never again attend any school in Fair Hills. This melancholy fact he seemed to know, on the morning of the first day of his new life.

BY 11:05 A.M. THERE HAD BEEN NO CALL FROM THE KIDNAPPER/KIDNAPPERS. Downstairs, the pleading/begging prayers of the faithful had passed beyond abject, fawning, desperate to fatigued.

Another time the ransom note was read aloud, by Reverend Higley. " 'The Eye That "Sees." ' Maybe it—he—is watching this house?"

This was a new thought. This was a profound thought. This was a disturbing thought. Bix Rampike lurched to his feet declaring that he would go outside, and investigate. He would drive along Ravens Crest Drive on the lookout for "suspicious vehicles." And so Bix Rampike left the house, driving away in the sleek new Jaguar coupe, and was gone from the prayer/phone vigil for approximately forty minutes.*

Returning to report he had seen no one "suspicious." The usual delivery vans, the mailman. If the kidnapper/kidnappers were watching the house, there appeared to be no way any private citizen could locate them.

"It may be that we have to call the police, after all," Reverend Higley said. "It may be that the 'Eye That "Watches" ' has no serious intention of contacting us, only of torturing us."

Just then, the phone rang.

Quickly Reverend Higley lifted the phone receiver, even as Betsey Rampike staggered to her feet, pressing a hand against her breast. Higley, hand cupped over the receiver, said in a whisper: "Betsey? It's a friend of yours—Mrs. Chaplin."

Mrs. Chaplin? *Trix?*

After so many months of not calling? Trix Chaplin, at such a time? For a moment Betsey hesitated as if about to take the call, then drew back, frowning; saying, with dignity, though her mouth trembled: "Please tell Mrs. Chaplin that I will call her another time. This is not a good time."

Now it was, Bix Rampike stood. Mumbled something inaudible and without a backward glance at his surprised companions made his way out of the room like a man in a dream determined to wake from the dream. "Bix? Where are you going? Bix—" Betsey called after him, unheard.

The time: 12:06 P.M. Reverend Higley would recall.

In the old butler's pantry off the kitchen where Bix kept reserves of liquor he paused to pour two inches of Dewar's into a shot glass to be downed in a single swallow. So fortified, he made his way then to the back stairs,

---

* *Forty minutes! Imagine all that Bix Rampike could accomplish in forty minutes, that no one investigating Bliss Rampike's death would ever know.*

and down the stairs to the basement—why? Bix would never be able to explain—a hunch, a premonition, a sensation like a hulking predator bird flapping its wings over his head—unerring he made his way through the ghost-Rampike-family room (never used by the Rampike family! never to be used and to be totally dismantled by the next tenants of the house) and past the (rarely used) "family fitness room" with somber stationary bicycle, treadmill, "Stair Master" and weights scattered on the floor like giant, discontinued coins, past the laundry room (in which, at this very moment, fresh-laundered bed linens and articles of Rampike clothing were tumbling gaily about in the oversized drier), past the drafty storage room (where the just-discovered broken window had been temporarily "mended"—a piece of cardboard wedged against it), and at the door to the furnace room he paused for a moment before pushing the door open and switching on the overhead light, stepping inside and this time advancing farther into the low-ceilinged room entered mostly by Valley Oil repairmen, and there, in the smutty corner behind the first-floor furnace, lay the small broken body.

"Bliss? My God."

(Hiding from Daddy? All these hours? When they'd thought she was kidnapped? How was this possible?)

He stooped over her, where she was wedged between the furnace and the concrete wall. He saw, or must have seen, the blood smears on the wall, and the blood, coagulated, yet still glistening, on the matted blond hair. Must've seen the stiffened arms awkwardly forced back behind the child's head, bound with duct tape and the badly wrinkled and stained crimson silk scarf. Must've seen the waxy face, the part-open opaque eyes and the duct tape over her mouth. The torn and stained nightgown, and the naked legs like stilts. Must've known that the child was dead but the cry erupted from him: "Bliss! Darling!" He ripped the duct tape from her mouth. He leaned close, he knelt on the sticky floor, he lifted her in his arms grunting with the effort, how strangely heavy his daughter had become, how unresponsive to his pleas, he staggered from the furnace room carrying her, staggered/stumbled/made his frantic way up the stairs and back into the family room where the others awaited him having heard his cries, and thinking he would revive her, even as the others were screaming in horror, tenderly he lay her on the floor, not on the sofa but on the floor, on the white Bolivian goatskin carpet, and why?—haltingly he would explain *She would need artificial respiration, a floor is more practical* while upstairs in his room hearing the adults' cries Skyler knew at once: his sister had been found.

Whatever he'd been preoccupied with, comic books, sketch pad, went flying. Lila, alarmed, tried to stop him: "Skyler, no! You must stay up here, with me. Your mother . . ." but already Skyler was running along the corridor, and Skyler was taking the stairs two at a time, risking another broken leg, or a replay of the original (twice) broken leg, and Skyler was panting running into the family room seeing his father crouched over something on the white fur rug, his mother wailing like a stricken cat throwing herself on whatever it was, on the white fur rug, and rudely Skyler pushed past the adults who were in his way, a sharp punch to the fat thigh of one of the white-haired church grannies who was always cooing over him, but no cooing now, no stopping Skyler now, Skyler was grabbing at his father's shoulder, trying to see, trying to see what it was his mother was lying on as if she'd fallen from a great height delirious and moaning and now Skyler saw, it was Bliss, of course it was Bliss, had to be Bliss, and Skyler shouted, "There's nothing wrong with her! It's what she always does, to get attention!"

POSTMORTEM II

WHEN WAS THIS? A LONG TIME AGO.

If viewed through a telescope, but through the wrong end of a telescope, it would be even more distant in time. And all who'd survived would now be vanished, like Bliss.

OUR PEDOPHILE I

"IT'S HIM. HAS TO BE."

In the waning years of the twentieth century in much of affluent rural-suburban New Jersey there was perceived to be, among professionals trained in such matters, a scarcity of known sex offenders: and so, in Morris County, the townships of Basking Ridge, Bernardsville, and Fair Hills were obliged to share thirty-four-year-old Gunther Ruscha, currently unemployed elementary school teacher/resident of 29 Piper's Lane, Fair Hills.

"Who else but Ruscha? Sad sicko pervert."

Poor Gunther Ruscha! Each time a Sex Incident was reported to local police, no matter that Gunther's cherished specialty was Pedophilia, a rarified sub-category of sex perversion, and no matter how greatly descriptions of the (alleged) offender differed from the description of Gunther Ruscha in police files, little time was lost before a squad car equipped with deafening siren, flashing blue light on its roof, BASKING RIDGE POLICE, BERNARDSVILLE POLICE, or FAIR HILLS POLICE emblazoned on its sides, and manned by husky police officers, shook the quiet of Piper's Lane to pull aggressively into the Ruschas' narrow cracked-asphalt driveway.

"Rusch-a! Gun-ther Rusch-a! Police."

That Gestapo pounding on the door, poor Gunther recognized like an old, familiar kick to the scrotum.

And there was Mrs. Ruscha screaming at him: "Gunther, what have you done now? For shame!"

Even those neighbors on Piper's Lane who were mostly sympathetic with, or pitying of, sixty-three-year-old Gertrude Ruscha the pedophile's mother, longtime resident of Piper's Lane and newly retired from her minimum-wage job in food services at the Fair Hills Medical Center where she'd worked since the abrupt and inexplicable departure of Gunther's father when the budding pedophile was but a toddler, could not resist a shiver of *Schadenfreude** while peering through their venetian blinds as the squad car pulled up to 29 Piper's Lane another time, with increasing frequency it seemed, as Sex Incidents were being more frequently reported to local police, at the clapboard Cape Cod invariably described in the *Fair Hills Beacon* as a "modest dwelling"; observing the lanky, red-haired, incongruously boyish-looking Gunther being forcibly walked, between grim-faced police officers, to the waiting squad car where he was made to stoop as he slid into the rear of the vehicle, a police officer's (gloved) hand pushing down on Gunther's head in a gesture you might almost mistake as friendly, to prevent the terrified pedophile from striking his head against the car.

"That Gunther! What has he done now!"

It was observed that our pedophile's face, unnaturally pale, with rubbery lips in a frightened smile, and stark staring glassy eyes, that more than one (female) observer believed to be "poetic"—often glistened with tears at such times. If police came for him without warning, as usually they did, Gunther was likely to be wearing nondescript clothes (khaki trousers, sweatshirt, baggy sweater) like any Fair Hills adult male, and not the "spiffy"—"show-offy"—"fag"—clothes (faux-suede, black leather, brightly colored scarf tied at his throat) in which he dressed when he left the house to drive away in his mother's weatherworn old Datsun or pedal away on his bicycle (with what destination: public park, children's playground, kiddie matinee, skating rink?); if police came for him in the night, a favored time, for it involved blinding spotlights illuminating the front of the Cape Cod, as on a movie set, Gunther was likely to be hauled outside in pajamas, without shoes; on the most humiliating occasion, Gunther was taken into police custody bare-chested and in white Jockey shorts: his legs were revealed as spindly and lacking muscle, like an ostrich's legs; his white Jockey shorts might have fit the groin area of a prepubescent boy; his narrow,

---

* Schadenfreude: *classy German term for being thrilled, usually secretly, by others' misfortune; unless the misfortune inconveniences you in some way in which case you "commiserate."*

concave chest was hairless as a young boy's, with berry-like nipples distinct against the sickly pallor of his skin. For you had only to glance at our pedophile, the pariah of Morris County, all knowledge of Gunther Ruscha's lurid past but a *tabbouleh rosa*, and a primitive warning signal would detonate in the frontal lobe of your reptile brain: "Sex deviate!"

More subtly tuned frontal lobes would detonate: "Pedophile!"

Yet, so strangely, you might say perversely, Gunther Ruscha seemed never to become adjusted to his situation. Having served only eighteen months of a three-and-a-half-year sentence in the notorious Sex Offenders' Unit of ghastly Rahway State Prison for Men, to which only the "most hardened" of New Jersey criminals are sent, and having lost all chance of being ever again employed as an elementary school teacher (specialty: music), as a consequence of having pleaded guilty to several counts of "sexual misconduct endangering a child," Gunther Ruscha yet displayed surprise and hurt, at times indignation, when given harsh looks by Fair Hills residents who knew his identity. And when, at the mall, hurriedly making his way with lowered head and eyes fixed to the floor, he heard in his wake the crude chant *Pedophile! Pedophile! Sicko pervert pedophile!* he never glanced around for fear of seeing a teenager known to him from the neighborhood where of all the world he wished to feel at home.

It was believed that, newly paroled from Rahway, Gunther had gamely tried to find employment, but with no luck: for who in his right mind would hire a convicted pedophile! It was believed that Gunther was fearful of leaving the only home he'd ever known, with silly Mrs. Ruscha who must have loved him for look at how she'd been supporting him for years, defending and protecting him for years, paying for sex therapists, psychiatrists, Gunther's short-lived effort to attend "beauty technician school" in West Orange, though Mrs. Ruscha's meager pension and Social Security checks must have been seriously strained to pay for her son's show-offy fag clothes. Why, observers wondered, didn't our pedophile move away from Fair Hills and out of the dingy Cape Cod on Piper's Lane? Out of cowardice, very likely; or, it may have been, if Gunther had tried to move into another community, anywhere in the United States including even the remote arctic wilds of Alaska, or the mossy/sultry/alligator-plagued settlements of the Florida Everglades, he'd have had to register with local police as a convicted sex offender/pedophile; and these police wouldn't have known Gunther as a wholly unthreatening if not pathetic sicko, requiring no more than two police officers to haul him in for questioning: no "backup" or SWAT teams or what's called "extraordinary force."

Female neighbors on Piper's Lane who'd become acquainted with luckless Gertrude Ruscha over the years spoke of the woman's "adamant" belief that her son was completely blameless of the crimes for which he'd been sent away to Rahway: poor Gunther, twenty-six at the time, had been the true victim; a group of "vicious" sixth-grade girls at Kriss Elementary where Gunther had been so happily employed for two years after graduating *summa cum laude* from the Rutgers University School of Education (Newark), had suddenly, for no reason, out of pure meanness accused their music teacher Mr. Ruscha of "saying bad things to them"—"touching them in a bad way"—showing them his "weenie" and asking "would they like to touch it?" Shameless girls shrieking with laughter over Mr. Ruscha's "weenie"—"such a teeny weenie"—"wrinkled and ugly like a mashed mouse"— and though it had seemed like a crude, cruel, silly joke of some kind or like a small fire that grew wildly out of control it happened that the girls' parents filed formal complaints and eventually sued the principal at Kriss Elementary, the Fair Hills public school board, and luckless Gunther Ruscha who wasn't insured for such a claim. And, in this way, Gunther became a known sex offender: *pedophile.*

Yet Gunther was continually surprised, disoriented and terrified when wakened from sleep by a pounding at the front door of his house, and shouts: "Rusch-a! Gun-ther Rusch-a! Police." And those blinding spotlights.

Though Gunther Ruscha was at least six feet tall, angular and sinewy as an eel, as soon as he was gripped by the officers' strong hands he seemed to shrink, and to become boneless; if you were a husky Morris County police officer you could feel little but manly contempt for the timorous/cowering/trembling/slouch-shouldered/flamey-red-haired pedophile who, shoved into the rear of the police vehicle, whimpered: "Don't hurt me! Please don't hurt me! I haven't done anything! Please believe me, whatever it is *I am innocent.*"

Hauling in Morris County's lone pedophile to police headquarters had become a routine, something of a ritual to which new police officers had to be initiated, over the past six years; yet Gunther Ruscha continued to be taken by surprise, and greatly agitated, as if in fact he was guilty. At the police station Gunther would be "interviewed" while his accuser was brought to observe him through one-way glass: "Him? That isn't him! I told you, the man who 'exposed himself' to my daughter was short, bald, looked like somebody's grandpa." Or: "Him? He's got red hair. The one I told you about has dark hair, he's 'swarthy-skinned' like Hispanic, Indian—" Or: "Billy? Open your eyes, honey. The bad man can't see you through the glass, he can't hurt you any more I promise. Billy? Please look, honey. You don't want that bad man to be let free, and come after you again, do you . . ."

Very rarely was Gunther Ruscha "arrested": most of his impromptu visits to the police station were but opportunities for questioning and attempts at identification. When, as happened from time to time, Gunther was arrested, and charged with a crime, the politesse of "interview" was replaced by the aggressive strategies of "interrogation"; the mild-mannered pedophile, accustomed to taking his nighttime medication (Zomix, Percodan) with a glass of warm milk and cookies at 10:30 P.M. most nights, and of being asleep in bed by 11 P.M., was kept awake at the police station through the night being "grilled"—as it's said on TV—often without knowing what the crime was for which he'd been arrested; nor was it clear who his accusors were. Gunther had learned not to request a lawyer: such requests merely inflamed police officers, like protestations of innocence.

"LET ME THROUGH! LET ME THROUGH! I HAVE TO SEE HER—BLISS! *LET ME through.*"

Even as two police officers had been dispatched to the dingy Cape Cod on Piper's Lane to bring in, as quickly as possible, convicted sex offender/ pedophile Gunther Ruscha for questioning in the apparent homicide of six-year-old Bliss Rampike, only just reported to the Fair Hills Police Department, it happened that, at 3:07 P.M. of January 29, 1997, there came the very man—white-faced, disheveled-looking, breathless—in a battered '93 Datsun attempting to turn onto Ravens Crest Drive that was barricaded to all but police and emergency vehicles, an ungainly floral display of white flowers on the seat beside him: "These are for Bliss! I heard the terrible news on the radio! The little angel has been injured! I can save her! I can take her away! She is my darling! I am her special friend! These flowers are for her, officer! Please let me pass." But the distraught flamey-red-haired youngish man with a redhead's milky pallor and stark staring green-gray eyes was turned back by a Fair Hills patrolman who had no idea that this was Morris County's pedophile, at that very moment being sought for questioning by Fair Hills PD; except that the driver in the Datsun had seemed "excitable"—"like he was high on some drug"—"with a big, weird bouquet of white flowers for the little dead girl." For Gunther Ruscha was not the only party eager to turn into Ravens Crest Drive that afternoon, to be turned away by Fair Hills patrolmen.

At 12:29 P.M. a 911 call had been placed (by Reverend Higley, stammering and nearly incoherent) summoning "emergency aid" to 93 Ravens Crest Drive; by 2 P.M. the first of the news bulletins were broadcast on local radio and TV; through the afternoon, "word spread" through Fair Hills and vicinity in a firestorm of emotion beyond even *Schadenfreude: Bliss Rampike had been killed? Murdered? That little ice skater? The skating prodigy? In her own home, in her own bed? In the night, when the Rampikes were sleeping? Someone had broken into the house? Someone had tried to kidnap the little girl, and had killed her instead?*

Fair Hills's first homicide in seventy years.

In the Rampike house and vicinity was a swarm of police officers both uniformed and plainclothed, crime scene technicians, emergency medics; in the Rampike driveway and on the road, numerous police vehicles, a crime scene van, a mobile command center. An officer from the Morris County Sheriff's K9 Squad arrived with two-year-old German shepherd Blazes to sniff with explosive energy and high hopes outside the Rampike house and on adjoining properties, around a drainage ditch and nearby sewers, and in the township-owned property at the rear of the Rampikes' two-acre lot, a strip of densely wooded land approximately fifty feet wide that ran parallel with Ravens Crest Drive, to block homeowners' views of the less-than-glamorous rears of properties on Juniper Pine Lane in the next sub-division. Blazes was a handsome dog with alert, intelligent eyes, a sleek dark muzzle, burnished-looking fur, a young dog's springy energy and a sharp bark, much admired by his handlers for his brilliant sniffing ability and indefatigable optimism, but Blazes was picking up no crucial scent in the woods, and was about to be urged back in the direction of the Rampike house, when he began barking fiercely: for there came, stumbling through the underbrush, an individual to be described by arresting officers as a Caucasian male, early thirties, height six feet/weight 150, red-haired, "excitable" and "belligerent," clumsily carrying a large floral display in a vase spilling water down the front of his trouser legs; commanded to stop by the police officer, as he was vigorously being barked-at by Blazes, the red-haired youngish man brazenly continued to press forward, as if, by sheer insolence, he might be able to push his way past Blazes and the police officer, in a high-pitched voice declaring: "I—am a friend of the Rampike family! I—am expected in their hour of need! I am Bliss's secret friend! Bliss is expecting me! I demand to see her! I have been in that house many times as a trusted friend! I have been in Bliss's room with her, as a trusted friend! I demand to see Bliss! These are calla lilies—for her. Not for *you*—" as the police officer, joined by another officer, grappled with him and the vase and calla lilies went flying, and Blazes leapt at the raving red-haired man, barking ferociously, knocking him to the ground, in underbrush glazed with particles of icy snow; though overpowered by two officers and a German shepherd weighing more than one hundred pounds, and though one of the officers was pressing his knee against his back and mashing his face against the ground, yet with maniacal desperation he continued to struggle even as his arms were wrenched behind his back, and Blazes's sharp yellow fangs tore at his left ear: "Bliss! Bliss! I love you, Bliss! I have come to save you!"

CUFFED AND DAZED AND BLEEDING FROM SEVERAL FACE AND HEAD WOUNDS, Gunther Ruscha was to be the first "person of interest"* taken into custody in the Bliss Rampike homicide investigation; so promptly, the Fair Hills police were to be universally praised, within an estimated twelve hours of the little girl's death.

---

*Our luckless pedophile! He was also arrested on charges of criminal trespass, disturbing the peace, refusal to obey a police officer's command, two counts of assault against a police officer, and one count of assault against a police dog. Bail was set at $450,000.

OUR PEDOPHILE II

"IT'S HIM. HAS TO BE."

Quickly it was discovered by Fair Hills police that Gunther Ruscha had been several times in the past three years detained by patrol officers for "suspicious behavior" on Ravens Crest Drive, where, according to complainants residing at 89 Ravens Crest, 65 Ravens Crest, and 47 Ravens Crest, he'd been reported to be riding a bicycle "repeatedly" on the curving road, to the cul-de-sac at the end of the road and back to the intersection with the Great Road; questioned by patrol officers called to the scene, Gunther was able to convince them that he was "only just bicycling" in the neighborhood because the road ended in a cul-de-sac and there was little traffic; and because this was a "beautiful, quiet neighborhood" with a "feel of holiness" to it. He was "cooperative"—"unarmed"—"a Fair Hills resident." Stricken with regret for having upset anyone, Gunther eagerly suggested to police officers that he be allowed to apologize in person to the complainants as well as to the family (name unknown: so the canny pedophile pretended) living in the Colonial at 93 Ravens Crest Drive: "Someone in that house might have seen me, too, and wondered who I was. And if I—if I offended— anyone in that family—a young child, for instance—little girls are especially wary of strangers!—I want to say how sorry—how sorry—how sorry I am."

Needless to say, Gunther Ruscha was not invited to "apologize" in person and warned to stay away from Ravens Crest Drive or he'd be arrested.

"THAT'S HIM. THAT MAN . . ."

Quickly it was determined by the Rampikes' housekeeper Lila Laong, brought to the Fair Hills police station to observe, through one-way glass, the sickly-looking/shifty-eyed/twitchy Gunther Ruscha, that this was the very man who had bicycled to the Rampikes' house several weeks ago, in early January, just before Bliss was scheduled to skate in a competition in Pennsylvania, bringing her a bouquet of flowers—a "large, beautiful bouquet of spring flowers"—and a hand-printed card signed G.R. Lila had thought it was "strange" that the flower delivery was made on a bicycle—and in such cold weather!—by this "youngish man, very pale"—"red-haired, with no hat"—"smiling so hard, his mouth looked stretched"—"not dressed right for a delivery man"; and this G.R. was the same person who'd brought a present for Bliss's sixth birthday the year before: "Oh it was so—unusual! At first, it was—very nice. Pretty stuffed birds inside a little glass box, a robin and a little female bird dressed like a groom and a bride, that Mrs. Rampike wouldn't let Bliss keep and had me throw away because it was 'disgusting.'"

Asked why the gift was "disgusting," Lila Laong said: "Because, Mrs. Rampike said, the birds were real birds, and hadn't been 'fixed' right, like you do with chemicals when you stuff a bird or an animal, and so the poor things were rotting inside their feathers . . . You could smell them." Lila shuddered, recalling the smell.

As soon as *The Marriage of Miss Finch and Cock Robin* had been disposed of, Lila said, Mrs. Rampike forgot it; Bliss had cried, because she'd wanted to keep the "special" present, but after a day or two Bliss forgot it, too; for Bliss received so many cards and gifts from strangers, and people were always wanting to see her, and Mrs. Rampike had too many things to think about managing Bliss's career: "Mrs. Rampike would never think that any of Bliss's fans would want to hurt her! They all loved her so."

Lila shuddered again, and hid her grief-ravaged face in her hands.

(THE HAND-PRINTED CARD FROM GUNTHER RUSCHA, SIGNED *G.R.*, ONE OF HUN-dreds of cards kept by Betsey Rampike in a half-dozen albums in Bliss's "trophy room," which the reader might remember from an earlier chapter titled, "The Marriage of Miss Finch and Cock Robin," would soon be discovered by Fair Hills detectives and "positively linked" to Morris County's pedophile. The noose was tightening around G.R.'s slender neck!)

"THIS MAN! THOSE EYES! SUCH EVIL IN THOSE EYES . . ."

In Fair Hills police headquarters, Mummy was being shown "mug shots" of Gunther Ruscha. As if overcome by sudden faintness Mummy swayed in her chair, clutching at her head, and Morris Kruk, who would never leave a client's side when police officers were anywhere near, leaned over her, and encouraged her to take slow, deep, calm breaths, and to try to remember if she'd seen this man before.

"This man": at the time incarcerated in the Morris County Men's Detention Center, in "quarantine" from other, non-sex offender/pedophile detainees.

It was the day following the day *it* had happened: *it* was a way of the Rampikes to speak, meaning ▇▇▇▇▇.

As, for some, *G-d* is a word not to be uttered. So ▇▇▇▇ is not to be uttered within the Rampike family.

Mummy, Daddy, and Skyler were at police headquarters. I think, yes Skyler was there.

Skyler had been brought by Mummy and Daddy and Mr. Kruk to the Fair Hills police station because wherever you might look, Bliss was not there.

Skyler was only beginning to comprehend. There was Bliss's remains, which had been taken away (where? Skyler did not want to know) but Bliss herself was gone and was not anywhere.

So strange! To look around, Skyler's narrowed eyes, Skyler's withheld breath, and *Bliss was not there.*

And the wicked thought came to Skyler that, the last time Mummy, Daddy, and Skyler had been alone together like this, without Bliss, had been long ago: before Edna Louise was born.

In a faint voice Mummy was saying: "—this man! I know this man. I've seen him at Bliss's skating competitions. You get to recognize their faces. His face!—I know him. He was very aggressive, videotaping Bliss. Video-taping us. The first time I'd seen him was years ago. At a skating rink here

in Fair Hills where I'd taken Skyler—not Bliss, Skyler—*he* can skate, too!—
and there came this stranger, pushing close to us, such eyes! such hair!
and around his neck a bright-colored orange or red scarf—and he asked if
my child was 'a beautiful little girl or a beautiful little boy' and I said, 'Skyler is my son.' And years later, when Bliss won her first title, Miss Tots-on-
Ice 1994, she was only four years old, and there came this same man up to
us, with a video camera pushing in our faces, I remembered him at once,
that red hair that doesn't look like a normal man's hair, and that wet rubbery smile, and around his neck he'd tied a bright crimson silk scarf that
was nothing a normal man would wear, and he said: 'The first time we met,
Mrs. Rampike, you had a beautiful little boy-skater with you, and now you
have a beautiful little girl.' Oh God! I was putting my own children at risk,
in the presence of a pedophile, and *I had no idea.*"

Bitterly Mummy began to cry. And now Daddy moved to comfort her,
stiffly like a man rousing himself from a stupor. For all this while, Daddy
had been sitting silent and stony-eyed staring into a corner of the
fluorescent-lit windowless interview room chill as an autopsy room as if
he wasn't listening to anything that was being said. Before entering the
police station (what an ordinary building!—single storey, resembling a
dental clinic, on Charity Street sharing quarters with the township clerk's
office and a small windowless courtroom of no more interest or intrigue
than a classroom at Fair Hills Day) Daddy had stood on the steps outside
staring at the sky smoking a cigarette, smoking in swift pleasureless
drags, Skyler did not remember Daddy smoking anytime before this and
so it seemed strange to him, and wrong. And it seemed strange to Skyler,
and wrong, that Daddy seemed not to see him but to *look through him* as
if Skyler was a ghost!—not Sky-boy, not Big Boy, or son, but—a ghost! And
now Daddy roused himself to comfort Mummy but with a look of strain
and distaste as if you might comfort a wounded or diseased creature at
whom you could not bear to look, Daddy's hand on Mummy's shoulder and
Mummy shivered not turning to Daddy as Mr. Kruk spoke quietly in
Mummy's ear. Poor Mummy!—so stricken by *it*. Who would never recover
from *it*. Who'd been taken by ambulance to the emergency room at the Fair
Hills Medical Center when she'd fainted and fallen to the floor of the family room striking her head hard and waking not knowing where, hooked to

a heart monitor and made to breathe pure oxygen and an IV needle in the crook of her right arm where an ugly bruise of the hue of rotted bananas had begun to bloom and where was Bix? where was Bix? where was her family? what had become of her family?—but now it was the following day and Mummy had been released from the medical center and here was Daddy beside her, and Morris Kruk was beside her, and Mummy was eager to cooperate with Fair Hills detectives who'd been so kind to her and Bix, in their somber faces you could see how shaken these men were by the terrible thing that had happened to Bliss, a "home invasion" here in Fair Hills, a kidnapping, or attempted kidnapping, a six-year-old child murdered in her very home while family members slept unknowingly in their beds: the stuff of nightmare! of frenzied tabloid headlines! Assigned to the case were senior detectives Sledge and Slugg,* longtime "veterans" (as journalists would note with varying degrees of respect/irony) of the tidy little suburban Fair Hills Police Department where the usual arrests were for traffic violations, drunk driving, underage drinking and drug sales (pot, "uppers") at Fair Hills High; and where no one could recall a homicide investigation, still less claim to have been involved in one. And so, Detectives Sledge and Slugg moved about the Rampike household with the clumsy caution of dumfounded cattle being urged to the slaughter, fumbling to take notes in small spiral notebooks, as they'd been trained; both took pains to address the grief-stricken Rampikes with respect for clearly these were prominent Fair Hills citizens, obviously very well-to-do; Bruce Rampike was, it seemed, a "high-ranking executive" at the megacorporation Univers, Inc., Betsey Rampike was a member of the Village Women's Club; both belonged to the ultra-exclusive Sylvan Glen Golf Club; they lived in a beautiful Colonial in a very expensive residential neighborhood; they belonged to the Trinity Episcopal Church, and were close friends of Reverend Higley and his wife; still more impressively, the Rampikes were friends with the Morris County district attorney Howard O'Stryker, for whom the Fair Hills PD worked; they were friendly with Chief Justice Harry Fenn, and their lawyer was the "brilliant" and

* *Clearly fictitious names bearing but the most oblique onomatopoeic relationship to the names of the now-retired New Jersey police officers.*

"controversial" criminal defense attorney Morris Kruk. And the murder victim herself: here was no "casualty" of impoverished/drug-addled parental negligence/abuse in association with the notorious incompetence of the New Jersey Child Welfare Bureau: no six-year-old child "of color" discovered abused, strangled, broken in an elevator shaft in a Newark tenement, or in a Dumpster behind a WaWa in Trenton. Here was a Fair Hills child. A Caucasian child. A six-year-old *famous child*! For already, to the distress of Detectives Sledge and Slugg, the normally idyllic Village of Fair Hills was beginning to swarm with intruders: TV camera-crew vans, journalists and photographers, brash emissaries from the "media" world with the terrible power to expose, humiliate, vilify the merely competent, the well-intentioned-but-inexperienced veterans who'd made their fairly frictionless way through the ranks of a small-town police department looking to retirement and generous public-service pensions and so if the unspeakable thing that had happened in the Rampike house was a kind of fire, it was a fire only just beginning, a fire on the verge of exploding into a conflagration, how desperate the wish of the veteran guardians of the law to *put it out.*

"Skyler? Do you recognize this man, son? Take your time answering."

Slugg spoke quietly. Or was it Sledge. Men of indeterminate age, older than Skyler's father by many years, faces drawn with unease, fatigue. Skyler was made to know that he should say *yes.* How powerful the wish, that Skyler say *yes.* Staring at "mug shots"—as on TV!—of a frightened-looking youngish man with stark shadowed eyes and a soft, bruised mouth. Longish hair, disheveled. Who was this? The "ex-convict sex offender" who'd broken a basement window in the Rampikes' house, crawled inside with the intention of kidnapping Bliss—but killed her instead? Heavily sedated Skyler (Serenex, Zomix) was having trouble thinking over the roaring in his ears. How many hours or days this was, after "it" had happened, Skyler could not have said. His heart was pounding hard and sharp as an ice pick in his chest, for all the adults in the room were staring at him and waiting for him to speak.

"—saw him at an ice rink? Did you?"

"—on Ravens Crest Drive? Outside your house?"

Skyler tried to think. He had seen this man somewhere: he knew. At one of the ice rinks? The staring eyes, the soft bruised mouth that felt like Skyler's own mouth for he'd been gnawing at his lips. The man's eyes were bulgy as Skyler's eyes and there was that stricken/guilty look *Please have mercy, I am your friend.*

Suddenly Skyler remembered: a horizontal mirror, a mirror spanning a wall in a men's restroom, above a row of sinks. In that mirror the rusty-red-haired man stood watching him, a smile stretching the rubbery lips.

Quickly Skyler shook his head, no.

"D'you mean—no? You don't recognize this man?"

Stubborn Skyler shook his head. *No.*

Mummy was staring at him, disappointed. Mummy's face swollen and discolored from crying. And Daddy, puffy-skinned and tired-looking rubbing a big-Daddy fist over his mouth.

No! Skyler didn't remember this man. No more than Skyler remembered *it.**

---

* *How puzzling this is! Though Skyler "remembers" having seen Gunther Ruscha in a men's room one evening, that memory is utterly inaccessible to me at age nineteen. Yet, I remember "remembering" it, though the original memory has vanished. And I have no idea why I didn't tell these adults that I'd seen him when it was the truth for why, at such a time, would I have lied?*

TABLOID HELL I

EX-CON PEDOPHILE CONFESSES
"I KILLED BLISS"
35-Yr-Old Fair Hills, NJ Sicko
Paroled After 18 Months of 3¹/₂-Yr Sentence

New Jersey Sentinel
February 10, 1997

"I KILLED BLISS TO SAVE HER"
CLAIMS EX-CON BABY RAPER RUSCHA
6-Yr-Old Skating Prodigy Slain
While Family Sleeps Upstairs

Star Eye Weekly
February 10, 1997

SLAYER OF 6-YR-OLD BLISS RAMPIKE CONFESSES
Ex-Con Child Molester Ruscha Indicted in Fair Hills, NJ
"I Killed Bliss Because I Loved Her"

The Trentonian
February 11, 1997

HOW VALID IS RUSCHA CONFESSION?

Fair Hills Police: "Investigation to Continue"

*The Star-Ledger**
February 12, 1997

* *Reader, repeat these headlines, accompanied by full-front-page tabloid photos of beautiful little Bliss Rampike and her purported slayer Gunther Ruscha, ad nauseam. And photos of Betsey Rampike, and Bix Rampike. And that Rampike family photograph taken for our 1996 Christmas card. If you can stomach this crap, fine. Not for me! Though it's true that I grew up in the seething penumbra of tabloid hell, and that the very name "Rampike" was borne by me as one might bear the ignominy of an obscene figure branded into one's forehead, I was able to shut it out. Mostly.*

OUR PEDOPHILE III

IN HIS QUAVERING HIGH-PITCHED VOICE BRAVELY HE DECLARED:

"I am the one. I am the murderer of Bliss Rampike. Only me."

How these words sprang from him. At Fair Hills police headquarters. In that fluorescent-lit windowless interview room. And no need for a lawyer. Insisting: no lawyer.

"What has been caused to happen by my hand, I must be punished for. I am that one."

So readily did Gunther Ruscha confess to Fair Hills police detectives, yet so incoherently, in more than thirty hours of taped, rambling interviews over a period of several days, it would prove very difficult for investigators to collate, distill, and verify this statement. Initially, Ruscha told detectives that he had come to the Rampike house to "spirit Bliss away"—confusing his attempt to bring flowers to her, when he'd been taken into custody, with approaching the Rampike house through the woods and entering it through a basement window on the night of the murder; it became clear that Ruscha had somehow confused the two incidents though when detectives questioned him, he seemed not to hear, repeating in a quavering voice: "I am the one. I am the murderer of Bliss Rampike. Only me."

How Ruscha's eyes shone! Greeny-gray glassy eyes with twitchy red-rimmed lids and pale-red lashes that looked as if they'd been partly pulled out. The pedophile, incarcerated at the Morris County Men's Detention Center, sequestered in a "quarantine" wing to prevent his being attacked by other (normal non-pedophile/sicko) inmates, had not shaved that morning nor had time it seemed to wash for his slender/snaky body smelled frankly of sweat, anxiety, guilt.

What could be corroborated in Ruscha's statement was his admission of having bicycled numerous times on Ravens Crest Drive and having come to the Rampikes' door twice; of having attended Bliss Rampike's skating competitions where he arrived early and stayed late and videotaped as many "precious moments of Bliss" as possible; of having written to her, cards and letters and "special little gifts," over a period of approximately two years.

There had been a "secret understanding" between Bliss Rampike and Gunther Ruscha, Ruscha claimed. From the first, they had been able to "send their thoughts winging" between them; they shared dreams—"That were more real, much more real!—than this is, or you"; it was when Bliss called to him desperately with her thoughts that he came to her, bicycling on Ravens Crest Drive, passing the beautiful Rampike house that was set back from the roadway, at the end of an ascending graveled driveway; tirelessly Ruscha pedaled to the end of Ravens Crest Drive and circled the cul-de-sac, returned then passing the Rampikes' driveway—"Many more times than people complained of"; and in the evenings, when he was rarely detected, Ruscha picked up "secret signals" from his darling Bliss inside the house at a second-floor window facing the road: "They had her captive in there. I don't think they were her real parents, I think they adopted her. They 'bought' her. These things happen. She was an angel on earth, the Rampikes 'bought' her. They did terrible things to her, Bliss told me! In the window Bliss would light a candle to signal me. Or Bliss would shine a flashlight and blink it: like Morse code. 'Help me Gunther—I am so lonely in this place Gunther—I am so afraid—don't leave me with these terrible people will you—Gunther?' "* Ruscha's voice broke, recounting such pleas. And at Bliss's skating competitions, in the midst of one of Bliss's performances on the ice Bliss would "lock eyes" with Gunther, seated always in the same approximate place in the arena; in Gunther's videotapes you could see how the astonishing little skating prodigy, even as she glided on the ice, turned, spun, twirled, leapt and "skate-danced," managed to cast her small, secret smile at him.

* *How strange this is! I don't like this at all. That the delusional ravings of Gunther Ruscha should so echo my sister's words to me. Which I know can only be meant for me.*

Asked by detectives why, if he'd loved Bliss Rampike, he had killed her, Ruscha became vague and agitated insisting at first that he had not meant to "harm" her but only to "spirit her away"—for they were "soul mates" regardless of their ages. Ruscha was vague about where he would "spirit" the six-year-old to, as he was vague, excitable and not very coherent telling detectives how he'd made his way through the woods to the Rampike house on the night of the murder, he'd been summoned by Bliss to her, broke a basement window, crawled through and made his way upstairs in the darkened house—"Bliss pulled me to her, in her thoughts. It was like one of our dreams." And inside the little girl's room, Bliss was waiting for him in her bed. Ruscha spoke agitatedly claiming that what had happened was an accident: "On the stairs, Bliss fell. I couldn't save her. So I hid her away, in the basement. I don't know why. On the news it was said—'brutal attack.' It was not 'brutal'—but an accident! Bliss fell from my arms and hit her head. She was hurt. She was bleeding. I saw." Asked why he hadn't summoned help if the little girl was hurt, Ruscha lowered his head, struck his forehead against the table at which he sat, muttering: "Because I am a coward. I deserve to die."

Yet next morning, Ruscha's story had shifted in tone, and become darker and more lewd, yet more romantic; for somehow in the night in his cell in the grimy interior of the men's detention center at Morristown, Ruscha was made to recall what he'd done to his darling Bliss Rampike differently: "Detectives, it was a suicide pact. We had decided, we would both die. To escape the world that would judge us harshly. The plan was that I would 'extinguish' Bliss's life—painlessly. And then I would kill myself. And so I did it. But then, it was so terrible to see my darling lifeless, I lost my courage to kill myself. I was a coward, I ran away. I ran away in the night. I left my darling behind, and ran away in the night. And I thought *Maybe this is a dream?*—it was so like dreams we had both had. But when I am executed by the State of New Jersey, I will make amends. I will be forgiven. Bliss will see that I have not abandoned her. Bliss will see that I killed her to save her. I killed her because I loved her. No one loved Bliss Rampike as I did! I love her now, I will never stop loving her. When I die, I will join her. I must be punished. This is fair and just. Momma must understand, and let me *go*."

Ruscha broke down, sobbing; yet his expression, preserved on the grainy Fair Hills PD videotape for posterity, was radiant. Here was the very glisten of madness: or, of one who has been, like the martyred Saint Sebastian, transfigured by suffering.*

"DISGUSTING."

A warrant was issued to allow Fair Hills police to search the Ruscha house on Piper's Lane and there, in Ruscha's private quarters on the second floor, which Mrs. Ruscha conceded she had not entered in years, the pedophile's secret treasure trove was discovered.

On the walls, nearly covering every inch of wall space at eye level, were photographs of Bliss Rampike in her dazzling skating costumes, smiling shyly into the camera or performing on the ice; on the wall close beside the pedophile's narrow bed (the covering of which, I am obliged to reveal, though not one reader among you would give a damn if I did not, or even miss such a trivial detail if it were not shoehorned in here, shamelessly parenthetically, when the reader's obvious wish is to move on, to see what the hell is on Ruscha's wall: this covering, faded and stained with God knows what pasty-crusty pedophile-sicko excretions, was a pale blue, emblazoned with boy-nautical symbols: compulsively repeated silhouettes of frigates, man-o'-war ships, leaping whales, anchors) mawkish and sentimental pastel drawings of Bliss Rampike as a little-girl-angel skater; neatly shelved in strict chronological order in a five-foot Ikea untreated pine bookcase, were videotapes of young girls' skating competitions, beginning in 1986 (when the pedophile was only twenty-three), long before

---

* *It is clear that Gunther Ruscha was a man consumed by guilt and shame and yet: the fact that in his thirty-plus hours of a rambling confession he never speaks of a "ransom note" or the crimson silk scarf used to bind Bliss's wrists above her head would seem to suggest that Ruscha is merely confabulating, and is not the killer. Yet, no less an expert than E. L. Lance of the FBI, commenting on the "snarled and botched" Rampike case years later, came to the conclusion that Ruscha followed the pattern of "the most devious and ingenious" of psychopath killers: one who "confesses" in such a way to suggest delusion, and therefore innocence, while shrewdly failing to address crucial facts that would substantiate his guilt. Following such a pattern, the psychopath killer would leave no trace of himself at the crime scene, which was the case with Ruscha. "In my mind, Ruscha was the abductor/killer of Bliss Rampike. Not the parents."*

Bliss Rampike's debut as a child skater. (And how fortunate these anonymous young-girl skaters were!) But with the spectacular emergence of Miss Tots-on-Ice Debutante 1994 on Valentine's Day of that year at the Meadowlands rink, the pedophile discovered his destiny, Bliss Rampike, and footage of other girl-skaters, though taking up some space on Ruscha's tapes, had the air of the incidental and haphazard.

"Disgusting!"

The shocking revelation was, Gunther Ruscha had been stalking Bliss since February 1994. How was it possible that the tall lanky rusty-red-haired pedophile had managed to tape hours of Bliss practicing at the Halcyon rink? (Must've been in disguise, or in disguises.) There was much footage of Betsey Rampike driving her daughter along Ravens Crest Drive, to and from town; there were numerous blurred mall scenes, and parking lot scenes; Betsey and Bliss and sometimes Skyler, climbing into/climbing out of Betsey's car or minivan; there was footage of the eye-catching Rampike family—big handsome smiling Bix, glamorous smiling Betsey, darling little children in Sunday clothes and polished shoes—entering quaint Trinity Episcopal Church amid a stream of other well-dressed Caucasian worshippers. (One day it would be startling for Skyler to see his young self with his family oblivious of being captured on videotape, for a lurid and unimaginable posterity: an ordinary-seeming little boy of seven or eight walking beside his father without any discernible limp which is weird because I know that I limped, and I know that my child's face was disfigured by scowling.) There was even a surreal shot of Mummy, Skyler, and Bliss being videotaped together in Sunday clothes, or maybe it was Mummy's birthday, Bliss and Skyler holding hands and Mummy behind us leaning over us and smiling happily, the three of us positioned on a hill in (I guess) Fair Hills Battle Park (where I haven't troubled to bring the reader since nothing of significance in this document ever happened there, I'd thought); videotaped, that is, by Daddy standing a few yards away holding his new camcorder, beaming with Daddy-love for his little family; and somewhere close by, hidden from view, the pedophile Ruscha was lurking, daring to videotape the Rampikes without their knowledge. (If Daddy had known? Had seen Ruscha? It is possible, *My Sister, My Love: The Intimate Story of Skyler Rampike* would never be written, and you, reader, and I, tangled together in its pages like the luckless Laocoön family in the giant serpents' grip, would never have come to know each other.)

How hard this is to comprehend, even for edgy/pessimist/paranoid Skyler, that for years the Rampikes were being observed by a stranger; moments of their lives were being snatched from them, and preserved on tape and on film; and that, in some of these scenes, so unexpectedly, Skyler appeared young, innocent, *a mere child*.

And yet: the reader knows, as I know, that this can't be true.

In glossy pink albums not unlike those favored by Betsey Rampike, Ruscha had lovingly inserted laminated clippings of interviews with Bliss from such publications as *People*, *New Jersey Lives*, *Galleria*, *The Star-Ledger Magazine*; newspaper stories of Bliss's skating triumphs: Miss Tots-on-Ice Debutante 1994, Little Miss Paramus Ice Princess 1995,* All-Star Girls' Figure Skating Champ (Junior Division) 1995, Little Miss Atlantic States (Regional) 1995, Tiny Miss Golden Skate Princess 1996, Little Miss Jersey Ice Princess 1996, Little Miss All-American-Girl Ice Jubilee First Prize Winner 1996. And more.

Always, in the life of a public figure, there must be more.

(Of Bliss's defeat and humiliation at the Hershey's Kisses competition, there was no trace. So protective was Gunther Ruscha, though claiming to have killed my sister!)

Yet more disturbing material was discovered in a musty-smelling alcove off Ruscha's room, where the pedophile had a kind of workshop, or studio; here, detectives found more pastel drawings, and portraits of Bliss Rampike in acrylic paint, weirdly glossy, at odds with the "poetic" subject matter:

> **—A very young (four-year-old?) Bliss Rampike posed en pointe on ice skates, in a daffodil-yellow tulle skirt and sequined top, lavender ribbons fluttering in her pale gold hair**

> **—A slightly older, less shy and "seductive" Bliss in the sexy red-sequined *Boléro* costume with the (just slightly) padded**

* *How strange, I hadn't remembered this title; there is no record of it in my manuscript; yet Gunther Ruscha remembered, and enshrined it here, lest it be lost.*

bodice and slit-skirt, peekaboo black panties beneath (which
the amateur artist had tried to represent, detectives discover
with revulsion, with a small patch of actual black lace)

—An ethereal "angelic" Bliss in a ballerina's costume of antique
lace fitting her small body tight as a glove, fluffy white tulle
skirt, a hint of white silk panties, white lace stockings, ashy-pale
hair plaited like a crown upon which a white-gold tiara rested

—Eyes closed, hands clasped on her chest, Bliss lying on her
back inside what appears to be an ivory-white casket, in her
Hershey's Kisses costume of dark-chocolate velvet with tinsel
trim; seemingly at peace, a small sweet smile on her pink-
rosebud lips; yet the eyelids were translucent, as if the little
girl was peering through them; if you stood close, you could
see the glimmer of a cobalt-blue gaze fixed upon *you*.

In all of Ruscha's likenesses of Bliss, the little blond girl was crudely
and yet tenderly depicted; her face, mawkishly sentimental, with exaggerated features, was yet recognizable as the face of Bliss Rampike.

"Jesus! What next!"

Equally repugnant to the detectives were Gunther Ruscha's florid
scribblings, kept in a leatherbound ledger labeled BLISS MY BELOVED:

BLISS MY BELOVED

You, my Destiny; and I, yours—
Never will I understand
The cruel ways of God to man—
You, a Child; and I, a Man—
This cruel fate, we dare not mate.

BLISS MY DESTINY

Summon me my darling, and I am at your side—
In the grave, you will be my bride—

Your little footprints in the snow—
Reveal to me, where I must go.

"LITTLE MISS JERSEY ICE PRINCESS 1996"

None is more beautiful than you,
None is more angelic than you,
None is more perfect than you,
None is so blessèd, to be you.

SONG OF INNOCENCE

Who dwells in beauty is a Child
Unknowing how Man's heart is wild
Who dwells in joy must one day weep
Such promises she has made, she cannot keep.

CRUEL ANGEL HEAR ME!

Ah, to be the Ice
Beneath your sharp Skate
In ecstasy's Vise
I am—thy Fate!

In disgust the detectives examined a few of the manuscript pages. Here were "rimes"—"poetry"? More than sixty pages of pedophiliac love verse but reader, I will spare you.

Fortunately, Ruscha owned no computer. The year was 1997, a little too early for the average pedophile to have realized the possibilities of the Internet for kiddie-porn. And so, reader, we are spared even more despicable crap.*

---

* Am I being too "harsh"—"judgmental"? Am I overstepping the tacit boundary between Author and Reader, and speaking too openly where I should try for subtler and more modulated tones? If there are pedophiles among my readers, can I afford to offend and alienate anyone? Let me say, then: for readers with a "scientific" interest in the ravings of the lunatic mind, The Collected Works of Gunther Ruscha—love verse, reproductions of "art-works"—is available in the teeming cesspool of cyberspace. Investigate at your own risk!

"Jesus. Will you look at *this*."

Yet more astonished, Fair Hills detectives discovered, in the ill-smelling basement of the Ruscha house, what appeared to be a taxidermist's workshop: on a badly stained and scratched table were a number of clumsily "stuffed" small animals (squirrel, chipmunks, mice, a young rat with a stiff pointed tail and bristling whiskers) and birds (primarily sparrows but also a bluejay, a cardinal, a mangled house finch); here was a powerful odor of formaldehyde, amid a more powerful odor of organic decay. Gunther Ruscha, long notorious as Morris County's pedophile, had been, all along, in secret, an amateur taxidermist as well? Inside several Plexiglas boxes were attempts at "artful" arrangements of stuffed creatures, and in one of these, seemingly Ruscha's favorite, for it was showcased on a pedestal table, was a bird of about the size of a cardinal, but with pale gold feathers that looked as if they had been painted; the little bird had ill-fitting glass eyes; on the little bird's tiny feet, tiny ice skates fashioned of tinsel. And on the bird's pert, uplifted head, a tiny tinsel tiara. The little gold-feathered bird was skating on one skate, on an aluminum foil surface meant to suggest ice, wings outspread, while at the sides of the Plexiglas box an audience of small birds, mostly sparrows, looked on, applauding with their wings. On the Plexiglas sides glitter dust had been sprinkled. The effect was both tenderly quaint and grotesque. The smell was unmistakable.

In silence detectives Sledge and Slugg stared at this hellish display, pressing handkerchiefs over their noses. For never had these Fair Hills detectives, longtime "veterans" of the force, seen, or smelled, anything so bizarre.

"You think? He was going to stuff her?"*

* If any among my readers think that this is funny, it is not.

Whether Sledge or Slugg made this remark is not known. Though neither would include this grisly speculation in his report, it quickly became part of the Gunther Ruscha legend, maintained in cyberspace by individuals convinced that GR was a budding and ingenious serial killer who had planned to kill and "stuff" his beloved Bliss.

OUR PEDOPHILE IV

"JESUS! LOOK AT THE FUCKER!"

At 6 A.M. of Valentine's Day, February 14, 1997, exactly three years after Gunther Ruscha had first seen Bliss Rampike, his lifeless body was discovered in his cell in the Morris County Men's Detention Center, in a "contorted and convulsed" posture on the floor beside his bed. Around his neck the confessed murderer had fashioned a crude noose made of a torn shirt, one end of which he'd knotted to the iron post of his bed; somehow, with desperate effort, he'd managed to choke himself to death, by repeated thrusts of his body downward. The medical examiner would declare Ruscha's death to be "self-afflicted"—the "most unusual suicide" in the history of the detention center, where inmates usually hanged themselves in showers or from lighting fixtures or, having fashioned crude knives out of toothbrushes and the like, slashing an artery.

Neatly placed on Ruscha's pillow was a handprinted note:

GONE TO JOIN MY BELOVED.

I AM "THE EYE THAT SEES."*

G.R.

---

* *"I am 'The Eye That Sees' " is a belated claim to have written the ransom note prompting investigators to wonder: had Ruscha only just heard about the ransom note; or had Ruscha, in fact, written the ransom note? Informed commentators on the subject are divided: 52 percent believe that Ruscha wrote the note, with materials (paper, pen) found in the Rampike house; 37 percent believe that Betsey Rampike wrote it; 9 percent, that Bix Rampike wrote it; 2 percent, "other."*

No attempt was made to revive Ruscha when his body was discovered, by either prison guards or emergency medics, for it was clear that Ruscha had been dead for hours.

Immediately the news was released to the public nationwide: the "confessed killer" of Bliss Rampike was dead, "by his own hand."*

BY THIS TIME, BLISS RAMPIKE'S "AUTOPSIED" BODY HAD AT LAST BEEN RE-leased by Morris County's medical examiner Dr. Virgil Elyse and had been buried in Trinity Episcopal cemetery. A private funeral had been held at the church to which only a "select" number of Rampike relatives and close friends were invited, yet the small church was jammed with mourners, including an impressive number of those Fair Hills residents once listed on Mummy's secret pyramid of names. And so many flowers! A deluge of flowers, most of them white, dazzling-white, lilies and other spring flowers, surrounding the heartrendingly small gleaming-white (closed) casket set before the altar.

The sweet sickly fragrance of calla lilies, suffused through the quaint little "historic" church like an expelled breath.

Outside on Highland Avenue, in this neighborhood of large old homes set back from the street with an air of patrician dignity, a crowd had gathered that would be called "unruly"—"comprised of mostly outsiders." This crowd of an estimated one thousand people had started to form as early as 6 A.M. Fair Hills police officers including the elite Equestrian Squad (five handsome horses, five police officers) were on hand to direct traffic and to maintain order. Though the Rampikes had been warned, and a small cadre of security guards had been hired to protect the family from the ever more intrusive media, as from grieving fans of Bliss Rampike, yet the Rampikes

*Do you believe this? Mrs. Ruscha never did: "They killed my boy. They made him 'confess' then they killed him." Soon after Ruscha's death it began to be said that he'd hanged himself in this awkward way "with an assist" from a guard or two; and that this "assist" had been a populist expression of the righteous loathing felt by the New Jersey community for the pedophile; in time, it would begin to be hinted that the "assist" might have been purchased by an agent of an agent of an associate of the canny M. Kruk. (Hey I know: I shouldn't be promulgating such rumors in this objective document, and yet: what if the rumors are true?)

were surprised by the size of the crowd, and the excitement their appearance provoked when they stepped from a black Lincoln Town Car and ascended the stone steps to the church. Cries of "Betsey!"—"Betsey!"—"Bix!"—followed in their wake.

Astonishing to Betsey Rampike that so quickly, in death, her beautiful daughter seemed to have achieved a degree of fame she had not had in life; and that she, Betsey, Bliss's grief-ravaged mother, seemed to have ascended to that hallowèd ground as well.

Like an annunciation, it was. And so quickly!

Ashy-skinned stony-eyed Bix Rampike stared straight ahead and did not acknowledge the crowd. Behind her dark glasses Betsey blinked back tears and smiled—wanly, bravely—lifting a gloved hand to the rapt faces and the eyes of strangers damp with tears that mirrored her own.

"Betsey! God bless you!"

"Betsey! We loved Bliss!"

"Betsey! Bliss is with Jesus!"

Badly Betsey wanted to pause, to take the hands of grieving strangers, to speak with them and to share their tears but there came Bix's strong fingers gripping her arm without sentiment and urging her forward.

Betsey wore stylish dark glasses to hide her discolored and swollen eyes, which she fumbled to remove when she entered the church. The grieving mother was swathed in black: black belted cashmere coat with a black mink collar and cuffs, mink-trimmed black hat, black leather gloves. Red lipstick like a gash in her pale-powdered face that seemed to have lost its shape, like uncooked bread dough. It was observed that Betsey Rampike seemed to have gained weight, as if bloated. And Bix Rampike, it was observed, had become strangely—"uncharacteristically"—grim-faced, distracted. Moving clumsily and almost wincingly like an athlete who has been stunned by defeat with no clear idea how seriously he has been injured. (And had Bix been drinking? Was Bix *drunk*?)

"Betsey! Bix! We are praying for you!"

In their front row pew the Rampikes were flanked by Bix's numerous relatives—brothers, sisters, uncles, cousins—Bix's mother Edna Louise who was now an elderly, infirm woman hunched like a turkey vulture, the lower part of her face frozen in a grimace of awe, hurt, astonishment as in the aftermath of a stroke; during Reverend Higley's funeral sermon, elderly Mrs. Rampike would whisper into Bix's ear, tugging petulantly at his sleeve. ("Who is that man? What is he saying about my granddaughter? Who has given him the right? Why are we here?") No members of the Sckulhorne family were present, for Betsey had rebuffed their eager wishes to drive down from Hagarstown in a minivan to attend. ("Not now! Now it's too late! You didn't know my beautiful Bliss in life, you will not know her and exploit her fame in death. Our grief is not yours.") An organist was playing Bach: "Jesu, Our Redeemer." A soprano sang "O Christ Who Art the Light and the Day" in a voice of thrilling certainty. The Trinity choir rose to sing "Hail to Thee, My Jesus Holy!" At this time it was known that the pedophile-murderer of Bliss Rampike had been swiftly arrested by Fair Hills police and had confessed; and the effort was now, as Reverend Higley said gravely, blinking back tears at the pulpit, to begin the task of "healing"—"helping to support the Rampike family" in this time of "unfathomable tragedy and pain."

In the quaint little "historic" Trinity Church, as in the snowy "historic" churchyard to the rear, where Bliss Rampike in her child-sized gleaming-white coffin would be "laid to rest" there were many tears, you can be sure. But none of then were Skyler Rampike's: why?

Skyler wasn't there. Wasn't at his sister's funeral. Skyler was in quarantine.

(In fact, did you miss Skyler? Was the runty kid's absence noted by anyone at all?)

Quick cut! Let's depart the solemn "church scene" tremulous with Trinity Church's show-offy organist (male, Brit) tripping and clattering up and down the keyboards emitting yet more deafening Johann Sebastian Bach that most classy of classics, now we're in an unidentified room, dowdy old "good" furniture, vaguely Skyler recalls through the cotton batting scrim of Serenex/Zomix haze that this is the room designated as "his" where he'd been brought to stay with Mummy in a dark-browed old English Tudor house smelling of mothballs, must've belonged to one of Mummy's rich-old-widow church friends, Frannie Squires or Adelaide Metz, who'd been eager to take in the Rampikes after *it* happened, for Skyler could not sleep in his room any longer, not ever again in that room where in the night in even the Zomix haze his sister Bliss barefoot and shivering in her nightgown pushed open the door pleading *Skyler? help me Skyler help me there is something bad in my bed* causing Skyler to wake screaming and thrashing and his runt-heart to race at twice its normal beat nor could Mummy sleep in that "accursed" house in which "Satan" had set foot for Mummy's heart was "torn to shreds" as Mummy had said weeping in numerous "exclusive" interviews. Certainly it was true and would be forever true that Skyler could not sleep in that house in that bed but Skyler could not sleep very well in any house or in any bed nor could Skyler eat without needing to puke up what he'd eaten nor could Skyler sit still for more than two or three minutes, nor would Skyler allow any doctor to examine him without panicking, kicking and screaming like a two-year-old except, as a two-year-old, Skyler had not ever thrown such tantrums, especially Skyler went ballistic ("ball-istic": way cool word in Skyler's dyslexic vocabulary) when a nurse tried to draw blood from his runt-veins, shocking to hear a child diagnosed as "withdrawn"—"indifferent to surroundings"—"mute"—suddenly cry *Nooo! Noooo! Nooooo!* piteous as a bawling calf. Most annoying to adults, Skyler refused to "meet their gaze" including such adults as Mummy, Daddy, Grandmother Rampike and the wedge-faced new Maria whom Mummy had hired to look after Skyler now that Lila Laong had decided to return to the Philippines unless maybe Mummy had had to "let Lila go"* (but why? Skyler would not have known) and Skyler missed Lila! Skyler missed Lila! Skyler cried missing Lila who'd been so kind to him even as he'd pushed her aside, scowled and spat and refused to allow her to bathe him, slapped her hands away when she tried to prevent him scratching so hard at his scalp, his nails came away ringed in blood, and hair began to fall from his head, how cruel he'd been to Lila *I hate you you let Bliss be hurt, hate hate HATE YOU* which made no sense (did it?) but Skyler remembers such accusations as Skyler remembers his

---

* *Poor Lila! I hope that, returned to her native island, a comforting distance from Fair Hills, New Jersey, this lovely woman has no awareness of how, in the most lurid recesses of cyberspace, the more lunatic Bliss Rampike Web sites entertain the possibility that, amid those who had "opportunity" and "motive" to have killed Bliss Rampike, the Rampikes' nanny/housekeeper remains, if not a prime suspect, a "suspect."*

throat shutting up tight so he could not scream at all, could not speak at all, choking/gagging possibly it had to do with his medication, after *it* happened Skyler's medication was naturally increased, new medications prescribed by the new pediatric psychiatrist Dr. Splint. And so, Skyler missed his sister's funeral. Skyler missed his sister's burial in a far corner of the old Trinity churchyard. Nor would it be explained to Skyler where his sister was "buried" for the crude word "buried" would not be uttered in Skyler's presence like such words as "die"—"dead"—"death." Nor such cruder words as "murder"—"blunt force trauma." Nor such a word as "suspect." And on that day, Valentine's Day 1997, there came Mummy to Skyler to wake him from his groggy nap in an unfamiliar room smelling of mothballs, Mummy's face was wet with fresh tears, and Mummy's eyes shone, and Mummy hugged Skyler so passionately, Skyler thought, in the confusion of waking from groggy sleep, that Bliss must have returned to them: was this good news?

Mummy pulled Skyler from his bed, that he and Mummy might kneel together. "We will pray for that terrible man's soul, Skyler. Jesus forgives him, he knew not what he did."

V

And After

"THE MURDER HOUSE"

NO ONE LIVED IN IT. "GHOST LIGHTS" BURNED INSIDE. A CARETAKER IN A pickup appeared from time to time. A FOR SALE sign appeared at the end of the long graveled driveway. A NO TRESPASSING sign appeared. After a sudden blizzard, snow drifted over the driveway and no private snowplow came to clear it. In time, movers came in an enormous Mayflower van, and took away the furnishings. Months passed. More months passed. There were no buyers for the beautiful old sprawling eighteenth-century Colonial at 93 Ravens Crest Drive in which a six-year-old girl had been murdered. Most "potential buyers" were but morbid-minded curiosity-seekers. Worse yet, journalists/photographers with a "new angle" on the Rampike story. Mrs. Cuttlebone did her darndest to weed these out! Mrs. Cuttlebone was a "personal friend" of the Rampikes and yes, she'd known beautiful little Bliss Rampike the "prodigy ice-skater" who had been murdered in her bed by a sex maniac/pedophile-psychopath dwelling in the very heart of Fair Hills: a sex-offender parolee who had served less than two years of a ten-year sentence for child molestation. The over-liberal judges of this Democrat-controlled corrupt state of New Jersey! It was enough to make you cry.

Sometimes, Mrs. Cuttlebone did cry. Startled clients stared as the handsome forty-year-old powdered face crinkled like a paper mask to reveal the grieving fifty-nine-year-old face beneath.

"We don't call it 'The Murder House.' Of course not!"

Realtors listed the house at 93 Ravens Crest Drive as a *breathtakingly beautiful part-restored 18th century Colonial. Price: negotiable.*

Skyler never saw the house again. Skyler would come to "forget" the house. Skyler would come to "forget" his room. Skyler would "forget" much that happened in the house. For Mummy did not speak of the house, and Daddy did not speak of the house. For a while, Skyler was an outpatient at Cedar Hills Children's Neuropsychiatric Treatment Center in Summit, New Jersey. And then, as his condition was said to be "progressing," Skyler was an inpatient at the Cedar Woods Children's Neuropsychiatric Treatment Center in Summit, New Jersey. In this way, time passed.

When was it, the house, at 93 Ravens Crest Drive was finally sold? Skyler never saw the house again.

Except so frequently, in dreams.

AMATEUR TAXIDERMY

DID SOME OF YOU SMILE, IN HAUGHTY DISDAIN, AT GUNTHER RUSCHA'S AMATEUR taxidermy? Mangled and misshapen creatures, lumpy fur, ill-fitting glass eyes and most shameful of all, that smell. For all Ruscha's effort at taxidermy (bloodletting, evisceration, "embalming" and "mummifying") his stuffed animals were but unconvincing "real" creatures set beside stuffed toy animals. Melancholy creatures that, in death, were cheated of death's dignity because their taxidermist was an amateur.

How I wish, for my sister Bliss Rampike, that she might be "memorialized" by a Homer, a Dante, a Shakespeare instead of *me*. And yet: Skyler is all that Bliss has.

Will you help me Skyler   Never leave me Skyler

Last night, writing "The Murder House," in a white-hot rush of inspiration and exhilaration, it came to me that, for all my good intentions, and my fervor, *My Sister, My Love: The Intimate Story of Bliss Rampike** is a kind of taxidermy, and much of it is botched in the way that Ruscha botched his. Reasons are:

—Both G.R. and S.R. are amateurs, and amateurs care too much.
—Both G.R. and S.R. are confounded by the "real."
—Both G.R. and S.R. "came too close to the flame."†

---

* *Must've typed this by mistake. But let it stand.*

† *What's this mean? Some kind of mystical bullshit? Yet, how otherwise to express the inexpress-*

And in the quicksand of my despair there appeared to me the man who asks to be known—unabashedly, and without irony—as Pastor Bob, urging me *Son speak what is in your heart love and not hate must guide you know that truth is beauty, son do not labor to create mere beauty.* How badly I want to believe Pastor Bob of the New Canaan Evangelical Church of Christ Risen!

It is irony I must give up. It is my own woundedness I must surrender. The smell of my own suppurating wounds. Pastor Bob is right. So what if this document into which I have spilled my guts isn't a work of beauty but a kind of fucked-up taxidermy? It is the best I can do.

As Gunther Ruscha's pathetic specimens were the best that poor bastard could do.

As in the most stylish of contemporary films let's just quick-cut to a poignant/enigmatic scene in a room in the dark-browed English Tudor home of wealthy-widow Adelaide Metz, one of the clucking sisterhood of elderly church ladies who'd competed with one another to help the Rampikes in their hour of need and who claimed to have loved Bliss "like a granddaughter." Here is Mummy charging into the room with the glowing/stunned face of one who has just won the New Jersey lottery with a purloined ticket, lifting Skyler so hard his ribs creak, next thing Skyler knows his mother has pulled him to the floor beside her and the two of them are praying together for the soul of Gunther Ruscha who—unknown to Skyler—had only just "committed suicide" in the men's detention center a few hours before in the most ingenious of ways, hanging himself from a height of less than thirty-six inches.

---

ible? For the fact is, both G.R. and S.R. remain "suspects" in the yet-unsolved police investigation into my sister's death. While it's commonly believed that Ruscha was the killer, no physical evidence was ever found by police linking Ruscha to the crime or even to the interior of the Rampikes' house; and no witness ever claimed to have seen him in or near the house at the time of Bliss's death. A small but strident cult has grown in cyberspace, like poisonous mold inside damp walls, insisting that Bliss's brother Skyler was her killer, which makes me sick to acknowledge, but I should acknowledge it, I know. (The last time I checked into cybercesspoolspace, about two years ago, I was high on trippy dextromethorphan [drugstore cough medicine] and only just laughed. Now, I am off drugs and so sensitive, it's like the outermost layer of my skin has been peeled off. And the exhilaration of last night's "white-hot rush of inspiration" has totally worn off. And worse yet—well no. I will save "worse yet" for another chapter.)

Why pray for the soul of the very man who'd hurt his sister? Skyler wondered. Yet Mummy insisted.

"Jesus hates the sin but loves the sinner. Only think, if Jesus can love that terrible man, how Jesus will love *us*."

AND SO IT WOULD BE TOLD TO SKYLER EVER AFTER THAT THE "BAD MAN" who'd hurt his sister would "never hurt anyone again" and yet perversely it seemed, Skyler took little comfort from the fact, who knows why?

These weeks, months, and years to come when Skyler would be medicated "for his own good."

In February 1997 Skyler was treated for PDD (Premature Depression Disorder) and for CAS (Chronic Anxiety Syndrome). Needless to say Skyler continued to be treated for such ongoing conditions as dyslexia, attention deficit disorder, et al., but soon after Skyler's tenth birthday in March the moody brat would be diagnosed by Dr. Vandeman as suffering from a disorder so new, yet so "epidemic" in the United States, that child mental health experts were only beginning to grasp the scope and breadth of its prevalence and pharmaceutical companies were only beginning to manufacture the (costly) psychotropic monoamine oxidase inhibitors required to combat it: ASD.*

Abruptly, Skyler had been withdrawn from school.

Headmaster Hannity concurred with the Rampikes, that the "traumatized boy" would be a distraction to his classmates and should avoid "stressful situations" for the next several months. (Yet in secret Skyler wore his hunter-green school blazer with his precious little gold H.I.P. pin in the lapel, of which he'd been so pathetically proud. In secret, Skyler smiled wanly at himself in the mirror recalling Headmaster's thrilling

---

* *"Autism Spectrum Disorder": Defined by the American Association of Child Neuropsychotherapists as "significant impairments in social interaction and communication and the presence of perverse behaviors, speech patterns, and interests." In 1997, a federal study revealed that one out of every three hundred American children was afflicted with ASD; now, it's one out of every one hundred-fifty. If the reader has persevered so far in this flagrantly "perverse" book, very likely the reader is afflicted, like the author, with ASD and should be taking, as the author no longer does, five hundred milligrams of Claritan thrice daily.*

words: " 'Skyler! Congratulations, son' "—" 'In the American meritocracy, Fair Hills Day is betting on you to go the distance for us.' ")

(Embarrassing! The reader, who has never smiled at him/herself in any mirror, still less murmured such piteous words of self-praise, is asked to pass by such revelations in silence.)

One good thing that followed from Bliss's murder: all Skyler's playdates ceased. Permanently.

A single card from an ex-playdate found its way to Skyler Rampike:

DEAR SKYLER,

   PLEASE ACCEPT MY CONDOLENCES FOR THE LOSS OF
   YOUR SISTER. I WOULD LIKE TO SEE YOU AGAIN BUT
   IT WOULD BE TOO SAD YOUR MOTHER SAYS.

SINCERELY,

E. Grubbe

ELYOT GRUBBE

Sometimes Skyler would recall his Fair Hills Day friends with a pang of nostalgia. Cool boys like Calvin Klaus and Billy Durkee who'd been his close buddies; and brainy Mildred Marrow who'd expressed the wish that Skyler might be her brother. But much of the time, in his dreamy medicated state, Skyler scarcely missed his sister.

Overhearing Mummy speaking with visitors in Mrs. Metz's house, from a stairway landing: "My son is adjusting. My son has suffered a terrible trauma as if that terrible man had laid his evil hands on *him*. We never speak of it."

In all, Mummy and Skyler would stay for several weeks as houseguests of the devoutly religious Mrs. Metz, and the house on Ravens Crest Drive was unoccupied, with but "ghost lights" kept burning in scattered rooms, to deter burglars. It was never entirely clear to Skyler where Daddy was for often Daddy was staying in a hotel—or a condominium—in Quaker Heights, which was a short commuting distance to Univers, Inc.; but Daddy also stayed at his apartment on Central Park South sometimes, where, it was promised, Skyler might visit Daddy soon, and Skyler and Daddy could attend a Knicks game; better yet, Skyler might "spend quality time with Daddy" in the city; then again, as both Daddy and Mummy agreed, with Skyler in such a "fragile mental state," how much more sensible for him to remain in Fair Hills with his mother; how much more sensible for him to continue treatment with Vandeman, Splint, and his new pediatric pain-management physiologist Yu Kwon who was always so cheerful and hopeful about Skyler's "healing."

Daddy had been badly shaken by *it*. Daddy was never to speak of *it* to Skyler. (Or to anyone? Skyler wondered.) Though Daddy had been granted an emergency leave from Univers, Inc. at the time of the tragedy, Daddy had returned to work on the morning following Bliss's funeral for Daddy had needed to throw himself into work at once: "More work, the better! *Sick transit mundi*."

Of course, Daddy tried to spend weekends in Fair Hills with the remnant of his little family. How Daddy's eyes brimmed with warm-Daddy tears when he greeted Mummy and Skyler: grabbing Skyler around the ribs, lifting him and kiss-nuzzling Skyler's sensitive face. "Skyler! Love ya, son." But Daddy's voice was hoarse as a frog's croak and the big-Daddy smile had less wattage. Daddy did not even loom so tall any longer for there was a stoop to Daddy's right shoulder as if he'd caught the weight of a falling object. At such times, Skyler thought it was strange that Daddy chose to stay with Fair Hills friends, usually Mr. Kruk, for always there was "legal business" to discuss with Mr. Kruk, and not with Mummy and Skyler in their rooms in Mrs. Metz's English Tudor mansion on the Great Road; but Daddy explained that he could not risk sleeping overnight in that house where the mothball smell was so strong, Daddy worried he might become "embalmed."

Was this a Daddy-joke—"embalmed"? Were you supposed to laugh? There were so few Daddy-jokes now, Skyler had forgotten how to respond.*

---

* *What a melancholy little chapter this is! I guess it must be because its kiddie-protagonist Skyler is "embalmed."*

RED SILK

WHOSE RED SILK SCARF WAS IT?

Tied around my sister's wrists that were tightly bound together by duct tape. And her thin arms forced up over her head, arranged in a "seductive pose."

And her bare legs, that were not so thin but slender and hard with muscle, an unexpected sight in a child so young, outspread, the stained flannel nightie bunched up beneath her hips.

The canny reader will recall the crimson silk scarf from my ground-breaking chapter "Sex Toys?"—I hope. Yet, as Mr. Kruk informed investigators, it was likely that the intruder had found the scarf inside the house, to use for his own purposes.

"He was wearing gloves. He came prepared. The roll of duct tape he took away with him. He left no sign of himself behind."

New Jersey Sentinel, Star Eye Weekly, National Inquirer, Up Close & Personal would publish countless "interviews" with "anonymous sources" close to the Rampikes alleging that Bliss Rampike had been sexually molested; and that this sexual molestation was the reason the child had been murdered. (For why otherwise would anyone kill a six-year-old?)

And yet: Morris County Medical Examiner Virgil Elyse reported finding no sign of sexual trauma on the child-victim's body. No semen on the body or in the furnace room.

And so the murder of Bliss Rampike had not been a sex crime—had it?

Yet: why had Bliss been positioned in such a "seductive" way, arms flung above her head and legs provocatively outspread, in the stained little-girl nightie . . .

Skyler! help me   *Skyler it's so dark in here*
Don't leave me   *Skyler*

In the tabloids as in cybercesspoolspace it was charged that Bliss Rampike was "almost certainly" an incest victim. "Anonymous sources close to the Rampike family" would so claim. "Anonymous sources" in the Fair Hills Police Department, in the county prosecutor's office, and in the county medical examiner's office. In most instances it was Bliss's father who was the abuser but in some instances, the brother.

In *Up Close & Personal*, a "former nanny" who'd been employed by the Rampikes claimed *It was the brother. Doing bad things to that little angel from when she was a baby.*

On one of the Bliss-cult Web sites a "former classmate" of the brother's at Fair Hills Day School claims *He was a real sicko! Showed us these weird cartoons like R. Crumb, him doing really weird things to his sister. Like, he's expecting us to say, "Way cool, man"?**

Reader, I am not teasing you! I am only just grimly reporting what is out there in Tabloid Hell where unlike the Rampikes you do not dwell. Digging at the stitches in my face. Picking at scabs until they bleed and the sensation of wetness on my dried and cracked nails feels good and this messed-up paper on which I'm writing another mangled chapter—"Red Silk": sounded so fucking promising—is speckled with my blood like squashed lice.

---

* *Who is this? Tyler McGreety? Spreading terrible lies about his old playdate Skyler Rampike?* Why?

"TABLOID HELL": A NOTE

JUST TO ASSURE THE READER: NONE OF THIS WILL EVER HAPPEN TO YOU. Never will you know how "anonymous sources" including your friends will spread terrible lies about you like bats erupting from their mouths and if asked why, why lie, why hurt another person, the answer is *Because I am anonymous, that's why.*

"YET WORSE"

THIS MORNING, ANOTHER LETTER CAME FOR SKYLER RAMPIKE, FORWARDED from the Pittsburgh law firm of Crunk, Swidell, Hamm & Silverstein, pale-apricot envelope with return address HEAVEN SCENT.

Don't! Don't open but already I'd opened it.

A single sheet of lightly perfumed pale-apricot stationery, the unmistakable lavender handwriting, making its claim—

February 14 2007
Dear Skyler—
Darling Please.
Your loving Mother
"Mummy"

"I will not. *I will not.*"

This time she hadn't mentioned surgery. Yet I knew.

Crumpled the pale-apricot letter and stuffed it into a pocket of my army-fatigue pants and stumbled outside into a bright winter sunshine. Must've been picking at my face, the way people looked at me leaking blood down my left cheek. I'd been supposed to return to the medical center to have the stitches removed but hadn't gotten around to it. A few blocks away church bells were ringing with lunatic fervor. If I could believe in God there was a place for me in that church but I can't, so there isn't. Along Pitts Street limping and cursing and wiping at my face, "Will not, I will not." Yet the fear came to me *What if she dies? What if it's cancer and she dies? And I did not see my mother one final time?* but I would not give into that woman, not ever again.*

---

* *The curious reader wonders: why is Skyler so frightened of a middle-aged woman who happens to be, or to have been, his "mother" for approximately fifteen years? What is the powerful "hold" this woman has over him, that reduces him to childish fear, and melts away his capacity for irony as a microwave oven would melt away a hefty icicle? What throws Skyler into a panic, that this woman holds the key to "his" memory; that this woman possesses knowledge about him, like some wise-guy oracle in a Greek tragedy, of which the brainy kid hadn't a clue of, himself? Read on.*

TV-MUMMY I

"THE GRACE OF GOD, AVIS. THERE IS NO OTHER WAY."

This first time he'd seen TV-Mummy he hadn't realized who the woman on the TV screen was. His eyesight was blurred and watery from his meds and in his ears there was a constant high-pitched ringing/buzzing that interfered with his thoughts. Must've drifted into the visitors' waiting room of wherever this was, Cedar Hills?—an area of the "treatment center" off-limits to patients. And why, he didn't know. He wasn't naive enough to expect that there might be visitors waiting to see him, for his last "visitor" had been weeks ago and then to his disappointment only just Grandmother Rampike badly aged, attended by her nurse/companion and in a weepy mood to kiss, fondle, hug Skyler who stiffened at the old woman's touch and refused to speak to her. And now scanning the faces in the waiting room and seeing no one for him. And on the lounge TV a familiar face, a warm urgent appealing voice:

". . . prayer, Avis, and humility in the face of God's inscrutable plan for us. No bitterness. No 'dwelling in the past.' My faith sustains me. Knowing that Bliss is with me always, and that her spirit abides with all who love her . . ."

Was this Skyler's Mummy? Was this Betsey Rampike? Being interviewed by another woman, on a TV talk show? Skyler was dumfounded. Skyler's slack little mouth went slacker still. Skyler wiped, rubbed at his eyes that leaked tears shameful to him for Skyler's fellow patients ridiculed him as a crybaby and damn, Skyler was not a crybaby.

In fact, Skyler never cried. As Skyler never spoke. And refused to "look into" adult eyes.

On TV, a bugle voice interrupted: "But Betsey! How does a mother survive such a tragedy? I know—and our TV audience knows—that you have 'given your heart to Jesus'—and yet: how can you 'forgive' such a sick monster as the pedophile who murdered your daughter in her very bed? How can you find it in your heart, when—" The interviewer was a hatchet-faced woman with hungry eyes and shark teeth that glistened in swift savage smiles. Her name was Avis Culpepper and she was the hostess of *Up Close & Personal with Avis Culpepper* which was an afternoon TV talk show associated with the tabloid newspaper *Up Close & Personal* which many on the Cedar Hills staff watched; for TV sets played continuously during the day at the Cedar Woods Children's Neuropsychiatric Treatment Center in Summit, New Jersey where Skyler at age eleven was a patient. (Why had Mummy and Daddy "committed" him? Because something was "malfunctioning" [Daddy's term] in Skyler's brain and "no expense would be spared" [Mummy's promise] in the effort of making right again what seemed to have gone wrong.) And there was Betsey Rampike—"Mummy"—on TV speaking in her warm urgent voice that contrasted with Avis Culpepper's shrill voice for Avis Culpepper was admired by her many fans for her very shrillness, her indignation, her jeering laughter that invited TV audiences to side with her. Skyler was relieved to see that the hatchet-faced woman seemed to like Mummy and spoke to her with sympathy. Beside Avis Culpepper, Betsey Rampike was soft-voiced as one yearning to be liked; with a girlish moon-face only just slightly raddled about the jowls, vividly made up for TV with highlighted eyes and glossy pink lipstick and her hair red-brown and springy as a wig and not limp and streaked with gray as it had been in the confusing and upsetting nightmare weeks following *it*. As Betsey spoke she continued to smile earnestly at Avis Culpepper as if the fierce woman were a figure of authority to be placated. Skyler saw that his mother was very attractive in a lilac dress of some crinkly material, low-cut in front to show the creamy swell of her breasts; around her neck, she wore a small gold cross on a gold chain; her plump beringed hands were clasped in her lap; how powerful the urge in Skyler to rush at the TV set, astonish the visitors in the room by climbing into the picture crying *Mummy! Mummy! Mummy! It's Skyler why don't you see me Mummy!* For Mummy had not visited Skyler in nine weeks though it was true, Mummy did telephone

Skyler at least once a week, and so did Daddy; and always there were promises of visits-to-come. Why was Mummy so busy? What was Mummy's "new life" about which Mummy spoke with such wistful hope? Avis Culpepper whose brassy hair was a glinting helmet like a Valkyrie's was holding aloft a book with a fleshy-pink cover and crimson letters for her TV audience to see—*Bliss: A Mother's Story* by Betsey Rampike*—and urging her viewers to rush out and buy it, or, if there wasn't a bookstore nearby, send a check for $26.95 to Avis Culpepper c/o Eagle News Network, Box 229, Cincinnati, OH: "If this doesn't break your hearts, and make you damn good and mad at left-wing legislators and radical-liberal judges giving overlenient sentences to vicious sex offenders proliferating in our midst, you can ask for your money back from me." As the fierce interviewer continued to ask Betsey questions the screen shifted to show a little-girl ice-skater: a doll-like blond child in a pale pink costume with a gauze skirt and "fairy wings" attached to her narrow shoulders: was this Skyler's sister? Was this Bliss, whom Skyler had not seen except in dreams, for so long? How beautifully the little girl was skating! Skyler had forgotten the "fairy wings" and he'd forgotten the song Bliss had skated to—"Over the Rainbow"—but he remembered the evening of Tots-on-Ice, the evening when it all began, at the drafty Meadowlands arena: Bliss Rampike's first victory, at age four. Now the scene shifted to Bliss at a slightly older age, sweetly smiling into the camera as with startling agility she skated out onto the ice in an upsurge of music—"Sleeping Beauty Waltz"—in a dazzling-white costume with a springy tulle skirt, peekaboo white panties and white eyelet stockings; and then the screen shifted again, and here was Bliss with upswept blond hair Las Vegas–style, little-glamour-girl Bliss Rampike in a hot bronze-orange lamé costume skate-dancing to thumping "Kiss of Fire"; next, little-angel-Bliss again with curly hair in ringlets, strawberry satin-and-sequins skate-dancing to the disco "Do What Feels Right" and now before a cheering crowd being crowned Little Miss Jersey Ice Princess 1996 by mammoth Jeremiah Jericho bursting out of his tux like an upright

---

* Bliss: A Mother's Story *by Betsey Rampike as told to Linda LeFerve (Simon & Schuster, 1998), 208 pp., $26.95. Though I have seen this* New York Times *#1 best seller in bookstores, I have not been able to bring myself to read it.*

whale. When the screen returned to Avis Culpepper and Betsey Rampike, the hatchet-faced interviewer made a show of wiping at glaring-wet eyes as she marveled at the "prodigy-ice-skating champion" who'd been snatched away by "pure hideous evil" at the age of six, yet who had already brought such joy to all who knew her, and would live forever in the memories of all Americans. Betsey was very touched by Avis Culpepper's words, carefully dabbing at her eyes, as, in conclusion, Avis Culpepper erupted in a fusillade of what sounded like prepared words on the subject of the "epidemic of sex offenders" sweeping the United States in the wake of "Godless atheism" unleashed by the radical-left-wing Democrats "Slick Willy" and his Women's Libber wife Hillary: "But hopefully as our Eagle News polls consistently show, this sickening state of affairs will end with our next Presidential election in November 2000. Betsey Rampike, thank you for joining us this afternoon on *Up Close & Personal* and speaking to us from the heart. What is your final word you wish to leave our viewers with, Betsey?" and Betsey blinked as if with startled pleasure, staring into the camera, seeking out Skyler's gaze: "Only just 'have faith in God.' As one who has 'walked through the Valley of the Shadow of Death' I can tell you *do not despair ever* for God loves us all, and remember to pray for Bliss, and Bliss will pray for you."

Quick cut to a loud advertisement featuring a cheery little brat spooning Nutty Nugget Krispies into his mouth.

During the interview, everyone in the waiting room had watched. And now Skyler at the rear of the room was stunned to hear a woman laugh meanly, "Can you believe that? That terrible Rampike woman? She murdered her poor little daughter herself, everyone knows it!" and a companion said, mildly bemused, "*Is* it 'known'? I always thought some 'sex maniac' killed Bliss Rampike."

At once everyone in the waiting room began speaking. These were predominantly women but there were several strongly opinionated men as well. One of them said angrily: "For shame! That poor woman *lost her daughter*." The first woman who'd spoken now said, jeering: "The Rampikes got away with murder because they're rich and connected, I have friends in Fair Hills and it's an open secret." As angry voices rang about him Skyler stood paralyzed hearing his name—*Ram-pike!—Ram-pike!*—harshly uttered as nails fired from a nail gun, and there came someone behind him to tug gently at his arm, a young black-girl attendant named Serena who was kind to Skyler whispering: "Skyler! You're not supposed to be out here! Come with me, it's time for your meds."

THREE DAYS LATER THERE WAS A "SUSPICIOUS FIRE" IN A BASEMENT STOR- age room at Cedar Woods that did considerable damage before it was extinguished. "Probable arson" was the cause but no arsonist was identified. Yet somehow it happened, within forty-eight hours of the fire Skyler was discharged from the treatment facility, whether his parents had wanted to remove him at that time, or Cedar Hills authorities had expelled him, Skyler was never to know, for no explanation was given to him; a black Lincoln Town Car arrived with a private nurse to take him away, scarcely an hour's drive to the Robert Wood Johnson Children's Neuropsychiatric Treatment Center in New Brunswick where Skyler's newly diagnosed IESD (Incipient Epilepsy Spectrum Disorder) would receive "state-of-the-art" treatment.

WANT YOU TO BE WELL AGAIN SKYLER YOU KNOW THAT DON'T YOU
Your Daddy and Mummy, nothing matters to us except you
The way you used to be Skyler! the power lies within you, and we will succeed

FAST-FORWARD TO A LATER TV-MUMMY SIGHTING WHEN SKYLER WAS THIR- teen and in what was called eighth grade at Hodge Hill School in Hodge Hill, Pennsylvania: "Nestled in the hills of Bucks County, boasting a thirty-acre wooded campus near the scenic Delaware River, Hodge Hill School (founded 1951) is a private residential school with an enrollment of 220 students. Hodge Hill has a tradition of academic excellence combined with 'special needs' instruction. On its staff are eminently qualified teachers, psychologists, and therapists in addition to a full-time resident physician. A full-service infirmary is maintained. The school is within twelve minutes of the Doylestown Medical Center and is approved by the American Association of Child Psychiatrists, Psychologists, and

Physiotherapists. Hodge Hill School provides a safe, secure, and stimulating environment for children aged 10–18 who have been diagnosed with social, emotional, psychological, and academic disabilities. Non-refundable full-year tuition required in advance."

By this time, in the fall of 2000, Skyler had outgrown "mute." Skyler was into "speech as aggression." Skyler's fawn-colored soft-kiddie-hair that had fallen out in clumps after his sister's death had grown back in coarse and weirdly zinc-colored. In his armpits and at his groin, were patches of kinky-zinc hair, that both repelled Skyler, and fascinated him.

Nor was Skyler a runt any longer. Though skinny, and scrawny, and couldn't run without limping, he'd grown to a height of five-feet-six and was one of the taller boys in eighth grade as he was, by default, one of the brainiest.

In a dormitory lounge, there was TV-Mummy.

An empty lounge, and the TV turned up high. Through Hodge Hill there were TV sets and during the day the TV sets were usually on and if you approached a room you couldn't tell if TV voices or "real" voices were chattering away inside.

". . . a pilgrimage into Hell, and back. Coming to terms with grief that seizes you like a demon's hand at your throat. But now I feel blessed, Zelda, at last able to speak to others in their hour of terrible need . . ."

Skyler stared. Skyler's cynical little jaw drooped. For here was TV-Mummy, less than five feet away.

Skyler's mother! Betsey Rampike! He'd had no warning that Betsey was going to be on TV that day—the last time he'd heard from Betsey, it hadn't been Betsey but Betsey's new assistant who'd called to tell him, in a voice of sincere regret, that his mother wouldn't be able to make the trip to Hodge Hill for Parents' Weekend after all.

Nor had Bix, unavoidably on his way to Seoul, South Korea, on business, been able to attend Hodge Hill Parents' Weekend.

But here, so suddenly, was Betsey Rampike being interviewed by zestful big-bosomed Zelda Zachiarias who hosted a lively women's-issue TV talk show, *WomenSpeakOut*, every weekday afternoon on CBS, much mocked and jeered-at by Hodge Hill adolescents. Skyler tasted panic at the sight of her: looking younger and more "radiant" than he remembered, with conspicuously lightened hair to her shoulders, and warm, rosy/"dewy" skin that looked soft as uncooked bread dough, that would retain the impress of your finger if you poked it. Betsey was wearing a fuchsia pants suit with a plunging V-neck that showed the powdered cleavage of her large breasts, and many rings, necklaces, and clattering bracelets which, it was being revealed by an admiring Zelda Zachiarias, Betsey had designed herself as a way of "keeping grief at bay" after the tragic loss of her daughter three years and eight months before. Smiling bravely, winning the hearts of Zelda's TV studio audience by wiping her eyes and faltering as she spoke, Betsey was answering the interviewer's probing questions about her six-year-old daughter's death, and about her family's effort to keep going, and continue with their lives; Skyler winced to hear his sister's name evoked so frequently, and by Zelda Zachiarias as well, who spoke with such familiarity, you'd have thought she had known the child.

At Hodge Hill, Skyler uneasily assumed that everyone knew who he was, or had been.

There were other students at the school with "known" names, in several cases "famous"/"infamous" names. It wasn't cool to allude to such distinctions, still less to bluntly ask the bearer *Are you related to*—? or *How does it feel*—? Worse yet, to request an autograph.

Skyler hey: c'n you just write your name on this paper? It's for my mom not me.

"—a bold, brave, courageous and truly inspirational memoir, Betsey. I've been giving copies to all my friends and relatives and now I'm going to start giving them these nifty Heaven Scent designs, I love the 'emerald' crosses, and the bracelets, so kind of funny, girlish and clattery." Betsey, deeply moved, held out her shapely arms to display her clattery bracelets which were all colors of the rainbow, and Zelda Zachiarias, with the maternal/mammalian generosity of the very best friend you'd never had held aloft Betsey's new book with a glossy rainbow cover and gold embossed lettering: *"Pray for Mummy": A Mother's Pilgrimage from Grief to Joy* by Betsey Rampike.＊

＊ "Pray for Mummy": A Mother's Pilgrimage from Grief to Joy *by Betsey Rampike as told to Brooke Swann (Basic Books, 2000), 192 pp., $21.95. Rather would I douse myself with kerosene and light a match than read this one.*

Skyler stared disbelieving. His face smarted with shame. If anyone entered the lounge, how mortified he would be! Yet he didn't switch off the TV, and he didn't run from the room.

"Mummy. *Oh.*"

The irony was: Skyler no longer called his mother by that silly name, if he could stop himself in time.

As Skyler never called his father "Daddy" any longer. Only, with a smirk (unseen by Bix: these were mostly phone conversations), "Dad."

Especially, Skyler hated "Mummy"—born of such weakness, childish longing. A shudder of revulsion passed over him, hairs stirred at the nape of his neck.

He was no God-damned child now: he was thirteen.

Not Mummy's *little man* but his own damn self.

"—the first year is the hardest of course—truly it is 'the Valley of the Shadow of Death'—the strain of mourning is exhausting as a physical illness. And the terrible things that were said in the media about my husband and me—and even our nine-year-old son. When it was known—worldwide, it was known—that my poor Bliss was abducted and murdered by a convicted sex offender who'd been stalking her for years without our knowing—the man confessed, and killed himself. And yet, as you know, Zelda, in the media, it's the most sensational 'twist' that sells." Betsey paused, dabbing at her eyes with a tissue. Zelda, who was leafing through Betsey's book, read a passage aloud about "closure" and asked Betsey to comment and Betsey said, recovering her composure, "I believe it was Freud, Zelda—Sigmund Freud the controversial pioneer of the Unconscious—who stated that we are 'melancholy' in mourning because we have taken the loved one into us and we have 'become' the lost loved one—" as Betsey hesitated, having become confused, Zelda Zachiarias winked at the audience to signal *She's losing me with these deep thoughts!* which provoked titters of good-natured laughter, and so Betsey apologized for becoming upset: "Zelda, I have been in therapy. And this happens in therapy—you think too much! You think too much about how life has wounded you, and that can be 'narcistic'—'narcissitic'—for you have swallowed up the lost loved one, and you must surrender the loved one to a Higher Power, and move on. 'Closure' is the goal. My memoir ends with

'Closure: Heaven Scent.' For my line of beauty products and services is truly 'heaven-sent'—it has saved my life. But such strain can spell the death of a marriage . . ." Here Betsey paused, momentarily stricken; Zelda Zachiarias took her hand, gently urging: "Will you share with our audience, Betsey, as you shared with me before the show, the newest development in your 'marital life' of fifteen years?" At first Betsey seemed incapable of speech then rallied, with a quivering little smile: "Yes. I will. My h-husband and I are filing for a divorce."

Divorce! Skyler listened, stunned.

Comforting Betsey, Zelda could not resist inquiring, as the audience listened eagerly, whose decision this was; and Betsey, in a moment of tender rapport, as a woman will impulsively share her innermost secrets with another woman with whom she has bonded, "Ohhh Zelda! I am so—heartbroken. I am just devastated. You know how fervently I believe that marriage is forever—'sickness unto death'—and so this has been a terrible blow to me. Since Bliss was taken from us, my husband has been what is called 'compulsive' in his pursuit of—other women. Younger women. A man's virility is so determined by fantasy, Zelda, the slightest blow to the male ego, he will suffer"—embarrassed, Betsey lowered her voice, though the microphone picked up every syllable—"impotence; and will blame the wife every time."

At this dramatic juncture, the studio audience, comprised solely of women, burst into applause, and ribald laughter. Zelda Zachiarias clapped as well, leaned over to Betsey Rampike to kiss Betsey's flushed cheek, saying that it was time for a brief break: "Please stay with us and we will continue this fantastic conversation with Betsey Rampike author of the new instant best seller 'Pray for Mummy': A Mother's Pilgrimage from Grief to Joy."

There followed then a succession of advertisements during which time Skyler sat paralyzed a few inches in front of the TV screen, that exuded an ominous heat. He'd begun scratching at his face and scalp, his nails drawing blood. How his skin itched! How he'd like to have clawed his skin off! In his ears was a roaring as of a sanitation truck ingesting trash into its belly.

Ending? The m-marriage? Mummy and Daddy? And no one had told Skyler? The panicked thought came to him *Neither will want custody of me.*

Skyler knew: he should switch off the TV and quickly retreat to his room before Betsey Rampike returned, or someone stepped into the lounge. For where, in Hodge Hill School, as in any of the private boarding schools to which Skyler was/would be sent, is there more safety, more sanity, than in one's room? To his room on the third floor of the residence Skyler frequently retreated, during even mealtimes, though he was one of the taller boys in eighth grade, and his teachers warily liked him, for amid so many misfits, losers, "mentally disabled," Skyler Rampike could not fail to shine; his grades were mostly A's, and he'd learned the knack of not-swallowing the most powerful of his meds; though he couldn't lock his door from within, he could barricade the doorway with furniture. Yet: Skyler remained in the lounge. Like a rodent mesmerized by a cobra swaying before him, Skyler remained in front of the television set until the program resumed, and Zelda Zachiarias re-introduced Betsey Rampike; this time, Zelda wished to evoke for viewers her guest's "tragic loss," and so there came footage of the skating prodigy Bliss Rampike onto the screen, familiar footage of Skyler's sister skating again on the ice, here was Bliss's famed debut to "Over the Rainbow" at the Tots-on-Ice competition; here again, Bliss in the dazzling-white ballerina costume; and, with glamorous upswept hair, in Las Vegas-sexy bronze-orange costume skate-dancing to gallumping "Kiss of Fire" for *it has all happened already, many times and there is no way out* for Skyler had seen this footage many times, since Bliss's death it was played, played and replayed on TV, by chance you might discover it at any time, day, night, on any TV channel, by sinister magic it had happened, and who knows how such things happen, that Skyler's little sister had become since her death the most famous six-year-old in American history and what did that mean, that this six-year-old was dead? had been killed? yet Skyler could not bring himself to switch off the TV even now, nor could Skyler stagger from the room for to stagger from the room would be to leave Bliss, and abandon her; another time, Skyler would abandon her; he would abandon her to Mummy; he would not save her; though she called to him *Skyler?*   *help*   *help me Skyler* yet he would abandon her, it was the irrevocable fact of his life.

"—Zelda, it has been so hard. It has been so very hard. Our son is a 'troubled' child. He has been in therapy for years for both neurological 'deficits' and 'borderline personality' issues. He receives the very best professional care but—believe me!—it has not been easy. Both my husband—formerly an all-American halfback, now a high-ranked executive—and my son—suffer from 'deflected aggression.' In Skyler's case, it is believed that the horrible loathsome deviate who stalked and murdered my Bliss preyed upon him, too—in some way he will not divulge, for such trauma is locked inside the hippocampus—the 'seat of memory'—in a state of denial. There are 'passive-aggressive' issues as well. A 'communication abyss' between us. Many in your audience, Zelda, may have had the identical experience—a trauma in the family, and the 'masculine dynamic' begins to disintegrate, even as the 'feminine dynamic' grows stronger of necessity. In this case, it was our troubled son Skyler who provided the 'tipping point.' Our marriage of fifteen years that might have withstood the trauma of our loss of Bliss was finally shattered by the post-traumatic-stress 'Oedipal masochism' of our son—"

Reluctantly, mournfully, yet bravely Betsey Rampike spoke. It is not easy to bare your soul on national TV. Still more the souls of others. Tenderly the camera dwelled upon Betsey's rosy flushed face. A flame erupted suddenly in Skyler's brain. Might've been an aneuryism in the hippocampus except the poor kid didn't pitch over dead but began to pant asthmatically and then to shout unintelligibly. Began to strike, punch, kick at the TV set stinging his hands. Bruising his weak hands. Shouted louder like a rising siren and someone came running into the room, one of the headmaster's burly assistants grabbing at Skyler, cursing: "Damn you, Ranpick! Down on the floor."

But Skyler like a panicked squirrel managed to elude the burly man for TV-Mummy was still speaking, TV-Mummy would never cease speaking, though Skyler was outweighed by fifty pounds he managed to throw off the attendant's grip and another time Skyler rushed the TV set now knocking it onto the floor and kicking savagely at it and at last the screen shattered and bits of TV-Mummy's face flew in sharp shards and slivers about the room including Skyler's hair, Skyler's eyelashes, Skyler's nostrils and inside Skyler's collar. A uniformed security guard now rushed into the room, as burly as the headmaster's assistant, grabbed the mutinous boy's head and near-decapitated him flinging him onto the floor, in the struggle overturning chairs, a massive floor lamp, stacks of Hodge Hill School yearbooks, still Skyler managed to scramble free shrieking like a deranged bat until overcome by sheer brute force, a combined weight of beyond a thousand pounds mashing his face against the grimy carpet and breaking and bloodying his nose, cracking several teeth at the gum line, knocking the wind out of him as you'd wallop a dust-laden carpet flung over a clothesline with a "rug-beater," and so the lurid tale would be told for years afterward how three husky attendants and two security guards with billy clubs had been required to subdue hundred-pound Skyler Rampike who'd not only fought them with fists, knees, and feet but with his bared teeth, "frothing and foaming" like a rabid creature forced finally into an inflatable "restraining jacket" and carried outside on a stretcher to be borne, via ambulance, with a shrieking siren, to the Doylestown Medical Center to be sedated and next morning transported to Allentown General Hospital for psychiatric evaluation.*

The Rampike kid? The one who might've killed his little sister? Went ballistic. Finito!

---

*See "Brother of Slain Skate Champ Bliss Rampike Committed to PA Mental Hospital," Celebrity Watch Weekly, October 4, 2000. A lurid cover story containing close-up photos of Skyler strapped to a stretcher, his face so contorted with rage it is unrecognizable.

MISADVENTURES IN "MENTAL HEALTH"

IN THE INTERESTS OF FULL AND SHAMELESS DISCLOSURE, FOR THE BENEFIT of readers with a morbid interest in psychotherapy, psychiatry, psychiatric psychopharmacology, ctc., here is a partial list of the shrinks to which Skyler Rampike was sent in the years following his sister's murder: Splint, Murdstone, Qualls, Schiskein, Roll. And here is a partial list of the diagnoses affixed to Skyler Rampike by these individuals: hyperactive anxiety disorder/narcissistic anality disorder/obsessive-compulsive disorder/dyslexia (chronic, progressive)/ADD + IEP/CAAD/amnesia/hyperamnesia/anorexia/agnosia/anosagnosia/aphasia/analgesia/CAAD + catatonia (intermittent)/ASD/PDD/bi-polar + "borderline personality"/echolalia/apotropaism/ASD + infantile aggression disorder/PMD + "phantom pain" disorder/hebrephrenia*/algolagnia/paranoia + SSD (schizoid spectrum disorder)/hysteria/anaclisia/hyperdependency + regressive disorder/infantile aggression disorder/Asperger's disorder—and more!

For each of these, a medical prescription of which some have already been listed in this document teeming with "sharply observed" details/facts like maggots in a decomposing corpse.

There was Dr. Splint. Through a sepia haze of pain, Dr. Splint a pair of oversized eyeglasses jauntily perched upon a beaky nose. "Skyler? Speak to me. You can speak to me. You are not mute, Skyler. There is nothing medically wrong with your vocal cords or your throat, Skyler. You know this. It is an 'hysterical' muteness, Skyler. It is not 'real.' You do not speak

---

* *Surprised? Don't blame you. This document hasn't exactly been a laff-riot nor anything like what hebephrenia (literal meaning: "ensnaring thicket of laughter") might suggest.*

to your mother or to your father, Skyler, and they are very worried about you but you may speak to me, Skyler: will you speak?"

Six sessions with Dr. Splint. (Female, big-boned. Big teeth clenched in smiles. Or was that Dr. Roll, to come?) Given Play Clay to "shape your thoughts" in the stubborn absence of speech and these emerged as snakes, mostly.

Except Doll-baby. At last emerged Doll-baby. After eight snakes of varying lengths and girths, ambition, and authenticity. Doll-baby was the size of a rat and fashioned of flesh-colored Play Clay, allowed to dry and then—so suddenly, Dr. Splint's big plastic glasses nearly tumbled from her face—*bang-bang-bang* against the table. Doll-baby's head *bang-bang-bang* against the table. And Dr. Splint lost her professional poise visibly flinching, drawing back behind her desk as if frightened of her raging ten-year-old patient, managing then to compose herself saying, "Skyler, you did not hurt your sister. You were not the one to hurt your sister," and Skyler laughed wildly continuing to shatter what remained of Doll-baby, pellet-sized pieces scattered across the table and the floor and onto the top of Dr. Splint's desk. For the first time speaking to the therapist, jeering: "I did! I killed her! I broke her head! I wanted to! I tied her arms, too! That was me."

This sixth and final session with Dr. Splint.

"THAT WOMAN! WITH A DEGREE FROM JUST RUTGERS. I SHOULD HAVE KNOWN better, a 'child trauma specialist' who is herself childless. And so overpriced, you'd think she was a *man*."

THOUGHTS CAME SLOW NOW TO SKYLER. DR. MURDSTONE REGARDED SKYLER at a distance. To Dr. Murdstone Skyler had haltingly/falteringly/stammeringly/dim-brainedly confessed that his sister came up behind him sometimes and teased him and asked him to help her, laughing at him because he couldn't see her, he could only hear her, but when he listened closely he could not hear her. Thoughts came slow to Skyler now in the sepia-drug-haze like those little stones you had to strain and squeeze and grunt and whimper in pain to expel from your hind-quarters ("hinder" was Mummy's word which was a nicer word than Daddy's word which was "asshole") and the effort hurt so! and sometimes afterward there was blood to be flushed down the toilet with the hard little nasty stones.

Dr. Murdstone was not a smiler like Dr. Splint. Dr. Murdstone sneered at Skyler for Dr. Murdstone possessed X-ray vision to see into the conniving little brat's brain: "Skyler, you know that your little sister is not 'there.' You are not being 'haunted.' You know that 'she' is but an auditory hallucination, this has been explained to you many times."

Had it? Skyler was made ashamed, Skyler could not remember.

In the mirror a little baldie boy with a bumpy scalp, enormous shadowed eyes, sallow and splotched skin. Could not keep from picking at his skin unless his medication was so increased, his hands were too heavy to lift to his face.

"Skyler!"—was this Dr. Qualls? Somehow, Skyler was in Dr. Qualls's office where someone must have brought him. Damp-sand-colored mustache, derisive flash of eyeglasses. Dr. Qualls advised: "Skyler, you are too old for such childish confabulations. You are ten years old and by that age fantasizing in children has about run its course and it has certainly exhausted the patience of adults in your vicinity."

And there was blunt pragmatic Dr. Schiskein (fattish male, psychiatric psychopharmacologist) who brushed aside Skyler's weepy/whiny tales of being haunted by his little dead sister and handily prescribed the new Wonder Drug Zilich (F.D.A.-approved "revolutionary" psychotropic drug for children afflicted with IED + PSSD [Paranoid Schizoid Spectrum Disorder]) and Skyler learned, as the reader would learn, that, medicated with three hundred milligrams of Zilich twice daily you will no longer hear phantom voices in your head *Skyler!* *there is something bad* *in my bed* you will not hear your own thoughts in your head for all that you can hear is the beat beat beat of pulses deep inside the brain stem.

AT THE VERHANGEN TREATMENT CENTER FOR DOOMED CHILDREN AND ADO-lescents in Bleek Springs, New York (fifty miles north of Manhattan, "breathtaking views of the Hudson") there was Hedda Roll, M.D., Ph.D.,

C.R.M.T. (Certified Recovered Memory Therapist) briskly urging Skyler to reveal to her the *secret hurt* he'd been made to endure through his pro-longed and protracted, indeed interminable childhood, session following session in that confused backwater of time following Skyler Rampike's luridly publicized departure from Hodge Hill School for it was an inter-lude when Skyler's mother (whom Skyler *would not* call Mummy!) was "away, visiting" in Palm Beach, Florida, with her dear friend wealthy old Mrs. Poindexter who owned an oceanfront Spanish villa there, and Sky-ler's father (whom Skyler *would not* call Daddy!) was "unavoidably unavail-able, feel like hell letting you down, son" though so far as Skyler could determine, Bix Rampike was still a "top exec" at Univers, Inc. though liv-ing much of the time in Manhattan, in the condominium on Central Park South which Skyler had yet to visit, as Skyler had yet to be taken to a Knicks game at Madison Square Garden. It was unclear to Skyler from whose "shaky, precarious, paranoid-schizoid" self the starker dimensions of Reality had to be kept at a calculated distance, whether his parents were "divorced" by this time or only just "separated" or "trying damned hard to work things out" for even before TV-Mummy on *WomenSpeakOut* Skyler had more or less given up trying to call his elusive parents for the numbers he'd been given for Betsey were never answered or "no longer in service" and there was no Rampike home any longer, for the sprawling old white clapboard eighteenth-century Colonial at 93 Ravens Crest Drive had been emptied of the Rampikes and, so far as Skyler knew, strangers lived there and were happy. When once he'd been able to get through to Bix Rampike at Univers, Inc., his father had been frank in telling him he loved Skyler "like hell" but was "sickened and disgusted" by the hideous cover story in *Celebrity Watch Weekly* that had, unconscionably, been picked up by numer-ous other publications including the *New York Post*, *The Star Spy*, and, in three brief paragraphs on an interior page of the Metro section the *New York Times*. Skyler's sessions with Dr. Roll were draining and exhausting, for Skyler seemed to be afflicted again with his old (hysterical, "reaction-formation") muteness in the presence of this woman looming before him quivering and shape-changing as a giant squid urging him to reveal to her the *secret hurt* he'd almost certainly been made to endure as a very young child, possibly even an infant, for sexual abuse of children can start at very young ages, when Skyler had been too young to resist and too young to remember the trauma inflicted upon him by his abuser or abusers he could not protect himself against who were—*who? Tell me Skyler who has abused you, who has molested you, who has interfered with your psychic growth stunting you as a result, what are you hiding from, Skyler? Why won't you look at me, and tell me: WHO ARE YOU PROTECTING?* On the table before the guiltily squirming fourteen-year-old there materialized an unclothed doll-baby of about the size of an adult Norwegian rat and at this object Skyler stared dry-mouthed and stricken with embarrassment for Skyler wasn't a child any longer! Skyler wasn't to be baited with such child-shrink props! Skyler was an adolescent however "under-developed" physically/socially/emotion-ally; yet here was a naked doll-baby, a boy-doll-baby, which is a very different matter from a girl-doll-baby; and its anatomical features were of unusual, indeed ominous frankness and clarity unlike any doll Skyler had ever had the misfortune to see, here was a boy-doll with a "penis" the size of a partially engorged slug, and here were accompanying "testicles" the size of Concord grapes, and, yet more alarming, here were realistic hind-quarters of a kind you would never see in an actual doll; in contrast, the boy-doll's face was bland and blank and Caucasian; its mouth was open-able for its small jaws had hinges, and there was a rosy-pink cavity inside, and even a discernible tongue; how terrifying this seemed to Skyler, who stared and stared; how terrifying (Skyler was remembering now: an am-nesia fog-patch lifted suddenly and there was revealed how at one or an-other of the "treatment centers" to which he'd been sentenced, that is, sent, by his "deeply concerned" parents he'd had to be "force-fed" by way of a tube thrust down his protesting mouth bruising his lips, tongue, mouth-interior, throat) and the boy-doll's head mockily resembled Sky-ler's baldie-head of several years before when the trauma of his sister's death caused his hair to fall out in handfuls so that, accosted by other kids his age, blunt staring little boys, he was asked *You got cancer? Taking chemo?* Worse yet, beside the hapless boy-doll there now materialized two adult dolls, several times larger than the boy-doll, with bland blank Caucasian features and similarly hinged mouths, naked adult dolls with hideous adult genitalia, Skyler shielded his eyes not wishing to see, a glimpse of sizable female breasts complete with berry-sized nipples, a glimpse of a male semi-erect rosy-pink penis of a size, relative to the doll's size, which Skyler's former boy-classmates would have called awesome. These doll-adults Skyler shut his quivering eyes against which provoked Dr. Roll to nudge them suggestively closer to the boy-doll and to Skyler saying in a gentle caressing voice *Skyler? Don't be shy! Take your time Skyler using these dolls to demonstrate what was done to your body, you have repressed for years. Skyler? Will you look at me, dear? Why do you protect your abusers? You are safe with me now.* Skyler shuddered. Skyler shivered. How badly Skyler wanted to please Dr. Roll, for always you want to please the adult in authority, yet Skyler could not bring himself to speak as Dr. Roll repeated her command leaning closer to him, quivering and shape-changing as a giant squid and Skyler dreaded the brush of her tentacles against his bare skin, Skyler dreaded the shock of being stung. In misery pressing both hands against his eyes, sending sparks into the interior of his head, underside of Skyler's battered head, numbly his lips moved in a mumble telling Dr. Roll that he guessed he could not remember being hurt by anyone when he was little. Could not remember being hurt at all. Now in a sharp voice Dr. Roll said *Skyler why are you protecting them, why are you refusing to cooperate, you will not begin to heal unless you cooperate with your therapist, you will remain stunted through your life, look at me, Skyler! and look at these dolls* for Dr. Roll knew that her guilty-squirming young patient was lying to her, of course Dr. Roll knew from years of recovered-memory experience that this was a grievously wounded/abused/sick child before her, yet stubbornly Skyler shook his head *no*, stubbornly Skyler would not touch the naked dolls nor would Skyler meet the glare of Dr. Roll's X-ray eyes for Skyler could not say *yes it was my father, yes it was my mother.* Could not say *They killed me. They killed my sister, and they killed me.* He could not. He could not. He could not.

"HSR"

FOR THE RECORD IT SHOULD BE NOTED THAT, AFTER DR. ROLL DISMISSED, IN disgust, Skyler Rampike as a patient, curtly informing his parents that their son was "encrusted in so extreme a state of denial, equivalent to metastasized cancer in all of his bones," she could not "in all conscience" continue to treat him, the vengeful woman affixed to his medical record, to follow the accursed kid through the remainder of his life, a new, grim Mystery Diagnosis: "HSR."*

Dr. Roll's bill, for less than six sessions, rendered through the venerable Verhangen Treatment Center, came to an astonishing $46,399.†

---

* "HSR"? Wonder what this disorder is? Skyler did, too.

† Of which canny Bix Rampike, by this time chief of (domestic) research development at Univers, Inc. did not pay a penny. Instead, Skyler's litigious father sued both Hedda Roll and the Verhangen Treatment Center for Doomed Children on grounds of "extreme malpractice" and "character defamation," for $13 million plus legal fees. (The lawsuit was eventually settled out of court for how much, Skyler was never to know.)

First Love, Farewell!*

A Teen Memory of a Lost Love

* *This inspired title I'd believed was original with me but now I'm vaguely recalling a book with this title, a paperback with a lush moist pink cover like a palpitating female organ, must've been one of my mother's romance novels she'd tried to hide from my father who was likely to tease/sneer in smug polymath superiority: "Jesus, Betsey! How can you read such crap?"*

I.

. . . love you, I guess.
Me, too.

• • •

Think I can't do it?

Think that I, Skyler Rampike, steeped in irony, *ressentiment*,
and chronic *sand fraud* like a squid steeped in ink, can't put
aside postmodernist strategies of "storytelling" for the naive,
raw, throbbing emotions of mere storytelling? Smugly you'd
believed that I would not be capable of presenting the death of
my sister nor the confused aftermath of that death but, though
severely constrained by my ignorance of all that happened, I
did; and so, I think that I can present the "bittersweet"—
"poignant"—"fated" story of Skyler's first love, that came to
such an abrupt and melancholy end.

For what is more challenging to the jaded postmodernist
sensibility than love? More challenging still, love between two
painfully inexperienced adolescents in a prep-school setting?

Read on.

"THERE SHE IS. 'HEIDI HARKNESS.' "

On the stone steps of Babbitt Hall the boys stood. Their
voices were low and sniggering and meant to be overheard by
the tall lanky-limbed girl in crumpled-looking clothes who
hurried past them, eyes averted. For "Heidi Harkness" was the
designated name of a new transfer student at the Academy at
Basking Ridge, New Jersey, who was known to be the daughter
of a recent celebrity murderer, a former major league baseball
player who had been acquitted the previous spring after a
lengthy, luridly publicized trial of having murdered his
estranged wife, the wife's alleged lover, and the wife's beloved

424

poodles Yin and Yang; "Harkness" was not a name that much resembled the original, but "Heidi" was a name not unlike the daughter's actual name.

Except, for my purposes in this document, I have made both "Heidi" and "Harkness" wholly fictitious names. As I have changed crucial facts and circumstances relating to Heidi's notorious father and surname.

Skyler   you won't write about me will you   please?

Skyler   I'm not sure if I can promise   I won't write about you

Exiting dour Babbitt Hall after ninety dour minutes of chemistry lab, there came Skyler Rampike now grown to a scrawny height of five-feet-ten, sulky-faced slouch-shouldered sixteen-year-old with "weird kinky-metal" hair lifting from his forehead like a mad rooster's comb, an adolescent Skyler the reader would be startled to behold: not a runt any longer, nor was Skyler's soul a runt-soul, for Skyler had learned at last the advantages of being a professionally afflicted kid of affluent background; amid the walking wounded of the Academy at Basking Ridge, Skyler held his own with some measure of defiance and dignity; Skyler's very limp, that used to mortify him, he'd begun to wield in some circumstances like a club, at will: walking heavily, thudding on creaky floors and stairs, lurching and plunging and forcing others to make way for him. And now lurching out of Babbitt Hall into the humid late-September afternoon, Skyler passed provocatively close behind two senior boys, "Beav" and "Butt" we can call this pair for their resemblance to two TV-cartoon cretins whose fame/infamy had peaked and waned within Skyler's adolescent memory; Skyler heard the sniggering voices and saw the girl being taunted turn away, and walk away; Skyler felt a rush of pure hatred, caught the taller boy Beav with the edge of his backpack as if accidentally and Beav whirled upon him—"Watch out, you"—and both Beav and Butt swung at Skyler, punched and shoved, kicked Skyler halfway down the stone steps causing him to lose his balance and fall hard on his knee (God damn, Skyler's right knee), Skyler tried not to wince with pain as the boys chortled in triumph above him: "How's it goin', 'Sly'? 'Ram-pole'—'Ram-pole'—" Chanting Skyler's synthetic name as Skyler adjusted his backpack and limped away.

And where was Heidi Harkness, Skyler had hoped might witness his bold assault upon Beav and Butt for her sake? Nowhere in sight.

AS CHASTENED/GLOWERING SKYLER LIMPS ACROSS THE "GREEN"—AN expanse of mangled and mutilated and mostly browning grass above which massive oaks loom, bordering Babbitt Hall, Skudd Chapel, McLeer Hall and The Monument—I should freeze the action, such as it is, to explain "Sly Rampole."

As "Heidi Harkness" is a fictitious name invented (by me) as a cover for a "real" fictitious name, and that fictitious name a cover for a "real" name of leprous celebrity, so too Skyler's name at the Academy at Basking Ridge, New Jersey, in fall 2003 when Skyler was enrolled as a new student in tenth grade, was fictitious: "Sylvester Rampole."

After the debacle at Hodge Hill School, and Skyler's expulsion, the elder Rampikes came to the conclusion that some attempt must be made to shield their troubled son from the "unjust, cruel, vindictive and ignorant" notoriety that accrued to the Rampike name: "At least while Skyler is still in school, and in such a fragile mental state." (Mummy's words! And Daddy concurred.) For since Bliss's death, no matter that her murderer, a convicted pedophile, had not only confessed but had killed himself as an expression of guilt and remorse, yet the insatiable news media, a "howling pack" of hyenas, jackals, and vultures, continued to pursue the Rampikes; and had no more shame than to try to approach poor Skyler, and to inveigle anyone associated with him (teachers, classmates, therapists)* into being interviewed about him. The Academy at Basking Ridge, the Rampikes were

---

* *For instance, Dr. Roll. In violation of professional ethics, to spite her uncooperative young patient, and for who knows how many thousands of dollars, this therapist at the Verhangen Treatment Center almost certainly had to be the "anonymous psychiatric source" for a lurid feature in* Up Close & Personal *titled "Repressed Memory Recovered: Did Skyler Rampike Confess to Killing His Sister Bliss?" (No! Never read it.) (Bix Rampike filed a $10 million lawsuit charging defamation of his [minor] son's name; a few months ago, the suit was settled out of court, for how much, how would I know?)*

assured by Headmaster Horace Shovell, had acquired a "national reputation nonparallel" for respecting the privacy of its "very select, very special" students: except by invitation, no members of the "press core" were allowed on campus, and all faculty and staff signed contracts forbidding them to give interviews and/or write about any Basking Ridge student, at any time. ("'At any time'? What about a statue of limitations?" Bix Rampike asked doubtfully, but Headmaster Shovell assured him, "We haven't yet been challenged, Mr. Rampike. But if we are, our legal counsel will assure that we will prevail.")

Located on forty wooded acres in the idyllic rolling hills north of the Village of Basking Ridge, New Jersey, the Academy at Basking Ridge was known for its high academic standards as well as for the high quality of its counseling and psychology staff; unlike most private schools providing educations for "special needs students"—the "mentally, emotionally, and psychologically challenged"—Basking Ridge also provided advanced placement courses in such subjects as Mandarin Chinese, Swahili, and Korean; there were "university-level" introductory courses in economics, investment finance, the sociology of property development, "bio-ethics and bio-engineering"; for minimal extra fees, the school provided intensive workshops to prepare students for SAT exams, as for "Résumé Building: Craft & Art" and "The Art of the College Interview." The Rampikes were assured that their son, despite his history of "difficult adjustments," would find a "warmly welcoming home" at Basking Ridge; except for Headmaster Shovell and his immediate staff, no one at the school would know his identity. "The school was originally founded in 1891 as a Presbyterian institution for the 'wayward sons' of distinguished New Jerseyans," Headmaster Shovell said, with an ingratiating chuckle, "and in recent decades, the school has not lost sight of its original mission, to provide a 'safe haven' for the sons, and now the daughters, of persons whose names are 'known' in a way to cause, in some quarters, distress. Please know that at the present time there are a half-dozen young people enrolled in the school incognito, and happily so." Headmaster Shovell paused, as if to provide the Rampikes with an opportunity to inquire, in all innocent curiosity, who these young people were: the children of disgraced politicians, financiers, *artistes* or showbiz folks?—but neither Bix nor Betsey rose to the bait, sensing how their query would be met by a prim shake of the headmaster's head. Shovell continued, "Skyler should be no exception, Mr. and Mrs. Rampike, provided he doesn't speak carelessly of himself, for sometimes children in such situations reveal themselves, who knows why? 'Adolescence is a foreign country, they do things differently there.' This sage remark of our founder, Reverend Elias Dingle, is as apt today as it was more than a century ago. And what is the name you have chosen for your son here at Basking Ridge, Mr. and Mrs. Rampike?"

Numerous names had been suggested by Skyler's parents, but Skyler had rejected them all. Confronted with the loss of "Skyler Rampike"—a name Skyler had believed he'd hated—Skyler felt a sick, sinking sensation, as one might feel peering over the edge of an abyss. For how could Bliss locate him, if Skyler were no longer Skyler? That faint mewing plea in the night in the dark in any bed Skyler found himself in dazed, exhausted and sleepless *Skyler?*   *help me Skyler*   *where are we, Skyler*

During the interview in the headmaster's study both Skyler's parents had avoided looking at each other; they'd arrived at the school in separate vehicles, and would depart in separate vehicles; Skyler had yet to be informed that his parents had "divorced" and yet not wanted to make inquiries.* Now Betsey said, with a reproachful glance at Skyler, and, past Skyler, at her husband who'd been surreptitiously glancing at the regal

---

* *The (mature, not-neurotic) reader will find it difficult to believe that Skyler, at sixteen, is yet so immature. That this boy who assumes a pose of scowling indifference, picking at his face as the adults discuss his future, is so hesitant to acknowledge what is, by this time, a* fête *accompli: for hadn't Skyler glimpsed a lurid banner headline on the cover of* SleazeWatch Week *proclaiming*

PARENTS OF SLAIN ICE-SKATE CHAMP BLISS RAMPIKE DIVORCED

Asked Is There Another Woman Bix Says: "No Comment"

Rolex on his brawny wrist, with the restrained-restless air of a man yearning to be elsewhere, "'Sylvester Ram-pole'—isn't it kind of—showy? Self-conscious?" but Bix said, with beaming-Daddy smile, as if rousing himself from a sleep of several years, "'Sylvester Rampole.' It's got style. It's got pizzazz. I like it. See, Sky-boy, you retain your initials—'S.R.' 'Rampike' is echoed in 'Rampole' plus 'Rambo.' Very clever, kid."

So Skyler was stuck with it. The joke-incognito he'd been sure his parents wouldn't allow him. Headmaster Shovell hadn't seemed fazed, either. From Bix Rampike he had received a cashier's check for a full year's tuition payable in advance and non-refundable.

IT HAD BEEN MY WRITERLY INTENTION TO "FREEZE" SKYLER IN THE act of limping across the campus green in pursuit of Heidi Harkness but in fact by this time Skyler is almost out of sight, having hobbled past The Monument, past Old Hill Hall, past "historic" cobblestone Founders House, downhill on the soggy-wood-chip path past Yelling West and Yelling East, beyond Craghorne (boys' dorm), beyond Clapp (dining hall), Clapp Gym, Clapp Stadium; past visitors' parking and past the heating plant and the "chilled-water" plant; past the tennis courts (occupied, noisy) and the soccer field (shouts, whistles, noisy game-in-progress), through the Great Meadow (visuals called for here: reader is directed to lavish color plates of autumn flowers notably goldenrod, Queen Anne's lace, blue-flowering chicory, toss in a cluster of dark red jack-in-the-pulpit berries, near the marshy edge of the field some cattails and un-identified sere grasses, to be handily located in *The Audubon Field Guide to North American Wildflowers*) in the direction of The Woods; stubborn and indomitable limping in the wake of the elusive "Heidi Harkness" whose incognito had no more shielded her from the smirks and stares and pitying smiles of strangers than "Sylvester Rampole" had shielded Skyler. *They know us. Our enemies. We have only each other.*

Following Heidi into the woods. At least, Skyler believed he was following Heidi into the woods because otherwise, where was she?

Often he'd sighted her, walking alone at the scrubby edge of the campus. For this girl to whom he'd never spoken he felt a stab of erotic yearning, or was it *Schadenfreude*: delicious German *harm-joy*.

Thinking *She is more famous than I am. More miserable.*

No *harm-joy* more exquisite/voluptuous/sensuous-brimming as the Germanic!

And it may have been that Skyler resented Heidi Harkness. Not for her fame/infamy/misery but for the annoying fact that, when Skyler had tried to speak with her, in the thunderous corridor of Babbitt Hall where both tenth-graders had classes, the shyly evasive girl had managed to elude him: *him!* Skyler Rampike who rarely went out of his way to speak to anyone, still less to smile at anyone. Heidi Harkness had snubbed *him.*

Inside each maladroit loser, like a hoagie falling out of its greasy wrapper, is a raving egotist. Especially at sixteen.

"'Heidi Harkness.' I want to be your friend."

Or, more forcibly: "'Heidi Harkness.' My name is Skyler Rampike and maybe you've heard of me? I want to be your friend."

More forcibly yet, hoping to pitch his voice low and compelling as in a movie close-up: "'Heidi Harkness.' Don't be afraid of me. I know what your life is. I want to be your friend. My name is—"

But where *was* Heidi Harkness? Skyler was beginning to sweat inside his clothes. His shoes were nearly soaked through. Tiny insects the size of punctuation marks, he had a vague idea were called *nats*, droned in a cloud about his spiky hair and stuck in his eyelashes. If the reader has not previously accompanied Skyler into idyllic "nature settings" it is because Skyler seems to have passed most of his life in airless, claustrophobic, and shrinking settings. Somehow the wood-chip path he'd been following had vanished in marshy soil. Something scuttled through the damp grass: a snake? *two* snakes? Thirty feet away was a shallow creek trickling over scattered boulders like misshapen vertebrae. Skyler was not lost for how could Skyler be lost?—even a boy unaccustomed to the outdoors couldn't have become lost so quickly. He had not walked more than a mile from the stone steps of Babbitt Hall. But Skyler was feeling the familiar choking sensation of panic* as if the reptile part of his brain wished perversely to believe that he was lost, and in danger.

(Away at school Skyler had grown careless, "unsupervised" and "on his own" and so he'd forgotten to take his morning meds [Zilich + Soothix] and deliberately he'd skipped his lunchtime med [Effexor] which made his mouth dry as an old sock, and his vision blurred.)

Promise me that you will take your medications as prescribed, Skyler, you know you will become sick again if you don't. So Mother pleaded.

Skyler had mumbled *Sure! I will.*

Politely adding *Sure I will, Mother.*

To her face he called her Mother now. No more Mummy! No more Mummy's *little man.*

Must've been the accumulative effect of so many drugs, so many years of so many drugs, Skyler had not frequently felt what are called *sexual urges.* Until recently.

Since being delivered to the Academy at Basking Ridge to make his "fresh start." Skyler liked it that he was "unsupervised" and "on his own."

Here in the woods, for instance. Why'd he come here? Wiping his face on his sleeve. God damn *nats.*

So far as he could see, he was alone. Yet: Heidi Harkness had to be here somewhere. Had she seen him following her, was she hiding from him?

From *him*? Skyler Rampike? Her only friend?

Skyler heard a sound, turned in alarm and there was Heidi Harkness less than ten feet away, staring at him with wild damp eyes. Her face was asymmetrical as if someone had twisted it subtly out of shape and her sallow skin was flushed as if she'd been running. Her chunky white front teeth overlapped like crossed fingers. Skyler could not have said if she was ugly or beautiful or some strange mixture of both. She was crouched,

* *"Panic": "Of, relating to, or resembling the mental or emotional state induced by the pagan god Pan who dwells in the forest in wait for the unwary." Like us!*

panting. Something glittered in her trembling hand: a blade? A *knife?*

Her frightened voice was low, abrasive like sandpaper rubbed against sandpaper: "Get away from me—stalker! Get away."

HOW COULD YOU THINK THAT I'D WANT TO HURT YOU! I LOVED YOU RIGHT away.

I didn't say you wanted to hurt me. I said you were stalking me.

But only because I loved you . . .

That's what stalkers say*

OF TWO HUNDRED FORTY-THREE STUDENTS AT BASKING RIDGE, "SLY" soon acquired a reputation for being "some kind of weird genius" in such difficult subjects as trigonometry, chemistry, and earth science. Quickly Sly hid his papers when they were handed back in class but you could see scrawled red A's: "Weird dude knows all the fuckin' answers." Sly was aloof, disdainful, preoccupied; in class, he looked straight forward at the instructor, and at the blackboard; he was taciturn, reluctant to speak, but could be counted on by his instructor to give correct answers to questions; though his voice was hoarse and halting as if infrequently used. He wore school clothing—mud-colored blazer, white cotton long-sleeved shirt, clip-on school tie—that was likely to be rumpled as if slept in. He never seemed to be watching where he was headed, frowning at the ground, or squinting into the distance; you had to leap out of his way, or, if you were one of the boy-jocks, you shoved him out of your way with a curse: "Watch out, asshole!"

Luckily, Sly was protected by his coveted P.M.E. deferment ("Perpetual Medical Excuse") which allowed him the luxury of avoiding gym and athletics altogether, and so he was spared

---

* *Flash-forward into the (near) future to collapse "cheap suspense"—the very coin of merely popular/best-selling fiction—and to assure the uneasy reader that Skyler's behavior was truly not what it seems to have appeared to be, to Heidi Harkness!*

combative physical activities in which the righteous wrath of his fellow boy-students would have been unleashed upon him: "Fuckin' lucky dude. Man!"

Sly turned up in class alone, and Sly left class alone; except for English class, where usually he left in the company of his single friend; as, in the thunderous dining hall modeled after some fabled mausoleum at Oxford, if Sly turned up at all he sat with his friend* at a table of losers/loners in a farther corner. Gregarious Bix Rampike had urged his sulky son to room in a "suite" and so enjoy the companionship of "suitemates" but more pragmatic-minded Betsey knew that it was far wiser to defer to their excitable son's vehement preference for a private room; for roommates/suitemates at previous institutions had not worked out well. And now, at sixteen, alarmingly tall and abrasive in his manner, and less inclined to take his daily meds as prescribed, certainly Skyler would be better off in a private room. So it happened, Skyler, that's to say "Sly," was allowed to live alone in a single room on the top, fourth floor of Old Craghorne, a creaking residence adjacent to (new) Craghorne Hall; where (new) Craghorne was made of buff-colored brick, Old Craghorne, a much smaller structure, was made of some darkly crumbling stone with a look of having been rained-upon for centuries. Where (new) Craghorne was the residence of the most popular boys, Old Craghorne was known to be the residence of losers/loners/freaks. Skyler's room, of the approximate size of two toilet stalls, was at the top of a steep flight of stairs that creaked beneath his meager weight (111 pounds at five-feet-ten: scrawny, eh?); though drafty, with ill-fitting windows and tilting floorboards, Skyler's room soon came to be, for him, a place of refuge. For hearty "jocks" from (new) Craghorne couldn't be troubled to make their way so vertically to harass "Sly Rampole" as in other circumstances they would have been delighted to do; and the boys of Old Craghorne were not up to the spirit of harassment, let alone the actions. These boys seemed to Skyler to have bonded together in a previous incarnation, having

* Could anyone have guessed? Skyler's old playdate Elyot Grubbe! Another time so cleverly I am avoiding the "cheap suspense" shunned by purveyors of Serious Literature.

attended Basking Ridge in the past, but they were not at all threatening, and all of them were shorter than Skyler. If he'd have liked, he could threaten *them*.

Noting how like a barely materialized ghost he passed through their somber stares hearing in his wake *That's him: Rampick*!

Or: *That's him? The guy who killed his . . .*

How blithely Headmaster Shovell had assured the Rampikes that no one at the school would know their son's identity! Yet it soon became clear to Skyler that everyone at Basking Ridge knew who he was, or that he was "somebody" to whom some measure of shame and scandal accrued. For how strangely they looked at him, how openly they stared at him behind his back, or smiled at him pityingly, and quickly looked away: even Rusty the cheeriest of the kitchen workers at Clapp Dining Hall, with his oily-dark skin and winking gold teeth; even Shovell's staff of mostly elderly prim-staring females having to restrain themselves from crossing themselves Roman Catholic style, as Skyler passed by. (As everyone seemed to know within a few days of her arrival that the new girl "Heidi Harkness" was the daughter of infamous "Leander Harkness.") Skyler learned to bear his affliction as one might bear a disfigured face or a misshapen body, with as much dignity as he could summon. "Hey how's it goin', 'Sly'?" was a frequent taunt, or query; possibly it was a friendly taunt, or a purely innocent query; "Sly" was not so bad a name; there was the macho example of "Sylvester Stallone"; you might argue that "Sly" was a sort-of cool name; and so "Sly" managed to smile a pained-grimace smile and to say: "Goin' okay, man: how 'bout you?"

Of Skyler's teachers he could not be absolutely certain who knew, and who did not. His chemistry teacher Mr. Badian regarded him with a perplexed gaze, at times; his French teacher Madame Du Mont seemed to take a special interest in him, amid so many bored and restless students; but there was unmistakably Skyler's English teacher Mr. Dunwoody who stared at him as if memorizing him, and feigned friendliness to "the new transfer student in our midst." Dunwoody smiled at his captive whom he'd seated in the first row (as he would seat

Heidi Harkness who began classes twelve days after the term began); he smiled at Skyler with moist pink gums, and briskly rubbed his pudgy hands together as a praying mantis might rub its forelegs together in anticipation of a feast: "'Sylvester Rampole.' You are new to Basking Ridge, Sylvester? And what was your previous school?" In his front-row seat Skyler would have liked to shrink into a dense hard object impenetrable to scrutiny as a chunk of Kryptonite. His newly sprung coarse hair that could not be flat-combed but lifted up from his forehead gave him an unnatural look; though Skyler wore the school uniform ("heather"-colored blazer with brass buttons, white cotton shirt, [clip-on] striped school tie) he stood out alarmingly; except for his scrawny body, you would not have thought him sixteen years old but much older. Since the incident at Hodge Hill School when Skyler had been beaten by security guards, he'd had dental surgery to repair some of the damage to his mouth, and his nose had healed with a small bony bump that gave him, he thought, squinting sidelong at himself in any flattering mirrored surface, the macho-guy look of a seasoned boxer. And now shielding his mouth with his hand Skyler answered the English teacher's taunting question in a mumble: ". . . Hodge Hell, Pennsylvania."

With the perky manner of a middle-aged twat accustomed to provoking mirth in cretinous adolescents, Dunwoody leaned forward cupping his hand to his ear: "Syl-vester? Excuse me? I'm afraid I cannot decipher rude mumbles."

A titter of laughter. Even the nicer girls, who ordinarily took pity on their picked-on classmates, couldn't help giggling.

Skyler had no choice but to speak a little more loudly, if sullenly, and unsmiling: "Hodge Hill, sir. School."

"Ah: Hodge Hill! Not quite of the academic/social caliber as the prestigious Academy at Basking Ridge, is it? One can see why you transferred here." Dunwoody, fattish-jowled guy in his mid-forties, faux-Brit manner, dry thinning hair and goofy-"sexy" tinted glasses with aviator frames, smiled at Skyler as a dentist might smile at a trapped patient. "And where is your home, Sylvester? Your sinus-clogged accent seems to suggest New Jersey, I think?"

His home! Where was Skyler's home!

Here was an unanswerable question. For Skyler could not say *I am from Fair Hills.* Could not say: *My home is Fair Hills.* For the fact was, Skyler no longer had a home in Fair Hills, at 93 Ravens Crest Drive. All that was finished, forever. Yet more shamefully, Skyler no longer had a home. Did Lionel Dunwoody know, and that was why he was asking? Skyler had not spent more than a few haphazard days with his mother in recent years, in one or another "temporary residence" of hers; he'd waited in vain to be invited to stay with Bix, in the fabled apartment on Central Park South, and to be taken to see a fabled Knicks game; the last "home" Skyler had stayed in had been Grandmother Rampike's big old house in Pittsburgh, where he'd been sent for a few confused days at Christmas 2002 . . . Elderly Grandmother Rampike was no longer on speaking terms with her "shameless" daughter-in-law; nor was Grandmother Rampike "very happy" with her son Bix's behavior; but, like most adult relatives in Skyler's family, she had not explained what she'd meant. Under Dunwoody's scrutiny Skyler felt his face burn. His mottled face, his battered face, sick-guilty-kid face. He'd been picking at a hard little pimple on the underside of his left nostril and now his fingernails drew blood and a little trickle ran rapidly down to his chin*; and, seeing he'd drawn blood, Dunwoody made a show of concern for his stricken student: "Oh my! What have we here! 'Sylvester,' here—quickly!—is a tissue."

But furious Sylvester pushed away the teacher's hand, stumbled to his feet and ran from the room—†

---

* *For those few readers with kinky-morbid-literary tastes, you might be interested to learn that just as sixteen-year-old Skyler's face began to bleed in Dunwoody's classroom, nineteen-year-old Skyler so picked and scratched at the stitches in his face, his face began to bleed onto* this very page.

† *Reader, I'm sorry! I can't continue this.*

Don't even know why I am writing about Lionel Dunwoody!

I'd meant to write about Heidi Harkness and somehow here I am writing about Lionel Dunwoody. As the reader should know from a long-ago chapter, it was Dunwoody who assigned our class E. A. Pym's notorious "The Aesthetics of Composition" in which it is stated that The death of a beautiful girl-child is the most poetic topic in the world. Out of pure sadism for "Sylvester Rampole," Dunwoody assigned this, knowing how it

At the farther end of the walnut-wood-paneled dining room modeled after some fabled mausoleum at Oxford, indifferent to the buzz, clatter, and hilarity of their fellows, the trio of exiles sat together beneath a high mullioned window: Harkness, Grubbe, Rampole. Young people disfigured by the infamy of their parents as by physical deformity.

Drawn to one another by temperament, and not, they would have passionately declared, by mere vulgar accidents of history, they were Children of Tabloid Hell.

Reader, this was my original opening for "First Love, Farewell!" Reader, I loved it so! I am ashamed to confess.

But some of you dislike such prose-poem artiness, on principle. Your sensitive eye, long habituated to the bland affabilities and predictable normalities of such fonts as Baskerville, Century, Bodoni et al. reacts negatively to such "distinctive"— "attention-grabbing"—fonts as the Lucinda Blackletter Bold of which the above is a sample: no doubt, you see it as "showy"— "overwrought"—"adolescent." I know that you are right, and yet: each time I read this paragraph, I am thrilled with its possibilities which seem to me two-fold:

Postmodernist: self-conscious/self-mocking/"weird"

Traditional: forthright/declarative/"linear"

Yet, the portentousness of the prose, the breathy solemnity with which "Children of Tabloid Hell" is intoned, would be very difficult to sustain for even the most virtuoso of stylists—which I am not.

---

would upset his student. This is the individual who would consent to an interview (in July 2004) with a reporter for No Holds Barred *as an "anonymous source" commenting in painful detail on the "psychological profile" of Skyler Rampike; asked by the reporter if he believed that the "troubled boy" might have been capable of murdering his six-year-old sister, he'd said: "When I gazed into those steely eyes, I gazed into an abyss. No further comment!"*

Yet it might be argued: *Skyler Rampike is in fact an adolescent.*

For much of this document, Skyler has been a young child: a *juvenile.* Now, lately he has morphed to *adolescence.* Yet, in his snarled little heart he is still a *juvenile.* The reader is perhaps aware of the latest neurophysiological findings, that, in the adolescent brain, the frontal cortex isn't fully developed; in particular, the frontal cortex of the adolescent male. (And how long does adolescence last, in our time? Well into a young man's twenties? Maybe—his thirties? Beyond?) The reader's habit of condescending to Skyler at age sixteen and the "overwrought" prose-poem that so aptly expresses his feelings is a mere consequence of the reader being older than Skyler, very likely decades older, so what is your prissy judgment worth?

Hey sorry: I didn't mean that.

I mean, I didn't mean to sound hostile.

I may be hostile as hell, just a festering petti dish of simmering/festering hostilities, but, reader, I don't mean to sound hostile; and if I have offended a few prissy middle-aged readers, sorry!

Skyler take care! There is a demon inside you Skyler yearning for nothing more than release.

II.

"GET AWAY FROM ME—STALKER! GET AWAY."

Unexpectedly there was Heidi Harkness confronting him. Naively Skyler had believed he would come up quietly behind her and instead, Heidi Harkness had come up quietly behind him.

In her trembling hand—what? Skyler couldn't determine if it was a strip of scrap aluminum foil she'd picked up from the ground, or a knife.

Skyler protested, "I wasn't s-stalking you. I—I wanted to h-help you. I saw—"

"'Help me'? How could you 'help' me? You can't help me."

The statement was flat, blunt, challenging. *No one can help me* this distraught girl seemed to be boasting.

Skyler wiped at his eyes. Nervous excitement made his eyes

mist over. Was it a small knife Heidi Harkness held threateningly, or a harmless strip of aluminum foil? The girl's nostrils were dilated, her eyes showed a rim of white above the iris. She was frightened, and she was combustible. Skyler could smell her agitation, and his own. Yet he dared to approach her, as if to calm her. Seeing that her eyes were a pale golden hazel like small spinning suns. Her eyes were finely threaded with blood, broken capillaries from sleepless nights, or weeping, Skyler understood. Yet her eyes were beautiful, Skyler could not bear to look at them. And at her left temple, a delicate blue vein pulsed. And at her hairline a scar-like area the size of a half-dollar where Heidi had been pulling out individual strands of her hair, as Skyler himself had once done. He would come to love Heidi Harkness's untidy hair, thick springy light brown hair like a broom, the identical color Skyler's hair had been before he'd gone bald at the age of ten.

Furiously Heidi said: "You! You've been following me! You and your hateful friends! Leave me alone."

Quickly Skyler said, "Not me! Not my 'friends'—I don't have any friends."

Impulsively then Skyler reached for the gleaming object in Heidi Harkness's hand. It might have been that, in that confused moment, Skyler had the idea he might calm her, protect and comfort her by disarming her. Instead, his fingers closed on something so steely-sharp he wasn't sure, at first, that he'd actually felt it. The surprise of it sent a tremor up his arm. Through his stunned fingers something seemed to be passing rapidly like a very thin wire that was scalding-hot. He felt something wet, oily in his hand. What was this? Blood? *His* blood? Had he been cut? Like a vengeful female figure in an Asian action film, part-human and part-animation, Heidi leapt backward wrenching the knife from Skyler's loosening fingers—it *was* a knife, with a sturdy four-inch blade—and tossing it in the direction of the creek.

Heidi stammered, "Are you c-crazy? What did you d-do? I—I might have k-killed you . . ."

Skyler stared at his bleeding hand. He'd been cut?

"It's okay, it isn't a deep cut. It doesn't hurt, much."

"But you're bleeding! It must hurt."

"Really, no. It's fine."

"I'm sorry! But you m-made me do it . . ."

With the magnanimity of a heroic man of action, and not a punk kid astonished and stymied by what had happened to his hand, Skyler tried to smile. Skyler assured the alarmed girl that his wounded hand was his own damned fault: "I provoked you. You were only defending yourself." Skyler examined his hand noting that several shallow cuts ran horizontally across the width of four fingers plus a nasty slash in the soft flesh at the base of his thumb. Skyler said, "Hey look: this isn't bad. My thumb might've been decapitated, but it wasn't." Weird and light-headed and transported by a powerful adrenaline kick to the heart and adrenaline coursing through his veins as Skyler hadn't felt in—how long?—since the meltdown in the TV lounge at Hodge Hill when a thousand pounds of brute macho force had been required to subdue a single skinny kid.

Female instinct roused Heidi Harkness to fumble to remove from a pocket a wadded pink tissue that looked as if it had already been put to use. Contritely she said, "This is all I have. Here."

"Hey, it's okay. I hurt myself all the time, worse than this."

"Please. Look how you're bleeding. Don't—don't wipe it on your blazer sleeve. Here."

Light-headed Skyler wasn't coordinated somehow, fumbled the tissue so Heidi was obliged to take hold of his shaky wounded hand, dabbing at the cuts with the pink tissue. Skyler stood very still and unresisting. Except for medics, nurses and physical therapists, and a quick handshake with his old playdate Elyot Grubbe who'd come up to him on the first day of classes at Basking Ridge, Skyler had not been touched in a very long time. A sensation as if he was standing at the edge of a precipice looking down into an abyss much deeper than he'd imagined . . .

Head bowed in concentration, muttering to herself in com-mingled alarm, sympathy, and exasperation, Heidi was obliged to stand close to Skyler. She was nearly his height, but downlooking now, her forehead creased with worry. Close up, he saw more clearly the coin-sized bare spot at the edge of her hairline. He saw that most of her eyelashes had been pulled out as well. The self-picker, self-punisher. Your favored nails were the sharp ones. *She is like me. She is one like me. She must know this.*

At sixteen Skyler Rampike—"Sly" in his new guise—gave off so sour and truculent an air that he appeared years older. Here was an individual whom others were not likely to approach. Surrounding him like a reverse magnetic field was a space which could not be invaded without upsetting Skyler considerably, yet now, in total obliviousness of this reverse-magnetic space, was a girl, Heidi Harkness, suddenly close. And so tenderly dabbing at Skyler's bleeding hand . . . The hostility in her fierce flushed face seemed to have vanished. She was speaking in wonderment, regret: "Oh God, I shouldn't have taken out that knife! 'Actions have consequences'—I know. That Swiss army knife—my father gave me. But he shouldn't have, not to bring here. 'The Academy at Basking Ridge'—I'm a 'probationary student' here. A knife is 'contraband' and I could be expelled. If anyone f-finds out about this—"

Quickly Skyler assured Heidi Harkness that no one would find out. He certainly wasn't going to tell anyone. She would not be expelled. If anyone inquired about his hand, Skyler would say he'd had an accident, he'd hurt himself. "I'm 'accident-prone' as hell. APSD—'Accident-Prone Spectrum Disorder'—it's in my medical file. They have our complete medical records in this place, 'the Academy at Basking Ridge' is a prep-school/clinic and we're all patients. We're all insured, if 'something happens.'" Skyler was deeply moved to see that Heidi Harkness had another tissue for him, to fashion a crude bandage for Skyler's hand, secured by a rubber band. Impulsively Skyler wanted to kiss the coin-sized bald spot at the edge of Heidi's hairline, but he laughed instead, a little crazily.

Reprovingly Heidi said, "What if the knife had gone into your—heart! You wouldn't be laughing now."

Skyler laughed, suffused with tenderness.

"Maybe it should've happened that way. *Couped-grass.*"

"You *are* crazy! Why do you say such—terrible—things!"

The tone of voice in which Heidi spoke, exasperated, confounded, seemed to Skyler a familiar tone: that of parental disapproval. Again he thought *She must know, she is one like me.* He heard himself say, like a magician drawing a shimmering crimson scarf out of the very air, "Some things are just 'fate.' Some meetings. See, our lives are 'contingent.'"

That means, not 'predetermined.' If you could rewind time—
turn time back to the start of 'organic life'—the first single-
celled life-forms—" improvising now in the voice-cadences and
with some of the bright-Jew-boy facial expressions of tutor Rob
Feldman, "—*Homo sapiens* would never emerge a second time.
This is so! Scientists say this! Too many factors are involved in
the evolution of so weirdly developed a species, and all of them
'contingent'—like the Ice Age, or asteroids crashing into the
earth. All you can say for sure is that what happens *is*. Life is an
acte gratoot."

Heidi Harkness smiled uncertainly. "'*Acte gratoot*'—is that
like '*acte gratuit*'—something that happens for no purpose?
Like, sheer accident?"

"That, too. Right!"

Mistrustfully Heidi Harkness regarded Skyler Rampike as if
she had never seen anyone like him before in her life. In her left
eyelid there was a twitch that mimicked, by pure chance, a
chronic twitch in Skyler's right eyelid. How beautiful Heidi
was! Those hazel-sun eyes, such beautiful eyes Skyler could not
look away from them. In so strange a state, a faint roaring
in his ears, and the throb of his wounded hand, he had but a
vague idea where he was. From somewhere close by, the trickle
of the creek through scattered and parched-looking boulders.
A nameless creek that flowed along an edge of the Basking
Ridge school property. High overhead in the tops of tall trees—
unnaturally tall trees they seemed to Skyler, with straight
smooth trunks, Skyler had no idea what such trees were called—
clumsy dark-winged birds were thrashing in the foliage,
emitting short sharp cries as in a drama of enigmatic intensity.
Skyler knew the names of no birds, Skyler was a stranger to
such woodland scenes. Thinking now in astonishment and
part-dread *Is this a nature scene, I have stumbled into? A nature
love-scene?*

He hadn't been marked for love. No one had loved him since
Bliss. And since he had abandoned Bliss, no one had loved him.
There was justice here, and logic.

All this while, Heidi Harkness stood regarding Skyler with
quizzical eyes. Her arms were crossed tightly across her
chest so that it looked as if she were hugging herself, to the

point of pain. It was a posture, a mannerism, unconscious, unnerving; like Heidi's furrowed forehead, and her way of gnawing at her lower lip. Like Skyler, Heidi was wearing school-regulation clothes: blazer, long-sleeved white shirt, tie. The blazer was "heather" in hue, the school tie "heather" with "royal purple" stripes. Like Skyler's clothes, Heidi's clothes looked as if they'd been flung on carelessly, without the benefit of a mirror. As soon as Skyler had left Babbitt Hall he'd tugged at his damned necktie, unbuttoned his shirt at the throat; and so had Heidi.

"Okay. I'm going now," Heidi said abruptly, "—good-bye."

Quickly Skyler said, "I—I'll walk with you," and Heidi said sharply, "I walk out here to be alone. I need to be alone," and Skyler said, "Well—me, too," and Heidi said, "I—I need to be alone if I am going to endure this terrible place," and Skyler thought This place? Terrible? Compared to what? though saying, "I know. Me, too," and Heidi said, "It's nothing personal, I just need to be alone. Being with other people too much confuses my head," and Skyler said, "Right! That is exactly right," and Heidi said, irritably, "I need to not talk to anybody. It makes me nervous to be talked to," and Skyler agreed; for Skyler would have agreed to anything this fascinating girl uttered. Thinking You can't stop me now, Mummy! No more little man. Heidi said, relenting, "If you want to walk with me and not talk, we could do that," and Skyler said eagerly, "Good. Let's go," but Heidi said, with a nervous flutter of her eyelids, "Except, I can't walk back that way," and Skyler said, perplexed, "You can't? Why not?"—for Heidi had indicated the way they'd come, directly from campus. Evasively Heidi said, "I just can't. Good-bye." The twitch in her lashless left eyelid had become more visible.

Then Skyler understood: this had to be one of Heidi Harkness's things.

If you were ROCD, or only just OCD, you had your things.

Things were rituals. Behavior-rituals. Making your way through the treacherous maze of each waking day without tripping a land-mine. The way might be a damned long way around but it was your way. Your thing.

Like being compelled to wash your hands—vigorously!—three

times. Like brushing your teeth—vigorously!—to the point of making your gums bleed—within minutes of having eaten (and if Skyler was prevented from brushing his teeth at such a crucial time, there teetered Skyler on the Brink of Ballistic). From Bliss he'd acquired the habit of walking exclusively on the carpeting on any floor that had a carpet, or on stairs; as there was a perfect way out onto the ice, that would make possible, though it could not assure, a perfect performance, so there was a perfect way into any space, and out of it again. Unlike Bliss, Skyler had learned to monitor his own bed and bedclothes. Defiantly slovenly in other regards, Skyler never failed to make his bed—vigorously!—with tight-pulled sheets and briskly shaken pillowcases—within a few seconds of getting up: for there is shame and disaster in an unmade bed. Unlike Bliss, Skyler had learned to prepare his school lessons carefully: assignments to be read no less than three times, homework always checked three times, long memorization-lists Skyler's specialty. And prayers to God in Whom you did not believe muttered under his breath a dozen times a day no matter where no matter when no matter the futility *Help me help help help me and my sister Bliss if only You would help us in the name of Your son in Whom I don't believe either AMEN.*

Skyler winced at the risky prospect of taking a different route back to the campus for Skyler's OCD thing took the, to him, supremely logical form of a compulsion to return to a place by the identical route you'd taken to get there: following such logic, how could you ever become lost? (You could not become lost!) (Not as Skyler had become lost, with such grievous consequences, in the labyrinthine corridors of Univers, Inc.) In the interests of accompanying Heidi Harkness, however, Skyler gave in.

Reluctantly, or was it shyly, Heidi Harkness extended her (right) hand, squeezed Skyler's hand and released it in virtually the same instant. Narrowing her eyes and in a flat voice saying, "And I am—'Heidi Harkness.'"

There was a clumsy pause. For "Heidi Harkness" was not this girl's name; and Skyler felt that he had to acknowledge the fact, without offending her. For like a skittish deer she was poised to flee through the woods at the slightest provocation, and Skyler

444

would have to limp after her. Trying for a confiding air he said, "'Sylvester Rampole' is the official—weird!—name they call me here. But 'Skyler Rampike' is my actual name. Maybe you've heard the name—'Rampike'?" Skyler's voice lifted in dread.

Heidi Harkness frowned. "'Ram-pike'? No."

Yet then some minutes later as they were making their way, with some difficulty, along an overgrown path beside the creek, through tall grasses and rank-smelling rushes, and vicious prickly bushes that tore at Skyler's clothing, suddenly Heidi said, in a neutral voice: "'Ram-pike.' Maybe yes, I have."

BATTA! AS BIG-DADDY BIX WOULD EXCLAIM.

Reader, I know: you are dismayed at this scene, for its lack of irony. All that has been recorded here took place in exactly this way on that afternoon in early autumn, in the scenic hilly countryside north of Basking Ridge, New Jersey. Two "teens"— mawkish, sentimental, silly-sad, and achingly real. As Skyler nervously foresaw, he and Heidi Harkness did become lost on their way back to campus; as Skyler might have foreseen, his wounded hand soon began to throb with pain. (For which his new friend kindly presented him with her "emergency meds"— two one-hundred-milligram capsules of the painkiller Oxy-Contin which Heidi kept carefully wrapped in aluminum foil, in a pocket—"I love Oxies. But it's a dangerous love. Oxies are for my rainy day.") Skyler, whose previous painkillers (Dopex, Dremzil) had been non-opiate, gratefully swallowed the Oxie capsules dry and imagined that, within a few minutes, the pain in his hand began to fade.

Pain fade out, love fade in.

They would return to campus late. Missing supper in the dining hall and so obliged to rummage up a meal from vending machines. By this time, it had been revealed to Skyler that, on the insides of his new friend's slender arms, there was a map of old/healed wounds and new/part-healed wounds, knife-cuts not unlike those knife-cuts in his fingers, like an exquisite Braille Skyler wished to draw his fingers over, to read.

And kiss. A few nights later.

· · ·

WHY'D SHE WANT TO HURT HERSELF—"CUTTING"—NOT JUST HER arms but (Skyler would discover) her belly, her breasts and the insides of her thighs—he had to ask though knowing why, for hadn't Skyler wished to hurt himself, in a fury wishing to hurt himself and in fact Skyler had hurt himself, and would hurt himself again *It's just something that feels right. Feels good.*

STAY WITH ME! BUT DON'T TALK.

DON'T LOOK AT ME! I'M UGLY.
  I'm ugly. Not you.
  You?—you're not ugly. You're beautiful.
  That's ridiculous. You make yourself ridiculous saying ridiculous things, please will you stop.
  It isn't ridiculous to say that you're beautiful and that I love you.
  Well. I love you . . . I guess.

I HATE IT, THEIR EYES. THE WAY THEY FOLLOW ME WITH THEIR EYES. Whispering together That's her! That's Leander Harkness's daughter.
  . . . the way they look at me thinking That's him! Bliss Rampike's brother.
  Do you want to talk about it?
  Do you?
  No.

YET ONCE, BURSTING INTO TEARS IN SKYLER'S ARMS, HOT STINGING tears that spilled onto Skyler, grabbing Skyler's neck as a drowning swimmer might grab the neck of her rescuer, Heidi spoke in a voice of childish hurt and grievance *He didn't! What*

446

they are all saying he did, he didn't! I will never believe he did.

(SO HEIDI HARKNESS BELIEVED THAT HER FATHER WAS INNOCENT! Skyler felt a pang of envy, he could've believed anything of anyone in the Rampike family including Skyler.)

THROUGH THAT AUTUMN AND THAT WINTER OF 2003 AT THE ACADEMY at Basking Ridge the young couple was observed: "Sylvester Rampole" and "Heidi Harkness" sitting together at mealtimes, with their fellow-exile friend Elyot Grubbe; side by side at school assemblies, programs and films; strolling together as if defiantly oblivious of their surroundings, fingers entwined, hips/elbows/shoulders lightly nudging, frequently kissing, in low urgent voices conferring. Yet it was so, as no one of their observers would have believed, that "Sylvester" and "Heidi" rarely spoke of their family disasters.

Murmuring *I love you.* A dozen times a day, uttered like an incantation *I love you.**

Skyler was protective of Heidi and would never have upset her by saying the wrong thing. Taboo subjects were many, you could tell by a stiffening of Heidi's jaw, the twitch like a frantic little pulse in Heidi's eyelid, the clenching of Heidi's fists. Nor did Skyler wish to bring up the taboo subject of his own family, the now-notorious Rampikes of Fair Hills, New Jersey. (From vague remarks made by Heidi, Skyler understood that she knew that something disturbing had happened in Skyler's past, when he'd been a little boy; but she didn't seem to know about Skyler's sister, or to remember. Like Skyler himself, Heidi had been only nine at the time of Bliss's death.) By contrast, the (alleged) murders of Heidi's mother, her (alleged) lover, and luckless pet poodles Yin and Yang, by Heidi's father, and the much-publicized trial in Nassau County, Long Island, had taken place just the

---

* *Does the prurient reader assume that Skyler and Heidi—in the crude vernacular usage—"had sex"? Maybe yes, maybe no. You won't find out from me.*

447

previous spring and still what Bix Rampike would call *O current* in the media.

In fact, Skyler knew very little about the Harkness case. He had not been a boy-baseball-fan, as we know. By the age of eleven he'd acquired the instinct to avoid so much as glancing at newspaper headlines; in stores that sold tabloid newspapers he swiftly looked away, as Heidi had more recently learned to do, from any display of such publications, full-page photos and banner headlines. In dark glasses, face grimly set, there was Mummy pulling at Skyler's arm *Don't! Don't look! It is Satan's revenge upon us.*

A few times, he'd looked. This had been years ago. Yes he'd been sorry.

Difficult to think of Skyler Rampike as an "American adolescent"—at least, difficult for me!—but more or less, that's what he was, and with little interest in that staple of adult conversation: News. Sixteen-year-old Skyler's awareness of what is called the "Mideast Conflict" was no more than the vague malaise a medieval European peasant might have felt for something called the Black Plague, or the Hundred Years' War, or a frenzy of witch-persecution rumored to be heading in the direction of his village. "Iraq"—"Iran"—"Israel"—"Madagascar" might've been squeezed into the same geographical space in northern Africa, or western Asia, or the steppes of Tibet, for all Skyler knew, or cared. At the schools in which he'd been enrolled, and particularly at Basking Ridge, history instructors discreetly avoided references to contemproary American history, foreign policy, and politicians since relatives of the most affluent students were likely to be involved in government, clandestine or otherwise; among Skyler's fellow students were sons and daughters of disgraced politicians and lawyers, businessmen, lobbyists, bribe-takers and -givers. Who these young people were Skyler didn't know and had no interest in knowing as the proverbial ostrich with its head buried in the sand shuns all interest in other ostriches with their heads buried in the sand.

Heidi was both fearful of and fascinated by TV, to which, to Skyler's disapproval, she seemed to be addicted. Of course, Heidi never watched "live news": the possibility of seeing a familiar face, or faces—including Heidi's own—was too great. She had a weakness for afternoon TV talk shows, with the sound muted; her favorite programs to watch were reruns; such programs as *The Young and the Restless, Only One Life to Live, St. Elsewhere, Sorrows of the Rich and Damned*; unlike Skyler, who avoided TV, especially late-afternoon TV, as one who has become violently ill from eating restaurant food avoids the restaurant in which he'd become ill, Heidi was capable of cutting classes, dreamily bloating herself with Diet Pepsi and watching TV reruns through the day: "Skyler, don't scold! These were programs my mother watched. And if I was sick, when I was a little girl I could stay home from school, and watch with her, and it was a happy time, and so nice to be sick! And now, so comforting to see how the stories turn out. This time."

Skyler kissed his girl. Heidi was likely to lift her arms to summon Skyler to her, in a cozy tangle of quilt, pillows, flannel p.j.'s, thick fuzzy socks sturdy as bedroom slippers on her long angular feet, to be kissed; and many times. In his girl's "down" mode—which alternated with her bright buzzy high-voltage "up" mode—Skyler had to be protective of her, and so he was. Yet not wishing to confide in her that his mother, too, had watched afternoon soaps, in a long-ago time of bliss-before-Bliss when Skyler was Mummy's own *little man* and what Daddy didn't know would not hurt them.

OF THE *TRIO OF EXILES* WHO SHARED MEALS IN A REMOTE CORNER OF Clapp Dining Hall, it was Elyot Grubbe who'd bravely, or was it brazenly, enrolled at the Academy at Basking Ridge under his own—"real"—name, and not a cover name. Somberly Elyot explained: "'Grubbe' isn't famous enough to disguise. Few people outside Fair Hills know 'Grubbe'—like they know 'Rampike'—'Harkness'.* You can see how people look through me here, as they did in Fair Hills when I was in grade school. And anyway, why should I care?"

* *Of course, Elyot didn't say "Harkness" but Heidi's actual name.*

Only the most obsessively observant of readers, as morbidly anal-retentive as this author, is likely to remember Skyler's playdate friend whom Skyler had wistfully imagined as a brother. (See the remote chapter "Adventures in Playdates II.") It had been a considerable shock to Skyler when, on the evening of the first, miserably interminable day he'd arrived at Basking Ridge in disguise as "Sylvester Rampole," a brisk compact boy with goggle glasses and magnified fish eyes approached him in the dining hall to say, *sotto vice*, "It's Skyler—is it? Rampike? Remember me? Elyot Grubbe."

A shock to Skyler, but a happy one. "Sylvester Rampole" had nearly burst into tears.

Implicit in the first handshake between the two child-casualties of Fair Hills was the promise *No one will know who we are*, or *once were*.

It was Elyot's custom, no doubt an affected-Brit custom, but one Skyler came to find comforting, to shake hands with Skyler when they met at mealtimes. When others were within earshot, Elyot never failed to call Skyler "Sly"; at other times, Elyot called Skyler "Sky"; so that, even if overheard by the sneering others who surrounded them, the privacy of "Sly"/"Sky" might be preserved.

Seven years since Skyler had last seen Elyot Grubbe! Seven years since he'd received the terse but touching letter of condolence from his friend:

DEAR SKYLER,

PLEASE ACCEPT MY CONDOLENCES FOR THE LOSS OF YOUR SISTER. I WOULD LIKE TO BE YOUR BROTHER AGAIN BUT IT WOULD BE TOO SAD YOUR MOTHER SAYS.

SINCERELY,

E. Grubbe

ELYOT GRUBBE

The domestic catastrophe that had befallen Elyot five years before was but vaguely known to Skyler who'd been (most likely) sedated at the time, and no longer living in Fair Hills, but Skyler understood the grim skeleton of the tale: Elyot's heiress-mother Imogene had been mysteriously murdered, "bludgeoned to death," in her bedroom in the Grubbes' mansion on the Great Road; somehow, Elyot's father had been involved; or maybe, since he'd been acquitted of all charges having to do with the murder, Mr. Grubbe had not been involved . . . ? Certainly, Skyler wasn't going to ask Elyot where his father was, or what his relations were with his father, any more than Elyot was likely to ask Skyler where his parents were, and what his relations were with them. *No one will know who we are, or used to be* had been sealed with a handshake.

(Skyler recalls: Mummy had started to tell him about "that awful thing" that had happened to Elyot's mother Imogene, as if to suggest to the broody brat there is plenty of misery to go around, and we are Christians who should know better than to give in to sorrow, but Skyler pressed his hands over his ears, screamed "Shut up, Mummy!" and ran from the room like a crazed little elephant.)*

This was Elyot's second year at Basking Ridge. Like Skyler, Elyot had missed lengthy patches of school and had, Skyler would learn, been "briefly incarcerated" in the Verhangen Treatment Center; still Elyot a year ahead of Skyler, and appeared settled in, to a degree. In the lapel of his Basking Ridge blazer was a small glittery-silvery snake upright on its tail to signify the honorific APS ("Advanced Placement Se-nior"); his duo-majors were science (that is, "pre-med") and music ("antiquarian"). In retrospect, Skyler supposed that, as a child, Elyot Grubbe had been heavily medicated, for he'd invariably seemed drowsy, with a slow drifting manner of speech and a dreamy smile; now, in adolescence, seventeen years old, Elyot was more animated, and certainly spoke more rapidly; the way in which Elyot's mouth twitched in anticipation of smiling suggested to Skyler the presence of "uppers" in his

---

* *Disturbing memory—"recovered" (I guess)—loosed and rising to consciousness out of the tidal muck, as S. Freud disdainfully called it, of the Repressed. Skyler must've been at least twelve at the time since clearly his "hysterical muteness" had vanished.*

bloodstream which Skyler himself had frequently been prescribed, in "bi-polar" mode; at mealtimes, Skyler sometimes saw his eccentric friend surreptitiously swallowing pills, quite a quantity of pills, and though some of the pills looked familiar (Prizzil? Xaxil? Vivil?) Skyler understood that Elyot would not welcome any commentary from Skyler; as, when Skyler rummaged through his pockets for his God-damned meds, cursing to himself when he could locate but used tissues and lint, Elyot pretended not to notice, or, fussily preoccupied with proofing homework, or listening to his Walkman, did not notice. Though the boys sat together in Clapp Dining Hall, frequently they passed entire meals without speaking more than a few murmured words. *Hi. H'lo. How are you. Okay, you?*

Yet Skyler felt (oblique, undeclared) affection for his old playdate friend. For Skyler had few friends, in fact Skyler had no friends, and certainly no "old" friends. In the intervening years Skyler had grown tall, angular, gangling, lopsided and, no other word, freaky; while Elyot had grown warily, to a height of five-feet-three; though compactly built, with the rigid-posture bearing and smooth cheeks of a boy-mannequin; he looked more like twelve than seventeen, a bright prepubescent with weakly intelligent eyes and a forgettable face like a smudge. How vulnerable Elyot would be to the Beavs and Butts at Basking Ridge, if he had not seemed to intimidate them, by some habit of bearing; and by the fact that, though "Grubbe" seemed not to be a known name at the school, "Grubbe" yet suggested an aura of wealth, family connections, and litigation.

And A. J. Grubbe had counter-sued! As A. J. Grubbe had filed a flotilla of lawsuits demanding financial restitution from publications, journalists, and private individuals who had "defamed" his name.

Elyot in no way resembled the fiery, flamboyant A. J. Grubbe whom Skyler had but glimpsed at a distance, at a cocktail gathering at the Rampikes'; poor Elyot resembled his unhappy-heiress mother Imogene who'd been one of those soft-boneless-mollusc females who quiver with emotion no one wants to share; an eagerly smiling wife/mother who senses that she will be mangled by life no matter how kindly—generous—"maternal" and "loving" and "good"—she is; for she is a wealthy heiress, and has attracted, fatally, the wrong kind of husband.

"And you have the most adorable little angel-sister, Skyler! How lucky your mother *is*."

One drizzly playdate afternoon at the Grubbe mansion on the Great Road there came Mrs. Grubbe stumbling downstairs in what appeared to be a Japanese kimono, that disguised her soft fatty folds, and in an exclamatory voice Mrs. Grubbe interrupted the boys' chess game, seizing Skyler's small-boy-face in pudgy-clammy fingers as an eagle seizes small-mammal prey in its talons; Mrs. Grubbe exhaled Chardonnay-sweet breath in Skyler's face, exclaiming over Skyler's sister, and marveling at Skyler's mother's luck. Afterward, with some embarrassment, Elyot had said: "Please excuse my mother. She has been diagnosed as 'tri-polar'—and she is medicated—but sometimes the medication fails, and she becomes excitable. I think that what Mother meant just now was that, if she were to lose me, she would have no child; whereas your mother, if she lost you, would still have your sister; and so your mother is 'lucky,' as Mother is not. But I doubt that Mother is capable of fully articulating such a thought, even to herself."

(Yes! Elyot Grubbe spoke in such grammatical little-pedant sentences even as a child.)

At Basking Ridge, the boys renewed their somewhat thoorctical friendship. Each was grateful for the other's company, though not excessively. Rarely did they see each other outside of mealtimes in clamorous Clapp Dining Hall where they sat at an unoccupied end of a table of losers/exiles, eating their meals mostly in silence. Elyot's usual mealtime practice was to eat slowly and distractedly while listening to music on his Walkman, and frowning over pages of elaborate musical notations; when Skyler first joined him, Elyot was making his way through the sacred music of Josquin des Prez; he then moved on to Bach's *Six Suites for Unaccompanied Cello*, performed by Yo-Yo Ma: "The most exquisite of composers, conjoined with the most exquisite of cellists." Skyler remembered that Elyot had been taking cello lessons in Fair Hills, but when Skyler asked him about music lessons, Elyot stiffened: "No longer. No." Skyler could see that Elyot didn't wish to elaborate, yet Skyler couldn't resist asking why he'd stopped taking lessons, and Elyot said, sadly: "Mother believed that I was something of a cello prodigy. I was not. But I had 'promise.' And so music became too important to me. Especially after—you know. I practiced, and practiced, and practiced and yet—I was not perfect. When I played for my teacher invariably I struck a wrong note. Sometimes I would make it to the very end of a lesson—and then my bow would slip, and I would make a mistake, and have to start over. And the same thing would happen again, and if my teacher didn't allow me to start over again immediately, I would become 'agitated.' We tried to defuse the situation by having me make a mistake—deliberately!—at the outset, and get it over with, but—" As Elyot spoke in his matter-of-fact glum voice, smile-twitches playing at the corners of his mouth, Skyler listened in sympathetic silence thinking *Worse than me! Poor bastard.*

Where Elyot immersed himself in exquisite music, Skyler immersed himself in Boring Things. No surprise—were you surprised?—that freaky "Sylvester Rampole" became an *A* student at Basking Ridge, for his courses provided a corncoopia of Boring Things for him to memorize, that he might, with clockwork precision, like few others at the school, regurgitate out on exams and quizzes. For example, Skyler excelled in his American History class by memorizing lengthy columns of dates: wars—battles—peace treaties; explorers—conquerors— territories; states, when admitted to the Union; dates of elections—inaugurations—deaths of Great Men; Whigs— Federalists—Democrats—Republicans—Free Soil Republicans— Abolitionists—Copperheads—"Tippecanoe and Tyler Too"; "Teapot Dome"—"We Stand at Armageddon"—"The Stolen Election" (1876).* Yet more comforting was the mind-numbing Periodic Table, for Skyler's chemistry class; lists of vocabulary words and verb declensions, for Skyler's French class; lengthy passages put to memory from *Macbeth* and *Julius Caesar*, to

*Is this comforting to know, or not-so-comforting? That, in the simmering cesspool of U.S. political campaign history, at least one previous election, (Republican) Rutherford Hayes vs. (Democrat) Samuel Tilden, was "stolen"?

confound Mr. Dunwoody who sprang frequent "pop quizzes" on his students, to keep them in a perpetual state of edginess, and who could not be dissuaded from believing that somehow, "Sylvester Rampole" had to be cheating.

Once Skyler met Heidi Harkness, and fell in love with her, his zeal for Boring Things quickly ebbed.

"Elyot? I'd like you to meet . . ."

Now there was a trio of exiles at the remote table beneath the high mullioned window. Skyler thought *We are all we need.*

But relations between Heidi and Elyot seemed always under negotiation, unsettled as a wind-sock. At first, when Heidi joined Skyler at mealtimes (which was unpredictably, for Heidi "hated food, on principle"), Elyot was unsmiling, and stiffly responsive; clearly he was dazzled by her, by the mere fact of her; what a shock, that Elyot's oldest/closest friend, whom surely Elyot had assumed was as unattractive to girls, and as unattracted by girls, as he was! On her side Heidi was wary of Elyot Grubbe whom Skyler had described as his oldest/closest friend from Fair Hills who'd had "something terrible" happen to him—in fact, to his mother—that wasn't to be talked-of, ever; and was "some kind of weird genius." Badly Skyler wanted his two friends to like each other, for he could not bear to shun Elyot, now that he had Heidi; and, given Heidi's moodiness, and unpredictable behavior (of which Skyler was only just beginning to learn), he was fearful of slighting Heidi . . . "Elyot likes you," Skyler told Heidi, who bit at her thumbnail until it bled, "—he's just shy, and isn't used to girls."

"I feel that he's judging me. He is this 'Eye That Sees'—judging me."

Skyler was startled by his girlfriend's words that had the air of being improvised, flung out on the careless shovel of her emotions. "'Eye That Sees'—what do you mean?"

"Well, two eyes. The way he looks at me."

"But why did you say—'Eye That Sees.' Where did that come from?"

"I—I don't know, Skyler. Things just come to me."

"Yes, but from where? 'Things come to me'—from where?"

"Skyler, I don't know! You're hurting me."

Heidi pulled away. Without knowing what he'd been doing

Skyler had gripped her thin wrist tight, might've been turning—twisting?—it. But not on purpose.

SEARCHING *SKYLER RAMPIKE* IN CYBERCESSPOOLSPACE. HAD SHE?

SHAME!

For there was Skyler in grungy black T-shirt, khakis, rotted Nikes and grimy baseball cap in the guise of a local high-school kid hanging about the 7-Eleven on the outskirts of the Historic Village of Basking Ridge. Sucking at a Coke, innocently eyeing the display rack of tabloid papers as he knew he should not, must not, like swallowing an unidentified pill, could be the worst mistake of your life, *do not do it*. Yet Skyler thumbed through pulp-paper *Star Watch*, *Star Weekly*, *US Spy*, where in October 2003 more than six years after his sister's death it wasn't unreasonable for him to assume—or was it?—that he would not come upon a photograph of Bliss Rampike another time, that heartrending little girl-skater captured in a graceful glide on the ice, glamorously made-up little fairy child, a glittery tiara in her curly blond hair Little Miss Jersey Ice Princess 1996 would not leap out at him another time, nor would he be surprised another time by a photograph of his ghastly smiling parents emerging from Trinity Episcopal Church flanked by their staunch Christian supporters Reverend Higley and Mrs. Higley, identified in red banner headlines BETSEY & BIX RAMPIKE: MURDEROUS MUMMY & DADDY OR BEREAVED PARENTS?—surely would not come upon, another time, the ghastly smiling likeness of his own child-self, SKYLER RAMPIKE: THE SECRET HE HAS NEVER REVEALED—nor those coyly juxtaposed photos of GUNTHER RUSCHA, CONFESSED PEDOPHILE-MURDERER and SKYLER RAMPIKE: RUSCHA'S FIRST SEX VICTIM? With a part of his mind monitoring the Indian clerk at the checkout counter at the front of the store even as he pages through sleazy *US Spy* trying to hold his breath against the sewage-stink of Tabloid Hell wafting to his nostrils, sickening sense of loss, sorrow, defeat, vanity of all human desire, utter helplessness of the kind the minimal consciousness of the ever-flapping wind-sock must feel, or the careworn Möbius strip turning, turning endlessly with the spinning earth around its sun in a remote galaxy near to collapsing upon itself to the point of a pin, fumbling to turn a page in *US Spy* to discover what he has been seeking: HARKNESS. Not RAMPIKE but HARKNESS. With vast relief thinking *Poor Heidi! But not me* for here is a six-page spread of mostly photographs, red banner headline SEXY EX-YANKEE LEANDER & SUPERMODEL STEFFIE: EXPECTING? Skyler studies the photos of good-looking Leander Harkness, on the pitcher's mound rearing back to pitch, World Series 1988; in another, Harkness has a shaved head, murk-colored eyes, sneering mouth; in another photo, in his Yankee uniform, he's leaning over to spit; there are photos of Harkness and his attractive blond wife Alina, and of Harkness's little daughter Heidi; Harkness, Alina, and Heidi at their town house on East 86th Street, New York City; another of Harkness and daughter Heidi at the waterfront house in Oyster Bay; how tender this Big Daddy is holding Heidi's little hand; how trusting the little girl gazing up at Big Daddy with an adoring smile; Skyler is struck by his girl's little-girl self, so very different from her angular, taut, wistful self; at sixteen, Heidi more resembles her murdered mother than she resembles the little girl in these photographs. And, on another page, an unflattering photo of Alina Harkness seemingly unaware of a paparazzo hovering near as, vexed-looking, decidedly dowdy, Alina emerges awkwardly from a car revealing a length of chunky leg: ALINA HARKNESS, 35. Cruelly close by is SUPERMODEL STEFFIE, 23: gorgeous, pouty Steffie with astonishing breasts, narrow waist and hips, near-naked and preening for the camera in a black silk "slip dress" for Armani. Steffie has satiny straight blond hair, bosomy lips and coy-candid eyes, a younger, slimmer, more beautiful sister of the slain Mrs. Harkness.

The feature ends with a heartbreaking photo of the poodles Yin and Yang peering up at the camera in expressions of doggy bewilderment above the caption *Master, no!*

Skyler has to laugh. As in the movements of a compass needle, that indicate, to the alert mind, the presence of a mysterious if invisible and inscrutable Authority beyond the world of mere appearance, so too one can discern, beyond the sludge and sewage of Tabloid Hell, the presence of an invisible, inscrutable, and malevolent Editor.

Skyler learns in *US Spy* that Leander Harkness, even while playing major league baseball for the Yankees, had been arrested several times by police in New York City, Oyster Bay, and St. Bart's; at the time of his wife's death there was a restraining order against him issued by a Nassau County judge, forbidding him to come within one hundred feet of both his wife and daughter, or to harass them in any way; Harkness had been tried on first-degree murder charges not once but twice in Nassau County: the first trial in late 2002 had ended in a hung jury, the second in spring 2003 had ended in an acquittal. No other suspects in the murders had ever been investigated and it seemed to be generally believed that, despite the jurors' decisions, Leander Harkness, acting alone, was the individual who had stabbed his wife to death (fourteen wounds to torso, throat, face) in the Harknesses' five-million-dollar home on the north shore of Long Island; Harkness had also stabbed to death his wife's alleged lover (eleven wounds, chest, belly, groin); and, in a macho spillage of rage, of the kind frequently exhibited during Harkness's high-profile baseball career, he stabbed to death the adorable poodles Yin (curly white fur) and Yang (curly black fur). During the murders, which took place in a ground-floor glass-enclosed room overlooking Long Island Sound, the Harknesses' fifteen-year-old daughter Heidi was upstairs in her room and would claim to have "slept through" the entire episode, though the murders had occurred at approximately 8 P.M. of a July night, scarcely dusk. Heidi Harkness would claim that she had not seen or heard her father in the house, or anywhere in the vicinity of the house; nor had she seen him drive away in what Oyster Bay neighbors described as Harkness's "distinctive" bronze Rolls-Royce coupe. At neither of her father's trials had Heidi Harkness testified, for "reasons of health." For fifteen weeks, Heidi had been an inpatient at the Verhangen Treatment Center in Bleek Springs, New York.

Shakily Skyler replaces *US Spy* on the display rack. Blindly Skyler staggers from the store.

Thinking *Poor Heidi! But not Skyler, this time.*

III.

"LOVE YOU."

"Love you."

As in twin mirrors reflecting each other to infinity.

HE WOULD BE PROTECTIVE OF HEIDI HARKNESS, SKYLER VOWED. WHAT he'd discovered in *US Spy*, Skyler would never reveal to Heidi. Not in their most intimate moments would Skyler suggest *You saw your father that night didn't you   you can tell me Heidi I will never tell a living soul*   for it was Skyler's responsibility, if he loved Heidi Harkness, to shield her from hurt. He was strong enough, he believed. This time.

IT WAS NOT UNCOMMON AT THE ACADEMY AT BASKING RIDGE WITH ITS population of variously "challenged" students for hired cars with tinted rear windows to appear on campus, to take away individuals at regular intervals, and to return them; and so each Thursday at 1 P.M. a black Lincoln Town Car turned into the graveled drive of the scenic campus, was flagged through by the uniformed guard at the kiosk, winding its way to the girls' residence Toll House, notable for its suite-sized private rooms with private bathrooms, and out stumbled Heidi Harkness in oversized dark glasses that hid most of her pale, taut face, a scarf tied in haste around her matted hair, and away to New York City two hours to the east she was borne to her weekly session with a Park Avenue psychopharmacologist whose specialty was, in Heidi's words, "fucked-up teenaged girls"; and sometimes Heidi would be returned to Basking Ridge by 8 P.M., and Skyler would be waiting for her, but at other, unpredictable times Heidi failed to return remaining in the city overnight and evasive about where she'd been telling Skyler with relatives, family friends, but Skyler believed that Heidi spent the night at her father's town house on East 86th Street, surely Heidi spent the night with her father if he was in the city; but Heidi never acknowledged these visits with Leander Harkness to Skyler, as Heidi never acknowledged the very existence of Leander Harkness and her connection to him to anyone at Basking Ridge. To Skyler this seemed an act of betrayal for how could Heidi have such secrets from him, if she claimed to love him? Weakly Heidi said, "But you have secrets from me, Skyler. We can't know everything about each other."

Skyler thought *You can't know everything about me. But I need to know everything about you.*

What offended Skyler was: Heidi didn't distinguish between him, and the others. If she loved him, he had to be special in a way no no one else was.

Heidi pleaded, "Skyler, don't. Don't push me. Just love me."

Beginning to cry. Hot tears splotching that pale angular face.

So Skyler relented, when Heidi cried he felt helpless, stricken with guilt, and the curious pleasure of guilt. Liking how the girl—Leander Harkness's daughter, who had lied for his sake—pushed her tremulous body against him, slipping her arms around his neck in a gesture of humility, need; yet womanly possessiveness, that excited him. "Hey. Don't cry. You know I'll take care of you"—for it was so, Skyler would protect Heidi Harkness from all harm even that inflicted upon her by Skyler Rampike himself.

WHAT DID YOU HATE MOST ABOUT THAT TIME?
Never being able to say anything true. And you?
Never being able to say anything true.

SHARED DIAGNOSES: DYSLEXIA/ATTENTION-DEFICIT DISORDER/CHRONIC anxiety syndrome/C.A.A.D./ROCD/HSR. ("'HSR'—what the hell is that, Heidi?" Skyler asked, for he'd never been told; and Heidi shivered, and snuggled in Skyler's arms, kissing his lower lip so Skyler couldn't see her eyes, saying, "Gosh. I don't know either.")

Shared I.Q.'s: Skyler's most recent testing, 139; Heidi's most recent testing, 141.

Shared meds: Skyler's Zilich, Dumix, and (newly prescribed) "junior antidepressant" Upixl, Heidi's Oxycodones, OxyContins. Shared clothes: Skyler's pea-jacket with zip-up hood, fingerless leather gloves, Outbound lace-up waterproof boots; Heidi's L.L. Bean cable-knit mittens, and Heidi's red cashmere muffler. Shared food: if Skyler peeled an orange slowly and sensuously and ate half of the segments, Heidi might consent to eat (very slowly) the other half. Ditto grapefruit, apples. Skyler's Hi-Protein Granola Bars. (For each bite Heidi managed to swallow, a big-brother kiss from Skyler.) (Hadn't Skyler so urged Bliss to eat, years ago? When Mummy wasn't watching.) (But could Skyler trust Heidi not to sneak away, stick a finger down her throat and vomit up everything she'd eaten at his bequest? As Bliss never had.) Shared joints: Skyler's grade-C, head-banger marijuana scored from a Basking Ridge senior whose source was a local high school kid with "Newark ties," Heidi's classy Acapulco Gold smuggled back to Basking Ridge from her mysterious Thursdays in Manhattan. Shared kisses. (Dreamy-dope-kisses! *Love love love you* lying coiled together like lazy amorous boa constrictors kissing/whispering/softly laughing/slipping into each other's dreams/hidden away in Heidi's room so much larger and more private than Skyler's room with a private bath.)

Shared music: Skyler's heavy-metal punk-rock bands Shank, Whack, Futt, Dream Bone, Heidi's esoteric "Estonian minimalist" Arvo Pärt. ("'Estonian minimalist'? You've got to be kidding." Skyler was unpersuaded by Pärt's music that was so slow, spare, still, almost you couldn't hear it; Skyler sweated, trying to hear; determined to hear what Heidi found so "beautiful"—"mystical"— in these small frugal notes that reminded Skyler of tiny mouse turds of the kind frequently found in his room at the top of Old Craghorne; if the value of music is its power to drown out demon-voices in your brain, Arvo Pärt was not loud, violent, crazed enough for the task and so Skyler became impatient with his girlfriend's attempt to turn him on to minimalist music: imagine Skyler's chagrin when, one evening amid the cheery cacophonies of Clapp Dining Hall his girl Heidi Harkness and his friend Elyot Grubbe share earphones to listen gravely to Arvo Pärt's *Alina* while Skyler sulked, devoured whatever was

461

heaped on his plate without tasting it, at last rising from his chair and walking away without a backward glance.)

"Skyler, are you angry with me? Skyler, why?"

And, "Don't be ridiculous, there is nothing between Elyot and me! You know there is nothing between Elyot and me. He's sweet, and so sad."

And, "Skyler, I won't do it again. Whatever it was, I won't. Only just love me . . ."

HE WOULD. HE DID. OOZING OUT OF HIM IN SLOW PAINFUL DROPS LIKE blood being squeezed from a wounded finger. *I can. I will. I am strong enough for both.*

". . . WHAT I HOPE TO DO WITH MY LIFE, I HOPE TO GET A DEGREE IN public health, I hope to work as a volunteer in an AIDS hospital in like Kenya, or Nigeria . . . I do! I want to redeem my name that has been contaminated, and I will."

Skyler was so moved by these words, halting childish words that fluttered like butterflies in the air about their heads, small fragile-winged butterflies of a species that lives for but a day, when Heidi asked Skyler what did he hope to do with his life Skyler could not think how to reply, his mind had gone blank, no idea how to answer except knowing he could not say *My life is over, fucked is what I am* nor even *My life is a Möbius strip, know what that is?—it can never be anything but what it is, and it never comes to any end.* In girlish excitement Heidi leaned forward to kiss Skyler on the mouth, one of Heidi's quick yearning kisses, and asked him again, what did he hope to do with his life, and Skyler heard himself say, ". . . seminary. Maybe Union Theological, in New York. I want to study in a seminary," and Heidi said, excited, "Skyler, you do? You want to become a minister, Skyler? I didn't know that you were religious, but Skyler, that is wonderful." Quickly Skyler amended, he didn't want to be a minister, he couldn't see himself preaching to any congregation or being a model for anyone—"I only want to know *why.*" For in fact this was true, so simple a fact it might be overlooked: Skyler wanted to know why; as Heidi Harkness wanted to know why, and Elyot Grubbe: *why*. Heidi said, "We can search for 'why' together, Skyler! You can come with me to Africa. You can be a 'man of God' in Africa, Skyler. Even if you don't believe."

AND THEN AT THANKSGIVING SHE WENT AWAY, AND LEFT HIM. FIVE days.*

And when she returned she was edgy and distracted and laughed more frequently, a nervous brittle laugh that irritated Skyler like a fingernail scraped on a blackboard. She was vague about where she'd stayed and where she'd had Thanksgiving dinner—"Skyler, just with relatives, family friends: women trying to make me eat, and me trying to escape them." And Skyler resented it, that Heidi Harkness who was supposed to be Skyler's girl was a stranger to him; her deepest loyalty was elsewhere, like a part of her tricky female body he could not reach. Shutting his eyes recalling the fantastical drawing of the female reproductive organs he'd stared at, maybe it had been in his playdate Tyler McGreety's bedroom, a medical text that opened to this page, *body of uterus, ureter, oviduct, ovary, cervical canal, mouth of uterus, mons veneris, hymen* looking to a young boy's eye like a highly detailed drawing of an Extra-Terrestrial with tendril-like oviduct arms. No mere boy-penis could truly penetrate such a maze, Skyler seemed to know beforehand.

"See what I've brought back for you, Skyler? For us."

In a Ziploc bag he'd thought must be some classy new type of dope, turned out to be (crushed) OxyContins.

---

* *Wonder where Skyler went at Thanksgiving? Skyler went nowhere at Thanksgiving. Nor was it so very lonely at Basking Ridge for there was a sizable number of his class-mates who had nowhere to go on this American-family-glutton holiday, including Elyot Grubbe; and Headmaster Shovell and his cheery wife Gwendolyn invited us all to Thanksgiving dinner in the Headmaster's house. As I am clumsy with warm, friendly, "nice" occasions, as with expressions of gratitude, I will pass over Skyler's Thanksgiving in silence.*

WHO'D TAUGHT HER TO MELT THE POWDER, WHO'D GIVEN HER THE sparkly glass pipes, Skyler inquired but Skyler was never fully convinced that Heidi told him the truth laughing and kissing him saying, "Oh honey, why's it matter? It doesn't."

"HEIDI, C'MON PLEASE."

Days in succession when Heidi would eat only mashed banana in plain unsweetened yogurt, like baby food. Washed down with cans of caffeine-laced Diet Pepsi leaving her dazed and drunk and bloated—feeling like, she said, being pregnant.

Skyler was worried about his girl so faint with hunger sometimes she could barely ascend a flight of stairs, pushing him away if he tried to steady her—"Skyler, hands off. I don't want people staring at us, and inventing ridiculous rumors." Heidi's grades were unpredictable because Heidi so often nodded off in class, in the midst of a test, laying her head on her test paper and drooling onto it; apart from the fame/infamy of her identity, Heidi Harkness had quickly acquired a legendary aura, the "brainy girl" who was capable of falling asleep on her feet while giving an oral report in a class, as the instructor looked on astonished. (Heidi quickly woke up, before she fell and cracked her head on the floor.) At mealtimes in Clapp Dining Hall, Skyler hated the way he and Elyot vied with each other trying to cajole Heidi into eating, offering her food from their plates as you might urge food on a willful child. Skyler knew it wasn't a good idea—"enabling"—yet as Elyot earnestly tempted Heidi with spoonfuls/forkfuls of food which, at times, like a fledgling bird opening its beak, Heidi ate, Skyler felt a rush of jealousy. *Here! Eat what I am offering you, God damn you I am your boyfriend not him.* In addition to mashed-banana-yogurt baby food, Heidi would (sometimes) consent to eat a few forkfuls of tasteless white rice, mushy tasteless cauliflower and zucchini, a half-glass of skim milk. Naive, boastful, Heidi argued for the purity of white foods: "If we have to eat at all."

Skyler laughed. Skyler scowled. Thinking *Your shit is the*

color as everybody's, stinks the same, can't purify that. This crude/shrewd Bix-insight Skyler knew better than to share with his friends who would have stared at him in dismay.

Hey I'm not a nice guy. I'm a guy who killed his baby sister. Maybe raped her. Why so surprised? I am Skyler Rampike.

Nervously watchful of Skyler, somehow Heidi knew. Heidi knew his moods. Even as Elyot gently chided Heidi in his prim med-school manner ("'Anorexia nervosa' is an addictive condition, a compulsion that becomes an illness, injurious to the brain, kidneys, heart, liver, resembles a misguided asceticism in a religion in which there is no God . . .") Heidi stared at Skyler who regarded her with a strange detachment, almost hostility, even as he stroked her thin wrist protruding from the loose sleeve of an oversized Basking Ridge sweatshirt. Those golden-hazel eyes like small spinning suns and the pert upper lip, the overlap of her two front teeth like crossed fingers . . . Skyler felt something clamp against his forehead, like a forceps: who was this girl, and why was she looking at him with such intensity?

Abruptly Heidi pushed away from the table, fumbled for her backpack that was heavy/bulky like something that might've been hauled by a mule, without a backward glance at Skyler or at gaping Elyot exited the dining hall.

"HOW CAN YOU HURT ME! I NEED YOU TO LOVE ME."
"I need you to love *me*."

". . . NEED YOU TO TRUST ME."
". . . need you to trust *me*."

SHE BEGAN LEAVING GIFTS FOR HIM. SOMETHING FRANTIC IN HER wish to surprise him with useless and unwanted little gifts coyly left in Sylvester Rampole's mailbox at Old Craghorne. "Hey Sly: Heidi was here"—one of Sly's fellow residents winked at him.

Sly scowled, not wishing to blush in embarrassment.

465

Sure he was touched, it was a sweet gesture on Heidi's part, but what was Skyler to do with, for instance, a tiny bouquet of tiny flowers that looked as if they'd been fashioned from tissue paper and spit, miniature roses, daisies, lilies they must have been made with a pair of tweezers, Skyler imagined Heidi working late into the night in that haze of obliviousness to the passing of time that is one of the doubtful benefits of OxyContin. And one evening at Skyler's usual place at the dining table in Clapp Hall there was an envelope with *S.R.* in elaborate script, and inside a greeting card JUST BECAUSE YOU ARE YOU, cartoon drawings of a figure with long legs, long arms and spiky zinc-colored hair and zinc-eyes made with something glittery like mica, and Skyler was impressed, the drawings were surprisingly skillful, and professional, in the way of a more benign R. Crumb. (But had Skyler ever told Heidi about his childhood infatuation with R. Crumb? He didn't think so.) And other love-tokens turned up in unexpected places, in a pocket of Skyler's jacket (little gold locket with Heidi's baby picture inside and a lock of hair, frazzled white lace presumably from a pair of Heidi's panties); in Skyler's backpack a small blue Tiffany box and inside a pair of expensive-looking silver cuff links engraved *S.R.* (Cuff links! For a sixteen-year-old who wore shirts that barely had cuffs.) (This useless gift, yet it was flattering, how Skyler would have liked to boast to Bix Rampike *See these cuff links, kind of cool aren't they?—guess whose daughter gave them to me. Retired Yankee pitcher, in the news a lot. Yes you'd know him, he's about your age.*) And one December day in Skyler's mailbox in his residence was a small jar of colored cut-glass and inside tiny red cinnamon hearts, spilling out onto Skyler's palm these little red hearts began at once to melt and to stain his skin and something swerved inside Skyler's head like a clumsily wrapped package containing a wedge-like weight *Skyler   will you make me a little red heart Skyler? will you make me a little red heart like yours   Skyler please* So clear this plaintive request, he hadn't been hearing for months yet standing now staring at the little red hearts staining the palm of his hand with a look that must've been more than ordinarily weird for a fellow resident of Old Craghorne was asking him, guardedly, yet not unkindly, if something was wrong? Calling him Sly, as if

"Sly" was his actual name, asking had he hurt himself, was his hand bleeding? But "Sly" sprang away like a large panicked bird and fled without a reply not knowing where the hell he was, or why.

Skyler! don't leave me Skyler

Skyler I am so alone here

He'd been neglecting his meds. God-damned meds he'd wanted to think he could take at whim. Rummaging now for Zilich capsules, in his pockets. Fucking Dumix, Upixl, one of Heidi's Oxies, anything he could get his hands on.

Make me a little red heart Skyler   like yours and he had done that. He had. He had done that and yet: it had not saved her. Skyler had not saved her.

That night asking Heidi why red hearts?

Heidi smiled warily seeing that her moody boyfriend was grinding his back molars, almost you could smell the smoldering teeth. Laughing thinking this had to be a joke Heidi said, "Red hearts? Little cinnamon hearts? Skyler, you are not angry with me: tell me you are not, this is too fucking weird otherwise." Skyler insisted he wasn't angry, only just curious why Heidi had left little red hearts in his mailbox, one of her cute silly little gifts, not that he wasn't grateful (face it: he wasn't grateful) but it was embarrassing to him, Heidi Harkness leaving mysterious little things for "Sylvester Rampole" in his mailbox, so that people saw, and talked about them; and Heidi said coolly if Skyler didn't want the damn candy just throw it away, why's it a big deal, why's everything so complicated with him, and Skyler said again he wasn't angry at her, it was a trivial matter and not worth being angry about except he had to wonder: why red hearts? Heidi said he certainly looked angry, and she wasn't in the mood to indulge Skyler's bi-polar moods, she had bi-polar moods to contend with herself, Heidi turned to walk away and Skyler followed after her, Skyler was upset that Heidi would turn her back on him and walk away, and Heidi threw off his restraining hand, Heidi said she was tired of loving someone who didn't want her love, someone who clearly hated her, and Skyler protested he didn't hate her! he loved her. And Heidi said, hot tears splotching her cheeks, incensed, indignant, you could see that this was Leander Harkness's daughter drawing herself up to her full height of five-feet-nine, cursing Skyler for his God-damned selfish ways, he had not kissed her or even touched her let alone thanked her for the candies, just attacked her like a predator bird crazed for blood, she was becoming afraid of him, the strange things he sometimes said to her and didn't remember afterward, and his jealousy about her overnight visits in New York, and his jealousy about poor Elyot who was so lonely, and so unhappy, and Skyler was so far from being an observant friend, Skyler might as well have been blind; she didn't want to see him any longer, she was finished with him, her mother had warned her, if a boy lays his hands on you just once, if a boy tries to bully you just once, and Heidi was walking swiftly away, half-running, they were on a soggy wood-chip path down behind The Monument, Skyler had no choice but to run after her, grabbing at her arm, her thin wrist he might've snapped like a sparrow's wing, now holding the struggling girl still, trying to comfort her, Jesus he was sorry, he loved her, never wanted to hurt her not ever but she upset him sometimes, seemed to want to upset him, like tossing a lighted match into something flammable, and Heidi protested she did not, she never did, and Skyler had unzipped his jacket, and Heidi's parka, so that they could press together, frantically they kissed, Skyler gripped Heidi's head in his hands to kiss her, forcing open her lips, his tongue kissing hers, they whispered together, Skyler kissed away Heidi's tears, Heidi's chill hands were inside Skyler's clothing, palms of her hands against his back that had broken out in pimples, he hoped she couldn't feel, and Skyler's hands were inside Heidi's clothing, inside her prim-starched Basking Ridge shirt, and on the hot skin of her smooth back, and her breasts, small soft breasts that made his breath come short, that were lightly scarred like Braille from old cuts, he wanted to believe that these were old cuts and not recent cuts, for Heidi had promised him she would not cut herself ever again, as Heidi had promised him she would eat and gain weight, she would regain the fifteen pounds she'd lost, in the shelter of an enormous oak tree with exposed roots, gigantic misshapen roots like legs they held each other like drowning swimmers for such a long time pressed together in the shelter of the massive oak tree as a light snow fell melting on their faces, in a delirium of sensation their knees began to weaken, almost they could have fallen asleep and each

inhabiting the other's dream on their feet clutching at each other
Love love love you for eternity.*

SKYLER YOU WON'T BETRAY ME WILL YOU SKYLER

Won't talk about me   write about me ever Skyler
Promise Skyler?   not ever

YET: THE TV IN HEIDI'S ROOM TROUBLED SKYLER. AFTERNOON TV AL-
ways on, muted. It was to keep her company, Heidi said apologetically. Even if she wasn't watching, to keep her company.
Those afternoons after classes were over for the day and Skyler
slipped into Toll House by a rear/forbidden entrance, a hefty
door all the girls used, for such purposes; and hand-in-hand
drawn by breathless Heidi up the rear stairs to her room on the
third floor where Skyler's first act was to snatch up the remote
control and switch the God-damn TV off.

And Heidi's dance magazines on display in her room, for
some reason these troubled Skyler, too. Dance-fetish he thought
it. Like Bliss's fetish for ice-skating. It was applause they
wanted, displaying themselves that they would be loved, and
applauded. And Skyler knew why. And Skyler wished only to
protect Heidi. Neatly positioned on Heidi's windowsills were
glossy *Dancer, Dance Spirit, Young Dancer, Pointe.* And on the
walls, photographs of young ballerinas, white tulle tutus,
slender waists and flattened bodices, uplifted bare arms and
beautiful mask-faces offered to the viewer: *Love me, or I die.*
Though Heidi was evasive about her childhood eagerly she told
Skyler about her dance lessons at the Manhattan School of
Dance on West 85th Street, her mother had enrolled her when
Heidi was three and from that age to the age of fifteen she'd
taken lessons, she'd danced each year in school recitals and it
was said of her that she was "promising"—"very promising"—

---

* *I know: the reader is offended by such heavy-handed irony. Yet the worst of it is, I intend no irony at all. Skyler and Heidi felt exactly like this.*

but then, when her life had changed the previous year, she'd quit: "I lost my body." And Skyler knew not to ask her more, Skyler knew only that Heidi wanted to be comforted, held in Skyler's arms. And so Skyler held her.

Love me, or I die.

What a quirky way of arranging clothes in her closet, by color! Skyler had to smile, how like a *girl.* But he didn't smile seeing that Heidi had arranged her books by color as well, not in alphabetical order, or by subject, as Skyler did, and as it was necessary to do. Seeing such disorder, Skyler began to feel uneasy, annoyed. "Heidi, what's this? Are you serious? Arranging books by the purely arbitrary color of a book's spine? Steinbeck next to Brontë—Poe next to Shakespeare—" Heidi explained that she couldn't stand visual contrasts—"wrong colors together"—because they made her nervous. Skyler laughed at her expression of actual distress, pulling books off Heidi's shelves to deftly rearrange them, in alphabetical order, and Heidi tried to stop him, laughing, then suddenly they weren't laughing for Skyler was becoming annoyed by Heidi's childish behavior, nor did he appreciate Heidi trying to stop his hands, her voice rising—"Skyler! Red can't be next to green, and these zigzag lines will drive me crazy, this is barbaric," and Skyler said reprovingly, "Heidi, it's barbaric to arrange books by a scheme so crude as color," and Heidi said, "Jesus! I can't believe this, you are trying to rearrange my books, I love my books," and Skyler said, jeering, "These are mostly 'young adult' girls' books, how can you read such crap," and Heidi protested, "These are my b-books! This is my r-room! You have no right." Skyler was bemused, how genuinely upset Heidi had become. And how this wanly attractive girl resembled Leander Harkness scowling and spitting. Heidi came at Skyler with a look of fury—"Fuck you!"— and Skyler laughed, "Fuck *you*"—and Heidi cried, "I h-hate you"—and Skyler said, "Bitch, I hate *you*." Skyler was only joking and yet: a flame seemed to pass over his brain, in a rage Skyler swept a row of Heidi's color-coordinated books onto the floor with his arm, Heidi cursed Skyler going now for Skyler's face, caught him with a sharp fingernail beneath the right eye, Skyler cursed her grabbing her flailing arms, pinning her thin wrists together, Skyler was surprised by the manic strength of this girl who scarcely weighed one hundred pounds, it was the strength of sheer willfulness and opposition to him that shuddered through her. But Skyler was stronger, and Skyler had Heidi pinned on Heidi's bed. This was the bed upon which Skyler and Heidi often sprawled sharing a joint, dreamily kissing and whispering together, coiled together like great amorous snakes except now there was nothing amorous about them. Heidi bared her teeth at Skyler as if to bite him, and Heidi spat at Skyler—"I h-hate you! Bastard!" Skyler laughed pinning her down, panting and grunting and hoping to hell that one of the Toll House RA's (resident advisors) had not heard the commotion up on the third floor and would rush up the stairs to knock on Heidi Harkness's suspiciously locked door demanding that she open it.

But it was 6 P.M. Everyone was at dinner. Loved the way ▬▬▬▬ and she ▬▬▬▬▬ O God so sweet ▬▬▬▬▬ slept coiled together in ▬▬▬▬▬▬ rumpled bed through supper waking dazed at 8:20 P.M. and would have to eat from vending machines, again.

READER: WARNING
The sensitive reader, if there is one, is advised to skip this next yet more lurid memory of Skyler's. Though I have acknowledged that this document is deficient in erotic encounters, as in so much else, yet the following scene is so distasteful to me, I am including it only reluctantly, because it happened to Skyler. In the interests of accuracy I am obliged to include it; but the reader is not obliged to read it.

"S-SKYLER? I N-NEED YOU."

A call on Skyler's cell phone. Quickly Skyler comes to Heidi. Climbing the rear stairs to Heidi's room where the door is unlocked for him to enter. In the dim-lighted bedroom there is no one, in the dim-lighted bathroom the part-naked girl is lying on a large striped bath towel where she has cut herself— beneath her left breast, in feathery criss-crosses like a bizarre calligraphy across her flat belly—with a razor. "Oh. Heidi. Oh God." Skyler kneels beside the girl half-conscious and wanly smiling up at him, in the dim light her blood looks black like ink, or smudged purple lipstick Skyler kisses and licks as Heidi grips his hair like metal quills in her hand.

"Oh Skyler. Oh oh."

Skyler takes the razor and lightly cuts his forearm, feathery-light strokes for Skyler wants only to draw a little blood to mingle with his girl's hot blood bringing his forearm against her hot skin beneath her small breasts, in the curve of her belly. Skyler jams his mouth against Heidi's mouth, his teeth against Heidi's teeth. Skyler can't bear it ██████████ Heidi seizes his hand and guides it between her ██████████ haunted for the rest of their mortal lives

IV.

ABRUPTLY, IT ENDED.

As the reader knew it must end, maudlin *teen memory of a lost love.*

Yet, ironically: Skyler walked out of Heidi Harkness's life, or what remained of that life, just three days before Christmas recess at a time when he'd been planning to accompany his girlfriend on a visit to relatives of Heidi's slain mother, in their house on the Gulf of Mexico at Naples, Florida. ("Aunt Edie is dying to meet you, Skyler! I've told her everything about you—well, almost everything.")

Skyler Rampike's first visit to a girlfriend's family, ever.

Skyler thinking elated and anxious *This is normal life. This is what people do. This is what Skyler will do. Hope I can make it!*

"SKYLER? COME IN, BE RIGHT WITH YOU."

Skyler likes the casual way Heidi waves him inside, door to her bathroom ajar, perfumy steam escaping. *Normal!*

Skyler has dropped by Heidi's room before supper, to help Heidi with her chemistry lab report. Shutting the door to the hall behind him in violation of school rules.

(Are they sleeping together, those two? Generally it is assumed *yes*.)

First thing Skyler does when he enters Heidi Harkness's room is take up the TV remote control to switch the (muted, yet distracting) set *off*, except this time, Skyler stands staring at the screen seeing a very young girl-skater with fairy wings attached to her slender arms, mesmerized Skyler switches the volume *on*. Quick cut to the girl-skater at a slightly older age, in white tulle ballerina costume, skating in long looping graceful glides and turns to dreamy "Skaters' Waltz"—quick cut to the girl-skater in a sparkly red-sequined costume with very short skirt, peek of white lace panties, upswept blond hair glittering with stardust, skate-dancing to hot-thumping *Boléro*. Entranced Skyler watches as the amazing girl-skater glides effortlessly backward on blue-shimmering ice, performs such graceful leaps, turns, twirls, Skyler is feeling light-headed like one who has ventured dangerously close to the edge of a great height . . . Almost, he'd forgotten what an astonishing skater his young sister was, how wildly audiences applauded her . . . Sudden close-up of Bliss's face, sweet wistful smile beneath the glossy patina of the adroitly lipsticked little mouth and, beneath eye shadow, eyeliner, mascara those cobalt-blue eyes fixed upon him

Sky-ler?   Sky-ler where are you   help   Noise in Skyler's head it's as if Shank, Whack, Futt, Dream Bone and Arvo Pärt are simultaneously blasting into his ears cranked up loud as his Walkman can take sound. Yet at a distance he hears what must be a TV voice-over, and Heidi is calling to him from the bathroom where she seems to be running faucets, washing her hair, while Skyler comes to squat in front of the television set he ordinarily scorns, watching as the beautiful little blond girl-skater is gliding, leaping, twirling, shy smile flashing, cut to wildly applauding audience, cut to Bliss Rampike in strawberry satin-and-sequin skating dress with a perky tulle skirt, fishnet stockings and a peek of white-lace panties, skate-dancing to sexy-peppy disco "Do What Feels Right" and there is Mummy hugging Bliss, kissing/hugging/weeping in ecstatic triumph, tears streaming down young-Mummy's flushed cheeks, a shock to Skyler who has not seen young-Mummy in years, as he has not seen his more mature mother Betsey in several months. Now six-year-old Bliss Rampike of Fair Hills, New Jersey, is being wildly applauded by an audience of mostly females, now she is being crowned by—is it mammoth Jeremiah Jericho, notorious/much-beloved Master of Ceremonies of girls' competitive amateur figure ice-skating in New Jersey and vicinity who'd been found dead "under mysterious circumstances" in Atlantic City the previous year?—yet Jeremiah Jericho is aggressively alive on the screen, fairly bursting out of his sleazy-satin tux with valentine-hearts cummerbund, with a broad smile placing the glittery "silver" tiara on the child-skater's blond head proclaiming "LITTLE MISS JERSEY ICE PRINCESS 1996"—"Go craz-zy for Bliss Ram-pike, folks!" Cut to Hawk News Channel's *Christians Speak Out* show host Randy Riley greeting studio audience and TV audience with the pugnacious magnanimity of a warlord, ruddy Irish face, bulbous nose and prying eyes like mica chips, military bearing, U.S. flag pin in his lapel, Randy Riley is the most popular news-talk-show host on U.S. cable TV. Skyler is shocked to see that Randy Riley's guest this afternoon is Betsey Rampike, naive of Skyler to be shocked, yet Skyler is shocked, giddy and light-headed as if someone has swiped at him with an ether-soaked sponge.

You would think that Skyler would know better (Skyler does know better) than to continue to watch this interview, it is forbidden for Skyler to watch TV-Mummy and yet: Skyler will watch TV-Mummy as a large powdery-winged moth is drawn to open flame, to be extinguished. Brawny Randy Riley is surprising in his warmth toward Betsey Rampike—"heroic Betsey Rampike"—"bravest woman I know, Betsey Rampike"— indeed Betsey Rampike is smiling bravely at the loudly applauding studio audience, bravely Betsey smiles into the TV camera at the vast American heartland, Skyler sees that his mother is looking just perceptibly older, yet still girlish and attractive with a new hairstyle cut to flatter her moon-shaped and somewhat jowly face, Betsey's hair has been "lightened" to a coppery hue like a new-minted penny; Betsey's eyebrows have been artfully reshaped, and are more delicately arched; as always Betsey's lush red lips are glistening and fleshy and kissable; all of Betsey is glistening and fleshy and kissable; glamorous/maternal Betsey Rampike in a revealing knit dress of purple zigzags with a low neckline displaying the ruddy cleavage between her breasts. Randy Riley is congratulating Betsey Rampike on her "brilliant, bold new book"—"gut-wrenching fearless prose"—Randy Riley holds up to the camera a Christmassy green-and-red book *From Hell to Heaven: 11 Steps for the Faithful*. Randy Riley speaks with Betsey Rampike about her new memoir, "intimate reminiscences" of her champion-ice-figure-skater daughter who'd died "so hideously"—"victim of a sex maniac paroled after an outrageously light sentence by secular-progressive Democrats in New Jersey." As Betsey speaks in her breathy halting way, Randy Riley nods vehemently. So true! So true! All that Betsey Rampike says, so true! Betsey speaks of her Christian faith that has never failed her in even the darkest of times, when her innocent six-year-old beloved daughter was taken from her very bed, assaulted and murdered in the Rampikes' very house while her family slept unknowing above: "'Though I walk through the Valley of the Shadow of Death' rang in my ears for many years, through the loss of my marriage and the estrangement of my troubled son . . . we all must walk through that Valley, Randy; and we all must emerge. It is God's plan for us, that we survive." How Betsey's voice quavers! A single lustrous tear leaks from her shining left eye to run down her rouged cheek and disappear into a crack at the corner of her mouth. Randy Riley, visibly moved, surprises his guest by naming her "Christian Heroine of the Week"—Betsey hides her face like a little girl, as the audience applauds. Quick cut to Betsey Rampike at a White House ceremony—"Spirit of America Authors Awards 2003"—Betsey's hand is being shaken by a beaming President Bush, beaming Mrs. Bush, hefty American Eagle medallions are presented to several best-selling "inspirational" memoirists, the California minister-author of *The God-Driven Life*, and sci-fi author Michael Crichton. Back to Randy Riley who shifts the subject to politics: for Randy Riley is incensed at the "proliferation" of sex offenders in the United States, convicted hard-core criminals paroled and allowed to prowl our cities, stalk our innocent children, what are these sickos but symptoms of moral rot, the true agents of Satan are those left-leaning judges across the country, left-leaning educators, news media—the "hot-bed" is in the Northeast—New York City, the "sicko liberal capital"—"godless left-wingers"— "mockers of family values"—"pro-abortion fanatics"—"Ivy League kooks"—"Ivy League Marxists"—a crucial need for "get-tough-on-crime" legislation— "three strikes and you are *dead*." Randy Riley has worked himself into a sweat of patriotic indignation, thanking Betsey Rampike for being "such a shining role model" for American girls and women, congratulates her on the "spectacular success" of her Heaven Scent Products— "Out of the ashes of tragedy, a harvest is reaped—that is the American way."

Betsey is invited to explain to viewers how she'd inaugurated Heaven Scent Products in 1998 as a way of "helping to heal the festering wounds" of her personal tragedy. On display are a number of Heaven Scent products: Heaven Scent Cosmetic Kit— Heaven Scent Perfumes—Heaven Scent Bubble Bath—Heaven Scent Christmas Chocolates—Heaven Scent Accessories (scarves, belts, bracelets et al.)—Heaven Scent Betsey's Special Recipe Christmas Fruitcake: all these items available for immediate shipping. Next, there's an admiring buzz in the studio audience as Betsey proudly displays a Heaven Scent Bliss Rampike Doll: a startlingly lifelike replica of Bliss Rampike in miniature, with vivid blue glass eyes that open and shut, a sweet rosebud mouth, ultra-realistic skin and fine blond shoulder-length hair, movable arms and legs, detachable doll-size ice skates for the tiny feet. The Heaven Scent Bliss Rampike Doll is available with a selection of wigs, tiaras, and skating costumes (ballerina tulle, pleated silk, chiffon, satin-and-sequins, Cinderella, Snow White, cowgirl, Las Vegas showgirl, ballroom, disco, flamenco et al.)— "'Bliss' is being offered pre-Christmas for a base price of just $99.99; with a complete wardrobe plus ice skates, for just an additional $49.99."

Betsey speaks earnestly, wiping at her eyes, holding the life-like Bliss-doll in her lap just as Heidi enters the room toweling her long damp hair—"Ohhh that woman! Who is that awful woman! She is so—so totally—utterly—*gross*." Heidi is laughing, that brittle edgy laugh that so irritates Skyler; as Skyler continues to stare at the screen, Heidi hovers over him, jeering—"That woman, I've seen her before, she had a little girl—like that doll—who was an ice skater, she dressed the little girl like a slut and some sex maniac came and murdered the little girl—isn't she *awful*? And him, that nasty pig-snout man 'Riley'—why on earth are you watching these awful people, Skyler?" Skyler stumbles to his feet, there is a roaring in Skyler's ears, like a zombie Skyler makes his way to Heidi's door, can't breathe, choking and can't breathe, has to get out, Heidi calls after him, "Skyler? What's wrong? You look so—" coming to touch him, but Skyler can't bear to be touched, Heidi Harkness is wearing an electric blue thermal undershirt, flannel p.j. bottoms, her thick scuzzy wool socks, Heidi's hair is damp, her eyes hurt, petulant, peevish and her oddly crossed front teeth glisten as if jeering, Skyler pushes away her hand, Skyler murmurs what sounds like, "—mistake," out the door and Heidi follows after him incensed and disbelieving, "Skyler? What is—? Why—" and Skyler hears himself say, in a flat cold voice, "—don't love you, never loved you, it was a mistake, good-bye." Heidi is so astonished Skyler can hear the sharp intake of her breath. Skyler doesn't turn to her but limps away. If he has hurt her, good! She should be punished, like Skyler. Blindly Skyler pushes through the door to the stairs at the rear of the residence, blindly Skyler descends the stairs and limps outside into a ferocious wind.

No idea where he is. Valley of the Shadow of Death, maybe.

AFTER BLISS, HE CAN'T LOVE. NOT ANYONE. NOT EVER.

A sweaty fistful of pills, capsules, tablets Skyler manages to swallow down with several glasses of tepid water before he begins to puke, leaking water through his nose and in a delirium of exhaustion collapses onto his bed like debris dumped into rushing black water ▮▮▮▮▮▮▮ while as in an arty split-screen film of the 1970s a quarter-mile away on the far side of the nighttime campus Heidi Harkness manages to swallow down nine large OxyContin tablets and sinks into a heavy sleep ▮▮▮▮▮▮▮▮▮▮▮ discovered comatose in her room, rushed by ambulance to the nearest hospital in Summit, New Jersey, where she is reported to be in critical condition as Skyler sleeps in sweaty, tangled, and soon urine-soaked sheets unable to awaken, sleeps through the morning in his cramped little room at the top of Old Craghorne until early afternoon at last waking groggy, dry-mouthed and stunned as one who has been struck a powerful blow to the head thinking *Am I still here? O Jesus.*

Eventually, Skyler would learn of Heidi Harkness. He would come to learn the meaning of HSR.*

V.

1 January 2004

Dear Skyler—

This is a letter of condolence on the death of our friendship. It is my decision after much thought that I do not want to speak with you ever again nor even see you.

---

* *The canny reader will have deciphered "HSR" in the previous chapter but for those others who, like Skyler, hadn't a clue, it means High Suicide Risk.*

I am not accusing you of provoking Heidi to act despairingly as she did because I do not want to know the extent of your guilt. I do not want to hate you for I do not believe in hatred, it is the curse of our species.

Skyler, good-bye.

Your former friend,

E. Grubbe

EPILOGUE: FIRST LOVE, FAREWELL!*

*Hey: down here. Skyler is down here. A long time then Skyler dwelt in footnotes at the bottoms of pages. After Heidi Harkness disappeared from Basking Ridge, and was never to return, in whatever "condition" Heidi Harkness was even the avid scribblers of Tabloid Hell were in disagreement, even where she was, if hospitalized, or somewhere "private" with relatives, or keepers—even after Heidi, Skyler Rampike was allowed to remain at the Academy at Basking Ridge though he no longer attended most of his classes, and the surreal-high grades of brainy "Sylvester Rampole" plummeted to the nether regions in which dwelt the most severely disabled/"challenged"/plain weird of his classmates. No need to inform the reader, Skyler scored plenty of drugs while dwelling in such nether regions. You would, too. Yet, unlike the other users at Basking Ridge, who craved one another's company like aphids, Skyler Rampike shunned the company of others. He did not ever hear from Heidi Harkness of course. (He may have believed she was dead. He didn't keep up with news.) He had lost his only friend Elyot Grubbe. (He did not make any attempt to reconcile with Elyot for he believed that Elyot's judgment of him was just.) (In any case, Elyot soon became friendly with another solitary boy, gifted like himself, and musically inclined; Skyler glimpsed them from afar sometimes, listening to music through twin earphones and frowning over a shared musical score.) It's reasonable for the reader to wonder why the Academy at Basking Ridge did not hurriedly expel Skyler Rampike and the reason is a simple one: Bix Rampike had paid the considerable tuition and room-and-board for his son through June 12, 2004, and had no intention of allowing Skyler to leave early; threatened with an enormous lawsuit, Headmaster Shovell quickly acquiesced. (For neither Betsey nor Bix Rampike wished to make a home for a chronically disturbed adolescent boy of five-feet-ten with sociopathic and possibly suicidal tendencies, do you blame them?) Later, Skyler would be recycled to yet another prep school. Or was it a treatment center. At which time prowling stores in which such publications are sold, Skyler was rewarded for scavengering in sewage by discovering, in an October 2004 issue of SleezeWatch Week, a tantalizingly blurry photograph allegedly taken at the Academy at Basking Ridge of Leander Harkness's daughter Heidi as she stood in the shelter of an enormous oak tree with exposed roots, in the impassioned embrace of an "unidentified male" believed to be an instructor at the "exclusive" prep school famous for "catering to" the sons and daughters of the wealthy disgraced. The photo was of Skyler and Heidi!—presumably taken in stealth by an audacious paparazzo as the unsuspecting teen couple hugged, kissed, whispered together in lightly falling snow. Shameless Skyler tore the page out of SleezeWatch Week without paying for the magazine, cherished this sole photograph of himself and Heidi Harkness for some time though eventually he lost it as Skyler lost most things.

VI

Pilgrimage to Hell and Back

THE SUMMONS

PLEASE COME!   SO LONG I HAVE PRAYED

we would be reconcilled   *darling*
soon to undergoe surgery   *pray to see you before*
loving Mother meant well   *Skyler*

He hadn't gone. Weeks ago she'd summoned him. And more recently, she'd summoned him. He had not gone to her. He had not. Yet now, he was going. He was going. He'd waked from a sleep leaden like death and now: he was going to her.

And if it's too late, and she has died. And if. She'd said *surgery*. That word and no more and like a knife it had cut him for his first thought was *cancer*.

Cancer was the thought. And *death*.

HE HAD PROMISED PASTOR BOB, HE WOULD GO TO THE WOMAN. HE WOULD GO to her. He would not forgive her but he would go to her. And Pastor Bob had said, A man is strong to the degree to which he can forgive those who injured him. A man is weak, to the degree to which he can't forgive. Crudely Skyler laughed. Panicked Skyler laughed. Skyler had a nervous habit of jamming a thumb nail between two of his lower front teeth as if to pry them out. Saying, Pastor Bob, fuck *forgive*, okay? I am trying just to comprehend what there might be required to forgive. My quest is epistemological,*

---

* *Classy word! Pertaining to "the study or a theory of the nature and grounds of knowledge, esp. with reference to its limits and validity." (Webster's Ninth New Collegiate Dictionary) Yet Skyler is correct in using it for there is no other so appropriate word as, when Skyler claims that*

before it can be moral. My quest is to know why I am so fucking confused, at the age of nineteen I will have to be told by the one who has destroyed me what it is I know.

HE HAD NOT SHOWN PASTOR BOB EITHER OF THE LETTERS HIS MOTHER HAD sent him. Not the letter received by Skyler weeks ago in January signed *Your Loving Mother Mummy.* Not the second letter which was dated Valentine's Day. (And why Valentine's Day? We know, Mummy and Skyler!) These handwritten letters on perfumy-peach-stationery Skyler had wrapped in newspaper sheets to block the powerful scent from his sensitive nostrils and to hide on a closet shelf. These letters he had not so much as glanced at since receiving them yet could not destroy. As the hapless reader can attest, he'd been preoccupied with spilling his guts out in these pages. Ever more lurid, these pages. Shameless tabloid-sewage, these pages. For Heidi Harkness had begged him not to write about her and in his desperation to purge himself of the poison in his guts, he has betrayed her. For in writing about Heidi in this way, Skyler has discovered that he loves her. That he has betrayed her, he loves her. That he is sick with guilt for having betrayed her, he loves her. *Heidi if you are alive and if you read these words Heidi forgive me.*

Hunched over his worktable, over these scattered pages like a deformed foot.

THIS FINAL SECTION OF MY HARD-WON DOCUMENT, TRACING SKYLER'S QUIX- otic pilgrimage to Spring Hollow, New York, will surely be much shorter than preceding sections, and will bring Skyler's "epic" journey to an end. For those readers who persist in believing that tragic art yields *katharsis* (Gr.)—at least, great tragic art—I will dangle before you the hope that *katharsis* will be achieved in the concluding pages of *My Sister, My Love.* If not . . .

Reader, I can't bring myself to contemplate *If not.*

---

he is so fucked-up he will have to be told by his mother what he already knows, he is essentially correct.

THE ARK

NOW HE HAD TO HURRY! NOW EVERY PULSE IN HIS BODY WAS THROBBING IN exultation, and in dread.

Ran/limped a quarter-mile to The Ark on Hurtle Avenue. "The Ark"— the barn-sized house/rectory in which Pastor Bob Fluchaus lived with an ever-shifting household of assistants, church volunteers, "family."

Skyler Rampike had been given to know *You are of my family, son.*

From the street, The Ark looked like an old sailing ship dumped in a city lot. It was a run-down old mansion of three floors and numberless rooms with steep slate roofs, Victorian turrets and trim, a front entrance framed by pillars like a Greek temple. Hurtle Avenue was a neighborhood of large showy houses now shuttered, abandoned, or converted to apartments and small businesses. Before Skyler had met Pastor Bob, well-intentioned New Canaan volunteers had begun painting the rectory as a gesture of good will for their much-beloved pastor but the daffodil-yellow paint they'd chosen for the house dried to a sharp mustard color and so only the front of the house had been painted, the sides and rear remained the original gunmetal-gray. From the pulpit Pastor Bob declared in his deadpan-comic manner: "Jesus would feel right at home in The Ark. 'The life is more than meat, and the body is more than raiment.'"

His ministry, Pastor Bob said, was for all who required healing. "In this way, I hope to be healed myself."

Pastor Bob was on the phone, on his feet in his office when Skyler arrived breathless and excited and eager to borrow one of the church vehicles to drive to Spring Hollow, New York. First thing Pastor Bob said was: "You may want a companion on your drive, son."

It was the way of the pastor of the New Canaan Evangelical Church of Christ Risen to confront excitable individuals with calm. For there was his young friend Skyler Rampike looking like a terrified diver on a high board about to catapult himself into space.

Quickly Skyler shook his head, no. Didn't want a companion.

Skyler's face was still bruised, weirdly swollen and discolored. Stitches in his left eyebrow and near his mouth were leaking blood. He had not washed in some time and smelled of his body. He had shaved for the first time in weeks and his jaws were scraped and splotched with tiny blood-beads. He wore a filthy pea-jacket, jeans and combat boots. His prematurely gray hair stiff as quills he'd slicked back damp and clumsily braided at the nape of his neck in a six-inch rat-tail.

Trying not to stammer Skyler stated: "I'm nineteen, Pastor Bob. I will be twenty next month. God damn *I am not a child.*"

Pastor Bob was not one to smile readily. Pastor Bob doled out his smiles with care. And when Pastor Bob smiled in a certain slant-way, a way of calculation, meditation, the burn-scar tissue on the left side of his face shone like scales. His large limpid perpetually damp eyes shone with something like sympathy, but not credulity. By profession he was a Born Again kindly-Christ sort of guy but by nature (you'd hear that Bob Fluchaus had been a sergeant in the U.S. Army in the 1980s, later a guard at Rahway State Prison) he had to laugh at bullshit. Like Skyler Rampike quivering before him claiming not to be a child.

"Son, we all need companions. In our hours of peril."

Skyler gnawed at his lower lip. *Fuck son. Who's a son.*

"I'm not in p-peril! It's only a few hours on the expressway. You know you can trust me, Pastor Bob. You've said you trust me." Skyler paused, hearing these words: were they true? "—I have a license and I've driven the station wagon already, I can drive it now."

This was so. Improbable as it might sound to the skeptical reader, who has assumed that Skyler has spent most of his time in New Brunswick holed up in his lurid rented room composing this wayward and unpredictable document, in fact Skyler had acquired a New Jersey State driver's license, with Pastor Bob's assistance, the previous summer. He had helped Pastor Bob out from time to time. For always at The Ark there was work to be done, and mostly volunteers to do it. Skyler had not been wholly reliable for he was one to appear, and then to disappear. In Pastor Bob Fluchaus's life as a volunteer counsellor at the Middlesex Rehabilitation Clinic and as minister of the New Canaan Evangelical Church of Christ Risen such abrupt appearances and disappearances were not uncommon.

Sometimes the disappearances were permanent. One day to the next, you never knew.

If (for instance) despairing Skyler Rampike had doused himself with lighter fluid and struck a match to himself not long ago in the chill city park overlooking the Raritan River. A flaming mannequin he'd have appeared to astonished onlookers, fiery and spectacular but short-lived and New Brunswick police officers would have contacted Bob Fluchaus over at New Canaan *Sorry Pastor: looks like another one of yours.*

Another of the good pastor's ex-junkie losers, lost.

If! But it had not happened, and Skyler was feeling damned good about that now. *HSR* means you have always the challenge of resisting your fate for a while longer.

In rehab, Skyler had told Pastor Bob about his HSR diagnosis, and many others. Skyler had confided in Pastor Bob to a degree to which Skyler would not have believed possible, and sometimes came to wonder if he'd spilled too much of his guts.

(Too many of his guts? Whichever.)

(Yet: the reader knows as much of Skyler Rampike as Pastor Bob was given to know. The fallacy being, the more you know of an individual, the less. As, knowing so much about yourself, reader, the less certainty with which you could summarize yourself. Yes?)

Clumsy Skyler trying to joke: "Pray for me, Pastor Bob? That I don't arrive at my m-mother's house too l-l-late."

Skyler smiled a sick-smirk-smile to signal to the frowning older man that for sure he wasn't serious, did not believe in prayer for *What is prayer?* but earnest deluded individuals talking to themselves and expecting to be answered.

Not Skyler! Skyler harangued himself virtually non-stop but didn't expect any answers.

But Pastor Bob didn't smile. Never smiled when such anxious jokes were made for one who has chosen to follow the path laid down by Jesus Christ knows that you can't help the walking wounded by laughing with them at the possibility that their wounds can't be healed. Especially the wounded know this, and are continually testing you.

"Will you call your mother first, Skyler? I'd advise it."

Pastor Bob was rummaging through a drawer, in search of the station wagon keys. Skyler took heart.

"I don't have a number for . . ." Skyler hesitated not knowing what to call the woman who was, or who'd once been, his mother. Mother? Betsey? ". . . her."

Pastor Bob cursed mildly searching through the drawer which contained numerous keys. His worktable was situated in the center of a cavernous room that might've been, at one time, judging from a tarnished chandelier overhead, a formal dining room of some pretensions. The wallpaper had been painted over but the ceiling was white stucco, intricately and beautifully molded. A bay window overlooking noisy Hurtle Avenue was comprised of leaded glass panes. Underfoot was a scuffed hardwood floor, missing a rug. The front foyer was large as the front foyer in the Grubbe house, or the McGreety house, had been, but its furnishings were utilitarian and there was no mirror to greet you.

"Son, here." Pastor Bob laid the keys onto the table but in so tentative a way, Skyler understood that some instruction would accompany them. A glimpse at Pastor Bob Fluchaus, you understood that here was a man to preach the Gospel: and what is the Gospel of Jesus Christ but *good news*? Even Skyler who could not believe in much beyond $2 + 2 = 4$ had to concede *All things are possible to him that believeth.*

For always Skyler was pleading with Pastor Bob, in yearning glances *I believe: help thou my unbelief.*

Pastor Bob was explaining to Skyler that, since he'd procrastinated visiting his mother, it might be the case that, by the time he arrived, she'd had the surgery, and was still hospitalized; or, and Skyler should be prepared for this—"The surgery might not have been successful."

Skyler wasn't hearing this. A buzzing in Skyler's head and he wasn't hearing much that Pastor Bob was telling him except the reiteration of *son/Skyler* which was both an irritant and a comfort to one who'd been spending so much time alone.

"Or, circumstances might have changed—and your mother isn't home. My impression is, Betsey Rampike is a very busy 'public' woman, and travels a good deal."

Skyler wanted to protest *But she has summoned me to her! She will be waiting for me.*

With childlike obstinacy Skyler said, "The last letter my mother wrote to me was dated February fourteenth. Today is the twentieth, that hasn't been so long."

"Son, today is the twenty-seventh."

Twenty-seventh! Skyler swallowed hard.

"You see, you've procrastinated. You've been afraid."

God damn Skyler would've liked to ease the car keys out from beneath the older man's hand like an audacious teenaged son taunting/flirting with his frowning daddy, but Skyler knew better. Pastor Bob could play with you, but you could not play with Pastor Bob except by his decree. Pastor Bob wouldn't have hesitated to pound Skyler's hand flat against the table with his fist.

Pastor Bob was a large intimidating six-foot-five barrel-chested man of some mysterious age—late forties? early fifties? older?—with a way of breathing heavily through his mouth as if his nasal passages were blocked and indeed his nose looked somewhat flattened, chastened. He exuded an air both rueful and dignified. His sculpted-looking head reminded Skyler of Roman busts he'd seen in a museum. Grizzled gray hair lifted from his head like brush-bristles. His mouth was distinct, chiseled. His eyes were what you'd call "piercing"—alert, avid. His voice was a thrilling deep-baritone that scarcely needed amplifying from the pulpit at the New Canaan church where on crowded folding chairs, for Sunday services, somewhere beyond eight hundred people often gathered. The entire left side of his face was layered in burn-scar-tissue like scales. You stared in fascination. You could not look away. The first time Skyler had seen Pastor Bob, when Skyler had been very sick, he'd stared at the ravaged man as a child might stare, rudely, naively, and Pastor Bob had chuckled saying: "Looks like a Hallowe'en pumpkin that caught fire, eh son? Want to touch it?"

In fact, Skyler had wanted to touch the big man's boiled-looking face. Pastor Bob took Skyler's hand and drew it slowly over the snarled-smooth scales, that were very warm, as if such a gesture was the most natural thing in the world.

Later, Skyler would understand that this was a gesture that Pastor Bob made frequently. Whenever anyone stared at him. There was something sweetly vain in it, boastful. At the county rehab clinic, everyone had wanted to touch the evangelical minister's fiery skin. Everyone had wanted to be "saved" by Pastor Bob. He was frank in confiding in them that he'd for sure wanted to die for a long time after his accident—though other motorists had been involved, the accident, on the New Jersey Turnpike, was "his"—but eventually he'd come round to accepting how he looked. He'd had eight operations on his face alone for he'd suffered second- and third-degree burns over 3o percent of his body and what remained with him two decades later was the wisdom of Burn Ward: " 'Some skin is a damn lot better than no skin.' Like, in matters of the soul, some 'soul' is a damn lot better than none."

Skyler had shivered. Such words stirred him powerfully. He was too enfeebled at the time for doubt, cynicism. Such intricacies of the spirit were exhausting, at such a time. When you're a near-drowned swimmer sunken beneath the surface of the water and someone extends a straw to you—skinny, bent, near-to-breaking—through which to breathe, you breathe.

And you were damn grateful. You didn't complain about the cheap quality of the paper straw.

You didn't complain of your rescuer. You adored your rescuer.

Pastor Bob was saying it wasn't the Dodge station wagon he was concerned about, it was Skyler who he didn't think should be driving alone right now. "I'd come with you myself except there's a family crisis I have to deal with here but if you could wait maybe an hour, I think I can line up someone to drive with you . . ."

"D'you think I'm using, Pastor Bob? You don't trust me?"

A fevered look to Skyler's face, something mismatched about his eyes. But Skyler is not using, Pastor Bob must know.

There came a woman named Miriam to set cups of coffee out for Skyler and Pastor Bob but Skyler was hesitant to lift the steaming liquid to his mouth, too hot, too strong. Caffeine would make him even crazier than he was.

Skyler's mouth was dry, he'd been swallowing compulsively.

Eyeing the keys to the station wagon, on the table. Badly he wanted to snatch them up, and run.

Nineteen. In a few weeks, twenty. And his life has come to this: ex-junkie loser, begging.

Pastor Bob was saying: "Your face, Skyler? Are those stitches? Did someone assault you? Kick you? It doesn't look as if those wounds are healing, son. You keep picking at them with your fingernails . . ."

Skyler touched his face in chagrin. His fingers came away damp: blood?

"Let Miriam look at you, Skyler. Miriam is a nurse."

"Pastor Bob, I need to see my mother. I have to see her now."

"Son, I know. But you don't want to put yourself in danger, or her."

Or her: what's that mean?

Does Pastor Bob think that Skyler is so distraught, he might try to harm his mother?

What a strange electricity there was to The Ark! Like the electricity in the New Canaan Church (formerly a food canning factory, remodeled as a vast meeting hall) when Pastor Bob roamed restlessly about the brightly lighted platform speaking earnestly and urgently and fixing each individual in each folding chair with his fierce somber gaze. Skyler was never equal to it. Skyler was frightened as hell of it. Though he'd flunked out of Basking Ridge—that is, doomed "Sylvester Rampole" had flunked out—he had learned in chemistry class that if you weren't sufficiently grounded—or was it, if you were grounded?—electricity ran through you and stopped your heart in an instant.

Charisma, it was. Big-Daddy Bix Rampike radiated charisma too, like sweat-drops shaken off Big-Daddy's handsome head.

Pastor Bob laid a hand on Skyler's shoulder. To comfort, or to restrain.

" 'The wind bloweth where it will.' All right. But let Miriam tend to you, son. And take a shower before you leave, and change into clean clothes. We can provide you with clean clothes. You can't go to your mother in her hour of need looking the way you do, son. You look like death, and you smell. You just can't do that, son."

With a show of sudden confidence, though very likely the canny evangelical minister felt a deep distrust of the situation and of his own complicity in it, Pastor Bob pushed the keys to the Dodge station wagon in Skyler's direction. A phone had been ringing, and Pastor Bob turned to answer it. "Yes? I'm here." His voice betrayed a mild exasperation tempered by hope. Skyler signaled *Thanks!* Taking up the keys, he had to believe he had earned, though made to grovel and plead like any supplicant son.

Skyler was led away by Nurse Miriam who chided him for having picked at his stitches. It must have been, Skyler and Miriam knew each other: Skyler hadn't paid much attention to the woman in this scene, as, in recasting the exchange now, I have purposefully omitted others who'd been coming and going in the background, as in a very amateur or very arty film; for always at The Ark, there were people; faces familiar to Skyler, and faces wholly unknown; there was even a nervously barking dog, somewhere at the rear of the house; phones ringing, footsteps on the stairs, cries of, "Pastor Bob? Got a minute?"—so resented by Skyler Rampike, who wanted attention exclusively on himself, they were virtually filtered out, and are vanished from my memory.

Except Miriam. Here was Miriam, one of Pastor Bob's "inner" family, living at The Ark, as Skyler belonged to the "outer" family. Many times since leaving rehab Skyler had eaten meals prepared by Miriam and others, and Skyler had helped out in the kitchen grateful to be included. For all her authority Miriam had the look of an ex-user, too. That guardedness about the eyes, that eagerness to be wholly *in the moment.* Miriam was younger than Betsey Rampike but had a soft raddled face like Betsey Rampike's face and a soft-sliding-voluptuous body like Betsey Rampike's body except Miriam in stained work-trousers, man's flannel shirt over a T-shirt, a kerchief around her head, was in no way glamorous like sexy-Mummy Betsey Rampike. Yet her eyes fastened on lanky-late-teen Skyler with a chiding-maternal intimacy: "These stitches! Lucky you aren't infected, the way you've been picking at them with dirty fingernails."

In his psycho-sick-kid career Skyler had come to believe that most ailments are psycho-caused: psycho-somatic. What exactly *is* an infection? Something in the blood, like an invasion? Could an infection be fatal?

Shamed Skyler was made to sit at a sink. Deftly Miriam removed the ghastly stitching with a small scissors. A torment of violent itching, he'd have clawed at with his nails except Miriam caught his hands. "No! Just stop." Miriam washed his face, that throbbed as if with fever, in lukewarm water; Miriam applied *All-Sterile 70% Isopropyl Alcohol First Aid Antiseptic* to his wounds, and covered them with oddly shaped starkly white Band-Aids. In a mirror Skyler gaped at himself, shocked: That was *him*?

"Pray your face will heal without scars. Try to keep your hands *off*."

Next, Skyler showered. First time in many days, shameful to admit. Without unraveling the rat-tail he managed to shampoo his straggly hair. How good it felt to wash himself, to stand beneath a pelting shower with his eyes shut, faint with gratitude. He loved Pastor Bob, who had treated him with such kindness. Almost, he loved Miriam who had bathed his wounds so tenderly. Of the great archetypes of which our spiritual lives are seemingly comprised, that of Father-Son/Mother-Son is ubiquitous. When Skyler blundered into The Ark that morning with his usual lack of foresight, like a naive swimmer diving into a ten-foot surf, he could not have anticipated a happy ending.

Here is what I have learned, from the effort of composing this document: Not all "symbolic" occasions are contrived. Some spring naturally from "life."

Awaiting Skyler after his shower were fresh-laundered clothes: baggy cotton T-shirt, boxer shorts, brown trousers that fitted him too loosely at the waist and too short in the legs, a wool flannel shirt of Pastor Bob's and heavy-duty white wool socks.

In the kitchen, Miriam insisted upon providing Skyler with a light lunch for the trip, since he hadn't wanted to eat breakfast at The Ark; she pressed upon him a Thermos filled with fresh-squeezed orange juice. As if Skyler were driving a thousand miles and not less than one hundred: Skyler stammered thanks. A sudden urge came over him, to seize the woman's hand and kiss it.

Miriam didn't know who he was. Only Pastor Bob knew. Skyler's secret was safe with Pastor Bob. He believed this.

Love love love you all! Someday, I will know how to show this.

But where was Pastor Bob? Not in his office? Skyler had hoped that the minister would still be around to say good-bye to him and to warn him about driving carefully but Pastor Bob had departed for his morning crisis. Miriam led Skyler through the rectory to a rear door opening into the garage where the battered old 2001 Dodge station wagon was parked. On its sides hand-lettered in bronze paint: NEW CANAAN EVANGELICAL CHURCH OF CHRIST RISEN.

"Skyler, we love you. Jesus will be your companion."

FREE FALL

He drove. On I-95 he drove. Gripping the steering wheel of the battered old Dodge station wagon he drove. In the right-hand lane of the thunderous Turnpike he drove. He drove at no more than the speed limit as eighteen-wheel trailer-trucks overtook his vehicle and passed him in derisive clouds of toxic exhaust. He drove! He drove bravely gritting his teeth. He drove sitting straight behind the wheel as the driver of a military vehicle loaded with explosives. Yet he drove fearless! He drove with determination and with concentration. He drove into the bright wintry-windy day. He drove into a bright wintry-windy day of a month/year he could not now have named. *Son, today is the twenty-seventh. Son, you don't want to put yourself in danger, or her.* He drove into wintry sunshine glaring from the chrome of hurtling vehicles. He drove beneath a fantastical sky of high-scudding white clouds beautiful as no clouds he'd ever seen except, as Heidi Harkness giggled and squirmed in Sky's ropey-muscled boy-arms, on the insides of his eyelids after ingesting a few grainy grains of exotic-named *foxy methoxy* his girl had smuggled back from a Thursday in Manhattan but why think of this now, now it's too late. Grimly he drove. Undaunted he drove. Not-thinking of Heidi Harkness and not-thinking of Elyot Grubbe required enormous concentration as he drove. At age nineteen years, eleven months and three weeks he drove. He drove in despair that he would live to his twentieth birthday. He drove in despair that he would ever make sense of his life. He drove now hunched slightly forward as if clinging to the steering wheel. He drove gripping the steering wheel of Pastor Bob's old Dodge station wagon tight in both big-knuckled hands as if expecting the wheel to twist suddenly and cata-pult the clumsy rattling station wagon emblazoned NEW CANAAN EVAN-GELICAL CHURCH OF CHRIST RISEN through the concrete median and into oncoming traffic and fiery oblivion. He drove thinking *It could be so quick.* He drove thinking *With Skyler's luck, it would not be quick.* He drove hearing Grandmother Rampike's sharp voice *Going to be a cripple? Going to limp, for life?* He drove with exasperating slowness in the right-hand lane for he was not a confident driver. He drove at less than sixty-five miles-per-hour for beyond that speed the station wagon began to shake and shudder. He drove past the exit for EDISON and at once his brain (hip-pocampus?) began to throw off sparks of Repressed Memory* quickly blocked. He drove past EDISON, and he drove past METUCHEN. He drove past such lyric New Jersey exits as RAHWAY†—ELIZABETH—NEWARK—NEWARK AIRPORT—UNION CITY—WEEHAWKEN—HACKENSACK. He drove with mounting anxiety not knowing why. He drove recalling the first time he'd attended prayer services at the New Canaan Evangelical Church of Christ Risen at Pastor Bob's invitation and how mesmerized he'd been by the minister's sermon to the mixed-race, mixed-age congregation on the "eternal good news" of the Gospels. Recalling Pastor Bob's weirdly scaly burn-scar face and deep-baritone voice he drove. In awe of the man's shrewd/kindly eyes that seemed to single out each individual in the hall he drove. He drove recalling his conviction *This is it, where I belong.* He drove hearing again the minister's voice echoing as in the aftermath of a powerful dream: " 'I am come a light into the world that whosoever believeth in me shall not abide in darkness.' " He drove wiping tears from his eyes. He drove without hope and yet—with what hope! Seeing GEORGE WASHINGTON BRIDGE 2 MI. he drove beginning to sweat inside his odd-fitting clothes. He drove beginning to think yes, probably it had been a mistake, this journey. To set off without having called his mother first, as Pastor Bob

---

* *Remember? Skyler doesn't want to recall how long ago Bix Rampike carelessly promised him he'd take him to visit the Thomas Edison museum here.*
† EDISON *has stirred dim sensations of hurt, loss, abandonment;* RAHWAY *reminds Skyler of Gun-ther Ruscha who'd served a brief prison sentence in the Sex Offenders' Unit of Rahway State Prison for Men. (No wonder Skyler will shortly blunder a crucial Turnpike exit.)*

had suggested. Yet he drove somehow convinced that he would see her, he could not be prevented from seeing her, for she had summoned *him*. Hearing his fumbling voice—"M-Mother: remember me? I am Sk-Sk-Skyler"—he drove. Rehearsing the words he would utter if a stranger greeted him at the door of 9 Magnolia Terrace, Spring Hollow, New York: "I am Sk-Skyler Rampike. I am B-Betsey Rampike's s-son." He drove unable to remember when he'd last seen his mother. Not TV-Mummy but in life. Two years ago? Three? In the life of an adolescent three years is a very long time for adolescence itself is infinity. After TV-Mummy and the break-up with Heidi Harkness Skyler could not bear to think of his mother and refused to accept any call from her even when he was summoned to Headmaster Shovell's office to accept such a call he'd refused *No! no I can't, not ever I hate her* and now he drove recalling these angry words with shame for had not Pastor Bob warned him *We must forgive those who have wronged us, Skyler lest our hatred turn to poison in our bowels.*

Distracted by such thoughts he lost his way. For a confused moment he lost his way. Having glimpsed an exit sign for GEORGE WASHINGTON BRIDGE impulsively he exited and discovered belatedly that he'd made a mistake, had no idea what he'd done wrong but it was wrong for now he was headed not for the bridge but for FORT LEE, New Jersey. And abruptly now in slow-congested traffic moving with the sluggish peristalsis of a blocked colon his speed was reduced to five miles an hour. Above, the sky was choked with clouds like distended/discolored tumors. Heavy stacked cumulus rain-clouds, shit-clouds shaped like hydrogen-bomb explosions. How had it happened, Skyler who was so anxious to arrive at Spring Hollow, New York, had missed the George Washington Bridge? How is it possible to "miss" so mammoth/magisterial a structure as the George Washington Bridge? Yet neither the "upper level" nor the "lower level" could Skyler approach for he was lost in Fort Lee, New Jersey: a rat's maze/sinkhole of narrow, one-way, dead-end and under-excavation streets. He would never get to Spring Hollow! He would never arrive at his destination! He began to sob in hoarse guttural sobs like choking. He began to curse—"Fuck! Fuck *fuck*!"—for there was no one to blame except Skyler himself, his own stupidity and ill-luck which is but a form of stupidity and yet: Skyler had no choice but to continue, had he? As the Möbius strip has no choice but to turn endlessly? In a slow crawl of exhaust-smitten traffic on N. Syke Street in Fort Lee, New Jersey . . .

POOR SKYLER! THWARTED MIDWAY IN HIS JOURNEY TO SPRING HOLLOW, NEW York, and for all we know, maybe he never arrives there. While Skyler is lost in *medias race* in Fort Lee, New Jersey, we can use the lull in the narrative to present a miscellany of items too unwieldy to have "worked into" previous chapters.

For instance, throughout this seemingly candid document Skyler has been purposefully reticent about his relations with his parents. The unsuspecting reader would think from "First Love, Farewell!" that Bix and Betsey rarely made any attempt to contact their troubled son, having more or less abandoned him to psychiatric facilities and "high-security" prep schools; the fact is, Betsey did telephone Skyler from time to time at the Academy at Basking Ridge; if not Betsey personally, one of Betsey's cheery female assistants at Heaven Scent, Inc., leaving messages for Skyler to please call back. (But Skyler never did.) Shortly before Betsey's appearance on the Randy Riley show, the first step in Betsey Rampike's twenty-city book tour for her new memoir *From Hell to Heaven: 11 Steps for the Faithful*, Betsey's Heaven Scent partner/financial advisor/romantic companion Nathan Kissler placed several urgent calls to Skyler in the hope of introducing himself over the phone to Betsey's son, of whom he had heard numerous troubling things, but of course Skyler had not returned these calls; Mr. Kissler had sent a lengthy, thoughtfully written e-mail to Skyler explaining his role in Skyler's mother's life as her "closest friend and advisor"; this e-mail Skyler had in fact received, jeeringly skimmed and deleted within seconds, as one might delete an obscene advertisement from the computer screen. Poor Mr. Kissler, deeply in love with Betsey Rampike and determined to be a "father, of a kind" to Betsey's problem-son, sent Skyler the hard copy of this e-mail, via certified U.S. mail; which Skyler accepted, imagining that the envelope might contain a check from Betsey and when it did not, tearing up the heartfelt letter in typical adolescent *pick*.

Reader, what was I to do? Believe me, if I had introduced this distracting material into the melancholy love story of Skyler Rampike and Heidi

Harkness, teen-exiles of Tabloid Hell who had, for a brief enchanted spell, "found each other" at the Academy at Basking Ridge, the result would have been as jarring as, let's say, a sudden eruption of John Philip Sousa into the ethereal musical meditations of Estonian Arvo Pärt. You would all have hated it, and reviewers would have savagely denounced such a blatant change of tone in all violation of Aristotelian unity.

Another omission from "First Love, Farewell!" is Skyler's silence on the subject of finances: who is paying for such exorbitantly expensive private schools as the Academy at Basking Ridge,* for the sulky Skyler; who is paying for Skyler's exorbitantly expensive medications, most of which, in defiance of doctors' orders, he refused to take, or—is the reader shocked?—sold to certain of his Old Claghorne fellow residents, who felt the need to self-medicate at any opportunity. (The reader will be shocked to hear that Skyler dealt the powerful antidepressant Zilich on a regular basis to a boy on his floor so physically and psychically impaired, the diagnosis HSR might have been branded on the boy's forehead; Skyler took from this "collateral kid"—as the offspring of disgraced public figures were called, by themselves as by others at Basking Ridge—as much as one hundred dollars per week, and felt little guilt, or none, when the boy overdosed, whether deliberately or accidentally, and was hurriedly removed from the school as, a few weeks later, Heidi Harkness would be removed. But not a hint of this shameful episode did you hear from Skyler, right?)

Though Skyler was rarely other than slovenly dressed at Basking Ridge, showered only sporadically and wore the same grungy clothes for days in succession, the reader should know that his parents, especially Betsey, provided him with a generous "clothes and living allowance"; neither Betsey nor Bix ever forgot Skyler's birthday in March, directing their assistants to acquire appropriate *happy-birthday-son* cards for him, that they signed *with love*, to accompany birthday presents: from Betsey, usually an expensive cable-knit pull-over sweater, and from Bix, a sports-related gift, for

---

* *Tuition, room and board and other fees at Basking Ridge were, at the time of Skyler's incarceration there, approximately $65,000 for a full academic year. Compare $40,000 to $45,000 at such venerable Ivy League universities as Princeton, Harvard, Yale; and such prestigious liberal arts colleges as Swarthmore, Williams, et al.*

instance a nifty genuine cowhide catcher's mitt, or a Canuck Red-Eye hockey stick with Skyler's initials branded into the wood. At the time of Skyler's withdrawal from classes at Basking Ridge, as we've seen, Bix insisted upon Skyler remaining at school with the hope that Skyler might "snap out of it" and "recover"; when Skyler failed to recover, and may have grown worse, Bix called several times personally to leave messages for Skyler in a grave voice: "Skyler! Headmaster Shovell has been telling me some very upsetting things about your behavior there and I am registering my extreme disappointment that you should let me down another time, son. He claims that you became involved with a girl there—the daughter of Leander Harkness!—and that this 'seriously disturbed' girl tried to kill herself—and drugs seem to have been a part of it. Your therapist there says you've stopped coming to see her, but I am still being billed. You had better answer this call, Skyler. Maybe you can manipulate your gullible mother, but you can't play your sick-psycho-kid tricks on your dad, got it? *Quid pro quod!*"

Another omission in Skyler's account of his Basking Ridge year has to do with the exact nature of his relationship with Elyot Grubbe; or, rather, Elyot's relationship with Skyler. For it must have become painfully clear as the weeks passed that while Skyler thought condescendingly of Elyot as simply a friend, Elyot thought of Skyler as something more than a friend; only a prig-homophobe could have failed to interpret Elyot's shy smiles and lovesick manner, which Elyot tried to disguise, not very convincingly, by listening obsessively to music on his headphones. And so it was a crude and cruel gesture for Skyler to bring Heidi Harkness into the picture, as if to flaunt his girlfriend to poor Elyot, and the fact that, unlike Elyot, beneath his weirdness Skyler Rampike was *a normal guy.*

Poor Elyot Grubbe, I.Q. 159, destination Harvard Medical School, made to be a hapless observer of those two love-smitten teens Skyler and Heidi so visibly hand-in-hand, whispering together, kissing; the most defiantly unattractive of couples, and both, to Elyot's chagrin, so tall; in the very throes of what the cool-headed reader with a Gallic flair recognized immediately as a *folie-à-do!** Worse yet, as we've seen Elyot seemed to have

---

*Folie-à-do: *one of those mysterious French phrases that apply so precisely to other people, yet never to oneself. Why?*

fallen in love with Heidi Harkness, too. (Fortunately, a *folie-à-trey* did not develop. Skyler saw to that.) No wonder that, finally, after Heidi's collapse, Elyot reacted against his self-involved insufferable friend who, though Elyot's oldest companion from idyllic pre-trauma Fair Hills days, frequently smelled of his body, and his breath; and wrote him a chill little note ending their friendship.

How proud I was of Elyot Grubbe, at that moment! I did not see this coming, but it felt just right. Guilt-wracked Skyler got exactly what he deserved in this succinct riposte.

And all this escaped even the canny reader's notice, didn't it? Do you know why?

For instance, not one of you was sharp-eyed enough to have noted how, in a silly-tender moment typical of teens, Heidi Harkness beguiled Skyler Rampike by playfully unlatching a pearly "cap" on her charmingly crooked front teeth: "See? My mother wanted my smile to be 'perfect'—so is it?"

Skyler laughed, swooping in to kiss.*

But no readers took note of this sweetly silly little incident since Skyler neglected to report it. In fact, most of what Skyler experienced, and continues to experience, since December 1991, beginning with the chapter "In the Beginning"—("In the beginning—long ago!—there wasn't Bliss") has been left out of this document. Most of Skyler's life has not been recorded, and has become lost; as all our lives become lost. And how much worse the situation if, like poor Skyler, the narrator seems to be locked in a consciousness ceaselessly under siege by what S. Freud so aptly called the *un*consciousness.

For Skyler does not know all that Skyler's brain cells know; and you, who are Skyler's readers, can know only what Skyler chooses to tell you. Though presumably I am the "author"—I, too, know only what Skyler can tell me.

---

* *In fact, Skyler is so stricken with a Repressed Memory at this moment, he quickly kisses his girl to disguise his emotion. Nor will he record the incident in this document since, in so eerily mirroring a similar gesture of Bliss Rampike's years before, Heidi's gesture might seem, to the more* O *current literary theorist, too transparently "symbolic" to be convincing. (Not all events that really happen can be made to seem "real" in prose.)*

For instance, Skyler has failed repeatedly to acknowledge the myriad consequences—legal, personal—following his sister's death. For the most part, the legal complications did not directly involve him, for Skyler was, of course, a minor at the time. Skyler has skittishly alluded to the crude reportage of Tabloid Hell, that has kept Bliss Rampike's glamorous-waif likeness in the public eye, as it has kept Bix and Betsey Rampike in its sights; but mainstream/legitimate publications and media outlets have also turned their sporadic attentions upon the Bliss Rampike case, as it has come to be known, as well. Not one but two grand juries had been convened in Morris County to investigate every aspect of the controversial case, that had come to a premature impasse of sorts when the leading suspect Gunther Ruscha suddenly died, and had languished under the jurisdiction of longtime district attorney Howard O'Stryker, in legal circles known for his reluctance to bring criminal cases to trial unless he was absolutely certain of winning. Succumbing to pressure from the public and from the New Jersey attorney general, Mr. O'Stryker finally convened a second grand jury in the fall of 2002 which met at regular intervals for three months, in utter secrecy; a succession of witnessses was called, Fair Hills police officers, the original investigating detectives Sledge and Slugg (now retired), local/state/FBI forensics experts, sex offenders and pedophilia experts, sepulchral Dr. Elyse ("Of all child homicide victims in my career as a medical examiner, it is Bliss Rampike who continues to haunt me. My fear is that I will die before that poor child's murderer is found"); numerous individuals (therapists, prison guards, fellow Rahway inmates, parole officer, relatives, neighbors, etc.) associated with Gunther Ruscha; Fair Hills neighbors, acquaintances, friends, former employees, Trinity Church associates of the Rampikes, and many others; yet not, ironically, Bix and Betsey Rampike, for their ever-vigilant attorney M. Kruk succeeded in blocking all requests for interviews with his clients, who had, by this time, both moved out of New Jersey. As no physical evidence or witnesses had ever placed either of the elder Rampikes at the scene of the actual crime, no subpoenas could be issued to force the Rampikes to cooperate with the grand jury; nor was Skyler Rampike, represented by a lawyer named Crampf, a partner in Kruk's law firm, served a subpoena. A majority of jurors may have believed that Gunther Ruscha who had confessed to the crime had told the truth in his confession, yet, as forensics experts claimed, there was no physical evidence linking Ruscha to the crime scene, nor even to the interior of the Rampike house, and there were no witnesses to testify that they'd seen him that night. And so, in December 2002, the second grand jury in the now-notorious Bliss Rampike case was dismissed by the district attorney of Morris County without handing down a single indictment, and without establishing that Gunther Ruscha was the murderer.*

In the media, particularly in tabloid papers and on TV, this second failure of a grand jury to reach any conclusions in the Bliss Rampike case was greeted with scarcely concealed derision, or, as in the *New York Post*, outright derision, as in this front-page banner headline:

N.J. GRAND JURY TO BLISS: "WE CAN'T HELP YOU"

In his defense, it should be said that Skyler was but dimly aware of the grand jury, as, in one or another treatment center at this time, Skyler was but dimly aware of the world of "news."

More mysteriously, Skyler failed to include in "First Love, Farewell!" this enigmatic episode:

One November afternoon in 2003, a summons came for Skyler in the midst of his fifth-period math class, to go immediately to Headmaster Shovell's office where, to Skyler's surprise, a middle-aged man who looked vaguely familiar to Skyler, one of Bix Rampike's golf-, tennis-, or squash-playing friends perhaps, greeted him with a smile and a brisk handshake: "Skyler! You've grown, I see. It has been a while—six years, four months to be exact—but I hope that you remember me: your attorney, Craig Crampf."

Skyler's attorney! Skyler had not given a thought to Crampf in the

---

* *The reader may be intrigued, or repelled, to learn that at least one other individual, also a "convicted sex offender" residing in New Jersey, had confessed to killing Bliss Rampike by this time. Who this was, how seriously Fair Hills police took the sicko's claim, or whether other "intruder" theories were investigated by the police, Skyler did not know, and did not want to know.*

intervening years. It was a shock to him that Crampf seemed still to be retained by Bix Rampike in the role of "Skyler's attorney."

Before Skyler could ask why Crampf was at Basking Ridge, another man stepped forward to introduce himself to Skyler: "Hal Ransom, Fair Hills PD senior detective." Mr. Ransom explained that he had recently been assigned to the Bliss Rampike case which was being re-opened another time, and he had a few questions to ask of Skyler that would not keep him very long. Skyler, beginning to be frightened, muttered what sounded like *Okay I guess* with a glance at Crampf who smiled at him consolingly. Shovell discreetly departed, and Skyler and the two men sat at a polished mahogany table. This was a time in Skyler's fevered-adolescent life when he was dazzled by Heidi Harkness, his first girl; yet all thoughts of Heidi Harkness vanished from his mind, like water down a drain. Skyler recalled Mummy warning him *Do not speak of it ever not ever not to anyone not even Jesus. Do not.* The interview would last perhaps forty minutes during which time Ransom asked Skyler a succession of questions ("What do you remember of the night of your sister's death?"—"When was the last time you saw your sister alive?"—"What was the last thing your sister said to you?") and as Skyler opened his mouth to speak, perhaps to stutter *I d-d-don't r-really r-r-remember much*, canny Mr. Crampf said, "Detective, my client declines to answer." Several times Skyler felt a sharp urge to speak, like an urge to sneeze, but canny Crampf quickly interceded, with the virtuoso ease of a Ping-Pong player who always outplays his opponent no matter how swift his opponent is, saying: "Detective, my client declines to answer." A faint flush of indignation came into the detective's face though he did not appear to be greatly surprised. At the end of forty minutes he handed Skyler his card which, in a gesture that might have seemed rude in a less poised individual, Crampf took from Skyler's fingers with the comment: "Thank you, Detective. Good-bye." Though Skyler had barely spoken during the interview yet Skyler could barely push himself up from his seat, he was so exhausted. Like pushing yourself up from the snaky-skinned gym mat where you have fallen, hard. Very hard.

"Son." Now in a kindly mode Crampf laid his hand on Skyler's shoulder. This was a gesture that should have reminded Skyler of his father but the memory went askew and was lost. ". . . remember: no one can touch you. 'You have a right to remain silent'—the cornerstone of justice in America."

And what does the reader make of this interlude? Is Skyler, at age sixteen, being investigated as a suspect in his sister's murder? Or is Skyler meant to be an informing witness, one who might name the murderer?

Whatever. Best remedy is to excise it from memory. By the time he met up with Heidi Harkness that evening at Toll House, he'd forgotten the episode entirely.

THAT NIGHT THRASHING AND GROANING IN SWEATY/SMELLY/SEMEN-STAINED sheets unchanged for a week Skyler felt his mother's consoling caress and heard her gentle yet urgent warning like the lyrics of a secret hymn *Do not speak of it ever Skyler not ever not to anyone not even Jesus. Do not.*

AND WHERE IS SKYLER? NO LONGER IN FORT LEE, NEW JERSEY BUT— approaching Spring Hollow, New York? Reader, I had not expected this!

While I was busily preoccupied in providing you with (crucial) background information, my intrepid teen hero seems to have driven out of the foreground of this narrative without my noticing.

"My n-name is Sk-Skyler Rampike. I've come to see my . . ."

Somehow, frankly I can't imagine how, Skyler managed to find his way off N. Syke Street in Fort Lee within a few minutes, capture his way back onto thunderous I-95 and so, on the "upper level," manage to cross the George Washington Bridge for the first time, as a driver, in his life. (Of which, being an insecure kid, Skyler would be enormously proud except in his state of wound-up nerves, mouth dry as ashes and heart clenched like a fist, pride is beyond him.) (Also, while crossing, in the right-hand lane, he dared not glance to the left or the right and had no more awareness of crossing the great Hudson River than he would have had of crossing a valley of rubble.) Equally unexpectedly, Skyler managed, on the New York side of the river, not to screw up another time and take a wrong exit, as you'd expect, but to negotiate an insidiously tricky lane-change onto the Henry Hudson Parkway North; from there, feeling a small charge of confidence, Skyler had no trouble exiting onto Route 9 North; scarcely needing to consult his hand-drawn map, Skyler drove at a steady speed through the suburban communities of Irvington, Tarrytown, and (quaintly named, redolent of Headless Horseman and demonic pumpkin) Sleepy Hollow; at last turning into Spring Hollow, pop. 2,800 where in a state of mounting excitement, or dry-mouthed panic, he stopped at a gas station to buy twelve dollars' worth of gas and stumble into the men's lavatory dazed and his head ringing, trying not to breathe in the foul odors of myriad predecessors telling the sickly-pale face in the splotched mirror above the urinal *Hey look: you can still turn back, okay? She doesn't know you are here.* Yet then returning to the borrowed Dodge at the gas pump looking like a junked vehicle newly charged with life, bronze-gleaming letters NEW CANAAN EVANGELICAL CHURCH OF CHRIST RISEN and so Skyler heard himself ask the gas station attendant for directions to Magnolia Terrace and was told in heavily accented English what sounded like *Two lights left, turn by the river.*

MAGNOLIA ESTATES IS A VERY NEW, CLEARLY VERY EXPENSIVE RESIDENTIAL community ostentatiously set off from a neighborhood of older, smaller homes: MAGNOLIA ESTATES 3 & 4 BEDROOM CUSTOM-DESIGNED LUXURY HOMES SOME RIVER LOTS STILL AVAILABLE. Here are narrow curvy lanes—Magnolia Drive, Magnolia Heights, Magnolia Terrace—like those Skyler recalls from Fair Hills, New Jersey; at 9 Magnolia Terrace, an antebellum plantation house with elaborate white wrought iron trim and a columned front portico, peach-colored like a confectioner's cake. At 11 Magnolia Terrace is a custard-and-cherry Colonial, at 7 Magnolia Terrace is a pistachio-raspberry Greek Revival. The houses of Magnolia Estates are smaller than they appear from the street for their showy two-storey facades disguise one-storey structures; while their lots appear long from the street, most of the property is at the front while at the rear the property is shallow, hardly more than a few yards; as in a cinematic dream-sequence, Skyler has a sense of shrinking dimensions. Trying not to panic. Scratching at his face. Light-headed with hunger but had not had any appetite to eat the lunch Miriam so kindly provided him and fumbling now in his jacket pockets for—what?—stray Zilich pills, one of Heidi's lint-covered OxyContins. Thinking *But I can still turn back! She hasn't seen me.*

All this while, Skyler has not wanted to acknowledge that something is very wrong in Magnolia Estates. Not just the showy, synthetic houses, a number of which appear to be empty, with LUXURY HOME FOR SALE signs in the front yards, but the fact that he has been seeing too many people, and the wrong kinds of people, for such a setting, in which ordinarily there would be no pedestrians at all, since there are no sidewalks. And there is too much traffic, not the sleek high-quality cars favored by well-to-do suburban matrons but an ominous preponderance of minivans. In the street across from the peach-colored plantation house is a motley, restless crowd of about thirty people: TV camera crews, photographers and reporters, "gawkers." What has happened? Why are these people staring at him? Calling to him? Panicked Skyler ducks to shield his face. So luridly bandaged, his steely hair in a rat-tail, he can't be identifiable as Skyler Rampike—can he? Yet photographers are eagerly aiming their cameras at him, a TV camera crew for WSRY-TV is eagerly taping, reporters call excitedly after the Dodge station wagon: "Wait! Are you 'Skyler'? Are you—the son?" Skyler sees that police barricades have been set up in the street to keep these aggressive individuals from trespassing on the lawn at 9 Magnolia Terrace and rushing up to the peach-colored house. Two uniformed Spring Hollow patrolmen are directing traffic. At the foot of the asphalt driveway two private security guards—both black, with dour expressions—stand beside a barricade with a sign attached PRIVATE   INVITATION ONLY. Several vehicles including a van marked WCBS-TV have been allowed past the guards to park in the driveway; in his most earnest voice Skyler explains to the guards that he is Betsey Rampike's son, and she is expecting him.

"You? Miz Ranpick's son? You are?"

"Y-Yes. I am. Mz. Ranpick's son."

"You some kind of—what? 'New C'nan Church'—minister?"

"No. I mean y-yes. I belong to a—"

"You comin' for some service, son?"

"Yes." Skyler shows the frowning guards his New Jersey driver's license. The first time in his life, Skyler is anxious to be identified as Skyler Rampike.

THE LOOK IN THE WOMAN'S FACE, A DARK-SKINNED MARIA IN A STARCHED white housekeeper's uniform, Skyler understands that he has come too late.

"You are who? 'Skee-ler'—"

"Where is my mother? Where is Betsey?"

Skyler has stumbled into a brightly lit foyer of mirrors and wallpaper sparkly and cheery as Christmas tinsel. Quickly the housekeeper backs off from him, her dark eyes veiled with pity. "Excuse me, I will bring Mr. Kissler."

Blindly Skyler follows the woman into a living room lavishly furnished in what must be "period" pieces. How long ago, in what a distant and improbable country of Mummy-*little man* romance, Skyler's young mother searched for "period pieces"—"antiques"—for the sprawling old Colonial on Ravens Crest Drive. Here, in a smaller but showier setting, like a store-window display, are plush velvet sofas, chintz-covered chairs bright as parrots' wings, oddly shaped floor lamps, brocaded wall hangings. On the velvet sofas are cushions large enough to smother an elephant. Underfoot is an Oriental rug thick as the snaky-skinned mats in the Gold Medal Gym, garlanded with flesh-colored cabbage roses and mustard-bright trim. How perfumy the air is! Skyler can scarcely catch his breath.

On the wall above a white marble fireplace, a large portrait of Betsey Rampike in the prime of her youthful beauty and Bliss in the crook of her arm, Bliss at about the age of five, very sweet, very blond and very pretty, with one of her silver tiaras on her curled and crimped blond hair. Though Betsey is a lush dark-eyed brunette, and Bliss is a fair-skinned blue-eyed blond, yet the painter, in the way of a kitsch-glamor-pop Renoir, has made the mother and daughter resemble each other to an uncanny degree.

Skyler backs off, shielding his eyes. Noooo.

All he'd been able to ingest that morning, the long heart-straining hours of that morning beginning in the windy dusk before dawn in the third-floor rented room on Pitts Street, so long ago he can barely recall it, has been a few mouthfuls of the fresh-squeezed orange juice kindly Miriam gave him, that had tipped over in the passenger's seat of the Dodge spilling sticky juice. So Skyler is dazed, and Skyler is not feeling so good.

Where is Betsey? Must be, by now the Maria-woman has told her that Skyler is here?

Through an archway of sculpted molding—a stark white frieze of nymphs, swans, girl-skaters—there is another, slightly smaller room in which, beneath blinding bright lights, and overseen by a team of a half-dozen individuals, a television interview seems to be in progress. A sofa has been pulled out at an angle from a wall, and other pieces of furniture artfully arranged as in a TV talk-show set; a glamorously made-up woman with a lilting exclamatory voice, whose face looks familiar to Skyler, is interviewing a middle-aged man with shellacked-looking black hair and a grief-stricken yet floridly tanned face. Seeing Skyler stumbling forward like a drunken boy the man quickly rises to approach him, interrupting the interview.

"Are you—Skyler? Betsey's son?"

"Yes. Where is my mother? I want to see my mother."

"Haven't you been told, son? Your mother—our beloved Betsey—has passed away."

"Passed away? Where?"

Skyler's voice is young and raw-sounding and edged with contempt. Skyler is concerned that this stranger, a man in his early fifties whom Skyler doesn't know, is extending both hands to him, and Skyler does not want to be touched.

"Skyler, I am Nathan Kissler. I think Betsey must have told you about me . . ." Kissler is Betsey's partner in Heaven Scent, Inc. Financial advisor, "companion." From somewhere, some surreptitious and unacknowledged glimpse into Tabloid Hell, Skyler seems to know that Kissler is Betsey Rampike's fiancé.

"Skyler? Son? Why don't you have a seat, here. We'll get you something to drink, you are looking very pale. Of course this is a terrible shock to you. A terrible, terrible shock for all of us who love—loved—our darling Betsey . . ."

"Mister, could you not talk so *much*. I want to see my mother."

Skyler gazes at Nathan Kissler with the derisive-male eyes of Bix Rampike. This dapper little man scarcely five-feet-six, Bix would tower over him, Skyler's mother's fiancé? And what does that mean—fiancé? Skyler is appalled at the thought that there might be something sexual between Kissler and his mother, isn't going to think of anything so obscene. Kissler is wearing a black silk shirt, a black silk ascot, black Armani jeans that fit his narrow waist and hips snug as the jeans on a male model thirty years his junior. Especially offensive to Skyler's sense of decorum is a black leather belt with a brass medallion buckle. And the man's face isn't tanned but has been expertly made up for the television cameras: pancake makeup with an orange base, eyelashes darkened with mascara. Sucking little fish-mouth, reddened.

Kissler is urging Skyler to sit down, the woman in the starched white uniform has hurried off to get him a glass of ice water, but Skyler eases away, doesn't want to sit down, too many eyes are greedily fastened upon him. The TV cameraman has turned his camera in Skyler's direction, little green light *on*. Kissler is saying gravely, ". . . passed away, Skyler, only this morning. After complications following surgery. The news has just been released and already there has been a deluge of—"

"But where is she? I want to see her."

Skyler has the idea that, though she has "passed away," Betsey is also somewhere close by, in another room in this house, preparing for a television interview. There are the bright lights, there are the cameras. Two cameramen. And the female interviewer whose face is familiar to Skyler. Why doesn't one of Betsey's assistants tell her *Skyler is here*?

". . . after the surgery, her heart couldn't bear the strain . . . She'd wanted the operation to be kept utterly secret . . . no tabloid 'leaks'! The funeral will be in two days, here in Spring Hollow."

"But I want to see her. I want to see her now. I have a right to see her, I'm her son and she invited me here."

Patiently Kissler explains: "Betsey's 'remains' are still at the hospital, Skyler. There will be a private viewing at the funeral home—"

Skyler interrupts: "She left me something, didn't she? Where is it?"

Quickly the TV interviewer intercedes, embracing Skyler warmly. Skyler is too stunned to resist, the woman is big-boned, fleshy, though glamorous she is a motherly sort of woman, with muscles Skyler can feel, and hard spongey breasts the size of hubcaps. Now Skyler recognizes this woman: Zelda Zachiarias of *WomenSpeakOut*. "Skyler! Please accept my condolences for your loss. What a brave woman your mother was, Skyler! We're preparing a special tribute to Betsey Rampike to be aired on Friday, and it would mean so much to us, as it would have meant so much to Betsey, if you would join us, Skyler. You see, Betsey spoke of you often. Betsey said, 'Every hour of my life I pray to God, and to Jesus: Look after my son.' Betsey believed without a doubt that you and she would be reconciled one day, Skyler. It was her great hope, and she had faith. Oh Skyler!—I can't believe that Betsey Rampike will never again be on my show, as a model for women—mothers—who have suffered the most grievous loss, and survived. Yes, and triumphed. Not a word did Betsey want uttered of her ordeal—you know what a private—'stoic'—person Betsey was—not a word of her struggle with—" The throaty voice drops solemnly, as if Zelda were trying to keep from bursting into tears, Skyler has to strain to hear what sounds like *cancer of the service.*

Cancer of the service? Skyler shudders.

Passionately Zelda Zachiarias continues, standing very close to Skyler, "Just before her surgery Betsey said, 'Pray for me, Zelda. God will do the rest.' So brave! For our TV audience, Skyler, will you just say a few . . ."

Skyler detaches himself from Zelda Zachiarias's grip. Tries to shield his face from the rapacious TV cameramen advancing upon him. Hateful little green lights *on*, Skyler knows what that portends: Skyler Rampike is exposed.

Close by Nathan Kissler has been speaking through a cell phone. He seems wary of Skyler now, not so friendly. The air of paternal warmth has been replaced by a slightly ironic chill. Skyler returns to the subject of what his mother left for him, and Kissler says, with a pained smile, "Skyler, your mother left a will. Certainly, Betsey left a will. In fact, she may have left wills . . . She was always changing and 'updating' her will as new friends came into her life, and older friends invariably dropped out . . . There will be a formal reading of Betsey Rampike's will in her lawyer's office, in time. But in the meantime—"

Skyler says loudly, "Where is it, what Mummy left me? Is it somewhere

here?" and Kissler says, "Skyler, please keep your voice down. The last thing we want is for those hyenas and jackals out on the street to hear us. This is a terrible shock for all of us, not just you. Our big spring launch is coming up in three weeks, and we have more than six million dollars invested in Heaven Scent spring products. If only you'd called first, someone could have prepared you," and Skyler says, "Where is it? My mother left me something. A letter, or a videotape . . . That was why she asked me to come here. What did you do with—" and Kissler says, "Skyler, there is no need to shout. We can hear you," and Skyler says, "You don't hear me! I'm asking, where is my mother? And where is what she left me? God damn you, I can look for it myself . . ."

Skyler tries to push past Nathan Kissler who, though shorter than Skyler by several inches, and older by three decades, is surprisingly agile, and strong; but Skyler manages to free a fist, and swing it, striking the older man on the bridge of his nose, and breaking it; there is a gratifying *crunch!* and a warm spurt of blood. But one of the private guards has appeared, a large dour-faced black man who calls Skyler "son" and gently but very firmly restrains him. Skyler is being walked somewhere, rapidly. As the guard grips his upper arms, Skyler walks rapidly, with buckling knees, like a cartoon character whose feet barely touch the ground. Now they are outside, in wintry air. Skyler struggles with the guard, but Skyler's strength is fading; not the black man's hands but something like a clamp, a vise, closes tight about Skyler's chest; his lungs open in the cold fresh air as if sliced by a knife but the slit is too narrow, Skyler can't suck in enough oxygen, overhead the sky is a mass of tumorous clouds, underfoot the frozen ground suddenly opens and Skyler falls through*

███████

---

* *Exactly like this! Would've fallen and cracked my head except kindly Evander Franklin (security guard) caught me. To Nathan Kissler's chagrin, Franklin carried me back inside the dollhouse-sized peach plantation house, as TV cameras across the street rolled. In a few minutes, I revived. Not wanting to call an ambulance for me, thereby "fanning the flames" of the tabloid jackals, Kissler called Bix Rampike, for the second time that day.*

ENTFREMDUNGSGEFUHL*

"SON. THERE HAS BEEN A TRAGIC HISTORY BETWEEN US. BUT MAYBE—NOW—
that will change."

These words! Skyler swallowed hard. *Now* had to mean *now that your mother is dead.*

The men were in a wood-plank booth in the Old Dutch Tavern in the historic old Washington Irving Inn in Sleepy Hollow, New York, where Skyler was spending the night after his mother's funeral, at Bix's expense. Since they'd entered the tavern, Bix had been speaking slowly and deliberately with what seemed, to Skyler's hyper-acute ear, a slight drag to his voice, like the all-but-imperceptible limp an athlete, or an ex-athlete, tries to disguise. To the normal eye, the limp is imperceptible. But Skyler had no more a normal eye, or ear, than he had a normal right leg (femur, fibula, knee).

The shock of his former wife's death seemed to have shaken Bix Rampike who seemed, to Skyler, less looming-tall and imposing than Skyler recalled. At the crowded *après-funeral* hosted by Nathan Kissler at the Sleepy Hollow Country Club, Skyler had noticed his father drinking. There was a wounded-shaggy-bison look to the older man, something gray-grizzled in his eyebrows, a baffled fleshiness to the lower part of his face. Must be, Skyler thought, he'd still loved Betsey?

A man never ceases to love the mother of his children, son. That's the bottom line.[†]

---

* *Handy German word for* fucking-unreal.

[†] *Fleeting frisson of child-memory: as, long ago, Skyler was transported by Daddy in the '97 Rogue Warrior SUV to one or another physical therapy session in Fair Hills. Probably, Daddy was only just musing out loud, with no intention that Skyler reply.*

"Son? You're listening, I hope."

Quickly Skyler assured his frowning father, certainly he was listening. "'Maybe—now—that will change.' You said."

As always in this man's presence, Skyler spoke with boyish optimism. Even in this time of shared mourning, for Skyler to be in close proximity to this man was to feel certain facial muscles, long dormant, stir to life: *Smile!* And a certain craven eagerness to his shoulders, leaning forward: *Yes Daddy?*

Skyler had noticed that Bix had brought into the tavern with him a briefcase of soft dark Italian leather, and now Bix lifted this briefcase onto the table between them, slowly and ceremonially; he seemed about to open it, but did not. How poignantly furrowed Bix Rampike's forehead was, how his soulful eyes glistened with a kind of brooding regret, yet resolve. Skyler's heart beat painfully. He thought *In there? Is there something for me?* He dared not hope.

Massively, Bix sighed. Lifted his heavy whiskey glass, and drank.

"Of course, son: it can't bring her back."

Numbly, Skyler agreed.*

SKYLER HAD BEEN PREPARED TO BE UNMOVED BY *SON*. TO SHRUG AT *SON*. BUT when his father uttered *son*, the ice encasing Skyler's gnarled-kid heart began to melt.

And the tenderness of certain of Bix's gestures, clumsy-warm-Daddy embrace that nearly cracked Skyler's ribs, rough-Daddy kiss smearing spittle on Skyler's inflamed cheek, squeeze of Skyler's hard little biceps, all took Skyler off guard. Heavy-breathing Daddy, tear-brimming eyes: "This is a sad time, son. 'Requiescat poor Betsey in peace.'"

Reader, forgive me: this is sentimental as hell. These many pages, Skyler has been bitching about his parents, now you're expected to be sympathetic with Bix, even with Betsey, and that is asking too God-damned much. And I am not expecting you to oblige. Yet, to be scrupulously honest,

---

* *But what is Skyler agreeing with? Does Bix mean "her" to be Betsey, or Bliss?*

as I have tried to be in this document, this is how Skyler felt when Bix Rampike came at once to 9 Magnolia Terrace, Sleepy Hollow, summoned by the distraught Nathan Kissler who had no idea what to do with his deceased partner/fiancée's nineteen-year-old son who'd not only showed up unexpectedly at the house, less than six hours after Betsey's death, but fainted just outside the door, on his way out.

"A SAD TIME, SON. AND YET: WE ARE TOGETHER."

(And how long had it been since Skyler had seen his father last? Two years? Two-and-a-half? And then, under awkward circumstances. After Skyler had "walked away" from a drug treatment center in East Orange, New Jersey, and New Jersey State police had been alerted, and Bix had appeared quivering with revulsion: "Skyler! How the fuck could you! Again.")

Now, Bix was looking older. And Bix was looking shaken, remorseful. Something hunched and crestfallen in the man's face as if his ex-wife's death was a personal blow he had not yet fully grasped. Saying to Skyler: "Son. We'll get you a place to stay here. And we'll get you a haircut, and some decent clothes. You will attend your mother's funeral, son. With me."

Feebly Skyler protested. He would attend Betsey's funeral but—he didn't want his hair cut, and he didn't want to wear a suit. And Bix dug his fingers into Skyler's stiff shoulders, and said, "You will not shame the Rampikes, son. No more than you already have."

The place to stay, two nights on Bix Rampike's credit card, was the quaint-historic old Washington Irving Inn, less than two miles from 9 Magnolia Terrace. The haircut was expensive, and made Skyler look near-normal from certain angles. The clothes, purchased on Bix Rampike's credit card in a single pragmatic visit to Hugo Boss at the Tarrytown Shopping Mall, were: charcoal gray wool-silk suit, narrow-waisted coat, pencil-thin sharp-creased trousers (adjusted by the resident tailor to accommodate Skyler's disproportionate frame); a long-sleeved dress shirt of white Egyptian cotton of the kind favored by Bix Rampike, and a dark-striped silk tie. Funeral attire for the grieving son! In a three-way mirror Skyler regarded his Hollywood-transformed self with mirth: "Me? Not."

From behind, Bix gripped Skyler's slouched shoulders forcing them just slightly back, and up: "Stand tall, son. No more of this flaky-kid crap. You're a Rampike—stand like one."

ALSO, BIX PROVIDED SKYLER WITH DARK GLASSES. VERY DARK GLASSES.

"Stare straight ahead, son. Don't so much as glance at the jackals. And don't smile, for Christ's sake. When they call your name, you don't hear. When they wave at you, you don't see. Just walk close beside me, try not to limp and remember you're a Rampike—deport yourself like one."

SKYLER'S FIRST "VIEWING."

In his new clothes (trousers tight in the crotch, starched white collar chafing his neck) Skyler made his way like a man in a dream not his own to the white-gold-gleaming casket at the rear of the chilled room, past strangers frankly staring at him, past tubs of lilies, steeling himself for what awaited him and in confusion relieved thinking *Not Mummy in the casket! Not Mummy* for this woman was no one Skyler knew. Thinking *There has been a mistake, I can leave now* except wiping moisture from his eyes it seemed to him, yes the female corpse in the casket in layers of pink chiffon, thick ropes of pearls around her neck, clam-shell-sized pearl earrings in her ears, did bear some resemblance to the Betsey Rampike he'd last seen on television in Heidi Harkness's room. Except the hair did not appear to be real hair, synthetic-glossy-maroon-red like a perky Heaven Scent Glamour Wig ($359.95). You would not have believed that the face was that of a woman of forty-four!—unlined forehead, full rouged cheeks, nothing fleshy visible below the chin. Serene-shut eyes expertly made up in several shades of eye shadow (taupe, silvery-green, silvery-blue) and ink-black mascara, Cleopatra style. The fleshy red-lipstick-lips that seemed to be about to smile, Skyler had to concede did look familiar. And if this was Mummy, was Skyler the *little man*? A sensation of abject fear came over him leaving him weak, light-headed. The horror was, Mummy's *little man* must kiss Mummy good-bye! Or was it to wake Mummy from her unnatural sleep, by kissing her on those red-lipstick-lips? As long ago he'd glimpsed his sister Bliss lying in a tangle of awkward limbs on the living room floor of their house, arms flung over her head and wrists bound together, eyes open and small wounded mouth slack and he'd been too frightened, and too cowardly, to run to her to save her: that boy was Skyler. Now to make amends Skyler must lean over the casket with its dazzle of white-gold, Skyler must balance himself carefully so he doesn't slip, and fall into the casket like a TV cartoon figure which (he knows, he acknowledges) he resembles in sexy new Hugo Boss attire, Skyler must kiss Mummy on those lips *now.* Yet—so strangely—unable to move as if paralyzed, staring helplessly awaiting the Cleopatra eyes to open and claim him, Skyler's breath now coming rapidly and shallowly and elsewhere in the lavishly decorated viewing room agitated Nathan Kissler could not think what to do about Skyler Rampike teetering over the casket in which Betsey Rampike lay "as if sleeping"—could not think what to do about his deceased fiancée's clearly psychotic son, finally daring to approach Betsey's ex-husband Bix Rampike who was stationed a little to the side of the casket, staring with glum fascination at the voluptuous female figure without coming nearer, and in a lowered voice Kissler said, "Mr. Rampike, your son," and Bix said, "What about my son," and Kissler said, "He does not appear well, Mr. Rampike. Please do something about him," and Bix said, jaw jutting in the way of a former all-American fullback, though in his mid-forties, going soft in the mid-section, still you would not want this six-foot-four/two-hundred-plus Alpha-male *Homo sapiens* specimen to tackle you, "My son is mourning his God-damned mother, 'Nathan.' That's a problem with you?" and Kissler said, shaken, dapper little man in prim-mannequin-mourning-attire, dark grays, black, shiny-dark-purple silk ascot disguising the wattles beneath his chin, trying neither to threaten nor to plead, "Mr. Rampike please I am asking you, please move your son away from Betsey, he has been standing there teetering for six minutes or more and he doesn't look well."

Must've been, Bix relented. Approached Skyler quietly and with gentle/ firm Daddy-fingers gripped Skyler's upper right bicep waking him from the eerie Mummy-trance in which poor Skyler might have committed an act of such unspeakable and irrevocable weirdness, to this very hour it would be posted on Web sites through galaxies charted and uncharted to the last syllable of recorded Time.

"Son. Come with me."

UNEXPECTED DEVELOPMENT, READER! TRULY I DID NOT FORESEE, ANY MORE than Skyler did, his being so readily "reconciled" with his long-estranged father of whom Skyler knew very little at the present time except: Bix Rampike was remarried, and the "proud new father" of a very young child (sex not known to [jealous? embittered?] Skyler); Bix Rampike was now CEO ("chief executive officer"—such grandeur deserves full recognition) of the Univers, Inc. subsidiary New Genesis BioTech, Inc., headquarters in New Harmony, New Jersey, one exit beyond Univers, eastward on I-80. (Yet, so far as Skyler could determine, Bix seemed to spend much of his time in New York City.) In a classic work of art that celebrates reconciliation, forgiveness, and a heartwarming reaffirmation of the human spirit greatly tested by adversity, Skyler and his father would be brought together more than merely temporarily by the occasion of Betsey Rampike's death, and so I will see what I can do to achieve this. For truly, for all my postmodernist cynicism I want this document to turn out "heart-warming"— "truly inspiring!" and not "the longest God-damned suicide note in the history of the English language."*

"SON. BEAR UP LIKE A MAN."

God damn he was! Skyler felt certain.

Next, the funeral service. Next morning at 11 A.M.

And here was the first surprise: Betsey Rampike's funeral service would not be a staid/solemn/"beautiful-but-boring-as-hell" Episcopal service but a fervent/impassioned/"smiling-through-tears" Assembly of God funeral. For it seemed that Skyler's mother had cast off the hoary old Episcopal formality she'd taken on when marrying Bix Rampike for the

---

* *"Longest suicide note on record" is* Will & Testement [sic] *by the minor American poet V. West-gaard (1841–73), an astonishing 999 handwritten pages. Reader, I am not able to match this.*

far more exuberant, "outgoing" and "joyous" Christianity celebrated by the Assembly of God worshippers. (Bix remained stolidly Episcopalian of course. Such was his "heritage." The Episcopal God was not one to interfere in the affairs of mankind as, ideally, Big Government should not interfere in the affairs of business-kind. Disapprovingly Bix commented to Skyler: "How could your mother 'convert' to Assembly of God, after the Higleys stood by us, in our hour of need! Damn selfish.") Skyler had to be impressed, if a little overwhelmed, by the showy mega-church that was several times the size of quaint old Trinity Episcopal in Fair Hills, with an alleged seating capacity of 2,100; beyond Wal-Mart, beyond Home Depot and Big Savings Bonanza at the traffic-clogged intersection of Route 9 and I-87 was a sleekly gleaming modern structure of white concrete smooth as taffy, sparkling glass and steel in a fantastical architectural design combining old-style churchiness with New Age flying-saucer uplift. Said Bix, in grudging approval: "Twelve million, bottom line. That's 'Born Again' for you."

Inside, the Assembly of God appeared even larger. The size of a football field, at least—two football fields?—Skyler had but a vague sense of such epic proportions. The altar was enormous as a rock-concert stage and above it, seemingly floating in air, eerily and wonderfully, was an enormous copper cross of about twelve feet in height. Much of Betsey Rampike's funeral service would be music: electric organ/synthesizer, twin white-robed "tabernacle choirs" singing, with great swoops of emotion, grief-stricken to joyous, dirge-like to pop-rock, the deceased woman's favorite hymns: "Nearer My God to Thee," "Christ Our Redeemer Cometh," "What a Friend We Have in Jesus," "Beyond the Sunset," "A Mighty Fortress Is Our Lord," "Onward, Christian Soldiers!" Unlike the singing in the New Canaan church which tended to be raggedy and off-key, the combined effort of hopeful amateurs, the singing in this dazzling mega-church was syrupy-smooth and accomplished. (In the program it was noted that these hymns were included in a newly issued Heaven Scent CD titled *Betsey Rampike's Most Inspiring Christian Hymns*, available for $26.95.)

Though Betsey's funeral was a private affair limited to Betsey's "intimate friends and associates," most of the seats in the vast interior, including even the soaring balcony, were filled. (Yet no Sckulhornes, Skyler's father informed him. And of the Rampikes, only Bix and Skyler seated in the front row close by Betsey's dapper little fiancé Nathan Kissler.) Pastor of Assembly of God was a leonine-haired Reverend Alphonse Sked, a man with a formidable bass voice to rival that of Pastor Bob Fluchaus, and a solemn-breezy manner like a TV actor. Arms tight-folded as a straitjacket across his chest in the expensive Hugo Boss funeral suit, Skyler tried to concentrate on the florid-faced preacher praising "my beloved friend Betsey Rampike who departed this world too soon"—"one of the most courageous Christian women of our time"—"triumphing over Evil and 'secular progressivism' "— "confirming the values of American family and freedom"—and not to stare at the white-gold-gleaming casket, now closed, that had been placed upon the altar like a gigantic jewel box. In a confluence of spotlights, the casket loomed even larger than it had in the viewing room.

"Son? Stand. Sing."

Bix nudged Skyler from his trance. Skyler stood, tried to sing with the others: "Onward, Christian Soldiers!" Skyler's lips moved numbly. He had no idea if the "much-loved" hymn was painfully silly or a rousingly beautiful song. Thinking how he had not been allowed to attend his sister's funeral. He had never been taken to visit Bliss's grave, that had to be in the cemetery behind the Trinity church. *Skyler I am so lonely in this place*   *I am so afraid*   *Skyler help me*

"Son. Here's a tissue. Get control of yourself, for Christ's sake."

L'APRÈS-FUNERAL, AS THE RECEPTION FOLLOWING THE FUNERAL WAS CALLED in the invitations, was held in the prestigious old Sleepy Hollow Country Club on a hill overlooking the Hudson River. Skyler was exhausted and drained of emotion by this time but his father insisted that Skyler accompany him: "*Nobles oblige* means if you are an aristocrat, you don't shirk your duty to your subjects." And so Skyler in dark glasses that gave him the look of a peevish beetle and in his now rumpled funeral-suit allowed himself to be led into the midst of a clamorous gathering of strangers eager to commiserate with him: "Oh is it—Skeel-er? Betsey spoke so warmly of you in her memoirs, and on TV! Please accept my heartfelt condolences!"—"Son, your mother was a rare woman. 'I believe in happiness,' Betsey told our book club, 'for my special angel is in heaven already, beckoning me to her' "—"Scooter, is it?—poor boy, you've been crying, let Aunt Madeleine give you a *hug*." Very soon, Skyler saw that canny Bix Rampike seemed to have slipped away, drink in hand.

Most of the mourners were women, middle-aged and older, with here and there a young woman, often overweight, or frankly obese; there was a scattering of middle aged and older men most of whom, unless Skyler in his mildly deranged state was imagining this, resembled dapper little Nathan Kissler. It was surprising how these people ate and drank with such appetite, given the solemnity of the occasion. Skyler saw a bevy of Christian teens stuffing themselves with food from the twenty-foot buffet table in the dining room: lobster croquettes, Tex-Mex chicken wings, sweet potato-marshmallow puffs, banana fritters and strawberry shortcake (recipes available in *Betsey Rampike's Honeymoon Homemaker's Handbook*, available from Heaven Scent Products, $22.95). Skyler saw no other person remotely resembling Skyler himself. No one remotely like Heidi Harkness. On wall-TV screens videos were playing photo-montages of the life of Betsey Rampike as in an art museum installation in which viewers shuffle gravely from screen to screen. Skyler stared up at fleeting images of his Fair Hills past: Rampike-family photos taken in front of the twelve-foot Christmas tree in which in miniature, so very young, Skyler himself appeared sweetly innocent, smiling. (Was it possible? Skyler could scarcely believe that that small child was him; or, that he had once been that small child.) In one of the photos, pretty young Mummy was hugging Skyler, who clutched a stuffed animal; in another, handsome young Daddy appeared to be guiding Skyler on a tricycle. Vaguely Skyler remembered the tricycle, but he had no memory of that child . . . And there was the baby in Mummy's arms: Edna Louise.

Hymnal music wafted in from overhead speakers. Amid the food odors was a powerful scent of calla lilies. Skyler drifted from room to room, staring at the TV screens. From a brochure handed to him by a Heaven Scent staffer Skyler learned that Betsey Rampike's "dream funeral" had been created by Betsey herself; in spring 2007, Heaven Scent Products was launching its new Heaven Scent Life Services Caterers whose motto was *It is never too early to plan for life's special occasions. Let us help you celebrate that special wedding, anniversary, christening, bat or bar mitzvah, graduation, funeral.*

Skyler was staring at a wall-TV screen on which, graceful and seemingly weightless as a butterfly, his very young sister Bliss was skating on the ice. He had seen this footage many times and yet, he dared not look away. Sweet little four-year-old Bliss in her white satin skater's costume, fairy wings on her shoulders . . .

"Why—is it 'Sky-ler'? Betsey's son? Oh please: can we take just a few shots of you and Bliss?—if you stand here by the screen—"

Middle-aged couple, doughy-animated faces, thrilled eyes, some sort of camera device in the man's uplifted hands, and Skyler heard himself say in a reptile voice: "If you don't turn that fucking thing off, I will strangle you both."

Sharp cries as of frightened waterfowl. Some commotion as of a firecracker carelessly tossed. There came Bix Rampike grim-faced to rescue the psychotic son gripping him by the upper arm and leading him from the room: "Son. This way. Out the back. And don't fucking *limp*."

IN THIS WAY, *DER ENTFREMDUNGSGEFUHL* DEEPENED.

"OF COURSE, SON: IT CAN'T BRING HER BACK."

The flatness in Bix Rampike's voice, the haggard look that, fleetingly, came into the big-boned guileless face, Skyler had no doubt now that it was Bliss to whom his father was referring.

Skyler nodded, grimly. Skyler was pressing an ice-cold glass of club soda against his heated and slightly swollen face.

It was early evening. The men were sitting across from each other in the musty-romantic Old Dutch Tavern of the Washington Irving Inn where Skyler was spending the night. Bix was on his second, possibly his third Scotch whiskey. And now thirstily Bix swallowed a large mouthful of this precious amber liquid. Almost, Skyler could taste the whiskey going down, lovely fiery comforting sensation. Almost, Skyler wished he'd been a drinker instead of a drug-user. Alcohol was legal, you had only to be old enough to buy it. Now that he'd pledged sobriety to Pastor Bob, it was too late.

Upstairs in his room Skyler had slept a stuporous sleep for several hours. Bix had brought him back to the hotel, walked him to his room, tenderly laid him on the bed and partly undressed him and left him to "sleep it off"—as if Skyler, and not Bix Rampike, had been drinking at the reception. Now Skyler's head throbbed with an obscure and ominous pain. He'd come downstairs to the Old Dutch Tavern to meet his father who had "something crucial" to tell him and (it seemed) to give him. Skyler was to have dinner that evening with Bix and Bix's "new" wife Danielle whom Skyler had never met and had little wish to meet but who was, as Bix said pointedly, "very eager" to meet Skyler who was "after all, her stepson."

Stepson! Skyler shuddered. So strangely thirsty, he'd finished his second bottle of club soda.

Brooding Bix leaned forward on his elbows, on the wood-plank table. Skyler saw how his father's eyebrows had grown thick and tufted as an animal's vestigial markings. There was a gleam of Daddy-affection in the soulful hazel-brown eyes, unless the gleam was Daddy-malice. "Son, you don't drink, eh? Not ever?"

Skyler shrugged. "Told you, no."

"Sure, you've 'told me'—but frankly, son, I find it a little hard to believe. The demographics on this subject are epidemic: your age-group drinks. And a kid with your background—'drug user'—'recovering addict'—hell, Skyler, let's not mince words, this has been one existential hell of a day." Seeing the alarmed look in Skyler's face, Bix relented, bared his teeth in a reassuring-Daddy smile, placed a heavy warm hand on Skyler's chill hand. "Just want you to know that you can talk to me, son. Your father."

Skyler muttered *Okay Dad*.

So long Skyler had determined to call his father *Father* and not *Daddy* nor even *Dad* and yet: in the man's presence, *Dad* came to Skyler's lips, irresistibly.

Bix was saying in the slow, dragging way that seemed new to Skyler that he, too, had a problem with "substance abuse"—in his case, alcohol—and he, too, had been "recovering" for the past ten years. "Son, when a man loves what he has lost, best—" Bix paused, and began again: "When a man loses what he has loved best—his soul is rent forever."

Skyler was shocked by these words. Never since Bliss's death had his father spoken to him like this. Skyler could scarcely recall his father speaking to him in any intimate way at all.

"Do you think of her often, son? Your beautiful little sister?"

Quickly Skyler shook his head to signal *yes*. Or was it *no*. Squirmed like a giant worm impaled upon a hook shaking his (bowed, guilt-stricken) head to signal *no*, he did not want to take up this subject, now.

Bix had moved the Italian-leather briefcase aside as if he'd forgotten it. Speaking so earnestly, he'd seemed to be pleading with Skyler. Out of a pocket he withdrew a wallet stuffed with credit cards and out of the wallet he withdrew several small photographs which he spread out on the table-top with tenderness and pride for Skyler to peer at: were these photographs of Bliss?—or photographs of the "new" family? Skyler's eyes filled with stinging moisture, only vaguely he could make out a curvaceous female figure, blond hair and clearly not Betsey, and there was a small child, possibly a little girl, blond also, smiling up at the camera . . . Skyler had no idea what his father was saying. From across the dim-lighted Old Dutch Tavern in the area of, possibly, the enormous fieldstone fireplace in which gas-fueled yule logs were merrily blazing, Skyler heard his father's words, a rush of urgent-Daddy speech, pleading-Daddy, righteous-Daddy, and through a scrim of headache pain he saw his father's jaws moving, a sudden pike-smile.

". . . hope you are happy for me, son. Could be, this is your 'new' family, too."

". . . OLD ARE YOU, SON?"

"In a few weeks, twenty."

Skyler spoke in the flat dread voice of one foreseeing a crash and unable to forestall it. For he knew that his father would say next *What have you done with your life?*

Instead, Bix signaled the waitress for another drink. Saying, with a massive-bison sigh, "You still limp, I see. How is your 'recovery' coming?"

Skyler laughed uneasily. "You mean my leg, or—?"

"Son, your recovery. 'Recovering' your life."

Bix hunched forward, like a sudden landslide. He was wearing a very expensive, elegantly tailored suit so dark a gray as to appear black in the dimly lighted Old Dutch Tavern; he'd removed the coat, to lay across the rear of the booth; he'd removed his necktie, and opened the collar of his long-sleeved white dress shirt. It occurred to Skyler that his father might have been drinking for much of the time Skyler had been sleeping upstairs.

Skyler told his father that his "recovery" was coming along very well. He rarely used a cane now. He could "run"—if not far, and not very fast. He did "experience pain"—but nothing he couldn't live with. He was off painkillers and he was off all "meds" and he'd been "sober" for forty-nine days.

"Son, that sounds good. That sounds damned promising. 'Sober' is how you look. I hear there's a high degree of 'redivicism' after drug rehabilitation, though."

"'Recidivism,' Dad."

"If I'd taught you to drink. There might not be this weakness in you. Drugs!" Suddenly Bix was snorting in bemused-Daddy contempt. Skyler recalled how scornful his father had been of Betsey's myriad tranquilizers and mood-elevators.

"I am sober, I said. And I intend to stay that way." Skyler spoke with more aggression than he felt. Through the headache scrim he saw his father shifting his shoulders ominously.

Now came their waitress to bring Bix another drink. And another club-soda-with-lime, Skyler didn't recall ordering. In keeping with the period-decor of the Old Dutch Tavern, their waitress wore what was intended to be a sexy-tavern-wench costume, ankle-length burlap skirt, waist cinched tight in a black leather strap, white lace-up corset baring the tops of her fatty breasts. She was an attractive snub-nosed woman in her late thirties with shingled glamour-hair and some prior knowledge of Skyler's father for she called him "Mr. Rampike" with a flirty-reverent flutter of her eyelashes. Skyler felt a pang of sexual resentment, that the waitress took so little notice of him, and only of his father. Between the two adults passed rapid-fire dialogue and gazes of the kind two would-be amorous dogs might exchange while being tugged in opposite directions by their owners.

As soon as the tavern-wench waitress left, Bix's smile faded. Reading his gangling son's mutinous thoughts he said, "This girl you were 'involved with' at Basking Ridge—Leander Harkness's daughter? What came of that?"

Quickly Skyler said he did not want to talk about Heidi Harkness. Not ever.

"Are you in contact with her, son?"

"No."

"When the girl left school she wasn't pregnant, was she?"

Skyler flushed. "Jesus, Dad. You sure are blunt, aren't you."

"Well, was she?"

"No."

"And would you know that, with certainty?"

Skyler bit his lower lip, mortified. He could not believe this conversation and yet, he seemed not able to push himself out of the booth, and escape. Something like a fistful of blood had rushed into his face. "Yes I would know. She wasn't. And I don't w-want to t-t-talk about it, Dad. I told you."

In fact, *was* Skyler certain? Had Skyler ever been certain of anything? Very likely there were ways for a girl to become pregnant of which naive/innocent/clumsy/ill-coordinated Skyler Rampike had had little knowledge at sixteen, as he'd had little experience.

For some minutes, Bix spoke of Leander Harkness. Marveling at the pitcher with the "demon arm" and "steely-cold nerves" and how "unjust" it was that Leander Harkness would never be inducted into the Baseball Hall of Fame and in this way the great American tradition of the Hall of Fame itself was "compromised" for Harkness's pitching skills were nonparallel and "after all" Harkness had never been found guilty of the crimes charged against him in any court of law.

Through this impassioned speech, Skyler cowered before his father looming above him like a death-dirigible. Bix Rampike had long been a Yankees fan and a particular admirer of Leander Harkness and so Skyler was waiting for his father to ask him if he had ever actually met Leander Harkness and (maybe) shaken his hand; and trembling Skyler prepared to say in the cool wry tone of a young film actor delivering a dynamite line to an elder *Hell no Dad, one murderer in one lifetime is enough for me.*

Instead, following a mysterious stream of associations, Bix took up the subject of his own life, about which Skyler had not asked him a single question; not only Bix's new family but Bix's "terrific" new job as CEO of New Genesis BioTech, Inc.

Skyler thought *He's hurt! He wants me to care for him.*

Grateful to be spared the ominous subject of Leander Harkness, Skyler obliged his father by asking about New Genesis BioTech, Inc.

For some minutes then, with something of his old animation, Bix spoke of the "exciting"—"revolutionary"—"state-of-the-art" research being done by a team of international scientists at the company's laboratory in New Harmony, New Jersey. With boyish pride Bix told Skyler that, of the numerous, very profitable subsidiaries of Univers, Inc., New Genesis was the "most heavily capitalized" and that he had been invited to head the new company by the CEO of Univers, Inc. himself—"That midnight call from Hank took me totally by surprise, Skyler. Has to be the *piece-resistance* of my professional life."

"Dad, that's swell!"

(Was "swell" still idiomatic? In his actual childhood Skyler had never uttered this childish expletive but he had the idea that, in the comic strips and cartoons enjoyed by Bix Rampike, "swell" remained an American favorite.)

". . . 'miracles of genetic engineering' . . . 'donor specimens handpicked to grow your new kidney!' . . . 'organ transplants soon to be common as dentures, toupees' . . . 'organ regeneration à la mode of self-replicating amphibian-lizard genus *Caudata* (your common lizard)' . . . 'VSP': 'Volunteer Specimens Project' . . ."

Something about this last item roused Skyler to bratty-adolescent curiosity. " 'Volunteer Specimens Project'? What the hell is that, Dad?"

In a grumpy-Daddy lowered voice, as if the Old Dutch Tavern with its scattered and inconsequential patrons might be avid to overhear the secrets of corporate America, Bix explained to Skyler that the "VS Project" was his particular brainchild. In "restricted environments" in the United States and abroad, individuals were "invited to volunteer" in New Genesis experiments, and were "pretty well-paid" for doing so.

Frowning Skyler asked what sorts of "restrictive environments" were these. He'd begun to notice that his father's words were just slightly slurred and a tic-like smile played about the Rampike pike-mouth.

"Prisons, treatment centers and psychiatric facilities, state hospitals and VA hospitals and some church-related hospices exempt from over-zealous federal and state regulations. As I said, 'VSP' has been my personal brainchild, son, and in our first twelve months of implementation, in Texas, Louisiana, Georgia and Florida alone—"

"Dad, wait. What do you mean, these are 'volunteer specimens'? Do they have any choice about 'volunteering'? Do you tell them that the experiments might be dangerous?"

A dramatic pause. At the bar, a tipsy female patron was laughing like a runaway zipper. Bix hunched his fullback shoulders and said, with the imperial air of a chief-executive-officer reciting a script to a vast audience: "New Genesis volunteers are duly informed of any risks involved in our projects. They are given waivers to sign, and these waivers have been thoroughly vetted by our legal team in strict accordance with federal and state regulations, when applicable. Under the current administration, there has been much-needed 'reform' of over-zealous regulatory legislation designed to hamper and place unnecessary financial burdens on business. Of course, foreign countries are another matter. And there are frequently beneficial side effects to our experiments, of course—the 'regeneration' of destroyed brain cells, for instance, or a diseased liver— and many more instances—in addition to the generous payments New Genesis volunteers receive for their participation in scientific progress."

"Jesus, Dad! Are these helpless, incarcerated people? Prisoners, psychiatric patients? Retarded people? 'Specimens' in hospices, on their deathbeds?" Skyler's hoarse voice rose in alarm. He had not been so excited in a very long time and had no idea what was happening except he saw that he'd spilled club soda onto the wood-plank table and had gotten his shirt sleeves wet.

Bix said furiously, "Keep your voice down, son. You are disgrace enough already to the Rampike name."

Bix Rampike's face glowered like a rotted pumpkin. In his displeasure with his son he brought the flat of his heavy hand down on Skyler's outspread fingers, like a mallet.

STUMBLED AWAY TO THE MEN'S ROOM. CONSIDERED HANGING HIMSELF IN one of the toilet stalls except (1) Skyler's luck, someone would come whistling into the restroom to piss into a urinal and discover him; and, (2) at Hugo Boss, Skyler had left behind his sexy newly purchased leather belt so he had not the means to hang himself anyway.

Thinking *Having come so far, my epic journey, I can't give up now. Can I?*

". . . WORLD MIGHT'VE THOUGHT, INCLUDING YOU, PRISSY SKY-BOY, HEAD UP your Ivy League ass, that your mother and I were not on the very best terms because of the divorce and the bullshit in the tabloids, but not so!—"

Badly Skyler wanted to nudge the Italian-leather briefcase toward his ranting father; or, with the childish audacity he'd never had as a child, appropriate it and open it himself.

". . . though it did hurt, have to admit, when Betsey went on those damn TV shows promoting her damn 'memoirs' and spoke of me, her ex-, like I'm the woman's beet-noir . . . as if our marriage ending was my fault alone. God damn, son, you're said to be high I.Q., if fucked-up as hell, so you know that things are never that simple. Onan's Razor—know what that is?—means that things have multiple causes. Like history, like why we fought the Civil War, or World War II, or the difference between asbestos and asbesteosis, it's 'over-determined.' Y'know what Freud means by 'over-determined' . . ."

Impatiently Skyler nodded yes! Yes he knows what S. Freud meant by "over-determined."

". . . anyway not true. Betsey and I remained in contact till the ghastly end. We had our 'troubled' son to deal with—we had joint lawsuits, like the 'KILL BLISS!'* outrage—we had 'copyright infringement' on the name 'Bliss Rampike' and her likeness. (The most repulsive, some sneaker company using Bliss's picture on girls' damn *footwear*.) Our lawyers are interbreeding, their kids are marrying! Naturally Betsey contacted me before she went into the hospital last week. 'Bix, I have written to Skyler again, I have pleaded with Skyler to come see me or at least speak with me but he *has not*.' I told your mother not to cry, not to judge you too harshly because there are reasons not to judge you like a normal American kid, or even a normal American fuck-up kid. Anyway, your mother and I were on close terms and nothing like the monsters those jackals and hyenas have painted us in the gutter-press. No one can understand how close we were, joined at the heart—when you have had children together with a woman, and when you have lost a child."

Abruptly Bix ceased speaking. A film of perspiration had broken out on his deep-furrowed forehead, Bix wiped on his shirt sleeve. When the waitress brought him his drink, Bix disappointed her by scarcely acknowledging her for he was staring broodingly at Skyler. "This 'fiancé'—'Nathan Kissler'—Betsey turned a deaf ear to my investigator, who'd turned up some frank evidence that Kiss-my-ass would've been arrested for embezzlement not once not twice but three times, some fund-raising scam he'd had going up in Darien, Connecticut, also a history of forged checks, but it's been elderly widows he's romanced, not the kind to 'press charges.' Anyway, Betsey contacted me to tell me that a 'precious document' was being sent to me by certified mail, which I could read 'if I so wished,' but I was not to speak to her about it, would I promise? and so, what the hell, I prom-

---

* *Popular video game first issued in 2000. The player is a pretty blond cartoon-Bliss, skating ingeniously/desperately to escape her potential killers who include GUNNAR and GUTHER (sex perverts), MOM, DAD, and SNIVELER (older brother). Bix and Betsey Rampike joined forces to sue for criminal libel and to remove the offensive item from stores, but sales continue on the Internet and are said to be "in the millions." (No, "Sniveler" has never seen this disgusting item.)*

ised. Betsey said the 'precious document' was a letter for Skyler, she had been wanting to write for years. And with the letter there will be a video: 'Bix, you remember.' "

Video! Vaguely Skyler recalled a video. Swallowing hard thinking *Maybe I don't want this after all. Maybe I am making a mistake.*

". . . y'see, son, this surgery of Betsey's, she had a 'premonition.' Betsey was a woman for 'premonitions'—most of which never came off—but this time, she was right. She'd had a half-dozen 'surgerical procedures' that I knew of, that were kept secret. This famous New York publisher who came to her, after that sex-pervert Roosha killed himself, offering Betsey an 'undisclosed sum' to write her memoir, not that Betsey had to 'write' it, they hire people to do the actual writing, like speechwriters, the crucial test is can you go on TV, do you pass the TV test, and damn right, Betsey Rampike did. But for TV, and these 'promotional appearances,' Betsey needed surgeries, for which the publisher paid the bill."

"Surgeries? Like for—cancer?"

"No, Skyler. Not for cancer."

"But it was cancer of the—" Skyler faltered, shy of the word *service*, "—that's what Betsey died of, wasn't it?"

Bix lifted his glass and drank. For a long bemused moment contemplating his son's anxious face. Then he said, with the air of one speaking to a very young child, "Sky-boy, no. It wasn't 'cancer of the cerxiv' or cancer of anything. Your mother's surgeries were all cosmetic. Back in Fair Hills, Betsey began with 'eyelid tucks.' Those injections—'Botox'—'collagen'—'laser wrinkle remover.' Her first face-lift, we were separated then, had to be 1999. The surgery that killed her, son, was the nastiest one: 'liposuction.' " Bix shuddered, and took another large swallow of whiskey.

" 'Lip-o-suction'—?"

"Of course, it was 'cancer' that was leaked to the press. Betsey's PR team is very skilled at 'leaking' what is said to be secrets, and the press just gobbles it up. See, if the press gobbles up a wrong factoid, they can 'correct' it in the next issue, or on TV. It's all bullshit, but it's lucrative bullshit, just between you and me, son, I have invested in some of these 'gutter-tabloids,' they do turn a profit and that's the bottom line. But the tragedy was, Betsey died of 'liposuction' and not cancer, and Heaven Scent is frantic to keep that secret. Because Betsey Rampike has been such a 'role model' for the Christian-consumer community. Poor Betsey was saying, she could not 'diet off' a roll of fat around her waist, and hips, God knows the poor woman did try, it was hell living with Betsey when she was 'dieting' . . . and if she did drop ten, fifteen pounds, it was the Dark Night of the Soul, and then the damn skin hung loose. I felt sorry for her, God damn. Like a part-deflated elephant-balloon, skin hanging loose. Poor woman's rear, that had used to be so smooth and bouncy, you would not want to have seen, Skyler. Some sights, like fallen-down tits, that'd once been stand-up beauties, you do not want to see, son. Your dad will shield you from such precocious knowledge. Anyway, the surgery went bad. Had to know it was a disaster, Kiss-my-ass called me. This conniving fucker, called *me*. 'The liposuction went wrong. Parts of Betsey's stomach got sucked into the vacuum. And some intestines . . .' Poor guy was bawling. Maybe he did love her. Maybe he hadn't gotten her to change her will yet. 'Bix, she isn't going to make it. The doctor says, the stress to her heart . . .' She was on life-support for three days. He was saying he was her business partner and fiancé but he didn't have power of attorney and I said, 'Look. I am not "next-of-kin" any longer, Betsey and I were divorced years ago.' Kiss-my-ass was in over his head. Two-bit embezzler, he'd fucked this up and knew it. Makes me sick, thinking of her and him in bed together, so I don't think of it, and advise that for you, too. See, son . . ."

Bix's voice had thickened. Tears swelled in his eyes and trickled down his flushed cheeks. Skyler was trying to comprehend the fact: his mother had not died of cancer but of "liposuction"—cosmetic surgery. His mother had died, and that was why he was here.

"Son, this is yours."

At last, Skyler's father opened the briefcase. With surprisingly steady hands he removed a peach-colored envelope, and what appeared to be a battered and water-stained videotape. "This material is yours, Skyler. Your mother prepared it for you 'in case God calls me' and it was her wish that you do with it whatever you want and, son, that includes destroying it which is what your dad recommends *toot sweet*. Betsey entrusted these items to me, she said, as the 'great love of her life'—or was it 'the great tragic love of her life.' You see, your mother and I agreed never to reveal what passed between us. That is, what happened to your sister on that terrible night. Though I was not present, I was responsible, as you will learn. I may be drunk right now and I may be a son of a bitch lacking a soul, but I readily concede an existential fact, that I am responsible for the tragedy of our family, for I believe in truth without flinching. Son, truth is the bedrock of the scientific method. And the scientific method is the bedrock of western civilization. That controversial pioneer of the Unconscious S. Freud has said, the female of the species is not so 'morally evolved' as the male and so it is the case, son, we males must take responsibility for female acts, at times. Though your mother and I were divorced and never appeared together in public yet we remained 'amicable' through the years—like nations with nuclear weapons poised to kill each other. Now that poor Betsey is gone, I can give you these in the hope that you, Skyler, will be granted a new lie—I mean, a new life—by what you discover here. I did not read every word of the heartfelt letter your mother wrote to you, Skyler: it was too painful. Nor did I watch that damned video again, that I'd seen years ago and that had so misled me about you, son. No need to reopen festering wounds! I hope, Skyler, that after you have examined these documents you will call me, and forgive me, son, for misjudging you, all these years; and I hope that we can be father and son again, as we'd been in Fair Hills, in happier times. I will pay your tuition at any university or college you can get into—if you stay sober!—and you are free to study anything you wish though keeping in mind the challenge of the future—'Ever evolving' which is the axion of New Genesis, Inc. How proud your old dad would be, son, if you took a course of study, molecular biology for instance, or gene-splicing, so you could join up with our New Genesis team. And I will buy you a new car: frankly I was shocked to see that piece of shit you're driving, pulled up into Betsey's driveway when I got there. My 'new family' will welcome you, Skyler, though probably you would not want to live with us which would be an unfair strain on Danielle but you are welcome to visit us often, in the condo on Central Park or at 'Harmony Farm' which is our two-hundred-acre country estate over in Jersey. Son?"

Skyler pushed out of the wood-plank booth. Had to leave! Now he had what he'd come for, both items in hand, he was damn sorry to disappoint his dad, sorry not to be meeting the "new wife," stammered thanks, thanks

Dad, shaking Dad's iron-grip hand, and when clumsy-drunk-Dad lurched partway out of the booth to hug him, and leave a snail-scum-trail of spittle on his left cheek, Skyler gritted his teeth allowing himself to be kissed, allowed himself to be hugged, one final time: "Son, remember your old dad loves you like hell."

"Dad, I know that. And I love you, too."

IN THE MURKY PART-TIMBERED LOBBY OF THE WASHINGTON IRVING INN LIMPing at a trot toward a cave of elevators Skyler was distracted by the sight of—was it Mrs. Klaus? Skyler's best-friend Calvin Klaus's coldly beautiful blond mother? But a closer look at the woman in the ankle-length sable coat dissuaded him, for Morgan Klaus was Skyler's mother's age, in her mid-forties; and this woman was considerably younger. She was on her way into the Old Dutch Tavern and her gaze—steely-blue, opaque—passed through Skyler like a laser ray. In the elevator ascending to his room on the fifth floor clutching the perfumy peach-colored envelope and the water-stained videotape to his chest he thought *Must be Danielle*.

"Your Loving Mother-Mummy"

February 21 2007.

Dear Skyler—

It was not intended that your sister would die. And yet—I am to blame.

How terrible is God's wrath & His ~~mercy~~—mercy—this is a true "Jest of God"—that the Person who loved Bliss most of all the Earth—her mother—was the unwished vessell of her death.

Skyler, please forgive me—I was fearfull of "confessing" what I had done—the ignomy of shame

of Mankind — Mother Rampike's
judgement — I could not bear.
   It was indicated to your
father that you — a child of
9 — was responsible — and so,
your father conspirred with
me, to shield you. It was love
for you — that your father cherished.
He believed — "What Skyler has
done was a child's act and
he must be proo tected." I had
led your father to believe that
you & Bliss were playing hide
& seek & a game of "tying
up" & by accident you struck
Bliss's head against that
hard wall. But the truth is —
your Mother was the instrument

of Death & this out of Vanity –
to make your father love me –
as he used to love me – that is
the reason my weakness allowed
a demon to enter my soul – this
demon of Jealousy – Jesus warned
me "Let your husband go and
he will one day return from
his whores but grab at him
and try to bind him and he
will not return." But in my
drunk blindness I could not
listen. The "ransome note" I
wrote as a joke – I think – it
would be waiting for your father
when he came for Bliss that
morning to take her to New

York City & he would be very
upset & would search for her—
& he would find her in the
furnace room where she would
be hiding—with arms & wrists
tied as in a game—& he would
be made to know that Bliss
was his beloved daughter he must
not abandon his family. At
this time I was "medicated" &
had also been drinking & could not
think clearly—I think—for
I did not forsee that Bliss
was not such a little girl now
but 6 yrs old & would resist
her Mother's plan of a "hiding
game"—very sleepy at first & I
was upset she had soiled her
bedsheets and thought to hide
them from me then I told
her—"We would play a funny

trick on Daddy" then in the
furnace room she rebeled & was
fighting me she said "Mummy
I dont want to be here" & she
said what was hurtfull to me —
"Mummy you are _drunk_ " — &
somehow then the demon siezed
me & I grabbed her shoulders &
a blackness came over me
Skyler — the wickedness was
done that could not be undone —
so then I went to you — &
planted the seed — that _you_
had hurt your little sister — &
I called your father to summon
him from his whore of that
time who would have no more
shame than to send flowers
& a card of condolence &

look me in the eye at Bliss's
funeral – she is the one & will
never forgive –

Your father then saw – what
had happened – that could not
be undone – & the video that
I had made of you Skyler &
am so sorry for – for then
your father would always believe
that you had killed your sister –
tho' when that "sex prevert"
Ruscha appeared – it came to
seem that he might be the
murderer – for he confessed –
that was very surprising to
me but it came to seem
– & so your father thought too –
that Ruscha was a "gift from
God" to the Rampikes in their
Hour of Need & many came to

believe that it was so – that
man had hurt Bliss there was
the wish to believe for in truth
G. R. was a sex prevert by his
own admission. & your father
said – "This will save Skyler."

I prayed to Jesus to forgive me –
I would allow an "innocent
man" to be maligned in my
place – & Jesus said "So it was
with me Betsey – an innocent
man to be crucified" & at a
latter time Jesus said "And
now you know Betsey – you are
crucified too – you have lost
your darling angel until you
are joined in Heaven."

Skyler if you can see it in
your heart to forgive me –
you will only read this if
"something has happened"

to me & then will you pray for your Mother who meant only to keep our beautifull family together & who has never stopped loving you.

Your loving Mother—

"Mummy"

As for the mysterious videotape—battered, badly water-stained, near-ruined: this would turn out to be the "lost" camcorder tape of seventy-two murky seconds Skyler's mother had taken of him shortly after Bliss's death, and later played for him, as it would be played for Skyler's father who would remove it from the Rampike house before police were summoned.

What a shock to Skyler, to see this old nightmare tape, he'd long assumed had been destroyed by his father! To see again, in sick fascination, the blurred figure of the child—"Skyler"—with his small pale sleep-stunned face, innocent tousled light-brown hair and flannel p.j.'s; to hear again the distraught, accusing, near-inaudible off-camera voice *Skyler tell where sister did you* as the stricken child-face began to break into particles, as Mummy's voice was breaking *Skyler please tell this house? hide and seek? where is will not be punished Mummy promises* and in the grainy underwater tape the guilty child is weeping as if his little demon-heart has been broken.

THE REVELATION

NOT GUILTY! **IN A STREAM OF GLITTERING HEADLIGHTS CROSSING THE GREAT** bridge above the Hudson River deceptively placid, near-invisible in darkness below and into New Jersey wiping hot stinging tears from his eyes. Thinking *I was not the one. I was not* astonished and stunned as if he'd been struck a blow over the head with a mallet, yet smiling to indicate he was not injured, he was in fact very happy. And he was blessed. Had to be blessed. For his miserable gnarled life had been handed back to him, transformed. Bearing left amid a confusion of traffic into the lane indicating NEW JERSEY TURNPIKE SOUTH. He was driving with more confidence now. Thinking *It was not me! I was never the one.* Approaching garlands of lights at Newark International Airport staring at aircraft descending out of the sky, unerring in their descent out of the sky and onto invisible runways behind the gigantic terminals and Skyler swallowed hard thinking *But it could be otherwise, that plane could crash in an instant.* Thinking *Any of these planes, at any time.* And yet, he'd been spared. So long he had believed himself damned, yet he'd been spared. He had not injured his sister. He had not struck his sister's head against a concrete wall and left her to die in the darkness of the airless furnace room. *Not me! never me* smiling, shaking his head as he drove, his night-vision blotched by tears. He'd had to check out of that hotel. Couldn't bear to remain in that room another minute. Knowing that his drunken father would want to see him, would come knocking at his door. And he could not bear to see Bix Rampike. Nor could he bear to be introduced to the "new" wife/"stepmother" unnervingly like a younger sister of Calvin Klaus's mother. He could not risk the tremulous flame of his new happiness threatened by the presence of others. For no one could know how powerfully *Not guilty! Not my sister's murderer!* pulsed through him.

In his impatience pressing down hard on the gas pedal. Not heeding that the station wagon was beginning to quake at sixty-six miles an hour for he was desperate to get back to New Brunswick, to his family there. For it was Pastor Bob whom Skyler loved, and not Bix Rampike. It was Pastor Bob whom Skyler trusted, and not Bix Rampike. How could his father have believed, these long years of Skyler's exile, ten long years banished from the family, that he, Skyler, was a murderer! Of his own sister he'd loved, a murderer! Never would he forgive Bix Rampike. Never would he see Bix Rampike again, if he could avoid him. He had a new family now, the old curse of the Rampikes had lifted. Why had Bix Rampike believed *her*, and not Skyler? Why'd he have faith in *her*, and not in Skyler? Such relief Skyler felt as if released from the death-grip of the giant serpents rearing out of the Greek sea with nightmare logic to clasp the priest Laocoön and his innocent young sons in their coils *O help us, God help us* is the terrible cry that breaks from the throat at such times but there is no help, there is no hope for it is by God's decree that the giant serpents have struck. On the day Skyler had set out on his pilgrimage to Hell he'd prayed aloud; " 'I believe: help thou my unbelief' " and this prayer had been answered. Though Skyler did not believe in a God who answered prayers yet it seemed to him, yes this prayer had been answered. Skyler's miserable mangled dwarf-life had been handed back to him, whole and transformed. *Not-guilty* he'd been designated. *Not-guilty* he'd been all along.

Now passing ELIZABETH in an eerie miasma of chemical smells pungent as rotted eggs. Outside the station wagon was a nighttime industrial landscape of wild winking lights, smokestacks rimmed in lurid red flames like tongues. Skyler's nostrils constricted, Skyler felt a tinge of nausea. And at the RAHWAY exit made to think *But the "prevert" died, died by her hand* and in that instant Skyler nearly lost control of his speeding vehicle, drifting out of the right-hand lane and almost struck from behind by an eighteen-wheeler bearing down upon him, panicked Skyler steered the station wagon back into the right-hand lane, chastened by a jeering horn, swallowing hard thinking *But I can't be cheated of my happiness, I have waited so long.* A flash of the weeping child-face in the ruined video, the skinny shoulders, narrow chest and utter helplessness in that body and yet: she had not taken pity on him, had she? She had sacrificed him, to save herself: his mother. A leaden sensation had begun to pass over him. A heavy booted foot on the nape of his neck for the fact was *Ten years of my life taken from me, and my sister taken from me.*

Just before the exit for New Brunswick, traffic was being routed through a single, very slow lane. Near the median there had been a spectacular accident involving several vehicles and here were flares and emergency vehicles, squad cars with flashing red lights, broken glass spread across the pavement through which Skyler had no choice but to drive wincing as if barefoot. Skyler tried not to look to the side not wanting to see the injured, if there were injured. Not wanting to see mangled corpses. He did see a grotesquely smashed and upended vehicle not unlike one of Bix Rampike's super-military S.U.V.s and for a delirious moment Skyler worried his father might have been driving that vehicle. And exiting for NEW BRUNSWICK he felt a stronger conviction, he had failed someone, he had not helped someone needing his help. Thinking *But all this time I have been alive, and Bliss has been dead.* It was not a new realization for Skyler was prone to such thoughts at any and all times and yet it struck him now with a fresh horror. By this time, the euphoria Skyler had felt on the earlier half of the drive had faded. Like dirty water draining from a tub, Skyler's happiness had drained away. He could not comprehend now why he'd been so happy . . . Gloating in the discovery that he hadn't killed his sister when he'd done nothing to prevent her being killed by their drunken mother. Pilgrimage to Hell this journey had been and Skyler had believed he was escaping Hell not understanding that Hell would be dragged after him for Hell was Skyler Rampike's natural habitation. *Demonic despair is the most intense form of despair: in despair the will to be oneself . . . In hatred toward existence, it wills to be oneself, wills to be itself in accordance with its misery.*

In his hoarse raw voice speaking aloud inside the rattling and (who knows? on the Jersey Turnpike, few have died in "spectacular" pile-ups who'd expected, taking a ticket at the toll booth, that such would be their fate) possibly death-bound vehicle: "I'm not strong enough for happiness. Despair is my only strength."

"SON? WAKE UP"

THOUGH EXHAUSTED BY HIS ORDEAL YET HE HAD TO RETURN THE STATION
wagon to the rectory garage. And in the garage, had to position the vehicle
in exactly the place it had been, when he'd backed it out the other day. A
vise gripped him tight, *had to*.

Inside The Ark he told them—he interrupted whatever they believed
they were doing to tell them—he had to speak with Pastor Bob that night.
And when they tried to dissuade him he repeated he had to speak with Pastor Bob that night.

Had to.

(And if not?)

Had to obliterates *if not*.

In The Ark they tried to dissuade the flamey-faced youth with twitchy
mouth and crazed eyes as often they dissuaded desperate individuals
drawn to the evangelical mysteries of the New Canaan church who were
convinced that they must, that very hour, meet with Reverend Bob Fluchaus
for the salvation of their souls; tried to explain that Pastor Bob had spent
the first part of the day visiting a distraught woman being held in the
Middlesex Women's Detention Center on charges of manslaughter, and
negotiating between the woman and her family of young children, and the
second part of the day he'd been at the bedside of a friend, a dying man in a
local hospice, wouldn't be returning to the rectory until late and when he
did return he would be exhausted, and Skyler listened or appeared to listen then saying he would wait for Pastor Bob in the church, not in the rectory but in the church where he could be alone with his thoughts; and
again they tried to dissuade him, Skyler Rampike who gave off a fierce ra-

diant heat like a throbbing artery, it was nearly 11 P.M. and why didn't Skyler go home for the night—wherever his home was—and return in the morning—and impatiently Skyler explained he had to see Pastor Bob that night, his life depended upon it. And by this time there came Miriam in sweatpants, pullover Rutgers jersey and flip-flops on her scrawny feet, Miriam's off-duty attire, frowning and fussing Miriam accompanied Skyler to the darkened church, unlocked a rear door, switched on a few lights for Skyler who stumbled inside so distracted he barely remembered to thank her.

"Help me, Jesus. Or—somebody."

How stark, how plain the interior of the New Canaan church at such an hour! Here was a space of no more romance or mystery than the interior of a warehouse. Except for the modest altar and the cross positioned above it on the wall and the many rows, shading off into murky shadow, of bleakly empty folding chairs of which it might be said by a neutral observer *No one of any significance or importance will ever sit on such chairs.* In a gesture of self-abasement Skyler knelt on the concrete floor. Skyler knelt despite his painful knee, intending to remain kneeling until Pastor Bob came hurrying in: he would punish himself yet more subtly he would punish Pastor Bob if Pastor Bob did not hurry to him. Yet—how uneasy he was beginning to feel, in the empty church! That sensation to which S. Freud affixed the term *uncanny* came over him. For never in Skyler's life had he seen any church except when there were people—"worshippers"—inside; never had he seen the New Canaan church except when it was crammed with people, and with life; for the congregation of the New Canaan church was what you'd call a hopeful and expectant congregation, of individuals who have come primed to hear good news. And Skyler had never been in this interior without seeing, at the front, like an upright flame quivering with heat and energy, Pastor Bob Fluchaus. Yet now there was no one. Except Skyler, no one. A shiver of dread came to him as he stared at the rows of empty folding chairs fading into murky shadow at the rear of the room *What if this is the afterlife? This!* Seeing that the plain wooden cross above the altar was considerably smaller than the majestic copper cross that floated above the altar of the Assembly of God. For here was a cross, as Pastor Bob said, of the approximate size of the "original" cross upon which Jesus Christ was crucified; as Pastor Bob told his congregation, "Our ministry is human-sized, flawed and imperfect for we are but God's creatures, we cannot be as gods."

Pastor Bob never spoke of Jesus's miracles, in his sermons or at other times. Pastor Bob did not believe that "miracles" were likely to occur in the vicinity of New Brunswick, New Jersey.

After only a few minutes Skyler could not bear the concrete floor against his knees. The bone-ache of kneeling on such an unyielding floor was beyond Skyler's capacity for self-abasement and humility and so he slouched in a folding chair dazed with exhaustion and yet determined to keep from falling asleep before Pastor Bob arrived. He had no doubt that the minister would come to him, in his hour of need. Crossing his arms tightly over his chest to keep from shivering convulsively and to contain his excitement so close to spilling over, like crackling electricity. He could not bear it, this sudden knowledge that he *was not* guilty; he was *not the one*; all these years, without his knowing *Skyler Rampike had not killed his sister*. This astonishing fact swelled like a balloon—swelled and swelled to the point of bursting—as Skyler rapidly spoke, gestured with his hands in the anxious/aggressive way of Bliss's old tutor Rob Feldman—trying to convince a vast audience of ominously silent strangers staring at him without sympathy. Shamelessly Skyler hoped to convince this audience, placate and seduce them with a combination of Rob Feldman's logic and the boyish-wincing smiles with which he'd faced his father in the Old Dutch Tavern revealed to Skyler now, abruptly as in a clap of thunder, to have been yet another anteroom of Hell.

"Son? Wake up."

A MAN'S HAND ON HIS SHOULDER, MORE OF A NUDGE THAN A CARESS.

There was Pastor Bob short of breath and short of patience looming over sleep-dazed Skyler, frowning. "What is it, Skyler? They told me at the rectory you had something to tell me that couldn't wait till morning."

This not-so-subtle reproach, *couldn't wait till morning*, Skyler chose not to hear.

Damn he was embarrassed! Would've wanted Pastor Bob to discover him on his knees praying, not slouched in a chair sleeping so hard he felt now as if his heart had lurched partway out of his chest. Neck stiff, head halfway to his crotch and a rivulet of drool across his chin.

Skyler began to tell Pastor Bob what had happened in Spring Hollow.

Something of what had happened in Spring Hollow.

His mother had died just a few hours before he'd arrived. He had gone to her funeral. The letter his father had given him from her, and the videotape Skyler had not seen in ten years and had assumed had been destroyed . . . Skyler was stammering so badly, Pastor Bob asked him to speak more slowly and clearly. Skyler fumbled to show him the handwritten letter from Betsey Rampike on eight sheets of perfumy stationery but Pastor Bob drew back with a frown saying, "Son, wait. I don't think that's a good idea. Your mother's letter was intended for you alone." And Skyler said, pleading, "But I n-need you to advise me, Pastor Bob. The way you did when I was sick, in rehab. When I wanted to die, in rehab. And you said, 'Skyler, there is more challenge in living than in dying. You must be a warrior of your own life.' But now it's like I am back in rehab, Pastor Bob—my thoughts are all broken. My skin is all itchy. I can't think past what's in front of me, I can't imagine next week, or tomorrow—an hour from now—Please help me, Pastor Bob?"

And Pastor Bob surprised Skyler for Pastor Bob was not smiling in a way to encourage Skyler but in a way to discourage him, as you might beat back an eager puppy jumping up against your legs; and Pastor Bob said, "Help you how, Skyler? You're not a child, you are almost twenty years old, what do you expect me to tell you?" And Skyler wanted to protest, hurt *But I am a child! I am a pigmy!* saying aloud, more reasonably, "What to do with the letter, and the videotape. Tell me, Pastor Bob." And Pastor Bob said, "Examine your conscience, Skyler." And Skyler said, "I—don't think that I have a conscience, Pastor Bob. I don't have a s-soul." And Pastor Bob said patiently, "Then you must acquire a conscience, Skyler. You must acquire a soul, for no one can give you one." Skyler said, "Pastor Bob! Should I t-try to think what J-J-Jesus would do? In my place?" And Pastor Bob said, "Why bring Jesus into it, Skyler? D'you think Jesus is a crutch?" And Skyler said, "This is evidence—this is a confession, in a criminal case—should I turn this 'evidence' over to police, or should I d-destroy it so that no one will ever see it?" And Pastor Bob said, "That decision you will have to make for yourself, Skyler." Removing from a pocket of his soiled nylon-polyester jacket a wadded tissue into which he blew his reddened nose, as Skyler persisted, now more defiantly, "—can't forgive her for what she did to Bliss, all of what she did to Bliss over the years, and will never forgive her for what she did to me." When Pastor Bob failed to respond Skyler said, "God damn I wish there was H-Hell, that 'Betsey Rampike' would suffer as she deserves," his voice rising furious and resolute, "—h-hate both of them, him and her, 'Bix' and 'Betsey,' wish there was fucking Hell for them to suffer in the way they made us s-s-suffer." And still when Bob, searching in his pockets for another tissue, failed to respond Skyler said, "—turn this 'evidence' over to the Fair Hills police, or to the FBI—to expose her— p-punish her," and when Pastor Bob still failed to respond Skyler's voice rose sharply, "—or maybe sell this shit. The 'Betsey Rampike Confession Letter'—the videotape making out nine-year-old Skyler to be a psychotic murderer—the tabloids will go crazy for this shit, they will pay millions, I'll throw in an interview with m-myself . . ." So Skyler ranted in the bleak interior of the church, and Pastor Bob listened, or appeared to listen, with strained sympathy; now sitting in a folding chair that creaked beneath his weight, and by degrees through the tears of fury in his eyes Skyler could not fail to see that the minister, a not-healthy-looking man of middle age, was clearly exhausted. Lines of fatigue in the ruin of his face like erosion in a rock facade. In the grudging and sallow light Fluchaus's burn-scars winking like scales and eyes bloodshot and damp and even in his frenzy of self-pity Skyler was made to understand how in the shallow sea in which the minister bravely waded there were schools of quick-darting piranha (like Skyler Rampike) eager to devour him, to assuage their terrible and insatiable hunger. A shallow sea, a mere man, and infinite hunger: and there was Bob Fluchaus unable to stifle a yawn, a yawn so immense it forced his face into rubbery-cartoon contours; now rubbing his eyes with his big balled-up fists; Skyler could smell—what?—alcohol?—on Pastor Bob's breath, and Skyler could smell beyond the panic-smell of his own body the older man's body, for Pastor Bob was a heavy man who perspired readily in even cool places and Pastor Bob had not showered since early that morning, possibly Pastor Bob hadn't had time to shower that day at all; as his heavy jaws were covered in a coarse silver stubble, and his hair was matted and tufted and grizzled, like his eyebrows; his nylon-polyester jacket, dark-purple, of the kind a high school coach might wear, was grease-stained, and his trousers were badly rumpled; fingernails broken and edged with grime as if Bob Fluchaus was, not a minister, not a "man of God," but a manual laborer, at the end of a lengthy shift. And Pastor Bob said, "Whatever decision you make, Skyler, it must be yours. It must come from a place in your heart, that is purely you." And Skyler said, furious, " 'Heart'—'conscience'—'soul'—what the fuck are these? I need you to tell me what to fucking *do*, my skin is so itchy I'm going to tear it off"—scratching at his face, his neck, his hands, until Pastor Bob had no choice but to grab his hands, to calm him; and Skyler allowed himself to be calmed; and Skyler said, "The letter is 'evidence'—that I am innocent. I should show this letter to the world, Pastor Bob, shouldn't I?" And Pastor Bob said, "But you must have known that you were innocent all along, Skyler, didn't you?" and Skyler said miserably, "No, Pastor Bob. I didn't know," and Pastor Bob said with a mirthless laugh as of a high school coach who witnesses one of his players fumbling an easy play, "For Christ's sake of course you knew. You are not a murderer, how could you think that you were?" and Skyler said, confused, "I-I-I d-didn't know. There's a difference between 'thinking' and 'knowing,' " and Pastor Bob said, "Did you need to believe that you might have been your sister's murderer, to spare yourself knowledge of who was?" and quickly Skyler said, "N-No," and again more emphatically, in the face of the older man's expression of bemused disbelief, "No." And Pastor Bob said, "But now you wonder if you should reveal this 'evidence' to the world, to 'prove' that you are innocent." And Skyler said, "But isn't it my duty? My 'conscience'? Gunther Ruscha—the 'sex prevert'—the man who 'confessed' and 'killed himself' in prison—should be proven innocent, too. Even if the poor bastard has been dead for ten years." And Pastor Bob said, "Whatever this 'evidence' you have, this letter from your mother—I'm guessing that it won't constitute legal proof of anything." And Skyler said, pleading, "Pastor Bob: tell me what to do. This is hell." And Pastor Bob said, "Yes, it is hell. Let me explain, son: my ministry is a ministry for those who dwell in hell. It is a flawed ministry, as my face and body are scarred so I stand before my congregation and before the world flawed, and I don't present myself as a 'perfect' man. I have plenty of sympathy for Pilate who said, 'What is truth?'—fuck if I know. Maybe you've heard rumors that I will be bringing my ministry to a cable TV audience—these rumors are false, for I have told would-be producers I'm a minister only of flesh-and-blood, preaching to flesh-and-blood individuals in the room with me. To appear on TV you must wear makeup to make you look 'like yourself'—what bullshit. Anything that isn't flesh-and-blood, eye-to-eye, it's bullshit. You've heard rumors that I'd been a prison guard before becoming a minister and these rumors I try to correct: I wasn't a guard at Rahway, but an inmate. 'Bob Fluchaus' served three and a half years of a seven-year sentence for vehicular homicide, son. Driving drunk, twenty-nine, with my young wife and three-year-old son. Driving drunk on the Turnpike—speeding—passing a tractor-trailer on the right and cut in too sharply and next thing I knew my car was skidding toward the median and spun around and struck another car, got hit by another truck smashing my 'economy car' like you'd smash a tin can with a sledgehammer. And my son died there on the spot, and my twenty-six-year-old wife I'd known since high school died on the way to the hospital. And another driver died, in the other car. And 'Bob Fluchaus' lived. On a life-support machine for two weeks, burns over thirty percent of my body, skull fracture and eleven bones broken and should've died and wanted to die but did not. Why in hell, who knows. So I pleaded guilty to all the charges they could rack up against me and they sent me away, to think things over. And not an hour a day now, I fail to think about my young wife and my little boy who'd be my wife's age if he'd been allowed to live. And I try to think why God spared me, if it was purposeful or just one more freaky accident on the Turnpike. Because my life sure feels like a freaky accident to me. Because I asked myself in the hospital, 'Why have I been spared?' and God said, 'You have been spared to live out the remainder of your miserable life in misery,' and I did not dispute this, but saw the logic of it, but later God said, 'You have been spared to bring forgiveness to the world, that you can't ever receive yourself from any source.' And I said, 'I don't believe in you, God. "God" is a crock of shit and "Bob Fluchaus" was created in that image,' and God laughed saying, 'What I am is not dependent upon your belief, asshole.'

Must've been high on Demerol in the hospital, never would hear God so loud and so clear as then. So at Rahway I had plenty of time to think, and there was a chaplain there, and we talked a lot together, and we read the Bible together, aloud we read the Gospels, and it seemed to me the Jesus Christ of the Gospels was a visionary crazed with his vision, made the mistake of falling for his own miracles seeing how the 'multitudes' were as little children craving all sorts of bullshit before they'd 'believe'—but he was a true seer, with a wildness in him, and no fear of torture, or death— and one day in my second year of incarceration I made the decision that I would try to carry the message of the Gospels to as much of the world that I could. For though I don't believe in much of anything I 'believe' in human- kind and our need to 'believe' which is a need like hunger. And though I'm not what you'd call a happy man, I'm blessed with the power to make others happy. And some of this I see in you, Skyler. In the rehab clinic, last year. If you'd speak what is in your heart. Son, you don't have to 'believe' in Christ if Christ is in you. If the crucifixion-agony is in you. And that is you, Skyler. Or so it has seemed to me. I am almost never wrong in my judg- ments of people, Skyler, let me boast a little, son, and say that I see in you something of me, at a younger age, except it is finer in you, or might one day be. Am I mistaken?"

By this time it was 2:20 A.M. Skyler would return with Bob Fluchaus to The Ark and in a spare bedroom he would sleep for twelve hours and when he awoke it was to a sensation of great happiness and calm realizing *Noth- ing has been decided. Yet.*

CONDOLENCES

FORWARDED TO SKYLER AT THE PITTS STREET, NEW BRUNSWICK, ADDRESS came a letter postmarked Cambridge, Massachusetts:

2 MARCH 2007

DEAR SKYLER—

PLEASE ACCEPT MY CONDOLENCES ON THE OCCASION OF YOUR MOTHER'S DEATH. BETSEY RAMPIKE WAS A TERRIBLE PERSON (IN MY OPINION) BUT SHE WAS YOUR MOTHER.

SINCERELY,

E. Grubbe

P.S. I AM NOW A JUNIOR AT HARVARD (MAJORS MUSICOLOGY, MOLECULAR BIOLOGY). MY E-MAIL ADDRESS IS EGRUBBE@HARVARD.EDU

Épilogue

HE FORGAVE. NOT FOR BLISS, HE COULD NOT FORGIVE FOR BLISS BUT FOR himself, he forgave them.

He burnt the letters. And the damn video.

Eight tissue-thin pages of sweet-perfumy peach-colored stationery he burnt, and the two previous letters she'd sent to him that he had hidden wrapped in newspaper in his closet, he burnt. And the damn video, that was harder to burn and gave off a sickening stink.

In the scrubby park by the Raritan River he burnt these items. On a wet-glistening gusty morning in March. Sky shimmering like washed glass, sun a smoldering dull-red coal behind shreds of Skyler's favorite cloud—"Altocumulus." It gave him pleasure to recognize the cloud type, and to speak it aloud.

He'd been a promising student at one time. He would return to that life again soon, he believed.

Your sister is dead. You are alive. And so what next?

So Pastor Bob said.

He'd purchased the materials for burning in the neighborhood 7-Eleven store. Where as soon as Skyler entered a wave of *déjà vu* washed over him leaving him breathless. *Not again! Not here! Not me.* For a moment he felt stunned, incapable of thought or volition.

Why was he so frightened? He had vowed to Pastor Bob, he'd made his decision.

There was the clock above the front entrance. Flat as a disc, glowering. Long black hand at eight, short black hand at eleven. In the digital era, "clock faces" would soon vanish Bix Rampike had predicted. But Skyler knew, this time it was morning.

Déjà vu! A faint sepia-tinged odor as of burning leaves, that made Skyler's nostrils pinch and stung his eyes.

Behind the cashier's counter stood the Indian clerk. Youngish but not young, courteous, wary. The clerk was just ringing up a customer's items, Skyler saw his wire-rimmed eyeglasses flash in Skyler's direction. Skyler paused to smile at him and to greet him with a casual upraised hand for at The Ark you learned to greet others with a smile, an easy upraised hand exposing your palm, outspread fingers. In Skyler the gesture was slightly awkward but well-intentioned.

"Hello!"

"Hello, sir."

Sir. Was this irony? Or just courtesy? Behind the wire-rimmed glasses the clerk's eyes were hidden by a glare of reflected light and his smile had tightened into something like a frown.

This time, Skyler knew exactly which aisle. Which shelf. Just two items: five-ounce container of Hercules Lighter Fluid and a single box of (small-sized) Five Star Kitchen Matches.

At the cash register deftly the clerk rang up Skyler's purchases. Hesitating then, like an actor who recalls his lines but has come to doubt them: "Anything else, sir? Cigarettes?"

Politely Skyler said: "No, thanks."

Pools of *déjà vu* at his feet. Toxic mists, now a flavor of burning rubber. Skyler brushed at his eyes, annoyed. Skyler thanked the Indian clerk more brusquely than he meant, forgetting to smile in his haste to get the hell out.

Quarter-mile hike to the park. Skyler knew shortcuts: alleys, vacant lots. Must've been one of his good days, Skyler was walking without a limp except: any sharp-eyed fellow-limper could discern, there was something wincing in his posture.

Still, it was one of Skyler's good days. Rejoice in that. And the other day, he'd received the letter from Elyot Grubbe meaning that Elyot had forgiven him.

Painful to think of Elyot Grubbe, for Skyler must then think of Heidi

Harkness. And Skyler did not want to think of Heidi Harkness, at this time.*

In eleven days, Skyler Rampike would be twenty years old. At The Ark, this event of dubious significance to Skyler would be celebrated. As Pastor Bob said wryly *Celebrate what you have. It might be a while before you have another occasion.*

Skyler was walking now through the park. Headed for the path above the river. *I hope I hope I can make it* came to him like a scrap of litter lifted in the wind, blown against his face. Or was it a line of music. *Hope! hope I can.* In this fierce bright March sunshine the Raritan River was choppy and scintillant like a river of small flames. The wind was raw and gusty out of the northwest and so did not smell of toxic-chemical-New Jersey. On the ground ice was melting in shiny rivulets. So flashy, you'd mistake them for cellophane/aluminum-foil litter of which, in the park, there was much. At the edges of things, in the shadowy crevices in the ravine, were coils of dirty snow like entrails slow-melting, shrunken. Skyler recalled from his childhood these early *faux*-spring days in New Jersey. A balmy taste to the air: the taste of (*faux?*) hope. There were others in the winter-ravaged park: young mothers pushing baby strollers, shouting children, teenaged boys, vagrants sunning themselves on park benches. And at the remains of the basketball court tall burly black boys in baggy-gangsta pants, T-shirts with ripped-off sleeves, tossing a basketball at one another and at the battered backboard above the lopsided bare rim—"Hey man!"—"Fuck man!" Skyler winced recalling the beating he'd been given, very likely among the exuberant basketball players were boys who'd stomped the white fucker's face and scarred it, but he couldn't be sure, and had no intention of making sure. Even Pastor Bob wouldn't have counseled Skyler to seek his assailants out, and forgive them.

As Daddy would say *Batta!*

Skyler climbed from the concrete walkway up into the shelter of an immense misshapen and graffiti-covered granite boulder. There seeing that no one was close by, no one seemed to be observing him, Skyler squatted

---

* *Fact is, Skyler has started letters to Heidi Harkness but never got beyond* Heidi can you forgive me, I love you *before he gave up in dismay and disgust.*

and removed from his pocket his mother's crinkly letters and the video-tape and these he placed between two rocks and doused them with lighter fluid and quickly before he had time to reconsider, not only the enormity of what he was about to do but that it was irrevocable, he struck a match, with trembling fingers struck a match, God-damned wooden match failed to light and snapped in his fingers so he tried again and with the second match a bluish-yellow flame leapt up and this match Skyler dropped onto the perfumy peach-colored pages and the videotape and with a small astonished *pouf!* the letters burst into flame and more grudgingly it seemed the videotape began to burn. Within seconds the tissue-thin stationery had gone up in flame and was reduced to ashes—*Your loving Mother—Mummy* reduced to feathery ashes; as the videotape burned, more sluggishly, ill-smelling smoke wafted to Skyler's nostrils, stung his eyes.

Then came a sudden shout, a loud male voice: "You! What the fuck're you doing there?"

Skyler woke from his trance to see a furious young police officer gesturing at him from the farther side of the ravine. Quickly Skyler stammered, "N-Nothing," and quickly amending, with the preppy instinct to grovel before authority, "N-nothing, sir." Like a figure in a TV cop show he raised his hands to show that they were empty, weaponless; he was harmless. The police officer could not have been more than five or six years older than Skyler but exuded an air of brusque no-bullshit certainty; his rough blunt face seemed to shine in the wintry air, like a boot. In disgust he told Skyler to put out the fire: "What d'you think this is, a garbage dump?" Skyler quickly obeyed kicking out the flames, holding his breath against the melting-plastic stink that was fouling the air. Skyler's alacrity in obeying police orders seemed to placate the young police officer for, disgusted, but not in a mood to walk all the way around the ravine to confront Skyler close up, the policeman turned away with a dismissive wave of his hand of the kind that signals, in any language, *Asshole.*

Skyler felt a pang of shame, mortification. How like Skyler Rampike to fuck up the most beautifully "symbolic" gesture of his young life.

Within a few minutes wind blew most of the feathery ashes away and the remains of the incriminating videotape, Skyler kicked into the ravine to mingle with the detritus of ages. Now no one would know with certainty who had killed his sister. Forever now, the identity of the killer would be unknown. No one would know what it had been, the Rampike family secret that had so bonded them, never to be uttered aloud even to Jesus.

"Fuck you I 'forgive' you. Both of you: 'Mummy'—'Daddy.' But not for Bliss, I don't forgive you for Bliss, only Bliss can forgive you for her. For Bliss, you can both rot in hell."

It came to Skyler then, since moving into The Ark, he had ceased hearing his sister's plaintive voice in the night *Skyler help* *help me Skyler*

Skyler was not crying. God damn Skyler was not crying.

Skyler leaned over the railing, above the river. Choppy leaden waves, a smell as of detergent, mysterious chemicals. Pastor Bob had such hopes for Skyler Rampike: seeing in Skyler someone whom Skyler himself could not see, and in which Skyler could not believe. He would return to school, he would resume something of his old, derailed life. He would not accept a penny from Bix Rampike, he would not. If Betsey Rampike had remembered him in her will, as very likely, stricken with guilt, she had, Skyler would not accept a penny of that blood money, God damn *he would not.*

He would contact Elyot Grubbe. Drive up to Harvard and visit Elyot in the spring. Resume their friendship for he intended to resume what was most valuable in his old life.

"M-Mister? Can you come help my mommy?"

A child of about four years of age was approaching Skyler cautiously, sucking at a forefinger. Her small face glistened with tears and snot. Her pink nylon parka was soiled, her sparrow-colored hair matted and uncombed. Bare-legged, in sneakers and tiny white ankle socks, she was too lightly dressed for the day. Not far away, a young woman who must have been the girl's mother was slumped on a park bench, looking dazed. When Skyler had first entered the park he'd noticed this young woman swaying on her feet, pulling her small child by one hand; behaving strangely, as if drunk, or drugged. She was shaking a cell phone, perplexed and angry that it didn't seem to be working; it fell from her fingers, and she kicked at it. She, too, was inappropriately dressed: in a short trim jacket of some fluffy purple material, a twisted skirt of some kind, bright green stockings or tights, red plastic wedge shoes with straps. Her streaked hair blew untidily in the wind. Her swollen lips moved, she was muttering to herself. She might have been in her late twenties or early thirties. Skyler believed that he'd seen her somewhere recently: in Pastor Bob's congregation, in Second Chance Books where Skyler sometimes hung out, possibly at the rehab clinic. Very likely, at the rehab clinic. There was that post-rehab look to the young woman, Skyler recognized. He had never spoken to her and she had never spoken to him and Skyler doubted that she had ever noticed him and even now, though her daughter was standing before him whimpering and pleading, she had yet to take notice of him. Every impulse in Skyler urged *Get the hell out. Run!* He guessed that the little girl had approached others in the scrubby park who had turned away. And seeing that Skyler had not, the little girl pleaded, "Mister? My mommy is acting strange, my mommy doesn't feel right . . ." Precisely what was wrong with this mommy, Skyler supposed he'd soon find out.

    I hope   I hope I can make it